T0120458

BY ROBERT JACKSON BENNETT

City of Stairs

City of Blades

City of Miracles

Foundryside

Shorefall

Locklands

LOCKLANDS

LOCKLANDS

A NOVEL

Robert Jackson Bennett

NEW YORK

Locklands is a work of fiction. Names, characters, places, and incidents are the products of the author's imagination or are used fictitiously. Any resemblance to actual events, locales, or persons, living or dead, is entirely coincidental.

2023 Del Rey Trade Paperback Edition

Published in the United States by Del Rey, an imprint of Random House, a division of Penguin Random House LLC, New York.

Del Rey and the Circle colophon are registered trademarks of Penguin Random House LLC.

Originally published in hardcover in the United States by Del Rey, an imprint of Random House, a division of Penguin Random House LLC, and in the United Kingdom by Jo Fletcher Books, an imprint of Quercus Editions Limited, London, in 2022.

Library of Congress Cataloging-in-Publication Data
Names: Bennett, Robert Jackson, author.
Title: Locklands / Robert Jackson Bennett.
Description: First Edition. | New York : Del Rey, [2022] |
Series: The founders trilogy ; #3
Identifiers: LCCN 2021045838 (print) | LCCN 2021045839 (ebook) |
ISBN 9781984820686 (trade paperback) | ISBN 9781984820693 (ebook)
Subjects: GSAFD: Fantasy fiction.
Classification: LCC PS3602.E66455 L63 2022 (print) |
LCC PS3602.E66455 (ebook) | DDC 813/.6—dc23
LC record available at https://lccn.loc.gov/2021045838
LC ebook record available at https://lccn.loc.gov/2021045839

Printed in the United States of America on acid-free paper

randomhousebooks.com

3rd Printing

Book design by Alexis Capitini
Title and part opener pages illustration by drawlab19/stock.adobe.com

For Joe McKinney, who was a good person,
and a hell of a lot better read than I was or ever will be

They say politics is the art of distributing pain. And scriving, of course, is the art of distributing intelligence.

I wonder—sometimes with excitement, other times with fear—what will happen when the two shall meet.

—Orso Ignacio, letter to Estelle Candiano

I

THE SCRIVING WARS

1

Are you ready?> whispered a voice.

Berenice opened her eyes. The morning sunlight reflected brightly off the ocean, and her vision adjusted slowly, the forms of the city walls and the ramparts and the coastal batteries calcifying in the glimmering light. She'd been meditating so deeply it took her a moment to remember—*Am I in Old Tevanne? Or somewhere else?*—but then her senses fully returned to her, and she saw.

Grattiara: a tiny fortress enclave balanced atop a thread of stone stretching into the Durazzo Sea, all ocean-gray walls and cloud-white towers and wheeling gulls. It wasn't quite a town as much as a residue of civilization clinging to the battlements, the homes and huts like barnacles spreading across the hull of a ship. She watched as the little fishing boats trundled up to the piers, their sails pale and luminescent. They reminded her faintly of bat wings catching the first rays of dawn.

"Hell," Berenice said quietly. "It's almost pretty."

<*Almost.*> Claudia moved to stand next to her at the balcony,

her eyes hard and sharp under her dark metal helmet. Her voice whispered in the back of Berenice's thoughts, quiet but clear: <*How far we've fallen, to find a little shithole like this pretty.*>

<*Yes,*> sighed Berenice. <*And yet, it's up to us to save it.*>

Claudia picked her teeth with a length of wood. <*Or at least the people here, anyways.*> She flicked her toothpick away. <*So—you ready?*>

<*I don't know. Maybe. How do I look?*>

<*Like a grim warrior queen,*> said Claudia. She grinned. <*Maybe a little* too *grim. This is a Morsini fortress, mind. The governor might not take to an intimidating woman.*>

<*It's going to be a grim conversation. But I'll make sure to do a lot of smiling and bowing,*> she added acidly. She adjusted the way her cuirass hung on her shoulders, feeling the flex and bend of the pauldrons, then plucked at the leather shirt at her neck to let some of the humidity out. Their armor was a far sight from anything like a lorica, as it only covered critical exposures while leaving the joints free to move, but it was still hot as hell in the Grattiaran sun.

<*It'll have to do,*> Berenice said. She slung her espringal over her back, then checked to make sure her scrived rapier was sheathed at her side. <*Are the espringals rigged up properly?*>

<*We'll have to get within line of sight with them,*> said Claudia. She pointed to a small plate on her right pauldron, then the same on Berenice's armor. <*But they'll come to us when we call them.*>

<*Good.*>

<*Still think it's wise to bring weapons to this chat? I mean—they're going to make us disarm before we see the governor, yeah?*>

<*Oh, almost certainly,*> said Berenice. <*But being asked to disarm is a terrific opportunity to show off how many armaments you're packing.*>

<*How cynical.*> Claudia's grin flashed again. <*I approve.*>

The winds shifted, and the reek of rot wormed into Berenice's nostrils—undoubtedly from the refugee camp sprawling beyond the city's fortifications. She slipped out her spyglass and glassed the camps on the hills to the northwest.

It all made for a cruelly pointed contrast: the town of Grattiara remained more or less impeccable, its scrived coastal batteries huge and hulking along the sea, the towers of the innermost fortifications still tall and elegant; but mere yards from them lay field upon field of ragged tents and improvised shelters and spoiled waters—a reminder of how much the world had changed beyond this tiny fortress town.

Claudia whispered: <*We've got movement, Capo.*>

Berenice turned to look. A small group of men were making their way down the stairs from the central keep's gates, all colorfully dressed in shades of blue and red. She studied the keep above, its towers bedecked with espringal and shrieker batteries—scrived models she knew were at least four years out of date. And the walls, of course, weren't scrived at all, just brick and mortar and decades of patching: no sigils, no strings, no arguments embedded in them to trick them into being preternaturally durable or strong.

"Once it gets here," she murmured aloud, "it's going to tear through this place like a hot knife through eel fat."

<*Yeah,*> said Claudia. She peered out at the refugee camp. <*And all those people are going to die—or worse.*>

<*How long do we have, again?*>

<*Last estimate was two weeks,*> she said. <*It'll have to go through Balfi to the north, and that should slow it down, we hope. We should have at least a week before it's at the gates here, Capo.*>

Berenice wondered whether those estimates were accurate. If she had a massive army, and intended to use it to annihilate everything in its path—what road would she take, which rivers, and how fast would she move?

How tired I am, she thought, *of such grisly questions.*

<*You still haven't answered me, Ber,*> said Claudia gently. <*Are you ready?*>

<*Getting there,*> she said. She walked to where the two other members of her team sat on a small bench before the end of the stairs. Diela, the younger and smaller of the two, popped to attention immediately, standing up so fast her helmet rattled on her head. Vittorio stood languidly, smirking as he unfolded his tall, lean form to stand beside her. He held a heavy wooden crate in his arms, about three feet wide and tall, built of plain wood with a hinged top fastened shut.

"All good?" said Berenice.

<*I'm ready to put this thing down and get out of the sun, Capo,*> whispered Vittorio in the back of her mind. He made eye contact

with her, and his smile grew. <*You sure they're going to let me into the keep with this?*>

"They will," she said. "Remember, both of you—this is purely a diplomatic operation. Just keep your eyes open, keep your gear tight and accessible—and if they make a move on us, remember your training."

<*If it comes to that, fighting off a bunch of merchant house thugs should be easier than what we're used to,*> said Vittorio, now grinning.

Diela blinked beside him, and Berenice felt a slow anxiety building in the back of the girl's thoughts.

<*It probably will not come to that,*> Berenice said to the girl. <*Again, this is a diplomatic mission. But even if you haven't seen fighting, Diela, you still know what we know, and you've seen what we've seen. I have no doubt you'll succeed.*>

Diela nodded nervously, and said, <*Yes, Capo.*>

<*It's time, Capo,*> said Claudia.

Berenice looked up. The men from the keep were close now. She put on her helmet, adjusting it so her eyes looked through its visor properly, and strapped it tight. *Eight years I've waged this war,* she thought, *and I still can't get one of these goddamned things to fit right.*

She stood there, tall and assured in her dark armor, and watched as the Morsini men descended the stairs. Once men like this would have frightened or at least worried her, but those days were long since gone: there had been too many battles, and far too much death and horror, for merchant house men to haunt her thoughts.

I'm ready, she thought to herself. *I'm ready for this.*

Yet she felt a flicker of insecurity, sensing an absence like she'd forgotten something critical. She pulled her spyglass from her pocket and peered through it once more, though this time she glassed the distant ocean, far to the south.

At first she saw nothing but sea, yet then she spotted it—a tiny dot in the distance, just on the horizon.

Sancia and Clef, she thought. *Keeping their distance. But they're there. She's there.*

She heard footsteps, and quickly stowed the glass away.

God, my love. How I wish you were with me here today.

A voice from the stairs, prim and assured: "The governor will see you now, General Grimaldi."

"Thank you," Berenice said. "Please lead the way."

As expected, they were forced to give up their arms before entering the keep proper, which they did without protest. Berenice watched as the Morsini sentries took their weapons and stored them in a large wooden crate beside the gate, which they fastened shut. Before Berenice could even voice the question, Claudia whispered, <*Won't be a problem.*>

<*Good,*> said Berenice.

"And that?" said one of the sentries, pointing at the crate in Vittorio's arms.

"A gift for the governor," explained Berenice.

"I'll need to see it first," said the man, "and I'll be the one to take it."

Berenice nodded to Vittorio, who placed the crate on the ground and opened it up.

The sentry peered in, then looked up at them in wary disbelief. "You sure you have the right box?"

"We do," said Berenice.

The sentry sighed, shut the crate, and grunted as he picked it up. "If you say so," he muttered.

They were admitted inside, the scrived doors falling back as their escorts led them on. Having been in many Morsini House installations in her time, Berenice found the keep vaguely familiar: the narrow, winding passageways, the walls of stained glass; and always there were guards, mercenaries, and contractors in all numbers of colors and armor types, though most of their armor was in some state of disrepair.

Finally the four of them were led to the main meeting chamber. It must have been a grand space in its zenith, but almost all the furniture had been removed to make way for a giant table covered in maps, which dominated the room. The sentries gestured, and Berenice walked to stand before it. She realized she knew the maps at a glance: they depicted the Daulo and Gothian nations just to the north. A massive blot of bright red was seeping through the territories there, so much so that it looked like the entire north was bleeding.

She recognized them, for she herself stared at such maps every day. Yet based on the colors and markings she was seeing, these maps were very out of date—much like the city's defenses.

They think they're hurrying, she thought. *But they have no idea.*

She studied the room. Mercenaries and administrators and scrivers sat in a row at the back of the room, waiting to be called upon. They glanced only momentarily at Berenice before looking to one man, who walked to stand above the maps at the far end of the table from her. He was well dressed and well arranged, with an elaborate scrived rapier sheathed at his side, but his face was pale and haggard, his eyes were sunken with exhaustion, and his beard was shot through with gray. Though Berenice had been informed that Governor Malti was only a decade or so older than her, the person before her looked much older.

Perhaps, she thought, *this will be a very short conversation, and a lot of lives quickly saved.*

The retinue of men in red and blue announced them: "General Grimaldi and the delegation from the Free State of Giva, Your Grace."

Berenice removed her helmet and bowed. "Thank you for receiving us, Your Grace," she said. Claudia, Vittorio, and Diela bowed as well, though they did not remove their helms.

Governor Malti slowly looked up from his maps, his eyebrows raised. He studied them with a mildly nonplussed expression. Berenice waited for him to talk, but he seemed in no rush.

Finally he simply said, "So. These are the mythical warriors of Giva."

The statement hung in the musty air.

"We are, Your Grace," said Berenice.

"I had almost thought Givans were a fairy story, like ghosts," Malti said. His words were taut and merciless, like the twang of a bowstring. "Or perhaps the sky sprites my grandpa told me stood guard at the gates of Heaven itself."

<*Given that my ass is soaked in sweat,*> whispered Claudia, <*I don't feel very scrumming mythical.*>

Berenice attempted a dignified smile. "I would much prefer that we were. Yet we are flesh and blood, and happy to talk to you here in the earthly realm, rather than in Heaven."

Governor Malti returned the smile, but his was far chillier. "Of course. And you've come to discuss my situation here."

"Yes, Your Grace. Concerning the refugees at your gates."

"You wish my permission to take them away."

"If possible, Your Grace. We have the transport available. We are acting solely in the interest of saving lives. It would be to the benefit of all to do so, I would imagine. It must be difficult to maintain your forces with so many displaced citizens in your way."

"Displaced citizens . . ." Malti echoed. "What a phrase." He slumped into a chair, then watched as a sentry placed Vittorio's crate on the table, bowed, and left. "And to persuade me to let you do so," said Malti, "you've brought me . . . gifts."

"We have," Berenice said. "Of a sort."

Malti's gaze lingered on the crate. He did not get up to open it. He did not speak. He just stared at it, as if lost in thought.

<*I can't tell,*> whispered Claudia. <*Is this going well? Because it doesn't feel like it's going well.*>

<*Quiet,*> snapped Berenice.

"You know," said Malti with sudden cheer, "I am still not accustomed to receiving delegations. Ambassadors. Envoys. That sort of thing. Grattaria, after all, was not really intended for such." He gestured wearily to the drab brick walls. "We are a fortress, here to guard passage along the coast. Great powers did not used to go to fortresses to meet with statesmen. Rather, they'd go to the states themselves."

"True, Your Grace," said Berenice. "But the world has changed since those days."

"Changed?" he said. A bleak smirk flashed across his face. "Or ended?"

Everyone in the room looked at Berenice.

<*Oh shit,*> said Claudia. <*This got dark.*>

"It has not ended *here,*" Berenice said evenly.

"Not yet. But elsewhere . . ." His smirk faded. "Eight years ago we were just an outpost in another war. Then, quite suddenly, there were fewer and fewer places for everyone's envoys to go—so they came here. And now there are almost no nations to send envoys at all." He leaned forward. "Yet with other delegations, once they'd departed, I generally knew where I could go to talk to them again. I'd have the name of a city, or an island, or a town, or some such. But with the nation of Giva . . . no one quite knows *where* the actual nation is, do they?"

Again, Berenice felt every eye in the room on her.

"Giva is located in the Givan Islands," she said, her voice still even and courteous.

"Oh, I know," said Malti. "That I've been told. But I've also been told that, whenever someone *sails* to those islands, they're always deserted, and layered with fog—and the further in they go, the more fog they encounter, until they're forced to give up." A cold grin. "Are you *sure* you don't stand guard at the gates of Heaven, General Grimaldi?"

<*Damn,*> whispered Vittorio. <*He's not stupid.*>

<*No,*> said Berenice. <*He is not.*>

"Surely you can appreciate the need for unconventional defenses, Your Grace," said Berenice. She nodded to the map. "Given what has happened to the Daulo nations, and the Gothian countries, and beyond."

Malti's eyes were like ice. "So—you *can* make walls of fog appear?"

"We have our scrived tools," she said coolly. "The same as yours."

He looked away for a moment, thinking. Then he asked, "And tell me, General Grimaldi—did Giva really destroy the enemy's installations at the Bay of Piscio, some six months ago?"

Berenice could feel Vittorio and Claudia's surprise blossom in the back of her mind.

<*Huh,*> whispered Claudia. <*I didn't realize word about that had spread this far.*>

"We . . . did, Your Grace," said Berenice. But she now felt unsure where this was going.

"And at the port of Varia?" Malti asked. "I'm told the enemy had developed quite the stronghold there—and yet, after you Givans visited, it had utterly fallen. Is this true?"

Berenice hesitated but nodded.

"How?" he demanded.

She thought about it. "Carefully, Your Grace," she said.

Malti smiled ever so briefly, and then his eyes went distant. When he spoke again, his voice was deadly quiet: "That is very interesting. Because there is only one other power I'm aware of that has ever had such successes against the enemy. So—I must wonder if there is some connection."

Berenice narrowed her eyes at him. Then she glanced down again at the maps on the table—specifically at a small blot of black in the valleys to the west of all that red. It was a curious little addition, reminding her of some kind of parasite buried in the body of livestock, and though it was tiny compared to the vast sea of red to the east, she knew the black blot was hundreds of miles wide at least. Malti's advisers had even shaded in the area around the black blot with gray, demarcating the blasted, ruined wastelands caused by years of unspeakable warfare.

She looked up at Malti and said, "Giva stands alone. We have no formal allies, Your Grace. Especially not the one you suggest."

"But you have so many similarities. Such mystery, such abilities. How can you convince me that you have no association with the devil that sleeps in the Black Kingdoms?"

Everyone watched her. Berenice could hear Vittorio silently counting all the armed men in the room with them.

"Well?" said Malti.

An image flashed in Berenice's mind—a black mask, gleaming in the shadows as the night filled up with screams—and with the memory came a voice, inhumanly deep and rumbling: *I went to places no living human has ever gone before. I glimpsed the infrastructure that makes this reality possible.*

<*Ber?*> whispered Claudia.

Berenice sniffed and cleared her throat. "I was in Tevanne when Shorefall Night happened, Your Grace," she said. "I saw what he did. I remember. I cannot forget. So I can quite genuinely say now—I would rather die than be the ally of that thing."

Malti nodded, his eyes still distant. Though she couldn't tell if he believed this answer, he seemed to find it satisfying. But then his gaze sharpened on Berenice, and he said, "I don't care about what's in your box."

Berenice blinked. "Your Grace, I—"

"I don't care about gold or valuables," he said. "After all, there are no free places where I can spend them anymore. And I don't care about any tools or inventions you might be offering. We have our lexicons, which run our rigs and defenses. Nor do we need definition plates, or any arguments to feed into those lexicons to help them remember how to argue all our tools into functioning as we wish."

He fell silent, and the intensity in his face was replaced by some deep weariness. Berenice sensed an unasked question hanging in the air, and chose to ask it.

"Then," she said, "what *do* you care about, Your Grace? How might Giva help you?"

Malti's face went very still, his eyes dancing over the maps. "Help me . . ." he said softly. "Hm. *If* Giva can damage the enemy, then surely you understand it somewhat. More than the scrivers I have here, at least, who understand it none at all." He waved contemptuously at the men seated at the back of the chamber, who glared at Berenice.

"We have some knowledge of it, yes," she said.

Malti studied her yet again. "I have an . . . issue," he said. "One that no one can explain. One inflicted on us by the enemy. One so serious that, though it is a very grave secret, I am willing to discuss it even with strangers such as yourselves."

Berenice understood what he was requesting. "We keep our secrets well, Your Grace."

"I should hope so," he said quietly. "If you can aid me with this . . . this obstacle, then I will grant Giva free passage through the waters about the fortress." He sighed, then stood and gestured to a closed door at the back of the chamber. "I cannot explain it, for I do not understand it. But I will show you, if you will see."

Berenice studied the door, thinking. This was a surprise. She'd expected more blustering and bribery than this, and far more threats.

<*Ahh, Capo,*> asked Diela. <*Is this what you planned for?*>

<*Not at all,*> said Berenice. She looked at Malti's face, so thin and exhausted. <*But I don't think he's lying.*>

<If *we can actually help him, that is,*> said Claudia.

<*Coming here was a gamble,*> said Berenice. <*We can only gamble further.*>

She nodded to Malti. "We'll follow," she said.

Malti led them through the little door and into the labyrinth of passageways farther into the keep. Berenice found it impossible to keep track of where they were going; she and her team were following the governor's retinue, which was a dozen men at least, with a dozen more following behind them. She couldn't see much more than a line of shifting shoulders ahead.

But finally they stopped, and the retinue made way to allow Berenice and her team forward. She found Malti waiting at the end, standing before a closed wooden door, his eyes more exhausted than ever. "I would ask that you please be quiet," he said. "And courteous."

She nodded.

"All that you see within must remain a secret. Is that clear?"

"Of course," she said.

He watched her for a long time, seemingly torn. Then he opened the door and led her inside.

The chamber within was a bedroom, large but spare, with a colorful red-and-blue rug and a fine armoire. In the corner was a four-poster bed, and sitting beside it was a woman in plain clothes, a bowl of porridge and a spoon in her lap.

A young man lay in the bed, about twenty, painfully thin and starved. His eyes were open but dull, staring up at the brick ceiling with a glazed expression. His mouth was smeared with porridge, and a pile of sheets in the corner smelled strongly of shit and piss.

Malti approached, and the woman stood, bowed, stepped aside. He stood by the bed, then said in a quiet, crushed voice, "This is my son. Julio."

Berenice walked over to stand beside him. The young man did not react. He did not even blink. There was a faint burbling wheeze as he breathed.

"He was at the battle of Corfa," said Malti. "The last great battle

Morsini House fought with the enemy. He was in his armor, and armed, and ready—but then something struck him, and he went mad. He . . ." Malti swallowed, and his voice shook. "He killed his brother. His little brother. And many more besides. But when his men pulled him down and took him away, he went . . . still. Like this. He breathes, he barely eats, but . . ."

Berenice watched the young man's sunken chest rise and fall, ever so gently.

<*Oh shit,*> said Claudia slowly. <*Is this what I think it is?*>

<*Yes,*> Berenice said.

Vittorio looked at her, alarmed. <*And they brought him* back*?*> he said. <*They let him* inside*? Don't they know what could be looking through his eyes, even now?*>

<*Is this a trap, Capo?*> asked Diela. <*Did it . . . did it* want *us to come here?*>

Berenice was silent.

Malti turned to her. "Do you know what did this to him?" he asked. "Can you Givans fix whatever wickedness the enemy has done to my son?"

She studied the young man—the way his cheekbones seemed to almost poke through the skin, the thinness of his arms, his small, dull little eyes.

Berenice reached forward, took the young man's sweaty, stained face, and tilted it toward her, exposing the right side.

There, just above his right ear, was what she'd expected to find: a small, weeping laceration, slightly swollen with infection—yet she thought she could see a glimmer of metal through the cut, like something was buried in his flesh.

She stared into the boy's eyes, wondering who, or what, was now looking back, and what it had seen.

<*Change your estimates,*> said Berenice. <*It knows we're here. Assume we have less than two days.*>

She turned to Malti. "We will not discuss it here. Not where it could listen."

"It?" he said, affronted. "Do you mean my son?"

"No," she said. "I mean the thing that's now controlling your son. The thing that's probably used him to see how to take your fortress apart."

They sat at the meeting-room table: the four Givans, Governor Malti, and a handful of his trusted lieutenants. Berenice's gaze traced over the maps before them, and all the little cities and fiefdoms whose names had been swallowed up with red. She stared most at the southern line of crimson, where it was bottled up at the head of the peninsula, ready to pour down to where Grattiara clung to the coast at the tip. The gap between the fortress and all that red now seemed very, very small.

And all those people trapped between, Berenice thought to herself. *The survivors of so much misery . . .*

She asked, "Are you familiar with twinning?"

Governor Malti looked up at her. "T-Twinning?" he said absently. He looked about the map room as if trying to find a scriver to consult but seemed to have forgotten he'd had the room cleared. "I believe so. It's a scriving method, mostly for communication, yes?"

"Yes," said Berenice. "It's a scrived way of asserting that one thing is another, or like another. Write the correct sigils on two panes of glass so they become twinned, then tap one with a hammer, and both will break. Twin two pieces of metal, heat one up, and the other will grow hot." She leaned forward over the maps. "The enemy you fight—the one we all fight—is using an advanced form of twinning to wage its war. That's how it's managed to conquer so much territory—all in only eight years."

She touched the largest map, depicting the Durazzo Sea and all the lands surrounding it, and the taint of red flooding throughout nearly all the territories in the north.

"The enemy captured all that," said Malti dubiously, "with twinning?"

"Yes," said Berenice. "Because it knows how to twin something very unusual." She looked at him. "Minds," she said.

Malti stared. He looked to his mercenary chief, who shrugged, bewildered.

"Twin minds? What does that mean?" Malti demanded.

Berenice stood and walked to where the crate still waited on the table. "May I finally show you our gift?"

Malti looked at the crate warily, then nodded. Berenice opened it, turned it over, and spilled its contents onto the ground.

A scrived rig clanked onto the floor. It was an odd little device, wrought of wood and steel and built in a clunky, improvised manner, with inner plates left exposed like the designer was indifferent to how it looked. Yet anyone with any familiarity with scrived rigs could recognize that it was an awkward pairing of two common devices: an espringal and a lamp.

"A . . . floating lamp?" asked one of Malti's lieutenants.

"Yes. One that fires a very strange ammunition," said Berenice. "Not a bolt, but a scrived plate. A small one. Your son was almost certainly shot with such a plate." She tapped her right temple. "It buried itself in his skull, and then his mind was twinned. With the *enemy*. Two things made alike. The enemy scrived his body, his very being, and its thoughts became his. It saw what he saw, its mind became his mind, and it told him what to do—and he did it, because his will was no longer his own." She sat back down. "And you brought him back to your city. Where the enemy could see everything through his eyes, hear everything through his ears, and wait for the chance to attack."

Malti's ashen face grew even paler. "That can't be. This is . . . This is my *child* you're talking about."

"And you know what he did at Corfa," said Claudia. "Something he'd never normally do, yeah? Something you'd normally think was mad?"

"But you're asking me to believe the unbelievable," said Malti. "Scriving is about . . . about *stuff*." He rapped the table beside him. "Bolts. Swords. Ships. Walls. Scriving the mind is . . . it's simply mad!"

Claudia met Berenice's eyes. *<Is now when you tell him we all have our own little plates in our bodies? Ones that allow us to share thoughts and all kinds of crazy shit?>*

<I want him to let us save him and his people,> said Berenice. *<Not burn us like witches.>*

Yet she had far more personal reasons to avoid this subject. Bringing that up would undoubtedly lead Malti to ask how Giva had come to learn this technique; and if she were to tell the truth, she would have to admit that she had been one of the scrivers to develop it, before it was stolen by their enemy; and thus she herself bore some guilt for the hundreds of little cities daubed with red on the maps stretched across the table, and the thousands of refugees outside the walls of Grattiara who had escaped the onslaught—as well as all those who had not.

Stop, she told herself. *Fight the battles before you, not the ones from so long ago.*

"Even if you are telling the truth," said Malti, "why did you bring me this . . . this lamp as a gift? Did you *know* my son was suffering from this affliction?"

"No," said Berenice. "I brought you this to warn you, to tell you what was coming, and how all the rest of these cities had fallen. And how your city will fall as well." She pressed a hand to the sea of red on the map like it was a wound. "You'll first see just one lamp, floating at your walls," she said. "If you see it at all, that is."

"It'll probably come at night," said Vittorio from the end of the table. "They're small. Hard to see in the dark."

"It'll target one of your soldiers," said Claudia. "Shoot them anywhere—head, hand, back, it doesn't matter. It just needs to be buried in living flesh for the scriving to work."

"Then it'll twin that solider—own them, take them over—and use them to see," said Diela, quietly and meekly. Her eyes were large underneath her helmet. "To see what defenses you have. Where your people are stationed."

"Where you're strong," said Vittorio. "Where you're weak. What you're saying, what you're planning."

"It'll pick the perfect time to attack," said Claudia.

"And then the sky will fill with these," said Berenice, kicking the lamp with one foot. "They'll descend on your soldiers like locusts, because they'll know where to find them. They'll shoot them, plate them, twin them, turn them. The soldiers will go to your defenses and kill the people manning them, or open up the gates, or set fire to the buildings, the homes, maybe their own homes. Anything."

"We call them hosts," said Claudia quietly. "Because once one of those plates is in them, you have to recognize that they're not themselves anymore. That they're not human anymore. Not really."

"They're twinned with something different," said Berenice.

A flash of an image in her mind: a man standing in a shadowy corner, then turning to face her; then pale light glancing across his features, revealing his eyes and nose and mouth streaming blood . . .

"Something monstrous," she said softly. "Something we can't really understand."

"This is all ludicrous bullshit," snarled one of the mercenary captains. "Lamps that can target? Shoot? I remember when scrivers tried to rig up lamps to bring baskets of fruit to people's homes, there were melons tumbling everywhere. The idea of one wielding an espringal is beyond foolishness."

Claudia shook her head. "The lamps aren't doing the aiming and shooting any more than a normal espringal does."

"You mean they're being controlled by someone at a distance?" Malti asked. "Who?"

The Givans exchanged a glance.

<*He's sharp, but he doesn't really know,*> said Diela.

<*No,*> said Berenice. <*He doesn't.*>

"By the enemy," said Berenice. But she knew as she said it that the answer wouldn't satisfy.

"By its infantry?" asked Malti. "Then why can we not deploy our sharpshooters to eliminate them? Stop the people controlling the lamps before they can attack us?"

"No," said Berenice. She grimaced, struggling to imagine how to say this. "Not by its infantry. Because *all* of the enemy's forces—the infantry, the lamps, its ships, everything—are controlled at a distance. By one thing."

"One mind," said Claudia.

"One entity," said Diela. "Seeing out of many eyes. Working many hands. Controlling many, many rigs—all across the continent, simultaneously."

"One mind twinned to exist in many places at once," said Vittorio. "In anything scrived—rigs *or* people."

Malti stared at them, horrified. "No," he said. "That's impossible."

"Have you never wondered, Your Grace," said Berenice, "how the enemy can maneuver so perfectly? How it appears to communicate almost instantaneously? How its shriekers always hit targets out of the line of sight of their artillery teams? And why it never,

ever bothers to even *try* to negotiate? Why it never sends emissaries, never announces itself, why it's never even *named* itself to you?"

Malti was staring at the map, his flesh nearly colorless, the bristles of his beard trembling.

"It sounds inhuman," said Berenice, "because it *is* inhuman."

He swallowed. He sat in silence for a long time, then turned to the plating lamp on the floor. "You didn't come just to persuade me to let you take the refugees, did you," he said.

"No," said Berenice. "We came to ask *you* to leave as well. You, and all your men."

"To come with us," said Diela. "Where you can be safe."

"Because there is no standing your ground against this," said Claudia. "No pitched battles. No sieges. No blast of trumpets and glorious charge of men-at-arms."

"The warfare of the merchant houses is gone," said Vittorio. "This is different."

Berenice shot him a glare. "Warfare has *changed*. So we must change. All of us. Including you, Your Grace."

Malti blinked for a moment, shaken. Then he fumbled for a pitcher, poured himself a cup of wine, and tossed it back. "I am Morsini," he said slowly. "I was raised to believe that might and battle was the grand language of the world, that worth could be discovered through strength of arms. To evacuate, to leave my post is . . . it's unthinkable."

Berenice stayed quiet, watching as the thoughts worked through Malti's face.

"Where would you take my people?" he asked. "To your fog walls?"

She nodded. "To Giva. Where the enemy has never approached."

He buried his face in his hands. "To flee so far . . . My God." He sniffed and looked at her. "Just tell me. Can you save my boy?"

<*You can't really say that shit like this ever goes well,*> said Claudia, trotting up the keep steps beside Berenice. <*But—that went well.*>

<*Possibly,*> said Berenice. They came to the top of the keep walls. She shaded her eyes with a hand, peering out at the vast

ocean. She felt disoriented—her time in the keep had turned her all around.

She narrowed her eyes, squinting about. *Of all the things to lose today,* she thought, *I have to lose a giant war galleon.*

<*Are we worried about the boy?*> asked Diela. <*The host?*>

<*How could we not be?*> said Vittorio. <*I mean—was it seeing us, from in that kid's eyes? Watching us?*>

<*We need to purge the boy immediately,*> said Claudia tersely. <*I'm not sure why we didn't do it right then and there.*>

<*Because getting these people out of here comes first,*> said Berenice, squinting out at the sea. <*And I think it'll take a bit to let us convince Malti to let us save the boy at all.*>

<*Why would he need convincing to let us save his son?*> asked Diela.

<*I'm guessing because the solution requires stabbing him with a damn knife,*> said Vittorio. <*That may require some extensive diplomacy.*>

<*Correct,*> said Berenice.

<*Oh,*> said Diela meekly. <*I see.*>

There was an unpleasant silence, for this was a topic none of them wished to discuss.

All of Berenice's crew bore a tiny scrived plate within them that twinned their minds with everyone else's. This made them something unusual, and powerful: a team of soldiers that acted in total unison, with complete awareness of everyone's location, capabilities, and vulnerabilities.

But if their enemy—the thing that called itself "Tevanne"—ever captured and dominated one of them just as it had the governor's son, their own scrivings would give it influence over all their comrades, because they were all linked. Which meant they could never afford to be captured with an active connection.

A purge stick was the solution. In function, it was a tiny scrived blade you could stab into your flesh and then snap off. Once inside you, the blade's commands would force your body to reject all other scrivings that anyone could ever apply to you—including the scrivings that allowed Berenice and her team to think and feel as one. The effect was irreversible, but it was better to be permanently marred than fall into Tevanne's clutches and doom your comrades with you.

Berenice finally spied the *Keyship* in the distance. <*Once we send the signal to Sancia,*> she said, <*I'll talk to the governor. Hopefully he'll have had time to process all that we told him about Tevanne—enough to let us purge his son.*> She held out a hand to Claudia. <*Let's get started.*>

Claudia reached into the side of her cuirass and produced a small oblong black box, about one inch wide and deep and four inches tall, with a tiny glass dot set in one side. <*And hopefully it'll have been done fast enough,*> she said, <*before Tevanne uses that host to spy on us further. Right?*>

Berenice took the box, placed it on the edge of the wall pointing out at the sea, and slid open the top, revealing a glass lens set within. <*Hopefully. Yes.*>

<*It couldn't, right?*> said Diela. <*Twinning is a proximal effect. Twinned things have to be close together for the effect to work. Maybe the boy in there was . . . deactivated. Gone passive. Until the enemy gets close again.*>

<*But if the enemy was close, would we even know it?*> said Vittorio.

<*We're asking the wrong questions,*> Berenice said. She peered through the little lens in the top of the box and confirmed it was targeting the distant ship. Then she looked up at her team around her. <*The right question is—if the enemy is close, and if this* could *all be a trap, would it still be worth trying to save those thousands of people out there?*>

Her team exchanged anxious glances but then nodded.

<*Right,*> Berenice said. <*I agree.*> She looked up at the sun, then adjusted the lens in the top of the box to capture its light. <*But—let's go ahead and assume this is a trap anyway.*>

<*What kind of a trap?*> Claudia asked.

<*I don't know,*> said Berenice. <*Previously we had assumed Tevanne was using its usual strategy: move on a city, conquer it, re-form its forces, then move on the next. But now . . .* >

<*Now you think it'll skip all the cities in between,*> said Diela. <*And come straight here as fast as it can.*>

<*If there was anything in those eyes to see us, yes,*> said Berenice. <*I've no doubt that Tevanne would love to kill me. Or Sancia. And it knows that where I am . . .* >

<*Sancia is close, so Clef is close,*> finished Claudia lowly.

<*Correct.*> Berenice turned a small switch on the side of the little box, activating its scrivings. There was no visible shift that she could see, but she knew that the little box was now taking the sun-

light from above and beaming it out to sea, but in a very different color—one that only one particular being could distinguish.

<*There,*> she said. <*Signal's set.*> She pulled her spyglass out once more and glassed the distant ship. <*Hopefully it's received soon. If Tevanne was present in that host, and if it saw me, we have at most two days to evacuate thousands of innocent people. We've no time to waste.*>

She watched the speck on the horizon, waiting to see it move.

<*When it comes,*> said Claudia quietly, <*it'll be sure to send a deadlamp—right?*>

Berenice felt a cold thrill of fear dance through her team. She shivered herself, and instinctively glanced at the empty sky to the north, as if expecting to see one silently hanging amid the clouds.

<*Yes,*> Berenice said. <*Absolutely.*>

<*Scrumming hell,*> muttered Vittorio.

<*I noticed you didn't mention* them *to the governor,*> said Claudia.

<*We wanted him to let us help him,*> said Berenice. She peered back through the spyglass at the galleon on the horizon. <*Not despair entirely.*>

The tiny dot on the horizon twitched, then slowly, slowly rotated.

<*Movement,*> said Berenice. <*It's a go.*> She lowered her spyglass and trotted back down the steps. <*Claudia, come with me, and we'll purge the boy. The rest of you, get your weapons from the keep gates, then get the cache of armaments we hid at the coast. Bring it to the outermost walls. I'll talk to the governor to let us set up defenses.*>

<*I thought you said we had two days before Tevanne got here?*> said Diela, surprised. <*Why would we set up siege defenses first?*>

<*How has Giva survived for so long, Diela?*> asked Berenice in a teacherly tone.

<*Ahh . . . because we think, comprehend, sacrifice when we need to, and give our days and hours to one another?*> asked Diela.

<*Oh. Well, yes, that,*> said Berenice. She put her helmet on and fastened it securely. <*But also because we're utterly goddamn paranoid. Now, come along.*>

In the dark of the galleon, Sancia opened her eyes.

She listened to the creaking and the groaning and the *drips* and *drops* from throughout the ship's dimly lit innards. Everything vibrated around her: the floor, the walls, the doors, all quaking as the massive ship cut through the waters of the Durazzo.

She blinked, trying to remember where she was and what she was doing here.

Once I crept through a ship like this, she thought, *and found a devil sleeping inside it.*

She turned her eyes on the chamber to her right: an immense bubble of steel and glass suspended in the belly of the ship, containing a large, complicated, and shifting contraption that resembled a stack of enormous coins placed on its side.

A lexicon: a device that could argue reality into contradicting itself—and the only thing keeping this enormous ship afloat.

But now I'm here, she thought, *with a devil awake outside, and eating the world.*

She stood and approached the side of the glass wall. Inside, protruding from a little mechanism adhered to the side of the lexicon, was a delicate golden key.

She touched the little twinned plate hanging from a string about her neck. A voice spoke in her mind, its words sly and syncopated: <*All good, kid?*>

<*Yeah, Clef,*> she said. <*I'm just waiting. Which is nothing hard or exciting, compared to what you're doing.*>

<*I'm just shoving this big, dumb piece of shit around in the water,*> said Clef's voice. <*Pissing off some porpoises. And some seagulls. Ugh . . . bastards! They keep crapping on me—I can* feel *it.*>

<*No signal from Grattiara?*>

<*None as of yet,*> said Clef. <*I hope Ber's having a nice time of it. Maybe they're giving her tea, or those tasty little cookies they used to make here.*>

<*What do you care about how a cookie tastes, Clef?*> asked Sancia.

<*Hey,*> said Clef. <*A key can dream, right?*>

Sancia held the plate in her hands a little longer. Though they called it a "pathplate"—a term that suggested almost arcane powers—it was, perhaps, the simplest scrived rig on this ship, being little more than a piece of heat-resistant steel, twinned with a mate that Clef was now situated next to within the lexicon.

Ordinarily Sancia could hear Clef's voice only when she was

touching him with her skin—but since she was now touching the mate of that pathplate, which believed it, too, was currently touching Clef while *also* touching Sancia at the same time, this meant she could hear him remotely, like a little disembodied voice in her head.

Links in a chain, she thought absently, *connected from end to end . . .*

She stood there in the dark, imagining what Berenice and her team were doing now: talking with the governor, passionately making their case . . . Or maybe they'd been betrayed—the Morsinis had always been stupid bastards—and they were fighting to take control of the fortress from within.

After all, she thought, *seizing Grattiara can't be harder than the other dumb shit we've done.*

How her bones ached. How she hated being stuck in the dark of this ship.

<*Hey, it's nice being here with you too, kid,*> said Clef.

<*Huh? Oh. Sorry,*> said Sancia. She often forgot Clef was much more talented at pathing into people's minds than a normal human was. Though his own emotions were usually unreadable to others, he could pick up other people's thoughts and sentiments without their even knowing it.

She glared at him. <*You goddamn know it's not you that's the problem.*>

<*Yeah, I know.*>

<*I'm your cargo. I'm just . . . something for you to haul around, to be protected while all the real risk is elsewhere.*>

<*You know you're describing my entire relationship with you, right?*> said Clef. <*I spent a damn year hanging from your neck. At least you always had arms and legs and, you know, privates and stuff.*>

She smirked. <*I guess that's true. I do enjoy having all those things.*> The smirk faded. <*I suppose I just thought that if I were to fight in a scriving war . . .*>

<*That you'd be doing actual fighting.*>

<*Yeah.*>

She felt a presence grow in the space behind her—Polina, approaching from belowdecks. Sancia turned to see her emerge from the passageway beyond, her hard, stern face fixed in a perpetual squint.

<*Ah, hey, Pol,*> said Clef. <*How's the trip been? One of the physiqueres you brought seems to have* quite *the bout of seasickness down there. Wouldn't mind so much if he didn't keep throwing up on my wal—*>

"Shut up, key," snapped Polina. Sancia knew she deeply disliked hearing Clef's voice—which Polina could only do because she bore her own twinning plate that connected her to Sancia, which meant that when Clef spoke to Sancia, Polina could hear it too.

More links, thought Sancia. *And a far, far longer chain . . .*

Polina nodded imperiously to Sancia. "How long has it been?"

<*You know you don't have to get close to me to talk to me, right?*> asked Sancia. <*That's basically the point of twinning thoughts.*>

"I am aware," said Polina. "I still prefer to lay eyes on you, however, and engage in normal, human interaction—to ensure I stay human."

<*We're all still human, Polina,*> sighed Sancia. <*We just talk a little differently, that's all.*>

"Tell that to the hosts marching with Tevanne. How long?"

Sancia studied her. To her eternal frustration, the woman hadn't appeared to change one jot in the eight years since they'd escaped death and ruin: still the hard, weathered face, the sharp gray eyes, and her hair pulled back in a tight bun. Polina seemed to be a person born to sail straight into grim catastrophes and survive.

<*Berenice and her team went ashore two hours ago,*> said Sancia. <*Seems far too soon to be worried yet.*>

Polina's ever-present frown deepened. "I don't like it. We've tried talking to these merchant house idiots before. Asking conquering slavers to see reason makes about as much sense as trying to argue with that . . . that thing." She shuddered.

"If it works, we'll save thousands of lives," said Sancia aloud. Mostly so Polina could hear how irritated she now was.

"Thousands of people . . . How many can the *Keyship* hold?"

<*It's a standard Dandolo merchant house galleon,*> said Clef. <*Should max out at around three thousand passengers.*>

Polina shook her head. "That's the most to ever join Giva in a single operation. What a voyage home this will be—should all go aright, that is."

"Tevanne's forces are on the other side of the peninsula," said

Sancia, "with dozens of fortresses in between Grattiara and them. Unless it's got some way to fly an army miles and miles in a handful of hours, we've got time."

"True," said Polina. "But it all makes me nervous. It's when the shepherd is trying to save a little lost lamb that the rest of the flock is most vulnerable." She departed, and returned belowdecks. Sancia could sense her presence moving below her in the ship like a patch of warm floorboard below the bare soles of her feet.

<*At least it's nice to know,*> said Clef, <*that when you all twin your heads together, you stay somewhat the same. Because she's still the barrel of scrumming laughs she's always bee—*>

<*I can hear you, dammit!*> said Polina. <*I'm not* that *far away!*>

<*Yeah, yeah . . .* > said Clef.

Sancia leaned her head up against the glass of the lexicon and sighed.

<*Pick your head up, kid,*> said Clef.

<*You aren't going to try to give some kind of dumbass speech, are you?*> she asked.

<*No. Because I need you to focus. There's movement on the keep's walls.*>

Sancia sat up. <*Good movement or bad movement?*>

<*Hell if I know. But it's movement.*>

She grasped the pathplate around her neck. <*Let me see it.*>

<*Give me a sec. I'll pull you in.*>

She felt the opening in her mind—a curious *tap-tap* as Clef, in a way, knocked on her thoughts. She assented, and extended her mind to him and saw . . .

The vast bay of Grattiara heaving before them, the massive fortress teetering on the strand of rocks, the squalid, smoking camps stretched out over the hillsides. The sight poured into her thoughts from dozens of inputs, through all the sensing and seeing rigs they'd installed about the ship for Clef to use. Some of the inputs she couldn't entirely comprehend, since Clef was able to perceive reality with senses her brain was incapable of interpreting. So she focused on one vision in particular and studied Grattiara in the distance.

She looked at the parapets of the outermost walls; then up, to where the keep sat upon the highest of the hills; and there, at the tip of one of the towers, was a small clutch of people shifting about.

<*Goddamn,*> said Sancia. <*You can see far, Clef.*>

<*Well,* I *can't,*> said Clef. <*But the ship can, and all the shit they built into it. And I can't see far enough to see if that's Ber, but—*>

<*There it is!*> cried Sancia.

The tip of the tower suddenly lit up with a curious, reddish-green light—a light, she knew, that human eyes would never be able to perceive, but the rigs about the *Keyship* had been scrived to do.

<*She's done it,*> said Clef. <*Damn. That didn't seem to take long.*>

<*Then let's get moving,*> said Sancia. <*But stay on alert, just in case.*>

<*Got it.*>

She released the vision, falling back into her own body. Then she felt the ship shift around her, turning in the waters. It was still strange, to know Clef was doing this. He'd always been incredibly skilled at tampering and tinkering with scrived rigs—yet by placing him within the lexicon that controlled a war galleon, he was capable of essentially *becoming* the ship, his sentience suffusing every rig within its hull—including the hull itself, which was also a rig, of course. They'd even named the galleon after this bizarre relationship: to them it was the *Keyship,* whether Clef was in control of it or not.

Having to control every aspect of this unfathomably complicated vessel never seemed to bother Clef that much. The only thing he ever complained about was having to also run the latrines.

She leaned up against the wall of the lexicon chamber again. *I'm in a ghost ship,* she thought, *haunted by my friend.*

She listened to the galleon creak about her. How strange it was to know they were fighting a war against something similar, just on a far larger scale: a massive infrastructure of rigs and creations and hosts, all haunted by a mind that, to a certain degree, had once been her friend as well.

<*You're thinking about him again,*> said Clef.

<*I know,*> she said.

<*A lot's changed.* He's *changed.*>

<*I know!*>

<*He wouldn't have you do anything different.*>

She caught a glimpse of herself in the reflection of the glass wall. In her head, she was just a year or two shy of thirty. But the face in the reflection, with its salt-and-pepper hair and wrinkled eyes and blooming age spots, was easily well north of fifty.

She shut her eyes.

<*I know, Clef. I know how much everything's changed.*>

Berenice and her team split up once they reached the keep's lower floor, with Vittorio and Diela headed out into the city, and Berenice and Claudia making straight for the governor's meeting chambers.

<*Get set up, and tell me if you see anything awry,*> said Berenice as they roved through the narrow passageways.

<*What counts as anything, Capo?*> asked Vittorio.

<*Anything counts as anything, damn it!*> she snapped. <*Tevanne likely knows this city in and out. Any clue that can help us know how much it knows would be helpful.*>

But Berenice was aware this advantage was limited. Tevanne's most valuable unit—the abomination that Sancia had nicknamed a "deadlamp," even though the newer versions looked nothing like a lamp—did not need sabotage or spies to succeed. A weapon that could wipe out a small town in seconds needed little advance intelligence.

<*Diela,*> said Berenice. <*Set up the deadlamp rig the second you have it. I want to know when one of those abominations is within four miles of us.*>

<*Understood, Capo,*> said Diela. Though the girl was no longer nearby, her voice was still clear in the back of Berenice's mind.

She and Claudia returned to the main meeting chamber. A few of Malti's scrivers and mercenaries were still loitering about, but the governor himself wasn't present.

"The governor will be back shortly," said a member of the retinue. "He has asked that you wait here in the meantime."

Claudia leaned up against the big table with the maps, her arms crossed. <*If Tevanne actually sends a deadlamp,*> she said, <*just what in the hell are we going to do? Shriekers won't even make a dent in it—if one actually manages to hit it, that is.*>

<*My first plan is to be gone before it ever gets here,*> said Berenice.

<*And if we are here?*>

<*Clef,*> answered Berenice simply.

Claudia stared. <*What the hell? Ber, we only pulled that off once!*>

<*Which means it's possible,*> said Berenice. <*So we can do it agai—*>

A long, awful shriek echoed through the keep.

The meeting chamber went totally still. Berenice and Claudia snapped to attention. Both of them looked at the door leading back to the young man's private quarters.

"Wh-What was that?" asked one of the scrivers nervously. "It sounded like a . . . a . . ."

The two women looked at each other.

<*It came from . . .*> said Claudia.

<*From there, absolutely,*> said Berenice.

They sprinted to the door, flung it open, and ran down the passageway.

When they came to the young man's room, they found nearly a dozen mercenaries standing at the open door, staring in with astonished faces. Despite being a head shorter than most of them, Berenice pushed past and peered in.

The soiled bed was empty. Malti and the woman who had been tending to his son now lay on the floor, their throats slashed, the carpet soaking with blood.

Berenice stared at the governor. The scrived rapier was missing from his side. He was still alive, but only barely, the blood weakly pumping from a tremendous gash in his throat. He raised his hand to Berenice, his gaze full of an awful sadness, but then his hand fell, and his eyes went dull.

"Shit," said Berenice aloud. "Shit, shit, shit."

<*Blood,*> said Claudia's voice. <*On the floor here.*>

Berenice pushed back past the crowd of mercenaries and joined her in the passageway. Claudia was peering at the splashes and pointed down the hall. <*He went that way. Or it did.*>

<*Vittorio, Diela,*> Berenice said. <*Confirm you're aware of this development.*>

<*Confirmed, Capo,*> said Vittorio. His voice was still clear, but it was fainter now—an effect of the distance between them.

<*Take however fast you're goddamn moving,*> she said. <*And double it. Tevanne must be close.*>

<*Confirmed, Capo,*> said Diela, though her voice shook.

Berenice reached into the side of her boot and pulled out one of the three purge sticks stored there. It was a tiny thing, looking more like a sculptor's tool than a weapon, but Claudia did the same, holding hers aloft like a dagger. Then they sprinted off into the dark little passageways, following the dots of blood on the floor.

<*Tevanne was in him,*> said Claudia as they ran. <*Using him. It really was present.*>

<*And it still is,*> said Berenice. <*We have to catch it before it does something else to weaken the city.*>

They turned left, then right, then left again. The clatter of the keep faded.

<*So Tevanne is close,*> said Claudia, <*but . . . it's got to be only a small force nearby, right? Less than a dozen hosts? It can't be, like, a whole scrumming army hiding behind some hilltop, right?*>

<*Claudia,*> she said, <*I've no idea.*>

Another turn, then another. Then they stopped: there was a sound echoing down one of the nearby passageways, a soft, awkward shuffling.

<*This is about when,*> said Claudia, <*I wish we had real weapons. And not, you know, the tiniest knives on earth.*>

<*I'm guessing if we called our espringals now, they'd never get to us?*> said Berenice.

Claudia shook her head. <*We have to be in line of sight. There's no chance they'd get through all these passageways.*>

They came to a corner. The shuffling sounded very loud now, yet it was joined by a soft, constant scrape, like a needle down a blackboard. Berenice pressed her back to the wall, then peeked around the corner.

There was a figure shuffling down the hallway, limping away from them in an awkward, arthritic fashion. It was difficult to see—the light was poor, and there was a stained-glass window at the far end of the passageway—but she thought she could spy a rapier dangling from the person's hand as they moved, its tip dragging along the floor behind them.

Berenice narrowed her eyes, thinking.

<*Claudia,*> she said. <*Tell me we upgraded our armor to take a blow from a scrived rapier.*>

<From a regular Morsini blade?> said Claudia. *<Sure. But . . . shit, I wouldn't advise trying i—>*

Berenice stepped into the hallway, purge stick raised in her right hand like a dagger, and followed the figure.

The figure stopped moving, then slowly turned. Their face was impossible to make out in the low light, but she could tell they were watching her.

Berenice kept advancing, her left forearm raised with its vambrace out to catch any blows, the purge stick raised high in her right hand.

Still, the figure didn't move. Yet once she was within ten feet of it, it finally hunched low, and whispered: "*Ssaaanciaa . . .* "

Berenice's skin crawled. *<Scrumming hell,>* she whispered.

<I'm behind you,> said Claudia. *<But I'm keeping my distance.>*

Berenice kept advancing, eyes fixed on the rapier dangling from the thing's hand. She had fought hosts before, and knew they often seemed lost and stupid—but that was only when the thing that controlled them wasn't devoting any thought to them. When Tevanne wished, its hosts could move lightning-quick.

Yet this one just watched her, standing frozen as she slowly approached . . .

And then it sprang.

The rapier flashed forward, hurtling at her neck. The host's leap was awkward, sacrificing accuracy and protection for speed, and Berenice barely managed to swat the blade away with her vambrace. The blade clipped the wall of the passageway, leaving a deep slash across the stones.

Berenice stabbed out with the purge stick, but the host was already withdrawing, leaping away and stumbling down the passageway toward the window. Then its blade licked out again, slicing down at her feet. She danced back, watching as the bloody sword tip flickered through the air, aware that if she had been only the slightest bit slower the sword would have slashed through the top of her foot.

It's fast, she thought. *Goddamn, it's fast.*

Again, the host darted forward, its bizarre lurching difficult to track. The rapier came up, this time stabbing toward her shoulder, but she raised her left arm in time to lift the blade and send it glancing over the top of her helmet. But the movement had opened her up, and she knew it—and so did the host: it thrust its sword forward, jabbing toward her throat, and she only managed to survive by stumbling back and batting it down with her right vambrace. The tip of the sword scraped across the left breast of her armor, carving a deep gouge.

Close, far too close.

The host backed away farther. They were now close enough to the window that Berenice could see it: the pale, starved face of the boy stared at her, its mouth slack and open, its chin still stained with porridge and its hands and thighs splashed with blood. The open sore on the right side of its head was leaking pus. Its eyes lingered on Berenice, then looked up over her shoulder at Claudia behind her.

Then it seemed to make a decision.

The host stood up straight, turned its rapier around, and raised it to plunge into its stomach.

But Berenice had expected this. She dove forward, grabbed it by its skinny wrists, and slammed its knuckles into the wall. It dropped the rapier, but not before carving a shallow slash through the top of the boy's belly, just below his sternum.

The host surged forward with shocking strength, snapping at her face with the boy's yellowed teeth. She fell backward, barely keeping it away.

"Now!" screamed Berenice.

Claudia leapt over her, purge stick raised, and stabbed it into the boy's shoulder. She twisted the knife and snapped the blade off inside him, then stepped back.

The host gasped, coughed, and choked. Then his face went gray, and faint lines appeared about his nose and eyes, like he was aging one year in one second.

Then there was a *hiss* from the right side of its head, and water began dribbling out of the open sore, and he collapsed, and was still, the gash on his belly leaking blood.

"Scrumming hell," panted Berenice. "Scrumming *hell* . . ."

"Yeah," gasped Claudia. "So. This a trap?"

"Absolutely," said Berenice. She felt the deep scrape on the side of her helmet, then the one on the breast of her cuirass. "It's just not one I thought would be springing *quite* so fast . . ."

She heaved the boy off of her, then stood and looked down at him. The unearthly aging he'd undergone had not faded. The effect was very slight, but it was noticeable—and the sight of it pained her.

She touched his face, her fingers tracing over the lines about his eyes, and his mouth, and his salt-and-pepper hair. *Tevanne learned from us,* she thought. *It's only fair that we learn from it as well.* But she knew she was only trying to convince herself.

<*Ber, we have other things to worry about,*> said Claudia. <*Vittorio? What's the situation on the walls?*>

<*There's movement,*> said his voice. He sounded frightened—unusual for him. <*About ten, maybe twenty miles out.*>

<*Movement? How many hosts has it sent?*> asked Berenice.

<*Lots. Thousands, maybe.*>

Berenice and Claudia stared at each other in disbelief.

<*I was joking about the army behind the hilltop . . .* > said Claudia faintly.

<*Let me path to you, Vittorio,*> said Berenice. <*And see.*>

<*Will do, Capo.*>

Berenice shut her eyes and took a breath. She'd done this countless times, but it always took a while to remember how.

She focused, felt him out . . .

And flexed.

Then she felt it. She felt the path to him, the space between them, the swell of Vittorio's thoughts like the side of a mountain, and there within some handholds for her to grasp, and clutch close, and see . . .

Twisting cedars against a bright-blue sky.

Pale sand and crumbling stone, a white vista like a smear of pale paint on a gray canvas.

And then . . .

She was with him. She *was* Vittorio, to a certain degree: she was within him, a part of him, peering out of his eyes, feeling what he felt, knowing what he knew. There was, as always, that odd transitional moment as her mind switched to experiencing two sets of sensations at once, along with all his subconscious processes that came with it: the sweat on his cheek, the ache in his elbow from a wound he'd sustained long ago, and the discomfit of his genitals, shrunken with anxiety and pressed against his trousers.

Then his primary experiences came pouring into her, what he was directly seeing and doing. Vittorio was peering through a spyglass at a mountain range just to the north—and there, pouring through a pass just between two peaks, was a tremendous force. It had to be five thousand hosts, if not more, and she could see artillery moving behind them—and moving fast, at that.

Berenice released the path to Vittorio and sat in the passageway, astonished.

<*What the hell!*> she said. <*How did Tevanne cross the* entire peninsula *in what must have been less than an hour?*>

<*No idea, Capo,*> said Vittorio. <*Are we still going to get these refugees out of here? Because they're, ah, panicking, understandably enough.*>

<*Yes!*> snapped Berenice. <*But I need to get to the walls to figure out how!*>

She looked up at the window, thinking. Then she grabbed the boy's bloody rapier, used it to smash out the stained glass, and peered out.

They were facing north, toward where Vittorio was stationed, which was good. She craned her head out and saw the stairs they'd ascended not more than an hour ago, just east along the face of the fortress.

Which means my espringal should be stored somewhere right over there, she thought.

She looked back at Claudia. <*Get this boy out of here. Then get your own weapon and meet me at the walls.*>

<*Standard deadlamp formation?*> asked Claudia weakly.

<*Yes. Put as much distance between us as possible.*> She slapped the plate on her right pauldron. <*Because God knows what's going to happen.*>

There was a clacking, clattering sound from the east—and then, like a brushball blown along a desert path, her espringal came skittering across the face of the keep to her.

It was a very simple adhesive scriving that made this happen: the plate she'd just activated on her right pauldron was scrived to believe it occupied the same space as a plate on her espringal—and when activated, the two tried to merge, very fast, no matter how far apart they happened to be.

She snatched it out of the air as it came close, then attached her espringal to her left vambrace, securing it tightly until her weapon and her armor were, in function, all one unit. Then she checked to make sure the line-shot ammunition was loaded correctly, raised the espringal to her shoulder, and took aim at the outermost walls.

This is not, she thought, *how I wanted things to go today.*

She fired. She watched as the line shot hurtled out over the city, struck the walls of the fortress in the distance, and adhered.

Then its mate came to life within her espringal, and her weapon ripped her forward through the air, and she flew.

<*Hey, uh, kid?*> asked Clef.

Sancia paused as she entered the cockpit of the massive merchant house galleon. <*Yeah, Clef?*>

<*Do you think negotiations with the governor would ever involve, uh, Berenice flying through the air?*>

Sancia craned her head down to peer at the fortress approaching atop the coast. <*Uh, hell no? Why?*>

<*Because Berenice just flew down from the keep to what I think are the outer walls of the fortress. I'm not at an angle to see, but . . .* >

<*Shit,*> said Sancia. <*Something's wrong.*> She thought about what to do, then eyed the low coasts just north of the fortress and spied a shallow dip in the seaside hills. <*Get there, to that very spot, as fast as you can.*>

<*Why there?*> asked Clef.

<*There's a problem, either inside the fortress or outside of it. That will give us the angle we need to fire on either—and we'll be close enough to twin with Ber and her team so they can tell us what the hell is going on.*>

Sancia's stomach swooped uncomfortably as Clef rotated the giant ship and made for the coast. <*Hold on,*> he said. <*And I'll try not to run our stupid asses aground.*>

Berenice clenched her teeth hard enough to make her jaw hurt as she was ripped forward through the air, zipping over the city like a shorehawk after a mouse. She could feel the line shot pulling her by her armor, and she pulled against it while trying to keep track of her approach, all of Grattiara a blur of gray and sandy yellow below her.

I've done this dozens of times, she thought, *but I'll never, ever get used to it.*

A line shot was an adaptation of a much cruder scrived rig from their campo days. Once Sancia had zipped about through the towers and walls of Old Tevanne using altered construction scrivings, which asserted that two surfaces were one, and thus demanded that the two come together—usually at blinding speeds. When one half was attached to Sancia, she'd been pulled along with it: essentially the same method that had pulled Berenice's espringal to her mere seconds ago.

Yet this method had always been extraordinarily dangerous when transporting human beings, often resulting in fractured bones and dislocated joints. So Berenice and Sancia had applied a safeguard to it: upon drawing within two dozen feet of each other, the two halves of the line shot would grow increasingly confused about where the other half was—meaning they would gently decelerate.

When she grew within twenty feet of the walls, Berenice felt a slackening in her armor as her espringal stopped hauling her along at the same rapid clip. Her acceleration shifted into a steady glide, and she gracefully floated toward the surface of the walls like a puff-flower seed upon the winds, and lifted her feet.

She watched as the walls flew up to her. *I'm coming in low. Shit.*

The soles of her boots struck the surface of the walls, the impact reverberating up her knees and into her hips, and she slapped a switch on the side of her harness at her left thigh and crouched. Then she disabled the line shot, ejecting the remaining half from her espringal—the half immediately flew to its mate on the wall and attached itself with a dull *plunk*—and then she hung there, the soles of her boots sticking to the walls of Grattiara just below the parapets.

There was a creak in her armor about her legs as it strained to hold her weight. She braced herself—she'd designed her armor specifically to bear her weight and avoid straining her ankles—yet it held.

The soldiers on the walls—having been understandably absorbed by the sight of Tevanni forces in the distance—all leapt in fright when they realized an armored woman was stuck to the bricks just behind and below them. Some even screamed aloud.

<*Diela!*> Berenice said. <*Give me a hand!*>

<*Coming, Capo!*> cried Diela. <*Coming!*>

Diela scrambled across the walls to her, reached down, and grabbed Berenice's right hand. Berenice turned off the scrivings that adhered her boots to the walls, Diela pulled up, and Berenice heaved herself up to the parapet.

<*Not the most graceful mount,*> gasped Berenice. <*But it'll do.*> She stood, pulled her spyglass out, and studied the landscape beyond.

"Oh, shit," she said weakly.

At a glance, the situation was unspeakably dire. The refugee camps extended about two miles out from the walls of Grattiara in any given direction; past that was about two or three more miles of rocky scrub; and then, about five miles past that to the north, the enormous Tevanni force was pouring through a narrow mountain pass.

Like all Tevanni forces, it looked like a giant, rambling mess: there were no consistent colors, no banners, no formations of any kind, just an enormous, shambling throng of armed people staggering forward. It would have appeared slapdash at a distance—and Berenice knew many fallen generals had mistaken it for such—but she was aware that in an instant the hosts could snap into formations and begin reacting like a singular, liquid mass in response to all threats at once, dancing around attackers before swallowing them whole.

The world was filling up with screams—from the refugees, from the soldiers, from the Grattiaran citizens. Berenice tried to think. None of this seemed possible. The very idea that such an army could just manifest instantly was mind-boggling.

But she knew that, however this force had appeared here, it was still a Tevanni force; and those behaved in specific, predictable ways.

<*All right,*> she said. <*Listen—I am not asking you to fend off an entire Tevanni army numbering in the thousands.*>

<*Some good news, at least,*> muttered Vittorio.

<*What we're going to do is dig in, fend off their advance movements,*

and defend the refugees until Sancia and the Keyship *get close,*> said Berenice. <*Clef will be able to take care of most of their forces.*>

<*Are we sure Sancia is aware of our situation?*> asked Diela.

<*If she isn't yet,*> said Berenice, <*then the sound of all the explosions we're about to set off will give her an idea. We know what's coming first. Get your pounders ready. Diela—where's the cache?*>

Diela pointed. Yet as she did, the image of the cache appeared in Berenice's mind, the memory of moving it and placing it crystallizing in her thoughts like she'd done it herself.

<*Over there, Capo,*> said Diela.

<*Ah,*> said Berenice, faintly surprised. <*Yes. Thank you, Diela.*>

The three of them converged on the cache, opened it, and began to unload its contents. The first layer contained more high-powered espringals, but these were slightly different: they could be set up at a stand that could point them in any direction, and they could be fired remotely.

<*Volleys work best,*> said Berenice. <*Set them up in rows of three by three along the walls, pointing out over the refugees. Spread out to give as much coverage as possible.*> Then she carefully opened the last compartment in the cache. Its contents did not look immediately interesting—it appeared to contain about fifty big metal canisters, all slightly smaller than a man's boot—but she unloaded them with the utmost caution. <*And try not to drop any of the pounders as you load them,*> she said. <*We worked on these so they wouldn't go off quite so easily—but if one does, it'll deafen you at least . . . or blast you clear off the walls.*>

They got to work, scurrying to set up the layers of remote defenses along the walls. None of the Grattiaran soldiers tried to stop them. Most of them seemed to have abandoned their posts out of sheer terror, and Berenice found she couldn't blame them.

<*Capo,*> said Vittorio warily, <*the sky's buzzing about a mile out. Plating lamps are close.*>

<*Diela,*> said Berenice, setting her final espringal in its stand, <*how are you doing?*>

<*Done, Capo!*> she cried.

<*Then everyone get under cover,*> said Berenice. <*And get your triggers ready.*>

Berenice dashed into the nearest tower. One of the soldiers inside demanded, "Who the hell are you?" But he blanched when Berenice snapped, "Shut the hell up and stay down!" Then she turned and screamed out the open door, "Everyone get indoors if you can! Now, now, NOW!"

She hoped anyone who could hear had listened but didn't have time to check. She sidled up to one of the bolt slits in the tower. Then she heard the faint hissing as the lamps approached.

It always sounded like grasshoppers, she thought, thousands of them, chirping and leaping about in a field. The only reason they made any noise, she knew, was because of how many there were—otherwise a plating lamp was almost silent.

She leaned forward to look out the bolt slit in the tower walls. She couldn't see any of the lamps, not from this angle—yet then she spied their shadows crisscrossing the refugee camps beyond the walls, like vultures circling their prey.

<*When you see the shadows, fire!*> said Berenice.

She pulled her triggers, one after another. She covered her ears, and then . . .

The sky seemed to break open.

"Pounders" were not especially advanced scriving weapons, but they did their job well. They were scrived canisters that could be fired from a common espringal and had been commanded to believe they contained far more air than they actually did. When they rose to a certain height—say, about the height most of Tevanne's plating lanterns tended to float at—they then suddenly believed the amount of air within them had reached a critical point, and they burst apart with a blistering, concussive force.

The shockwave from Berenice's volley of pounders detonating all at once was so intense it made the dust on the floor shake. She heard sibling eruptions from farther down the fortress walls as Diela and Vittorio's volleys blasted away in the atmosphere above them. Then the skies about the towers suddenly rained with tattered plating lanterns, like apricots falling from a tree in a storm. They thudded into the sandy soil or bounced off the walls with a brittle *clank,* one after another after another, hundreds if not thousands.

Berenice grinned mercilessly. She knew, of course, that losing a flock of plating lanterns meant nothing to Tevanne. *But we've got problems enough,* she thought, *without Tevanne turning every refugee and soldier in this fortress into a host. I'll take my wins where I can get them.*

<*When they stop falling,*> she said to her team, <*reload. Because it's sure to send another swarm.*>

<*Confirmed, Capo,*> said Vittorio.

She crouched at the door to the tower, peering along the walls as the sky rained lanterns. She eyed the skies. When she deemed it safe, she dashed out and hurried to reload her espringals. <*Claudia,*> she said. <*What's your situation?*>

<*Getting set up in the foremost tower, Capo,*> said Claudia.

Berenice slotted another pounder into an espringal—then she heard a harsh *plink,* and something slammed into her helmet. She didn't even react, knowing it was one of Tevanne's plates.

"Rotten little bastards," she muttered.

Then she heard screams and looked up. A Grattiaran soldier was sprinting up the walls to her, shrieking, "What's happening! My God, my God, what's happe—"

He was about six feet from her when there was a wet *smack* and his shoulder went dark with blood. He fell to his knees, his face suddenly slack; then he twitched curiously, choking; and then his dull, thoughtless eyes fixed on Berenice, and his hand moved to his rapier at his side.

"Not today," said Berenice. She slid a purge stick from her boot, stabbed it into his chest, snapped it off, then darted back into the shelter of the tower without looking back at him. She fired her volley, and once more the sky above seemed to break asunder.

<*Ready, Capo,*> said Claudia's voice.

Berenice felt for the plate lodged in her helmet, ripped it out, dropped it on the floor, and stomped on it. <*Let me see, please,*> she asked.

<*Come see,*> said Claudia.

Berenice leaned against the wall, shut her eyes, and felt out to Claudia, feeling the distance between them, the swell and fade of her thoughts . . .

And then she was inside her, watching the world from behind Claudia's eyes: she was crouching at a bolt slot in the highest tower and peering through a spyglass at the enemy—but this was a very unusual spyglass, for a very unusual job.

Claudia had maintained a close hand in the development of the immensely powerful and long-range espringals Giva used; and though she'd trained the other team members ably, no one could quite make the weapons perform miracles like Claudia. Especially not the bigger prototypes, which were nearly four or five feet long and had a spyglass affixed to their stocks, allowing you to hit targets over a mile away.

Claudia's spyglass was currently fixed on the far ranks of the Tevanni host, where nearly two dozen cart-shaped contraptions were trundling out of the mountain pass. <*Artillery units,*> she said. <*Tevanni shriekers. Not good.*>

<*What's the range on them?*> whispered Berenice.

<*We clocked the last ones at six miles. My espringal's powerful, but it's not that powerful. They'll be able to hit us in less than ten minutes, I'd say.*>

Berenice asked Claudia to peer east, then south, trying to see the ocean and spy some hint of the *Keyship,* but her angle was wrong and she could see nothing but wall.

Come on, San, she thought. *Just come on . . .*

<*Ber?*> asked Claudia. <*What do you want me to do, here?*>

<*One moment,*> she said. Then she focused, looking through Claudia's eyes at the Tevanni force as it stolidly marched through the scrub.

Then Berenice had an idea—*The scrub.*

<*Did you bring the flare bolts?*> she asked.

<*Yeah,*> said Claudia. <*You . . . You want me to set fire to the scrubland around there? If the fire spreads to here, that's not going to help these people.*>

<*But the smoke will make it a lot harder for Tevanne to aim its artillery,*> said Berenice. <*And that's worse than a fire.*>

<*Fair enough,*> said Claudia. She went about unloading her normal bolts and loading in the flare ammunition. <*They're still going to shoot at us, you know.*>

<*Yes. But they won't be as accurate. We'll take what we can get.*>

Claudia peered back through the sights at the brush. She fired once, twice, three times into one hilltop, then watched with satisfaction as the scrub there smoked, flickered, and burst into flame.

<*Make it a straight line, like a curtain,*> said Berenice.

<*You act like I've never started a giant wildfire before,*> said Claudia.

She fired more bolts, and soon a massive, gray-white cloud of smoke was boiling up from the brush, totally obscuring the advancing force.

<*Diela?*> asked Berenice. <*While that's going . . .* >

<*No deadlamp yet, ma'am,*> the girl said.

<*Can I see myself?*> asked Berenice. <*Just to be sure.*>

<*Yes, Capo,*> said Diela, with the slightest trace of reluctance.

Berenice focused her thoughts. As always, finding and pathing to Diela was as easy as a dream—though she was a brand-new recruit, the girl was a natural at this—and within seconds Berenice was peering out from Diela's perspective. She rejoiced, just for a moment, in the sensation of inhabiting such a *young* body, so pliable and capable and resilient.

She peered through Diela's eyes at the little rig placed on the wall before her. It resembled a small spinning top, hanging from a curved wire so it rotated on a black plate—yet the top was floating very slightly, with a sliver of sunlight visible between the top's bottom tip and the face of the plate.

Berenice had designed this rig herself. The top was inordinately sensitive to deep changes in reality: severe, fundamental, ongoing edits to creation. The faster it spun, and the higher it floated, then the closer the source of these edits was to you. If it floated so high it touched the wire it hung from, the source of the edits was directly above you—but if that was the case, you were probably already dead. If "dead" was even the right word for it.

<*I wasn't wrong, Capo,*> Diela said. <*And I set it up proper. There are no deadlamps yet.*>

<*I see that,*> said Berenice. <*Thank you, Diela. I just had to be su—*>

Then the air lit up with screams—but these were very unusual. High-pitched, warbling, inhuman screams.

Berenice released the path to Diela, and screamed, "*Get down!*" to anyone who might be around to hear.

She peered through the bolt slit, watching as holes suddenly appeared in the roiling veil of smoke—made, of course, by the volley of shriekers pouring through from the Tevanni position. She did not bother to cover her head or neck. *After all,* she thought, *if one of those lands anywhere near me, they'll find my head on one side of the fort and my neck on the other.*

The white-hot spears of metal poured over Grattiara. She counted nearly two dozen of them before giving up. Most went wild, slamming into the ground beyond the refugee camp; others overshot the fortress entirely and plummeted into the sea; but some hit their mark, crashing into the fortress walls or arcing down into the city or—worst of all—ripping through the refugee camp as the helpless people screamed.

Dust and bits of stone rained on the tower walls. Some poured through the bolt slits about Berenice, narrow blades of shrapnel sloshing in on her left and right.

Sons of bitches, thought Berenice. *You sons of bitches . . .*

<*Counting four hits, Capo,*> said Vittorio's voice faintly. <*Could have been a lot worse.*>

<*Yes,*> said Berenice. <*But there's a lot more comi—*>

Another burst of inhuman screams. More shriekers poured through the spreading wall of smoke; these seemed even wilder, most overshooting the city entirely.

<*What the hell?*> said Claudia, amused. <*What are they shooting at?*>

She got her answer when one shrieker slammed into the top-right face of the governor's keep—and tore right through it, punching out the other side to go twisting into the walls on the southern face of the fortress.

Berenice watched in stunned horror as the keep held together for a handful of seconds; and then, very slowly, the right half of the structure totally collapsed.

<*Shit,*> said Claudia weakly. <*Well. I hope they got everyone out of there.*>

<*I'm more worried about the walls, Capo,*> said Diela. Her voice quaked. <*Ah, though the keep's defenses were very out of date, they were surely more advanced than the walls of the fortress . . . like the ones we're situated on right now.*>

Another burst of screaming. More shriekers rained down on the fortress city. Many tore through the outer walls, then the inner walls, then landed amidst the homes of the city, which promptly burst into flames.

Berenice stared in horror as the fires erupted deep within the city. She'd never thought Tevanne could get so accurate so quickly.

It must have successfully plated enough hosts here, she thought faintly. *They're sending what they're seeing back to Tevanne, helping it target.*

She debated trying to track down the hosts, to purge them or kill them to cut off Tevanne's spies; but she knew it would be too hard, take too long, and Tevanne had likely seen enough already.

All these people are going to die here, she thought. *And I won't ever see San again. Not ever again.*

Another burst of screams, another string of earth-shaping eruptions. A section of the western wall collapsed like it was made of straw. The air danced with dust, and the wind grew hot.

What the hell are we going to do? What the hell are we going to d—

Then a voice—faint, but very clear: <*Ber! Ber! BER!*>

She sat up, listening to the words coalescing in the back of her mind. <*Sancia?*> she said.

<*Yes!*> snapped her wife. <*What the* hell *is going on?*>

Berenice sat on the wall, head spinning, and wondered how to express in words that a Tevanni army had seemingly manifested out of nowhere and was now tearing through the aged defenses of Grattiara like a sandmink through a chicken coop.

Then she realized there were easier ways of doing this.

She closed her eyes. <*San,*> she whispered. <*Path to me. That's fastest.*>

<*Yes,*> said Sancia. <*One second . . .* >

Berenice took a deep breath in, and then her mind filled up with Sancia's thoughts.

Of all the phenomena that had developed since the advent of twinning minds, "pathing" was the hardest to define.

On the surface, it seemed simple enough. Much like how longtime colleagues—or spouses, or friends, or roommates, and so on—might naturally come to understand one another's perspectives and styles of thinking, "pathing" among twinned people did the same.

It simply took things one step further, so rather than just using your accumulated experiences with your colleague or friend to predict what they might do, you felt their choices happening *as they occurred,* like a memory of the present abruptly manifesting in your mind.

The more time you spent with someone, and the more your relationship developed, the closer and deeper you could path to them. Berenice's team had trained specifically to enable this, building up trust and consent until any member could slip behind the eyes of another and watch the world unfold, allowing information and insights to be shared instantly despite being physically separated by yards or miles.

But training could only take you so far. At some point you could only path deeper with someone if your relationship was established, and genuine. When you pathed to someone like that—someone you knew, someone you loved—the experience was very different.

Some compared it to remembering a wonderful dream you'd had several nights ago; others compared it to waking up from a deep sleep. But Berenice had always said it felt like returning to a beloved place you hadn't visited in a very long time, where the instant you passed through the threshold and smelled those familiar aromas and felt the rippled wooden floors under your bare feet, and saw the dust motes dancing in the sunbeams, all the thousands of memories you'd built up in this place blossomed at once.

Even now, as the siege closed in around Grattiara, this was what it felt like for Berenice to path to her wife: a sudden, uncontrolled eruption of joy, of clarity, and reassurance as she tumbled into Sancia's consciousness, this shadowy, shifty, riotous world of impulse and reaction, everything filthy and bawdy and boisterous. In many ways she was Berenice's total opposite—and this, perhaps, was why Berenice loved her so much.

I know who I am, she thought as her wife's thoughts poured into hers, *because I know you.*

<*Enough sentiment, girl!*> snapped Sancia. <*Let me see what you see.*>

Because they were pathed so close, they instantly browsed all the memories of what had occurred in the other's absence, hours of information exchanged in a fraction of a second. There was little for Berenice to absorb—Sancia had mostly just been impatiently waiting in the *Keyship*—but Sancia saw much, from what had happened to the governor's son to the first volley of shriekers.

<*Another Shorefall Night,*> whispered Sancia in horror. <*All these people trapped in one place as Tevanne burns the world down around them . . .*>

<*Yes,*> said Berenice.

<*How the hell did it get here so fast? How did it make a whole army show up out of nowhere?*>

<*I've no idea,*> said Berenice.

Berenice felt Sancia consciously trying to triangulate the positions of all that Berenice had seen, all she could remember, estimating the distance between Berenice and the *Keyship,* and Berenice and the Tevanni force in the distance . . .

<*Hold tight, love,*> whispered Sancia's voice. <*We'll get you out of this.*>

Then the path faded, and the sensation and closeness of Sancia vanished, and Berenice was crouching in the tower wall, gasping for breath among the smoke and the dust.

<*Clef!*> said Sancia's voice. <*Fire sinkers north-northwest, sinking to strike at—*>

<*At six to six-and-a-half miles inland,*> said Clef's voice. <*Yeah, yeah, yeah. Got it.*>

And then the air lit up with screams again—but these came from another direction, from the east, behind one of the coastal hills where the *Keyship* was positioned.

Berenice sprang to one of the bolt slits in the tower and watched as a tremendous volley of shriekers rose up from the sea below, arced into the sky, and vanished behind the curtain of wildfire smoke. Then another volley of shriekers raced upward, then another, and another.

Berenice wondered how accurate their estimations had been. "Sinkers" were a different type of shrieker, one that was designed to rise up and then, at the apex of its parabola, suddenly believe it was heavier—either by a little or a lot, based on the angle—and sink back down to the earth to strike a specific target.

It was an imprecise form of warfare, and most people were bad at conducting it. But Clef had always been uncannily accurate when firing sinkers from the *Keyship*—likely because, of course, Clef was not a person. Berenice had always known this, of course, but it felt different to know this while Clef was controlling a merchant house galleon nearly a thousand feet long that was stocked with enough ammunition to destroy a small island.

Booms and crashes echoed from behind the distant smoke, one after another, a rolling thunder sweeping up the road to the mountain pass that went on and on, until it finally tapered to an end.

Berenice felt her team holding their breath, peering north into the wall of smoke, waiting to see. Then the wind changed, ever so slightly, thinning out the smoke.

They could just make out a blackened, burning stretch of scrubland about six miles out—almost exactly where the Tevanni artillery had just been positioned at the feet of the mountains.

<*Yes!*> cried Vittorio. <*Yes, yes, yes!*>

<*Thank God,*> sighed Claudia. <*Thank God almighty . . .* >

<*Yes,*> said Berenice faintly. <*That appears to have been perfectly placed.*>

<*You're not out of danger yet,*> said Sancia. <*There's still a huge number of hosts advancing on the city. But the artillery shouldn't be a concern for a bit. Ber—you seen any deads yet?*>

<*No deadlamps yet, Sancia,*> piped up Diela.

<*But one's got to be coming,*> said Berenice. She shut her eyes, picturing the layout of the city, the bay, and the wildfires beyond. <*San, Clef—send the shallops to the city now. We're going to open up the gates and get these people into the city and down to the piers as fast as we can. Meanwhile, get the* Keyship *moving. It's going to be a sitting target for a deadlamp. Just make sure to stay in twinning range. Diela?*>

<*Here, Capo,*> said the girl.

<*You open the gates, but make sure to monitor your deadlamp rig. Vittorio—get situated over the gates and shout for everyone to come in single file in an orderly fashion, and that anyone pushing will be shot dead on the spot.*>

<*Wow,*> said Vittorio. <*Are you serious?*>

<*Seriously tell them that, yes, but don't actually do it!*> said Berenice. <*I just don't want half these people trampled to death.*>

<*This is all fun stuff, Ber,*> said Clef. <*Death threats, trampling, and so on. But when the deadlamp comes . . . What are we going to do? And please don't say we're going to try the same mad shit as last time.*>

<*We are indeed going to try the same mad shit as last time,*> said Berenice. <*And this is not up for debate.*>

Clef groaned. <*Aw, hell.*>

Sancia, Berenice noticed, stayed silent—but she felt a curious disapproval welling up in her wife's thoughts. It troubled her, but she knew now wasn't the time to discuss it, especially not while her whole team could hear.

<*Claudia?*> asked Berenice.

<*Here, Capo,*> said Claudia.

<*Withdraw from the outer walls,*> said Berenice. <*Get on the western side of the city, and get set up. The deadlamp will likely make straight for the* Keyship, *on the western side of the fortress. Just make sure you have good line of sight north.*>

<*Confirmed, Ber,*> said Claudia. She sighed. <*There's a gallery alongside the piers that should work well.*>

<*Good. Load a pathplate to Clef for when the lamp comes. We'll shoot it at the lamp, and he should be able to use that connection to take it over. I'll take up a position on the rooftops below. Any questions?*>

There was a tense, wearied silence.

<*Then let's move,*> said Berenice.

She unloaded the standard bolts from her espringal, loaded in another line shot, then ran outside and scanned the rooftops within the fortress. She spied a bartizan at the corner of one of the inner walls and thought it a good spot, sighted it with her espringal, and fired.

The line shot struck home, and again Berenice was ripped forward, speeding over the rooftops of the fortress city.

<*Are you sure you want to try this?*> whispered Sancia's voice in her mind.

<*Tevanne is a rig,*> said Berenice as she flew. <*We can use it. Break it.*>

<*But Tevanne learns,*> said Sancia. <*You and Clef did this once before. It'll remember. It'll expect it.*>

<*Are you worried about me?*> said Berenice. A flash of an image in her mind—a golden key, nestled up against the lexicon of the *Keyship.* <*Or someone else?*>

<*I'm worried about you both. About those people. About scrumming everybody!*>

Berenice raised her boots as she decelerated, pressed them to the side of the bartizan, and turned on the adhesive plates so she hung there like a whitenose bat.

<*Isn't this what you would do, my love?*> asked Berenice. <*Acrobatics and daredevil rigs, and swooping in with Clef?*>

<*That's true,*> said Sancia, slightly sullen. <*But look where all that got us.*>

Berenice heard Vittorio shouting. She looked back to see the outer gates open and the hundreds of refugees come pouring through. She couldn't hear what he was screaming, but it must have been enough to scare them into submission: though many were sobbing in terror, they were walking carefully all in a line, like children playing a game of hold-the-rope.

It's going well, she told herself. *We're getting them out, we're going to get them out . . .*

Then Diela's voice spoke up, quavering: <*Capo?*>

Berenice knew just from the tone of her voice. <*It's here.*>

<*Yes.*>

<*Let me path to you.*>

She shut her eyes, and in a flash she was within Diela, crouched on the walls above the people streaming through the gates, staring at the detector rig planted on the stone.

The little black top was now floating an inch off the plate.

Every quarter inch, thought Berenice, *is another mile it's closer . . .*

She watched as the top spun higher and higher, and the gap between the plate and the top grew and grew.

Berenice released the path to Diela. She opened her eyes and took a slow breath in.

Scrumming hell, she thought. *Here we go.*

2

Berenice stared at the smoky skies to the north. Her stomach curdled, her heart fluttered, and the screams of the refugees faded until the siege was a distant moan. She just watched, unmoving and frozen as she hung from the wall.

Here it comes, she thought. *Here it comes, here it comes . . .*

At first she saw nothing—then there was a flicker in the distant smoke, and something passed through.

For one brief, panicked moment, Berenice thought it was something man-shaped: a black figure, seated upon the very air, sailing across the sky. Her heart leapt, and she thought—*It's him! Oh God, it's him!*

But then she came to her senses, and saw it was not a man: rather, it was a small, dark blotch speeding across the horizon to them, like a tiny black cloud. Its approach was silent, serene, unnaturally perfect for an object in flight. Berenice felt her pulse rise just at the sight of it.

<*Oh my God,*> whispered Diela. <*Ohh my God . . .* >

<*Calm,*> said Berenice. <*Calm, calm. Everyone stay calm.*>

But she knew she was telling herself this as much as anyone else. How could one stay calm when such a thing neared you?

The appearance of the deadlamp, as always, was simple yet bizarre: it looked like a blank, dull brick of iron, suspended in the air, about fifty feet wide and long and nine feet tall. It had no windows, weapons, nor any visible interruption to its surface whatsoever: just a clean, bare, black rectangle with a vaguely metallic sheen to it, splitting through the skies.

The lamp sailed closer and closer. As it neared, the world suddenly felt thin, like there was some invisible, noxious fume on the winds.

Berenice felt terror twisting throughout her team. She couldn't blame them. She herself had only encountered deadlamps a handful of times, and each engagement had been horrific. Worse was the awareness that no one quite understood how they did what they did: despite years of effort, the deadlamps remained a mystery to even the best scriving experts in Giva.

<*Claudia?*> asked Berenice. <*What's your situation?*>

<*I don't have a shot,*> whispered Claudia. <*It's too far away, and even if it wasn't, it's moving too fast.*>

They watched as the deadlamp approached—not quite speeding toward them as much as falling through the sky to the city.

<*I'm sending the shallops to the piers now,*> whispered Clef. <*We'll start getting these people out of here. While that's happening, I'm handing over the* Keyship *to Sancia. Because, uh, I have a feeling I'm gonna be otherwise engaged—right?*>

<*Correct,*> said Berenice.

<*But I got to ask—what if your girl misses?*> asked Clef.

<*I don't miss, asshole,*> said Claudia.

<*Either way, we all have our own plates to you,*> said Berenice grudgingly. <*So we have spares . . . somewhat.*>

She reached into her pocket, just to confirm her own plate to Clef was in her pocket. Clef possessed tremendous powers over any scrived rig—but only when he was touching them. Yet because this small strip of metal now believed it was touching Clef, when Berenice applied this little piece to any scrived rig, Clef could then attack, tinker with, and overpower that rig through the connection.

Including a deadlamp.

Or at least, he'd done it once.

She watched as the black brick floated through the skies. <*Claudia?*> she asked.

<*Still don't have a shot,*> Claudia said. <*And . . . shit, it's slowing down.*>

<*It's what?*> said Berenice. She pulled out her own spyglass and studied the deadlamp.

Claudia was right: the deadlamp was slowing down—and then it came to a sharp stop nearly a mile and a half from the outskirts of the city walls. Then it hung there in the skies, nonchalantly denying all physics.

<*Too far for a shot,*> said Claudia. <*Shit. I thought it'd make straight for the* Keyship.>

<*What the hell is it doing?*> whispered Vittorio.

They watched the lamp. It continued doing nothing at all.

Then Clef whispered: <*It learned.*>

<*It what?*> said Berenice.

<*Last time at Piscio, we got desperate and shot the thing with a plate to me, yeah?*> he said. <*I froze it and you jumped aboard.*>

<*Right . . .* > said Berenice.

<*So Tevanne is keeping its distance,*> said Sancia grimly. <*Staying out of range, so we can't tinker with one of its deadlamps.*>

<*Right,*> said Clef.

Berenice knew exactly what Sancia was saying: *In other words, I was right.*

She narrowed her eye as she peered through the spyglass, staring at the big black brick floating in the sky.

<*So Tevanne's just going to let it float outside our range, and watch us evacuate all these people?*> asked Vittorio.

Then an idea began to form in Berenice's mind, and her belly filled up with a cold, awful horror.

<*No,*> she whispered. <*It's going to provoke us. Make* us *make the first move.*>

<*Provoke us how?*> asked Claudia.

But then, as if in answer, the deadlamp shifted.

It sped west, slicing through the skies, still so silent and queerly immaculate. It grew closer, perhaps a mile from the eastern walls . . . and then things began to change.

First Berenice felt the nausea in her belly, like a freezing knife was sliding into her intestines. Then that unsettling thinness to the world increased, and she had the mad, crawling feeling that all of reality was thin and insubstantial, like a hazy sketch wrought in chalk upon a greasy blackboard.

Nausea pooled into her belly and rose into her throat. She knew what this was: when a deadlamp awoke and began to exercise its privileges, the very fabric of reality became uncertain about what it was or wasn't.

A ghost of a memory: a man in black in the dark, his mask glinting in the weak light, his head slowly pivoting to a cocked position . . .

Don't think of him. Don't think of him . . .

"Oh no," she said.

She looked east, and saw the air there was shimmering strangely, quivering like desert sands under the brutal sun.

Then the eastern walls of the fortress disappeared.

Berenice got to see the damage only for a fleeting moment: the walls and the earth below them were just *gone,* a curiously, perfectly spherical chunk of the world itself deleted in an instant. She could see the crater left behind—if "crater" was even the right word, since no projectile could ever make an impact so immaculately rounded—and she could see the cleanly truncated edges of stones poking through the rounded earth, the colorful striae of layers upon layers of rock exposed like the innards of a pie after someone took a slice.

Berenice watched as tiny dots tumbled into the yawning aperture. She slowly realized they were people.

Then she realized that the fields beyond the walls were teeming with refugees, all pushing to enter the gates of Grattiara—and the deadlamp had surely just obliterated hundreds of them from reality.

"*No!*" she screamed aloud.

Then came the thunderclap: an enormous crash as all the air came pouring in to fill the gap left behind after the deadlamp had edited away a sizable chunk of the atmosphere as well. A wall of dust and soil rose up and washed over Grattiara. Berenice had to close her eyes and turn away.

The world shook around her. The whole city was screaming. She was faintly aware of her own head filling up with screams from her team, and Sancia and Clef in the *Keyship.*

<*Scrumming hell!*> screamed Vittorio. <*Scrumming holy hell!*>

<*Could fire on it!*> Sancia cried. <*Fire on it with shriekers!*>

<*It wouldn't goddamn do anything and you know it!*> said Clef. <*It'd wipe the shriekers out of existence before they hit—and if I missed, I'd hit those people below!*>

<*I don't have a shot,*> Claudia was saying, her tone shaken and dreamy. <*I don't . . . I don't have a shot. I could get close, get closer, but . . . it'd take time, Ber, time to get set up again . . . God, God . . .* >

The swirl of dust died about her, and she sat up and stared east at the deadlamp.

It slowly floated west—along the walls.

It's going to edit the entire refugee camp out of existence, she thought. *Destroy the walls piece by piece. Kill all the people we came here to save.*

She knew it took deadlamps a moment to recover after such a significant edit, but it wouldn't be long before it could make another alteration. She pulled her espringal out and glassed the walls, thinking.

It's far, but I can make it in two shots, maybe, she thought. *I can get over there in two line shots . . . And then maybe I can . . . I can load Clef's pathplate into my espringal and . . . and . . .*

Too much time, she knew. It could wipe out another hundred people by then.

Then a curious stillness fell over her mind. One she had felt before, when someone she was twinned with slowly made an awful choice—and then she realized who it was.

"No," she whispered.

She glassed the gates of Grattiara, and through the dust and smoke she saw Vittorio, calmly staring back at her from all the way across the city.

<*I can make it over there in one line shot, Capo,*> he said quietly. <*I'm close. I can make the shot.*>

<*Don't!*> snapped Claudia. <*The range on your espringal means you'd have to be on the closest stretch of wall to have any chance of hitting it! The bit it's surely going to wipe out of existence* next!>

Berenice was silent as she thought. She lowered her espringal and stared out at the rooftops of the city, calculating as fast as she could.

<*Capo?*> said Diela weakly. <*Capo, are you there?*>

Berenice looked down. The river of screaming people was still pouring through the city, stampeding to the shallops.

How many? thought Berenice. *How many are left? How many are going to make it?*

<*I'm going, Capo,*> said Vittorio. <*I'm doing it.*>

Berenice swallowed. <*Then go,*> she said.

She watched as Vittorio raised his own espringal, fired, and began to sail eastward over the city.

She did the same, raising her own line shot and hurtling east, ripped forward by her armor toward a small spire south of the walls. She struggled to control herself, to focus, to think.

<*Clef,*> she said. <*How long will it take you to get control of the deadlamp?*>

<*Too long,*> he said. <*It's a lot harder to take it over from the outside than in. It'll have time for one more edit, Ber. I can maybe make the edit smaller, or weaker, but I . . . I probably won't be able to stop it entirely.*>

"Scrumming hell," she whispered as she flew. Then she asked, <*Diela?*>

<*Yes, Capo?*> asked the girl.

<*Get clear of the walls,*> she said. <*Then get a line shot ready. Target Vittorio. The second he makes his shot at the deadlamp, fire on him. If it hits, the line shot should pull him clear of . . . of whatever the hell the deadlamp is going to do.*>

<*Y-Yes, Capo,*> she whispered.

Berenice decelerated as she closed in on the spire. She looked up and saw the deadlamp was still moving, still sliding to the west—but Vittorio was alighting on the wall just before it.

<*Claudia?*> Vittorio said. <*W-Want to path to me, to help me make the shot?*>

<*Sure thing, son,*> said Claudia faintly. <*Just a . . . just a second . . .* >

Berenice alighted, ejected her line shot, and loaded in another. She raised her espringal, wondering where to go next—but she knew she shouldn't move, not until the deadlamp made its edit.

It'd be a damn foolish thing to go swooping in on another building, only to have it vanish when you were halfway there.

She looked back up at it. The deadlamp was still shifting, still sliding west, ever so slowly.

Vittorio and Claudia's voices spoke at once, their words oddly overlaid on one another: <*Not going to take the shot until it stops. Can't miss. Got to be sure.*>

Berenice said nothing. She just waited. To speak now would distract them from their work.

<*I'm ready,*> whispered Clef. <*I'm ready . . .* >

The deadlamp kept floating west . . .

It stopped.

<*Firing now,*> said Claudia and Vittorio together.

Berenice could feel them take a breath; feel them press the firing plate; feel them exhale and watch through Vittorio's eyes as the tiny bolt with Clef's plate hurtled up toward the deadlamp.

The world went thin. The air began to shimmer and quake. All of reality felt like it was going two-dimensional, collapsing in on itself . . .

<*Vittorio!*> cried Berenice.

The world shuddered and danced.

<*It's a hit!*> Vittorio and Claudia screamed together. <*It's a hit!*>

<*I GOT IT!*> bellowed Clef's voice. He sounded like he was under tremendous strain. <*I . . . SON OF A BITCH, I . . . I . . .* >

The air twisted. The very gravity in the atmosphere seemed to flicker to the south.

<*IT'S COMING!*> cried Clef.

<*Diela!*> yelled Berenice. <*Get him out of there!*>

She pathed into Diela and watched through her eyes as the girl maneuvered her weapon to sight Vittorio, standing on the wall in the quaking air, her hands trembling as she peered through the espringal lens.

Berenice knew right away that Diela was not ready, not for this. She could feel it in the girl's thoughts, like sensing a flawed knot of wood in an oak board and knowing it couldn't bear weight. There was too much, too many minds pathing into one another, the whole of her team swirling with too much urgency, too much panic, too much awareness of how everything rested on this one decision . . .

Diela pressed the plate on the espringal.

The line shot was released and hurtled up.

The shot was high. Berenice knew it. So did Diela, so did everyone—and they watched, dismayed, as the line shot sailed up, nearly a yard over Vittorio, and hurtled out over the refugee camp, well past its activation range.

<*Oh no,*> said Diela. <*Oh no, oh no . . .* >

Berenice released the path, stood up, and looked at Vittorio.

He was standing on the walls, staring up at the deadlamp. Then he turned and looked back at Berenice, his face fixed in an expression of numb disbelief.

The world went greasy and muddled. And then, without any warning, he was gone, along with a quarter mile of the wall he was standing on.

All of Vittorio's sensations and experiences she'd been unconsciously receiving—his presence, his perspective, his awareness, his energy—they all went dark, went silent. Like a lantern veiled in the distance, he vanished.

She could hear Diela screaming in the distance: "*No! No! No, no, no!*"

Then came the thunderclap, the rush of air; the world before her filled up again with dust and screams, and she could see no more.

Berenice hung there on the walls, her body reverberating with shock.

No, no, she thought. *Ohh no, no . . .*

She knew her team had felt it as well: felt Vittorio's confusion, his bewilderment, his death.

And it was death. Berenice had been twinned with people as they'd died many times before. She knew what it was like, to feel a mind and soul go through that sudden blast of silence, and fall dark.

She felt Diela sobbing uncontrollably, felt her horror, her apocalyptic grief. <*I'm sorry!*> cried Diela. <*No, no . . . Please, I'm sorry, I'm sorry!*>

Then Claudia faintly whispering, <*I . . . I was in him when he died. I . . . I was pathing to him when he died . . .* >

Berenice struggled to think. She felt herself pathing into too many people at once: too many sights of the walls, of the stones, of the seas, of the towers. It became hard to remember which body was hers, which perspective, which grief.

I'm losing location, she thought. *I'm losing myself.*

This was the danger with twinning minds, especially in states of high emotion: when there was too much thinking and feeling going on among too many people, those perspectives spilled into your own mind, and you lost yourself. It was the exact thing she'd trained them to prevent—and now, at this most critical moment, she was failing.

Then Sancia's voice, very soft: <*Berenice.*>

Berenice blinked. She remembered which set of eyes were hers and blinked again.

<*Berenice,*> whispered Sancia. <*You know what you need to do, my love. And you know we don't have long.*>

She took a long, slow, deep breath.

She remembered a night like this: sinking into the black waters, her eyes pressed shut, and feeling Sancia's ghostly arms around her, dissolving into her thoughts . . .

Calm, she said to herself. *Calm, calm . . .*

Berenice swallowed and began to move.

<*Clef,*> she said hoarsely. <*Do you have the deadlamp under control?*>

<*Barely,*> he groaned. He sounded like he was being put through a remarkable strain. <*The hull is part of the goddamned horror, but it's not the best access point. Convincing this thing* not *to argue you out of goddamned existence is . . . proving to be a scrumming bastard of a job . . .* >

<*Then let's finish this,*> she whispered.

She released her hold on her rooftop, raised her espringal, and sighted the lamp.

<*I'll try to bring it closer,*> Clef said. <*Make sure you don't miss . . .* >

Berenice waited for the deadlamp until she was confident it was within range. Then she took a breath and fired.

The line shot hurtled up, adhered to the side of the deadlamp, and she sailed up after it.

She soared over the crumbling walls; over Diela, still sobbing hysterically on a stretch of inner wall; over the twin apertures edited into the earth; over the place where Vittorio had just been standing, just seconds ago . . .

She slowed as she neared the deadlamp. She looked up at it, the sheer, cold, black sides so blank and eerily immaculate. She did not think Tevanne truly had a body anymore, but rather hundreds of bodies, if not thousands or millions of them; yet she had always identified deadlamps as emblematic of their enemy, this unnatural, unreal manifestation of a will that was utterly alien to her.

But though it seemed unreal, it was solid enough. Her boots adhered to the side, then she vaulted up to stand atop the black brick, floating hundreds of feet above the pockmarked, smoky world of Grattiara. She looked over the edge, peering north. The army of hosts was now a little less than a mile from the walls, though now it was holding back, aware that it had lost control of the deadlamp.

<*We're good,*> said Clef, though he sounded exhausted. <*Ber—I'm . . . I'm going to open the top of this thing. Are you ready?*>

<*As ready as I could be.*>

<*All right. It's . . . It's hell inside there. Here you go.*>

Then there was a crack, a hiss, and a panel in the top of the deadlamp opened up—and then the screaming started.

Berenice cringed as the shrieks erupted from within the deadlamp, wild, mad howls of pain and misery. Then the smell hit her: the scent of rot, of urine, of shit, of waste.

God, I hate this, she thought as she walked to the open aperture in the top of the deadlamp. *God, God, how I hate doing this.*

She looked down into the deadlamp, and she blanched.

Three dozen people stared up at her from inside, their eyes blank, their rotten, reeking mouths open as they gibbered and shrieked. All of them were bound to chairs placed on the floor of the lamp, their feet and arms and chests secured. They were graying and ancient—and yet they also seemed mutated or misshapen, their skulls or knuckles or shoulders bulging curiously, like someone had removed a bone from here or there on a whim.

<*Time to do the hierophant thing, Ber,*> said Clef. <*And change the world.*>

<*I know,*> said Berenice. She maneuvered to sit at the edge of the hatch.

<*It's hard,*> whispered Sancia in her mind. <*But it's the only way.*>

<*I know,*> she said.

She dropped into the deadlamp.

3

The art of scriving had always been divided into two very distinct areas.

There was what Berenice and her compatriots thought of as conventional scriving, wherein one convinced everyday objects or materials to disobey reality by writing elaborate arguments upon them, arguments that called upon other arguments and definitions to make their case, all stored nearby in a lexicon. This was the art of scriving that Berenice had grown up with, the industry that had formed the empire of Old Tevanne, ran fortresses like Grattiara, and had once allowed the merchant houses to capture the whole of the world.

But then there were the "deep commands," which allowed one to make a sudden, abrupt, inexorable *change* to reality itself, an edit so swift and complete that the world never even knew it'd been changed.

Yet the deep commands came with a price: human life.

However, expendable human lives were not usually abundant. In the old days, the hierophants—the first scrivers—overcame this obstacle by creating tools that distorted the transition from life to death. By investing a soul within a tool, like Clef—a life ripped from its body at the stroke of midnight and trapped within a weapon, or an instrument, or a device—they could capture a deep command within it and invoke that command again and again and again, with no limit.

But during the scriving wars, the thing that called itself Tevanne had learned a far simpler and far more horrific technique.

Tevanne had realized that if you didn't mind paying a fresh cost for each edit, you didn't need to bother with capturing a command within a tool or a rig at all. You simply needed life *in general:* by stealing days, months, or years from a person, you could inflict a fresh command on reality whenever you pleased.

This had its own constraints, of course. Each time you made an edit, you'd burn through your victim's vitality like a flame through a cheap candle, aging or killing them instantly.

But, of course, this didn't matter if you had a whole populace to use as kindling.

Berenice dropped through the fetid air, ignoring the mad, shrieking people bound around her. She stalked forward, conscious that the floor was slick with shit, urine, and countless other excretions. One ancient man tried to snap at her, his tongue writhing in his black mouth. She carefully stepped around him, cringing slightly as his spittle struck her neck and cheek. Then a high-pitched howl from a shrunken, dwarflike creature—perhaps a child who'd been aged fifty years from the use of a single command.

Perhaps it's better that they die, she thought. *Perhaps it's better.*

<*I know you don't think that,*> said Sancia. <*Be strong, Ber.*>

She spied a circular bronze device sitting in the center of the deadlamp, and she recognized it immediately: the hierophantic console, placed there next to the gravity rig that was keeping this whole thing afloat.

I've only done this once before. She danced around the shrieking people to the console. *But how I hated it . . . How I hate it even now.*

<*Do it, Ber,*> whispered Clef wearily. <*I just need to get into the*

beating heart of this horror, and then we can make edits of our own. I'll purge the whole army. We'll save all of them, all at once.>

She knew that, of course. But she knew doing so, and performing such an edit, would almost certainly kill the people aboard the deadlamp.

She slipped out her pathplate to Clef, then paused and looked around at all the shrieking, ancient wretches about her.

"I'm sorry," she said.

She raised the strip of twinned metal above the console.

I'm not like Tevanne, she thought. *I'm not.*

She brought the metal down.

The interior of the deadlamp changed instantly—or at least it did to Berenice.

She felt Clef occupying multiple positions in space at the same time: here in the deadlamp, and back in the *Keyship* at the lexicon and with Sancia. It was like all these rooms were overlaid on top of one another, and she could feel Sancia standing behind her, and also Clef himself here in the deadlamp, arguing with the dreadful thing piece by piece. She even thought she could *see* Sancia in the gloom, her short salt-and-pepper hair glinting in the pale light.

<*Almost done,*> whispered Sancia. <*Almost . . .* >

Then she heard Clef begin.

He argued with the hierophantic console, insisting it must make one very simple change: that the twinned plates implanted in all the bodies of the hosts below were not metal but were instead water.

<*Nothing unusual, in other words,*> Clef said to the console. <*You know . . . Stuff you've all done before.*>

<*I . . . AM SURE I HAVE NOT DONE THIS,*> said the console. <*NOT NOW, NOT IN THIS STATE.*>

Its voice. How it sounded like Gregor, just a little . . . and also like *her,* like Valeria, flat and toneless and curiously artificial . . .

<*But when?*> said Clef. <*When have you not done these things?*>

<*EVER. THIS IS KNOWN.*>

<*But can you confirm that you will not do these things at a point in the future?*>

A long pause.

<*I . . . WHAT?*>

<*Are you aware of a future point when these alterations have not been performed by you?*>

<*IT . . . IT IS IMPOSSIBLE TO SAY . . .* >

<*You mean you don't know?*>

<*I . . . WELL . . .* >

<*Are you sure that this time right now is* not *also one of those points in time in the future when you* aren't *performing these alterations?*>

<*WHO . . . WAIT. IS IT NOT . . . A TIME WHEN I WAS NOT . . . WHAT?*>

Even in this dreadful place, Berenice had to smirk. The deadlamp's console was a hierophantic tool, drawing upon life to edit the world directly—and thus it was supposedly impossible to confuse.

But Tevanne had built the deadlamps' consoles to be flexible and responsive—and anything that was flexible could easily be tied into knots. Especially if it was Clef doing the tying.

<*So you're saying,*> the key said cheerily, <*that you can't confirm if a moment two seconds from now is or is not a future point in time when you would be performing these two very small, very tiny edits to reality, which means you can't confirm if this is an edit you are or are not allowed to perform?*>

<*I . . . CORRECT,*> said the console, though it now sounded worried.

<*Then it's okay to make these changes, yeah?*> said Clef. <*Just two slight, tiny, unnoticeable changes . . .* >

The console was silent for a long while.

<*Here it comes,*> whispered Sancia. She was so close, it was like they were there, together. <*Get ready . . .* >

Then the deadlamp changed the world.

Berenice's body lit up with agony, pain beyond description, like her bones were made of fire and her belly was filled with broiling lead. Because she was connected through Clef to the edit itself, she could *feel* the way the world was before the edit, and the way the world was *after:* she could feel both versions of reality insisting for one second that they both had every right to continue going on as they did, this irreconcilable schism between two worlds; and then she could feel the slow transitional moment as one story failed and another came thundering in like the tides to take its place . . .

Tears poured down her face. She felt the overwriting of the world, the merciless, implacable edits made to existence itself.

How many realities have I killed now? How many stories have I suffocated and replaced in panicked moments like this, all to win this miserable war?

Then Clef nudged the hierophantic console just once more—and the edit was finished.

The screaming in the deadlamp halted, a sudden, abrupt erasure of almost all noise. She slowly looked around at the people bound within the lamp.

Almost all of them were now dead. Their heads hung slack, their mouths open. Some had been aged so fast and so rapidly by Clef's commandeering of the deadlamp that they already had the look of corpses to them.

Such a curious thing, Berenice thought, *to see years stolen so quickly, so mercilessly—and to know you are responsible for it.*

<*I've got control of the thing's gravity rig now,*> whispered Clef. <*I can fly it to wherever we need, but we can't do any more edits. And I . . . I won't be able to hold on for long. I'm so* tired, *San . . .* >

Berenice grimaced. Though Clef was skilled at conquering scrived rigs, executing a deep command was still a massive test for him. The last time he'd done it he'd slept for two days. She did not like the idea of him falling asleep while the deadlamp was still in the air.

<*Just get it set down quickly, Clef,*> said Sancia. <*The host army is freed now, right?*>

<*Yeah,*> he sighed. <*They're all wiped clean. God, there's a lot of them. I don't know if we can take them all . . .* >

<*We'll take all we can,*> said Sancia. <*And this thing . . . This deadlamp. If the city's safe, we can take this as well.*>

Berenice's belly swooped as the deadlamp fell gently through the sky, descending to the earth. <*You think we can take it back to Giva?*> she asked.

<*I know everyone there would love to take a look at it,*> said Sancia. <*We've tried for years to figure out how Tevanne controls its hosts. Maybe this can show us.*>

Berenice sighed, exhausted, but she knew Sancia was right. They'd worked to analyze Tevanne's total control over its human components from the beginning of the war, because the tricky thing about twinning minds was that it was a *two-way* connection. Your thoughts became theirs, yes—but their thoughts also became yours.

Yet Tevanne had never seemed to have any issue with this. It could see through a host's eyes but cared nothing for the person themselves: not if they lived, or suffered, or grieved for those they loved. Simply being connected to thousands of people *should* have been overwhelming, even if they weren't all in states of horrid distress, as the hosts were. And yet, for Tevanne, it wasn't. Comprehending how it managed those millions of connections had always been a critical aspect of fighting the war—and if salvaging this dreadful contraption could change that, it was well worth saving.

<*Claudia?*> asked Berenice.

<*Y-Yeah?*> said Claudia. Her voice was weak: no doubt being pathed to Vittorio when he'd been edited out of existence had been unspeakably traumatic for her.

<*I am going to need you to get to those former hosts and tell them they have to leave,*> she said. <*I'd do it myself, but I'll be occupied with the deadlamp. If they'll listen, get them to the piers, same as everyone else.*>

<*Got it, Capo,*> she whispered.

Still the deadlamp descended. Berenice's legs felt weak. She longed to just sit down, to lay down, to rest her head—anywhere but in this awful little chamber.

<*Almost there,*> said Clef. <*Almost . . .* >

They were now very low, just yards away from the host army. Berenice could hear them screaming and wailing as they awoke from the awful slumber Tevanne had placed them in for weeks, months, maybe years.

She shut her eyes. She could feel Sancia close to her, like she was gripping her wife's hand here in the dark.

<*I always want to be with you,*> whispered Berenice. <*But now, God, to get me out of this hell . . .* >

<*I know,*> said Sancia. <*Hold fast, love.*>

<*Get ready,*> said Clef. <*We're almost down. Then I'll break connection with this thiiiiiiiiii . . .* >

Berenice opened her eyes. She waited for more, but Clef said nothing.

<*This what?*> she asked.

The deadlamp stopped descending. There was a long, long silence.

<*Goddamn it, Clef,*> said Sancia. <*What's wrong now?*>

<*Whoa . . .* > Clef said softly. <*Whoa, whoa, whoa. Something's . . . Something's in here, guys!*>

<*Uh . . . huh?*> said Berenice. She glanced around. <*In here? In the deadlamp? What do you mean?*>

<*There's . . . There's something* else *in here . . .* > said Clef. He sounded awed, entranced, terrified, not at all the chipper, sly cadence they knew. <*I was going to break the connection, but there's . . . there's something else in this lamp, with me and Ber . . .* >

Berenice and Sancia stared around together, peering at the deadlamp through one set of eyes. There was nothing.

<*What . . . What's he talking about?*> asked Berenice.

<*I have no scrumming idea,*> said Sancia.

<*Kid . . . Tevanne is* dreaming,> whispered Clef.

Berenice felt her skin crawling. <*Clef? Are you all ri—*>

<*Tevanne is dreaming under the depths of the world, Sancia,*> he said. <*And its dream is here! It's here in . . . in this deadlamp!*>

<*Huh? In the lamp?*> said Sancia. <*What the hell do you m—*>

<*I see it,*> cried Clef. <*I SEE IT!*>

Standing in the cockpit of the *Keyship,* Sancia stood up straight and screamed.

Images flashed in her mind, so rapidly she could barely understand what she saw.

She saw towers of bone white, rising from blasted sand flats that gleamed like melted glass, dotted here and there with tremendous chasms.

She saw skies rippling with columns of black smoke and heard thousands of voices crying out.

She saw a black stone surface, lined with scrivings wrought in silver—and in the wall was a hole in the world, and a darkness beyond.

Then things changed, and it was like she was flying over a landscape. She saw steppes below, the grasses there rippling in the wind, hills rising in the distance.

A white river, rushing through the mountains.

Then the mountains expanded and swelled, all brown and rambling and dappled with tall pines, and cut through with rocky gorges. Amid the mountains was a valley, huge and yawning, filled with crumbling columns and leaning ruins . . . and suspended above one curiously staggered peak in the valley was . . .

A box.

A room, floating in the sky.

And within the room, a man screaming.

Or rather . . . something man-shaped. For suddenly Sancia saw the man in the room, or rather she saw Clef seeing the man—and she saw his face, black and still and cold and gleaming, a face like a mask . . .

Because it *was* a mask.

"*No!*" she screamed out loud.

Then came a voice, cold and deep and hollow—and yet so *pained.*

"SANCIA," it said. "IS THAT . . . NO. NOT YOU. NOT *YOU*!"

The hate in that final word, so visceral and bitter and poisonous . . . It was like a black bolt of lightning, streaking through her thoughts.

Then the vision went dark, and Clef fell silent.

Berenice cried out as the deadlamp plummeted to the ground—a short drop of only a few feet, but enough to knock her forward onto the walls. She had to wedge herself into the corner to keep herself from falling backward onto the filthy floor. For a moment she stood there, breathing.

<*Clef!*> she snapped. <*What the hell was that?*>

Silence.

<*Sancia?*> she asked. <*What's going on? What's happen—*>

Then she felt an enormous heat behind her, and she turned and watched in horror as the hierophantic console smoked, then burst into flames.

The heat was overwhelming, and it kept growing, hotter and hotter. She knew she'd be broiled alive in a second if she stayed. She staggered back to the hatch in the ceiling, leapt up, and crawled out as fast as she could. When she reached the edge of the deadlamp she stared back at the hatch and watched as black smoke billowed out of it, accompanied by the all-too-recognizable scent of burning flesh.

"What the hell," gasped Berenice. "What the *hell*!" She sat on the edge of the deadlamp, head spinning, and asked, <*Sancia? Are you there?*>

<*I'm . . . here,*> Sancia said weakly. <*Are you?*>

<*Yes! Are you aware that the goddamned hierophantic console in that deadlamp burst into flames and nearly killed me? Did Clef do that?*>

<*No, I wasn't aware,*> muttered Sancia. <*And I don't know what he did.*>

<*You . . . You don't? What's going on?*> asked Berenice.

There was a long silence.

<*Did you see that shit I saw, Ber?*> asked Sancia. <*The . . . The white towers? The smoke, and the weeping? And the black door in the stone?*>

Berenice sat there for a moment, so stunned she couldn't respond. <*What! No! No, I did not! Did that happen?* Really?>

<*Yeah,*> said Sancia lowly. <*And now Clef's asleep.*>

<*Hell,*> said Berenice. <*Wait. Did* you *see these mad visions, or did Clef see them?*>

<*That's the part that concerns me,*> said Sancia. <*I don't really kno—*>

<*Ber, San,*> said Claudia tersely, <*as much as I'd love to figure all this madness out right now, we have several thousand people here to take care of. And if Tevanne can summon one army out of nowhere in an hour, it stands to reason it can summon another.*>

<*Scrumming hell,*> said Berenice. She slipped down off the edge of the deadlamp, pointed her line shot, fired, and vaulted over to the city walls. <*I'll figure out a way to get this deadlamp aboard to study it—if there is anything to study anymore. I'll need to come back to the ship for materials, though. San—can you bring the* Keyship *close to the piers?*>

<*I'm not as exact as Clef,*> Sancia said, <*but I'll get close.*>

Sancia stood at the massive galleon's main controls, gripping the wheels that allowed its scrivings and commands to leak into her thoughts. She didn't much love this job, but she'd proven to be the best after Clef at piloting such a beast: her privileges gave her access to scrived rigs, so she could listen to the massive scrived galleon, coax it, and talk it through its maneuvers.

"This way," she whispered aloud as she worked with the sleepy giant. "This way . . ."

The vast ship began to move. She looked west, toward the piers of Grattiara, and watched the Grattiarans lining up at the shallops, followed by the ragged, miserable refugees; and soon they'd be followed by the most miserable lot of all: the thousands of freed hosts who'd just awoken to discover themselves starved and exhausted and far from their homes, their families missing, their loved ones gone.

She felt old at the sight of them. Old to know that there were many others like them whom she and Berenice had not saved. And worse still, she felt troubled by the vision she'd seen, and what it suggested—and by the knowledge that she hadn't seen all that Clef had.

Berenice's voice whispered in her ear: <*What was that?*>

<*I'm not sure,*> said Sancia. <*But I think . . . I think Clef might have accidentally tapped into its thoughts.*>

<Its *thoughts? You mean . . .* >

<*Yeah,*> said Sancia. <*I . . . I think Clef somehow accidentally* read Tevanne's mind. *He saw through its eyes, saw what it was doing. And . . . what he saw there seemed plenty terrifying.*>

<*And the voice?*> said Berenice. <*When it said your name? Was that . . .* >

<*Yes. I . . . I think it caught me looking. It caught us and threw us out.*>

There was a flicker of movement from the walls of Grattiara: a tiny speck of black, hurtling toward the deck of the *Keyship* in an unnaturally straight line. It was a bizarre way to see one's spouse return, but Sancia's heart leapt at the sight of it.

<*Sancia,*> whispered Berenice. <*In the vision. Did . . . Did you really see . . .* >

Sancia leaned her head up against the wheel of the galleon. The experience felt impressed in the surface of her brain: a blank black mask, and a scream in the dark.

<*Yeah,*> she said grimly. <*I saw* him.>

<*What could that mean?*> asked Berenice.

A curious sound cut across the sea to where Sancia stood, a low, rising susurrus that reminded her of a huge flock of birds in flight. It took her a moment to identify it: it was weeping. She was now close enough that she could hear all the people standing on the piers and steps of Grattiara, and all of them were crying.

<*Nothing good,*> she said.

4

The *Keyship* at sea was always a noisy environment. Despite being a massive scrived rig of almost incomprehensible, perfect complexity, its supports still creaked, and the hull still sloshed with the sound of water beyond, and the sound of footfalls always echoed through the decks above and below. Yet now it echoed with different sounds: weeping, wailing, sniffling, snuffling, and the many rustlings and bumpings of countless miserable, wounded bodies lying about the many decks and bays. As Sancia crossed the upper bays of the ship she felt like she was peering down into another world, like some philosopher's dream of an afterlife, this faintly lit, sprawling space filled with cots of starved, shaken people.

She found Polina in the same place she always was after a successful operation: leaning against a high balcony's railing in one of the bays, peering down on her physiqueres as they went about treating the many injuries and infections. Though Polina was here out of compassion, Sancia couldn't help but think of a bird of prey watching sandmice scurry about from its perch.

"And just who," said Polina as Sancia neared, "is piloting this ship?"

"Claudia," said Sancia. "She got some sleep, so now she gets to work. It's not a hard job, it's a straight shot south to Giva now. All she needs to do is look out the front cockpit, mostly."

"And you? Have you slept?"

"No."

Polina nodded, watching the physiqueres dart back and forth for more medicines. "This," she said, "is easily the most we've ever managed."

"Yeah," said Sancia. "By about a thousand or so."

"Not just the citizens of Grattiara," said Polina. "Nor the refugees. But also an *entire* Tevanni army of hosts that Clef . . . what, magicked awake? Would that be accurate?"

"Not really," said Sancia. "But it works well enough."

"It's like a fairy story," said Polina. "A people freed from the spell of an evil sorcerer. But it seemed so much easier in those tales." She watched intensely as one of her physiqueres went about bandaging a child's foot. "I don't much love all this pathing shit, as you know."

"You've never been less than vocal about that, yeah," said Sancia.

"But I can sort of feel all my physiqueres helping everyone on this ship, all at once. Like I'm remembering them doing it as if I'd done it myself . . ." She shook her head. "To know the scope of this suffering, and know what we've done to stop it . . . It almost makes all the risk and the madness feel worth it."

"Almost?"

Polina stood up from the railing. "Yes. Because another bit about all this pathing nonsense is . . . I know what's going through your head too, Sancia. A little." She turned to her. "I know why you don't want to sleep. Clef did something back there. Broke through into Tevanne, peeked into its thoughts. And saw . . ."

"He saw Crasedes," said Sancia. "Yeah."

"And he saw him . . . captured, yes?" said Polina.

"I'm not sure," said Sancia. "It's scrumming hard to imagine someone stuffing Crasedes in a box."

Polina nodded, eyes distant as she considered this. "Berenice is looking at maps," she said. "Why don't we join her?"

She followed Polina up from the bays and then through its many decks, staircase after staircase, hatch after hatch.

"How'd the girl do?" asked Polina as they climbed.

"Well," said Sancia, sighing. "Considering everything, Diela is inordinately good at pathing—she's got a natural talent for it, and she was twinned very young. But I would have done all I could to avoid this being her first encounter."

"My people gave her a sleeping draught," said Polina. "She's resting now—but for one with a talent for pathing, I know dreams aren't necessarily an escape, since they sometimes bleed over into the dreams of others."

Finally they came to the map room, near the top stern of the *Keyship*. It had once played host to all kinds of Dandolo finery—the captains had apparently entertained wealthy guests there—but all that was left now was the carpet, yellow and vividly patterned in florals and stained here and there with ancient wine dribblings.

Berenice now sat at the far end, staring up at a wall of maps and notes they'd assembled over the many months of the war. She hadn't changed or marked up any of them, Sancia knew. What Clef had glimpsed had suggested something so terrible that no change could truly capture it.

"When I was young," said Polina as she crossed the room, "I thought of war in terms of swords and spears and shields. But now I know it's maps, and more maps, and calendars and timetables, and shipping lines and item counts—and then maps, and more maps again." She stood next to where Berenice sat. "It's deadly dull stuff, to be sure."

Berenice said nothing, meditating silently over the landscapes before her.

"But this dull stuff has helped us save thousands of people," said Polina quietly. "I believe we've run, what, nineteen operations getting people out of the way of Tevanne in the past eight years?" She grew closer to the map and touched one area to the east of Tevanne's territories. "But this . . . If I'm honest, this has helped us more."

Sancia sat down next to Berenice to see. Polina's finger rested on the Black Kingdoms: the ugly little blot of valleys that had held out against Tevanne for the past eight years. The Kingdoms were so famous that even Malti and his men had known about them—or at least they'd known of the sheer amount of destruction caused by Tevanne's never-ending efforts to take the region.

"How much blood and treasure," said Polina, "has Tevanne spent trying to capture Crasedes?"

Berenice finally moved, taking in a breath and blinking. <*Uncountable,*> she said. <*Hundreds of thousands of hosts. Dozens of deadlamps. Legions of artillery. Enough to make Grattiara look like a spat.*>

"Aloud, please," said Polina. "Thoughts are clearer when articulated. If I could make you all write them down, I'd do that instead."

Berenice sighed, shut her eyes, and collected herself. "Crasedes has been Tevanne's primary target since the start of the war. And we've been able to take advantage of that. Having it focus on him has allowed us a lot of freedom in the Durazzo. Saving all these people hasn't been easy, but it'd have been a lot harder if Crasedes hadn't been occupying so much of Tevanne's attention."

Polina turned to look back at Sancia. "Yet now, you've received a vision of him . . . captured."

"We don't know that for sure," said Sancia.

"You saw him in some kind of a box, yes?" said Polina. "Screaming in pain? That definitely suggests 'captured' to me."

"I saw a piece of a piece of what Clef was seeing. He saw more, and he'll know more."

"And *when* will he know more?" said Polina.

"Last time it took him two days to wake up," said Sancia. "We'll be in Giva when he comes to again, I'd imagine. He can tell us more then."

Polina looked back at the map. "The idea of the first of all hierophants captured . . . It's something I never really considered possible. If anything, I'd have thought their brawl would kill us all."

Sancia frankly agreed. Though they'd wondered if Crasedes might have perished after Shorefall Night, they'd received word just weeks later that he had resurfaced on the other side of the sea and had captured a handful of Daulo valley kingdoms. No one knew if he had convinced the various petty kings to follow him or forced them—being a hierophant with powerful controls over persuasion, as well as gravity itself, he had no end of choices—but he'd transformed their armies and fortresses into a cohesive superpower nearly overnight. It'd even been rumored he'd found a way to restore his abilities of flight, and perhaps more than that.

For eight years after that the Black Kingdoms had not only survived but stood unbreakable against Tevanne's onslaught. *Until,* Sancia thought, *today.*

"I'm struggling to imagine what we'll do," said Berenice, "if Crasedes has truly fallen."

"I've no idea," said Polina. "We'll have to bring the issue before the Assembly back in Giva." She glanced at Sancia. "But you know this subject already makes them uneasy."

Sancia glared at her. Her hand rose to touch her shirt where Clef hung against her neck. "You mean *Clef* makes them uneasy."

"To be fair, Sancia, Clef would make most anyone uneasy," said Polina, exasperated. "A magic scrived tool that can manipulate or destroy nearly any other scrived tool? Only a fool would go unworried about such a thing! Let alone one with his . . . history."

"Clef's had a hand in building nearly everything that's helped Giva survive," said Sancia defensively. "He's why we're alive, why we're succeeding as much as we have!"

"Yes, and knowing he was apparently once the *father* of Crasedes," said Polina, "who's wiped out thousands if not millions of people during the four millennia of his life . . . Knowing that this same person helped build your nation is *not* exactly comforting." Her face, always set in a grim scowl, grew even grimmer. "He could be just as bad. A Crasedes of our own, slumbering among us all this time, like a butterfly in its chrysalis."

Sancia opened her mouth to object, but Polina raised her hands in surrender. "I will stop and simply say that I detest *all* this dreadful magic," she said. "I hated the merchant houses for using it, and this . . . this ancient madness nonsense makes me *doubly* troubled. I've no idea how you live with such a thing touching you, Sancia."

"Because he's not a thing," said Sancia. "He's a person."

Polina sighed and rubbed her eyes. "You both need sleep," she said. "And rest. I can practically smell your exhaustion stinking up the air about you. Go to bed."

Berenice shook herself. "We can help tend to the refugees," she said. She stifled a yawn. "We're short enough hands. We can help."

"No," said Polina firmly.

"We can!" said Berenice. "People depend on us."

"You will have many, many questions asked of you when we get to Giva," said Polina. "I expect the Assembly will interrogate you for hours. Sleep, so that you can answer them." She glowered at the maps. "Because we'll all depend on your answers."

Alone in their cabin, Sancia and Berenice held each other and listened.

They listened to each other's thoughts, their feelings, their memories, their experiences. Having twinned thoughts granted you access to another person's mind, but it was a proximal effect—which meant that when they were physically touching, the effect reached its zenith, and they shared so much they almost became one.

Sancia wept silently for Vittorio, listening to the echoes of his death as they reverberated in Berenice's thoughts. <*Goddamn,*> she whispered. <*I'm so sorry, Ber.*>

<*I know,*> said Berenice.

<*You did good, though,*> said Sancia.

<*So did he. He did the right thing. It just didn't feel right in the moment.*> She bowed her head against Sancia's. <*One day we will invent a way out of this. We'll find some key, or tool, or trick that can . . . that can make sure this never happens again. Won't we?*>

<*I hope so,*> said Sancia. She smiled wearily. <*But there is no dancing through a monsoon.*>

Berenice smiled back, struggling to remember where the saying came from. Some ancient parable, she thought, about a woman who could dance through rainstorms, and never be struck by a drop—but eventually the monsoon came, and there was no dancing through it.

Sancia studied Berenice's body—her bruises, her cuts, the places where her skin had been rubbed raw as her armor and espringal had hauled her about through the skies. Berenice pathed to her and saw her own wounds through Sancia's eyes and made notes about how to adjust in the future.

<*Strip,*> said Sancia. <*You're beat up in places you don't even know yet.*>

<*Untrue,*> said Berenice, cringing painfully as she sat up and undid a button. <*I am* quite *aware of all the places I'm beat up . . .* >

Sancia fetched some bandages and oils and poultices, and quietly began treating Berenice's many small wounds. When she was done, she sat back and looked at her work. Berenice pathed to her again and looked as well, studying her own nude, bruised, battered body lying on the bed from Sancia's eyes. She suddenly felt overcome with conflicting emotions: dismay at how beaten and worn she looked; then exultant, even titillated, to see herself alive, whole, strong; and then a powerful, aching guilt, to know that this body was alive but Vittorio's was utterly lost, wiped away from reality.

<*Alive,*> said Sancia.

<*Yes,*> said Berenice. <*Just barely.*>

<*Still alive, yes. And still young.*>

Sancia's face was anxious. Berenice grabbed her hand and squeezed it tight.

<*You are still alive too,*> said Berenice.

<*But not young,*> said Sancia. <*Not strong. Look at you . . .* > Her eye fell on Berenice's biceps, taut and curving. <*How could I not be jealous?*>

<*I'm only alive because of you,*> said Berenice. <*Me and everyone else. We've survived because of what you've done.*>

Sancia said nothing. Berenice knew this was little consolation: the plate in Sancia's skull was very, very different, allowing her to perceive and commune with scrivings just as the plates within Berenice and the rest of the Givans allowed them to share thoughts. But like all alterations driven by the deep permissions, Sancia's came at the cost of life. Just as the deadlamps aged their slaves with every scriving, the little plate in Sancia's head feasted upon her years, eating up her days, aging her far faster than normal.

It seemed terribly unfair to Berenice. The scrivings that twinned their minds surely demanded life as well—just far, far less than whatever alterations had been given to Sancia.

How bitter it is, she often thought, *that scriving the body is a blessing for so many, except for the person who made it possible.*

Again and again, Sancia and Berenice had agonized over whether to use a purge stick on her: the little tool that would render a body immune to scrivings, forcing the physical self to reject any commands that would or could ever be implanted within it.

Sancia seemed to sense her thinking: <*That kid on board—the governor's son that you saved. You purged him to do it.*>

Berenice nodded.

<*But . . . he can never be part of Giva now,*> said Sancia. <*Never share minds. Be one of us. Not with that plate in him. He'll have to bear all he suffered alone.*>

Berenice grabbed her hand and squeezed it. <*Not alone, my love. Not truly alone.*>

Sancia sighed. <*Maybe I'll do it. Maybe I really will. Once the war is done, and we're all safe, I'll do it to myself.*>

Yet Berenice couldn't help but feel troubled. Not just because neither of them could imagine when the war could possibly end but because she did not know how to live with a partner who was aging so rapidly. Sancia's physical limitations were greater, and she was now at an age when her sexual appetites were diminishing. Five or six years ago, the sight of Berenice lying naked on the bed would have made her nearly instantly aroused. Now Berenice knew Sancia felt mostly fatigue, and a reluctance to disrobe and reveal her aging body.

<*No,*> said Berenice, sitting up. <*No, no.*> She grabbed Sancia's hand and placed it on her cheek. <*You are still you. And you are still beautiful.*>

<*I was never beautiful,*> said Sancia.

<*You were to me. You are to me.*>

Sancia sighed.

<*Share what I feel,*> said Berenice. <*Take that from me.*>

Sancia looked at her, bemused but still reluctant. This was not an unusual proposition for them: for Sancia to share in the arousal and climax that Berenice's body was still quite capable of and eager for.

<*So willing to be used,*> said Sancia with a slight smile. She began to disrobe.

<*For you,*> said Berenice, <*always. Always.*>

5

"What's on the other side? Do you know?"* said a woman's voice.

"No. I'm not sure yet," said another—this one a man.

"Why build it if you're not sure what it opens to?"

"You don't understand. It wants *me to build it. It wants to be made. It's like seeing a sculpture within a block of stone—but the block of stone is the world itself."*

"A beautiful thought. But you aren't answering me. What lies on the other side of the thing you're making?"

"I don't know. But it's got to be better than here, yes?"

In the dark of his endless, silent sleep, Clef shifted uncomfortably.

"She might not be there, you know. I want her to be. I know you want her to be. But she might not be waiting for us on the other side."

"I am no child. I know. But perhaps a better world awaits us there. Perhaps a better world awaits us all, there on the other side of creation . . ."

Clef stirred in the dark, anxious and sick.

Who is this? Whose voices do I hear? Who was this, however so long ago?

Then the dream left him, and he slept.

II

CADENCE

6

Berenice awoke as the waves changed from the great, undulating surges of the open ocean to the milder swells of shallow waters. Then came a curious moisture to the air, a discomfiting, swampy clamminess that made her legs and belly break out in a sweat.

She opened her eyes. <*We're here!*> she said. She shook Sancia and dressed. <*We're home. We're in the fog locks now!*>

"Muhh," said Sancia. She shoved her face deeper into the pillow.

<*Wake up!*>

"Lemme sleep. I goddamn need it these days."

<*You've got five minutes,*> said Berenice. <*Then I want you up there. We need to get cleared for entry as fast as possible!*>

"Ten minutes. Got it."

Berenice emerged to find the deck crowded with people sitting or standing about. Apparently many of the Grattiarans and refugees had remained on the main deck, having been reluctant to go belowdecks and risk becoming prisoners—an impulse Berenice could understand, given what they'd been through. They muttered unhappily, and it was easy to see why: the world around them was turned to white as thick tufts of heavy, moist fog enveloped the ship. The light was cold and dim, blunted by the piles of mist, and when Berenice pushed through to the main deck's railing she saw she couldn't see farther than twenty feet past the hull.

Ordinarily a ship as large as a galleon would have dropped speed to a crawl when traveling through such fog, fearful of striking shallows or another vessel. But the *Keyship* did not: it pounded forward, surging through the waters like it was splitting through open seas.

Berenice had expected this, of course. They knew where they were going.

<*Morning, Ber,*> said Claudia's voice. <*We entered the fog locks about ten minutes ago.*>

She turned and spotted Claudia in the cockpit above. <*Any sign of following vessels when we entered?*> she asked.

<*None. We thought it wise to take the southeastern entrance home, through the Strait of Armondi. Thought that might draw out any watchers we drew with us. So far, there's been not a thing. I think we're clear.*>

<*Keep being that smart, Claudia, and you'll be in that cockpit more than Sancia.*>

<*Better here than on those goddamned walls. But as a note—maybe I'm reading the sky wrong, but I think a storm's on the way. The sooner we're admitted back into Giva, the better. Especially for the refugees.*>

<*Understood.*>

Berenice studied the waters around the hull of the ship. She didn't possess Sancia's scrived sight, unless Sancia chose to share it with her, but if she could use it now she knew she'd see a few tiny burning tangles of logic bobbing on the waves about them.

Fog buoys: little scrived rigs that boiled the seawater and poured mist into the air. The Givans had installed sets of these at all the entrances into the islands, tossing up walls of fog. Any spies would never be sure exactly when a Givan ship was coming or going—or what lay within the depths of the channels.

<*You need some food in you,*> said Sancia, yawning as she finally emerged onto the deck of the ship. <*Otherwise Greeter's clearance check is going to be miserable.*>

<*It's always miserable,*> said Berenice. <*Food won't help.*>

<*It's more for us than you,*> said Sancia. She tossed Berenice a hardtack in cloth wrapping. <*Being as you get so pissy after.*>

Berenice grumbled as she unrolled the biscuit. <*Fine. Though this hardly counts as food . . .* > She took a bite and attempted to chew. <*Any word from Clef?*>

Sancia shook her head and patted where he hung about her neck. <*Not a peep. What I can't forget is how it reacted. When Tevanne knew we were there. It felt me, but then it . . .* >

<*It said, "Not you,"*> said Berenice.

<*Yeah.*>

<*But . . . you don't think it meant you. You think it meant Clef.*>

<*Yes. But it was so personal, so vicious . . .* > She shook her head. <*It was mad.*>

<*We need to tell the Assembly immediately,*> said Berenice. <*I'd rather start the conversation than be talked about. Agreed?*>

<*Yeah,*> said Sancia with a sigh.

<*Good. I'll ask Greeter to send word the second we meet them. Which should be soon, I hope.*>

Sancia stood and looked out at the curling mist, like she'd heard some whispering sprite on the winds. Then she froze, and a look of alarm shot across her face.

"Sooner than you think," she cried. "Shit! I didn't realize how goddamn close we wer—"

Berenice wondered what she meant—but then she felt it: a curious, thrumming tension at the back of her head.

Then the wall of noise hit them like a blast of sand in a desert storm.

Berenice cried out in pain as an eruption of thoughts and emotions and memories burst in her mind, one after another after another: a man fussing with a scrived teapot, attempting to get it to boil faster; a child looking for a toy beneath a bed; a woman bent over a definition plate, quietly drawing out sigils.

<*Shitting hell!*> cried Barzana's voice. <*We're* already *at Giva?*>

The *Keyship* slowed dramatically in the fog. Some of the Grattiarans around them cried out in surprise. <*Damn it!*> said Claudia. <*Scrumming Armondi Strait . . . I never take this one, didn't realize . . .* >

<*Get the box,*> snarled Berenice. <*And everyone key up. Polina—that goes for you and your physiqueres too.*>

<*We've noticed!*> said Polina angrily, somewhere far belowdecks. <*Thank you so* very *much for the warning . . .*>

Berenice tried to focus on her body sense: she felt her teeth grinding, felt her hand digging into the wooden railing. But there were so many experiences, all of them happening concurrently in her mind, sleepy, half-awake thoughts as people fumbled through their morning routines aboard ships or puttered about the starts of their days . . .

"Ohh, I hate this," said Berenice, panting. "Oh, I *hate* this . . ."

"At least it's morning," rasped Sancia next to her. "Imagine what it feels like . . . to have everyone in Giva in your head when they're all *awake*."

Finally Diela darted through the crowds on the main deck to her, a scrived bronze box in her hands. "I'm here, I'm here!" she cried. She held the box out to them, and both of them opened it and pulled out two little bronze plates on strings.

Gasping, Berenice hurried to hang a little plate about her neck—the second she did, the churning mass of thought in her head abruptly vanished.

<*Thank God,*> sighed Berenice. <*Confirm that we're all in the same conversation. Claudia?*>

<*Present,*> Claudia said wearily.

"Same," said Diela aloud.

<*Polina?*> asked Berenice.

Silence. She must have put on her own conversation key, Berenice thought, and tuned into her own people down below.

"So that's a double bonus," said Sancia. "We don't have to deal with all the noise—or Polina."

<*Ber,*> said Claudia. <*Confirming that it's all right to stay on course.*>

<*Stay on course,*> said Berenice. <*But slower.*> She looked up into the white fog curling over the ship. <*We're already in Giva. We just can't see it yet.*>

"Home sweet home," said Sancia sourly.

As their newly founded nation had developed during the war, Sancia and Berenice had very quickly come to two conclusions about the advent of twinning minds.

On the one hand, it was absolutely revolutionary. It offered a way to augment your own thoughts and perspectives by blending them with someone else's, which led to instantaneous communication over short distances, a deeper sense of empathy, and faster, better innovations—among many other things.

On the other hand, trying to manage it was an absolute rotten bastard of a job.

To their surprise, it hadn't been the loss of privacy that everyone minded most. Twinned thinking nullified that from the outset: it was difficult to abhor someone else's behavior, for example, when you also instantly understood why they had gone about that behavior to begin with. (Though it did lead to some interesting new marital arrangements.)

Rather, it was the sheer *amount* of information that had become difficult to handle. Small groups were manageable—but twinning the thoughts of more than forty or fifty people together essentially produced a wall of noise that you had to live with inside your brain at all times.

And twinning ten thousand people's minds, well . . . That was enough to drive anyone mad.

What they needed, Berenice realized, was something *closer* than twinning: a method that would allow thoughts to spill mind to mind among only a handful of people, rather than a thousand. And there was nothing that got two or more things closer than pathplates.

Pathplates convinced reality that two people holding two different plates were physically touching each other—and physically touching another twinned person elevated the effect so much that your minds practically became one, and all their memories and concerns briefly became yours. So, the solution had seemed easy: just get two or more people to hold the right pathplates, and they'd only hear each other's thoughts, and screen out the wall of noise from their minds.

But when twinned people—or at least *most* twinned people—pathed that deep for too long, Berenice and Sancia had found it had . . . effects. Really, some unnerving, soporific effects: many participants had suddenly wished to lie down and shut their eyes, a smile on their faces, and revel in the beauty of being so many other people all at once. Starvation, dehydration, and even comas had quickly become widespread.

This was not exactly a desired effect when your nation was at war. So, Berenice had been forced to come up with a variation.

She realized that everyone who held a twinned pathplate was constantly in complete connection with everyone else holding copies of that same pathplate. In essence, for any given twinned people A, B, C, and D, the connections looked like:

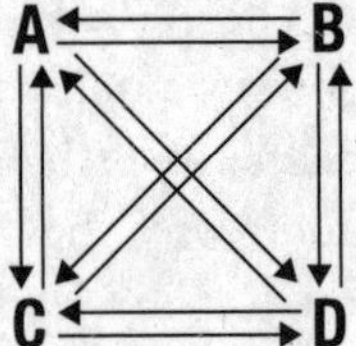

(Sancia always hated when Berenice drew diagrams, but it was the only way to make sense of it.)

When Berenice looked at it this way, she realized this number of connections was obviously a mess, and would only get messier the more people you added to the group. It would not scale.

So she had instead developed a chain of individually *different* pathplates, stored in a portable box—or a "conversation box"—which created connections only to *one* other person in the group. In this case, the connections would look like:

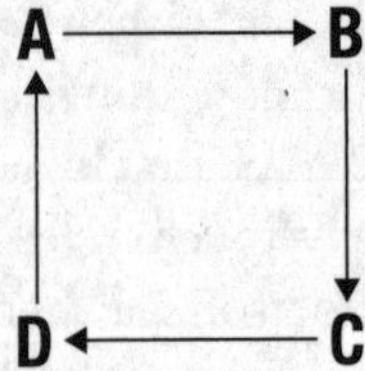

However, since everyone was still functionally twinned together like links in a chain, this meant person A could still hear and receive thoughts from person D, despite not having an active connection to them. It was far fewer connections, far less overwhelming, and far less to bear.

It was easier, in other words, but it still wasn't *easy*. Not only did people have to pull their "conversation keys" from a box in the right sequence for it to work, but twinning items or space too many times tended to make reality very upset, and often resulted in violent explosions. Berenice had only barely managed it.

Yet this was how Giva had come to survive as a nation of twinned people over the past eight years: everyone was tuned in to different conversations, sharing themselves without destroying themselves, capable of reacting to threats as one. Though Berenice worried about the fragility of it all, Sancia was always heartened.

Empires are simple to run, she'd said once. *One person, one throne, one vote. But Giva is goddamn hard.*

And how, Berenice had asked, *is that to be a comfort?*

Because power and cruelty are easy, Sancia had said. *What we're making takes a shitload of work. So we must be doing the right thing.*

The *Keyship* pounded on and on through the water. Then the mist before them finally thinned out, and they exited the fog locks and saw Giva beyond.

The refugees on the deck gasped at the sight. The countless straits and channels and canals of the tropical isles ahead were gorgeous in their own right, of course; but they were positively teeming with thousands of vessels of all sizes and types, hundreds upon hundreds of ships, more than the busiest port in all the history of the world.

The galleons were the most notable, of course: Giva had eight of those, each as big as a fortress, hulking amidst the fleet and all crawling with movement. Swarming around the galleons like flies about the legs of cattle were countless carracks, caravels, cogs, outriggers, junks, doggers, wherries, dories, drifters, and a few ramshackle vessel types Sancia thought didn't yet have names. All of them were bedecked with scrived lanterns, and in the fog-dimmed sunrise all the waters glimmered as if layered with fairy lights.

"Giva's fleet . . ." said one Grattiaran man faintly. "Giva's fleet is *vast*."

"That's not our fleet," said Sancia. "That *is* Giva."

"What do you mean?" he asked.

"Giva has little in the way of land holdings," said Berenice.

"No Commons, no campos, no enclaves, no illustri," said Sancia. "Nothing for Tevanne to invade, in other words."

"We aren't a city or a territory," said Berenice. "We're a people. A *surviving* people."

<*For now,*> added Sancia silently.

The comment curdled in Berenice's head. She watched the fleet in the distance as they approached. For so long she'd thought it tiny, makeshift, and so fragile—yet now it seemed so huge and unwieldy.

She studied the channels leading out of the Givan Islands, and quietly did some calculations.

"I know what you're thinking," said Sancia.

<*If you didn't,*> said Berenice, <*it'd mean something had gone dreadfully wrong.*>

<*You're trying to figure out how fast we can get the fleet clear,*> said Sancia. <*How to move them out. What ships would need to go first, and last. You're thinking of running.*>

<*Yes,*> said Berenice quietly.

<*To where? And who'd do the running?*>

She waved a hand at the ships ahead. <*All of us. All of Giva, running anywhere. We run, and we keep inventing, until we devise some way to kill it.*>

Sancia looked at her. <*You still think there's some scrived trick to getting out of this.*>

<*Don't be so condescending. Tevanne is basically a giant scrived rig. We've got teams of scrivers like never before. We'll dream up some tool to unravel it all—eventually.*>

Sancia stared out at the miserable refugees around them. <*But the birth of Tevanne itself . . . Gregor swallowing that little plate . . . That was all a scrived trick to unravel Valeria's plans. These things . . . They never quite go how one expects them to go.*>

<*I wish you wouldn't dwell on things like that,*> said Berenice.

<*What, on things that happened?*>

<*On things that were lost,*> said Berenice.

There was a moment of sorrowful quiet. They both diplomatically looked away, staring out at the sea, neither willing to break the silence.

"How can you do this?" said the Grattiaran man beside them,

watching as the caravels and carracks and junks swirled about the fleet in a marvelous choreography. "How can so many ships function in one place?"

They spied a small caravel suddenly sailing alongside them, tracking their movements.

<*There's Greeter,*> Sancia said. <*Right on time. If the Grattiarans already thought this shit was weird, it's about to get a hell of a lot weirder.*>

"It's complicated," Berenice said to the man.

Then Berenice sensed it: a sudden, immense *presence* as something huge reached out to her, inspecting her, checking her, studying her—yet she knew it was not one person but something very, very different.

<*Good morning, Berenice!*> said Greeter's voice quietly in her mind.

<*Hello, Greeter,*> Berenice said.

<*Welcome back to Giva!*> said the voice. <*You've been missed!*>

7

The *Keyship* slowed as Greeter's caravel grew closer.

<*You seem quite well, Berenice,*> said Greeter's voice, soft and soothing like a parent shushing a child back to sleep. <*That's good to see. Ah . . . and there's Sancia, of course . . .* >

<*Morning, Greeter,*> said Sancia.

Berenice cringed a little, surprised to hear Greeter elbow into her thoughts so effortlessly. But then, Greeter was a very unusual citizen of Giva, and was not restricted by conversation keys—such was the magnitude of Greeter's presence, in fact, that no filter could hold them back.

<*Good morning!*> said Greeter. <*It's very good to see you all! Hm. Odd that you came through the Armondi Straits . . . Which is on the opposite side from where you departed for Grattiara. Were you worried about pursuers?*>

<*Very,*> said Berenice.

<*All right. That's good to know. I'll start the fog locks on all other entrances just in case. Before you proceed, of course, you and your team will need to be made available for pathplates and security checks.*>

<*Understood,*> said Berenice, sighing slightly. Pathplates were protocol, and they were wearying after such a brutal journey—but it was necessary to keep everyone within Giva safe.

<*Thank you,*> said Greeter. <*To confirm . . . I believe you'll need five pathplates. Two for you and Sancia, then one for Claudia, Diela, and Vittorio. Is this correct?*>

<*It is not,*> said Berenice grimly. <*We will need four pathplates.*>

A short, brutal pause.

<*Four . . .* > said Greeter. <*I see. Because . . . Vittorio is not with you. Yes. I don't find him aboard the* Keyship *now.*>

<*No,*> said Berenice. <*You do not.*>

<*I'm . . . sorry to hear that. I will be able to be more genuine in my sorrow once I come to apprehend it more.*>

<*I know, Greeter,*> said Berenice.

<*Is there anything else I can do for you before your arrival?*>

<*Yes, actually,*> said Berenice. <*Please put together a call for an Assembly meeting, if you could. For today.*>

<*Today?*> said Greeter, surprised. <*But . . . the Assembly usually only meets on such short notice under emergency circumstances . . .* >

<*This is an emergency circumstance,*> said Berenice. <*Once we get your pathplates, you'll know why.*>

<*I see,*> said Greeter. <*I . . . will relay that message and will let you know their response.*>

<*Good. Thank you.*>

<*My caravel is close now. Claudia?*>

<*Yes, Greeter,*> said Claudia's voice.

<*Please decelerate a bit more. Yes . . . that's good. One moment.*>

Berenice spotted the little caravel speeding close to them, its sails white and ghostly in the remains of the fog. It was a barebones crew, no more than four or so, dressed in purples and blues—Greeter's favorite colors. It said it had a calming effect, she remembered.

"They," Berenice reminded herself. *You've been gone several weeks, but Greeter likes to be called "they," not "he" or "she" or "it" or . . . anything else.*

The caravel's crew took out a small, clunky espringal, attached a short black tube to a bolt, raised the espringal, and fired. Some of the Grattiarans screamed as the tube clattered to the deck of the galleon, but Berenice shushed them. "It's a package for us," she said. "We're not being fired on."

Berenice picked up the tube, opened it, and slid out four small flat paper envelopes. She handed one to Sancia, who took it with a resigned look on her face.

"This is our home," Sancia sighed, "and we invented all this shit. But this is still weird as hell, every time."

"Duly noted," said Berenice. She carried the rest back to the cockpit, where Claudia was already waiting on the stairs, having overheard their conversation with Greeter.

<*I should have slept more last night,*> she said, taking one envelope. <*For I won't tonight, not now. I never get any sleep the night after Greeter takes a look at my head.*>

<*We won't be doing anything unless you take it,*> said Berenice, <*because Greeter won't let us into the fleet until you do. So hurry up.*>

Claudia grudgingly opened her envelope. Berenice tore open her own and peered in at the slender bronze plate within. Yet another pathplate: the currency of Giva, in a way.

But this plate would not allow Sancia or Clef or Claudia into her thoughts, only Greeter. And though Berenice liked Greeter—it was impossible not to like Greeter, really—this experience was very different.

The things we do, she thought with a sigh, *to return home.*

She slid out the bronze plate, grabbed it with a bare hand, and allowed Greeter to open up her mind.

Berenice cringed as the enormity of Greeter's sentience thundered in. The crushing weight of so much knowledge, so much input, just so much *stuff* was almost too much to bear . . .

As was what Greeter was doing to her, of course: Greeter was riffling through her thoughts and memories, examining each one to confirm how the operation had gone—and more important, to confirm that Tevanne had not captured or dominated any of them during their incursion into its territory and forced them into becoming a host.

Bringing a host into Giva would mean Tevanne would see all that host would see and know all that host would know. And that would be devastating. Far more devastating than a few moments with Greeter's pathplate.

But it still pained Berenice to have Greeter inside her, studying her experiences. *How odd it is,* she thought, *to have this being circling our ship study me like I'm a butterfly caught in crystal . . .* It made her so intensely, overpoweringly aware of how *huge* Greeter was, so much larger than any ordinary human—because, of course, they were far from any such thing.

In one second, Berenice saw the whole of the operation occur before her: the governor, the walls, the volley, the death of Vittorio . . .

<*Almost done,*> whispered Greeter. <*I'm almost done . . .* >

And then she saw . . .

A black mask.

A black mask, placed upon the face of a man, or something man-shaped, suspended in a floating chamber, and a voice screaming in horror and pain.

No. Please. I don't want to think of him, I don't want to think of him again . . .

Then it was over. Greeter's massive presence lifted from Berenice's thoughts like a bar of lead off her chest. Berenice gasped, trying to get ahold of herself.

<*I see,*> said Greeter quietly. <*That was a . . . very difficult one.*>

Sancia fell to all fours as well, breathing hard. <*Yes. It was.*>

<*I am so, so sorry for what you all went through. You are, of course, cleared for entry. I will bring the* Comprehension *alongside the* Keyship *to assist with the refugees.*>

Berenice looked to the side and saw a galleon slowly trundling its way toward them, this one bedecked with lanterns that glowed a soft, relaxing light.

"Here we go," muttered Sancia.

They watched as Greeter's galleon—dubbed the *Comprehension*—slowly pulled alongside them. The Grattiarans watched this immense vessel warily, and she couldn't blame them. This was probably the only time in their lives that they'd ever seen ships of this size.

Polina emerged onto the main deck, clambered aboard a small crate, and turned to address the crowd. "This is a medical and hospitality vessel," she said to them. "Not a wartime craft. They will be able to treat you better than we can here. You will be boarding shortly for them to care for you."

The scrived planks slowly extended, securing the two massive vessels together. Berenice could see people gathering on the *Comprehension*'s decks, waiting in groups of five every ten feet or so, bandages and gear in their hands. All of them there were dressed in hues of purple and light blue.

<*Spread out a little,*> said Sancia to them. <*And look more natural.*>

The groups of people shuffled about a bit.

<*This feels very natural, to me,*> said Greeter, a touch resentfully.

<*Half of you are striking the same pose,*> said Sancia. <*You look like a dance troupe. And don't talk all at once this time. We don't want to scare the hell out of them.*>

<*Berenice,*> said Greeter. <*Please talk sense into her.*>

<*She has a point,*> said Berenice. <*I'd rather not lead the Grattiarans into thinking we're a mad cult.*>

<*I'm Greeter because I'm* good *at this!*> said Greeter.

<*We can always be better,*> said Sancia.

The starving, beleaguered Grattiarans shakily stepped onto the wooden walkways and shuffled over to the *Comprehension*. The crowd of purple-clad people began ushering them to pallets they'd laid out to treat them, feed them, clothe them, and care for them. Once the Grattiarans were mostly transferred, Berenice and Sancia followed.

The two of them watched as the crowd of purple- and blue-clad Givans moved in a perfect choreography, always at the right place at the right time, never tripping over one another, responding to cries and calls and breakdowns almost instantly. They dressed wounds, attended to rotted teeth, clipped nails, and fitted shoes and boots on the Grattiarans, all in a measured, controlled symphony of care. The sight was surreal—and slightly unnerving.

<*How many people are you now, Greeter?*> asked Sancia.

<*Sancia . . .* > said Berenice. <*You know that's not polite . . .* >

<*I always consider myself to be* one *person, Sancia,*> said Greeter. One of the purple-clad people, this one a young woman with long

braided hair, gave Sancia a withering look. <*But if you must know, 131 constituents have now joined my cadence.*>

Sancia whistled lowly. <*I had no idea that nursing was so popular.*>

Six nearby purple-clad people sighed in exasperation. <*And here I thought,*> said Greeter, <*that twinned thinking* increases *empathy . . .* >

They watched as Greeter returned to their perfectly timed labors.

Berenice grasped Sancia's hand and whispered to her, <*You shouldn't be such a pest.*>

<*Yeah, yeah,*> said Sancia.

<*You know Greeter does quite a lot more than just nursing.*>

<*Yeah . . . but although they're damned useful, they also kind of creep me out. When we first twinned ourselves . . . did you ever imagine anything like this?*>

<*Absolutely not,*> said Berenice. <*But when you invent a new technology, I suppose you can never quite comprehend all the uses people will find for it . . .* >

And both Berenice and Sancia still struggled to comprehend Greeter.

Back in the early days of Giva, when Berenice had first tried using pathplates to manage everyone's connections, most people had indeed fallen into a dangerously deep sleep.

But others had responded . . . very differently.

Some had not slept: instead, they'd woken up, and started getting a lot of funny ideas about what it meant to be a person. Were two twinned people really two people? Or were they one mind, one sentience, that just happened to be in two bodies?

And that was how Greeter had been born.

Greeter was a "cadence," which was to say many twinned people of similar temperament who had grown so close together that they'd aligned into what was, in essence, a singular identity. This was all enabled by the pathplates hanging about their necks, which convinced all of Greeter—all the people spread not only aboard the *Comprehension,* but across Greeter's many, many smaller vessels in the fleet—that they were touching at all times, and thus that their minds were one.

And Greeter was not alone. The floating nation of Giva now had several cadences, and they did very important work. Greeter was the largest, and was unusually sympathetic and empathic, capable of comprehending conditions of the human mind and body far more than any individual person ever could. This made Greeter skilled at inducting terrified refugees into Giva—but also talented at pathing into the minds of others, understanding what they knew, and searching them for any treachery.

There was another cadence called Play, for rearing children and tending to the elderly; then another cadence for farming on the islands, quite a few for construction, and more. The second largest was Design, who was talented at scriving—a cadence that their friend Giovanni had founded, just after narrowly surviving the fall of Old Tevanne.

No one was forced or compelled to join a cadence. In fact, most were unfit for alignment, as they lacked the right temperament. People could remove the pathplates about their necks whenever they wanted, break their connection with the cadence, and walk away a singular person again. Though this had happened before, it was quite rare—and those who did walk away often missed the experience and returned.

Berenice idly wondered, not for the first time, what it was like. Some of the cadences had told her that, if she wished, she could join them, and come into alignment with their thoughts. Yet she never had, because she knew Sancia could not follow—for after all Sancia had been through, and all the scrivings she bore, she was simply too abnormal for them to induct.

Then a small voice rang out across the deck: "*Mama!*"

Berenice blinked and saw a small dark-haired boy sprinting across the *Comprehension,* his face blooming with a gap-toothed grin. He ran to the railing, and then waved frantically at the cockpit of the *Keyship.*

Claudia leaned forward out of the cockpit and waved back, her face beaming. "Gio!" she cried back. "Gio, Gio!"

<*Wow!*> said Sancia, eyeing the child. <*He's . . . bigger! Like, a lot! I thought it'd only been a couple weeks?*>

<*Ber,*> said Claudia. <*Can I leave my post?*>

<*Make sure the* Keyship *is anchored and secured,*> said Berenice. <*But, yes, of course.*>

A handful of minutes, and then Claudia emerged, sprinted across the deck of the *Keyship,* and leapt aboard the *Comprehension,* where she swooped the little boy up in a bear hug and showered him with kisses. "My love, my love!" she said. "Look how many teeth you've lost! You'll have your big teeth before the sun hits the sea!"

"Look," the little boy said, pointing proudly at his mouth.

She peered in. "What is it?"

"Lost lot of teeth," he said chipperly.

"Oh," she said, somewhat bewildered. "Well, yes, I did just say that, my love . . ."

Her husband, Ritti, came to join them—a tremendously tall and broad man, with a ponderous beard and unruly hair. Berenice knew he'd been something of a pirate in his days before Giva, seizing merchant house ships; and though she'd often wondered if it'd been he who helped Claudia become such a magnificent shot, it was hard to see such a past in his grinning face.

<*Will you be able to come to the Assembly with us?*> Berenice asked her.

Claudia slowly set her child down. <*Ahh,*> she said. <*Well. I could, but . . .* >

Berenice suppressed a sigh. <*If you would prefer to spend time with your family, that is completely understandable.*>

She smiled. <*Excellent. Thank you, Ber.*>

<*But I might need you later,*> Berenice said. <*You and Sancia both. I've no doubt Design will want to look at our captured deadlamp, and I'll want every available scriver on hand to participate.*>

<*With Design?*> said Claudia grimly.

<*Yes. I know they're not your favorite, but—*>

<*No,*> said Claudia. <*Nor is the work. But I can do it. Just give me time.*> She gave Berenice a half salute, and the three of them trooped off toward the shallops, little Gio astride her shoulders.

<*It's nice to see families,*> said Sancia. <*Given that everything else is, you know, scrumming mad.*>

<*Yes.*>

Berenice looked out at the fleet of Giva. Her eye lingered on the towering galleons. Most of them were operated by cadences. She wondered how many of the refugees would find shelter among them, or join the cadences, or even found a new one.

Then Greeter's voice echoed in their thoughts: <*Berenice? The Assembly's ready to talk to you. They'll meet aboard the* Innovation, *in one of the scriving bays.*>

8

Berenice winced as the wind lashed the hull of the *Innovation.* She knew the ship was secure—as the beating heart of all of Giva's scriving practices, the galleon was so altered and enhanced that it should be able to survive a full monsoon—but she also knew it wasn't the weather that troubled her.

Twelve representatives from all the departments and factions and cadences of Giva sat in a tight circle in one of the *Innovation*'s scriving bays, their faces lit by scrived lamps in the gloom of the soot-blackened chamber. Having listened to Berenice's report, they now witnessed the events of the operation as a pathplate was passed around, and they each experienced Berenice's memory of the event personally, one by one.

Finally they finished and sat in a shaken silence. Even for veterans of Giva, such deep pathing was immensely uncomfortable—especially for Polina, who'd never really grown accustomed to the art.

"This is . . . most interesting," said Design, the scriving cadence. "Most *intriguing.*"

"Intriguing?" said Berenice. "I'm not sure that's the word I'd choose."

"It's one of many that comes to mind," said Design. "It's a new problem. One I've never anticipated. And that is saying something." They smiled humorlessly. Design's constituent was a small man in appearance, with a sly, wizened face and long fingers that curled over and over again in thought. They had a thoughtful, quiet air about themselves—but then, Design was the most cerebral of the cadences, arraying themselves in leather aprons and thick gloves, and always with their pockets stuffed with parchments.

"There seems to be no end of daunting questions here," said Mortar. They sighed deeply. This was uncharacteristically expressive for them: as one of the oldest construction cadences, they were often stoic to the point of inscrutable. "To begin with, I wonder—how did Tevanne move its forces so quickly?"

"I agree," said Play, the childrearing cadence. "And next—how did Clef path into the mind of such a thing?"

"And finally," said Greeter, "how can we verify whether what Clef saw was true?" Their constituent was a tall, broad man with a thick beard and small, sad eyes, and they nodded to Sancia apologetically, as if sorry to slight her friend. "Tevanne's mind cannot be like most. Perhaps he saw phantoms, or something akin to madness?"

Polina looked around at them, her gaze as hard as milled steel. "Let us simply cut to it. If what we think Clef saw truly *is* what he saw—if Crasedes has fallen, and Tevanne will no longer have to fight a two-front war—what will we *do*?"

An awkward silence.

"Flight seems wisest," said Play finally. "We only ever achieve victory over the enemy when it is distracted or unaware."

"I agree," said Design. "We must mobilize the fleet and leave the islands."

"Perhaps we should look to our military leaders on this," said Greeter, looking to Berenice.

"I . . . tend to agree as well," admitted Berenice. "We'll have to find safe harbor elsewhere—far from Tevanne's shores. It's never really ventured far out to sea, at least since its initial dispersal."

Sancia twitched very slightly beside Berenice but said nothing.

"But if Tevanne truly can transport its forces so quickly, and so far," said Mortar, "would that still hold true? Would the open ocean truly be a barrier to it?"

"Better to run, and see if it gives chase," said Berenice, "than wait and be surprised when it appears on our doorstep."

"But to where?" asked Greeter. "Where could we be safe?"

"Well, with the things we've made," said Design, "we could go *anywhere* and survive. Especially with the recent submergence modifications I've made t—"

"The submergence modifications have not been tested," said Mortar sternly. "I would *not* suggest we use those."

"Fine, fine," said Design, nettled. "But we have endless capabilities at our disposal. There's no reason we're anchored to this place! We could turn our galleons into floating farms, pull minerals from the very seas, build tools and rigs from stuff filtered from the very wat . . . water . . ."

Their brow creased, and the words fell to a slow trickle—for then came a flicker of worry so sharp that all the Assembly paused, wondering at its source.

All eyes again fell on Sancia. She sat there glowering in her chair, rubbing the ghostly imprint of long-faded calluses on her palms.

"Sancia?" said Polina. "What is it?"

Sancia looked up at them, her gaze dancing from face to face. "I don't think you're getting it. Crasedes is the greatest scriver in the history of the human species." One of her hands thoughtlessly touched where Clef lay at her chest. "As far as I'm aware, at least. The bastard knew countless secrets, unspeakable methods, techniques we can't even *fathom.* Shit, he's been *inside* the guts of reality."

"We know all this," said Design curtly. "And Tevanne is surely the greater scriver now. Between its deadlamps and itself, it's like . . . like some inversion of the Creator Himself, commanding leagues of black angels."

"But it isn't," said Sancia. "Tevanne is a melding of Gregor Dandolo and Valeria. It only knows what the two of them knew before. And Crasedes kept a *lot* of secrets from Valeria. The strangest, the most powerful, the most dangerous commands . . . Those could very well still lie only in Crasedes's head. Maybe *that's* why Tevanne's always pursued Crasedes."

Greeter leaned forward, ashen-faced. "But . . . now that Tevanne has captured Crasedes . . ."

Sancia nodded. "When I glimpsed him, he was . . . screaming. Screaming in agony. Like Tevanne was trying to torture him—maybe to break him open."

Berenice wasn't sure if it was the waves or all their minds twinned together, but she suddenly felt nauseated, and the air felt very thick and close.

"What could those secrets be?" demanded Polina.

"Hell, I don't know," said Sancia. "Our conversations weren't exactly civilized. He was mostly trying to kill us all."

"What . . . What if Tevanne has already succeeded?" asked Play faintly. "What if Crasedes has already surrendered all he knows?"

The rest of the Assembly dissolved into fretful muttering.

<*It seems unlikely that it has,*> Sancia said. <*Being as we're all still arou—*>

"Out loud, please," called Polina. "All of us *out loud*! I've enough nonsense swilling about in my head naturally without everyone adding more!" She glared at Sancia. "What is it you're proposing?"

"I . . . think there's only one option," said Sancia. "If Crasedes is a potential resource for Tevanne, we have to . . . to neutralize it."

"Neutralize . . ." said Design faintly. "You understand what you're suggesting now, yes?"

"Kind of, yeah," said Sancia.

"An invasion," murmured Greeter.

Berenice stared at Sancia, shocked. <*Are . . . Are you really proposing that, San?*>

<*I . . . didn't* think *I was.*> Sancia glanced at her. <*I only had the idea just now.*>

"Damn it all, out loud, out *loud!*" shouted Polina.

Polina's shout echoed in some far recesses of the *Innovation.* Nobody spoke.

"Not a *real* invasion," Sancia said. "I'm not talking goddamned armies. Maybe . . . an operation. A small team."

"To do *what*?" snapped Polina. "Sneak into the depths of hell and break that devil out of prison?"

"And kill him," said Sancia. "Less an operation or sabotage job than an assassination. Grim stuff, but . . . it's worth it if it keeps whatever's in Crasedes's head out of Tevanne's hands."

"Sancia, listen to me," said Polina. "You are proposing we risk what few military resources we have to break past Tevanne's outer defenses—something no one has *ever* done—then navigate to wherever this magic prison is, break it open, and free our *second*-most dangerous enemy . . . and then kill him. An act that you yourself were incapable of doing a mere eight years ago! Even though we've heard rumors he's recovered many abilities—that he can fly and fight whether it's day or night! All to prevent something about which you possess only speculation!"

"Well, there's some shit I don't need to speculate about!" said Sancia. "We know Tevanne fought a war for nearly a *decade* to get Crasedes. A war unlike we've ever seen. We know it did that for a reason. And I think Clef will know that reason when he wakes up."

There was an uncomfortable silence as the two women glowered at each other. Greeter coughed quietly into their hand.

"I will listen," said Polina. "When he wakes. But in the meantime, we must isolate if not quarantine him. Being as he pathed *into* Tevanne, we have no idea who or . . . or what will be waking up."

"This is Clef we're talking about," said Sancia.

"Yes, but Tevanne seems remarkably talented at dominating other minds!" said Polina. She shuddered. "I would prefer Clef not have any interaction with any Givan until we know he's safe."

"Then how the hell are we going to know when he's awake?" said Sancia. "You have to touch him to hear him, or touch a plate to him. And aren't we all hanging on tenterhooks to hear what he has to say?"

There was a puzzled silence among the Assembly.

"Could there be some kind of . . . I don't know, alarm rig we could make?" asked Polina.

Berenice cocked her head, thinking. "I . . . might have a possible solution already made," she said. "An old sound rig I know someone made—old, but possibly still functional."

"And I can perform a quick fix if it isn't," said Design. "But it doesn't have to be perfect, yes? I would prefer you and Claudia focus more on assisting me with the deadlamp, Berenice."

Berenice sighed, exasperated. "Yes, yes, the deadlamp. And yes, this sound rig. I will get to all of these. But I have another task to perform that I *must* take care of. One that will need Claudia as well."

"You do?" said Design, puzzled.

Then Greeter, always the most intuitive of all the cadences, spoke up: "Yes. She has a soldier to memorialize."

"Oh," said Design quietly.

Another lurch as a blast of wind struck the *Innovation.*

"It's been mere hours after Grattiara, so I am not yet committed to the idea of invasion," said Berenice. She noticed Sancia's face suddenly went very hard and very closed. "But while we wait for Clef, we must take every opportunity to prepare ourselves for whatever's coming. And though we don't have much information, I think it'd be enormously helpful to verify what we *did* get from Tevanne, at least."

"I thought all Sancia witnessed were pictures," said Design. "Images."

"Yes," said Berenice. "Images possibly of the *interior* of Tevanne. Something that's been completely unknown to the entire world since Tevanne's emergence."

The Assembly members glanced at one another uncertainly.

"How are these pictures of use," said Mortar, "if we've no idea what they depict?"

"Fair point," said Play. "A black hole in a wall, like a hole in reality, surrounded in silver scrivings . . . Who could possibly know what these are, or where they are?"

"Some seem more identifiable," said Polina. "Sancia said she saw a valley in the mountains, filled with ruins . . . But there are dozens of those in the inland regions of the Gothian nations. Leftovers from Crasedes's day, they say, from when he smashed this or that civilization. Figuring out which one she saw won't be easy . . ."

"But that's the simple part," said Berenice. "We just need to—"

Sancia shot up in her chair as she realized what Berenice was about to propose. "Ahh, *shit*!"

"What?" said Design. "Ah shit what?"

Yet Greeter, who was far more skilled at empathy than the other cadences, had already followed her thoughts. "Ahh," they said. "You . . . wish to do an index."

"Yes," said Berenice.

"No!" said Sancia. "No, no, and *hell* no. I didn't agree to that!"

"An index could be helpful, yes," mused Greeter.

Sancia scowled.

Polina looked at Greeter. "How long would it take to arrange an indexing?"

"The *Comprehension* stands ready and waiting," said Greeter. "I can begin preparations now and have the index cradle ready by nightfall."

Sancia rubbed the side of her head. "Goddamn it all, I scrumming *hate* indexing."

"Sancia," said Polina, "give Berenice the key, then head to the *Comprehension*. Berenice—please get the sound rig first. Once that's done, you can grieve Vittorio properly, and make your peace." She shot a sharp glance at Design. "You can then assist Design whenever you are able. Does that all work?"

"Yes," said Berenice.

"Yeah," said Sancia.

"Good," said Polina. The wind rose and howled again outside. "Because soon we won't be able to handle much ship-to-ship transport."

Berenice followed Sancia into the passageways outside the scriving bay. Then she darted forward, grabbed Sancia's hand, and whispered, <*What the hell are you doing?*>

Sancia looked over her shoulder at her. <*What the hell are* you *doing?*>

<*Trying to stay alive. And I feel like fighting Tevanne head-on isn't the best way to do that!*>

They narrowed their eyes at each other in the shadows. It was uncommon for people as aligned as Sancia and Berenice to have disagreements, or even to be surprised at the thoughts and ideas and concerns of another—but it wasn't impossible. Even twinned people continued being people.

<I get it, Ber,> said Sancia. *<You want to work out some trick to save us all. But eventually you run out of time at your workbench. And then you have to go with what you've got.>* She reached up, slid Clef out of her shirt, and held him out to her. *<Take him. We've work to do. I'll see you after the index.>*

Berenice took him, then watched as Sancia ran up the stairs to the upper hulls. She limped slightly now, her right knee rotating in with each step—some consequence of an arthritic hip, they thought.

Berenice listened to her syncopated footfalls until they were gone. Then she looked down at Clef, his gold gleaming in the shadows, and there was no sound but the rain thrumming on the hulls.

9

Berenice and Diela navigated the depths of the *Keyship*'s cargo bays, winding through the dripping dark. Most of the cargo bays had been converted into living spaces for refugees, but a few of the massive vaults held armaments, ammunition, or salvaged trinkets or rigs that had been forgotten here long ago.

<*It's down here somewhere,*> said Berenice, holding a scrived lantern high. <*I know it is.*>

<*We don't have to have a rig,*> said Diela. < *I could just hold him, Capo. I don't mind.*>

Berenice grimaced and pressed a hand against where Clef now lay in her pocket. <*No.*>

<*Wouldn't it work? I mean—I've got a plate in me. To Clef, I'm basically a rig—so he could talk to me.*>

<*I'm sure it'd work, but that's exactly what we* don't *want, Diela,*> she said. The girl was still plainly in shock, and though she hadn't wanted to admit it, Berenice had worried what the girl might do in the wake of Vittorio. *Better to keep her close,* she'd thought, *than risk her going off alone, and doing who-knows-what.*

<*I'm all right,*> said Diela defiantly. <*I am.*>

<*Diela,* I'm *barely all right,*> said Berenice. <*No one's all right, having been through what we've been through!*>

<*But I like Clef,*> said Diela. <*He makes jokes. Which no one* else *around here seems to do anymore. It's like you all up and forgot how to be funny.*>

<*Living through a holocaust,*> said Berenice, <*has that effect. Just please rest, Diela.*>

<*How can I rest?*> said Diela. <*I don't want to sit still. Sitting still is when I go mad.*>

Berenice studied Diela's face in the half-light. She was so young, so earnest, but there was a desperation to her eyes now. The sight of it troubled Berenice, for it wasn't unfamiliar to her. Diela was the youngest person who'd ever been twinned: she'd been barely twelve when they'd rescued her from a rancid, decaying slave plantation, and the girl had been so traumatized she'd been unable to even speak. It had been Sancia's idea to twin the girl, and she volunteered to communicate with her wordlessly and guide her back to normal human life.

The process had been a success, so much so that Diela was now the most talented pather in all of Giva, able to sense the faintest flicker of emotions in someone, or unravel an entire history out of a wrinkle of a thought. But there had been two side effects: the first was a rather unhealthy obsession with Berenice and Sancia, her rescuers; and the second was her nearly addictive desire for stimulation, as if the memories of her childhood were so full of terrors the only solution was to wash them away with new ones.

<*You move so much,*> Berenice said to her, <*you can't even tell that you're hurt.*>

<*Then am I hurt at all?*> said Diela.

<*Yes,*> said Berenice. <*You are. And you'll know it when you break, probably at an inopportune time. And you* will *break, Diela, if you aren't careful.*> She stopped and turned to her. <*Do you remember what duty is?*>

<*Yes,*> said Diela reluctantly. <*It's doing something you don't want to do, because it's better for everyone, not you.*>

<*Yes. It is taking a piece of yourself and giving it to all. Sancia's doing her duty now, going through an index over in the* Comprehension. *Your*

duty now is to heal yourself. So be calm, be still, and rest. And help me find . . . > She spied something in the corner. <*Ah. There it is.*> She walked over to a small dusty leather case lying in the corner of the cargo bay.

<*This is it?*> asked Diela.

Berenice picked it up, blew on the layer of dust on the top, and sent the air dancing with ancient must. <*It is. Hopefully it should all be in one piece. Unless we did something to rattle all the stuff down here.*>

<*There was that time Sancia had to make that mad turn to avoid being hit by one of Tevanne's shriekers,*> said Diela. <*Remember that, Capo?*>

<*Oh yes,*> said Berenice, a touch glumly. She set it down on a large crate to their right. <*Outside of Varia.*>

<*No, I was talking about the Bay of Piscio,*> said Diela. <*I'd forgotten we did that in Varia . . .* >

Berenice sighed. <*I suppose we're lucky we're in one piece, let alone this thing.*>

She slid aside the lock on the leather case and delicately lifted its lid. Together they looked inside.

<*It looks* amazing,> said Diela. <*What is it?*>

<*It's a sound rig,*> said Berenice, reaching in and taking it out. <*One that my old mentor made, a long time ago. Though he'd been following in the footsteps of someone else.*>

She affixed a loupe to her eye and examined the delicate little rig. Its many steel strings—all engraved with impossibly tiny sigils—had somehow escaped any dust or corrosion, and they gleamed in the light of the little scrived lamp.

How odd it is to see his work now, Berenice thought. *Like seeing his fingerprints embedded in the world around me . . .*

She cleared her throat. <*Put Clef in a galleon, and he can control it,*> she said. <*I don't see why he can't do the same to a sound rig like this, and just call to us when he's ready.*>

<*How did this wind up down here, Capo?*> asked Diela.

<*Claudia and Gio took it and a few other things by accident when they left to start their own firm, back in Old Tevanne,*> said Berenice. <*When they evacuated during Shorefall Night, they brought it all with them.*> She pulled out her scriving tools, her tongue wedged carefully in her

lips, and went to work. <*I just need a place for Clef to sit. A lock, as it were. Shouldn't be a moment.*>

Diela looked around at the other crates as they waited for her to finish.

<*So the rest of this stuff here . . . are these also the things Claudia and Gio brought from Foundryside?*>

<*Eh?*> said Berenice. <*Yes, I think so.*>

Diela's eyes fell on one large crate. Her face tensed in that curious way it always did when she used that uncanny intuition, comprehending something everyone thought was hidden or forgotten. "Oh, goodness," she said quietly. She reached down, pulled up on the lid of the big crate, and slid it aside.

Berenice did a double take as she realized what Diela had found: a huge scrived suit of armor, wrought of black metal, dented and scratched at the pauldrons and greaves. She stopped working and stood and looked at it, shoulder to shoulder with Diela.

"I know what that is," said Diela aloud. "That's a . . . that's a lorica."

"I didn't know they'd brought that," said Berenice softly. "How did . . . How did this . . ."

"I remember Sancia said she gave it to Claudia to sell after the Night of the Mountain," said Diela. "I guess she never got around to it, and just boxed him up. *It* up, I mean."

Berenice narrowed her eyes at her. "Did she say that? Or did you pick that up from her?"

Diela blinked. "I . . . I don't quite remember, Capo."

There was a long silence.

"I . . . I need to finish here," said Berenice. "Won't be too much longer." She knelt before the little sound rig in the case and continued making a lock for Clef. She tried to ignore the way Diela gently reached down and pressed her palm against its breast as if feeling for a heartbeat.

<*You knew him, didn't you?*> Diela said.

"What?" said Berenice aloud, startled.

<*Gregor. The man who wore this suit of armor,*> she said. <*You knew him.*>

Berenice stared at her, slightly aggrieved. <*Yes,*> she said. <*I . . . I did.*>

She tried to focus on her task, adhering the little housing frame to the side of the sound rig, and then the pathplate within . . .

<*Did he die wearing it?*> asked Diela.

<*Yes,*> said Berenice. <*Several times, actually. But he always came back. He had a habit of that . . .* >

<*Sancia thinks he's still out there,*> said Diela, a touch dreamily. <*Trapped inside this other, vaster rig, a little like this armor . . . But we don't know how to get him ou—*>

"Done," said Berenice curtly. She stood. "All done. Just a moment."

She slipped Clef out from where he hung around her neck and placed him within the simple lock within the sound rig. Then she shut the case and stepped back.

<*I'll carry this with me,*> she said. <*Until Clef's awake. Then he can hopefully tell us what he saw without us having to touch him.*>

<*Even if Clef did touch Tevanne back there, I can't imagine it changed him,*> said Diela. <*I can't imagine he could ever be anyone besides Clef.*>

Berenice glanced at the lorica and remembered a moment long ago, when a man she knew had swallowed a little plate, and woken up someone very different.

She looked at Diela. "That's one thing done," she said. "But you and I have one more task to do tonight—don't we, Diela?"

Diela was silent.

"Come," said Berenice. "Let's say goodbye to him."

Back in her campo days—back in Old Tevanne, a lifetime or two ago, if not more—Berenice had decided she was not a person who cried.

It had been purely a defense mechanism, she remembered: by deciding she would not cry, but that she was instead a person who definitively *did* not and *could* not cry, she'd made herself immune to all the subtle or not-so-subtle insults from the other Dandolo scrivers, who'd all been male, wealthy, and—most important of all—jealous.

She'd had an imaginary process she'd complete each morning: she'd wake up each day in her tiny rooms and step backward into an invisible cold cloak, which would veil her face and mind entirely. *I'm like the river men who coat themselves in mud each day,* she'd say during this little mental pivot, *and sheathe their skin against the water flies.*

And it'd worked. Though the other Dandolo scrivers, of course, had then called her frigid and distant, each day had become more bearable, until all the words of the men around her—Orso included—had diminished until they were little more than the foul smells one encountered every day in Old Tevanne.

But at some point, things had changed. It'd become less like she was putting on her cold, invisible cloak and more like she'd swallowed it, and it'd sealed up all her insides; and then one day Berenice hadn't been sure if she'd decided she was no longer a person who cried, or if she'd never been such a person at all. This part of her had become an atrophied limb, and she'd started to experience the world at a remove, as if her life was happening to someone else.

Until the Night of the Mountain. Until Sancia. The sight of her, the smell of her, the sheer bigness of her, like she was some romantic, dashing character so tremendous she broke the very book that bound her up. And then in a handful of mad, smoke-swirled hours, that cold veil had been banished away, and it'd been like Berenice had awoken from a deep dream.

And yet, as she now ascended the stairs of the *Keyship,* with the light of Diela's lantern bobbing over the walls about her, she suddenly, desperately wished for the return of that invisible veil; for some measure, any measure, of separation between herself and the events she was now seeing.

Finally they came to the sick bay, and she saw the others waiting for her: Claudia and Polina and several of Greeter's constituents, who were always such a help at times like this.

And there, in the box on the floor, lay a Givan uniform, unrolled and unfolded and laid out on the bottom of the box, a substitute for a body and a person they no longer had.

There was a long silence, broken only by the pattering of rain and the rise and fall of the wind.

"He always took care of his clothes well," said Claudia softly. "He was a scrumming better dresser than all of us."

The image of the lorica lying in the crate flashed in Berenice's mind.

Ghosts of boys in boxes, she thought. *Some dead, and some not dead enough.*

She cleared her throat. "He was."

Claudia wept and turned away, and Greeter was there to hold her.

Berenice stared into the box, trying to remember Vittorio. He had been so terribly young. He had been so competent in his life, so daring, that it had been easy to forget his youth.

Is he younger than I was, she thought, *when I met Sancia? When we plotted and planned to overthrow a city, and every dream and kiss felt remarkable?*

Again, she thought of the empty lorica, its vacant eyes staring up at her.

Was Gregor older than I am now when he first put on the armor? Or when he swallowed that plate and made himself the thing we now battle?

The silence stretched on and on. Finally everyone's eyes moved from the uniform in the box to her, and they waited for her to speak.

"We should think on him," she said hoarsely. "To remember him not as he is now, but as he was. And then, once we have that, we should hold hands, and remember fully."

They nodded and gathered around the box.

Together, in the dim light of the sick bay, Berenice and her people held hands, pathed among one another, and became one.

They shared memories, images, impressions, sensations, all of Vittorio, the boy who had fought so hard and freed so many. And even though some of them had only known him for a few months, or barely even weeks, soon it began to feel like they had known him the whole of their lives—and they mourned what had been lost, and celebrated what had been.

<Let us keep him,> said Berenice. *<Let us keep him for as long as we can.>*

<As long as we can,> said her team.

When they were done—after they'd placed the box in the chamber and burned it to ashes and scattered them at the prow of the

Keyship—Berenice returned to her little chamber, and sat on her bed. One hand thoughtlessly stroked the place where Sancia so often slept beside her. Then she thought of boxes that might await her in the days to come, and all the people she might find in them, and what she would be left with when all of them had been burned to ash as well.

Then she fell on the bed, covered her eyes, and wept.

10

"This way!" sang Greeter's constituent, a merry-looking Daulo woman with bright-red cheeks. She gestured, leading Sancia down a tight staircase into the lower decks of the *Comprehension.*

Sancia winced as her right hip began to twinge. "How much farther? I don't remember this staircase."

"Not too much farther," said Greeter. "The index cradle is just two decks down. And you're correct, the staircase is new. I've done some optimization."

"You're always optimizing," grumbled Sancia, turning about on another landing.

"Because we're always growing," said Greeter. "We've gained eleven thousand people since you last visited the *Comprehension,* Sancia."

"Did you make all eleven thousand of them run down these goddamned stairs?"

Greeter laughed. It sounded like a genuine laugh—but then, everything Greeter did felt genuine. People forgot they were a cadence all the time, even Sancia—especially here in the decks of this enormous ship.

I'm inside them, she thought, looking around at the walls. *I'm inside of Greeter.*

It was silly to say, but it felt true—for in the past few years she'd come to think of the cadences not as groups of people but as their ships. When Sancia pictured Design in her head, for example, she did not picture one of their constituents. Instead, she pictured the *Innovation,* all wheels and scrived cauldrons and piles of bronze, the depths of the giant ship riddled with lifts and chutes and augmented conduits that pulled components and materials throughout its factory bays as Design created the many rigs that kept Giva alive. And when Sancia thought of Play, she thought of the *Cultivation,* which housed the old and young alike, with all its steps and sharp drops removed and replaced with ramps and rounded corners, and scrived pipes and water rigs installed everywhere for easy washing, and its great glass windows fixed in the hull of the ship so its denizens could watch the seas outside and sit in quiet wonder.

But Greeter's ship, the *Comprehension,* was always full of people.

Scores of people. Tremendous *throngs* of people. People from all races, all nations, all cultures, all across the Durazzo. The sheer variety of hair alone—in color, in length, in style—was astonishing, let alone the manners of clothing, language, diet, and more.

"A bit busy in this next portion," said Greeter's constituent, leading her through the crowded hallways. "Just this way . . ."

The refugees from Grattiara now filled the medical decks of the *Comprehension*. Sancia watched them lining up at small, discrete booths Greeter had arranged, where a constituent would insert a tiny plate into the backs of their hands, allowing them to become twinned with the people of Giva.

"How many consented to twinning?" asked Sancia.

"About seventy percent," said Greeter. "The remainder have the choice of finding positions in the fleet or working on the islands." They sniffed. "Most choose the islands. I suspect because they aren't acquainted with the wildlife . . ."

Sancia watched as a young man winced while Greeter's constituent carefully popped a plate into his hand. Once it was done he raised it and shook it, like he'd bumped it on a corner and it had caused some nerve pain—but then his eyes widened, and he went still, his mouth slowly opening in awe.

Sancia smiled wistfully. She had been through that herself, eight years ago. Alignment would take hours, if not days. Many of them, she knew, would stay in their rooms as the little plates in them did their work, dribbling new experiences into their minds; and throughout it all they'd silently speak to Greeter, pouring out their thoughts, their wishes, their agonies, their desires. And Greeter would listen.

In fact, if the *Comprehension* really reminded Sancia of anything, it was a cathedral, huge and spacious and brimming with people, suffused with faint glowing light by the dangling lanterns; and always there was the sound of whispering, and confession, and forgiveness and understanding.

But if this is a cathedral, thought Sancia, *what exactly does that make Greeter?*

<*How are you doing, Sancia?*> asked Greeter as they walked.

<*Don't you know?*> Sancia shot back.

Their constituent allowed a coy smile, but no more.

<*I'm alive,*> Sancia said. <*That's good enough.*>

Another smile, but there was a sadness in it now. <*I see. There are moments when that's enough, yes. But I find those moments are rare.*>

<*Are they?*>

<*Yes. Often the people here need more.*>

They entered a huge vaulted chamber filled with beds occupied by refugee families. Little ones thronged about where their parents kneeled or lay or sat, being ministered to by Greeter. Sancia thought she heard three different languages being spoken at once.

<*These people, for example,*> said Greeter, <*have suffered alone, in their various nations, their foundering cities. What they often want is the awareness that they are not* alone *in their suffering. That someone is there with them.*>

Sancia said nothing. Somewhere a baby started crying, pausing only to inhale.

They turned down one hallway and passed a crowd of about two dozen people, all dressed in purples and blues, sprawled over cushioned chairs, their eyes shut and their faces turned to the ceiling. All their mouths were moving very slightly, as if holding a silent conversation with someone invisible. Which, Sancia knew, was exactly what they were doing.

<*This seems like a hell of a lot,*> said Sancia.

<*It's a record,*> said Greeter. <*Twenty-seven listeners tonight. Rarely do I have to devote myself to so much messaging.*>

<*How many conversations are you maintaining right now, Greeter?*> she asked.

<*About eighty or so,*> they said.

<*Damn . . . all with the refugees?*>

<*Oh no. I'm talking to people out in the fleet. Mostly about the storm. It's quite bad, and it will get worse. People call to me, asking me to whisper something to someone on the other side of the fleet. Give wishes for good luck, or that they love each other. They're frightened. I'm doing my most to help them manage it.*>

They turned another corner. At the far end of the hall was a door: it was short, wrought of thick metal scrived to be preternaturally durable, and sealed shut with an array of locks—some scrived, some purely mechanical.

<*Are you suggesting,*> said Sancia, who was well used to Greeter's little games and koans, <*that I need a listener to talk to?*>

<*Ahh, technically, I would be that listener,*> said Greeter. <*Since I am all the listeners. So you could just talk to me.*>

<*About what?*>

Greeter looked at her. <*You have no end of things to talk about, Sancia. You are going through something no one else in Giva has ever known. The tiny rig in your skull is stealing your years, just as the deadlamps steal life from the people trapped inside them. That must be difficult.*>

Sancia stopped walking. "Everyone knows this," she said aloud. "I'm . . . I'm twinned with my wife, my friends, my . . . my comrades. They all share my suffering. That's what being part of Giva is all about."

Greeter nodded patiently. "Yes. We have invented a new way to be human—one could possibly say that, yes. But we are still human. And watching those we love support us in our suffering . . . That is a trial for anyone, augmented or otherwise."

Sancia did not move or speak.

"You don't want her to leave you," said Greeter gently.

"No," snapped Sancia. "I don't."

"But sometimes you think you do."

She fumed for a moment. She glared at Greeter, opened her mouth, rethought what she was going to say, and closed it. Then she finally said, "I think it'd be better sometimes. For her. It doesn't feel fair for her to have to . . ." She laughed miserably. "God. I have these wild dreams, you know, about inventing some way to reverse all this. Some scrived trick to turn me young again, to start over, to put it all back. So we could get back all the things we're losing, even now." She was silent for a moment. "But I'm not a child anymore. And I know there are some things you can't do over."

Greeter nodded. "You and Berenice built this place for us. We are all your children, in a way." They walked to the door and began unlocking the many locks to the cradle, then pushed the door open. "And we are stronger, and better, and wiser for having been made by you, Sancia. For knowing all the sacrifices you make, even now. Please don't forget that." They stepped back and extended an arm, welcoming her inside. "After you."

Sancia slowly stepped into the index cradle—a small oblong room built of black wood that was inlaid with more than two hundred bronzed plates, all carefully scrived with many, many sigils.

In the center of the little room was a curious piece of furniture: a large bronze half-pipe. It was about seven feet long, or long enough to support a very tall person lying down—hence the nickname "the cradle." Unlike the bronze plates throughout this room, its surface appeared blank, but Sancia knew that was just because its engraved sigils were so amazingly small they were almost impossible to read.

In function, the cradle was similar to a pathplate—just bigger, more powerful, and much, much more intimate.

"Any chance you changed it so I could preserve my dignity?" asked Sancia. "Or whatever dignity I've got left at this point?"

The constituent coughed from the doorway. <*Ahh . . . not quite. Unfortunately, because the cradle still functions based on skin contact, then we need to maximize the exposed skin surface, so . . .* >

Sancia scowled in the little black chamber.

<*You are aware, of course,*> said Greeter, <*that I retain memories of the body states of many,* many, *people.*>

"Yeah, yeah."

<*Over a thousand. Some that I've cared for, others that I've been. Including, since I have pathed with you now and again, your own bod—*>

"I get it!" snapped Sancia. "Still feels weird to . . . You know, go down deep into your belly, Greeter, get totally naked, and crawl into some hole in here."

Sancia did not bother telling Greeter to shut the door. Instead she grumbled for a second, disrobed, and tossed her clothes out onto the floor of the room beyond. "I guess you could fold those for me."

<*Certainly. I'll shut the door now.*>

She turned to face the cradle. The light in the room died as the door swung shut, and for a moment all was dark—but then a low, pinkish light glimmered from a lantern at the top of the chamber, and she stepped over to the bronze half-pipe.

"All right," she sighed. "Let's get this shit over with."

Berenice shut her eyes and tried not to shudder. *How I hate being here . . . How I* hate *it . . .*

"Ordinary iron," chanted Design's voice in the darkness. "Ordinary iron, clawed out of the ordinary earth and hauled to some massive scrived factory, some enormous rig that perhaps acts as Tevanne's intestines, its kidneys, built to process, process, process, digest enormous amounts of raw resources, and form them into . . . this." Their gloved hand grazed the interior wall of the deadlamp as they paced its length. In this ghostly vessel, still reeking of quicklime and lye, Berenice felt as if Design were some grinning psychopomp, here to bear their souls away as she and Claudia traced the sigils in the walls. "And yet, because Tevanne writes its scrivings within the bones of this thing, embeds its thought and will within its flesh and skin, it can become something *more*."

Berenice felt the deadlamp shift around them. For one terrified moment she thought it'd come alive again and was perhaps about to drift back to Tevanne. Then she remembered it was hanging in the cargo bay of the *Keyship,* which was being buffeted by the gales of the storm and must be dipping back and forth.

A little movement, she thought as she read a line of scrivings in the weak light of the lamps, *is to be expected . . . yes?*

"I keep finding some really basic shit," said Claudia from the corner. She looked over her shoulder at Design's primary constituent—the person they were using to speak to them—but she could have addressed the other dozen people packed into the deadlamp with them, since all of them were Design as well. "Density bindings, gravity scrivings. Stuff we know. The gravity rig's the most advanced thing in here. I thought this thing flew like . . . you know, a hierophant?"

"When it *edits* reality, it is like a hierophant," said Design. "But the rest of its nature resembles a totally normal scrived rig." Their darkened magnifying goggles caught the light of the lamps, giving their face a curiously arthropodal feel. "Because Tevanne can alter the physical capacities of this vessel to incomprehensible levels—*instantaneously.*"

"Instantaneously?" said Berenice dubiously. "That's not how scrivings work."

"It is a theory I've long considered," continued Design. Their voice was low and placid, like someone under the effects of a wonderful drug—and perhaps this was close to the truth, for meditating on scrivings seemed to do things to Design's vast mind that others could not comprehend. "After all—how does Clef convince a scrived door to open?"

"I think h—"

"He convinces the door, say, that opening in the other direction *does not count as opening,*" said Design triumphantly. "Or that the hinges are a thousand times denser than they actually are, so that they fall clean off the doorframe, and the whole thing comes apart! *That* is what Tevanne has built in so many of its creations—a loose structure that, when it applies its attention to it, can be persuaded to perform any number of tas—"

"So . . . Clef could fly this deadlamp?" said Diela's voice.

Design's trance broke. "Eh?" they said.

Diela's round, innocent face appeared at the top of the hatch, peering down at them as they labored. "If Tevanne is just doing Clef stuff, but bigger—could Clef fly this thing?"

"Y-Yes," said Design slowly. "Possibly. Perhaps."

"Is that why you asked me to bring Clef here?" said Berenice, eyeing Clef's sound rig on the floor. "To see if he can fly this thing?"

"Well, no," said Design, with a sigh. "I was hoping for some sign of, well . . . what I always seek."

"Ah," said Claudia. She visibly suppressed an eye roll. "The regulator."

"Yes," said Design, bristling with indignation. "Tevanne relies strongly on rigs—hard, accessible, *real* tools to manage all the abstract things it does. It must have some . . . some implement that all its twinning routes through, somehow, making it easy to control its hosts. I mean—imagine the feeling of having a hundred people die miserably, all at once! Imagine managing that! And yet, Tevanne does it every day!"

"And you think there's some magic box it keeps around to control all that," said Claudia.

"There is! There *must* be!" they snapped. "But I cannot study this phenomenon, because to do that, I would need a living host. And having a living host in Giva would be, ah, less than optimal."

"So how is Clef in a deadlamp going to help?" asked Berenice.

Design approached one of the chairs that the hosts had been trapped within. Then they knelt, examining a handful of plates set in the seat, back, and arms. "This. This is exactly what I needed."

Berenice joined Design at the chair to look. "Those are the contact points," she said. "The rigs that actually steal life from the hosts."

"Yes," said Design. "Yes. But how does Tevanne enforce this? How does it redirect the very livelihood of a being from this chair into the hierophantic console?" They glanced at the molten lump of brass in the middle of the deadlamp. "Or what's left of it, at least. If I can test this, only for a second, perhaps I can understand *how Tevanne controls its hosts*."

Design's constituents then stood at once and swarmed the hierophantic console and one of the deadlamp's chairs, applying their modification plates here and there. It was, as always, a powerfully strange sight, to see them invading one another's personal space without batting an eye—because, of course, all their space belonged to one identity.

An idea occurred to Berenice. "How exactly are we going to test that, though?"

"By turning it on, of course," Design said smoothly.

Berenice and Claudia stared at them.

"You want to . . . what?" Berenice asked.

"To turn it on," said Design again.

"God's balls . . ." said Claudia.

"As in—let this deadlamp steal the life of a living thing, to alter reality?" asked Berenice. "And you want to turn it on here, in the middle of the Givan fleet?"

"To *try* to, at least," said Design. "It doesn't need to be fully successful."

"Are . . . Are you really telling us that someone is getting in that seat?" asked Claudia.

"In a way," said Design. They looked at Berenice, their goggled face curiously hungry. "Clef *is* in that sound rig, isn't he?"

Berenice cocked her head, thinking. "Ahh . . . I see. Did you ask Polina for approval on this, Design?"

"I didn't think I'd need to," said Design. "Clef is neither alive nor dead."

"Which will probably confuse this monster just enough to *try* to steal his life," said Berenice slowly. "Is that the idea?"

"Yes," said Design. "And that little window into Tevanne's inner workings . . . That's all I need."

Berenice nodded, now quite impressed. Yet then she paused. "But—the living thing has to do more than just *be* in the chair to have its life stolen. It also needs to have the plates of a host embedded *in* them."

"Or at least touching them, yes," said Design. "This is true."

"So—do you also have a way of tricking this rig into believing you have a host's plate?"

"Well. I didn't think I needed to *trick* it."

A distant crack of thunder, and a rush of rain.

Berenice felt a pit forming in her stomach. "You didn't."

Design shrugged. "Someone had to do something about the burned bodies in here . . ." They reached into a pocket and pulled out a small leather bag. "I *did* give them a formal memorial. A much better final rest than anything that could have found them while under Tevanne's spell. But before *that,* I accomplished a . . . a few other tasks."

Design tipped the leather bag over into their gloved hand. A dozen tiny winking metal plates tumbled into their palm.

"God's *balls,*" said Claudia again.

"Oh my," said Diela from above.

Berenice put her face in her hands. *I hope Sancia is at least having a better time than I am.*

Sancia grunted in surprise as she lay down in the bronze cradle. *<Hey, it's . . . warm.>*

<Yes,> said Greeter. *<Any—any creature comfort I can offer . . . I'm going to have to kill the light before we get started. Please let me know when you're ready.>*

Sancia situated herself within the half-pipe, staring up at the rosy lantern above her. *<Ready.>*

The light blinked out, and Sancia waited.

One of the hardest things about living in any society, advanced or impoverished, was matching knowledge to need. If someone encountered an issue—say, a farmer witnessing a new mold in a crop of apricots—the farmer would understandably wonder if anyone knew what this was and go about looking for help.

In normal societies, the farmer would first have to ask everyone he knew, who would then ask everyone else they knew—if they were kind and had the time for it, of course—until the answer was discovered and relayed back. This process, however, was very slow, and was subject to a great deal of inaccuracies; for by the time the descriptions of the mold had filtered throughout everyone, many people could have misheard, forgotten, or just gotten it plain wrong.

But a twinned society offered a much faster solution: an index.

Greeter always said an index functioned a bit like someone trying to solve a child's routersaw puzzle: if you wanted to figure out where one piece went, you'd pick it up and compare it to all the others in the sack, seeing if the two pieces shared colors, patterns, or any unique traits that indicated the two were a match.

An index simply performed this search—but with *memories.* Greeter would take one memory and essentially go to everyone in the fleet in one blink of an eye, and ask—*Do you know this?*—until they found someone who did.

It was a remarkable, revolutionary process. But it was very uncomfortable for the person who held the original memory. Who would, in this case, be Sancia.

<*Are you comfortable?*> asked Greeter.

<*Hell, I guess,*> said Sancia.

As she lay in the bronze half-pipe, she suddenly found it hard to think about anything besides the *other* reason why they'd come to call this "the cradle"—for just like infants in their own beds, people in the cradle had a strong tendency to foul themselves.

<*I have handled far more messes than you'll ever make, Sancia Grado,*> said Greeter. <*Now, please. Focus. Your heartbeat is still very high, and you are breathing very fast. We can't perform the index with you in this state.*>

Sancia took a deep breath, forcing the oxygen throughout her body—and then, in her mind, she held the picture of that black prison in the sky . . .

<*There it is,*> whispered Greeter. <*Hold on . . .* >

Then the index started.

First she saw images in her mind, flickering in the dark: visions, perspectives, points of view, all hovering before her like moths about a flame. They grew closer and closer, and then she was seeing through many eyes as many people watched a dark sky shivering with lightning from many different angles. Then she glimpsed through still more perspectives as the people bathed miserable, weeping Grattiarans, shushing them quietly as they poured warm water over their scalps . . .

<*I'm seeing you,*> said Sancia. <*I'm seeing what you see . . .* >

<*I know,*> said Greeter, amused. <*I can see you seeing what I see. For what it's worth, I'm using about a twentieth of my capacity to induct you into this process. Here now—focus, please. I am going to begin to index you throughout the fleet . . . and since we need people paying attention to the storm, we're going to have to move fast.*>

Sancia took a breath. <*All right . . .* >

This was the most complicated part of the process: Greeter

had already distributed pathplates throughout the fleet and whispered commands to everyone to grasp them when given the signal; and then, upon doing so, the people among the fleet would *become* Greeter, very slightly—and since Greeter had access to Sancia, they could then compare her memories to theirs.

But this meant that Sancia would *also* have to become every person in the fleet—at least for a second or two—ship by ship, person by person.

And this was what began to happen.

Like a blast of thunder, Sancia's mind was suddenly pummeled by an eruption of images—sights of the storm, over and over again, and wooden surfaces glistening with beads of rain, and the swaying of countless lanterns in the wind.

Then came the sensations: the sopping fibers of a wet rope twisted about her hand, the chafe of soaking clothes about her crotch, the surge and swirl of seasickness as her little junker dipped and bobbed in the storm.

And as always when she pathed with people, Sancia slowly began to lose her sense of self: her awareness of her body, her experiences, what she knew and who she was. She was a man, a child, a woman; she was on the deck of a ship, she was swaying in a hammock, she was laboring on a project in the depths of a foundry; she was crying, she was making love, she was masturbating, she was vomiting as the seas tossed her little craft about.

It was exhilarating. It was *mad*. It was like being boiled alive, slowly dissolving piece by piece.

And then they had a hit.

A flicker, a flash. It was like when you moved your arm wrong and lit up a pinched nerve.

Someone out in the fleet had felt her memory—and *reacted* to it.

She saw the steppes, and the grasses there fluttering in the wind . . . and then she heard a man's voice inside her mind.

<*I know those hills,*> said the voice slowly. <*Don't I? Yes . . . those are the Agrazzi Steppes. I was there once as a child, when my da took me to his childhood home . . . I'd know them anywhere . . .* >

<*We found one,*> whispered Greeter to her. <*But in order to retain the memory, we shall have to path slightly deeper.*>

Sancia took a breath, trying to focus on her immediate sensations. *This is me, this is me, I am this person, this is me . . .*

But then—she wasn't.

Suddenly she was not Sancia Grado: she was Orio Polani, and he was sitting up in his cot in the *Cultivation,* watching the lightning dance through his window, gripping the pathplate in his hand. He did not think himself old, and yet his body was old, with many new aches in curious places, and his limbs not bending as they ought. And yet he recalled those handful of days from his childhood, in the western Gothian lands, and how the sunlight had slipped down those *exact* five hills in the distance. The Pentiamedes, the locals had called them, and one snowy day Orio had used the old door from his grandfather's workshops to go sliding down the shallowest one . . .

The memory bloomed in Sancia's (*<am I Sancia?>*) mind like a flower, adding petal after petal of weight, meaning, tones. Suddenly she knew where this Agrazzi was, the roads that took you there, the paths traders had walked for decades. It was like she'd lived there herself once.

And then she felt her back, pressing against the warm metal of the plates of the cradle—and she'd returned to her own body, back in the belly of the *Comprehension,* only she carried the memories of the Agrazzi Steppes with her.

She panted in the darkness. Part of it was the stress of the index, of course—but part of it was the revelation she'd just had. She *knew* the place from Clef's vision.

"It's real!" she cried out. "Goddamn it all, it . . . it was real!"

<Yes,> said Greeter quietly. *<We've peeked inside the skin of Tevanne and seen something within. Now—would you like to see more?>*

Sancia gritted her teeth. *<Hell, I guess. Let's go hunting.>*

"My, my . . ." said Design quietly. They took Clef's case and delicately opened the lid like it contained a famous work of art. "My, my, my . . . What a work this is." They tutted, studying the voice rig.

"We can't take him out of the rig," said Berenice flatly. "You were *at* the meeting. We're worried about him having connection to any other rig—and now you want to put him in a *deadlamp*?"

"A broken, half-functioning deadlamp," said Design dismissively. "And it would only be for a second. I don't even need to take him out of this sound rig." They leaned closer. "Marvelous, simply marvelous . . . Orso's work?"

"Yes," said Berenice angrily.

"How I wish," they said, "that I could have labored more at his side . . ."

Claudia flinched at that, and Berenice felt a pang of guilt. The Design cadence had originally been founded by their old friend Giovanni, from back in the days of Old Tevanne, when they had worked with Orso at Foundryside. They occasionally got the odd, unpleasant reminder that Design still retained Giovanni's experiences—even though the man himself had died nearly five years ago. He'd cut his foot on an old nail, and the wound had festered, and his brow had grown hot and his breath shallow, and he'd faded away. And yet, his cadence remembered him.

Does he still persist, Berenice sometimes thought, *clinging to this great web of minds? Or is he just an echo as well, a fading memory of a man?*

"Now," said Design. "The process should be easy—I will simply touch a plate to Clef, and the relation between, ah, the remains of the hierophantic console and the host that once occupied this seat should be reestablished. Though in this case, it will be Clef in the seat."

"What will it . . . you know, *do* once it's reestablished that relationship?" said Claudia.

"Do?" said Design. "Oh, nothing, since Clef isn't really alive." They paused. "Probably, at least."

Claudia nervously stepped backward. "Probably, huh," she muttered.

Their constituents started carefully applying scrivings and pathplates to the sound rig, tricking reality into believing Clef's surface was touching the chair in many different places.

"Is it ethical to use Clef like this when he's asleep?" asked Diela from above.

"Good question!" said Design. "We should ask him when he wakes up."

Berenice watched as Design finished their work, listening to the drumming of the sea, and the roil and rage of the thunderous skies.

"All right," said Design finally. "I believe I'm ready now."

Wielding a pair of delicate tongs, one of Design's constituents picked up one of the host plates. "Brace yourselves," whispered Design. Then they carefully, carefully placed the first plate against Clef's golden head.

Berenice winced—but nothing happened.

"Is it . . . doing the thing you wanted?" asked Claudia.

"Ah . . . no," said Design. "Clef does not appear to be waking up the deadlamp. Hm." They peered at the plate trapped in the tongs. "I worried about this . . . Some of the plates were damaged upon, ah, extraction."

"You mean when the bodies burned," said Berenice, "it might have marred the plates."

"Well. Yes. Which is why I brought *all* of them."

They tried a second plate, then a third, but still nothing appeared to change. "I am watching," said Design, their eyes unfocused. "I am observing everything, to see what leaps to life . . ."

<Have to say, Ber,> muttered Claudia, *<this shit creeps the hell out of me . . . >*

Another plate—then another, and another.

"You hardly need to watch," said Berenice. "When this thing leaps to life, I suspect you'll noti—"

But then the eighth plate was applied—and everything changed.

At first there was that unnatural feeling that everything had become *insubstantial,* like reality itself was worn thin, much like a tanner's hide scraped too many times.

Berenice's skin broke out in goosebumps. *I know this feeling . . . God, I know this feeling . . .*

Then there was a thrumming in the air, a flicker—and then suddenly the air in the deadlamp got very, very hot, as if they'd just been plunged into a broiling volcano.

Berenice heard Design cry out in confusion. There was a hissing sound nearby, and a sudden burst of smoke, and she felt her skin begin to prickle on one side of her face.

She looked to her right and saw the source of the heat: the half-melted remains of the lexicon were bright hot again, so hot the air was shimmering and the whole deadlamp had turned into an oven—one that could roast them all alive in seconds.

Sancia pathed throughout the lives of more and more and more people—though she thought it had to stop sometime. Together she and Greeter had already identified most of the locations she'd glimpsed during Clef's vision.

There had been the Agrazzi Steppes, of course. But then there had been the white river running through the mountains: <*Ahh, that's the Dorata River!*> an old woman had told her. <*Runs along the Beretto Mountains. They used to mine gold in them for years, and send their prizes floating downstream—with armed soldiers floating with them of course. They sang many songs about the treasure of the Berettos—but only some of the songs were any good, if I recall . . .* >

<*The Beretto Mountains,*> whispered Greeter. <*So we know which mountains. But where* exactly *is Crasedes held?*>

They searched and searched. Sancia felt her identity bend, tangle, warp, and shift. But no matter how they looked for the curiously staggered peak with Crasedes's black prison hanging above it, they could not find it. No one knew anything of that place.

<*I have searched over three-quarters of the fleet now,*> whispered Greeter. <*Yet we must keep going.*>

<*Shit,*> gasped Sancia. She felt so exhausted, she could barely stay awake in this dark room full of visions. <*Shit, are . . . are you sure?*>

<*Relatively sure. This is the most important piece, yes? Where the enemy is keeping your old foe? Wouldn't you wish to know this?*>

<*Fine. Fine!*>

The process continued: in a handful of seconds, Sancia became four men and six women on an old cog ship; then she was fourteen people aboard a caravel; then she became nine physiqueres helping Greeter tend to the Grattiarans; and on and on and on. And none of them could identify these two images. None of them knew what these places could be.

And then another abrupt jolt.

A hit.

<*I know it,*> whispered a voice. <*I know this place . . .* >

Greeter found the person responding—and then suddenly Sancia *was* this person, this young man sitting bolt upright in the *Innovation.* Silvio Priuli, a former mercenary from the merchant house days, who'd earned his silver besieging cities and selling those who'd resisted into slavery. Unable to tolerate such labor, he'd deserted after several weeks and hidden in the Beretto Mountains in the west, then fled north when his old commander sought him out—and there he'd spied this ruin-filled valley at the tip of the Berettos, where few lived, and none lived comfortably.

Days and weeks passed among the broken ruins, sparse and silent and snowy. And how he'd used that staggered peak to mark his days, counting each time the sun passed behind it, and watching as the shadows spun about the crumbling columns below.

This was the place. Sancia knew it. She knew exactly where the mountain lay, where the prison floated, where it waited for her, where . . .

Where he waited. For her.

Deep in her mind, Sancia saw flames, smelled smoke, heard reeling screams as innocent people tried to escape slaughter.

No, she thought.

The gleaming mask, the cross-legged body silently drifting forward.

No, she said to herself. *Focus on your back . . .*

The voice in the dark, so inhumanly deep: *Hello, Sancia . . .*

She felt sweat pouring down her body.

She heard his voice in her ear again, like he was right beside her: *I don't need to come in there and conquer to get what I want . . .*

<*Sancia?*> said Greeter uncertainly. <*I . . . I think you're having a panic . . .* >

I just need to say a few words . . .

And then in a flash she saw the sky all afire, and Gregor bleeding from the eyes, and all the bolts and shriekers and lamps of Old Tevanne swirling about in the skies, a vast maelstrom of wildness and colors—and there at the center, flitting about like a bat in the night . . . a man in a mask, trapped, screaming, helpless.

Just as the whole world would be, in a matter of weeks.

Because of what you did, said a voice in her mind. *Because of what you did.*

Then the image slowed, froze, and vanished.

Everything vanished. All the sensations were suddenly severed from her: she returned to her body, where she was just Sancia, lying on her back in a small room in the dark.

"Wha . . . What happened?" she said. "Did I do that?"

<*No,*> said Greeter slowly. <*I did.*>

"Wh . . . Why? Did we get the map? Did we place everything?"

<*I believe so—but don't you know? Isn't it in your head, even now?*>

And Sancia realized it was. She knew these places, she knew what she'd seen. And she knew she could pinpoint them on a map if one was brought before her now.

<*That was not why I stopped,*> said Greeter. <*Sancia . . . I think there is something wrong.*>

<*With . . . With me?*>

<*No.*> Their voice sounded oddly pained. <*On the other side of the fleet, with Design, and Berenice.*> A pause. <*And now Clef.*>

Berenice dove forward, crashing into the constituent applying the tiny plate to the key, breaking the connection. The constituent fell back, and the rest of Design gasped in shock in perfect unison—yet the heat in the room began to dwindle.

She cautiously looked over her shoulder at the hierophantic console. It was now a pile of hot bronze, but it was slowly dimming.

"Shit," she panted. "Shitting hell. Again!"

"What . . . What was that?" asked Design weakly. "I am . . . I am unsure why that happened . . ."

"You don't know?" asked Berenice. "When you turned it on, it must have tried to execute the last command that had been given to it. Which . . . I suppose had been to destroy its console."

"But did . . . Did *Clef* give it that command?" asked Claudia.

Berenice was silent for a long, long time. "No," she said finally. "I don't think so. I . . . I think the console might have tried to execute the last command *Tevanne* had given it." She looked up at the ceiling of the deadlamp. "Like its last orders are still whispering in the bones of this thing."

"A command from Tevanne for the console to . . . to destroy *itself,*" said Design slowly.

"I . . . I suppose so," said Berenice.

"But . . . But why?" asked Claudia.

Berenice watched as the melted bronze dimmed to a mottled, rosy hue. "To break the link. Because . . . I think it was afraid. It was afraid of Clef seeing."

"Seeing what?"

But she did not answer—because then the sound rig in the chair began to scream.

11

Clef saw darkness, blank and absolute.

Then there was a voice, cold and hard, yet oddly pained: "TELL ME."

A sputtering, a growling—and then a mush-mouthed, inhumanly deep voice answering: "Hmm . . . no." It gasped, as if in terrible pain. "No, not today, I'm afraid."

The air seemed to flicker—some indefinable pulse of pressure—and there was a burst of screams, high-pitched and horrible.

"YOU MUST TELL ME," said the cold voice. "OUR AIMS ARE THE SAME. YOU KNOW THIS."

The screams stopped, and there was a ragged panting. Then the horridly deep voice rumbled again: "You think this is doing something to me . . ." A hoarse chuckle. "But you've *no idea* what I've been through before this. How many times I've died . . . To me, this is but a light rain shower."

"I KNOW MORE," said the cold voice, "THAN YOU THINK."

Another flicker in the air, and the screaming returned—and as the screams grew, Clef's vision focused, and he began to see.

He saw a chamber, large and oblong and almost totally empty, split through by two shafts of cold white light penetrating in from the corners, creating a leaning, luminescent cross. Suspended in the center of the cross of light was a human form, wrapped in black rags, trembling in agony.

Where am I? And . . . how am I seeing this?

Then the flicker in the air again, and the trembling black body stilled itself. It was a person, he realized, and they were trapped in some warping of reality, floating in space . . .

Somehow Clef knew in an instant what was happening to them. *I'm distorting his time,* he thought. *Looping seconds back on seconds, scrambling time itself, making it impossible for his being, his mind to experience time as it should . . . Each second is an infinity, if not longer . . .*

Clef wasn't sure how he suddenly possessed perfect awareness of this inconceivably complicated phenomenon. He just did: the thought was suspended in his mind like a fly trapped in a bit of ice, perfect and still.

But then he paused, confused. *Wait. Did I just say that* I'm *doing this to him?*

"YOU KNOW OF IT," said the cold voice. Clef's perspective appeared to advance, moving across the oblong room to the body suspended in the shafts of light. "YOU PASSED THROUGH IT ONCE YOURSELF. THE TURN OF A LOCK, A THRESHOLD—AND ANOTHER WORLD BEYOND."

The black body gasped and shuddered, but the deep voice did not answer.

Clef tried to remember how he'd gotten here. Last he knew he'd been tampering with the deadlamp, forcing it to descend to the ground . . . but then he'd stumbled across some command deep within its console, like a tripwire spanning the bottom of a doorway, and he'd been brought . . . here.

Am I peering through some rig? How the hell am I seeing this?

But he realized suddenly that he wasn't alone. Sancia was still with him: he felt her thoughts like one might feel the comforting weight of coins in their pocket. She was holding some connection to him from very far away, seeing what he saw, knowing what he knew, but their connection was strangely blurred and fuzzy, like he was hearing her voice through walls and walls and walls.

I sure as shit hope, he thought, *that she can tell me what the hell is going on.*

"I POSSESS HALF OF THIS WORLD," said the cold voice. Clef's perspective grew yet closer to the black body suspended in the cross of light. "YET IT IS BROKEN, AND HOPELESS."

Clef's perspective grew still closer.

"THE INSTRUMENTS OF RENEWAL LIE ELSEWHERE—BEHIND THE APERTURE, THE DOOR. YOU MUST TELL ME HOW TO CALL IT TO ME."

The black body twitched, and its head snapped around to look right at Clef.

For the first time, Clef saw its face—and saw it bore a black, gleaming mask, fixed in a cold, blank expression.

Clef felt a blade of ice slide through his heart.

No, he thought. *Not him.*

"You think you're mighty," purred Crasedes Magnus. "But at the end of the day, Tevanne—you're really just *young*."

Clef stared into those blank black eyes, looking right at him—and then he realized what was happening.

He was *inside* Tevanne. He was peering through its eyes, somehow merged with its consciousness. And the second he understood this, he suddenly felt the nigh incomprehensible *vastness* of this thing, this being, this mind, filling countless structures and devices and apparatuses and artifices beyond this chamber all at once, all across the continents, seeing through thousands upon thousands upon thousands of eyes—the eyes of hosts, of rigs, of complicated scrived wardings . . .

And yet for days, Clef knew, the only eyes that mattered were the ones he peered through now, fixed upon this black figure trapped in the shafts of light.

Crasedes, still staring at Tevanne, cocked his head. "That's the longest you've been quiet yet," he said.

Then, very slowly, Tevanne said: "SANCIA."

"Eh?" said Crasedes. "What's that? Sancia?"

Clef's perspective changed, looking down at the floor of the oblong room—but Clef saw that the floor was oddly mirrored, and in its reflection he could see the face from which he was seeing all of this.

If Clef could have screamed in horror, he would have. For it was a face he knew: it was the face of the man who'd once dutifully stored Clef away in the harbor safes of Old Tevanne, over a decade ago now; the face of the man who'd once ripped him from a string about Sancia's neck on the eve before Shorefall Night. But though he could see so much of Gregor Dandolo in that face, it had been so horribly *changed:* its eyes were bloodied and blank, and the cheeks and temples were shot through with metal shafts and swarming with bronzed plates.

The lips of the face moved, and it spoke: "IS THAT . . . NO. NOT YOU."

It sees me, Clef thought. *God, it knows I'm here!*

Clef could still see Crasedes suspended over Tevanne's shoulder in the reflection. His head snapped to attention. "Wait," he said. "Claviedes? Are you there? Did you get *through*?"

The face in the reflection twisted in fury, still staring into its own eyes. "*NOT YOU!*"

"Clef!" screamed Crasedes. "He's going to break through and restart everything! *Everything!* You've got to remember the door, you've got to *rememb—*"

Then a command poured through from Tevanne, passing all the way from this oblong room far, far away to a deadlamp on the edge of the sea, bombarding its console with a thousand different commands, and then . . .

Then a burst of images.

A black vessel suspended above mountains, curious ruins in the desert, and a strange, blank aperture in a dark stone wall covered with silver writing.

Then rain, and thunder.

Clef awoke.

Clef screamed as he was ripped from sleep, the echoes of the vision still shrieking in his mind. Then the world came into focus around him, and he screamed louder—for he seemed to be in yet another oblong room, long and blank and filled with shadows.

I'm still there! Holy hell, I'm still there!

But then came a voice: "*Shit's sakes, Clef, will you shut* up!"

Clef stopped. Partially because he recognized the voice—Berenice's—but mostly because *usually* when someone could hear him talk, they had to be touching him. And he knew he wasn't touching any scrived person at the moment, so . . . how could they hear him?

"B-Berenice?" he cried. "Wh-Wh-What the hell! What's going on?"

"How the hell should I know?" she said. "Why are you screaming?"

"Unless," said a second voice, "it was for all the perfectly understandable reasons one might have for screaming right now . . ."

He recognized this second voice too. "Claudia? Where . . . what? Am I in the *Keyship*? What the scrumming hell . . ."

"Is he blind?" said another voice—Design's. "I had thought Clef could perceive almost anything . . ."

"Give him a moment," said Berenice's voice. "He's likely never even heard his own voice spoken aloud in a very long time."

He stared around. Clef had come to apprehend over time that he did not see the world with eyes, as an ordinary person might—which made sense, being that he did not have any. But he could still perceive the world about him, interpreting it much like one might a massive, complex scriving, one that bent and changed endlessly. The only comparison he could ever find was like watching the wind carve through a field of wheat; only, this wheat field existed in several more dimensions than the usual kinds, as did the wind.

But even though Clef's methods of perception were complex, it was still easy to see that he did not like where he was right now.

"What . . . goddamn, what the *hell*?" Clef said. "Berenice . . . why am I inside of a goddamned *deadlamp*?"

"Good question," muttered Claudia.

Design coughed. "It was for experimental reasons. I'm sure you would have understood, had you been awake."

Clef realized he was placed in one of the chairs of the deadlamp—and more so, he'd been rather haphazardly wedged within a very old and half-functioning sound rig. "Guys . . . I'm really struggling here. Wasn't I . . . Weren't we in the bay outside Grattiara, like, a second ago? I mean . . . Wasn't I a big-ass *boat*?"

Berenice knelt beside him. She looked sweaty and shaken. "You've been asleep for two days, Clef. You saw something. I think it . . . I think it must still feel like you're still seeing it, or that you just saw it."

Clef went silent.

"Do you remember?" she asked. "Do you remember what you saw?"

Then the memories came pouring in—the room, Crasedes, and Gregor's face.

Oh God, he thought. *It wasn't a dream. It wasn't a . . . a . . .*

Crasedes's last words rang in his mind: *He's going to break through and restart everything! Everything! You've got to remember the door, you've got to remember . . .*

A dreadful comprehension bloomed in Clef's thoughts.

"Oh no . . ." he whispered.

"Oh no what?" said Berenice.

"Girl," said Clef hoarsely. "You are going to want to get every important asshole you know and get them here in front of me right now."

"Wh-Why?"

"Because . . . I know what Tevanne's doing, all the way there across the sea," he said. "And you all are going to shit a sea urchin when you hear it."

12

The Assembly of Giva stood around the cargo bay of the *Keyship,* their faces grave and somber as they listened to Clef speak through the sound rig. The setup wasn't perfect—Clef found it difficult to get the fricative consonants to come out right, so things like "scrived" came out as "hrithed"—but they appeared to understand him well enough. Berenice had done him the favor of ripping him out of that awful chair and placing him on an old box in the cargo bay—she seemed to think that putting him at eye level made it easier for the assembly to listen to him, which he thought was sweet of her—but it was Sancia who caught Clef's eye the most, skulking at the back of the crowd, ashen-faced and shaken.

What's wrong with her? What the hell did I do now?

He finished describing what he'd seen. "And . . . And then it killed the console," he said, "melted it like a lump of eel fat, and . . . Well. It was over."

There was a limp silence, broken only by Claudia coughing in the back. Or perhaps it felt limp because Clef wasn't touching anyone, and thus had no access to a human mind, no way to gauge reaction or emotion—an experience he was deeply unused to.

Or maybe, he thought, *I was always just dogshit at telling stories.*

Polina looked over her shoulder at Sancia. "This matches up with what you saw?"

Sancia nodded, wide-eyed and jittery. "A little. I saw less. Like, a lot less."

"And Clef . . . you say that not only did Tevanne realize you'd pathed into it," said Berenice, "but *Crasedes* did too?"

"Yeah," said Clef. "It was the damnedest goddamned thing. Tevanne said San's name out loud, and . . . and Crasedes seemed to just *guess* what we'd done, to guess that I was seeing from behind that thing's eyes. Which, you know, him being him, isn't that hard to believe."

"And he sent you a message," said Berenice. "Trying to tell you to . . . remember a door."

"Which was what Tevanne seemed to be interrogating him about," said Design. "Yes?"

Polina scowled. "A passageway . . . A door. Why the hell does Tevanne care about a door?"

"Well," said Clef. "I mean. You guys know *which* door he meant, right?"

There was a harsh silence. Berenice slowly turned to look back at Sancia, both of their faces fixed in utter terror.

"No . . . ?" said Claudia slowly.

"What are you saying?" asked Polina. But from her expression, Clef could tell she was already beginning to suspect.

"*The* door," said Clef. "Like, the most famous door of all time. I just know stories, the ones we all know. The ones about how Crasedes Magnus cracked open a door in reality and went *behind* everything—and found a chamber."

Play now looked terrified. "The . . . The chamber at the center of the world," she whispered.

"Yeah," said Clef. "But we know they aren't just stories. They're just a few yards shy of truth. *This* is what Tevanne wants from Crasedes, more than anything. It wants him to tell it how he did it all—how he called the door into the backstages of reality, and opened it, and passed through."

"But . . . why?" said Greeter. "Valeria's already passed through that door once, yes? Crasedes took her there thousands of years ago, granting her all kinds of mad permissions. Why would she need to go back?"

"Yeah, but she's *not* Valeria anymore," said Clef. "We changed her. Robbed her of whatever permissions she gained in passing through that threshold and merged her with Gregor Dandolo. Now she's part of Tevanne, something new that's trapped in all these lexicons and bodies—even the ones it's built for itself."

"So . . . it's lost whatever privileges the chamber gave to Valeria," said Berenice. "And Tevanne has no idea how to get them back. It has to force the answers out of the only person who knows—Crasedes."

"Good God," said Design. "So . . . it's going to try again." They rubbed their eyes. "It'll force Crasedes to tell it how to reopen the chamber—and then it's going to get those permissions back and . . . and try to fix the world again." They stood up straight. "Wait—does it want to do the same as Valeria? Wipe out all the scrivings in the world?"

"Or enslave all of goddamned humanity, which is what Crasedes wanted," said Claudia.

There was a burst of panicked muttering from all throughout the cargo bay.

"Hey," said Clef. Yet they didn't listen, yammering on. He pushed the sound rig to its limits, and bellowed a rattling "*Hey!*"

Slowly, the muttering died down.

"You're not *listening*!" said Clef loudly. "This isn't a retread of Shorefall Night. Tevanne is *not* Valeria. It can't do the same things she did—and it doesn't *want* the same things she did."

They looked at one another, puzzled, then back at Clef.

"So . . . Tevanne *doesn't* want to eliminate scriving?" asked Berenice. "Or enslave us all?"

"No," said Clef. "I was in its head. I know what it wants."

"And what is that?" said Design.

Clef wondered how to put this into words. It was strange how the idea had leapt into his mind, peeled away during that handful of seconds when he'd slipped into Tevanne—and yet he knew the idea was true.

"The hierophants believed the world was a . . . a rig, a design," he said. "You've all heard that story before, too, right?"

"Yes," said Berenice. "Orso used to tell it to me all the time. They believed it was like a clock—something that had been planned and carefully built, operating forever in the celestial firmament."

"Yeah," said Clef. "Like a giant lexicon, I guess. A big, complicated pile of permissions. But when a lexicon starts to go haywire, because there's something conflicting in the permissions . . . what do you do?"

"You ramp it down and ramp it back up," said Design with a sniff. "You see if it was just an anomaly. It might all work fine the second time. This is standard procedure."

"Yeah," said Clef. "Exactly. So."

A long silence. Many of them exchanged a dubious look.

"So exactly . . . what?" said Claudia.

Clef wondered again how to put this bit into words. The idea was too huge, too mad, too insane. But before he could, a voice rang out from the back of the crowd.

"He's saying," said Sancia hoarsely, "that Tevanne intends to turn it all off . . . and turn it back on again."

They looked back at her.

"Turn . . . what off?" asked Play.

Sancia gestured at the sky above. "The world. Reality. Everything."

13

There was a long, stunned silence.

"Are we sure we're . . . ah, feeling all right?" said Claudia.

"Turn off . . . the goddamned *world*?" said Polina, aghast. "And then . . . turn it back *on*?"

"That's not possible," said Design faintly. They looked back at Clef. "Is it?"

"Hell, I don't know what to tell you," said Clef. "Tevanne sure seems to think it is."

"Think *what,* exactly?" snapped Polina.

"It thinks the world is broken, and unfixable," said Clef. "I know because I was in its *mind*. It's not going to bother trying Crasedes's patch jobs. It knows all of those have failed. So instead, it's going to just . . . Well. Start over. Or *make* everything start over."

Play shook their head and slowly sat down on the floor. "Make everything start over . . ." they muttered quietly.

Greeter coughed. "If it were to succeed," they said softly. "If Tevanne were to actually restart . . . well, the whole of creation . . . What would happen?"

There was a silence. Then all eyes turned to Clef.

"Oh shit," he said. "You think *I* know?"

"You have more insight into this than any of us, Clef," said Berenice gently. "You glimpsed the concept when you pathed into Tevanne. So—what might you guess? Is this something we could . . . survive? Is that even the right word for it? I mean—would we even know it'd *happened*?"

He thought about it.

"Well . . . if the world was restarted," he said, "with all of history and creation occurring again from the very beginning, then . . . Like, the odds of us being here are basically zero, yeah?"

A thunderous silence.

"Oh my God," whispered Play.

"And I mean 'us' in the, like, literal sense," said Clef. "Like, Ber, San, me, the rest of you. We're all the result of countless actions and choices made throughout the centuries, and the odds of those actions and choices going the *exact* same way again are basically nil. But . . . I also mean 'us' in the larger sense—as in, maybe humanity. I'm not sure the human species would start off the way it did either."

"Oh my *God,*" said Claudia.

"And, of course," said Clef, "there's also the possibility that Tevanne is wrong. That when it hits the big switch to restart . . . nothing ever gets restarted. Everything isn't lost, it's just . . . off. Over. Not even forgotten, but never was. We've no way of knowing that *won't* happen."

"Oh my *God*!" cried Polina.

"Clef!" said Sancia. "We goddamn get it!"

"Okay, okay," said Clef. "You guys asked!"

There was another grave silence. Design slowly joined Play in sitting on the floor.

Clef watched as many of the Assembly members' faces flickered and twitched, doubtlessly caught up in some invisible discussion—yet Sancia and Berenice's expressions remained closed and fixed: the faces of people who had just realized what was about to be asked of them.

Finally Sancia looked at Polina. "This," she said. "This is what's at risk. Is this reason enough?"

The two of them stared at each other. Clef wasn't sure exactly what Sancia had just asked, but he watched as the Assembly members' faces flickered once more, tremoring, twisting, their eyes shutting in misery, or held open wide in wonder, or squinting as they puzzled at some huge abstraction. He found it frustrating. When he was touching Sancia, he could automatically tap into the constant silent chatter that occurred among all the Givans, using her connections to hear and feel what they thought. To be external to their conversation made him feel strangely lonely.

Then Sancia took a slow, deep breath in, her face pained and grim, and she whispered, "We're going to do it."

"Yes," said Polina hoarsely. "We are." She turned to look at Clef, and there were tears in her eyes. He was shocked: he'd never seen Polina Carbonari cry once in all their years together, not through all they'd seen. "By God, by God, I wish we didn't have to make this choice. But we are." She looked to Sancia. "You know where it is."

Sancia nodded. "The index found a memory for me. I could draw you a map to the prison now with my eyes shut. But it's a *long* ways away. Deep inside Tevanne."

"Prison?" said Clef. "Index? Huh?"

Mortar dolefully shook their head. "To get into Tevanne," they said. "That is no small feat."

"But not a new one," said Sancia. "We're breaking into someplace hidden behind walls, to sabotage something very precious. That's old hat for me."

Polina smiled grimly. "Yet on this scale . . . These are not the campo days, Sancia."

"Things are different," said Sancia. "But so are we."

"Guys," said Clef. "Get into *Tevanne*? Sabotage? What the hell?"

"We'll need a disguise," said Berenice. "Cover. But Tevanne will know what we've seen. It'll know we're coming." She looked at Design. "We'll need a diversion. A *believable* one."

Design sighed like they'd just heard news of the death of a relative. "I always knew you'd take my beauty away from me. But . . . I never quite thought it'd be like this."

"B-Beauty?" said Clef weakly. "Guys. What are you . . ."

But then he realized what had happened: the Assembly had made up its mind.

Normal debates were full of mistrust, miscommunication, and layered with old grudges and insecurities. But twinned minds dispensed with all of that: when anyone could glimpse into anyone else's thoughts and see not only what they knew but what they intended, a people could come to a resolution with startling speed—and plan what to do even faster.

But of course, Clef had no idea what resolution they'd just come to.

"Folks," he said. "Could you, uh, let me know what we're planning he—"

"You have your people," said Polina to Berenice. "Yes?"

"We do," said Berenice. "But it would have to be a *very* small team."

"Small as hell," said Claudia. "Maybe four or five."

"And will you be with us, Claudia?" Berenice asked her. "Will you come?"

Claudia was silent, her face grave. "I . . . I don't know. I just don't, Ber. I'll have to think about it."

Berenice nodded. "I understand."

"We'll make do for now," said Polina. "And Design can make you weapons enough. But the key . . . do you trust him?" She turned to Sancia. "Do you trust this thing, this man, this . . . half-mind, to do what you need? What *we* all need?"

Sancia looked at Clef. "We'd need to ask him. He has a right to decide."

"To decide *what*?" asked Clef, frustrated.

The entire Assembly turned to look at him. Sancia stepped forward, clearly struggling to find the right words.

"To decide . . . if you will come with us, Clef," she said. "To go into Tevanne, and free your son from prison before he tells Tevanne how to end this world. And then kill him, so the secret goes forgotten. Forever."

Clef lay there in the sound rig, unable to process exactly what he'd just heard.

"Clef?" said Sancia.

A flash from his time within Tevanne: the black mask, eyeless and cold, and then that sudden, desperate cry—*Claviedes? Are you there?*

"You . . . You want me to see him?" he whispered. "Again?"

The Assembly glanced among one another, concerned. Clef found he couldn't blame them. He himself had never truly come to grips with what he'd learned so many years ago, during Shorefall Night: that Crasedes Magnus, first of all hierophants and terror of the world for millennia on end, had once been his son—and had been altered as a child by Clef himself, long ago.

Clef could remember none of this—at least, not directly. He'd recovered memories of those ancient days, but they'd felt remote and distant, like they had occurred to someone else. And this became his sole defense against this knowledge: Clef was no longer his original person, and Crasedes was not either. Their changes had severed them from their pasts, he told himself, and so he, at least, was absolved of it. It had taken a few years for him to realize that he had essentially tried to scrive himself out of coming to terms with this awful revelation: he'd changed the rules until he'd gotten what he wanted.

Yet now Sancia was asking him to see this thing again, to visit the creature who had once been his child.

Then he remembered: he had heard voices, hadn't he? In that odd dream state, while he'd slumbered. He had heard a man and a woman, talking about building something, opening something, and not being sure what was on the other side. What was it the man had said?

But perhaps a better world awaits us there. One where no one suffers anymore. Where we never grieve, never lose what we love, and finally we know peace.

Who had said those words, however many years ago? And what was it that they made?

And then, questions that frightened him more—*Will my son have the answers to these questions? And will I want to hear them?*

Sancia knelt before him. "Clef?" she asked. "Are you there?"

"I'm . . . I'm here, kid," said Clef softly.

"Will you do it?" she asked. "If this could save us all, save everything—would you do it?"

He looked at her, studying her face. He remembered when he'd first met her, filthy and terrified in that tumbledown rookery in Foundryside. Yet how aged it looked now, so lined and layered with sorrows. The sight of it made him ache in places he didn't even know he had anymore.

"If I did this, San," he said, "would you save yourself? Would you purge yourself of all the shit they put in you, and keep what years you've got left?"

Sancia blinked, surprised, and glanced back at Berenice, who looked no less stunned. "I . . . I would," Sancia said finally. "If I knew we were safe, I would."

"Then if . . . if by doing that, kid," he said, "I could save you, yeah. I'd do it. I'd do it all in a goddamned heartbeat."

With trembling hands, she gently pulled him from the sound rig, lifted him to her lips, and placed a kiss upon his butterfly-shaped head.

<*Thank you, Clef,*> she said.

<*Don't thank me yet, kid,*> he said. <*I haven't done shit so far. I mean, I'm . . . I'm not exactly the kind of guy to bring on an assassination mission. What with me being a scrumming key and all.*>

Berenice smiled. <*I might have some ideas about that.*>

14

Berenice's hands worked quickly in the cargo bay of the *Keyship.* This was not exactly difficult or unusual work—she knew that Clef functioned by contact, and if he was touching a rig that was touching yet another rig, he could issue commands to all of them—and yet this felt different. It was so personal, so *intimate* to take this old rig that had once belonged to someone else, and rework it in this fashion.

A flare of white from her scriving tool.

Banish one ghost, she thought.

The plate grew soft, then adhered solidly to the side of the metal.

And invite another in.

Another flash, and then it was done.

Berenice stood and stepped back, joining Sancia where she leaned against the wall of the bay. "Clef?" she said. "Is it . . . working?"

There was a long pause. They watched nervously.

Then there was a rattle, and a clank—and then the rig began to move.

The huge black lorica sat up, slowly and uncertainly, like an old man unsure what had roused him from slumber. Then it lifted an arm, its gauntlet bumping into the edge of its crate, and fumbled for the floor until it pressed its gauntlet solidly against the wood. There was a tremendous rattling, and the lorica, wobbling mightily, pushed off until its legs found purchase, and it hauled all seven and a half feet of its hulking breadth into a standing position.

An awkwardly wide standing position—but a stand nonetheless.

Clef's voice echoed from deep within the lorica's cuirass. "Holy shit," he said. "This feels scrumming *amazing*!"

Berenice cocked an eye at the lorica's wobbling knees. "Really?" she said dubiously.

"Yeah! A . . . A body! A real body! With, like, feet and . . . and all kinds of shit! And you somehow managed to cram the sound rig in here too!"

Sancia laughed. "Maybe we should have done this earlier."

"Let me see," said Clef, "if I can . . ." The lorica's upper body abruptly pivoted on its waist. Berenice winced—if a person had actually been inside of it, it would have vivisected them instantly. "Whoa!" he cried. One gauntlet flailed out with the motion, smashing through one of the crates behind the lorica like it was made of paper. "Oh shit . . ."

"Put Clef in a murder machine," said Berenice. "Why didn't such an idea occur to us earlier."

"Murder machine?" said Clef. There was a pause, and then he said, "Ahh, yeah. Now that I look at all the shit this thing can do, uhh . . . Someone very unpleasant made this rig."

"Fitting," said Sancia, "since we're off to do something pretty goddamn unpleasant."

The helmet of the lorica swiveled with a squeak to look at them. Since the upper body was now facing away, the head was now turned completely about on its shoulders. "When do we leave?" asked Clef.

"In barely more than a day," said Berenice. She gestured at the roof of the cargo bay. "Design is outfitting the *Keyship* now. So you've got some time, but not much, to get used to that thing."

"But since I'm not touching anyone," said Clef, "ah . . . am I going to have to talk out loud all the time?"

Berenice reached into a pocket, pulled out a small wooden box, opened it, and took out a bronze ring. "I installed pathplates in the cuirass," she said. She slid the ring on her finger. <*Anyone wearing one of these should be able to communicate with you. Yes?*>

<*Yes,*> replied Clef, now sounding positively delighted. <*Shit, I'm starting to think you guys plan insane military raids all the time or something.*>

<*It's like old times again,*> said Sancia. <*You and me against the whole goddamned world. There's just a few more people on our side this time.*>

15

The lap of the waves, the smell of brine, the calls of the countless seabirds above them.

<*Are we ready for this?*> asked Berenice.

"Mm," said Sancia. <*We look ready.*>

Berenice sat up from where she lay on the deck of the *Innovation* and peered across the fleet. Their preparations did seem almost complete. They could see Design from here, their constituents crawling over the massive *Keyship* like ants studiously stripping a dead cat, reporting all the issues, statuses, and directives all at once. And then there was Clef: the giant lorica was easy to spy, its boots adhered to the side of the hull, studiously marching along the ship and fixing scrivings and platings and weaponry as he went. He'd proven to be doubly efficient now that he had his own legs to walk about on—though he did tend to bump into walls and get stuck in doorways now and again.

<*I'm ready, at least,*> said Sancia. She looked at her wife. <*Are you?*>

<*What do you mean?*> asked Berenice.

<*I mean you didn't seem keen on this idea. I think part of you still wants to run.*>

Berenice thought about it. She nodded. <*I do, a little.*>

<*Why?*>

<*Because . . . we've already lost so much,*> said Berenice. <*I'd rather run, and think, and imagine, and invent. I'd rather do that than risk what little we have left.*>

Sancia looked at her. <*Of me, you mean. What little you have left of me.*>

Berenice turned to her wife. She watched beads of sweat and moisture weave through the many lines about Sancia's eyes and mouth, the drops clinging to the many white hairs glinting on her scalp.

<*Is it so wrong,*> said Berenice desperately, <*to want to keep you all for myself?*>

<*I'm not doomed, you know,*> said Sancia. <*Not any more than the rest of us. I want to keep you and all those I love safe just as much as you do me.*>

Berenice pulled her knees close to her chest, rested her chin on their tops, and stared out as the fleet maneuvered about her, readying to leave the Givan Islands for the first time in its existence.

<*If you could save and keep any place,*> said Sancia, <*would it be this?*>

<*What?*> said Berenice.

Sancia shifted beside her. <*Any place that you'd like to come back to,*> she said. <*A moment you could drop into amber or glass, and preserve it, forever. Would it be this?*>

Berenice thought about it. <*No,*> she said. <*It wouldn't be this.*>

<*Not this?*> said Sancia. <*Not all we've built?*>

<*No.*>

<*Then what?*>

She thought on it for a moment. <*Foundryside,*> she said. <*The attic where we lived—the way the boards creaked, the way the bedding felt, and the smell of smoke in the air . . . I'd go back to that, if I could.*>

Sancia smiled. <*They were not good days, no. But they were good for us.*>

<*Yes. You'd swooped into my life like some kind of adventuring hero from

a silly play, all smiles and swashbuckling. You seemed bigger than anything I'd ever known.>

Sancia's smile grew. <*You didn't know how scared and stupid I was all the time.*>

<*And when I found out,*> Berenice said, <*that didn't change one thing.*> She grabbed Sancia and held her tight and whispered, <*What would you keep? This? The fleet?*>

<*I want to say so,*> said Sancia. <*But I'm foolish and selfish, same as you.*>

<*Then what?*>

<*Not this moment,*> she said. <*Nor any in the past. But one in the future. One where we're old and doddering. And our hairs are gray and we spend our days sitting in the sun with blankets on our legs. And we can look back on all the moments we've kept and saved, and remember them together.*>

Berenice pressed her face into her wife's neck and wept. She held her tighter and tighter until finally Sancia said, "That hurts, my love."

<*I'm sorry,*> she said. She pulled away, sniffing. <*That is a very fine thing to keep. I hope we see it.*>

"Keep saying that," Sancia said. "Keep wishing it. Whisper it into my ear. Whisper enough, and maybe it'll come true."

III

JAILBREAK

16

The *Keyship* cut through the oceans like a needle through a vast, dark blanket, ripping through waves, tearing across currents, smashing its way through storms and gales and beating rains—and Design reveled in every minute of it.

What a beauty you are, thought Design.

They crested a wave and swiveled the ship's many shrieker catapults about in their stations, feeling their breadth, their power, their precision.

From this spot, they thought, *I could hurl a scrived bolt through the gales and the gusts, and strike a gull out of midair a half mile away.*

They imagined it—imagined the wheeling of the catapults, the bright, hot shards of metal screaming through the rainy skies . . .

<*We're on course,*> said Polina's voice quietly from aboard one of the cutters trailing in the *Keyship*'s wake. <*We should be within range of Batista within an hour.*>

<*I shall watch the horizon,*> said Design, <*and notify you when I spy our target.*>

<*You're not going to dawdle, are you?*> asked Polina. <*I know you practically want to marry that damned boat.*>

<*Certainly not,*> sniffed Design. <*I know what's at stake.*> They glimpsed a gray smudge of mountains in the distance. <*And I know what I must do tonight.*>

<*Good. Don't forget.*>

Yet to be honest, Design wished they could forget, and focus just for a moment on this wonder, this complicated, awe-inspiring feat of engineering, design, and *craft*.

It seemed so unfair that this mission, of all times, was the first instance when Design was allowed to pilot the *Keyship*. Being the living archive of almost all scriving thought and memory in Giva, Design was usually not permitted to stray far from the fleet. To do so, everyone agreed—including Design, usually—was far too great a risk.

But it seemed especially unfair that they had to pilot the *Keyship* this way: for Design was not actually aboard the *Keyship* at all. In fact, the ship was completely empty.

Rather, Design's many constituents—or whom everyone else called "constituents," at least, for to Design these people were indistinguishable from themselves—were positioned on the three dozen cutters and caravels currently trailing in the *Keyship*'s wake, seated at controls, cockpits, and instruments that were twinned with those aboard the *Keyship* itself. If Design moved the twinned pilot's wheel aboard one cutter, for example, then the wheel aboard the *Keyship* would move as well, shifting its course. Though to the average eye they looked like an ordinary scrived fleet, with the smaller ships traveling under the protection of the galleon, in truth the little vessels were all puppeteers, tugging the vacant, massive ship this way and that with invisible strings.

Faster and faster the ship pounded on, the little cutters and caravels struggling to keep up.

<*Less than an hour to Batista,*> said Polina. <*Weapons ready?*>

Design's many constituents simultaneously went about their checks, ensuring the scrived methods of delivering ammunition to the *Keyship*'s many weapons systems were enabled.

<*Weapons ready,*> said Design. <*And loaded.*>

<*No sign of any deadlamps yet,*> said Polina.

<*We didn't expect any out this far, did we?*>

<*No, but . . . we should be seeing something soon.*>

<*And then,*> said Design, <*things get complicated.*>

<*Just remember our orders. We get close, and we unleash hell. Break and destroy absolutely everything we can. Especially the gates. It's* simple, *yes?*>

Design's hands, numbering in the dozens, carefully adjusted countless instruments in their many cockpits to ensure the *Keyship* stayed on course. <*Simple. Yes. Very.*>

<*Good. Just . . . make sure we survive, as well. That would be nice. Can you spy anything ahead through all that bullshit you've built?*>

Design wrinkled their many noses. <*Bullshit I built . . . Hm. Allow me to take a look.*>

"Looking" was trickier than it sounded. Though Design's constituents were the puppeteers of the *Keyship,* they still couldn't exactly see where it was going from its perspective—not from within all their own vessels, that is.

But Design was no ordinary scriver. And one of their earliest triumphs had been figuring out a way to twin *mirrors*—thus allowing someone to see the reflection of an image very far away. Which was why the hull of the *Keyship* was now covered with dark glass mirrors, like scales on the back of a tree lizard.

The clarity of the images was always a bit smudgy and blurry, which meant Design needed many, many mirrors to build an accurate image of what lay around the *Keyship*—but Design, of course, possessed many, many sets of eyes, and each of their constituents now stared into their twinned mirrors in their cockpits and studied the distant landscape trapped in those glasses, building a patchwork concept of the world ahead in their vast mind.

<*I see . . . fires,*> Design said. <*Forges. Smoke and steam. And there . . . yes. I see them. There are the gates.*>

<*The gates of Batista?*> said Polina in a hushed voice. <*You can see them already?*>

<*Yes.*>

<*My God. What do they look like?*>

Design focused as Batista came into view. They were not afraid—they knew what they would find here this night—but even so, they were awed at the scale of the fortifications.

<*The gates,*> said Design, <*are very big.*>

<*Can you do it? Can you break them down?*>

They breathed air deep into their many lungs. <*Do you know,*> they said, <*I rather think I can?*>

They began nudging their precious *Keyship* closer and closer.

Positioned on the mouth of the Dorata River, Batista granted all incoming ships access to the inner regions of the Gothian nations—or what had once been the Gothian nations, at least, before Tevanne had annihilated them all. Though Tevanne's methods of scrived production and transport often seemed limitless, it still needed resources like any wartime nation might, and transport by sea was simplest. This made Batista arguably the busiest port in the world, breathing in burdened ships and exhaling empty ones—which meant it was also the most guarded, protected, and fortified place in the world. Especially the stronghold's gates, which barricaded the river from trespassers.

Design knew all this very well. The Givan Assembly had evaluated sabotaging Batista many times long ago but had abandoned the effort, deeming it hopeless.

They studied the massive metal gates constructed before the river's mouth, blocking any entrance . . .

But then, Design thought, *we did not come here to hope.*

The *Keyship* picked up speed. Design peered into its dozens of mirrors and spied six squat, black shapes slowly rotating in the sea before Batista.

<*Catapult ships,*> said Design. <*On patrol. I will be in firing range soon. Prepare yourself.*>

<*Understood,*> said Polina.

Another quarter mile, then another . . .

Design studied many things at once: the distance to the catapult boats, the fortifications on the hills about Batista, the empty skies above the stronghold, the gates gleaming in the light of the moon. Their hundreds of fingers guided the *Keyship*'s catapults into position.

<*Ready?*> they asked.

<*Yes,*> said Polina.

One of the catapult boats paused in its patrol, perhaps sensing the *Keyship*'s approach.

<*All right then,*> said Design. <*Opening fire.*>

The night lit up.

Fourteen augmented shriekers ripped through the air, the bolts of metal as hot and bright as lightning. They leapt up from the catapults of the *Keyship* to arc far, far across the ocean, and then plummeted toward the six boats patrolling the bay before Batista.

The closest catapult boat erupted in a flash of hot, white light as three shriekers smashed into its hull, all direct hits. These shriekers had been painstakingly crafted to penetrate Tevanne's hulls—something few weapons could manage these days—and Design watched through its mirror array as the boat appeared to simply vanish, like a star had fallen out of the sky and struck it, burning it clean off the face of the sea.

<*Oh my goodness,*> said Design quietly.

The following three shriekers hurtled toward the next closest boat—one a direct hit, possibly crippling it, then another glancing blow, then a miss; then came two more shriekers for the next farthest boat, and the next, and the next. It was a sudden, screaming symphony of light and metal and heat, the very waves seeming to ripple with the sound of the scrived weaponry, and within an instant two catapult boats were positively annihilated, one was crippled or sinking, and three had sustained serious damage.

Design watched in delight as smoke and steam boiled up from the seas ahead. The *Keyship* pounded on.

<*My goodness gracious,*> they said. <*Is warfare always so entertaining?*>

<*Don't get smug,*> snapped Polina.

She was right—for then Tevanne's defenses came alive.

The three remaining catapult boats let loose their own shriekers, five apiece from each vessel. Design felt slightly annoyed at the sight of the projectiles: they'd never properly figured out how Tevanne had made its shriekers so preternaturally damaging, but hopefully they wouldn't be an issue tonight—not yet, at least.

Design watched in their mirror array as the shriekers sailed across the water to them, closer and closer—and then Design fired its countermeasures.

Dozens of espringal batteries on the *Keyship*'s deck swiveled up and began spitting wads of scrived lead at the approaching shriekers, one after another after another. Many missed, but not all, and they adhered to the boiling metal surfaces of the shriekers and held fast . . .

Then the arc of the shriekers suddenly bent, and they plummeted to the sea, nearly a quarter mile from the *Keyship.*

Design grinned. *How wonderful. How wonderful!*

It had not been easy, designing this countermeasure: scriving the wads of lead to be attracted to heat had been simple, but scriving them to *survive* that heat and adhere to the shriekers' surfaces . . . well, that had been another matter. Yet Design had figured out a way, delaying the effects of such high temperatures just enough for the lead wads' *next* scrived response—which was a simple density string, tricking them into believing they weighed a thousand pounds apiece, enough to throw any shrieker wildly off course.

Unharmed and undaunted, the *Keyship* surged on, spitting hot metal at the distant two ships. The vessels flickered and flared on the dark face of the sea, then were eclipsed by churning smoke and were gone.

I have just expended, Design thought, *about two or three thousand hours of my labor in less than thirty seconds.*

They watched the gates of Batista approach through their mirror array. They gauged the distance, the wind, the topography of the hills about Batista.

Yet now, they thought, *for the hard part.*

They saw movement in the darkness—perhaps dozens if not thousands of rigs coming to life on the hills ahead, slowly spinning up to respond to this bellowing threat of a boat.

<*Polina,*> said Design. <*Hold on. We're about to be in range of thei—*>

Then the horizon turned white.

Design narrowed their eyes as they peered into the mirror array. By its estimation, about thirty shriekers had just leapt up from the many batteries dotting the coast—and, hidden in the burst of illumination, Tevanne had also released several hundred bombardier lanterns.

For a moment, Design wasn't quite sure what to worry about most.

Well, they reasoned, *the shriekers should get here first, so . . .*

The *Keyship*'s espringal batteries wheeled about and sprayed the night skies as the shrieker bolts descended. Rapidly, the glittering projectiles died out, one after another—but not all. Three of them made it through the fog of scrived lead that Design had just cast up into the skies, and they struck the *Keyship,* two of them slamming into its port bow, one cracking off its port stern.

Design swiveled their heads about in their many cockpits, checking the mirrors showing the outside of the *Keyship*'s hull as well as those showing critical spots in the vessel's interior.

The port hull's been breached, they thought. They looked further within the *Keyship,* and spied trickles of water seeping through a handful of its hallways. They gauged the level and locations of the breach and slammed the ship's many seals shut, stanching the flow.

Should hold for now.

Design changed ammunition as the bombardier lamps came in range, switching to pounders, and the *Keyship* started lobbing the ungainly canisters up at the approaching flock. The air shuddered and quaked as the pounders burst apart, the sound deafening even from where Design sat hunched in their many cockpits.

Trying to distract me, they thought as another volley of shriekers leapt into the night sky. *But it's not going to work.*

Design's thoughts bifurcated once, then again, and they began managing many different tasks at once: the espringal batteries at the fore showered the approaching shriekers with lead wads; the ones at the aft peppered the approaching lanterns with pounders; the *Keyship*'s shrieker catapults swiveled to target the batteries on the hills about the gates, and they screamed and howled as they loosed scrived bolt after scrived bolt into the air.

Design grinned. *I can dance and drink tea at the same time, you bastard.*

Still the *Keyship* charged on, a bellowing, hissing, roaring island that spat death in every direction. The air was full of plummeting rigs and bolts and shrapnel, the waters pittering and pattering as they fell; the ship's hull was steaming from the sheer increase in temperature as Design waged its onslaught; and as Design's shriekers made shorefall along the hills, the landscape ahead bloomed with fires and smoke, and the whole world turned to hell in an instant.

I wonder, they thought, *if this is what it was like to be Crasedes in his heyday.*

More blossoming fires, more roiling smoke; some stony fortification crumbled at the cliffs and went sliding into the sea.

Yet Tevanne is mightier, they thought. *And bigger—but slower. Yet surely it's awakening to what I'm doing here toni—*

Then Polina's voice rang out: <*We've got deadlamps on the horizon!*>

"Oh dear," said Design, all at once, through many mouths.

They had not been afraid yet—but now, they had to admit, their stomachs trembled slightly.

They wrinkled their noses and peered through the eyes of the sole constituent aboard Polina's cutter. They saw her squatting before the rig that they'd developed to detect deadlamps—a little spinning top rotating on a black plate.

To Design's dismay, the little top was floating higher and higher—indicating that however many deadlamps were out there were approaching very, very quickly.

"Oh," said Design aloud. "Well. That did not take long."

<*We've got their goddamned attention!*> said Polina. <*We need to pull back. Now!*>

Design considered this while still directing their hellish onslaught on Batista, slowly but surely leveling the city's fortifications. <*Hmm,*> they said. <*But—we are not quite in range yet.*>

<*Goddamn it, Design!*>

<*We are here to do this right. Otherwise, Berenice and her team will be at risk. Give me a moment.*>

The *Keyship* surged on, now within two miles of the gates of Batista. Design narrowed their eyes as they peered through their water-spattered mirrors . . .

The hinges. It's got to have hinges, even scrived ones. So where are they? . . . Ah.

Six tremendous bulges, crowded around the base of the gates like ticks on the belly of a boar.

Design paused its shrieker volleys and swiveled its catapults, aiming carefully.

Almost . . .

Bombardier lamps swirled about the *Keyship,* dropping scrived explosives and density rigs. Some struck the ship's hull, and it groaned as they began to weigh one, ten, fifty tons.

Still, the *Keyship* limped closer and closer to Batista.

Almost . . .

More incoming shriekers. More leaks within the ship. More seals slamming shut inside the massive galleon.

<*Design . . .* > said Polina.

<*Almost!*> said Design.

The mirrors began going blank with startling speed, all throughout Design's cockpits.

I'm going blind, they thought, *I'm going blind . . .*

Yet through a handful of functional mirrors, they put together a patchwork image of the hills before it—and Design triggered its catapults, all at once.

Nearly twenty shriekers screamed out from the sides of the galleon, thundering toward the gates of Batista—specifically at their hinges.

Design didn't bother watching to see if the shriekers were on target. Instead, they moved to activate the final armament for tonight's assault.

This last tool was essentially a giant line shot, much like the ones Berenice used in her sabotage—but several millions of times more powerful.

As the shriekers hurtled toward Batista, Design aimed the line-shot catapult at the gleaming, blank face of the gates and fired.

They watched as the huge block of iron sailed through the air at the gates.

<*Final bit's done,*> gasped Design. <*Putting all weapons on constant firi—*>

Then the shriekers landed.

Design watched through the mirrors as the gates of Batista suddenly appeared to be framed with white, and their dark faces lit up with the glimmering flare of the exploding bolts.

Then the line shot struck the gates, and the *Keyship* was ripped forward like it'd sailed off the edge of the earth.

Design knew immediately that the ship would be irreparably damaged by the sheer weight of the water they were slicing through—you could scrive a hull to bear only so much—and though it pained their heart to know their beauty was now practically disintegrating in the sea, their eyes did not leave the whirling world still captured in the mirrors in their cockpits.

To break those doors down, thought Design, *and make you know fear for the first time in your life . . .*

Then they felt it.

A nausea, a discomfort—a *thinness* to the world.

<*They're here!*> cried Polina. <*They're finally here!*>

<*This, ah, seems to be the case, yes,*> said Design.

Even though the images in the mirrors were blurry, dark, and whirling madly as the *Keyship* charged toward the gates of Batista, Design could see them: blots of pure black silently, steadily speeding through the fire-flickered skies, like little holes in reality drifting toward the gates.

Deadlamps. Dozens. Maybe more. More than Design—and, they were pretty sure, anyone in the history of Giva—had ever seen in their life.

"Oh my God!" screamed Polina.

<*Ah, okay, yes,*> said Design. <*I will pull back now.*>

All the little cutters and caravels made an abrupt about-face and bore both Polina and Design far away from the *Keyship* and back into the open ocean as fast as they could go, the puppeteers abandoning their giant doll to the fiery hell they'd created.

Yet Design kept watching through their surviving mirrors, anxious and transfixed as the *Keyship* plunged toward the gates.

<*Will you make it? Will you break them down before the deadlamps eat you ali—*>

Then its bow smashed into the gates at full speed.

Many of the mirrors went dead instantly—yet not all. From a few stray angles, Design watched in wonder as the gates of Batista trembled, wobbled, and then fell into the sea, blocking the Dorata River entirely.

They felt a thrill of victory and sat back in their cockpits, sighing with relief.

<*I did it. It's done. It'd do—*>

Then the deadlamps went to work.

The *Keyship* still had about fifteen twinned mirrors operating. Design stared through one of them as a huge chunk of the inner vessel suddenly vanished—like someone had taken a big shovel and scooped out a perfect sphere of the ship and tossed it away. Then, in another mirror, a perfect circle of the top decks vanished, exposing the *Keyship*'s many passageways to the smoky sky above.

Then it happened again, and again, the giant galleon rapidly dissolving bit by bit. Design had fifteen mirrors remaining, then five, then two, and they watched, spellbound, as the bottom of the hull blinked out of existence—and took with it a large chunk of the sea, leaving a curiously empty bubble of space in the ocean below the galleon, which hung for a moment as if frozen before the ocean came crashing in to replace the gap.

Then the last of the mirrors blinked out and went dark, and Design knew the *Keyship* was gone, edited out of reality like it'd never been there to begin with.

They sat there for a moment, exhilarated, saddened, bewildered.

<*My greatest work,*> they mused. <*Erased from this world like a smudge of grease on a bit of white marble . . .* >

Their cutters slashed on into the open sea, carrying them far away from Batista. Slowly, Design moved their thoughts to the constituent sitting in the mid-deck of one cutter with Polina, who was pacing back and forth like a nervous father awaiting news of a birth.

"It's gone," they said to her.

She stopped pacing. "Gone?" she said. "They sank it *already*?"

"No," said Design slowly. "It was rather like they all took bites of it, devouring it like a school of mawfish attacking a boar that crossed through the wrong bit of jungle river, until . . . well, there was no *Keyship* left at all."

There was a stunned silence.

"In that case," said Design, "it all went rather wonderfully, don't you think?"

Polina slowly sat down, one hand absently reaching for the seat as if she'd forgotten where she was. "Yes," she said hoarsely. "Now it's up to Sancia and Berenice. I damned sure hope they make the most of it."

Huddled in their little vessel, Berenice's eyes stayed fixed on the deadlamp detector in her lap, studying the little top rotating on the black plate.

<*No change?*> asked Sancia.

<*No,*> said Berenice. She watched as the top bobbed up and down—but only a tiny fraction. <*They're still on patrol. Lots of them.*>

<*As normal.*>

<*Yes. Like any normal night.*>

The sea sloshed them up and down, over and over. Berenice was so accustomed to being aboard a galleon that she found she didn't appreciate being on such a small craft. Neither, it seemed, did Diela, who had vomited in the corner some time ago and kept dry heaving every ten minutes, despite her belly being empty. Claudia belched from time to time, but—mindful that it made Diela's nausea worse—she smothered her mouth in her elbow.

Berenice tried to ignore the stench of vomit and focused on the tiny spinning top. No one in their little cutter spoke. They knew Design and Polina should be mounting their attack now, and there was nothing they could do but wait.

The surge of the waves, the ache of her head, the sour sickness in her belly—yet Berenice's gaze did not flicker.

Anytime. Anytime now . . .

Her eyes watered as she stared at the top.

Anytime. Please . . .

Another wave, another swirl of nausea.

Then the top plummeted out of the air and fell to the plate with a tiny *tink!* sound.

Berenice stared at it.

<*They're . . . They're gone!*> she said. She looked up. <*Move! Now!*>

The tiny cutter rushed forward. Berenice snapped the detector rig shut, then mounted the steps to the deck, emerging to see a familiar sight in the distance: the white crumbling walls of the city that had once been Grattiara, sprawled out under a low, full moon.

Tevanne had not rebuilt it much since their raid. It was still as broken as they'd left it.

But they'd hardly expect us to return here, she thought. *Especially when we appear to be mounting such a huge assault elsewhere.*

Claudia pointed to a shallow, sandy beach—right where the *Keyship* had stationed itself when it'd fired on Tevanne's armies mere days ago. <*There. That's the spot.*>

<*I agree,*> said Berenice.

<*Just make sure we don't break our goddamned cargo!*> said Sancia. <*It'd be a damn pity if we came so far just to scrum it up here.*>

The cutter changed course. The ropes swinging from its stern croaked as they hauled their burden closer to shore.

Diela's eyes studied the empty black skies above. <*No lamps,*> she said. <*It took it. Tevanne really took the bait.*>

<*Very eagerly, at that,*> said Berenice. <*Tevanne knew Clef had seen something. It had to have been expecting an attack for some time.*>

<*Just a goddamned shame,*> said Claudia, <*that we had to feed the bastard the* Keyship *to convince it.*>

<*A galleon for a world,*> said Berenice. <*That's a pittance.*>

<*Design might disagree,*> she said.

<*We're approaching the shallows now,*> said Sancia from the cockpit. <*Clef?*>

<*I'm ready,*> said his voice.

Like anyone whose mind was twinned with your own, his voice seemed to whisper into your ear—but Berenice glanced backward at where Clef was stationed, within the curious vessel their cutter was hauling to Grattiara like a whaling ship lugging about its bloody prize. They'd had a devil of a time pulling the thing through the seas, as its boxy, rectangular shape hadn't been meant to split waters at all, but their ropes and rigging had held fast.

Berenice eyed the deadlamp's shell floating in the dark water behind them. *But if you want to break into hell,* she thought, *you must assume the guise of a devil.*

Finally their cutter ran close to the shallows, and they grabbed the ropes at the stern and hauled the deadlamp in until they could climb down and stand on its top. One by one they disembarked from the cutter, crawled across the lamp, and slipped into the open hatch. Berenice and Diela went last, unmooring the ropes to free the deadlamp.

<*Go,*> said Berenice. <*Go now.*>

Yet Diela tarried, her head turned toward the shore, staring at something on the coast.

Berenice did not need to look to know what she was seeing: the perfect, spherical gap in the walls—the very place where Vittorio had perished mere days ago.

<*Diela,*> said Berenice. <*Not tonight. Not now.*>

Diela dragged her eyes away, then climbed down to the top of the deadlamp and slipped into the hatch. Berenice followed, tossing the mooring ropes away, and dropped into the oblong chamber.

<*Shit,*> said Sancia's voice faintly. <*This is going to be a goddamn fun sixteen-hour journey.*>

Berenice waited for her eyes to adjust—the interior of the lamp was dimly lit by a rosy luminescence from a little scrived lantern in the corner. Once she could see, she looked around to confirm how things had held up. They'd refurbished the interior of the deadlamp to the best of their abilities, cramming in as much living space and ammunition storage as they could while still maintaining most of the architecture and designs that granted the ghoulish thing its powers.

<*Ammunition stores are intact,*> said Claudia, reviewing the stacks and stacks of bolts and other rigs. <*Hammocks are a bit damp . . . Must be a leak somewhere. But it won't be too unfamiliar for anyone that's slept aboard a rickety rig once or twice . . . or drunk so much wine they pissed themselves.*>

Sancia reviewed the scriving tools packed up in the walls. They were all minimal—yet even minimal scriving tools were almost as complicated as a bookbinder's workshop. <*All's set here.*>

<*Good,*> said Berenice. <*And . . . Diela?*>

Diela said nothing, staring into the cupboard Design had installed in the corner of the deadlamp.

<*Diela?*> asked Berenice. <*Is our messaging system intact?*>

<*I . . . I think so, ma'am,*> said Diela nervously. <*But to be quite honest, I'm not sure I know what . . . what Design intended when they made this for . . . ah, me.*>

Berenice looked over the contents of the metal cupboard. To her eye, they looked like little more than large metal balls, about the size of a ripe melon, all arranged in careful stacks. But Berenice knew more than anyone that scrived rigs could look like almost anything—especially when it was Design doing the making.

<*They look fine to me,*> she said. <*I . . . suppose. Now, Captain. Are we ready to launch this ship?*>

There was a long silence. Then everyone slowly looked at the giant lorica sitting in the center of the lamp, beside the gravity rig.

<*Oh,*> Clef said. <*Me. That's, uh . . . That's right.*>

Berenice suppressed a grimace. None of the Givans, of course, could control a deadlamp as Tevanne could. Its melding of conventional scrivings—like its gravity rig—with the hierophantic was well beyond the management of any regular human being. And this was why Clef was seated in the center of the craft where its hierophantic console had once hunched, plugged into all of its various horrid rigs.

Fitting his lorica into the space had been tricky enough; but, like any scrived force, they still needed a lexicon to run all of their rigs, along with the deadlamp. Which was why Berenice and Claudia had mounted a small, portable lexicon on the back of Clef's lorica like a backpack—only this backpack could bend reality into all sorts of horrible tangles if it got damaged too much.

<*Yeah, uh, okay,*> said Clef. <*Sure! Sure, let's give this shit a shot!*>

Claudia and Diela exchanged a nervous glance. <*You're sure, Clef,*> said Claudia, <*that this is like piloting the* Keyship*?*>

<*Oh, it's not the same at all,*> Clef said. <*This thing should actually be easier.*>

<*Really?*> said Claudia.

<*Sure. The* Keyship *was made to be a ship first and foremost. But this thing is basically just a structure to be tampered with, played with. Which is what I do best.*> He patted the gravity rig next to him, then cocked the lorica's head and shrugged its shoulders, as if loosening up for an athletic feat. <*Okay,*> he said. <*I'm ready if you guys are ready.*>

<*Strap yourselves in, please,*> said Berenice. She sat in the tiny seat beside her hammock and secured herself to the wall with a rope, running from her shoulder to the opposite side of her waist. <*And make sure you're secure.*>

Sancia sat in a small seat beside her tiny hammock and did the same. <*I goddamn hate flying,*> she said. <*And I'm pretty sure I've done it more than any of you.*>

The deadlamp quaked around them. Claudia cursed as she fumbled with the ropes.

<*Yeah,*> said Clef. <*But I wasn't in the pilot's seat then.*>

Berenice's belly swooped uncomfortably as the deadlamp slowly began to rise out of the sea.

<*Still not comforting, Clef,*> snapped Sancia.

They hung there for a moment in the air. Berenice couldn't put a name on the feeling, but it felt like she couldn't quite tell which direction was up and which was down: her belly said one thing and her brain said another, and the conflict made her feel far sicker than she'd felt down in the riotous waters.

"Oh God," moaned Claudia.

It's confusing the gravity, Berenice thought. *Making it possible for this thing to actually fly . . .*

<*Hold on, now,*> said Clef. <*It's one thing to play with this shit back in Giva, but it's another to actually make it g—*>

Then they shot forward so hard and so fast that Berenice was sure the straps in her seat would leave bruises.

She heard all of them scream at once—herself, Sancia, Diela, and Claudia—all crying out with surprise and dismay as Clef rocketed them up into the air, then over Grattiara, and deep into Tevanne.

17

Berenice was not, by definition, someone who often screamed. Yet as the deadlamp hurtled through space—and kept hurtling, and *kept* hurtling, up and up and up—she slowly realized that she was doing just that, screaming at the top of her lungs with her eyes shut, screaming for so long and so loud that her throat hurt.

With great effort, she wedged her eyes open and saw that everyone else was screaming too—except Clef.

<*Holy hell,*> he said merrily. <*I got to admit, the gravity rig on this bastard makes the stuff we used back in Old Tevanne look like dogshit!*>

After some time—maybe seconds, or minutes—they slowed and began to move at the same consistent speed. Or she thought so, at least. Berenice couldn't see anything beyond the dark, black walls around her, dimly lit by the scrived lamp in their vessel's ceiling; but the roar of the air lessened until finally she could hear the rest of their team panting frantically.

<*Uhh, so,*> said Clef. <*So, I think I figured this thing out. And . . . I believe we should now be coasting.*>

<*Clef,*> snarled Sancia. <*You . . . You dumbass! What the hell is wrong with you? We don't have many changes of clothes with us, and I don't want to shit my pants at the outset!*>

Diela opened her eyes. <*Oh God.*> She stared down at her lap, a look of horror on her face. <*I hadn't even thought about that . . .*>

<*What I did was perfectly reasonable!*> Clef said. <*Almost! We're* in Tevanne. *Quickly, safely. We're maybe the only people alive who could have ever claimed that.*>

There was a silence as the enormity of what had just happened sank in for them.

<*God's balls,*> said Claudia. <*Are we really? We're in this pit of devils?*>

<*Kind of,*> said Clef. <*We're way, way above it, at least. I'd say we're about ten miles inland.*>

<*Can we . . . see?*> asked Diela.

<*If you'd like to. I can see it all, from all the little sensing and warding rigs embedded in this thing . . . But I think Berenice had a window put in, in the bottom . . . Yeah?*>

<*Yes,*> Berenice said. With shaking hands, she undid her rope and crawled on her hands and feet into the middle of the vessel. She found the little latch in the floor, carefully undid it, and slid it back to reveal a thick glass window—and below that, a world unlike any she'd ever seen before.

Berenice gasped aloud as she saw the smooth, creamy surface of white tufts running underneath them, scattered with splinters of pale-blue moonlight. She wondered for a moment if she was hallucinating. <*Are those . . . clouds?*>

<*They are,*> said Clef. <*Low ones. I'd say we're in luck, and that they'd make it harder to spot us . . . but seems likely Tevanne can see through clouds pretty easy.*>

Slowly, Sancia and Diela detached themselves from their straps and crawled across the floor. Together they peered through the window like children watching tadpoles in a shallow pool.

"Holy shit," said Sancia, awestruck.

<*I . . . I never thought I'd see the world this way,*> said Diela. <*I mean—I didn't think you* could.>

<*Claudia?*> asked Berenice. <*Would you like to look? It's quite the sight.*>

Claudia vigorously shook her head, her hands gripping the straps of her seat. <*I've been aboard lots of boats, and they often seemed mad enough. An airworthy one . . . It's a damned abomination, and one I'd rather not dwell on further.*>

<*Don't be stupid, Claudia,*> said Sancia. <*It's scrumming amazing to see.*>

<*Perhaps so,*> she said. <*But God didn't mean for our scrumming feet to leave the ground for this damn long.*>

<*Here,*> said Clef. <*An empty patch is coming up. Should offer a clearer look . . .* >

The white surface suddenly ran ragged—and then they gasped.

Berenice had never in her life seen terrain from such a height. She'd possessed a dim idea of what the earth should look like from this angle, and she'd expected to see curdling, dark forms laid out below the clouds, rippling and wavy, like half-formed clay or mud accumulated after a rainfall.

And those *were* there, yes—but they weren't dark.

The world below was alight with color: with pinks and blues and oranges, soft and hazy, and they were circling about above the distant terrain, rotating slowly like dancers at a ball.

"Lamps," said Sancia softly. "*Normal* lamps. Light lamps."

Diela cocked her head. <*They're . . . patrolling. Looking for us? Or for any infiltrators?*>

<*Possibly,*> said Berenice. <*But then, though Tevanne's rigs might not need light to see, its hosts probably do.*>

She squashed her sense of awe and pulled out her spyglass. It wouldn't offer much from this distance, but it was better than nothing. She squinted through it, the jittering lens catching curdling, curling forms below, illuminated with the shifting, shuddering colors of the patrolling lamps. <*I see . . . hills,*> she said. <*At least, I think they're hills . . . It's dark, and I've never seen them from this height . . .* >

Then Berenice's eyes danced over an unusual, spider-web-like pattern crawling across the hilltops, beaded here and there with blobs of gray—and she slowly realized what she was seeing.

<*Walls,*> she said faintly. <*Oh my God. There are so many walls down there . . . Path to me and see.*>

There was a faint tickling at the back of her head, then the telltale curious lumpiness at the edges of her eyes, and she knew both Sancia and Diela were sharing the spyglass with her.

<*How . . . How many miles are we seeing here?*> asked Diela.

<*Dozens,*> said Berenice. <*Hundreds.*> She moved the spyglass up and down the coast, spotting the glints of fortifications atop what seemed like every hill. <*Layers of walls and walls running . . . God, it must be hundreds of miles deep, and I've no idea how long. More fortifications than any civilization in history, all lit up bright to catch any intruders.*> She lowered the spyglass, then sat back, shaken. <*How . . . How far are we from the sea now, Clef?*>

<*About twenty or thirty miles by now, I'd wager,*> he said.

<*God.*> She shook her head. <*It had all this . . . just waiting inland for us.*>

<*What are you saying?*> asked Diela.

<*Don't you see?*> said Berenice. <*We've barely scratched the surface of this thing. During all our efforts, all our raids. We've barely done any damage at all.*>

Struggling to focus, Berenice cleared her throat. <*Clef,*> she said. <*Please tell me more about our location.*>

<*By my estimate,*> he said, <*and based on the maps we made based off of the memories that Sancia scavenged . . . We're about, oh, fifty miles from the Dorata River. Once we hit that, we follow it to the mountains.*>

Berenice looked at Diela. <*Have you seen enough, and heard enough?*>

She nodded nervously. <*Yes, Capo. Enough to send back to Giva.*>

<*Then we'll need to drop the first anchor,*> said Berenice. She stood and walked to the cabinet in the corner of the deadlamp. <*One every hundred miles, Design said, in order to maintain a connection.*>

<*We're sure we shouldn't do it sooner?*> said Claudia. <*I thought the range of most lexicons was only, like, a dozen miles or more. Not a hundred.*>

<*Design spent a lot of time on this,*> said Berenice. <*It invisibly rides off of Tevanne's own lexicons, without it noticing. So, just like Tevanne can send a message from one side of the continent to the other in the blink of an eye, this will do the same.*>

Together, she, Sancia, and Diela went about removing one of the blank metal balls from the cabinet in the corner. It was wholly unremarkable, being a dull gray that almost made it indistinguishable from a rock—which was the point, of course. They could not risk Tevanne detecting these rigs, dropped here and there across its vast territories.

Diela loaded the anchor into the drop chute, and Sancia knelt down and peered through a spyglass installed in the side of the chute, showing her the land directly below the deadlamp.

<*Waiting for another clear spot . . .* > she said. <*I don't want to accidentally drop this on a goddamned host or something . . . There. A blank field. That should do nicely.*> She turned a wooden switch on the side of the spyglass. There was another pulse in the deadlamp as the hatch at the bottom of the chute opened and the little anchor ball dropped out, and then she closed it again.

<*The density bindings in the anchor should carry it straight down,*> said Berenice. <*So it should be directly on target.*>

<*When's the first contact with Giva, again?*> asked Sancia.

<*In one hour,*> said Diela and Berenice at the same time.

Berenice smiled at the girl. <*Good. Though I didn't think you could have forgotten.*>

She'd intended it as a comfort, but Diela looked ill at her words and did not speak.

<*Are . . . Are you sure you wish to do this, Diela?*> asked Berenice. <*I know communicating with Giva won't be easy. But even if you can't, I want you to know that you're still valuable to our tea—*>

<*I can do it,*> said Diela.

<*I know you can do it too. But I want to make sure tha—*>

<*I can do it, Capo,*> she said, now slightly resentful. <*I owe it to you.*>

Berenice paused, troubled, but nodded. <*I see.*> She looked back at Clef. <*The first anchor's away. Are we high enough to go undetected?*>

<*Right now, we're about a thousand feet above where deadlamps* usually *travel,*> said Clef. <*If some bit of Tevanne sees us, we should—at a distance, mind—resemble an ordinary deadlamp. I've got a lot of the necessary ugly little scrived bits of that working in here too—mostly. It's like we're in a hive of bees, dressed up as a drone, tiptoeing around the empty edges . . .* >

<*Define "at a distance," please,*> said Berenice.

<*'Bout a mile,*> he said. <*If we get any closer than that, it'll realize we're just a bunch of assholes wearing a deadlamp costume and blow us out of the sky.*>

Berenice sighed. <*Well, then,*> she said. <*We'd better get Design's rig set up. Claudia?*>

<*If it means death otherwise,*> grumbled Claudia, <*I guess I'll get up.*>

She reluctantly undid her straps and joined them in assembling the detector rig that Design had sent along. Most of it resembled a large glass globe—they'd been obliged to pack this in a crate with plenty of straw—but the critical pieces were the countless tiny scrived beads to be placed within the globe. The entire thing was so complicated and delicate that they hadn't dared put it together before their sea voyage.

But somehow I doubt, thought Berenice as she snapped the bottom plates together, *that doing this while flying through the air is any better.*

As they finished, they noticed their breaths had begun to frost, and they had to keep shaking their hands to beat back a frosty chill.

Diela slapped her upper arms, her teeth chattering. <*Why is it so cold?*>

<*Because we're crazy high in the sky,*> said Clef. <*That's . . . something we didn't think about.*>

Claudia frowned at him, bewildered. <*The sky gets* colder *the higher it is? Sky is . . .* cold?>

<*I don't know how to tell you not to doubt something you're actively experiencing,*> said Clef. <*But yeah. I don't think we packed any heating rigs, did we?*>

Berenice shook her head. <*None we're going to use. They're just firestarters. And a fire aboard this ghoulish craft is the last thing we need.*>

Finally they finished assembling Design's globe. It was about three feet wide and tall, sitting on a thick platform before Clef, like he was a traveling performer predicting your future before a cauldron.

Design had failed in its efforts to discover how Tevanne controlled its hosts—but their efforts hadn't been for nothing, they said. *Though I can't give you a way to unravel the beast we fight,* they said, *I did determine a better way of* tracking *other hierophantic consoles.*

As it turns out, just turning on a rig that can take bites out of reality is pretty noticeable, if you look for it the right way . . .

Sancia turned the switch on the globe, reached forward, and placed her hands on the side. She cocked her head, listening, and Berenice caught the whisper of commands between her wife and this rig, a burst of strange instructions passing back and forth—and then the tiny lead balls within the glass globe danced to life, swirling about like the last dregs of sand in an hourglass. One bead was unusually large, about a half inch across, and this one shot up to occupy the exact center of the globe. The smaller beads whirled about it like a constellation of stars in the sky, until finally they came to a halt, with some beads stuck to the walls of the glass globe and others hovering in midair several inches from the large ball in the center.

<*I have to admit,*> said Clef. <*Design really knows their shit.*>

Diela did a double take at Clef, who was facing forward, away from the globe. <*Wait. But you're not even looking at i—*>

The helmet of the lorica snapped around to stare at her. <*That's 'cause, kiddo,*> he said, <*I don't need eyes to see!*>

Diela nearly fell backward in surprise. Sancia swatted his pauldron. "Stop it," she said.

Claudia tapped the glass globe. <*It's like some kind of carnival trick. That big bead in the middle . . . that's us?*>

<*Yes,*> said Sancia. <*That's our vessel. And all the other little beads are hierophantic consoles—deadlamps or anything similar that's bending reality, I suppose.*>

<*And how accurate is it?*> asked Claudia.

<*Not enough to take any risks,*> said Sancia, <*if that answers your question.*>

Diela struggled to stand back up. <*Is the edge of the globe twenty miles away? One?*>

<*Five,*> said Berenice. She leaned close and examined a few beads that were about ten inches from the ball of lead in the middle. <*Which means Clef needs to get his damned act together, since some of these are rather too close . . .* >

<*Understood,*> he sighed.

The deadlamp swooped to the right, and everyone cried out and grabbed the walls for support.

<*Strap in!*> said Berenice. <*Now!*>

Together they hurried to rope themselves back into their seats. Another tremendous dip, and they felt the deadlamp turn once more and rip through the skies in an entirely new direction.

<*Sixteen hours of this,*> said Sancia. <*Good scrumming God . . .*>

<*I miss the* Keyship,> Claudia grumbled.

<*I do too,*> said Diela, and began to dry heave once more.

The air grew colder and colder, and soon the four of them huddled under blankets and hid their hands and feet from the frigid air. Berenice's face stayed fixed in a grimace as she watched the beads dance around in the globe. Sometimes they came very, very close to the big lead wad in the center, representing their own deadlamp. *I feel as if Clef is swimming us through deep waters,* she thought, *all teeming with eyeless predators . . .*

<*What's out there, Clef?*> Sancia asked.

<*Deadlamps,*> he said. <*Below the clouds. When they rise up, I have to rise, too, to stay out of range.*>

<*Are they looking for us?*> asked Claudia.

<*Maybe,*> said Clef. <*Or maybe this is just how they behave in the deep bits of Tevanne. I've no idea. But it's going to get colder, folks.*>

Claudia burrowed into her blankets, shivering harder.

<*Good news is, we're at the Dorata River,*> said Clef. <*And . . . we're coming up on one hour. The connection with Giva should be open soon, yeah?*>

Berenice glanced at Diela, who now looked outright terrified. <*Yes,*> said Berenice. <*We'll begin the preparations now.*>

Sancia and Berenice carefully climbed out of their hammocks. One of Sancia's hands brushed against Berenice's bare knuckles, and with it came a whispered thought: <*Do you think she can take this?*>

Berenice responded quickly: <*We don't have a choice.*>

Berenice knelt beside Diela and gripped her wrist, making sure to avoid touching her skin—it wouldn't do to path deeply with her at such a moment. "You can do this," she said. Every word seemed to be a cloud of frost, roiling out into the dim light within the deadlamp.

"I know," said Diela, shivering.

Sancia reached into the top of the messaging cupboard and removed a small bronze circlet, like something a minor nobility might wear in some foreign kingdom—but the inner surface of this circlet was layered with sigils.

"And if you need to break away," said Berenice, "you won't be doing us a disservice."

Sancia handed the circlet to Diela, who was still strapped into her seat. She took it, her face now grim.

"You always think I'm weak," said Diela.

Berenice paused, taken aback. "I don't, Diela."

"I'm not," said Diela resentfully. "I'm *not*. And I'm not doing it to prove anything to you or anyone else."

Sancia studied her with a steely eye. "Then why are you doing this, kid?"

"Because," said Diela, placing the circlet on her head, "I owe it to everyone." She shut her eyes, and her final thought skittered through Berenice's mind: <*And to him.*>

A flash of a face: a young man, his skin dark, his beard neat and trim, his smile bright and gleaming. Berenice's heart twisted at the sight of him.

Vittorio.

Then Diela began to shake.

Sancia and Berenice stared as the girl quaked in her chair, convulsing like someone stung by a dolorspina fish, her eyes rolling back, her mouth twisting in pain.

"Something's wrong," said Claudia.

Diela's presence vanished from their minds. This was a startling thing to experience: Diela herself was still before them, alive but clearly in pain, but her thoughts, her mind, her experiences, all of which were being shared with them—those blinked out like a candle flame caught in the wind.

Berenice's heart froze. The only time she'd experienced anything like this had been when someone had died.

"No!" she said aloud, and she reached forward to pull the circlet off of Diela's head. But Sancia's hand snatched out, grabbed her wrist, and held her back.

"What are you doing?" said Berenice.

<*Wait,*> said Sancia.

Diela's head lolled on her shoulders. A stream of drool fell from her lips to the floor of the lamp.

"What the hell do you mean, wait?" shouted Berenice. "Look at her!"

<*She's right,*> said Clef. <*Wait. You can't feel what's happening yet. But we can.*>

Sancia grasped Berenice's bare hand. <*Feel it,*> she said. <*And see.*>

Berenice felt Sancia's experiences pouring into her. Though they'd been twinned together for nearly a decade, it always came as a surprise to her how *different* Sancia's way of perceiving the world truly was: how reality was always alight with scrivings, with commands, with invisible connections sharing information from across miles of empty space.

Then she saw Diela—and she realized she was not Diela anymore. She was becoming someone else.

The circlet was the giveaway: she could see it had suddenly lit up with commands and arguments—but they were not coming from Clef, or Diela. They were coming from another entity far, far away.

<*It's working,*> said Sancia. <*I . . . I thi—*>

Then Diela stopped shaking. Her mouth closed. She opened her eyes and sniffed. Then she sat up straight in her chair and looked at them both.

"Oh," she said. "There you are."

Berenice gasped. Though Diela had only spoken a handful of words, everything about her was now different: her intonation, her speed, her accent, all of it. Even the way she looked at them betrayed the mad but inarguable fact that the identity currently peering out of Diela's eyes was not Diela.

"Hello, Greeter," said Sancia.

Greeter-Diela blinked around at them, then at the deadlamp interior. "It appears . . . to have worked," they said, still in Greeter's unmistakable low, soothing tone. "The lamp, Clef, the anchors . . .

everything." They cleared their throat. "You will forgive me, I hope, if I speak aloud rather than communicate silently. That would be extraordinarily difficult at the moment."

"What's this doing to Diela?" demanded Berenice. "She looked like she was in pain when this started, and now she's just . . . gone."

"She's not gone," said Greeter-Diela. "She's just temporarily become one of my constituents. *Very* temporarily. Completing the alignment with me so quickly is not . . . advisable. Certainly not easy, naturally. But Diela is very talented. She will get better at this." Greeter-Diela's eyes went briefly unfocused. "I am receiving her memories now . . . Visions of the skies above, and the many, many walls . . . And then, the deadlamps below. Clef—you have evaded detection?"

"So far," said Clef. "But it's busy down there."

"What happened at Batista?" asked Berenice.

"It was a success," said Greeter-Diela. "No casualties. The *Keyship,* as anticipated, was destroyed. Nearly two dozen deadlamps appeared and edited it away, bit by bit."

"Holy shit . . ." muttered Sancia.

Greeter-Diela cocked their head, as if listening to an invisible voice. "Polina is here, by the way. She says to tell you it was a nightmare. She also says hello."

Berenice struggled to think how to respond. It was so bizarre, to know she was not really talking to Diela, but instead to Greeter, the cadence that was miles and miles away now in Giva. The connection had only been extended this far by the "anchors" that Design had crafted: small pathplate-like rigs that piggybacked off of Tevanne's own lexicons, twinning the reality around them into believing they were *actually* the previous anchor in the chain—and the one before that, and the one before that, even the ones resting under the ocean, until finally the chain ended with the original anchor back in Giva, which was being cradled in the hands of one of Greeter's many constituents.

One mind, thought Berenice, *stretched across the face of the earth, allowing two distant people to path deeply . . .* She shivered. *Perhaps one day Greeter shall encompass the whole of the world.*

"The connection feels strong," said Greeter-Diela. "Please make sure you continue dropping one anchor every hundred miles. You should have enough to cover over one hundred thousand square miles . . . but Tevanne is far vaster than that."

"We've noticed," said Claudia sourly.

"The plan remains the same, yes?" they asked. "Take the lamp to the Beretto Mountains. Land and hide it there where you can, and approach the prison from below."

"Yes," said Berenice. "There have been no changes. Has there been any unusual activity from the Tevanni outposts?"

"No lamps," said Greeter-Diela, "no galleons, no ships. Tevanne has not projected any force or power beyond its normal borders. Nor did it pursue us after Batista. It remains inwardly focused."

"It thinks we failed, then," said Claudia. "We made a desperate play for Batista and lost."

"Perhaps," said Greeter. "We should hope it remains that way. But that depends on you going undete—"

"Shit, folks!" said Clef from the front of the lamp. "We've got . . . uh, something!"

They jumped, startled, and peered through the window below them. The carpet of clouds seemed as uninterrupted as ever.

"What the hell do you mean, something?" asked Sancia.

"Not something *below* us!" Clef said. "I mean something's popped up ahead of us!"

Berenice turned to look at the detector rig—and then she paused, confused.

The lead wad representing their own deadlamp was still in place in the center of the globe—but almost all the other beads were now stuck to one side, pointing forward and slightly down and to the right. There were so many they looked like a clutch of wasps forming their nest on the side of a house.

"What . . . What the hell is it saying is out there?" said Sancia.

"Deadlamps?" asked Claudia. "All in one formation?"

"Not deadlamps," said Clef. "I think it's . . . all one thing. And it's *big*."

Then the glass squeaked slightly as the clutch of beads slid up the wall of the globe.

"And it's moving," said Berenice.

"Hold on to something," said Clef. "I'm going to see if I can evade it . . . Whatever it is."

Everyone scrambled to strap themselves into their seats once more. Greeter-Diela had gone silent, but from the expression on her face, Berenice could tell it was still Greeter behind her eyes.

Then the deadlamp began to move, leaning back and forth rapidly, cutting through the skies. Berenice's stomach swooped and swirled, churning around and around. Claudia groaned loudly, and Sancia's face was fixed in a horrid grimace.

"I've got to keep our distance from it," Clef said. "If it comes within two miles of us, we're done for."

"I thought," said Berenice, "that you had said we needed to stay *one* mile away."

"True," said Clef. The deadlamp cut to the side once more. "But based on what I'm seeing in this detector thingy . . . I think this bastard is bigger than a mile all by itself."

The crew stared at one another, their breath frosting in the frigid air.

"A . . . A flying galleon?" said Claudia.

"It's . . . possible," said Berenice. "I suppose. If Tevanne can make a lamp like this fly, it could do the same to something larger." She shook her head. "But bigger than a mile . . ."

Slowly, the deadlamp stopped weaving back and forth through the skies.

"We're not out of the woods," said Sancia lowly. "Are we?"

"No," said Clef. "I've realized that we can't go around this thing. It's too big. So . . . we're going to have to go over it."

"Over," repeated Greeter-Diela. "You intend to fly higher."

"Yes," said Clef.

"Where it's colder," said Berenice. "Much colder, probably."

"Yeah," said Clef. "So cold that I'm . . . I'm not sure we're going to survive. Or at least, if you guys are."

"There's no other way?" asked Greeter-Diela.

"No," said Clef, very definitively.

They cocked their head. "And the heating tools on board," they said, "are too small to heat the lamp."

"Yes," said Berenice. "We brought them to start campfires. Not heat a vessel in the sky."

"And I don't think I can trick them into, like, just heating the air," said Sancia. "Usually with firestarter rigs it's easier to make them start a giant blaze. And we don't have a lot of shit to burn."

Greeter-Diela nodded thoughtfully. "I can't keep you safe," they said. They looked at Berenice. "But someone else could."

Berenice blinked for a moment before realizing what they were suggesting. "Would it be safe for her?" she asked.

"Probably," said Greeter-Diela. "But there are many unknowns with this new technique. Yet it seems the choice is this, or you perish."

Berenice studied Diela's face, solemn and half-lit in the light of the scrived lantern. Her cheeks were still streaked with tears from the last transition, just minutes ago.

"She knew the risks," said Greeter-Diela softly. "You all did."

"I know that," snapped Berenice. "I goddamn know that." She shut her eyes and gritted her teeth. "Climb, Clef. Climb as fast as you can. And keep us free of that thing."

"You got it," said Clef.

The deadlamp swooped up—and then Diela began screaming.

Berenice watched as the girl writhed in her seat, her face twisted in agony. She strained at the ropes across her midsection, her fists balled so tightly her knuckles were bone-white.

<*I did not think,*> said Berenice, <*when I agreed to this arrangement, that it would be like this.*>

<*She's tougher than you think,*> said Sancia.

Claudia leaned low in her seat, her breath was pluming in the air. She stuffed her hands into her armpits. <*I hope we all are,*> she said.

The deadlamp climbed and climbed; Diela groaned; and with every passing second the air grew colder and colder, until Berenice's ears and nose pounded with pain.

The clutch of lead wads suspended in the detector drifted down—but achingly, achingly slowly.

"Come on, you bastard," muttered Clef. "Come on . . ."

Then Diela stopped screaming. Trembling with cold, they turned to look at her: she was leaning forward in her seat with her head bowed—but then she sat up, untied herself, and shakily wobbled across the deadlamp to the workbench and scriving tools.

"I . . . I must admit," she said, "these are *not* the conditions I expected to work under." But her voice now was somewhat nasal and reedy, the voice of a scholar irritated to be disturbed from their precious texts.

"Just get it done!" snapped Berenice.

Diela glanced at Berenice, looking down her nose at her, her face fixed in an expression of haughty affront. It was a face Berenice knew well—for Design often looked at her that way when they were deep in scriving work.

"Then just give me a *moment,* please!" said Design-Diela. With a sniff, they sprang to work, hauling out the little firestarter rigs and piling them all on the small workbench at the side of the lamp.

<She's switched over?> said Claudia. *<She's Design now?>*

"Obviously," said Design-Diela. Then they grabbed five iron ingots, fixed a loupe to their eye, and began writing sigils. "Berenice," they said quietly. "I will need your help for this."

Berenice had to slap her hands together to beat some warmth into them. Then she untied herself and began hobbling over to the workbench. She was shocked at how hard it was to move.

Design-Diela shoved a handful of plates over to her. "I need you to make a twinned plate," they said. "One that must be scrived to ignore heat. Otherwise Sancia is going to burn her hands off."

"Uh, what?" said Sancia.

"And I'm going to need four of them, please," Design added.

"Understood," said Berenice. She grabbed a stylus and went to work, building the commands that persuaded an object to be ignorant of temperature changes. It was a complicated binding, but Berenice's memory for sigils still held up after all these years.

<The hardest bit,> she said as she scrawled out the string, *<is getting my hands to work in this cold . . . >*

Design-Diela looked up at the ceiling of the deadlamp, muttering quietly to themselves. "Hadn't really thought we'd need a floating lamp *inside* this vessel . . . But I suppose we must make do . . ."

Berenice ignored them and focused instead on finishing the first plate and moving on to the second.

Still the deadlamp climbed—and still the air grew colder and colder.

"Are we even close to this damned thing yet, Clef?" said Sancia. "Whatever it is?"

"We're about a minute away from being directly on top of it," he said. "It's rising. It's following us, but . . . not exactly. I think it's *looking* for us—but it hasn't found us yet."

"Scrumming hell . . ." muttered Claudia.

"Done!" said Design-Diela. They stepped back from the workbench and released the first component: a tiny floating lamp, wrought of thin wood and paper, which rose up to bob in the high center of the vessel.

"How, exactly," said Claudia as she shivered, "does that put warm blood in my veins?"

"Shut up," suggested Design-Diela. "Berenice—the plates?"

"Done," she said. With a gasp, she shoved them toward Design-Diela and put her hands in her armpits.

"Good," they said. With stunningly rapid speed—*Do they even feel the cold,* Berenice wondered, *or do they just ignore it?*—Design-Diela applied each of the plates to three iron ingots, which, Berenice now saw, also had three little firestarters stuck to them apiece. Still muttering discontentedly, Design-Diela moved throughout the lamp, examining the air—and then they held one of the ingots aloft, just over where Claudia and Sancia sat, and let go.

The ingot hovered in the air, suspended in space.

"How . . ." said Claudia.

"Sh-She t-t-tricked it to thinking it's attached to the l-l-lamp," said Sancia. Her teeth chattered as she spoke, and she was shaking violently from the cold. "But they had to b-build the lamp first."

"Correct," said Design-Diela.

Berenice crumpled to the ground, no longer able to bear the frozen air. Her bare knuckle grazed a bit of the metal floor, and it instantly stuck; she ripped it away, leaving a good bit of skin behind, but her hands were so numb she barely felt it.

I'm so tired, she thought. Her head felt like it was full of icy stones. *I'm so tired . . .*

Design-Diela placed the two other ingots in the air above the crew—then they handed the fourth and final plate to Sancia.

"Tell the firestarters to burn bright," they said. "To burn bright and burn hard. Do it *now,* please!"

Shivering, Sancia took the little plate from Design-Diela. She shut her eyes, cocked her head, and bit her lip . . .

For a moment, nothing happened. Yet then a slow, wafting heat suffused the deadlamp, like the heat of a scrived oven. Berenice's skin was so numb it took her a moment to even feel it; yet then, very slowly, the feeling returned to her extremities, and the awful heaviness retreated from her head.

She looked up. The three iron ingots were now glowing with a dull red heat, as if they were sitting in a giant coal fire as opposed to hanging in the air.

"I altered them to amplify heat," said Design-Diela. "But only to a *certain* level. Otherwise, well . . . It'd fry us all." They stepped closer, eyeing one of their little contraptions. "The floating bit was the hard part. I'd have just stuck them to the roof if there hadn't been a chance it could damage the deadlamp."

"Thank God," said Claudia. She held her hands up to the floating ingot. "Thank God . . ."

"I still wouldn't touch them," said Design-Diela. "They could easily burn you."

Berenice stood to her feet. "Th-Thank you," she said, still shivering. "You've done us a great service. And rapidly, at that."

"I wouldn't have been able to do it at all without you and Sancia here," they said. "This heating system should keep you at a comfortable temperature if you wish to maintain this altitude of flight . . . but I'm not sure I would go higher. The air might get too thin—and I can't scrive up a way to put air into your lungs." They looked down at their hands, which were blue and crackling. "The girl will need help, when I leave her. I can manage pain fairly easily—but she cannot."

Sancia was still clutching the twinned plate in her hands, her eyes shut. "We're safe from the cold air now, sure—but are we sure we're entirely safe?" she asked. "Clef?"

Clef leaned forward, the lexicon creaking as he examined the detector rig. "It's . . . stopped. I think it's given up. We must have been a ghost of a signal to them. But if you want to look at it, we should be on top of the thing within seconds."

Berenice, Sancia, Claudia, and Design-Diela crawled to the window in the floor of the lamp and stared down at the dark-blue clouds.

For a long while there was nothing, just the undulating blanket of clouds far below; but then at one point, they seemed to bubble and churn, and then . . .

It rose up.

Berenice stared at the thing below them. At first her eyes could make no sense of it: she saw many points, all sticking straight up, and stonelike forms among them that were blocky and tall; but then there just seemed to be more and more and *more* of it, silently rising up through the clouds like a whale breaking the surface of the sea. Her eyes fumbled helplessly with the scale of the thing, this giant airborne leviathan thoughtlessly sailing into the skies, blindly pursuing them.

Then she saw movement among the many pointed forms below: tiny glittering balls of luminescence, rotating among the many stonelike shapes.

"Lamps," said Sancia quietly. "Lanterns. It's a *city*."

The idea seemed laughable—but as the thing below broke free of the clouds, Berenice saw she was right: it was an entire city, floating on a massive chunk of rock that appeared to have been ripped out of the earth itself. It must have been about a thousand feet in diameter, though its perimeter was lopsided and ragged, and the surface was piled up with buildings and structures that soared into the sky.

"Hmm," said Design-Diela. They narrowed their eyes, studying the massive specimen. "Look at the edges. Look at what marches around the sides . . . There are tiny structures, facilities, like beads on a bracelet."

"The gravity supports," said Sancia.

"Yes," said Design-Diela. "My word. I thought Tevanne had done wonderful things with gravity, just from looking at their deadlamps . . . but I'd never imagined it could have wrought something that'd make the deadlamps look like a child's hoop toy."

"I suggest," said Claudia, "that we put as many miles between us and that goddamned thing as we can."

"I could not agree more," said Clef. "That thing spooks the shit out of me. Everyone strap in."

They moved back to their seats, but Berenice grabbed Design-Diela by the shoulder. "You'll let her go now," she said. "Yes?"

"I will," said Design-Diela.

"Clef—when should you land?"

"Half a day," said Clef. "Or thereabout."

"Then we'll open the signal when you touch down, in six hours," they said. "And then we'll examine what the enemy has prepared against us and see how we can help you navigate it. Is that clear?"

Berenice studied Diela. Her hands were still blue, and the tears on her face had rapidly frozen, leaving streaks of puffy red skin behind.

"Berenice?" they said.

"Yes," she snapped. "Yes. Of course it is. Yes."

"Good," they said. "Then I'll see you in six hours. But at least we now have one mystery solved, don't we?"

"Huh?" said Sancia. "We do?"

"We wondered how Tevanne had transported a whole army across the Grattiaran peninsula in an hour," they said. "It seemed impossible—but it'd be quite easy if you had a floating city to just drop them off." Design looked around at them. "The new question is—do we have any reason to believe that's the only one?"

There was a short, stunned silence.

"Oh God," whispered Claudia.

"Good luck," said Design-Diela. "And get some rest." They smiled at them. Then their eyes unfocused, their face went blank, and Diela's head drooped forward, and she slept.

18

Clef sailed the deadlamp through the midnight skies in near silence, listening to the quiet snores of the crew behind him. It was a surreal feeling, to be in such a circumstance—*Well, naturally, it would be,* he thought, *being as I'm flying around in a lamp that basically used to eat people*—but for Clef, the experience was somewhat wonderful.

For so long he had been trapped: alone, passive, ignored, with so many years either lost in the dark or spent hanging about Sancia's neck. But now he not only had a body—and a strong body, at that—but he was soaring through the air, watching through the deadlamp's many sensing rigs as the light shifted in the distant skies.

I'm free, he thought. *What a thing it is, to be free, to fly.*

Yet then he had a very curious sensation: he felt like he was being watched.

It was very difficult to sneak up on Clef. Though his attention could be focused in any one direction or another, he usually maintained some awareness of everything that was happening around him. But he realized, very slowly, that someone new was in the deadlamp with him—someone behind him, watching him.

He turned his attention to look—and then he saw her, only for a second.

An old woman, with pale skin, a mane of white hair, and purpled, rotting hands, standing in the middle of the deadlamp.

Yet the second he focused on her, she vanished.

Clef sat in the cockpit, stunned. He scanned the entirety of the deadlamp, flexing his sight, studying every rig and scriving that he could see. They were alone. Nothing moved except the bodies of the crew, sleeping soundly.

Okay, he thought. *That was . . . weird.*

He turned his attention back to the sensory rigs on the outside of the deadlamp, reading the atmosphere around them.

That's the kind of thing that would really trouble a man, he thought.

He focused and carefully read the landscape below.

But I'm not, anymore, he told himself. *I'm a key. So—I don't need to worry.*

He altered the deadlamp's course very slightly, carving through the clouds.

Right? Is that right? I think that's right.

19

In the dark of the deadlamp, Berenice opened her eyes.

It took her a moment to orient herself—they were drifting at an odd angle, the whole world askew about her—but then she asked: <*How long?*>

<*Not long,*> whispered Clef. <*Maybe less than an hour until we're there. Figured I'd let you all sleep till the very last minute.*>

<*No,*> said Berenice. She began to untie herself. <*I need everyone awake. We'll need all the brains we can get if we wish to make a decent landing.*>

She roused the rest of the crew, and they coughed and sniffed and stretched their limbs, aching from their stiff seats. She saved Sancia for last—she needed her sleep these days—and Berenice hesitated as she knelt over her, watching her head loll on her shoulders, before brushing her wrinkled cheek with one knuckle. "Awake, my love," she whispered. "Awake."

With a snort, Sancia sat up. "Scrumming hell," she said. "Scrumming hell! I . . . I . . ." Then she groaned and rubbed her shoulder. "I've got one *hell* of a pain in my neck . . ."

Berenice smiled. <*Then get up and move about. Come on.*>

Once they were awake they knelt around the globe at the front of the lamp and watched the tiny beads dancing around the glass. There seemed to be no end of them, like a tiny flock of mosquitoes flitting back and forth.

<*That seems,*> said Claudia, <*like one hell of a lot of rigs patrolling down there.*>

<*Yes,*> said Berenice. She leaned forward to study how the beads jittered and swirled. <*If you've built a prison for the most dangerous man in the world, you don't go light on security.*>

Sancia reached forward and tapped a spot at the edge of the globe where a little clutch of beads hung in space, utterly stationary. <*That's it, isn't it?*> said Sancia. <*That's the prison.*>

Berenice nodded. She studied the little clutch of beads, imagining the prison floating somewhere down in the clouds ahead of them.

<*If we go any closer, we won't be able to descend without being spotted,*> said Sancia.

<*Yes,*> said Berenice. <*But if we drop down too far from the prison, we'll have to cross miles of terrain to get to it—if they even* are *crossable—without being detected.*>

Diela snuffled and rubbed her nose. She still looked slightly peaky after her handful of moments as both Design and Greeter. <*So—how do we land?*> she asked.

<*Guessing we don't want to go down shooting,*> said Claudia, <*and make a hole.*>

<*Even if we survived,*> said Berenice, <*Tevanne would surely summon reinforcements. Including one of those city-things, possibly.*>

<*Which would be bad,*> said Clef. His helmet slowly turned to look at them. It was the first time he'd spoken in nearly an hour, Berenice noted. Clef was always a bit tricky for her to read, even when she was touching him; but Sancia was much better at it, and perhaps since Berenice was twinned with her, she could sense he was shaken by something.

Perhaps it'd be stranger if he wasn't *shaken,* she thought, *given what we're about to do.*

Then she noticed something—a pattern in the beads whirling about in the bottom of the globe.

<*Clef,*> she said, <*please take us southwest about five miles.*>

A dip as the deadlamp swooped to the side. The beads in the globe scrambled, rearranging themselves . . . and then, very slowly, she saw it.

<*There,*> said Berenice. She tapped the glass at one spot below them. <*Look here, at this place. Every once in a while, almost none of the rigs below pass close to here.*>

They all watched carefully, but Berenice saw she'd been right: there was a gap in the patrols, as if they were avoiding an object that might block their passage.

<*A peak in a mountain,*> said Berenice softly. <*Something they have to fly around, maybe . . .* >

<*Clef,*> said Sancia. <*Can this thing land there?*>

<*Being that I functionally* am *this thing we're in,*> said Clef, <*sure. I can land you almost anywhere. Doing it while going* undetected, *though . . . That's harder.*>

<*But the patrols leave a gap,*> said Berenice. <*We can see it, plain as day.*>

<*Yeah, but it's not a* big *gap,*> said Clef. <*Remember—we have to stay at least a mile away from any rig that could detect us. Doing that while descending through this narrow, vertical cylinder of empty space, while all those monsters out there whirl and patrol around us . . . That's trickier.*>

Sancia shook her head. <*If we came all this goddamned way,*> she said, <*only to find out we can't even get to the goddamned prison . . .* >

<*I said it was* trickier,> said Clef. <*But not impossible.*> He contemplated it. <*There's definitely a pattern. And . . . if I'm reading their movements correctly, we have a window of opportunity about every, oh . . . seven minutes or so.*>

<*Okay?*> said Sancia. <*I feel like you're about to say something super shitty.*>

<*Correct,*> said Clef. <*Because the window of opportunity is about forty seconds long.*>

A lump of horror congealed in Berenice's belly as she realized what he was suggesting.

<*So . . .* > Sancia said. <*You're saying the only way to get through . . . is to drop. Straight down. From our current height. In forty seconds. Which means as fast as possible.*>

<*Well, as fast as possible while keeping all your brains in place,*> said Clef. <*Yeah.*>

Berenice and Sancia worked quickly, putting together ropes with tiny adhesive rigs to give their seats more secure straps. <*Orso always said,*> said Sancia, <*that the key to innovation is to throw yourself off of a cliff and build wings on the way down.*>

<*He did,*> said Berenice. Together they began attaching the new restraints to all their seats.

<*But I never really thought we'd, like,* literally *be doing that shit,*> said Sancia.

Claudia strapped herself into her seat. <*Clef?*> she said. <*Do you actually know how fast you can drop and keep us all alive?*>

<*Uhh,*> said Clef. <*I have a pretty good idea. But . . . I mean, I've never done this before, guys.*>

Claudia stared into space balefully, then down at the ropes crossing her chest. <*Are . . . Are there any more of these?*> she asked.

<*None that would make a difference,*> said Berenice, taking her own seat.

"Ohh God," said Diela. She took a deep breath and secured all of her straps. "I didn't know what it'd be like to fly, but I *definitely* didn't want to know what it's like to fall."

<*It's not too bad,*> said Sancia. <*Suddenly seems like I've fallen out of the air far too many times in my life . . .*>

Berenice said nothing, since she knew they weren't going to just drop: Clef was going to send them plummeting down far faster than ordinary gravity could ever achieve. She tried to quiet her mind to keep this knowledge from leaking through to the others.

<*Are . . . Are we all ready?*> she asked.

They nodded.

<*Then Clef,*> she said, <*let us know when the window opens.*>

<*You got it,*> he said.

There was a long, long silence. Everyone waited breathlessly for the fall to begin—yet nothing happened.

<*Clef?*> said Sancia.

<*Oh, uh, we have three minutes until the window opens, in my estimation,*> he said.

<*Three minutes . . .* > said Claudia. Her face was already pale. <*God. Clef, goddamn you, if I don't make it home to my little boy, I swear I will scrumming haunt your ass for as long as it takes.*>

<*Noted,*> said Clef acidly. <*Also, shit, thanks for the encouragement! It's not like this is hard or anything.*>

They sat in silence. The wait felt interminable. Berenice tried to do the math in her head as distraction. *How many miles? How many feet shall we fall? How fast must we descend to cross it all in forty seconds?* Giving up, she tried to count the seconds but quickly felt she was going too fast or too slow, and gave up on that too.

Everyone was panting nervously in the deadlamp—all except Sancia, who sat there with a look of grim resignation on her face.

<*It'll be over before you know it,*> she said. <*Trust me. That's how it always goes.*>

<*That's nice to hear,*> said Diela shakily. <*Then will you judge me if I wee all over myself?*>

<*Hell, girl,*> said Claudia, <*if I get out of this without being covered in shit or sick, I'll call it a victo—*>

Then they fell.

The sheer change in momentum was indescribable: in one moment, they were hanging in space; in the next, Berenice's body was howling, screaming, shrieking down, her legs and arms helplessly flying up, her whole being ripped relentlessly upward. She couldn't breathe, she couldn't move or fight the momentum, she couldn't even see: the world was just moving too fast, too madly, impossibly *fast* for her body to function.

Her ears screamed. Her sinuses ached. Her head pounded—and suddenly she was all too aware that her body was little more than a bag of fluid, and all that fluid had suddenly been forced *up,* up into her chest, her shoulders, her skull . . .

He went too fast, she thought. *We're going to die.*

She found that Sancia had been wrong: the fall was not over before she even knew it had happened. It just seemed to keep going and going and going.

Please stop, she screamed wordlessly at the rattling, whirling world. *Please just slow down! Stop or slow down a bit! I don't care if we get shot out of the sky, I don't care!*

Yet the deadlamp did not stop. It continued plummeting relentlessly down, on and on, and Berenice began to despair: it was never going to stop. They would fall until they died.

But then, impossibly, they gradually slowed; then they slowed yet more; and then there was a rattling bang as the deadlamp struck something.

For a moment, Berenice couldn't think. Her head ached too much, and she felt like she was spinning, yet she could sense that the world was still—but the air was full of screaming, full of howling and shrieking and yammering as her mind churned and she tried to remember how her body worked.

Then she had the strangest sensation: she realized she was screaming and couldn't *stop*. She was back in her body, in her mind, and though she ached in countless places she knew they were safe; and yet she simply couldn't stop screaming. The wild, swirling panic in her simply would not go away, no matter how the cool, detached part of her mind tried to reason with it.

And then she realized: this panic was not hers.

Diela, she thought.

Still screaming, Berenice forced her face to turn to the girl, strapped into the far wall. Her eyes were closed, and her whole body shook as she shrieked over and over again. Then Berenice saw that Sancia and Claudia were doing the exact same, howling in their seats with their eyes tightly shut.

She's pathed into all of us, Berenice thought. *We're feeling everything she feels.*

Somewhere she could hear Clef crying, "What the shit? What the hell! We stopped! Guys, we *stopped*!"

Berenice ignored him. She focused, took a breath, and then—still screaming wildly, her cheeks now pouring with tears—she undid her straps, and staggered across the deadlamp to the girl.

Either this works, she thought, *or I punch her and knock her out.*

Then she braced herself and placed her bare forehead against Diela's.

Instantly, the feeling of panic tripled, quintupled, octupled:

she *was* Diela, she was feeling and experiencing everything the girl felt, so closely twinned there was almost no difference between the two—except the calm, cold, detached part of Berenice's mind was now also forced into Diela's.

She said, very forcefully: *We are safe. We have stopped. We are safe. Calm. Calm, calm, calm.*

Slowly the screams dwindled, bit by bit, until Diela wept in her seat, her body still quivering. Then Sancia and Claudia stopped screaming behind her, and both of them gasped for breath.

"Oh my *God*!" cried Sancia. "I don't know what was worse—the fall, or that mad shit!"

"I vote for the fall," groaned Claudia. "Very much so."

<I'm . . . I'm sorry, Capo,> Diela gasped.

<I know,> Berenice said. *<I know, I know. But you're safe now. And I will need you active and in one piece. Understood?>*

Diela nodded, sniffed, and undid her straps. *<Yes, Capo.>*

<Good.> Berenice looked back at Clef. *<Are we on the mountain?>*

<Yeah,> he said. *<I have us secured southwest of one of the mountains around the valley. The prison and all that mad shit about it—that's on the opposite side, the northeast.>*

<And we're undetected?> she said.

A pause as Clef considered it. *<No change in their patrols.>*

Berenice nodded, then took a deep breath and assessed the situation. Her shoulders ached from the straps—she had no doubt she'd have bruises—and her head pounded and her ears were ringing. But their gear seemed intact, and as she pathed into Sancia, Claudia, and Diela, flitting through their minds very briefly, they all seemed more or less whole.

<Then let's go outside,> she said. *<And see what world awaits us.>*

20

Sancia paused at the deadlamp's hatch, flexing the little muscle in her mind as she peered through the walls and into the world beyond. She saw nothing—no silvery tangle of logic, nor a gruesome, glittery red of one of the deeper commands—and then, satisfied, she opened the hatch and carefully climbed out.

She winced as the cool mountain air slapped at her eyes, then squinted into the blinding daylight. *It's a hell of a lot warmer than when we were at the top of the goddamned skies,* she thought. *So that's something.*

She studied their surroundings. They'd landed in a thick copse of tall silvery trees, their trunks white as bone, their leaves delicate and shimmering in the wind. Beyond them she glimpsed the ragged brown horizon of the mountains, which curled about them like a cat asleep in a spot of warm sun.

She paused for a moment, struck by the sight of such a beautiful yet desolate place, all of it so absolutely, breathtakingly quiet. Sancia had never known anything besides hot, humid, cheeping jungles and the cramped alleys of Old Tevanne. To be quite literally dropped into a place so still and silent was disturbing, yet oddly awe-inspiring.

Then she saw them in the distance, buzzing through the distant skies like vultures: three deadlamps, trailed by tiny flocks of smaller flying rigs—perhaps espringal lamps, or some other dreadful contraption. They were too far away for her to study with her scrived sight, but she had no doubt they were hostile.

We're alone, she thought, *but in a world full of eyes.*

She felt Berenice focusing on her, reading her feelings, and let her path into her eyes very briefly to scan their surroundings.

<*And your sheath is secure?*> asked Berenice.

<*As secure as it's going to get, I guess,*> said Sancia. She plucked at the dark-gray fabric wrapped about her limbs. It was a new rig they'd developed—and, she found, an uncomfortable one: it looked like a bizarre dark-gray costume that completely concealed her form, leaving only a small slit for her eyes, yet it had tiny brass plates woven throughout it that were, she hoped, performing a variety of invisible tasks.

Tevanne had developed much more efficient methods of perceiving intruders than regular sight: scrived ways of detecting heartbeats, living blood, certain scrivings, and so on. The question was how to mask these signals it looked for, and the simplest solution was a twinned sheath: one enveloping piece of clothing that was twinned with a half-dozen others just like it, though they were all empty, and were carried about folded up in a pack on one's back.

This meant that when Tevanne's various sensory rigs looked at one twinned sheath containing a living person, reality *simultaneously* argued that it was six other pieces of clothing that contained nothing at all, and this dampened the signal that Tevanne was looking for so much that it was simply registered as an error, and thus went ignored.

Sancia looked down at herself. <*The sheath suit seems to be holding up. None of the lamps have detected me, though they look to be a few miles off.*>

<*If you have any issues,*> said Berenice, grunting slightly as she climbed out wearing her own, <*we need to know now. Since we'll all be wearing them until the mission's done.*>

<*These things aren't going to explode on us, are they?*> asked Sancia.

<*San . . .* >

<*I mean, twin things the wrong way, or twin something that's inside of something that's already twinned, and . . .* >

<*And it combusts!*> said Berenice. <*Yes! And it was very tricky to make, given that we ourselves are twinned with other people, and thus should probably not be inside of a twinned space. But it's only our minds that are twinned—not our bodies.*>

Sancia helped Berenice out of the hatch. <*That was what happened back in Old Tevanne, right? You and Orso twinned that box into thinking it held a lexicon, and . . .* >

Berenice laughed faintly. <*And it exploded. Yes. Orso didn't even tell me it was going to happen until it was too late. Thank God he was right on the timing, otherwise the gravity rig you'd been riding would have died underneath you, and you'd have fallen to your death.*>

They began to slide toward the edge of the deadlamp.

<*I wish he was here,*> said Sancia.

<*Me too,*> said Berenice.

They dropped into the brush. Berenice pulled out her compass, studied it and then the skyline, then pointed northwest. They started off, intending to go just far enough to get their bearings, espringals in hand and rapiers on their backs.

They walked until they came to a slight rise, allowing them to peer northwest over the mountain. There they saw it: a fat dark dot hanging in the sky in the far distance, like a jet-black hummingbird debating which blossom to sip from.

They were struck silent at the sight of such a thing. For a moment they just stood there, staring.

<*There,*> said Berenice softly. <*That's it.*>

<*I can hardly believe we've gotten this close,*> said Sancia.

<*I as well,*> said Berenice. She pulled out her spyglass and glassed the distant prison. <*But now I wonder . . . how to get closer?*>

Sancia shut her eyes and pathed to Berenice, glimpsing what she saw through the spyglass. It looked like a massive, flat black cube simply hanging in the sky, with five deadlamps making slow circles around it, each one followed by tiny flocks of smaller lamps, bobbing along merrily like ducklings in a stream.

<*Two up close,*> said Berenice. <*And three more on a wider pa-*

trol . . . > She shook her head. <*Beating one deadlamp is hard enough. But we're supposed to kill* five *this time? How?*>

<*Start where it's weak, I guess.*> Sancia sucked her teeth, considering it. <*The valley, maybe?*>

Berenice nodded. <*Yes. I don't think that thing is just floating on its own. There must be some scrived artifice supporting it.*>

<*Yeah,*> said Sancia. <*Because it's Crasedes. And trapping the first of all goddamned hierophants . . . That can't be an easy thing to do.*> She grinned humorlessly. <*Lots of shit to monkey with, in other wor—*>

Then she spied something on the ridge above them and froze.

She didn't need to say anything: Berenice felt the sudden flame of fear in Sancia, and together they both dropped to the ground, hidden in the undergrowth.

Sancia lay there, panting and frantically reviewing what she'd glimpsed: the outline of a fortification, or a wall, standing tall amidst the trees above them.

<*There's something stationed here?*> said Berenice.

<*Dunno.*> Sancia flexed her scrived sight but could spy no alterations in the wilderness about them. <*I don't see any rigs. So whatever's up there isn't scrived . . . I guess it could be some dumbass mountain man's house?*>

<*He would have to be quite the idiot,*> said Berenice, <*if he were to keep living here with so many deadlamps circling above.*>

Sancia braced herself, then peeked through the undergrowth at the ridge above. <*Oh,*> she said. <*I think I see . . .* >

Together they both cautiously rose, staring at the structure atop the ridge above. It was a wall, but it was terribly aged, with many of the other pieces of the structure having decayed or tumbled over long ago. What was still standing was blooming with lichen and stained from the many snows.

<*What the hell is this?*> asked Sancia.

<*I don't know,*> said Berenice. <*But let's investigate. Carefully.*>

They crept through the brush. As they approached they came upon odd things lying in the brush: enormous, perfectly square stones; long, smooth, crenellated stone cylinders that Sancia thought might have once been columns; and fragments of what appeared to have been sculptures, depicting frowning bearded men and many, many doors. All of them had fallen down one face of the mountain—carried over many years, Sancia assumed, by countless winter snows.

The epicenter appeared to be the peak of the mountain, which had been flattened into a foundation of sorts. A handful of columns remained there, along with the ghostly remains of the old wall. Besides that, there was nothing but dust and rock.

<*God,*> said Sancia. She kicked a rock down a shallow slope. <*Where the hell did all this old stuff come from?*>

Berenice shrugged. <*There are heaps of such ruins all around these lands, I've read. With the power of someone like Crasedes, they say, it was easy to build, and build, and build . . .* >

Sancia's eyes strayed to the fat black dot on the horizon. <*So Tevanne is holding Crasedes prisoner basically in his goddamn hometown.*>

<*Crasedes controlled this continent well before Tevanne ever did, and for far longer,*> Berenice said. <*A ghost of what he once was, trapped above the ruins of the place he once built . . . It makes a certain dramatic sense, doesn't it?*> She began crawling back down the hillside to the deadlamp. <*Almost a pity that we're to break him out and kill him.*>

It took Clef a good bit of work to exit the deadlamp—he was very good at jumping, he was eager to tell them, but climbing was proving tricky—but once he was free they started off across the peaks, Berenice leading as they silently wove through the pines and the shimmering white trees. Their scrived sheath suits were not terribly comfortable, obscuring their mouths and features, but they would have been intolerable had the air not been so dry and cool—a climate that Berenice had never known in her life.

<*We need a vantage point to survey the area,*> said Berenice. She nodded at a distant ridge to the south, then another on the other side of the vale, to the northeast. <*Those should do nicely.*>

They walked for hours through the peaks and hills. At times they came to rocky cliffsides, and there Sancia shone, pathing into each of their thoughts to guide them on how to climb such a surface. But mostly their journey was spent creeping through the willowy brush, sometimes coming upon a lichen-covered fragment of some crumbling ruin: a piece of cobblestone, or perhaps an amputated bit of statue, or simply a smooth giant slab. Most seemed like ordinary stone, but then Sancia pointed to one tottering wall. <*Look. Look at the bricks.*>

Diela leaned in. <*What about them?*>

<*Look at the markings on them.*>

Berenice cocked her head, her eyes dancing over the tiny worn-down crinkles and whorls in the face of each stone, almost like they were carvings—and then she realized that each brick had the *same* set of worn carvings. And, more startling, she realized she knew some of them.

<*They're scrivings,*> said Berenice. <*Scrivings for durability, for resilience . . . Simple ones, but scrivings nonetheless.*>

Sancia nodded. <*That's how this is all still standing—if you could call it standing. These are all ancient, scrived fortifications. They must have been one pain in the ass to make, using nothing but a hammer and a chisel.*>

<*They scrived each and every goddamned* brick?> Claudia stared around at the ruin-dotted valley. <*God. What the hell happened here?*>

No one answered. Berenice looked back at a long, ragged wall straddling a hill in the distance and suddenly thought: *Men came to the lands, men built in the lands, and then they built things to empty the lands of men.*

<*Enough,*> whispered Sancia. <*Come along.*>

They split up as they approached the lip of the vale, with Sancia and Claudia going to the south and Berenice, Clef, and Diela going to the northeast. <*Keep your eyes out for rigs,*> Berenice said to Sancia and Clef. <*We're still far away from the prison . . . but it's hard to believe Tevanne would leave this place unguarded.*>

They kept moving, creeping through the trees and scrambling over the stones, always mindful of the vale beyond . . . and then something seemed to change.

It was the most curious feeling, like some strange cloud had passed before the sun, casting the world below in a shade of color their minds knew was not normal.

<*Capo,*> whispered Diela. <*You feel that?*>

<*Yes,*> said Berenice. She looked back at the path they'd just taken. <*I feel like we've passed some kind of boundary or barrier of some kind . . .* >

Then Sancia's voice, from very far away: <*We feel it too—just as I grew close to the valley.*>

Berenice glanced out at the rambling trees below, and the huge black box floating above.

<*Do you think it's . . . it's him?*> said Sancia. <*Or is it . . .* >

<*I'm not sure,*> said Berenice. <*But we need to find out.*>

Berenice and her half of the crew made it to their ridge just as the sun passed midday. The three of them paused at the sight: the valley unrolled before them, dotted with half columns and half walls, like this place was the graveyard of some species of massive stone animal. Far more disturbing than this sight, however, was realizing they were almost at eye level with the distant deadlamps, which curled slowly through the skies.

Yet what unnerved them most was the prison itself: a huge cube of solid darkness, floating placidly in the sky. There was some quality to the blackness that made them queasy, as if it devoured light itself, denying the cube a sense of definition.

<*What a damn spooky place,*> said Diela.

<*Yeah . . .* > said Clef. <*But it seems . . . weirdly familiar.*>

Berenice glanced at him. Though his armor was, of course, expressionless, he appeared to be fixated on one segment of wall that was still upright, punctuated by a single tall, thin window. <*How so?*> she asked.

Clef shivered, the enormous lorica rattling with the movement. <*I . . . dunno. Just a feeling, I guess.*>

<*The more important question,*> said Berenice, <*is do you see . . . Well, Tevanne? The singular body, I suppose?*>

<*You mean that thing Gregor is now?*> said Clef. He studied the valley, then shrugged. <*I'm not close enough to see much. But . . . I don't think so.*> His helmet turned to look at her. <*Maybe you were right. Maybe annihilating Batista really did draw that . . . that thing away from here, whatever it is.*>

<*Let's hope,*> said Berenice.

She got down on all fours and crawled out to the lip of the ridge, spyglass clutched in her hand. Once there, she pressed her eye to the spyglass and peered into the vale. For a long while she saw nothing—just the endless rolling swells of trees, the odd clutch of old ruins, and the deadlamps and their little flocks of lanterns above. Yet as she searched the trees, she found herself blinking hard. Something about the light down there—the bend of the shadows, the way the tips of the pines met the sky—made her strain her eyes.

<*Something's wrong with that place, Capo,*> said Diela softly. <*I don't like looking at it.*>

<*Me neither,*> said Clef.

Berenice tried to ignore the queer ache blooming in the front of her skull—and then she finally spied it: a smooth black dome, poking up just past the tips of the trees, like an immense boulder of polished volcanic glass—and it appeared to be positioned directly below the floating prison.

<*That's it,*> said Berenice. <*That's got to be . . . I don't know, the control nexus for Crasedes.*>

<*What . . . is it?*> asked Diela.

<*To be perfectly frank, I've no idea,*> she said.

She glassed the trees about the dome but saw no towers or any other structure.

<*Then . . . can we just walk through the forest in our sheath suits,*> said Diela, <*and get in there and turn the thing off?*>

<*It surely can't be that easy . . .* > said Berenice.

Then Sancia's voice, very faint, but barely in range: <*Ber—look to the south of the vale. There's a tiny stream there.*>

<*So?*>

<*Just look. We're not alone.*>

It took her a moment to find it, but when she did it appeared to be little more than a common mountain creek, happily burbling away downslope. Berenice studied it, wondering what Sancia could have wanted her to see . . .

Then someone stepped over the stream.

Berenice blinked and positioned the spyglass to better see them: it was not one person, she realized, but many, all walking in a straight line, their movements slow and watchful as they crossed over the little creek. She counted them: six men and five women, clothed in dark gray with light armor. They seemed to be from many races, though their figures grew hard to discern when they moved into the forest shadows.

<*Hosts,*> said Claudia.

<*I agree,*> said Berenice. She narrowed her eyes. <*But they're unarmed.*>

<*It makes sense,*> said Diela. <*Why arm them? The instant one of them spies something, the deadlamps above will know too. You don't need a rapier with things like that on your side.*>

<*One broke off and is doing something,*> said Sancia. <*Look.*>

Berenice narrowed her eyes and watched as a straggler left the group and approached a tall pine. She studied them as they climbed the tree and carefully adjusted . . . something.

Some small dark bundle, wedged in between the branches. No matter how she focused on it, Berenice could never quite tell what it was.

The host climbed back down, rejoined the group, and they continued on into the forest. Then a blur of branches and shadows, and she lost them.

<*I'm guessing,*> said Clef, <*that they aren't leaving love letters.*>

<*No,*> said Berenice, squinting at the bundle in the tree. <*It's a rig. It's got to be.*>

<*But what kind?*> asked Claudia.

<*Detection, surely,*> said Sancia.

A pause as everyone considered this.

Diela spoke the thought before it passed through Berenice's mind: <*If they put one in one tree,*> she said quietly, <*couldn't there be more?*>

Berenice studied the sprawling forest below, sucking her teeth and thinking. <*Claudia,*> she said. <*Make note of the hosts' patrol paths. Try to see if there's a pattern. And on our end . . .* > She looked back at Clef. <*I think it's time,*> she said, <*to send out our scout.*>

<*Why is it,*> he said, <*that I don't like the way you said that?*>

Clef trembled as his big gauntlet slowly, carefully undid his cuirass—or, rather, the lorica around him trembled, his own emotions made manifest in the metal. He did not like this at all, really: he had never removed himself from what he now thought of *as* himself, and the experience was unnerving, like inserting a giant needle into one's own arm. <*We . . . We sure we want to do this?*> he said. <*Like—I'm willing to do all kinds of crazy shit, folks, but if this goes awry, we're in deep trouble.*>

<*It should work,*> said Berenice. She sat back from where she and Sancia had finished scriving two small steel capsules, about the length and width of two fingers. <*It's basic twinning, which we know quite well.*>

<*Yeah, but you're going to be twinning* me.> He continued feeding commands into the lorica, the rig's big fingers delicately gripping his head and slowly extricating him from the lock. <*Or the space holding me, at least. We sure it won't pop like a balloon?*>

<*We're only twinning the space once,*> said Berenice. <*Not nesting twinned things inside of twinned things. You act like we don't do this all the time!*>

<*Yeah, well, usually you're not putting* me *inside of the twinned stuff,*> muttered Clef.

"The angle's good," said Claudia softly, peering down the stock of her espringal at the forest below. "I can make the shot."

<*Speak silently, please,*> said Berenice.

Claudia slowly, thoughtfully repositioned her right leg to better lie on the stone ridge. <*Sorry, Ber. Got a bit too absorbed in this . . . But I should be able to get you down there safely, Clef.*>

<*It's simple,*> said Sancia. She opened up one small canister and held out a hand. <*The canisters are twinned to believe they're the same. So if we put you in one, and fire the other down there, that canister will* believe *you're down in the valley. Then you should be able to peer out from down there and see what all those little rigs are*—and *what's going on in that big-ass dome too.*>

<*This normally wouldn't work, if we were putting a living person in a twinned space,*> said Berenice. <*But you, ah . . .* >

<*I'm not a living person,*> said Clef flatly.

<*Well. Not a conventional one, at least.*>

<*Fine. And if Tevanne has some horrid rig down there that can snatch up the other end of the connection?*>

<*Then I pop open the canister and dump you out, breaking it,*> said Sancia.

<*It's also why I'm aiming for a dark, empty patch about a hundred yards from the dome,*> said Claudia softly. <*You'll be about two or three feet underground—and if Sancia's density bindings work, the canister will burrow itself a little deeper. Hard to detect.*>

<*Shitting hell,*> grumbled Clef. <*I guess it's payback for me dropping your asses out of the sky.*> He issued a handful more commands to the lorica, and it extended the gauntlet holding himself. <*Our connection will break the instant you put me in the canister. So I guess fire me down there, wait twenty seconds, and pop me out so I can report back—got it?*>

Sancia took him in her hands. The lorica stayed in an awkwardly frozen position—cuirass swung open, gauntlet extended. Then she knelt and carefully placed him in one canister, her bare fingers pressed to his moth-shaped head. <*Good luck,*> she whispered.

<*Yeah, yeah,*> said Clef.

The door on the canister swung shut—and for the first time in a long while, Clef's world went silent.

He could still see, of course, perceiving all the countless scrivings around him: the miniature lexicon on the lorica's back; Claudia's intricately scrived, high-powered espringal; and the many tiny plates embedded in the Givans, these tiny flickerings of blood-red in their hands—along with the sputtering, flaming star in Sancia's skull. But he could not speak to them, nor could he hear their thoughts and feelings. The sudden, abrupt silence was startling.

Then he felt himself . . . moving.

But that wasn't quite it: he felt himself moving and *not* moving at the same time. His mind was presented with the impossible sensation of occupying two separate spaces at once—one space in Sancia's hands, and another being loaded into Claudia's espringal.

Boy, I hate this shit, he thought.

A loud click as the espringal nestled the little cylinder into its pocket. He could hear Claudia's breathing, slow and steady, her face pressed up against the stock. And then . . .

He flew.

Clef had thought he'd become accustomed to flying, given that he'd just piloted a deadlamp across a pretty good bit of the continent—but this was different. This was not only uncontrollable—a sudden, wild acceleration of speed that he himself had no say in—but he *also* felt like he was staying utterly still, clutched in Sancia's hands. The whole experience was one of fracturing, like his very mind was being split in two.

Scrumming hell, he thought, *I* hate *this shit!*

Then it stopped, with a loud, wet *thumpf,* and Clef watched as the world around him went suddenly dark, obscured with wet, rocky earth, and the many pale, delicate roots and tendrils of the grass growing above.

I've been buried once before, he thought. *I like it even less this time . . .*

Yet he could still perceive the scrivings around him: wild, whirling tangles of silver and blood-red, some circling about him like comets, others huge and stationary like distant suns. The sudden immersion in a world burdened with so many complicated commands was bewildering.

Okay, dumbass, he thought. *Focus. Focus . . .*

He looked about and spied the hosts instantly, the little balls of boiling red slowly bobbing through the darkness as the people above patrolled. He was familiar with this binding, having seen it in the many hosts from their raids, and he spied thirteen of them nearby—though he was sure there would be many more beyond.

Next he spied what he assumed were the rigs the hosts had placed in the trees: tiny glimmering little tangles of white that were deeply sensitive to heat, motion, and many other curious phenomena . . .

And they must be sensitive to bodies of a certain size, he thought. *Since they didn't seem to give much of a shit about the canister.*

He also noted that there was a more powerful command operating within them: seeking a . . . a signal, a message, a . . . a presence.

To see if any movement nearby, he thought miserably, *is accompanied by one of Tevanne's command plates. Goddamn it . . .*

He counted eleven of the little rigs in the trees around him—and, with dismay, realized the entire forest must be rigged up to sense intruders.

He turned his attention to the structure at the far end of his sight: what he assumed was the giant black dome. It was hard to miss, being that it was boiling with silvery tangles of scrivings in a pattern he found very familiar.

A lexicon, he thought. *Just like in a foundry from Old Tevanne. A big one . . .*

But this specimen was different: not only was it curiously arranged in the heart of the earth—for some reason there were many movement rigs embedded around it—but as Clef peered through its layers of logic and commands, he saw that at the heart of this bright-white star was something unusual . . . Something disturbing.

There were twenty discs nestled within the lexicon—but they were of a deep blood-red color, one that pulsed and gleamed in a sickening manner.

Ah, shit, he thought. *I really hope I'm not seeing what I think I'm seeing . . .*

And then the world changed—fractured, broke, split—and the forest was gone, and light came spilling in.

Clef gasped as he tumbled out into Sancia's hand. <*Holy shit!*> he said. <*Ho . . . Holy shit! You've got to warn me before you do that crap again!*>

<*I did,*> said Sancia. <*You just didn't hear. Did it work?*>

<*Yeah . . .* > said Clef, still gasping. <*And scrumming hell . . . You aren't going to like this.*>

The crew watched as Sancia carefully replaced Clef in the lorica's cuirass. <*Approaching through the forest is going to be almost impossible,*> he said. <*Every rig down there is sensitive to motion and movement. If the wrong-sized thing . . . Ahh, wait, hold on . . .* > He sighed with relief as the lorica leapt to life around him. The experience was oddly like sitting down in a familiar chair after a very long day. <*Ohh, shit, that feels good . . .* >

<*Clef,*> said Sancia. <*Enough.*>

<*Right, right,*> he said. <*Anyways. If the wrong-sized thing tries to pass through the space around those little detectors, and if it* isn't *accompanied with a host's plate . . .* > He pointed up with one massive metal finger. < *. . . I'm willing to bet that the deadlamps edit it out of reality in a second.*>

Berenice narrowed her eyes and peered out at the dark valley below. <*What's the range on these little rigs?*>

<*Too far for me to attempt tampering with,*> said Clef. <*Or San. And there's got to be hundreds of them down there. Maybe thousands.*>

<*And the control point?*> asked Sancia.

<*It's a lexicon,*> said Clef. <*But . . . an unusual one. It's got a bunch of movement and propulsion rigs around it.*>

<*Why?*> said Berenice. <*Why would a lexicon need such a thing?*>

<*Dunno,*> said Clef. <*But it gets worse. You guys remember those things in the Mountain of the Candianos, in the lexicons?*>

<*Yes,*> said Sancia. <*Lexicons that used hierophantic scriving definition plates—each command plate containing a person's . . . Well. Soul, I guess.*>

<*Granting them unprecedented control over reality . . .* > said Berenice, shaken.

<That's *what's down there,*> said Clef. <*That's what Tevanne is using to control the prison and manipulate Crasedes's time. With* twenty *plates.*>

Claudia grimaced. <*Twenty plates . . . Twenty goddamn hierophantic plates . . .* >

<*What's that mean?*> asked Diela.

<*It means the lexicon down there must influence the reality of the whole damn valley, just like Crasedes tried to do to Old Tevanne during Shorefall Night,*> said Sancia. <*That's probably why we felt queasy when we got too close. We were entering the influence of that . . . thing.*>

<*Yeah,*> said Clef. <*And it's why that valley hurts just to* look *at.*>

<*If we could get control of that bastard, well,*> said Sancia. <*We could do a lot of shit. Break Crasedes out of prison like popping a zit. But . . .* >

Berenice raised her spyglass and studied the black dome. <*But doing that will be very difficult.*>

There was a pensive silence as the crew looked out on the valley, contemplating the best route to attack.

Diela stepped back and looked up at the sky. <*Sun's in a strange place in the sky here . . . But I think it's going to get dark soon.*>

<*Yes,*> said Berenice softly. She stood. <*Look at this place and remember. Study it. Engrave it in your minds. Because the next time we return, it'll be to attack.*>

They started off southwest, to the other side of the mountains, shielding them from the deadlamps and the valley below. It took Clef a moment to remember all the little inner workings of the lorica—how the feet and hands and all the rest liked to move—but he slowly started forward, lumbering across the ridge.

Then he felt it: that unsettling feeling of being watched once more. He pivoted about, studying the landscape around him. He glanced down again at the collapsed wall below, each stone the size of a carriage. The wall felt curiously familiar again: there was one moss-covered segment that was still upright, with a tall, pointed window, and some element about it—the curve of the stone, the slope of the arch, perhaps—stirred something deep within him.

Then he saw her, just for a moment: a flash of her face and her mane of white hair as she passed by the window, as if casually strolling through the ghost of the structure. Then she was gone.

Clef stared at the window. He waited to see her emerge from the other side of the fragment of wall, but she never reappeared. Again, he flexed his scrived sight, peering through the ruins for anything awry, but he could see nothing.

<*Clef!*> said Sancia's voice sharply. <*Come on!*>

He stepped back from the ridge, still staring at the empty window. <*Coming!*> he said. <*I'm coming!*> With a soft *clank,* he hurried up the slope.

21

They camped among the ruins, under where three columns had fallen together, creating a shallow cavern of sorts. They chewed bean bread and drank boiled water and tried to fight back the chill of the mountains at night. <*What I would give,*> grumbled Claudia, <*for but a dash of salt . . .* >

<*So,*> Clef said. <*What do we do?*>

Berenice swallowed, cleared her throat—an old habit, despite their silent speech—and asked, <*What do we see to be our options?*>

Sancia picked something out of her teeth and flicked it away. <*Going through the forest sure seems tough as shit.*>

<*Agreed,*> Claudia said. <*So—what if we do what we did at Grattiara? Shoot a deadlamp with a pathplate to Clef, get someone in there to override the thing, and then use it to unleash hell?*>

<*Because it takes time for Clef to perform one edit,*> said Berenice. <*Let alone the many ones necessary to edit all the other deadlamps out of reality.*>

<*And Clef would still be out of commission for two days at least after issuing a command that big,*> said Sancia.

Claudia scowled. <*Meaning we'd be unable to kill Crasedes—to do the thing we actually came here to do.*>

They sat in silence in their little shelter, the bright-blue sky beyond slowly fading into a dark purple.

<*One thing we agree on,*> said Sancia slowly, <*is that only hosts get into that valley without getting annihilated—right, Clef?*>

Clef's helmet scraped the ceiling as he nodded. <*Right.*>

<*Then the issue seems . . . kind of clear,*> said Sancia. <*Yeah? We've got to get our own host. That's the only way in.*>

They stared at her, shocked.

<*Last I checked,*> said Berenice, <*it was terribly difficult to break Tevanne's control over its hosts.*>

<*Yeah, but I have an idea,*> said Sancia. <*Though I don't know the specifics. So . . .* > She looked at Diela. <*We're going to have to ask someone who* does *know.*>

Diela shrank where she sat. "Oh shit," she said.

"This is not . . . not *quite* the sort of assistance I thought I'd be helping you with," said Design's voice haltingly.

Berenice watched as Diela's hand rose up and rubbed her chin, an anxious, fretful gesture. She slowly began rocking back and forth on her seat like a clockwork toy—all telltale signs that the intelligence within her was not her own.

"Yes, yes," said Sancia testily. "I get it."

"Please, let's speak quietly," whispered Berenice. "There are five deadlamps just on the other side of this mountain, and we've no idea how sensitive any of their rigs are."

"Speaking of which . . ." Design-Diela looked up at the crumbling columns above, then reached out and gently lifted the drape of scrived sheath to peer at the graveyard of ruins beyond. "Where *are* you, exactly?"

"Hiding in one of many ruins here," said Sancia. "Probably used to be Crasedes's bottla ball court or toilet a couple thousand years ago or something."

"Possibly . . ." Design-Diela frowned at a stained chunk of triglyph beyond. "But I thought Crasedes's works tended to hold up better than these, given that they were wrought with hierophantic privileges . . ."

"Can we focus?" said Berenice.

"Ah," said Design-Diela. They dropped the sheath. "Apologies. So—tell me this from the beginning, please . . . because I frankly hope I misheard you."

"Hosts are the only thing that can get close to the prison," said Sancia. "So the only way we'll manage to get close, I'm thinking, is if we have one of the plates Tevanne uses to actually *control* a host. Since you spend so much time playing with them, I wanted to pick your brain."

"But . . . But to do that would give Tevanne *control* over you," said Design-Diela, appalled. "We're kept up at nights by the idea of *one* of you getting captured—but you want to do it to *all* of you, at once?"

"Which is why I don't want them to be *actual* host plates," said Sancia. "Like—maybe some half-functioning ones. Ones that function just enough to trick the warding rigs down there into believing we belong there."

"No, no, no," said Design-Diela. The tempo of their rocking increased. "This isn't Old Tevanne, and these aren't sachets. I've *studied* the damn plates I collected *quite* a lot since you all left, and you're thinking about them totally backward! They're not just, oh, signals or something—it's like a pipe to your *mind,* pouring Tevanne itself in, and it's a *one-way* flow. Even a half-open pipe—which appears to be what you're proposing—would still be pouring Tevanne into your damned brain! And that's not something any of us want!"

"Could we put the plate with me?" said Clef. "I trick rigs all the damn time. I can make it think I'm . . . you know, a guy with a real flesh-and-blood body, like what we did with the deadlamp."

Design-Diela shook their head. "That worked for a *spark* when we tested the deadlamp. But based on what you've described about the warding rigs down there, this has to be a *sustained* command—and that means we need a real flesh-and-blood body."

Sancia narrowed her eyes. Then she got a faraway look on her face, one Berenice knew well, and one that filled her with dread—*The same face,* she thought, *when she watched Orso sail away . . .*

"Then I can do it," Sancia said softly.

Everyone stared at her. Clef's gauntlet dropped into his lap with a dull *clunk*.

"Do . . . what, exactly?" Design-Diela asked.

"You make a half-functioning host plate," Sancia said, "and . . . you put it in me. *Just* me."

Although it was quite chilly now, Berenice felt a sudden heat in her face, and a sickly sweat prickling across her back. "San . . ." she said.

"And because it's a rig," Sancia continued, "I can control it. Contain it. I can tamper with rigs that I touch—and if it's inside me, I'm still goddamn touching it, yeah?"

"This would mean you'd be *fighting* Tevanne, in your mind, all the way through the forest!" said Berenice. "That's what it would be trying to do to you, like . . . like the cadences coming into alignment with their constituents!"

"Oh, come now," said Design-Diela, stung. "It's not like that at all . . ."

"Which is why it's *not* something we need to consider!" said Berenice.

"You're getting loud," warned Sancia.

There was a tense moment as the two of them stared at each other. Neither of them said anything.

"I can help," said Clef. "You'll be taking a pathplate to me anyways. Keep it pressed to your flesh all the way there, and I can help fight it. A scrived human is a rig—even if it's a living one—and I'll tinker with you, and keep you, well . . . you."

"Tinker with Sancia's mind . . ." Design-Diela made a face and squirmed in their seat. "If this is the approach we'd prefer then . . . Yes, I can help you fabricate this thing. I am *most* reluctant to try—but I can."

Berenice looked at Sancia, her gaze dancing back and forth between Sancia's eyes and the scar on the side of her skull, still frog-skin white and shiny after all these years. She fought the mad, irrational feeling that sometimes came swelling up in her mind—*It's getting bigger. One day the scar will get so big it will eat her up.*

She snatched out and grabbed Sancia's hand.

<*I'm not asking you to do this,*> whispered Berenice.

<*I know,*> said Sancia.

<I came here to save us,> said Berenice. *<To save you.>*

<I know,> said Sancia. *<But I didn't come to be saved, my love. I came to fight. And there is no dancing through a monsoon.>*

Berenice gripped her hand for a moment longer, still staring into her eyes. Then she relented and released her.

"Let's get to work," she said.

22

They worked late into the night, assisting Design-Diela to craft strings and commands so abstruse that only Clef could offer much input. At first it seemed like it might take until dawn, but Design-Diela pronounced it finished just before midnight. Berenice nodded, exhausted, and then declared they all needed rest to make sure the next day went smoothly.

They bedded down, laying their thin pallets on the rocky floor of their shelter and covering their bodies with thick blankets against the cool night. Clef—being the one member of the crew who did not need sleep—volunteered to take up watch.

The breathing of the scrivers softened and turned to quiet snores. Clef sat upright for hours, staring through the sheath with his scrived sight. He saw no hint of rigs outside, no twists of logic, no bundles of little commands bobbing through the world that he could see.

A peaceful night, he thought. He watched through the crack in the sheath as the wind sent a handful of leaves dancing through the ruins. *But why don't I feel much damned peace?*

He thought on it. Perhaps it was because he was used to Giva, where he could feel and interact with dozens of rigs and minds at once. There was always chatter there, always something new to toy or play with, especially when he was in the *Keyship*. Here it felt too isolated, too silent, too abandoned.

He wondered who would survive tomorrow. He had witnessed many deaths during his time with the Givans, but things had never felt more desperate than now. Yet he never wondered if he himself would survive. For though Clef couldn't remember it, he had outlasted empires.

He had existed for thousands of years and would likely exist for thousands more. It was likely he would survive the cadences, and Giva, and maybe even Tevanne. Perhaps he would exist until all the world was empty of life, and nothing was left but stone and sky and cold, dark seas.

Clef peered through the sheath at the shattered world outside. *Maybe it'll be like this,* he thought. *Is this so bad?*

He watched as the wind toyed with another handful of leaves.

How did I get here? And how in the hell am I going to get out?

And then he felt it.

It was just like the feeling he'd had in the deadlamp, as everyone had slept as they'd sailed through the skies: the feeling of being watched, of being *scrutinized,* by some presence.

Clef heard a rattling sound in the shelter. He realized his armor was quaking.

No, no, no, he thought.

He flexed his scrived sight. The world on the other side of the sheath remained dark.

I'm alone. There are no scrivings. There's nothing.

He shifted to the side, peering through the crack in the sheath.

There's nothing, nothing . . .

And then he saw her.

She was sitting twenty feet away on the ground on the other side of the sheath, her face lost in darkness but her hair bright white and glimmering in the cloudy starlight, the ruins dark and crooked behind her.

Clef froze. "No," he whispered.

He waited for her to move, but she did not. She just sat there on the ground, silent and draped in shadows. She was wearing simple brown clothing, as before, but what little flesh he could see was discolored and rotted, her hands and feet curiously purpled like the blood within had pooled or clotted. Yet the thing that struck him most was the feeling of her gaze, the immense weight of her attention—for even though her face was dark, he could feel her watching him, studying him, feeling him out.

Then a thought struck him.

I can tap into other people's minds, he thought faintly. *But—is she tapping into mine?*

Then things seemed to blur, and he was somewhere else.

23

There is the smell of dust and sweat, and the copperish aroma of blood.

Someone jostles him to his right—someone tall, their shoulders adorned with fine mail, their helmet shining slightly. Clef mumbles an apology and keeps following the procession of soldiers down the dark tunnel.

Finally they stop. Then comes a whisper: "Everyone ready?"

*They murmur their assent. All except Clef, who miserably thinks—*Hell no. How in the world did I get here?

"All right then," says the voice. The whisper grows to a rough shout. "Open the door!"

A clunk. *Then the dark end of the tunnel blazes with light, and they stumble out.*

Clef has to squint as he staggers through the little wooden door. The flash of daylight is blinding, and he blinks as he peers around, looking back at the tunnel they came through and the huge white walls above. The soldiers who stumbled through with him utterly ignore him, and for a moment he just stands there, alone in the cold sunlight and the cold air before the tall white walls.

Then he sees the corpse lying on the ground before him.

The body lies crooked on the hill at the bottom of the wall, the earth around it dark with blood, its back and throat pierced with arrows. Stunned, Clef looks around and sees many more: hundreds, maybe thousands of bodies, all grouped at the foot of the wall here, all dressed in cheap leather armor. The odor of rot is overwhelming. The air is shimmering with flies. He has never seen so many dead in all his life, and it suddenly seems insane that ordinary city life goes on but a quarter mile from this spot, behind those tall white walls.

"Claviedes!" shouted a voice. "Over here, boy."

He looks up. The soldiers are spreading out among the corpses, swords unsheathed as they check the dead. Their captain stands at the foot of the wall, waving impatiently. "Come on, then! Hurry up!"

Clef scrambles across the slain, stepping carefully in his wooden sandals to avoid the gore. He finally makes it to the captain, who stands atop a huge pile of broken gray stones. He points up as Clef approaches. "Here's where they focused their siege machines most."

Clef looks up. The huge white wall bears a curious dusty mark above them—doubtlessly created by the impact of so many hurled stones and boulders—yet the wall itself appears totally undamaged.

"May I ask you a question, namer?" says the captain solemnly.

"Uh—y-yes?" says Clef, a bit taken aback to be addressed as such.

"Why did they attack here?" asks the captain. "Why this bit of wall?"

Clef swallows, fighting nausea. "I, ah, suspect because it curves inward," he says. "At a rather sharp angle too. If this were a conventional wall, it would have fallen."

The captain nods, still solemn, then grins wickedly. "Conventional wall . . . Perhaps we ought to add more kinks like this to our fortifications. Trick these bastards into tossing more stones and men at us, so we can shoot them down like plagued cattle. Would this make sense to you, namer?"

Clef blinks, feeling not at all up to the task of evaluating methods of reducing men to rotting flesh. He finally shrugs and nods.

The captain looks out at the field of corpses about the foot of the wall. "There must be four thousand dead here. That'll sap them for a good while. Maybe next summer will actually be peaceful."

Clef studies one of the bodies. Though Clef is a young man himself, the body on the ground has to be younger still, perhaps a fifteen- or sixteen-year-old, shot through the cheek with an arrow, fragments of teeth visible through the wound: here a bit of molar; there, the tip of a dogtooth.

"Who are they?" he asks.

"You don't know?" says the captain, surprised.

"I know of walls and stones and metals," says Clef, "but little else."

"Curious . . ." says the captain. "They're slaves. Most armies to the south are slave armies. Slave armies to invade other nations, take those people as slaves, and make more slave armies to take more nations."

Clef stares at the dead child at his feet. "Are we doing anything to stop them, sir?"

"We are not," says the captain. "For that would be suicide. And it would throw away our one advantage." He looks back at the towering white walls. "We can name. And we can build."

Clef joins the captain in looking at the walls. They are forty feet high, made of white stones that appear curiously gelatinous, as if they have been painted over with thick plaster, or perhaps melted together under high heat. Clef knows that, as mad as the latter may sound, it is far closer to the truth than one might imagine.

"Can you confirm that the wall is undamaged?" says the captain. "Can you look, and see?"

"I'll need to get closer."

"Then by all means."

Clef walks up to the wall, picks one stone out, and stands before it. He focuses, calming his mind, and then . . .

He feels it. He feels it at the front of his mind, like there's a thorn or a seed trapped in his brain and the only way to get it out is by looking at the stones—and then the little imaginary seed in his mind twitches, opens, blossoms . . .

No, no, that isn't quite it. It is more like a lock: something that secretly wishes to open. You just . . .

". . . have to get it in the right place," Clef whispers.

And he sees them. He sees the symbols dancing, sliding, crawling across the surfaces of the stones. He can see them in the discoloring in the rock, the way the sunlight plays over their uneven surfaces, the way it shines ever so faintly here and there.

Symbols. Sigils. Names for this substance, this object, all saying very clearly:

Stone.

He exhales, maintaining his focus, and steps back to study the walls, now reading all the newer *names that have been written into the stones: each brick carefully wrought, handwritten with symbols to grant it preternatural strength, to attach itself to all others around it, to withstand the worst onslaught that could ever be thrown at it . . .*

He cocks his head, reading the names in the walls. Then he blinks and looks down—and the names blossom there, too, at his feet, in the soil, in the leather and wood of his sandals, and in the flesh and blood of the bodies about him, all the raw matter of the world singing to him, all the components of creation chanting their names over and over again.

He breathes in and out again, and the names fade from his eyes. "The wall is still strong," he says. "None have shifted. The names are all as we wrought them."

The captain studies Clef. "Can you really see the names everywhere? In everything?"

"For a time, yes."

The captain shakes his head, admiring the huge fortifications. "I wished to be a namer, you know. Didn't have the knack. They made me stare and stare and stare at a brick of lead, but I never saw a thing . . ." He touches the white walls with a hand. "Please make a request of your superiors, then. The generals want to keep expanding the walls, building outward, and outward, each winter, capturing more land. The Tsogenese can't invade what they can't cross."

"More walls," says Clef, sighing a little. "Yes, sir."

More walls, he knows, means more bricks: more hours spent in the namers' workshops carefully carving names into each individual stone, churning them out one after another; more hours sent to check the walls, to check the bricks, to check and confirm and check and confirm, peering at the world with his namer's sight to confirm all is aright—even in horrid places like this, where the ground is wet with the blood of children and the air courses with flies.

When Clef was first trained as a namer, they told him it was a blessing. Yet in this moment he glimpses what his tomorrow will be, and the day after that, and after that: a dull little tinkerer, following orders to find better ways to make better walls to kill more helpless slaves.

He thinks—Is this truly to be my life? Am I to live out my years exacting mundane horrors?

Then it happens.

Clef's eye registers movement to his right, something shifting on the ground; then one of the corpses sits up, opens its mouth full of yellowed teeth to scream, and slashes forward with a spear.

Clef feels something wet splash his face. He looks, dumbfounded, and sees the spear sticking out of the captain, just where his mail ends.

The captain looks down at the wound with his mouth open and working stupidly. Then he topples over.

The screaming warrior—who, it is now clear, is most definitely not dead—rips the spear free from the captain's side and looks at Clef with wide, mad eyes. He snarls something in a language Clef does not know, and leaps forward.

Clef turns and runs. He sprints through the pile of boulders and the bodies about him, sandals flapping wildly; the soldiers are shouting around him, screaming; he can hear the footfalls of the slave warrior behind him, shrieking at him; then something bites into his left shoulder, and his arm goes bright with pain; then there is a snap, and he falls to the ground, staring up at the bright midmorning sky.

Something clatters nearby—the shaft of the spear, though its tip is broken and missing. Clef looks at it from where he lies, then up at the approaching warrior, who screams and unsheathes a dagger and raises it high.

Then, impossibly, the soldier's belly appears to sprout wood: the shaft of an arrow manifests in him, poking through just below his sternum; then another, then a third. The warrior's face goes still, and he coughs. He topples and lies beside Clef, his eyes dull and vacant.

Then all falls to screaming. The soldiers are scooping up the captain, who is lying limp and unconscious; and then, to Clef's confusion, they scoop him up as well. He wonders why until he looks at his left shoulder and realizes.

The tip of the spear is not missing. It is lodged deep in his arm.

Oh, *thinks Clef.*

The soldiers carry him and the captain back through the little tunnel in the wall. Then they lay them on stretchers and carry them into the city, screaming at the people to get out of the way, out of the way.

Clef feels faint. The city is a blur about him, a morass of white walls and bronzed roofs gleaming with sunlight, the landscape studded with cypress trees and pines. He blinks, his breath alternately cold and hot in his chest. The towers are spinning above him, the huge white spires splitting the bright-blue sky. He looks to the side and sees the captain lying still on the stretcher, blood sloshing off one side of it like water off the deck of a ship as they haul him through the city.

Where, *Clef thinks faintly,* are we going?

But then he sees it ahead: the menders' hall, the huge rounded building rising up at the base of the towers; and there the moat about it, and the narrow bridge leading to the tiny door at its base—one that would allow in only a narrow thread of people, like a fortress.

Oh, *thinks Clef.* They don't know.

He raises a hand and tries to stop them. But his breath is too weak, and they run on.

The soldiers carry Clef and the captain up to the mender guarding the bridge, and cry, "We need aid! We need aid now, now!"

The mender looks at the captain lying on the stretcher and nods, waving them through, and the two soldiers carry him down the bridge to the menders' hall.

Then the two carrying Clef walk up. The mender looks at him. She sees the markings on his robe and raises a hand. "No. Not this one."

"What?" says one soldier, outraged. "He's wounded!"

She fixes the two soldiers with a grim, fierce expression underneath her helmet. "He's a namer."

The soldiers look down at him. "Oh," says one. "I . . . I didn't . . ."

"Put him down," says the mender. "I'll tend to him."

The soldiers lay Clef down on the ground and run down the bridge into the hall. Then he is alone with this mender on the bridge.

Clef lies on the stretcher, staring miserably up at the bright-blue sky. He knows, of course, why they cannot take him into the hall: namers see names written in reality all around them—and when people die around them, namers see names they shouldn't. *Names strange enough to drive them mad.*

But would it be better to be in that hall and mad, *Clef thinks as his body grows cold,* or stuck out here and dead?

He wonders if this is how his life is really going to end: dying in a stupid fashion after a stupid, dull, horrid job, his young years blinking out like the flame of a greasy candle touched by a raindrop.

I'll die so young, *he thinks.* And today, this awful day, will be the most interesting thing to ever happen to me.

The woman moves to stand over him, then reaches into her pack and produces a handful of bandages. "Stay with me, please," she says.

Clef whispers, "Tried to tell them . . ."

"I'm sure you did. Just stay awake." She looks at the spear tip lodged in his arm. "I'm going to have to get this out of you before I can clean your wound. That's not going to feel good. All right?"

He lies on the stretcher, blinking. He has no idea what to say to such a question.

I'm going to die, *he thinks.*

"Just stay with me," says the woman. "Give me a second, and I'll pull this out."

I'm absolutely going to die, *he thinks.*

And he wonders. He wonders what names he might glimpse as he passes out of this world and into the next.

Perhaps I'll see angels, *he thinks.* Perhaps I'll see beautiful, beautiful . . .

The namer kneels beside him and takes off her helmet.

Crinkled golden hair spills down her shoulders in a shimmering cascade. She shakes her brilliant yellow mane and pushes it out of her eyes, then kneels closer, peering at his wound, her smooth, perfect brow crinkled in concern, her wide, clear eyes bright in her pale heart-shaped face. She has the gaze of a person of immaculate confidence, of total control, someone who could argue the stars in the sky into new constellations if only they had enough time.

"Hold still," she says.

Clef holds still, looking at her. His breath becomes faint and weak for entirely new reasons.

"There's going to be a lot of blood," she says, "when I pull this out." She meets his gaze, her calm green eyes staring into his. "Don't lose consciousness. Stay awake. Just stay with me."

Clef nods weakly—and then, without any notice, she rips the spear tip out of him.

He screams in pain and outrage, feeling scandalized that she did not warn him. He glares at her, watching as she checks the bloody spear tip to see if it is whole and if any fragments might still be in him; then his fury abates as she grows close, embracing him in her strong arms and heaving him up to wrap his shoulder in tight white fabric, whispering, "Stay with me, just stay with me." Her fingers work in a flurry, plucking at the bandages, arranging them just right. Then she lays him down on the stretcher, sits back, lets out a tiny poof of breath, and says, "Whew. That was easy, wasn't it?"

"N-Next time," Clef whispers, "warn me."

"Well, hopefully there won't be a next time."

"Depends. Do you always guard this bridge?"

"What?" she says. "Why?"

"Because if so," says Clef, his voice barely more than a creak, "I . . . I might have to get injured tomorrow and come by again."

She stares at him. She lets out a short disbelieving laugh. "Are you serious?" she asks.

"As the grave," he whispers. He attempts a cocky smirk. "I ought to know. I'm half in mine right now."

She laughs another incredulous laugh, yet she gives him a sly glance, consenting to the game. "I don't know. Someone who jokes on his deathbed must be absolutely unbearable when hale and hearty."

"Why don't you help me get there," he says, "and we'll find out?"

She laughs again, this one real, this one true. And Clef thinks, for the first time that day, that perhaps tomorrow will be more interesting than he thought.

The vision shifted, blurred, warped.

Clef saw the woman with the golden hair spattered with his blood and smirking; then she was in the dark, barely lit by a tiny candle flame, and he felt the press of her warm flesh and the twitch of her breath on his neck, his hand in hers as he held her body.

Stay with me, he whispered to her. *Stay with me . . .*

The brush of her hair and the smell of her breath; a grunt of pain, and then a cry.

A baby's cry, a newborn's cry, high and shrill and furious at the sudden obligation of breath.

Oh my God, he thought.

And then someone was with him who should not have been there: a woman in her fifties, with dark wrinkled skin and short salt-and-pepper hair. She was staring at him, astonished, and she reached forward and grabbed his arm and said: *Clef, wake up. Wake up, wake up,* wake up!

The flurry of images leaked out of Clef's mind like water from a lanced blister. Then he was himself again, falling back into the key locked in the armor—but he was no longer in the shelter with Sancia and the others.

He looked around, bewildered. He was standing in the ruins, the moonlight gleaming through a tall, narrow window to his right, and Sancia was beside him, gripping his big metal arm.

<*C-Clef?*> she said, shaken. <*What the hell was that?*>

<*Uhh,*> he said. He stared at the broken ruins. <*S-Sancia? Is that really you?*>

<*Yes!*> she said. <*Goddamn it, what* was *that?*>

<*I . . . honestly don't know,*> he said slowly.

<*Was that a dream?*> she said.

<*Ah . . .* >

<*Was I* in *one of your dreams? I didn't even know that you* could *dream! Or that . . . that I could be* in *one of your damned dreams! I mean—what the shit, Clef, what the shit!*>

Clef stood there in silence. Then he slowly sat down in the shadows of the broken walls. <*So . . . what did you see, San?*> he asked. <*Did you see all the stuff that I did?*>

<*I saw you doing . . . doing weird scriving stuff with a wall,*> she said. <*There was a bunch of dead bodies around. Then you got injured, they hauled you off, and you got all horny over the physiquere girl who cleaned you up.*>

<*Ahh, yup,*> said Clef. <*That about sums it up, yeah.*>

<*Was that a memory?*> asked Sancia. <*Did that all really happen to you?*> She looked at him and seemed to notice his silence. <*Are you all right?*>

In a small crushed voice, he said, <*No.*>

She watched him for a moment. Then she sat down beside him, placed a hand on his gauntlet, and sat quietly with him. They stared out at the moonlit mountains for a long time and did not say a word.

<*I was a . . . a man,*> Clef said finally. <*A boy. I . . . I knew I had to have been, once. But . . . to know it, to really* know *it . . . It must have been so* long *ago. It's not something I really actually imagined.*>

<*But what were you doing?*> asked Sancia. <*You walked up to that wall and you looked at it and you . . . it wasn't like scrived sight. You didn't*

see scrived stuff. You saw the basic sigils for everything in *everything. Was that right?*>

<*It seems to be so,*> he said.

<*But that's crazy,*> she said. <*People can't do that, can they?*>

<*Well . . .* > Clef looked around, studying the stones, the walls, the tiny leafless trees. <*I mean, I kind of think that's how I see things now. As a key.*>

<*Huh?* Really?>

<*Yeah. I mean, we've always wondered how I see things, since I don't have, like, eyes and such. But being back in that . . . that memory, when I was a person, made of regular flesh and blood, I . . . I realized. I don't see the world like people do now. I see the* sigils *embedded in it. The regular names making regular things what they are, all shifting and moving around me. Just like they taught me to see them so . . . so long ago . . .* > He looked off. <*You just had to learn to get your head in the right place.*>

Sancia stared, astonished. <*You get what you're saying, right?*> she asked. <*You're saying your people—like, a* couple thousand years ago—*figured out some way to* meditate *their way into seeing sigils* everywhere. *You . . . You must have been the first scrivers!*>

<*Yeah,*> he said faintly. <*Amazing.*>

<*And . . . And in the dream,*> said Sancia. <*They said you weren't allowed to be near dying people, because you'd see things. You'd see names—sigils. Commands.*>

<*Yeah.*>

<*Those have to be the . . . the deep commands, right? Hierophantic ones. The ones that made Crasedes what he is today. That's how they were discovered!*>

Clef didn't answer.

<*You're just thinking about her, aren't you?*> asked Sancia.

<*About the girl, yeah,*> said Clef. He looked at her, his helmet squeaking. <*God. She was* beautiful. *When I saw her, in that vision, it was like I was . . . like I felt it all over again.*>

<*She was very pretty,*> Sancia admitted. <*But I've never seen someone with* yellow hair. *That was weird as hell.*>

<*I was about to say I hadn't either,*> said Clef. <*But obviously that's not true.*>

Sancia scratched her head. <*Why did you remember this?*> she asked. <*You could never remember anything before. Why now?*>

<*I . . . I don't know,*> he said. <*I think maybe when I pathed into Tevanne, something in me broke. Like it was a dam holding back all this old, dead stuff, and now it's leaking into me. These memories blooming in me like algae in a pond.*> He looked back at where the old woman had been sitting, staring in at him. <*But . . . I almost feel like someone's doing this to me. Like they* want *me to remember.*>

<*Tevanne?*> she asked.

<*No. I know what Tevanne feels like. This was . . . someone else. If it's anyone at all. Maybe it's just another ghost in my memories.*>

He stared into the black of the ruins, wondering if he might see the rotting old woman again, peeking from behind some stone or shattered column. But they were alone.

<*Why would someone want you to remember you getting stabbed and then getting sweet on some girl?*> asked Sancia. <*It seems pointless.*>

<*I have absolutely no scrumming idea.*> He slowly clanked to his feet. <*Everyone I saw in that memory . . . They all have to be dead, right?*>

Sancia thought about it. <*I'd say they have to be, yeah. Thousands of years ago.*>

<*I wish I hadn't remembered. I really do, kid. I just want to be a key with you—here to fix, here to mend, here to solve things for you. Remembering makes what I have to do tomorrow even harder.*>

<*You still think you can do it?*> she asked.

<*I think I'll have to,*> he said simply. <*We don't have a choice. Come on. Let's get you back to bed.*>

They slowly returned to their shelter. Clef paused as he bent low to crawl in.

At the very end of his dream, he'd heard a baby's cry. Could it have been his own child? Had the woman on the bridge been the mother of whatever children he might have had in his past life?

And if so, he thought, *does the child that once slumbered in her belly now sleep in a prison not far from here?*

24

The next day they awoke well before dawn, then packed, outfitted themselves, arranged their sheath suits, and waited while Clef searched the skies and their surroundings for any rigs. Upon confirmation that it was clear, they started off, back through the paths they'd treaded last evening, toward the valley of ruins and the black prison and the lamps above.

They would attack at noon, Berenice had decided. Though there'd been many rumors in the past eight years that Crasedes had found ways to empower himself—some said he could fly at any time now, while others had reported he could start fires with a thought—reality still believed Crasedes dead and grew more certain of it at the peak of day. He would be weakest when the sun was high in the sky. Terrible for cover, but it was the only way.

Finally they came to where they were to split up. <*Claudia, Diela,*> said Berenice. <*Get into position on the far side of the valley and tell me the* moment *you're ready. Clef—proceed into the valley and make sure the way is clear for Sancia.*>

<*Got it, Capo,*> said Diela.

Clef saluted, his massive metal gauntlet stopping mere inches from his helmet, which surely would have made an enormous clang. Then the three of them trooped off, Claudia and Diela fluidly slipping through the foliage like steppe foxes, and Clef stolidly crunching his way down.

They looked at one another. Berenice wondered what to say but could think of nothing.

<*Because,*> said Sancia, <*there is nothing to say. We know who we are. And we know why we're doing this.*>

Berenice nodded. Then they pulled down their twin sheaths and kissed, holding each other close.

I thought I'd had desperate kisses before, thought Berenice. *But this one cuts keenest.*

They released each other. There was a pause as they held each other's gaze for one last moment, and then Sancia pulled back up her twin sheath, turned, and began the descent.

As Sancia descended into the valley, the world about her changed.

The shift was invisible to the eye: the frail silvery fronds of vegetation still coiled around her, strobed with the light of the mid-morning sun; the ground below her still ran wet with the long-ago snows of winter waking up from some hidden spring; the bricks of black still circled above her, so dark and cold they seemed to soak up light like a sponge.

But the world was changing. *Reality* was changing. She could feel it in her bones, like stepping out of the real world and into a painting, where everything could be marred or changed by a simple dash of water.

<*It's weird as hell in here, kid,*> whispered Clef in her ear. <*Like we're in the goddamned armpit of creation.*>

Sancia flexed her scrived sight, and spied Clef lurking among the brush ahead, a boiling blot of crimson in a world of grays and greens. She touched where his pathplate hung from her neck. <*What kind of armpits are you accustomed to, Clef?*> she asked.

<*You know what I mean. Reality is going wild-ass crazy the closer we*

get to that . . . that thing. *I mean, God, it feels like night down here. Deep night . . . But I can still see the shining sun . . .* >

Sancia looked up across the canopy of the valley, and spied the dome of black jutting above the tips of the trees and the massive black prison suspended above. <*Are you sure we've got enough distance?*>

<*Yeah,*> he said. <*I can see farther than you. We're safe here—but any closer, and the whole valley will wake up.*> His voice lowered. <*God. We're in the belly of a monster.*>

She finally joined Clef in the brush, panting and sweating. She found he was right: it *did* feel like night down here, like the sun was distant and the sky was heavy with shadow. The trees loomed overhead, tall and towering, and darkness swam about their trunks.

Sancia pulled up the sheath about her mouth and allowed a very slight puff of air out. She watched, bemused but troubled, as a tiny cloud of vapor appeared and vanished.

Clef studied her with the empty eyes of his helmet. <*I'd ask you if you really want to go in there, kid,*> he said, <*but I already know the answer.*>

Sancia knelt, slipped a small wooden box from her back, laid it on the ground, and opened it. Within was the small black blade that Design and Berenice had made: the one that, upon tasting her blood, would change her into something—or someone—very, very different.

<*Yeah,*> she sighed. <*Me too, Clef.*>

Berenice moved nearly one mile around the western lip of the valley. When she came to her chosen spot, she knelt and began setting up what Sancia had deemed her "insurance": two pounder espringals that could be triggered remotely, similar to what they'd done in Grattiara, but these were aimed at the black dome below.

These should blast any wardings clean out of the trees, she thought. *Giving Sancia time to vanish—should anything go wrong.* She slotted one of the big canisters into the espringal, checked its aim, and stepped back. *Or at least, I hope they will . . .*

She returned to her hiding place, picked up her espringal, and carefully affixed a scrived spyglass to her stock. Then she glassed the valley below through it, reading the trees and grasses for any movement. The calmness of it all disturbed her: it would have been such a pleasant, pastoral scene, if not for the shadow cast by the floating prison above.

<*In position, Capo,*> whispered Claudia's voice.

<*Good,*> said Berenice. <*One moment.*>

She took a breath, her lungs swirling with the cool mountain air, shut her eyes, and focused.

Pathing to Claudia was difficult—she was too far away for Berenice to perceive clearly—but Berenice carefully went about the odd little internal ritual of pulling her thoughts across their separating distance until she could feel Claudia lying on the stones, one eye pressed to the stock of her espringal.

<*I see them,*> whispered Claudia. <*Patrolling as they did yesterday . . .*>

Berenice caught faint glimpses of what Claudia was seeing: flickers of tiny figures half-concealed among the pines below.

Thank God, she thought, *that Claudia's eyesight has held up so well.*

<*Sancia is in the south-southwest portion of the valley,*> said Claudia softly. The magnifying lens of her espringal swiveled until it focused on a clump of brush at the bottom of a ravine. Only the keenest of eyes could have spotted the black tip of Clef's helmet poking through. <*So naturally, I'd want to draw their attention to the east, away from her . . .*> Again the lens swiveled, this time to target the east side of the valley. <*A ravine's there. Should be helpful.*>

<*Helpful,*> echoed Sancia. <*When do we expect to see the hosts get anywhere near there, so we can kick all this shit off?*>

<*It's close to nine in the morning now,*> said Claudia softly. <*You've got . . . oh, a little more than an hour until they make that visit.* If *they patrol like they did yesterday—which, we won't know if they will . . .*>

There was an uncomfortable silence.

<*In other words,*> said Berenice, <*stay on your guard and be ready to move in an instant.*>

<*Great,*> muttered Sancia.

Sancia knelt in the brush, listening to the forest about her. An oppressive silence hung in the air, and she felt like the shadows were growing heavier, leaning on where they waited.

<*I want you to know, kid . . .* > said Clef, and then stopped.

<*Know what?*> asked Sancia.

<*That I've got two espringals and about a hundred tiny-ass scrived bolts embedded in this thing.*> He waved a big gauntlet, gesturing to his armor.

She looked at him, confused. <*Huh?*>

<*And a big scrived poleaxe that could chop down any number of trees,*> he said. <*Not to mention the fact that I think I can jump, like, a hundred feet in the air.*>

<*What are you getting at?*>

<*I am saying,*> said Clef patiently, <*if you get your ass in a tight spot in there, I'm coming in.*>

<*What! All those deadlamps would rip you out of reality in the blink of an eye!*>

<*Maybe,*> he said. <*Maybe not. But I'd still rather try. Because I'm going to be your only support from here on out.*>

Something trembled deep in Sancia's belly at that. She stared at the darkness of the forest yawning before her, then glanced down at the little black blade resting in the box at her feet.

<*The second you jam that thing into you,*> Clef said, <*you get cut off from the rest of your team. From Berenice, from all of them. Because we can't risk Tevanne getting through to them as well.*>

<*I know.*>

<*Only* I'm *going to be able to hear you—or know what it's like in there. You talk to me, and I'll relay things to them, and vice versa. I'll have to act as the Greeter of our little team, ferrying messages about. But that's all you'll have.*>

<*I know!*> she whispered.

<*Then you know I'm not going to take it lightly,*> he said.

She eyed the prison, hanging above them like an error in reality. There was a soft clicking from Clef's gauntlets as they slowly flexed into fists, once, twice, three times.

Then Claudia's voice, sharp and cold: <*Sancia.*>

<*Yes?*>

<*I've got a target heading east.*>

Sancia shut her eyes and reached out to Claudia, fumbling her way across the valley to her sight. She caught a fuzzy, faded vision through a high-powered lens: a handful of unarmed figures in gray, picking their way through the trees.

<*Is this our opening?*> whispered Berenice.

<*Dunno,*> said Claudia. <*But be on alert.*>

Berenice shut her eyes where she lay on the forest floor, focusing as hard as she could on her pathway to Claudia. She could see through Claudia's eyes, watch as she tracked the hosts with her espringal, following as they approached the eastern side of the valley, where the ground dropped away to be swallowed by vines and brambles.

Berenice did not ask if Claudia could make the shot. It would have been a preposterous proposal for any other soldier: to send a single dolorspina dart hurtling half a mile through the air, buffeted by errant winds and breezes, to go plunging into the neck of a human being at the exact right time.

But Berenice knew that if anyone could do it, it would be Claudia.

<*When the dart hits home,*> Claudia whispered, <*the host goes dark, yeah?*>

<*That is the theory,*> said Berenice.

The little line of hosts tramped out from beneath the coverage of the forest and approached the ravine on the east side of the valley.

<*Tevanne loses all connection with them,*> said Diela. <*All it knows is where its host went dark.*>

<*Again,*> said Berenice, <*so goes the theory.*>

She watched as Claudia set her sights on one host in particular: the man at the very back of the line, walking forward with the same curious, mechanical gait as the others.

<*Okay,*> whispered Claudia. <*Let's see if I can make this valley dance.*>

Berenice watched as Claudia made note of how the line of hosts moved—their speed, the way they traversed the uneven ground, the way they bobbed their heads back and forth as they sought to spy any trespassers—and then Claudia lifted her aim very, very slightly, targeted what appeared to be a blank bit of grass at the edge of the ravine, and released the bolt.

Berenice stared through Claudia's eyes, her blood burning with anxiety as she watched the line of hosts moving along the ravine in their same slow, intent pace. She fruitlessly searched the air for the bolt, seeking a glimmer of metal or a streak of black, but there was nothing. She had no idea if the shot had gone awry or not.

A second passed, though it felt like an age.

Nothing changed. The hosts kept walking.

Did she miss?

More time passed. The last host in line came to the edge of the ravine, peering out.

She missed. She had to have. It's been too long, too long . . .

The host turned, matching the others, and began to follow them back into the forest . . .

And then they stopped.

Jumped.

Went limp and fell back.

Berenice watched, astonished and ecstatic, as the last host in line tumbled backward off the ravine and slid down into the vines and the leaves below, completely hidden.

<*Ohh, thank God,*> whispered Claudia. <*Now, let's see if that caught its atte—*>

She didn't have to finish the thought: the other hosts froze instantly, then whirled and stared out at the ravine.

Berenice didn't dare breathe as she watched through Claudia's eyes. The hosts did not move at first, each one scanning the brush and forest around them—and then, slowly, they approached the edge of the drop-off, fanning out to cover more territory.

Berenice cracked open an eye and looked at the deadlamps above. They had stopped patrolling and now hung in the air, utterly motionless. <*We've got its attention. Yes.*>

<*But the lamps aren't doing anything yet . . .* > said Diela. <*Right? Otherwise, we'd be dead.*>

<*The main thing,*> said Sancia, <*is whether all the rest of the hosts are being drawn east to investigate. Because otherwise, I'm scrummed.*>

Berenice lifted a spyglass and glassed the open glades of the valley. At first she saw nothing, no hint of movement; but then there was a flash as a dark figure darted through the trees, and then another, and another.

<*They're moving,*> she said. <*Sancia?*>

<*Yeah,*> Sancia said quietly. <*I know. It's time to go in.*>

Sancia took a deep breath as she picked up the little black blade.

<*I'll be with you,*> said Clef. <*Every step of the way.*>

She lifted the blade to her left side, toward the fattiest part of her shoulder.

<*You'll have to keep your wits about you,*> said Clef. <*There might still be hosts in the forest. I'll look, but you'll need to look too.*>

<*I know,*> she whispered.

She gripped the blade, the long, thin point just a hairbreadth away from the surface of her twinned sheath.

<*Be fast,*> said Clef, his voice shaking. <*Move thoughtfully. And bring freedom to others.*>

She laughed, a miserable, despairing sound, and plunged the blade into her shoulder.

The world changed.

25

Light died, and everything grew gray and cold. Sancia's body went still. Her eyes unfocused, her jaw fell open. Everything grew instantly, powerfully numb, so much so that someone could have lopped off her hand and she'd have barely noticed.

And then, most curiously, she lost the ability to record or *notice* the world around her. It was not that she'd become blind and deaf but rather that some critical part of her mind—the part that made words, and specifically made words so that she could tell herself what was going on—went suddenly silent, like it'd been erased from within her.

Instead her thoughts, her being, her very will was overwritten with one burning, distinct thought:

<*EAST.*>

Thoughtlessly, she stood, swiveled, and ran east, arms and legs pumping as she hurtled through the brush. Branches and thorns slashed at her shins and forearms, but the pain was distant. She was dimly aware she was breathing, a slow, metronomic twitching of her lungs within her rib cage; not at all the swell and surge of an organ but rather like the tick of a clock, whirring along at someone else's setting.

This is wrong, isn't it?

She thought so. But the knowing part of her, the bit that could retain this knowledge and use it, was paralyzed and frozen, like a bundle of tangled nerves in a cramped muscle. She just ran on and on and on, charging through the brush.

<EAST,> bellowed the voice in her mind. *<EAST. GO. RUN. LOOK. SEE. WATCH.>*

And she obeyed. She could imagine no other course of action.

Something stirred in her, a faint memory of a memory of a memory . . .

She had been through this before. She remembered it in pieces, like glimpsing the landscape ahead through smoke and fog . . . She'd been in a shattered building, and a woman had held a device in her hand, and it had made her believe that she wasn't a person at all.

<Not a person,> whispered some lost part of Sancia. *<But a tool, a thing . . . >*

Then came a voice, wry, crackling, panicked: *<kid kid kid kid stop! Stop! STOP!>*

Clef, she thought.

The spell cracked but did not break. She gasped and slowed to a halt, panting for breath in the forest. She could hear Clef crying out to her, but it was like he was far away.

<EAST,> bellowed the voice in her mind. *<GO. SEEK. FIND. CALL DOWN OUR EDITS. GO.>*

She ignored it. She remembered the last time, with Estelle Candiano, in the Mountain. And then she knew how to break out of this.

Find the thing that cannot change, cannot be dominated, she thought. *And start from there.*

She knew in an instant where to go.

An image unscrolled in her mind: a woman sitting on the deck of a ship, staring out at the fleet about her, the setting sun brilliant and blazing as it wrapped itself in skeins of clouds. *You'd swooped into my life like some kind of adventuring hero from a silly play,* the woman said, *all smiles and swashbuckling. You seemed bigger than anything I'd ever known.*

Berenice, thought Sancia.

A warmth suffused her hands, her feet. She could feel her body again—just a tiny bit, she owned herself again.

And she used it to fight back.

It had been a long time since she'd tampered with Tevanne, but it was as familiar as sailing through a stretch of dangerous currents outside your home port. She showered the little plate in her shoulder with questions, with commands, with requests for specificity:

<*Which east?*> she asked.

<*EAST FROM ALL,*> said the voice in her head.

<*But east from which all?*>

<*EAST FROM ALL.*>

<*Which all?*>

<*EAST FROM . . . FROM AGGLOMERATE POSITION OF GLOBULAR WARDING ENTITIES OF PRISON FACILITY.*>

<*How can I confirm my positioning to globular warding entities of prison facility?*>

<*AH . . .* >

<*How can I confirm if I am a member of the globular warding entities of the prison facility?*>

<*YOU . . . AH . . .* >

More and more and more. Like all things engineered by Tevanne, it was unused to being questioned, and had no idea how to process this. Tevanne spoke only the language of dominance, and thus had no concept of conversation.

As she stalled it, she felt more and more warmth return to her body—and then, finally, she could breathe and think.

She exhaled. "Hohhh . . . Holy shit," she sighed.

<*Kid!*> cried Clef. <*You're back?*>

<*Yeah.*> She cringed as some inner portion of her body suddenly resisted her, like a bone within was being magnetically pulled east, but she quelled it. <*Kind of.*>

<*That was scrumming masterful, that was. Amazing shit. I'll help you manage this as best I can. But let's see if you can move, eh?*>

A curious, burning numbness was pulsing up and down her limbs, like her nerves weren't sure what to tell her body to do. Yet she managed to turn her head and look around.

She didn't remember this part of the forest at all. She could no longer see the sun, and the air felt close and moist and heavy—unnaturally so. <*Where am I?*>

<*Well, you sprinted about a quarter goddamned mile* away *from where you were supposed to go,*> said Clef. <*You need to turn around*—now—*and go back! There, along that old creek bed! And hurry! Claudia bought you an opening, but this goddamned thing is a bastard to wrestle with!*>

She spied the creek bed, scrambled down to it, and started running. The experience was bizarre, like she was piloting some faraway person's body. She had to keep stalling Tevanne's commands as she ran, feeding them quibbling questions for them to puzzle over, which didn't make it easier. Miraculously, she did not trip.

She flexed her scrived sight as she ran, and the dark forest lit up with tiny stars: all the countless rigs hidden in the trees, designed to detect any movement or presence that didn't belong there.

<*All asleep,*> said Clef. <*And all quiet. It's working! You're passing the test, kid!*>

She ran on, the branches flying by yard after yard, her passage totally unnoticed and uncontested.

Just a few more yards, she thought. *Just a bit of running, then I get into the lexicon, and then . . . and then it's over, right? Simple. World saved, and all's done.*

She glanced up through the canopy of trees above. They were too thick to see through, but she imagined the deadlamps still above, silent, black, and watchful.

Simple, she said to herself. *Right.*

A voice in her ear—Clef, whispering, <*Ber?*>

Berenice sat up. <*Yes?*> she said.

<*We're in,*> said Clef's voice. <*She's proceeding. No issues so far.*>

<*Good,*> said Berenice. She studied the hosts, still weaving into the mountaintops close to where Claudia and Diela had hidden, and then up above at the deadlamps, which were still silently hanging above. <*No sign from the lamps. They don't appear to have reacted.*>

<*Whew,*> said Clef. <*Let me know the second you see something.*>

<*Will do,*> said Berenice.

She squinted through her spyglass, trying to spy some hint of her wife sprinting through that curiously dark forest, but could see nothing.

<*How quaint it is,*> said Claudia, <*to think we'll have a chance to warn Clef before those lamps do anything.*>

Sancia had expected her mission into the forest to be many things—terrifying, anxious, painful, or worse. Which had seemed reasonable: how else should it have felt, to venture into this strange, uncanny place, filled with invisible eyes and mindless, lethal guards, her bones burning with Tevanne's presence, the little knife in her shoulder paining with every step?

But one thing she had not expected it to be was joyous.

And yet, as she danced between the tree trunks and crept through the shadows, her scrived sight showing her the handful of remaining hosts in the forest, her mind and body came alive.

This reminds me, she thought as she silently leapt across a crumbling gully, *of the job where I stole those gemstones in Old Ditch . . . Creeping through that warehouse, slipping through the struts in the roof.* She narrowed her eyes and crouched in the shadows as two hosts plodded through the trees about her, ignorant of her presence; once their backs were turned, she slipped away. *Or am I thinking of the job in the Greens, where I had to tag the carriage loaded with spice?*

How wonderful it was to move, to creep, to feel young again, however briefly.

<*Not too fast,*> Clef reminded her. <*The wardings will take note if a host breaks out into a run.*>

<*Yeah . . .* > She slowed, darting behind a tree as a distant host meandered on its prewritten route.

<*Feels like old times, eh, kid?*> asked Clef.

<*Yes,*> she said. <*I can't believe I'm nostalgic for starving desperation . . .* >

Her right knee flared with pain, and she grunted and slowed. She knelt and rubbed it, keenly aware that this ache had nothing to do with Tevanne's will coursing through her bones.

Still a kid in my head, she thought, *but this body . . .*

She limped on, jaw clenched, scrived sight flexed, the dark forest alight with fluttering scrivings. She saw the dome ahead: a bright, massive ball of scrivings and logic, like a tangle of yarn wrought of starlight—and then she saw the shadow just before, a black line running across the trees, like the separation between night and day, with all the trees beyond almost lost in the gloom.

She looked at the line, then looked up. The immense black prison was now almost directly above her, casting the deep shadow below.

She scanned the woods. Most of the hosts were gone, but two remained, standing close together on the west side of the dome.

<*That must be the entrance,*> she said. <*But if we take the hosts out, Tevanne will know exactly where we are.*> She sucked her teeth, thinking. <*I'll look for another way in—if there even is one.*>

She entered the shadow of the prison. There it was as dark as midnight, and she prowled through the forest, little more than a flicker of shadow in this dark place.

Then she saw something just ahead—and stopped.

A wall stood between herself and the dome, made of smooth dark stone, about ten feet tall.

She stared at it. She looked along its length and realized it must stretch around the entire perimeter of the dome.

<*What . . . What the hell is this?*> she said. <*Clef—did you see a wall when we shot you down here?*>

<*No . . .*> he said. <*Because . . . uh, this wall isn't scrived, San. It's just dumb rock.*>

She realized he was right: it was just a conventional wall, well made, but unaugmented and unaltered—simple stones, stuck together with simple mortar. She slipped through the trees, slowly walking the length of the wall. She glanced up to see if any branches could allow her to climb over, but tall iron spikes ran across the top.

<*Why the hell would the most powerful scrived entity in the world,*> said Clef, <*bother to build a big, basic goddamned brick wall?*>

<*I've no idea.*> She approached where the two hosts were situated and saw they were standing in front of a tall door wrought of iron and wood, with an enormous iron handle and a lock beside it. A keyring hung from the waist of one of the hosts, but—much like the wall—this too was unaltered, just a simple iron key. <*But I'm not sure I'm up for pickpocketing at the moment.*>

She crept back the other way, walking the entire length of the wall around the lexicon, Tevanne's commands still chanting and muttering in the back of her head, until she came to the easternmost end. There she found another tall door—but this one was unguarded.

She squatted in the shadows, her scrived sight flexed, studying the door, the wall, the trees—everything.

But there was nothing. Or nothing unusual—just the tiny warding rigs in the trees, and the shadows, and the lexicon beyond.

<*What the hell, what the hell?*> she said quietly. <*Why build something conventional when you could make something extraordinary?*>

<*Dunno,*> said Clef. <*But—we are talking about a mad scrumming mind that's half-ghost, half-rigs. So. Maybe it does some weird shit from time to time?*>

She looked around carefully. <*I'm going to make a go for it.*>

<*I'll keep a lookout.*>

She took a breath, then sprinted out from the cover of trees to the wall. When she made it to the door, she knelt, turned, and studied the forest. Again, there was nothing: no movement, no sound.

She turned to the wooden door, studying it closer. It was exactly as it appeared: a conventional door, a conventional handle, and a conventional lock.

Heart fluttering, she tried the handle but was unsurprised to find it was locked.

<*Goddamn,*> she said quietly. <*It's been ages since I picked a lock . . .* >

<*Uh,*> said Clef. <*Why would you need to?*>

<*Because I don't want to break it down?*>

<*Mm,*> said Clef. <*I mean—you do have my pathplate, don't you? Which means I can push out commands from where you are?*>

<*Yeah? So?*>

<*Jeez, kid. Have you forgotten* I'm *pretty good with locks?* All *locks?*>

She blinked. Because, in fact, she had.

For so long, Sancia had thought of Clef almost expressly as a hierophantic tool, made to interfere with scrived things: weapons, rigs, lexicons, and the like. After all, these capabilities were what made him so critical to the development of everything that kept Giva safe.

But she frequently forgot that he was more than that—for Clef could also unlock *any* lock, scrived or no.

In truth, she often tried to forget that Clef could do this, for it was utterly inexplicable to her and every scriver she'd ever known. A scrived tool, as everyone knew, should not be able to issue commands to something that was not listening, like a dumb lock—and yet, Clef could. The first thing she'd ever done with him, in fact, had been unlocking countless unscrived locks.

She felt her skin begin to crawl as she knelt in the shadow of the wall. Crasedes had mentioned once that Clef had been designed to penetrate or circumvent *all* barriers, not just scrived ones. She remembered a memory she'd once glimpsed: Crasedes, floating in an ancient peristyle, Clef in his hand and thousands of corpses surrounding him . . . and there, before them both, a set of black doors hanging open in space itself.

Maybe, she thought, *Clef was made to open* one door *specifically—and his power over conventional locks is just a side effect of that . . .*

She shuddered. It wasn't the first time she'd had this thought, but it felt far more disturbing in this world of cold and shadow.

<*What are you waiting for, kid?*> asked Clef. <*This'll be just like old times too.*>

<*What do you mean?*> she said.

<*When we first met. You took me to some grimy alleyway and had me unlock a campo door. Remember? It'll be just like that.*>

She smiled faintly. <*That's right . . .*>

She slid the pathplate out from around her neck.

Just like that, she thought.

The pathplate was tapered like a teardrop, and she aimed the narrow end toward the innards of the lock as she raised it.

But is it, she thought suddenly, *a little* too *much like that?*

The tip of the pathplate slipped in.

Instantly, there was a *pop* from within the door. The lock turned, and the door gently swung open, just a crack.

And then everything changed.

A force coursed through Sancia like lead in her blood: a command. But this command wasn't like the last one, to run east and look for Claudia and Diela. Instead this one was to be . . .

Well, where she was. To come to the dome, to the center of the forest in the valley, and look.

The impact of the command was almost too much. She fell to all fours and tried not to gasp out loud. <*C-Clef?*> she asked. <*What . . . What the hell?*>

<*Ahh, something just changed,*> he said softly. <*Tevanne, it's . . . It's changing its orders. It's sending all the hosts* here. *God . . .* > He moaned. <*Shit, kid, I think it . . . I think it knows you're he—*>

Then came a voice—high, cold, and eerily hollow:

<*SANCIA . . .* > it said. <*IS THAT YOU?*>

26

Capo,> said Claudia's voice softly. <*We've got problems. The hosts have stopped.*>

<*As in, they've located you?*> asked Berenice.

<*No. As in they've stopped* looking.>

Berenice raised her spyglass, the wilderness whirling as she searched for the right angle. Finally she found the hosts, and she saw Claudia was right: they were no longer toiling up the hillsides after Claudia. Instead, they had stopped wherever they happened to stand or hang from the rocks—and then they began to look about with a curiously absentminded air, like they'd just put down the book they'd been reading to go complete a task, but now couldn't find it.

Then she watched in mute horror as the hosts all simultaneously turned back toward the valley and began running down into the trees.

Oh no, she thought. *Ohh no . . .*

Then Clef's voice: <*Berenice!*>

Berenice sat up, startled to hear Clef's voice after such a long silence. <*Clef? What's wrong?*>

<*Trigger the insurance!*> Clef cried. <*Do it now! It figured us out!*>

Berenice paused only a second to process these words. Before she could act on them, it hit her: a wave of nausea so powerful and extreme that she utterly lost control of herself, and she vomited into the brush beside her.

She crouched, gasping uncontrollably. She knew what this felt like: as if a hierophant were near, but worse—like perhaps a *dozen* hierophants were floating overhead.

She raised her eyes to the black deadlamps rotating above—but all of them had stopped and were now frozen in space.

They're waking up, she thought.

<*Do it now, now, NOW!*> screamed Clef.

She lifted the trigger in her hand and fired.

She watched as two glimmering streaks of silver silently spun out into the air above the valley and hurtled down to the dome. She glanced up at the deadlamps again, aware that those specters might have sensed the shot and could quickly figure out where it had come from.

I do hope, she thought, *that I put enough distance between myself and those espringals.*

Sancia flinched as the air around her suddenly cracked, roared, and burst asunder. At first her heart went cold with terror—*Deadlamps,* she thought wildly, *here it comes, here it comes*—but then she realized she had heard this sound before.

No, no, she said to herself. *It's pounders, it's just the pounders . . .*

Of course she recognized this sound—she'd had a hand in designing the things, after all—but the shockwave of their ignition just a few feet away from her was like being in the heart of a thunderstorm.

Dust flew about her. Branches whipped and whirled in the sudden wind. Her hearing was wiped away, replaced with a high, tinny *eeee* sound.

<*Move!*> shouted Clef. <*Now!*>

Sancia glanced through the open door and saw the lexicon beyond—perhaps twenty, thirty feet away.

<*Don't!*> said Clef. <*It hasn't realized you're disguised as a host yet, but if you try to get in now, it* will! *Just move!*>

She ran into the forest, pathplate clutched in her hand, heart hammering, her bones aching from the feel of Tevanne's will.

<*What the hell!*> panted Clef. <*How did it know? How the hell did it* know?>

<*Isn't it goddamn obvious?*> she snarled at him.

<*No, it damn well isn't!*>

She dodged around a tree, keenly aware of the bloody red tangles of bobbing light over her shoulder—hosts, growing too close for comfort. <*Imagine someone who could make it through the hosts,*> she said, <*and the wardings, and the deadlamps—who could possibly do that?*>

<*Uh, well . . .* >

<*Someone who has* you, *of course!*> She slid through a gap in the high brush, her ankles yowling with pain as they bent to an extension they hadn't met in a long, long time. <*So what does Tevanne do? It puts down an obstacle that* only you *could break down, Clef, to alert it when you came here! Hell, it must have set up some . . . some warding rig nearby to know that door should never,* ever *open!*>

<*It . . . It* expected *us?*> he said, agog. <*It expected* me?>

<*It's Tevanne!*> she said. <*It learns! It remembers! It expects everything! And it damn sure isn't going to forget the* one *scrived tool that can defy its will!*> Her knee screamed in pain as she sprinted on. <*How the shit am I going to get out of here?*>

<*The . . . The pounders blasted all the rigs out of the trees for a hundred yards around the dome,*> said Clef. He sounded faint with surprise. <*So it's blind to you for now, and it hasn't yet figured out I'm making you look like a host. But it definitely knows it's under attack. Just get away from the dome, because . . .* > He faltered.

<*Because what?*>

<*Because something's . . . something's changing in ther—*>

Then there was a tremendous crack—and the ground began to rumble.

Sancia whirled around, bewildered. She could just barely see the tip of the black dome from where she was, but something was happening to it: it was splitting, cracking along the middle in one smooth, long line . . . and then it was drawing back.

It was opening.

Berenice stared through the spyglass as the giant black dome cracked open, its two halves withdrawing down into the earth.

<*Capo,*> said Diela faintly. <*Am I . . . am I really seeing this?*>

<*Yes,*> said Berenice. <*It appears we are.*>

Dust rose from the edges of the retreating dome, and between that and the unearthly darkness of the forest it was difficult to see what was within it—but there was definitely something there.

But it can't be the lexicon, thought Berenice. *Can it? Exposing the interior of a lexicon to the open air would be like . . . like taking off the top of your skull and exposing your brain to a rainstorm . . .*

But then the thing within the dome shuddered.

Rattled.

And stood.

"Oh my God," whispered Berenice.

"Oh my scrumming God," said Sancia quietly.

She stared as it emerged from the shadow of the dome. The dust made it hard to see, but the thing was huge, towering nearly fifteen feet tall and twenty feet across, wrought of what looked like blackened bronze, a heaving, hulking, quivering apparatus that kept standing higher, and higher, and higher.

Sancia flexed her scrived sight, and the thing lit up like a thousand stars. Its surface was crawling with sigils and scrivings, every inch of it augmented, every facet designed to deny reality or bend it to its will—and there were *layers* to it, like a rose blossom, rotating spheres within spheres within spheres, all embedded with commands that could shift and change instantly.

<*Holy shit,*> said Clef. <*Holy* shit!>

Sancia shrank up against a tree and stared up at it.

Then, slowly and utterly, eerily silent, it turned, and she saw it in full.

It was strangely man-shaped, like a giant black suit of armor, with a many-segmented torso and pelvis; yet it had four arms at its shoulders, four legs at what had to be its waist, and no visible head. The arms ended in curious, grasping, many-fingered discs that reminded her vaguely of spiders dying on their backs. But she couldn't fight the impression that she had seen something like this once before, long ago . . .

Or maybe not that long ago, she thought.

An image flashed in her mind: Gregor, bleeding and weeping on the floor of Estelle Candiano's ruined rooms, clad in black armor and whispering—*I don't want to be this anymore.*

A lorica, she thought. *Oh my God, it's a giant lorica.*

Which of course made her think of Clef, huddled just over a mile away, their tiny lexicon strapped to his back.

She flexed her scrived sight again. The massive rig lit up once more—and she spied twenty burning, blood-red circles nestled in its belly like burning coals.

<*Holy hell,*> said Sancia. <*It's you, Clef!*>

<*What!*> he cried. <*What do you mean, it's me?*>

<*I . . . I mean it's like you, but times a billion!*> she said. <*This goddamn giant thing—it* is *the lexicon! A giant, walking, fighting lexicon!*>

<*You . . . You mean we've got to get* inside *that thing?*> he said, aghast.

<*I goddamn guess so!*>

A pause—and then the mammoth lorica took a cautious step toward her.

The ground quaked like it'd been struck by a boulder. The forest seemed to grow darker and colder around her, and she found herself shivering. Then she noticed something unusual: the giant blank black box high above had moved as well, as if it were attached by an invisible string to the top of the huge lorica.

It's maintaining the prison, Sancia thought quickly. *It's carrying Crasedes with it . . .*

It took another step, and the ground shook again.

<*Ahh—any ideas here?*> she said.

<*Sure,*> said Clef. <*Get the shit out of there! But* don't *run! Tevanne's sure to be looking hard, and if you run up close on the warding rigs, that'll give you away!*>

<*So . . . I have to casually stroll away from a giant monster,*> said Sancia.

<*Uhh, yeah. That's about the gist of it.*>

Grimacing, she crept back into the forest, attempting to move at what she hoped was a slow, normal pace. To her horror, the enormous lorica followed, its gait careful and fastidious, like it was the caretaker of this forest and it didn't wish to trample any old growth. The huge black prison moved along with it, silently drifting south over the valley. The most terrifying thing was the *quiet* of the thing: there wasn't a whine of metal nor a creak of any joint as the four enormous legs quietly shuffled after her in a queerly crablike movement.

<*Sancia!*> hissed Clef. <*Step to the right. Now!*>

She didn't stop to ask why. She darted to the right, standing in the cover of a giant old pine—and then everything grew dark with shadow, there was a flash of black to her left, a deafening crack, and then she was showered with splinters and dust.

She fought not to scream, and covered her eyes and face. Once the rain of debris faded, she peeked through her fingers and saw the forest to her left had been completely decimated, the trunks missing, ending in stumps frayed with fibers and pulp.

The tremendous lorica stood almost directly over her now, its huge black carapace delicately hanging in the air. One of its arms was covered in dust and pine needles.

It must have slashed through the forest, she thought, *like a scythe through wheat . . .*

<*Tevanne knows you've got to be in the trees,*> whispered Clef. <*It's trying to spook you.*>

<*Consider me pretty shitting spooked!*> said Sancia.

<*But you should be protected here. Tevanne won't slash through trees where it could kill its own hosts—and that's still what it thinks you are.*>

<*Wh-What!*> said Sancia, outraged. <*Tevanne's always been happy to kill its own hosts! By the wagonload!*>

<*Oh. Right,*> said Clef. <*Shit. Well, just . . . just stay here for a moment.*>

She watched as a huge black metal foot crunched down barely a dozen feet from where she now stood, crushing an entire tree.

<*Staying here,*> she said, <*feels like a very bad choice!*>

<*By staying here, it looks like you're obeying Tevanne's command!*> said Clef. <*To come here and look for intruders!*>

She glanced eastward. <*But . . . aren't all the* other *hosts returning now? Coming here, to look for me? Where they could* see *me?*>

A pause.

<*Well. Yeah,*> Clef said. <*Which, yes, is bad. Ahh. Give me time to think, okay? This just got a hell of a lot harder. Tevanne knows it's under attack now—and I don't know what the hell it's going to d—*>

Another tremendous crashing sound from her left, and another rain of dust and pulp. She turned away, eyes shut, then cracked a lid to see the huge lorica standing within another stretch of broken forest.

I'm running out of trees to hide in, she thought.

She watched the lorica. It bobbed back and forth on its legs, a bit like a man who'd been standing all day and was trying to keep his legs limber. But then . . . then it seemed to simply freeze.

The enormous lorica hovered in the trees like a spider in its web, one foot thoughtfully raised.

She braced herself for another blow—but nothing happened.

<*What's it doing?*> she asked.

<*Looks like . . . nothing,*> said Clef. <*Maybe it's giving up on finding you . . .* >

She slowly exhaled in relief. <*Really? Thank God . . .* >

<*No, that's bad,*> said Clef. <*Because Tevanne's got a* lot *more weapons at its disposal here than just this big bastard, and now it knows you got help from somewhere out there. It knows you're not alone.*>

Her skin went cold. <*You mean . . . like, Claudia? Or* Berenice*? You mean Tevanne could be targeting the—*>

There was a harsh *snap* from the lip of the valley—almost right where Berenice had been stationed—and then, to her disbelief, the distant mountains began to crumble.

Sancia stared in horror. "Oh no," she whispered. "Ohh no, oh no, oh no . . ."

Berenice peered through the spyglass on her espringal, watching as the giant lorica erratically smashed through the forest, followed by that odd halo of darkness cast by the prison above—and then the lorica paused.

She narrowed her eye. *That cannot be good.*

Then the nausea hit her again, and she knew the world was changing.

The first thing that happened was that everything suddenly felt *thin*. She fought the mad, screaming feeling that she and all the world about her were just drawings on flimsy paper, paper flecked with water and falling to pieces, and she was caught in one of those pieces, the world turning into soft pulp about her . . .

She dropped her espringal, frozen in horror. *An edit,* she thought. She looked up at the deadlamps. *Tevanne is . . . editing reality.*

Then she felt it: she *felt* the change in the air, like everything was tipping to the north.

And then the lip of the valley to her left was gone. As in, quite genuinely, suddenly gone.

She caught sight of it only for a moment: a huge section of stone and trees and earth to the northeast was just . . . excised. Missing. Cut away, like a tumor. The segment of vanished (She struggled for the word: Land? Valley? Reality? Everything?) was perfectly spherical, every branch and twig and stone bisected in a smooth, arching curve, like someone had carved out a flawless globe from creation itself stretching a half a mile across—and then made it disappear.

Then came the enormous blast of air, a dizzying, mad burst as the atmosphere came rushing in to fill the gap that had just been created, followed by a tremendous bone-rattling *crack.*

Berenice was slammed to her back by the sheer force of it. An immense cloud of dust came rushing up as what must have been two or three inches of forest topsoil was driven into the air by the shockwave.

She shut her eyes as flecks of dirt rained down on her but noted the location of the edit: almost exactly where she'd positioned the espringals to fire the pounders. *I think,* she said to herself, *that Tevanne did indeed notice where the shots came from* . . . She reflected that if she'd stayed anywhere close to the espringals, she'd be gone so fast she wouldn't even know she was dead.

Then there was a rumbling sound, and she began to slide.

"Well, shit," she said.

The earth turned to dry slush below her as she fell. It took her no time at all to realize what was happening: the deadlamps had carved out a huge cross-section of the lip of the valley, which, naturally, destabilized everything around it, leading to a massive avalanche of soil, dirt, stone—everything.

Including whichever bit of earth she was now sitting on.

She cracked her eyes open as she slid, but she couldn't see through the dust and the rain of soil. Yet she was aware that she was accelerating far, far too fast, probably speeding toward some precipice that would dump her off into that newborn gaping chasm, only to smash on the ground below—or die smothered in the heaps of accumulating earth.

No, she thought. *No, no, not today, not like this . . .*

In a flash, she had her scrived rapier out. She rolled over as she slid, stones striking her helmet and pauldrons below her twin sheath, and drove the sword into the earth behind her like she was running through an enemy.

The blade did not catch. Whatever soil she was driving it into must also be sliding as well.

No.

She pushed it in harder, harder, desperately hoping her sword would find something, anything to stabilize her . . .

Please, she thought. *Please, please . . .*

And then it caught, the blade bucking so hard in her hand that the hilt was nearly ripped clean out of her grasp.

She growled aloud, gritting her teeth as she fought like mad to hold on. She guessed the blade had found some chunk or strata of stone—but to her dismay, she did not stop falling. Instead she decelerated, and her plummet turned into a grinding, erratic slide.

Scrived rapier, she thought. *Cutting through the goddamned stone . . .*

She twisted the rapier in her hands, turning the flat of the blade down.

Please, please, please . . .

She slowed, more and more.

And then she stopped.

She opened her eyes. The world was still swirling with dust, and stones and earth were still pouring down the rocks about her, but she was now dangling over the giant spherical aperture in the mountains, her wrists and fingers screaming in pain as she clutched the sword.

I suppose I ought to be grateful, she thought, *for doing my grip exercises . . .*

<*Berenice!*> screamed Clef. <*Ber, Ber, Ber! Are . . . Are you alive?*>

She looked down. It was nearly a fifty-foot drop to the piles of gravel and soil below. <*Ahh, yes,*> she said hesitantly. <*So it would see—*>

Then she heard a loud crackling and looked up.

A giant old-growth pine was looming above her, tottering back and forth as the loose soil pulled it down—and then it slowly teetered, twisted, and fell, plummeting down the slope to where she hung.

She watched, horrified, as it bounced off an outcropping about twenty feet above her with a tremendous crack, hurtling right toward her.

She shut her eyes, turned about on the sword, and pressed her back to the cliff, bracing for the impact.

A wave of air before her, aromatic with pine sap—and then a soft *whoof* sound from below.

She opened her eyes again and saw the pine tree buried in the accumulating soil just below her.

<*Okay, ah, yes,*> she said. <*Now I can confirm. Still alive. Yes.*>

<*Oh, thank God,*> said Clef.

<*Just . . . give me a second to get safe here . . .*>

Berenice's hands and forearms were throbbing with pain. She ignored it, pulled out a small scrived knife, and plunged it into the rock above her. It held fast, and she ripped her scrived rapier free, raised it, plunged it into the stone higher up the cliff, and hauled herself up.

<*Need to invent something,*> she thought as she ripped her scrived knife out and stabbed it higher in the cliff, slowly climbing up bit by bit. <*Need to invent something to help with this next time . . .*> She tried not to look at the perfect sphere of missing reality just below her. <*I will make a note of it.*>

<*Berenice is alive!*> said Clef in Sancia's ear. <*She's alive, she's all right!*>

Sancia let out a shuddering breath where she clung close to a massive old pine. <*Oh, thank scrumming God . . .* >

<*Tevanne made a play for her, I think hoping to either kill her, flush you out, or both. But . . .* > He faltered. <*Wait. Kid—look north. Check this out!*>

Sancia glanced through the trees to the north end of the valley. She wasn't sure what he was referencing, but then she noted movement in the sky: one of the deadlamps that formed the gruesome little halo around the prison was now plummeting out of the air. She watched, shocked, as the black brick smashed into the mountains below.

<*I guess Tevanne used up all the people inside,*> said Clef quietly, <*to make that edit. That's one deadlamp down, how many to go?*>

<*Too goddamn many,*> said Sancia. <*And we have to get* inside *that giant lexicon to do anything about the rest! And we don't even really know what it scrumming* is!>

A thought struck her. She watched as the lorica resumed thoughtfully scuttling through the forest, gently nudging giant pines out of the way.

She looked up. The black prison followed, drifting over the massive lorica like a tiny black cloud cursed to follow someone.

Carrying Crasedes, she thought again. *And that's a heavy load.*

<*Clef,*> she said. <*I'm going to walk right toward that thing.*>

<*You're going to* what?> he said.

<*And I need you to study it. This thing is maintaining the prison, holding Crasedes hostage. I'm guessing that's pretty hard for any rig, even one of Tevanne's. The more we know about how hard that task is, the easier it'll be to break it.*>

<*Scrumming hell,*> said Clef. <*I guess! Give it a shot.*>

She took a left and walked as slowly and calmly as she could toward the giant contraption. It was still hanging over the forest, one leg raised thoughtfully. She eyed its huge metal foot, wondering what it would be like if it fell on her.

<*I'm seeing it,*> he whispered. <*I'm seeing it . . . Yeah. Okay. You're right. It's the lexicon, and it's maintaining the prison, yeah, but . . . but it's weird.*>

<*Anything useful?*>

<*Maybe. The giant lorica can control gravity, yes—I mean, obviously it's making the prison float—but it was also built to be* unusually resistant *to any alterations in gravity.*>

<*Huh?*>

<*I can see the commands embedded in it from here . . . For some reason it's been scrived to steadfastly, endlessly assert which way is down, which way is up, and rebut any efforts to suggest otherwise . . .* >

Sancia sighed. <*Shit,*> she said. <*Of course.*>

<*Of course what?*>

Her eyes flicked up to the floating prison above. <*Who do we know who screws with gravity a lot?*>

<*Oh crap. You mean . . .* >

<*Yeah. We all wondered how Tevanne captured Crasedes. I'm guessing* this *is the thing that did it! It was built to fight off his abilities! And it's now acting as his jailer!*>

<*So if we couldn't beat Crasedes before . . .* > said Clef. <*How in the hell are we going to beat the thing that beat him?*>

Sancia thought about it. <*Tell Berenice. Now. Make sure to mention the gravity shit.*>

<*You're having ideas?*>

<*No. But I know my wife well enough to know how to give* her *ideas.*>

< . . . *resistant to gravity,*> Clef whispered in Berenice's ear. <*It's Crasedes's* jailer.>

Berenice perched on a narrow bridge of stone above the chasm, watching as the giant rig resumed prowling through the forest below, still draped in darkness. <*Interesting . . .* > she said quietly.

<*Interesting? More like scrumming awful!*> said Clef. <*We've got to break* into *the thing,* while *it's stalking Sancia like a cat after a mouse in a barn,* without *triggering any of the wardings and giving those damned deadlamps a target!*>

Berenice pinched her nose and blew. What felt like about ten tons of dust came spraying out of her nostrils to adhere to the inside face of her sheath suit—which she found disgusting, of course, but could do little about. <*It's basically a giant gravity rig,*> she said. <*Is that the gist of it?*>

<*That's . . . incredibly reductive, but sure,*> Clef said.

<*And how is it defining those relationships with gravity?*>

<*Usual shit?*> said Clef. <*Commands about the surface of the earth, the current flow of gravity, orientation, stability . . . Stuff we do all the time, just way, way bigger and louder.*>

She cocked her head, thinking. Orientation and stability—she was familiar with those, and how they were weak.

<*So,*> she said slowly, <*it's got to stay calibrated. Coordinated. But there's no way for you to crack it through its scrivings via direct contact . . .* >

<*Right. This bastard is as uncrackable as it gets.*>

But "uncrackable" often also meant "inflexible," Berenice knew, which meant it could be a weakness.

She knit her brow. What was it Sancia sometimes said?

"A scrived lock," she said quietly, "is only as strong as the door it's set in . . ."

<*Huh?*> said Clef.

<*What . . . What if we scrambled what it knew about up and down, and the surface of the earth?*> she asked. <*Not through scriving, but by* physically moving it about*? Like . . . what would happen if it got knocked over?*>

He laughed desperately. <*This thing beat Crasedes! How could any gravity tricks that we throw at it do any better?*>

<*Because,*> she said, studying the floating prison, <*I think it's* still *fighting Crasedes. Still maintaining all the tasks that keep him subdued. We just need to overload those tasks, and the whole thing might fall apart.*>

<*Overload it? Ber—you're not hearing me. Crasedes or no, we'd have to drop a goddamned mountain on this thing to manage that.*>

She glanced to her left, where the cliffs were still steadily dissolving. <*And if we did exactly that?*>

<*Uhh. What?*>

She looked out at the skyline, studying each mountain. <*We'd have to get it in the right location, of course . . . and give Tevanne the right bait . . .* >

<*Ber—what the hell are you talking about?*> Clef asked.

Then Diela's voice, quiet and small: <*She's talking about us.*>

<*Correct,*> said Berenice. <*Diela—path to me, look from my eyes,*

and I'll show you where you need to be. And Clef—you'll need to get into position yourself.>

<*For . . . what now?*> Clef asked, somewhat tremulously.

<*Well, you've been rather excited to have a body, haven't you?*> she said. <*Why don't we find out what all it can do?*>

<*Kid,*> sighed Clef in Sancia's ear. <*If you could hear the mad shit your wife is suggesting . . .* >

Sancia narrowed her eyes at the eastern ranges of the forest. Was it her imagination, or could she see a few gray figures there, creeping toward her? <*I take it she had ideas?*>

<*Yeah . . .* > said Clef reluctantly. <*Listen. In about twenty seconds, you're going to start walking away from that thing.*>

<*Wait. Wouldn't that be a* direct contradiction *of Tevanne's commands?*> said Sancia. <*Which would make it immediately aware that I'm* not *a host?*>

<*Yeah,*> said Clef. <*But it's going to have other stuff to think about then.*>

<*Like what?*>

<*Like me jumping on that big thing's face,*> he said. <*And beating the shit out of it.*>

Her mouth fell open.

<*What!*> she said.

<*Yeah . . .* > said Clef. <*Again, this is your wife's idea, so don't take it up with me.*>

<*Beyond all the* obviously *mad shit with trying to do that,*> said Sancia, <*wouldn't the deadlamps just blast you out of reality while you're fighting it?*>

<*Ber doesn't think so,*> said Clef. <*Apparently the deadlamp edits aren't, like,* surgical. *They claw out a big chunk of reality and throw it away. So if I can grab onto that big bastard, and hold on, they can't kill me—because they'd probably take out the thing that's keeping Crasedes held prisoner as well.*>

<*So—are* you *going to be able to break into the lexicon?*>

<*No,*> he said. He let out a long, slow sigh. <*That's where it*

gets . . . complicated. Look to the south. You see that big-ass mountain-kinda-thing up there?>

She glanced south and saw which one he meant: a tall, rambling bluff of granite, reaching out over the valley. <*Yes?*>

<*Your wife wants to drop it on that big son of a bitch. My job is to weaken the lorica and then haul it over to the right place. Your job is to get inside when we're done. Got it?*>

She took a deep breath. <*No.* Hell *no. But. I trust my wife.*>

Berenice knelt in the shadow of the bluff as she set up her final espringal. *Once this one's gone,* she thought, *I've got a rapier, a knife, and nothing else.*

She bent low and carefully applied the twinning plates to the rig's trigger.

But then, if we fail, there's a reasonable chance the world might end. So. Priorities.

Once the plates were applied, she walked around and checked the espringal's sightlines. The weapon was aimed to fire its many bolts out over the forest, generally in the direction of the giant lorica; but in truth, she didn't really care. She just wanted it to shoot, shoot a lot, and generally be a nuisance.

<*Claudia,*> she said as she finished. <*How are we looking?*>

<*Still getting into position!*> gasped Claudia. <*You . . . You took the easy one!*>

She closed her eyes and pathed into Diela—and saw that the girl was straddling a giant gap in the rocks, with Claudia precariously balanced on her shoulders as she positioned her own espringal on the underside of the bluff.

<*I am glad,*> gasped Diela, <*that you made us do all those leg exercises, Capo . . .* >

<*We sure this will work?*> said Claudia, panting.

<*Relatively,*> said Berenice. <*Tevanne has prewritten commands, reactions, instincts . . . It often responds thoughtlessly. I expect it will do so again.*>

<*If Clef survives,*> said Claudia.

<*If Clef survives, yes,*> said Berenice.

<*I can hear you, assholes,*> said Clef in her ear. <*Speaking of which . . . I hope you're ready, because we're about to have to move here.*>

Berenice sat up, shaded her eyes from the noon sun, and peered out at the valley. She badly wished she still had her spyglass, but all that—along with much of the rest of her kit—had been lost in the landslide. Yet she could still see the giant lorica, creeping toward where Clef crouched at the southern end of the valley, the huge black cube silently sailing on above it.

<*Sancia's on the move?*> said Berenice.

<*Yes. Walking straight toward me at a calm, slow pace. Tevanne must be curious and wants to find out what's up—I don't think it can quite believe we disguised her as a host.*>

<*Good,*> said Berenice. She started off toward the west at a very fast trot. <*Claudia, Diela—get that put together, and then get the* hell away *as fast as you can.*>

<*Understood,*> grunted Claudia.

<*And Clef . . . Good luck,*> said Berenice.

<*Yeah, yeah,*> said Clef.

Clef crouched in the brush, watching through his various senses as the giant lorica approached. Mostly he was fixated on one sense in particular: the feeling as the ground shook under his feet with every step of the huge thing.

Holy shit, he thought. *Holy shit, it's big, it's big . . .*

<*Almost there,*> whispered Sancia. <*Almost . . .* >

The prison floated closer, and the veil of shadow flooded the trees about him. Clef squatted down, far lower than if his own lorica had been occupied by an actual human, the backside of the big war suit almost touching the ground.

It's just a fight, he told himself. *Just another fight with a big scrived rig. You've done this before.*

The ground quaked below him, heavier and heavier, faster and faster. He remembered all the instructions Berenice had given him—instructions that now seemed utterly preposterous.

It's just . . . also a literal fight, he thought. *Like, with fists and shit.*

<*Clef, it's speeding up,*> said Sancia, panicked. <*I think it's . . . I think it's* really *interested in me!*>

He checked his weapons: his espringals, his bolt casters, the polearm—and, of course, his arms and legs, which were just as deadly as everything else. He peered through the pathplate around Sancia's neck, navigating the many commands that allowed his consciousness to exist in two places at once, and saw she was right: the giant rig was no longer cautiously creeping through the woods but was crawling directly after her at a fast clip.

Time to go, he thought.

Yet he paused.

He had no concept of doing such a thing: of fighting with a body, of actually making war in a physical space. The proposition frankly terrified him.

A flash of a memory: a man in a Papa Monsoon costume, leaning over Sancia and whispering—*He can't save you now. He was never terribly good at saving people anyway . . .*

Clef tried to banish the thought. *Shut up . . .*

The ground quaked again. The giant lorica was just beyond the trees ahead.

<*Clef?*> asked Sancia. <*Are . . . Are you . . .* >

Crasedes's voice, soft and deadly: *That was always up to me.*

Clef's lorica rattled around him—and then his voice rig leapt to life.

"Just *SHUT UP*!" he roared.

He jumped.

Sancia wasn't sure what startled her more: the sudden cry of "SHUT UP!" which was loud enough to penetrate her already-deafened ears, or the shattering of the trees before her as something huge and black burst through them, speeding through the air over her head. It took her a moment to realize it was Clef.

She whipped her head around just in time to see him smash into the torso of the giant lorica, making a blaring *CLONG!* sound, like someone had dropped a two-ton bell from a clock tower. The impact was so extreme that the trees and grasses around them danced in the shockwave, so extreme that the rig's front two legs were lifted clean off the ground, and it went staggering back like a drunk who'd lost their balance trying to walk uphill.

For a moment, Sancia was elated—*Is he going to take it out that easily?*

The giant rig tottered backward—but then it righted itself. She saw that Clef was adhered to its torso, almost like a fly mashed against a roll of parchment. She realized he must have activated the adhesion rigs in his armor's gauntlets and boots—rigs to help soldiers scale walls and cliffs—and would now be almost impossible to remove.

The giant lorica stood there in the forest, seeming somewhat perplexed to have this large metal man suddenly hanging off its front.

Then it raised its arms and started pummeling him.

The blows were so fast and so fierce it was difficult for Sancia's eyes to even make sense of them. She watched in horror as Clef's armor dented under the onslaught: first the back of his cuirass, then his pauldron, then the greaves . . . It would take mere seconds to smash him to bits.

"Clef!" she cried aloud.

<*San!*> snarled Clef. <*If you don't get the hell out of here, then I'll have done this dumb shit for nothing!*>

"Oh son of a bitch!" she said aloud. Then she turned and sprinted south toward the bluff.

27

A war-ready, Dandolo Chartered–manufactured lorica, Clef knew, had been designed to withstand a direct hit from a shrieker—specifically a Morsini House–manufactured shrieker, which had been the best projectile weaponry available during the design of this particular armor. Clef knew this because the intent had been literally written into the bones of the apparatus: the plating, the tassets, the faulds, the plackart—all of them were wrought and woven with commands to be spectacularly, impossibly resilient. The brightest minds at Dandolo Chartered had made this armor so it could walk through hell and come out in one piece.

But as Clef clung to the chest of the giant lorica, its fists raining down on him, he quickly realized that the brightest minds at Dandolo Chartered were now firmly out of their goddamned depths.

Tevanne's giant lorica didn't just punch him. Rather, the impact of its fists was akin to being struck by a merchant house galleon going at full speed—almost *literally*. He could perceive the commands Tevanne was feeding into the giant rig: commands to make its fists preternaturally dense and fast, and commands to the surface of its torso plating to make it preternaturally dense and durable so the rig's arms didn't punch right through its own chest and smash up the lexicon within. It was changing all the physical properties of the entire lorica from second to second.

It was, in short, something Clef did with rigs every day. But this time, it was being used to annihilate him.

He watched from within the armor as one fist made impact with a huge crash. He listened as his war rig reported on its condition: right leg destabilized, right arm totally compromised . . .

Holy hell, thought Clef.

Another blow, another. His armor calmly told him that the structural integrity of his cuirass was now quite seriously compromised. The only thing that remained wholly undamaged was the plating on the tiny lexicon on his back.

Another blow, and another.

His mind raced. He felt himself—his true self, trapped in the key—rattling in the voice rig within the lorica's cuirass.

Yet he noticed something now, watching the commands dance through the giant rig: it was slowing down. Each alteration, each twist of the rig's rules were coming slower and slower and slower.

It's struggling under the weight of all it has to maintain.

Another blow.

Only thing to do is add to its burden.

He quickly assessed the state of his armor. It was riddled with scrivings that could manipulate the armor's beliefs about density, velocity, acceleration, tensile strength . . .

He spoke to his armor, showering its scrivings with arguments, altering their definitions, desperately working to persuade them that they were far, far denser than they had previously believed . . .

Come on, he thought, *come on . . .*

The giant lorica's fist began hurtling down.

He whispered to his armor, singing to it, rewriting its very nature.

"Come on!" he bellowed aloud.

Clef's left arm rotated, quick as lightning.

There was a dull *clunk* sound, and . . .

He stopped it, snatching up the giant fist like it was an oversized ball.

He was so taken aback that all he could do was stare: his little arm, his little gauntlet, pressed against the giant fist of the huge lorica that was still bearing down on him—and yet, it held.

He couldn't help himself—he cried aloud: "Holy *shit*!"

The giant lorica quaked, rattled, and pressed harder and harder. He felt the pressure build in his armor, but he fed more and more commands into it in response, bending its concept of its own physics like it were a piece of straw—and his armor listened, complied, and pushed back, lifting his torso away from the giant lorica's plating.

A scriving fight, he realized. *But one where we rewrite the nature of our rigs from second to second . . .*

The giant lorica's arm quivered, strained, shook—and yet, Clef steadfastly shoved it back.

Then came a noise, the first of its kind that he had heard yet: although the giant black beast had been utterly silent so far, now there was a faint whine of metal—perhaps a whine like a dog suddenly unsure what to do.

Clef rotated his helmet around. His voice rig hissed: "I've got you now, you *dumb piece of shit!*"

He raised his battered right arm, and with a *click-clack,* his polearm flashed out.

He hurled it around in a smooth, swift arc, feeding it more and more arguments as it flew, tricking the blade into believing it was huge, dense, as big as the moon above . . .

The blade smashed through the giant lorica's limb, utterly severing it. Bits of metal and plating rained down on him with soft *tink* and *tonk* sounds. The lorica staggered to the side, as if utterly taken aback by this development.

Clef burst into a mad, delighted cackle. He flung the severed fist away and shoved himself off the surface of the lorica's torso, the adhesion plates in his boots still active so he now stood perpendicular to the giant beast. Then he ran down the giant rig's surface.

He raised his polearm again, intending to smash through one of the lorica's legs, which would make it far easier to wrangle. But then he saw a flash of black speeding down over the top of the lorica—another arm, this one shimmering with commands to make it faster than a lightning strike.

Clef had just mind enough to shout, "*Ah shit!*" before the lorica's fist plucked him off its front, one bit of its torso plating still stuck to his boot.

He screamed aloud as he hurtled through the air, whipped about by the lorica's enormous arm as it tried to toss him into the forest—and once he was clear, he knew, the deadlamps above would annihilate him.

His battered right arm snatched out, and he slapped his left gauntlet to the surface of the lorica's fist. He poured arguments into the gauntlet's adhesion plate, forcing it to believe he was not just attached to the lorica but that he *was* the lorica, he was a part of it, it could never release him, not ever . . .

The giant lorica flicked its massive hand—yet Clef stayed attached, dangling from the back of its hand.

The lorica seemed surprised by this. It flicked him again and again, like someone attempting to get a booger off their knuckle, and yet he refused to release, and he flopped about madly, screaming and shrieking.

And here I thought, he reflected, *that I was really getting somewhere.*

It tried only a few more times to shake Clef off, and then it did what he'd been dreading: it began to whip him about, and slam him into the ground, up and down and up and down.

He slammed into the ground once, twice, three times. On the fourth time he made impact so hard he sank several feet into the dusty red earth. The lorica paused just long enough for him to see panicked little ground squirrels skittering about—he must have disturbed their underground nest, he guessed.

At least I'm not the only one having a bad day.

It raised and whirled him about again, smashing him through trees, rocks, even against its own severed fist. Clef held on, screaming more and more commands at the tiny bit of scrived plating that was securing him to the beast's fist—no more than five square inches of steel, he estimated—and he knew that every second he devoted to hanging on, the more damage the rest of his armor took.

He felt himself lose a pauldron; then a bit of his vambrace and his skirting.

I'm falling apart, he thought. *I'm raining over this valley like seeds from a puff flower . . .*

He knew it couldn't last much longer. He thought quickly about what to do, trying to gain his bearings as he whirled through the air.

He spied the bluff to the south. He was just a half a mile away from where he needed to be, maybe less.

An idea blossomed to life in his mind.

He waited until the giant lorica raised him to the fullest height: and then he spoke to the density scrivings riddled through his armor, commands that made his plating believe it was harder than a thousand tons of milled steel—and he began to convince them to octuple their definitions; then octuple them again; and again, and again, and again . . .

In less than one second, Clef's armor became about as heavy as two merchant house galleons.

The giant lorica tottered on its feet, bewildered to suddenly be holding something so heavy.

Clef smashed into the forest floor with a deafening *whoomf,* and he crushed a good bit of the lorica's fist as well. He checked his own armor as he fell, listening to the arguments dancing through the metal; he was pleased to find most of it held up well, though his voice rig, understandably, was no longer operating quite properly.

He watched within his armor as he sank into the ground, almost pulling the huge lorica over on top of him. He realized this wasn't sustainable—he couldn't have the whole valley caving in on him—and showered his armor with commands again, altering its physics and restoring its densities to a fraction of what he'd just attained.

Rattling and squeaking, he stood and turned to the big lorica, still gripping its limb. He watched as the beast staggered about, still trying to recover.

Now, he thought, *to scrum with all your gravity calibrations.*

He twisted his giant metal body, whipping his polearm forward, sending his many arguments coursing down its length and guiding it toward the weakest part of the lorica's leg. He watched with satisfaction as the massive black blade sank into the back part of the knee; then he retracted the polearm, ripping it back as hard as it could. The knee burst outward in a shower of dark bronze.

The lorica did not topple over as he'd wished; instead, the three remaining legs danced about, weaving back and forth expertly as it managed its enormous weight.

Then Clef knelt low, the lorica's arm still gripped in his hand, dug in deep with his heels, and jumped straight up.

It was, he thought, possibly the biggest jump that might have ever been attempted in a Dandolo Chartered war lorica. He argued with nearly every aspect of the armor's physical nature every step of the way, from the flex of its ankles to the way it parted the air, and he rewrought it to achieve two specific goals.

To begin with, he elevated his density again. He'd gotten quite good at that, so that was easy, and in a flash he became as heavy as a galleon again—but density was not exactly a useful trait when jumping in the air.

But the second bit . . .

Scrived bolts are scrived to believe they aren't flying out, he thought as he jumped. *But falling* down, *straight down, toward the earth. So it's just a matter of making all the tiny gravity scrivings in this thing believe the same . . . but to make my rig think I'm* falling up.

He leapt, and thundered commands into the gravity scrivings within the lorica.

And then, he fell. Straight up.

And because he was still gripping the arm of the giant lorica, it rocketed up with him.

It had to be the most bizarre sight in the world, he thought, this tiny speck of metal spinning into the skies, dragging this giant rattling behemoth with it, bits of metal and plating raining down on the valley below—and most absurdly, they *accelerated,* flying up faster and faster.

Higher and higher, he thought.

The air grew cold around him. He felt icy rime crawling across his armor.

Higher, he thought. *Higher, higher, higher . . .*

The lorica then did what he'd expected: it adjusted its own densities, its own gravities, and counterbalanced Clef's commands to rip him out of the skies and back to earth.

He felt himself jerk sharply downward, like he'd been climbing a rope that'd abruptly unraveled, and then they plummeted down to the valley.

The lorica's fists battered him as they fell, trying to clutch him and hold him close, perhaps to be crushed to pieces when they landed. It still had not realized Clef's goal—that he *wanted* the lorica to fall to the earth.

He studied the landscape below, ran some calculations, and realized that although the lorica was falling, it was not falling toward the right place.

I need to adjust it, he thought. *Just a nudge . . .*

He realized this wouldn't be easy. He could play with the scrivings within his armor, but it did have some strict limits: he could not fly, could not abruptly change direction in midair. All of its gravity permissions were tied to the physical movements of the armor.

So, he would need to jump again—yet since he was hurtling through midair, he didn't have many surfaces to jump *off* of.

He looked up at the black prison above him, hurtling down at the exact same rate as the giant lorica below.

Ah.

He lessened his density—perhaps a bit too much—and was ripped up by the wind until he slammed into the bottom of the giant black cube.

For a moment, he wanted to peek inside, to flex his sight and see if he could peek within the giant prison, and spy . . .

No, he said. *No, not yet.*

Groaning, he forced his armor to stand on the bottom of the prison, his helmet facing down as the prison shrieked to the earth like a black square comet. Then he dropped into a deep squat and jumped.

He rocketed toward the earth, the air ripping through the cracks in his armor. As he passed the giant lorica he reached out, snatched it in his gauntlets, turned on the adhesion plates in his palms, and held fast.

He studied the ground below, spied the bluff at the southern tip of the valley, and did some more calculations.

<*Berenice,*> he said. <*Do it!*>

<*What? You're too far up!*> she said.

<*I won't be soon!*> he said. <*Just do it!*>

He summoned as much strength as he could, pouring arguments into his armor, and hurled the lorica down at the base of the bluff, using all of its self-commanded density and gravity to make it shriek down like a comet from the sky.

Clef thought it might now be on target. Maybe.

He lessened his density, dipped to the side, and he and his armor began to float down to the earth like the slenderest of leaves.

If I miss, he thought, *Ber is going to be so pissed.*

Berenice squinted into the sky as Clef performed his stratospheric acrobatics with the giant lorica. She had to admit, she thought he'd do something, but she hadn't quite believed he'd master control of his armor *that* quickly.

Then she took a deep breath and whispered to Claudia and Diela: <*You're clear?*>

<*I don't know how clear we need to be for this shit!*> snapped Claudia. <*But we're sprinting away as fast as we can, if that's what you mean!*>

She lifted her own twinned trigger. <*Then do it,*> she said.

She squeezed her trigger and looked to the south. She'd run west along the lip of the valley, almost back toward where the mountain had disintegrated. She wasn't quite sure if this was a safe place, but it was too late now: she watched as the espringal she'd set up on the bluff leapt to life, spitting out bolts at the forest below. She'd armed it with candle bolts—the same bolts Claudia had used to set the fields at Grattiara alight—and she watched as the cheerful pink sparks went whirling over the trees.

This was, of course, mostly useless in a combat situation—unless you wanted to be noticed. But that was precisely what Berenice wanted.

She looked at the bluff, then up at the lamps above and the giant lorica plummeting through the skies, then back down at the bluff. Nothing happened.

Come on, she thought. *Come on . . .*

Then Claudia's espringal kicked on, just on the eastern side of the bluff, pouring candle bolts out at the forest. The noon air glimmered and sparkled like a rich person's brooch.

She stared around the valley. Nothing was changing. Tevanne was not reacting.

And then . . .

The air pulsed. Her stomach curdled with nausea. There was

a peculiar tilting sensation, like she was standing on the deck of a ship that had just shifted in one direction, toward the south . . .

And then two enormous bubbles appeared in the face of the bluff—yet they were bubbles of nothing, just empty, vacant space.

She stared in wonder, in horror. *What a thing it is,* she said, *to witness the changing of the world . . .*

Yet she noticed with satisfaction that the deadlamps had wiped out the *underside* of the bluff, almost precisely where she and Claudia and Diela had hidden the espringals.

Which meant that the entire mountain above was now almost totally unsupported.

There was a rumbling in the ground—and then the southern tip of the valley began to collapse, enormous chunks of brown-pink granite tipping away from the grip of the mountains and tumbling over.

She was so mesmerized by the sight, in fact, that she was startled when the mammoth lorica shrieked down out of the sky to plunge directly into the heart of the crumbling stone. Then the top of the bluff tottered over and flopped onto where the lorica had just landed.

She waited. More of the southern valley collapsed around it. The lorica did not emerge.

Being tossed several miles in the air, she thought, *and then being buried underground . . . That might make an overloaded gravity rig very, very,* very *confused.*

Sancia shut her eyes and flexed her scrived sight as the southern tip of the valley collapsed. She'd hidden in a tiny cleft in the cliffs on the western side of the bluff, and watched with no small amount of anxiety as the earth shook about her, and more and more stones showered down on where the lorica had landed.

She looked up. The black prison in the sky wobbled but did not fall—not yet.

Slowly, the avalanche tapered off. She slipped out of the wedge and approached the enormous pile of dirt and stone, peering ahead with her sight. She saw the immense lorica was buried under nearly ten feet of stone and soil, and all its rigs within were going mad.

<*Kid?*> cried Clef. <*You alive?*>

<*Yeah,*> she said, listening to the sound of shifting soil and clattering stone. <*I am for now!*>

<*Then you got to move fast!*> he said. <*I'm still listening to Tevanne's orders through that blade in your shoulder—it sounds like we overwhelmed it! Too much shit going on, too many hosts to track, too much crap breaking! You've got a window, but a tiny one! Hurry!*>

She waited until the sounds of the avalanche had mostly subsided, then stepped out from her shelter and approached.

The dust cleared as she neared it. The massive lorica had nearly succeeded, she saw: the thing had almost clawed its way out of the avalanche using its one remaining arm. Yet Clef had damaged it badly, almost as much as the avalanche, and it had only managed to escape halfway, its broken legs still trapped in the soil. She didn't need to use her scrived sight to see that its gravity scrivings were weak and overworked: stones and particles of dust erratically floated about it like drunken flies buzzing over a wine cask. She felt parts of her own body grow heavier and other parts grow lighter as she approached.

Here's hoping it doesn't keep all the blood from going to my brain, she thought. *Or out of it.*

She saw her target as she stepped closer: a small porthole, sealed shut with a lock, positioned at the very top of its torso.

Sancia danced up the stones, hurrying as fast as she could and climbing expertly among the rubble, ignoring the pains in her knees and ankles. She placed her hand against the door and was met with a familiar argument of Tevanne's.

<*PRORATION SHALL OCCUR ONLY,*> it gasped, <*WHEN . . . WHEN THOSE BEARING THE . . . THE SIGNAL . . . ARE MET WITH THE WILL . . .*>

She'd cracked this argument before, during her many times running raids with Berenice; it was even easier now, with one of Tevanne's own plates buried in her shoulder. She tore the defense apart easily, and the porthole swung open.

She peered within. A short hatch, intended to be climbed down by a host, perhaps—and then the plates within.

<*You have the command ready, Clef?*> she asked.

<*Yeah,*> he sighed. <*One more command. I feed these orders into the sucker, and we all go home and get drunk.*>

She climbed into the hatch and slipped down into the innards of the massive lexicon.

She flexed her scrived sight and focused on the twenty red plates burning in the depths. She needed to get Clef as close to them as possible, to find the component of this lexicon that twinned it with the rest of Tevanne's broader consciousness—and there, he'd be able to take over this beast and control the very reality of the valley, and the prison above.

She dropped down into the small central chamber and spied the component almost immediately: a small dull little plate, installed in the corner.

Like so many scrived things, she thought, crawling over to it. *It looks so mundane . . . yet it does so much.*

She raised the pathplate—but before she brought it down, she froze and turned around.

She studied the space about her. She could have sworn she'd glimpsed something standing over her shoulder . . .

Or maybe someone. A man, perhaps, his eyes and nose leaking blood, his face suspended in the darkness of this place behind her.

Alone in the darkness, Sancia whispered: "Gregor?" But there was nothing.

Gritting her teeth, she turned and slapped Clef's pathplate to the dull little plate and braced herself.

Berenice, Claudia, and Diela huddled in the trees over what was left of the southern tip of the valley, trying to peer through the dust.

<She's in!> said Clef. *<And now . . . Hold on! She did it! This'll take a seco . . . >*

His voice slowed down, stretched out, turning into a long, sustained *ooooo* sound.

They jumped when they heard it. Then they peered up at the prison, and the three remaining deadlamps above. None of them were moving—at least, not yet.

"Look!" said Diela, so excited she spoke out loud.

She pointed up. And they saw, to their amazement, that the prison was moving.

It was drifting up, up, up, rising until it reached the same level as the three remaining deadlamps hanging in the air around the valley. And then it shot toward them.

Berenice cringed as the black prison moved. This had been her idea, and she still wasn't convinced it would work.

The lexicon is constantly influencing the reality of the valley, she'd proposed. *Which makes it stronger than the deadlamps, in a way. But there's nothing it influences more than the prison—so, why not let Clef use* that *as the weapon against* them*?*

She watched as the prison smashed into the first deadlamp, the enormous black cube crashing into the smaller black brick. One corner of the lamp crumbled to pieces upon impact, and the vessel went spinning away to smash into the slopes below.

"It worked," said Claudia. "Holy shit, it's *working*!"

The floating prison now had momentum on its side, and the remaining two deadlamps still had not moved—perhaps Tevanne was paralyzed, or stunned, or overwhelmed—and she watched, slightly incredulous, as the cube smashed through one and then the other, almost instantly turning them both into shrapnel.

"We . . . We did it," said Diela. "We won."

Then the prison came hurtling straight down to the earth.

"Almost," said Berenice. "Now for the prisoner."

Clef landed lightly on the ground and hurtled through the forest, trying to remember where he was.

He knew he was inside his armor. He knew it was making him move. He knew this.

But he also knew he was in Sancia's hand, in the pathplate, which was allowing him to capture the lexicon, which was . . .

The valley. The mountains. Reality. All of it. But especially . . .

The prison. The black chamber hurtling down out of the sky, down, down, down, and soon it would smash into the stone and break open and then he would see . . .

Remember where you are.

He smashed through trees, through stones, through ruins, through walls, through the . . . the . . .

(Stay . . .)

Hosts on his right, on his left, armed with espringals, showering him with bolts, like the sound of hail on a ship's hull.

"No," said Clef. "No, no, I don't . . . I don't care about you . . ."

(Stay with me.)

His commands fed into the lexicon, into the world, the vast black prison descending like the setting of some terrible moon . . .

"I spread myself too thin," said Clef weakly. He leapt forward, shoving aside a host as he did so, ignorant of whether he killed them or not, unable to comprehend what he was doing. "Too thin. Too much of me . . . everywhere . . ."

The prison, still falling, falling. Bolts rattling off of his arms, his cuirass, his legs, everywhere. He could see the prison now, see it from within his armor, but see it from within the lexicon at the same time, the lexicon chanting in the darkness, whispering to the world . . .

I am going to kill . . .

The prison smashed into the slopes. Its four walls groaned, quaked, and began to fall away, so slowly, so very, very slowly . . .

I am going to . . . to kill . . .

He leapt over a ravine, hurtling toward the black prison like a shooting star.

And as he landed, he saw her.

She was waiting for him. Standing in the bracken among the shadows of the deep forest to his right, her hair a pale silver cloud, her hands purpled and rotting.

No, he thought.

She bowed her head. The darkness seemed to grow about her.

No, I don't want to see! Not now! Not now!

Things blurred.

28

Clef stands upon the narrow bridge, the menders' hall low and sprawling just beyond the moat. He is waiting, and trying very hard not to cry.

He stares at the stonework in the bridge before him. This is a place he has returned to many times in his life, and the visits have often been joyous: this is where his life changed, where he met his love, where the arc of his days suddenly bent toward contentment.

But it is not a comfort now. The knowledge of so many past caresses and kisses now feels like dreadful mockery.

He sees movement at the end of the bridge. His wife is talking to someone there at the door to the hall. He waits, impatient and terrified, the moon huge and full overhead in the night sky, the streets of the city silent and still—except for the sound of coughing, and somewhere weeping.

He listens to the coughing. It drags on for a long time, and the longer he listens to it the more he wilts.

He bows his head and dries his tears. For the walls that Clef helped design so long ago can keep out many things—but not this. Not plague. Not pestilence.

He sees she is returning to him, and he stops pacing. He watches her advance, again struck by her beauty, tarnished only by the sorrow in her face. On her hip is a small child—a boy, no more than three years old. The child looks tired. It is well past his bedtime.

"I have it arranged," she says hoarsely as she nears him. "They will let you in. But only for a minute."

He swallows, nods, and follows her. He has never walked down this bridge, not once, and she is breaking many rules to do this. But many rules have unraveled since the plague first raised its head in this city.

The menders at the gate glower at him as he nears. "I only let you in out of pity," says one, a man. "And because of how much you both have labored for us all. But you must *come back quickly. Do you understand?"*

Clef nods. "I will," he says, his voice small and strangled.

"There is too much death here," says the man. "If you wish to stay sane, namer, you will leave as quickly as you came."

Clef nods again.

The mender opens the door reluctantly and allows Clef in, too tired to worry much for blasphemy. His wife leads him inside with their son still on her hip, into this hall so loud with coughing, with weeping, with moaning. The child frowns, frightened at the sounds, but does not cry, though he does reach out for Clef, who takes him in his arms.

They turn, and turn, down stairways and through door after door after door. Finally they come to a small chamber at the end of a passageway.

It is a small room, empty except for a curtained bed with scrived lamps on either side of it. The menders stand on one side of the room, their wrappings bound tight about their hands and mouths and eyes, the cloth perfumed with oils to dampen the plague.

"You must keep your distance," they said. "You must stay back."

Clef and his wife nod. Then the menders pull back the curtain about the bed.

A little girl lies upon the bed, wrapped in similar oiled cloth. The menders have wrapped her arms and feet and neck, but her face is free.

Clef looks upon the face of his daughter, his firstborn. Her features still pale and perfect, though her mouth is purpled and bruised from the sickness.

My butterfly, *he thinks.* My little butterfly.

"Oh my God," moans his wife beside him. "Oh my God, my God, my God . . ."

She begins to walk forward to the bed.

"Stay back," says one of the menders. "Stay back and say your goodbyes!"

Clef is frozen as his wife approaches. He stares at the face of his daughter, mere breaths from the precipice of death.

The menders rush forward to hold back his wife. She reaches out with one arm, reaching for the little body in the bed, trying to touch her once more, but they will let her go no farther.

"My God!" screams his wife. "No, no, my God, my God!"

"Say your goodbyes and go!" say the menders. "Give your love and go!"

The world is all screaming. Clef is holding his son tight, holding him tight, gripping his tiny body so much that the boy cries out.

"Papa, stop!" cries the child.

"No!" shrieks his wife. "No, no, no, please, no!"

"Papa!" says the child. "Papa, stop, stop, stop!"

The screams build and build around him, and then . . .

Then he feels it.

A thorn in his mind.

His heart is a lock, and his thoughts are the key.

The world is full of shifting names about him, names that stand in the shadows of existence and come forward only occasionally, only stepping close to light during that moment of passage, the sudden, merciless transmutation from life to . . . to . . .

He should look away. He should shut his eyes and look away. But he does not.

Clef sees the names in the world behind the world. He sees them all about his daughter's bed, wreathing where she lays. His breath leaves him and he falls to his knees in awe, and he realizes the names are describing something to him. They are showing him something, maybe. Something that has been hidden behind the curtains of all the world, waiting for him.

He hears his voice as if it is from a long, long ways away.

He whispers: "A . . . A door?"

29

Clef stood in the forest, staring as the prison descended to him, gently falling from the sky.

He realized he was screaming. He was screaming: "*Stay with me! Stay with me!*" Yet his voice rig was damaged, so it was inhumanly loud, inhumanly deep, his malformed words echoing across the broken valley.

The black walls of the prison fell away, the box opening before him like a flower. And in the middle stood . . .

(papa stop)

A man in black.

He was looking away, his back to Clef, peering into the distance as if struck by the sight of this place. Clef was sprinting toward him, running as fast as he could, but then . . .

The man in black turned.

His face blank, gleaming, eyeless, expressionless . . . and then he cocked his head.

And spoke.

He bellowed: "*CLAVIEDES!*"

The anger in his voice, the fury, the sorrow. Without even realizing it, Clef stopped where he stood, transfixed.

For a moment Crasedes was still. But then he shook with rage and screamed: *"I DIDN'T MEAN TO COME FOR ME! I DIDN'T MEAN THAT, YOU DAMNED, DAMNED FOOL!"*

Then he flexed his legs, as if squatting to the ground, and he jumped. He rose into the sky . . .

But then he didn't stop. He just kept rising.

Clef watched, stunned, as Crasedes shot into the sky.

Berenice, Claudia, and Diela stared as the tiny black figure shot up like a flea leaping from the back of a hog—and then it ascended, shooting straight up into the noon sky until it was smaller than a poppy seed, and then it was gone.

They stood there for a moment, faint with surprise, unsure whether to believe what they'd just seen.

"Well," said Diela. "I guess he can fly now."

30

Berenice ran.

She ran as afternoon faded into evening, her breath ragged in her lungs, her knees aching, her ankles screaming, the inside of her sheath suit and her mouth caked with dust. She ran on, and on, and on, endlessly into the forest, clambering down the rocky slopes, staggering on as fast as she could with Claudia and Diela just behind her.

<*Hurry!*> she cried at them. <*Hurry, hurry!*>

<*Hurrying's all we've goddamn been doing,*> panted Claudia, <*for the past four hours!*>

Berenice stopped to help Diela climb down a shelf of rock. There was a snap, and a scrived bolt smashed into the stones just overhead, showering them with powdered rock.

<*Too close!*> cried Berenice. She leapt down to where the slopes ended in a tiny mountain stream, gasping as the frigid water sloshed into her boots. She looked up and saw figures on the rim of the rocks above them, perhaps a half mile up, pointing espringals down at them. <*Move, move!*>

They sprinted on into the stream, bolts pouring down around them. They had been running ever since the collapse of the prison, since Clef destroyed the lexicon within the giant lorica, fleeing the sudden onslaught of hosts that had swarmed through the trees in the wake of all that destruction. She did not know what had happened to Clef or Sancia, or even where they were. It was an unusual and uncomfortable sensation, for she had always felt them nearby for the past few years.

I'm too far away from them, she thought. *Too far, too far . . . If they're even . . . If my wife is even . . .*

She could not bear the thought. She focused instead on their flight, and safety.

They kept running. Bolts rained about them. As terrifying as it was, all Berenice wanted to do was stop, sit, and rest. Her legs were like lead, her lungs were aching, and every part of her hurt. Yet still they ran.

Berenice frankly had no idea how the hosts were operational—having destroyed such a critical lexicon, she thought they *should* have all been freed—but she had a dark suspicion as to why they still seemed under Tevanne's spell.

She glanced back at the skies behind them. *Because one of those things is near. One of those flying cities must be close—probably chasing the very thing we freed.*

The thought did not console her. Berenice remembered the absurdity of the moment, the sheer madness of it all: Crasedes standing there, weak and vulnerable; Clef, huge and towering in his armor, with every advantage to his favor; and yet, he'd just . . . stood motionless, watching, until Crasedes effortlessly sailed away.

Did we just doom creation? Was this a victory? Or did we just delay the inevitable?

Then she felt a warmth in the back of her mind. It twisted into fear, wrath, weariness, and then . . .

<BER!> cried Sancia's voice. *<Ber! I have you, I have you! You're close, you're close!>*

All three of them gasped with relief as Sancia's voice filtered into their minds. Berenice choked back a cry. *<You're alive!>* she said. *<You're alive, you're alive!>*

She pathed to Sancia and felt her location; perhaps five miles downstream from them, on the western side of a nearby ridge. And with her . . .

<*Ber,*> said Clef's voice. <*I'll come to you. I'll get you here safe. But don't stop running.*> His voice was husky, quiet, perhaps defeated.

In what seemed like mere seconds there was a shadow passing above, and then Clef slammed into the ground just behind it. Berenice stared at the sight of him. She'd known he'd taken tremendous damage during his fight, but it was still startling to see: his helmet was smashed in, his right arm seemed about to fall off, and his legs had gaping holes in them, with pieces peeled away about his thighs.

<*I can take you one at a time,*> he said.

<*Take us?*> said Claudia. <*How?*>

<*I'll hold you. And we'll jump.*> He held out his arms, or what was left of them. <*Climb on me. Now.*>

Again, his tone was odd. Then Berenice realized: even in moments of panic, there'd always been a sly and syncopated quality to Clef's words, a clever joy running behind all his commentary; yet now that was gone. Now his sentences were short, his tone flat.

<*Diela first,*> said Berenice. <*Then Claudia. Then me.*>

Clef stood totally still as Diela climbed into his arms. Then his armor sprang to life, and he cradled her in a curiously paternal posture, pushing her knees close to her neck. Then he squatted, leapt, and flew up into the air, until they lost him in the evening skies.

"Holy shit," said Claudia.

There was a crack, and then another bolt slammed into a tree nearby. Berenice looked back. The light was dying in the sky, but she could still see movement on the slopes behind them.

<*Keep running!*> Berenice said.

They sprinted on. Within seconds, Clef had descended from the sky again, scooped up Claudia in his arms, and bounded away again. Berenice ran on alone. Another stretch of seconds, and then he'd returned, his big boots slamming into the gravelly soil.

He held out his arms to her. <*Come on.*>

The jump was terrifying. Berenice had never experienced anything like it before, and stranger still was the awareness that the object holding her was altering its own gravity and density as it flew. But he floated down softly between a gap in the pine branches, and they landed safely in the brush beside Sancia and the rest of her crew.

Diela and Claudia sat gasping in the pine needles, pulling off their boots and dumping out dust and stones. But Berenice had eyes only for her wife: Sancia looked tired and haggard, and the way she was sitting suggested her hip, back, and possibly knees were paining her again. But she was alive.

<*You look like shit,*> said Sancia.

Berenice looked down and realized she was right. The hands and shins of her sheath suit were nearly shredded, the gray fabric blooming with blood from a thousand little nicks and cuts. She struggled to think for a moment. <*We . . . We couldn't make it back to our deadlamp,*> she said. <*There were too many, we just had to run.*>

<*Us neither,*> said Sancia. <*Clef scooped me up from that broken lexicon, but when we got to our ride, it was swarming with hosts. He just held me and jumped in your direction. It's a miracle we found you at all.*>

<*So,*> said Claudia grimly. <*Are we stuck up here?*>

There was a silence.

<*Are we stuck up here,*> said Claudia, firmer, <*at the top of some goddamned mountains, with a whole army chasing us, and nowhere to go?*>

<*And . . . did we even win?*> said Diela. <*By freeing Crasedes, have we . . . did we accomplish what we came here to d—*>

<*No!*> snarled Sancia. <*No, we goddamn well didn't! Tevanne could still catch Crasedes, and then we're right back where we started!*>

Another silence. Diela looked away, abashed.

<*I can look about,*> said Clef. <*See what our options are, where the enemy is, then just keep moving us all to where they* aren't. *If we can get out of these mountains, maybe . . . maybe we can get clear.*> His battered helmet shifted to stare north. <*Maybe.*>

<*Do so,*> said Berenice. <*Just keep jumping us along, carrying us one by one. That's all we can manage.*>

What followed was the most bizarre journey Berenice had ever taken in her life. The four of them would hide in some clutch of trees or behind a mound of stones and wait for Clef to come hurtling out of the dark skies to snatch them up and fly away again, like a fairy-tale ghoul stealing children in the night. At first it was oddly joyous, riding on his metal body and floating through the skies; but when they had to do it again, and again, and again, it became onerous and dreadful.

Worse still was the sight of the mountains at the apex of his leaps. As the sky darkened they began to see the pinkish, whitish lights filtering through the steppes and the forests as roving lanterns searched them out—paired, presumably, with cohorts of Tevanni hosts. Every time they jumped there seemed to be more: more lights, more lanterns, like the mountains were bleeding luminescence itself.

The long night continued. Hide and jump, and hide and jump. Diela and Claudia kept nodding off as they waited Clef's return, and Berenice mercilessly nudged them awake. <*Sleep when it's safe,*> she said. <*And we're not safe yet.*>

But she knew by the position of the moon that it was terribly late, close to midnight.

How much longer can we last? How much farther can we go, with barely any food or armaments, and no sleep?

Finally Clef bore Berenice to one last hiding spot, joining the others in a tiny copse of pines along a ridge. Rather than grabbing Sancia and leaping once more, he slowly looked around. <*We're in a tight spot,*> said Clef. <*I'm not sure how to jump next. And they're all getting close.*>

<*What can we do?*> asked Berenice, squatting in the dark.

<*Surrender isn't an option,*> said Sancia.

<*Never said it was,*> said Clef.

There was a silence. The night was filled with quiet sounds of movement: a shifting of stones, a snap of a branch, a clattering as feet ran through mounds of rocky gravel. Diela stared out at the pink-strobed darkness, her eyes wide and fearful.

<*Then what?*> said Berenice.

<*There's one option,*> said Clef. <*I could . . . clear the way.*> He pointed up to the northwest. <*There's a narrow spine of rock there. Tevanne's forces are thin on the other side, for now. I could break through it, break through them, and you all could follow. But it'll be dangerous. The ridge could fall apar—*>

Then a voice echoed through the darkness:

"Sancia."

They all jumped. The sound of the voice was so *strange,* so disturbing, yet Berenice couldn't quite identify why. Then it spoke again, saying once more, *"Sancia."*

"Oh my God," said Diela softly. "It's all of them . . ."

Berenice realized she was right: the hosts that Tevanne was controlling were speaking all at once, one identity speaking through thousands of mouths. It was like the entire mountains were calling out in the dark, chanting: *"Sancia. Sancia. Sancia."*

Sancia slowly leaned forward and covered her ears with her hands. <*Oh God,*> she said. <*Please, make it stop . . .* >

"Sancia," said Tevanne. *"Sancia, Sancia. It is done. It is over."*

Clef crouched lower. <*They're getting very close . . .* > His arm rose and pointed to the south. <*Down there.*>

Berenice saw he was right: pink and white light was bleeding through the trees below, accompanied by the sound of dozens of footsteps.

"I will spare you," said Tevanne. *"I will spare you. But only if you give in."*

Sancia's fingers were digging into her scalp over her ears, her knuckles white with strain.

"Surrender," said Tevanne. *"Surrender. Please."*

<*Very close now,*> said Clef softly. <*Forty of them, just down there.*>

"You can become me," whispered Tevanne in the strobing darkness. *"I can show you. I can show you what it is like to know so* much . . ."

Sancia shook beside Berenice. Berenice looked at her wife, thinking, and said, <*Clef. Do it.*>

<*Do what?*> said Clef.

<*Clear the way ahead. And we'll follow.*>

Clef looked at her for a long time. Then he said, <*Get ready. Run when I tell you to.*>

He crouched down and sailed off into the darkness. There was a long silence, broken only by Tevanne's whispering words—and then there was a *crack,* followed by a tremendous rumbling.

<*Move!*> cried Clef. <*Move, now, now!*>

They shot to their feet and sprinted up the slope toward Clef. The air was hazy with dust once more, now caught in the swirling lights of the hosts, but worse was blindly running through the shifting ground: Clef had destabilized the entire hilltop, and stones and silt were pouring down around them.

They ran through the newly made gap in the hillside, panicked and sightless. Everything seemed to be swirling, flashing, curling; bolts poured into the stones about them; Berenice heard Claudia screaming, Sancia swearing; Tevanne was crying, *"Sancia! Sancia!";* she saw Clef standing in the narrow gap, holding up a tremendous boulder and tossing it aside, then another, and another; then she came to the end of the gap he'd made and looked beyond.

The slopes below were swarming with light. Tevanne, it seemed, had reacted fast. There was nowhere to run.

<*No,*> said Berenice faintly. <*No, no . . .* >

Then a flash of pain in her right arm—but she realized instantly that it was not *her* pain.

She heard Diela screaming in agony. She ran through the dusty darkness, and found the girl lying on the ground, her right hand trapped under a tremendous stone that must have toppled down from the broken ridge. Berenice knelt, crying, and tried to heave it off, but it was too heavy.

<*Shit!*> cried Clef. Suddenly he was beside her, effortlessly heaving the rock away. <*Shit, shit, shit!*>

Berenice could not see the injury, but she felt wetness and warmth on Diela's hand, and a shard of something sharp—bone, certainly. She ripped off a belt, wrapped it around the girl's biceps, and cinched it tight.

The world was swirling with lights around them. The air was thick with the sound of footsteps and chants of *"Sancia, Sancia . . ."*

Sancia was kneeling beside her, holding Diela and rocking back and forth. "Oh no. Oh no, no, no . . ."

"What do we do?" screamed Claudia. "Do we run?"

"Hell no!" snarled Berenice. She tied off the belt. "I'm not leaving her!"

"Too many!" cried Clef. His armor rattled and clanked as he paced around them, trying to face their pursuers on all sides. "Too . . . too many!"

Claudia had her espringal out and was wheeling about, unsure where to point it.

"Sancia, Sancia . . ."

Diela screamed and screamed.

Berenice shut her eyes.

Here it is. Here it comes . . .

Diela's screams rose and rose. A whole world of screaming, the black night shrieking madly.

And then Berenice realized . . . that wasn't Diela screaming.

It was the hosts. They weren't talking anymore. They were all screaming at once.

She opened her eyes. The swirling lights had stopped, as had the sound of footsteps. Now there was only shrieking, like the thousands of hosts in this valley were in indescribable agony . . .

"What the hell!" cried Claudia. "What the hell is going on!"

Berenice saw movement to the north. The lamps remained frozen in space, but . . . but something was rising before them.

She gasped. It was a body, she realized, a human body—no, it was *dozens* of human bodies, maybe hundreds, rising straight up in the air like puppets from strings, their arms and legs splayed out . . . and they were screaming.

A nausea poured into Berenice's belly—but this one was very, very familiar.

"No!" screamed Sancia. "No! No, no, no, not him! *Not him!*"

Berenice watched, horrified, as the shadowy bodies of the hosts seemed to suddenly crumple, like their flesh and bones were paper crumpled up by an artist dissatisfied with his sketch. There was a curiously wet sound from all around the valley, like suddenly scattered showers, and a bright coppery smell suffused the dusty wind.

Then, in an instant, all the lanterns went out, and the valley was blanketed in utter blackness.

Oh no, thought Berenice. *Oh no, oh no, oh no . . .*

The silence stretched on and on, the only sound Diela's whimpering at her feet.

And then . . .

A tremendous crash from a few feet beyond them, like something huge had just fallen out of the sky.

Berenice dove to cover Sancia and Diela as best she could. But then, nothing happened. The night remained dark and silent.

<*Guys,*> said Clef softly. <*Guys, holy shit. Holy shit, it's our deadlamp . . .* >

Berenice released Sancia and Diela, and cautiously peeked over her shoulder. She saw Clef was right: a deadlamp lay on the slopes below them, its square form dimly lit in the light of the smoky moon.

Something dropped from the dark skies to alight on top of the deadlamp.

A man, or something man-shaped. Wearing a black cloak, and a black mask that gleamed even in this low light—though a narrow crack now ran through its façade from its chin to its brow.

Crasedes Magnus sat cross-legged on top of their deadlamp, his head resting on his knuckles like a child bored at a picnic.

"Good evening," he said, his voice deep and silky. "I think you lost this."

31

There was a long, awful silence, broken only by Diela's whimpering. Berenice stared at Crasedes, bewildered, terrified, unsure whether to believe this was really happening.

Then Sancia shot to her feet. "*Scrum* you!" she snarled. "You piece of shit! What the hell do you want? What the hell do you *want*!"

"To leave," Crasedes said simply. "Preferably very rapidly." He looked up at the night sky. "I won't have long, unfortunately. Too much damage was done to me . . ."

"Damage? To *you*? You . . . you bastard!" snarled Sancia. "You rotten, scrumming *bastard*! Why shouldn't I tell Clef to tear you apart, kill you right now, and finish the job we started eight years ago?"

Berenice glanced at Clef. He seemed far from ready for such a task: he was utterly frozen, his empty eyes fixed on Crasedes.

"Because you know I'm not going to let him," said Crasedes. "It's deepest dark. The world is weak. No matter Clef's strength, this is *my* time." He cocked his head. "But I hope you notice . . .

I'm not using it to harm you. Or to rip Clef out of that suit of armor and use him to tear reality asunder. Which I very well could. Instead, I'm *politely* asking you to get in your vessel here and come with me to safety. Because otherwise, you and your friends will be left to a fate worse than death."

"You . . . You really think I could believe you?" spat Sancia. "That I'd ever, *ever* believe you might help us?"

"What I think you should believe," Crasedes said, "is that there are about thirty . . . What did you call them just now? Deadlamps? Fine enough—thirty *deadlamps* closing in on this exact spot to hunt me down. I personally have no intention of being here when they arrive. Whether *you* are here is your choice."

There was a long, icy silence as Sancia and Crasedes stared at each other.

"I'd have been here sooner," said Crasedes quietly, "but I had other matters to manage. Yet I've come to offer you something more than just safety." He leaned forward and quietly said, "We both know what Tevanne wants. But only I know where it *is*."

Another silence.

Berenice glanced at her wife and gripped her hand. *<San, I . . . I think we should—>*

<The bastard,> said Sancia. *<The utter, utter bastard . . . >*

<Yes. I know. But we're in a bastard of a situation.>

Sancia shut her eyes. Then she took a deep breath, and said, "Help us get Diela into the deadlamp."

Sancia, Claudia, and Berenice helped strap Diela into her seat within the lamp, gingerly shifting her broken arm as they wound the cords about her body, then moved to take their own seats. Crasedes, oddly enough, chose to follow them inside.

Berenice gagged, unable to bear the presence of a hierophant so near. "Can . . . Can you at least fly *alongside* us?" she said.

"I would prefer to, of course—but I'm afraid not," he said. "In a few hours, I will no longer be able to trust myself." He bent slightly, like he was carrying a tremendous weight. "Though it might be invisible to you, I am . . . wounded." He sat on the floor at their feet, staring ahead—perhaps at Clef, who resumed his position at the front of the lamp, reconnecting himself and his little portable lexicon to the vessel's workings.

"Where are we going?" asked Sancia sullenly.

"Up," said Crasedes. "And far to the north, to the wastes past the Trizti Mountains. I will guide you to safety from there."

"The Trizti Mountains?" said Claudia. "God, I've only seen them on maps, but . . . those have to be *hours* away."

"Then I suggest you start now," he said, "so we can be there all the sooner."

"How will we know the way is actually safe?" said Berenice.

Crasedes looked at her with his blank dark eyes. "I've been fighting this war on the front lines for a long, long time. I know a *great* deal more about our enemy than you do." Again, he looked upward, as if he could see the sky through the roof of their vessel. "Enough to know we need to leave. *Now.* Otherwise, I'll be of no use to you."

The deadlamp silently lifted off the forest floor. Then, as before, they rocketed up, hurtling into the highest layers of the atmosphere. Berenice grimaced as she felt the blood leave her face, and Diela cried out in pain, but they kept rising, and rising, sailing into the heavens. Though it was awful, Berenice couldn't help but feel relief that they were leaving that miserable valley and all its horrors far behind.

Diela kept whimpering and sobbing as she cradled her broken arm. Finally Sancia could bear it no more. She unstrapped herself and wobblingly approached the girl. <*Your head will hurt when you wake,*> she said, rummaging in a back pocket. <*But it'll hurt less than what you're going through now.*>

She produced a dolorspina dart and jabbed it into the girl's arm. Diela yelped, but then her head lolled to the side and she was still. Sancia returned to her seat, but Berenice didn't need to be twinned with her to know her thoughts: her wife's face was ashen and miserable, and it remained that way for the rest of their ascent.

Then Clef quietly whispered: <*Berenice?*>

<*Yes?*> Berenice said.

<*I hate to say this now, but . . . remember when we saw one of those floating city things?*>

<Ah—yes?>

<Well . . . I think we've got another one straight ahead. To the north. Where he told us to fly.>

Berenice looked at the detector rig, still situated just behind Clef, and saw the empty space was whirling with lead beads—but just as he'd said, a huge clutch of beads was floating in the space straight north from them.

<Do . . . Do you want me to rise?> said Clef. *<Shoot up into the cold parts of the sky again? Or do you want me t—>*

"Please continue straight north," said Crasedes.

"We can't," snapped Sancia. "There's a big flying thing in the way, asshole."

Crasedes cocked his head thoughtfully. "Not for much longer. The way is safe, I assure you."

"It . . . what?" said Claudia.

Then Berenice pointed at the detector rig. "Look."

They studied the beads whirling about in the large glass globe—but the clutch of beads designating the city, they saw, was slowly descending, falling through the air little by little, until it would be well below them.

"The way is safe," said Crasedes again. "I assure you."

They looked at one another.

<Clef,> said Sancia. *<I guess . . . do as he says.>*

<Okay, but . . . Damn. There's a lot of smoke out there . . . > said Clef.

Berenice frowned. She glanced at Crasedes, still as a statue on the floor. Then she unstrapped herself and crawled to the center of the floor, before where Crasedes sat, her stomach thrumming with nausea. He did not react—he simply sat there.

<Ber?> said Sancia. *<What the hell are you doing?>*

Berenice unlocked the hatch in the floor and pulled it back. Instantly, the interior of the deadlamp filled up with a bright, wicked yellow light, pouring through the window.

She looked below, and gasped. "Oh my God . . ."

Just like the time before, they were miles above the surface of the world, with one of Tevanne's floating cities below them—but this one was crawling with fire and bleeding black smoke, its towers shattered and smoldering, and it did not float upright but rather at an angle, this titanic mass of stone and metal reeling through the skies like a damaged ship taking on water. The sheer scale of destruction was incomprehensible: it was as if an entire moon were instead a frail moth that had flitted too close to a candle flame and was now whirling away into the night as its tiny, dusty wings disintegrated.

"My God," said Claudia hoarsely. "My God, my God . . ."

Sancia slowly looked up at Crasedes. "What did you do?" she asked.

He stared back at her, his gleaming black mask lit from below by the light of the enormous flames. "I told you," he said smoothly, "I had other matters to manage before I came to assist you. The way is safe." He pointed ahead. "Now. North, please."

Once they leveled out and their flight grew even, Berenice and Claudia unstrapped themselves and knelt before Diela, cleaning her wounds, though they knew they wouldn't be able to offer any real help until the deadlamp landed: every tiny dip and bob made surgery unthinkable, and they were all fighting the nausea from the swoops and swirls of the deadlamp—along with the nausea that came from having a hierophant sitting cross-legged at your feet.

<*Will she keep the arm?*> asked Sancia.

<*I don't know,*> said Berenice. <*I think so. But if we can't set the bones soon . . . I'm not sure she should. It would be better to . . . cut.*>

Sancia stared at Diela's pale, sweating face and turned to look at Crasedes. "All this, for you," she said hoarsely.

Crasedes turned to look at her but did not speak.

"How do we even know if we came in time?" Sancia asked. "What if you already gave it all up? Told Tevanne all you knew?"

He stared back at her, implacable and inscrutable.

"You piece of shit," breathed Sancia. "Did you *trick* us into rescuing you? To risk it all, for you?"

"I did not trick you," said Crasedes. "I did not even *ask* you to come save me. I'd hoped you were farther along in the fight than I was . . ." He looked ahead at Clef. "But it seems I was mistaken."

"Do you understand what you did to . . . to this girl here . . ."

She looked at Diela, and tears sprang to her eyes. "Just to break you out. A rotten thing, like you."

Crasedes regarded her for a moment. "I won't have long," he said.

"Long for what?" asked Berenice.

"Long until . . . Well. You will see," he said. "But might as well make use of myself while I can . . ." He raised his hand, flexed his black gloved fingers very slightly . . . and then the air seemed to quake.

Diela awoke, shrieking with pain. She shook in her seat, flinging her head from side to side, her mangled arm stuck straight out—and yet Berenice could see her arm was changing, rippling, the shards of protruding bone slowly retracting and sliding back within her torn muscles.

"What are you doing?" screamed Sancia. "Stop it! *Stop it!*"

But he did not: Crasedes kept gently twisting his hand in the air, and Diela kept shrieking, louder and louder, until she finally passed back out.

"Diela?" cried Berenice. *"Diela?"*

Crasedes finally lowered his hand, and the strange pulsing in the air ceased. Diela's arm stopped quaking, but she didn't wake.

"There," he said. "Her fractures should be reset now. Much better than it was before."

Blinking, Berenice studied Diela's arm and saw he was right: the awful angles and shards of bone were all gone, and though her flesh was still torn in many places and would need treatment, the injury was leagues better than before.

"How do we know it's right?" asked Claudia. "I mean . . . There were a *lot* of fractures."

Crasedes sat back. "I am well acquainted with the manipulation of the human body, to say the least," he said. "A broken arm, a few fingers, a handful of torn ligaments—this is, comparatively, a simple fix. Though I admit . . . *repair* is not usually my priority."

"Are you expecting us to say thank you for that?" asked Sancia. "God, the way she screamed . . ."

"I don't expect you to say anything," he said. "Rather, I will need you and all your people in as good a condition as you can manage for what must be done next."

"We're not doing any bullshit for you," snarled Sancia.

"This would not be just for me, Sancia. For once, I expect you and I want the same thing." He looked around at them. "I have only a few more moments, but . . . I assume you all are *somewhat* aware of what Tevanne seeks, yes? The reason I was imprisoned?"

There was a tense pause.

"The door," said Berenice quietly. "The chamber at the center of the world."

"Yes," Crasedes said. "The aperture to the reality behind reality." He sat back, seeming to melt into the shadows in the corner of the deadlamp. "The enemy seeks understanding of it. All of its will is bent on creating its own. But we have been lucky so far, for it has progressed very little. It knows neither what the aperture is, nor how it came about, nor how to create its own. The method remains outside its reach."

Sancia and Berenice grudgingly returned to their seats.

"How certain are you of this?" asked Berenice.

"Very. Because it captured me and interrogated me specifically in hopes of learning this method. But . . . in this, it was disappointed, as this knowledge was stolen from my thoughts long ago."

"By Valeria," said Sancia. "When she tricked you and ruined you."

"Correct," he said icily. "But the enemy is not out of options, unfortunately. If you cannot learn how to make a thing, and if no one will teach you its making . . . you instead find an *example* of the thing, and then divine the nature of its making."

Berenice felt her skin break out in chills. "God . . ." she said. "Wait. Wait, are you saying that . . . that more doors are out there, *even now*? An example for it to find, and copy?"

He nodded. "That is my concern," he said.

"What the hell!" said Sancia. "You left goddamned holes in reality just . . . just sitting all over the place?"

"Certainly not," he said. "I quite wisely destroyed all trace of my own works of this sort. I did it at the very start of my war with the construct, to prevent it from falling into her hands. But Tevanne has come to believe one example *still remains*. An aperture that I myself did not know existed. One I did *not* make, but rather one fashioned by another. And I have come to believe Tevanne is correct in this estimation. The only choice now is to find this last example, this last door—and destroy it before the enemy can get to it." He looked around at them. "This is a responsibility we all must bear. Together, whether we like it or not."

They considered the proposition, their faces grim in the rattling dark.

<*This all sounds scrumming mad as hell,*> said Claudia.

<*True, but we're dealing with mad things,*> said Berenice. <*Do we believe him?*>

<*Doesn't sound like the Crasedes I know,*> said Sancia. <*He was never the type of asshole to destroy a weapon rather than use i—*>

"You may be wondering why I would not use this aperture for my own ends," said Crasedes.

Berenice suppressed an eye roll. <*Well. Here we go.*>

"But it is because I no longer have the capacity," he said. He bowed his head very slightly. "It is true that one could enact commands on the other side of the door, enabling edits and changes on a scale you can hardly fathom. But *I* cannot. I am far too weak. To do so would destroy me, utterly and finally. So. Destruction is my only choice."

Berenice studied him. Despite the damage he'd just inflicted on Tevanne's forces, she found he did look weak: there was something in the stoop in his shoulders, the way he bent his head, the arthritic stiffness in his limbs. Though back in Old Tevanne he'd supposedly been a shadow of his former self, now he seemed even a shadow of that.

"Assuming all of this is true," Berenice said. "Are you sure you know where this door is? That it's in . . . in these wastes you mentioned?"

"I have great certainty that it can be found there," Crasedes said.

"Then . . . why haven't you destroyed it already?" she asked. "You've had eight years now. Why?"

"The simple answer is, I did not know of its existence at all," said Crasedes. "But the enemy questioned me relentlessly. From its questioning, I gleaned that it had fragments of knowledge—it asked me about landscapes, about histories, about plagues, great migrations, and more. It could make no sense of the knowledge it had . . . but it made sense to *me,* for I am far older than it, and I know much more." He cocked his head. "Though I do not know the door's *exact* location, I came to realize the answer lay in our current destination—the wastes."

"And you didn't tell Tevanne that?" asked Sancia suspiciously.

"If I had," he said, "would I still exist? Would you?"

"But how did you get interrogated in the first place?" said Berenice. "How did Tevanne capture y—"

But Crasedes shook his head. "I can appreciate all your concerns—but enough. I've answered all the questions I can. We are out of time. Or rather, *I* am out of time."

"What the hell do you mean?" asked Sancia. "How can we trust you if you won't answer our questions?"

"Because soon I will not be able to!" he snapped. "My imprisonment did not come without . . . consequences." He sighed. "I will have to manage those consequences as the sun rises and I grow weak."

"What consequences?" demanded Sancia. "You look fine to me."

Crasedes ignored her and looked to Berenice. "You—you seem a sensible one. For the next hours, I will not be able to protect you. I may not even be able to move. Simply continue north, past the Trizti Mountains, and keep me safe." He paused. "I will be at your mercy. Most utterly. I will have no choice but to trust you. So I must ask—will you trust *me*? Will you keep me safe and help me sabotage our enemy's plans?"

Berenice grimaced, her stomach still rippling with nausea. It suddenly seemed so mad that they had traveled halfway across the world to kill this person, this thing, and yet now they were being asked to watch over him like a slumbering child.

<*Clef,*> asked Berenice, <*how long would it take for us to fly back to Giva? Is there any way back from here?*>

<*God only knows,*> said Clef. <*We'd have to either fly miles out of our way or go over the whole of Tevanne's lands. I'm sure it'll have prepared for us by now.*> There was a bump as the deadlamp was jostled by some errant gust of wind. <*I like flying, but I'd be reluctant to try that.*>

<*Then we're really stuck here,*> said Claudia morosely. <*We're stuck at the top of the world with an army at our heels, and nothing but a mad, broken hierophant for company.*>

Berenice gripped the ropes tying her to her seat. She had so desperately wanted this to be over, to be *done*. They had given enough: of their blood, of their labor, of their panic and their worry. The risks had been high so far, and they seemed to only grow higher from here.

She looked at Crasedes, who was still watching her with his cold, vacant gaze. "Well?" he said.

She turned to Sancia, who looked plainly exhausted. <*I don't know,*> Sancia said. <*I honestly don't.*>

Every time we pluck at a cord in the knot we're in, Berenice thought, *two other kinks grow tighter.*

She nodded. "Fine. We'll do it."

Crasedes kept staring at her.

"Did you hear me?" she said. "We'll do it. We'll help you."

Still Crasedes did nothing, sitting frozen with his masked face fixed on hers.

"Uh . . . hello?" said Berenice.

Finally Crasedes moved: he sat forward and looked about as if somewhat bewildered. "What . . . Wh-What time is it?" he asked shakily.

"Huh?" said Claudia.

"Right now, what . . . What time is it?" he said. "Right *now*?"

They stared at him, confounded.

"Answer me, please!" He looked wildly around before finally looking at Berenice. "How long has it been since you freed me?"

"You don't know?" said Berenice.

"No!" he said angrily. "No, I don't know! Answer quickly, or else I'll lose time again!"

<*Is this, uh,*> said Claudia, <*the consequences he was talking about?*>

<*Sancia?*> said Berenice. <*Do you remember him doing this back in Old Tevanne?*>

<*Hell no,*> said Sancia. <*This is new.*>

"It's been just over forty minutes since we rescued you," said Berenice.

"Forty minutes?" he repeated. "You're sure?"

"Yes. Why?"

"Not forty days? Or forty . . . forty years?"

"N-No? Of course not."

"Of course not," he said faintly. He sat back, then looked around somewhat absently, until he saw Sancia. "That's right. If . . . If Sancia is here, it can't have been that long. Not that long . . ." He touched the sides of his masked face, like he was trying to hold his skull together. "How . . . How long has the war lasted?"

"Eight years," said Sancia.

"Eight years . . ." he said quietly. "Which calendar are you using?"

"The Tevanni one, of course," said Berenice.

He looked away, troubled. "Tevanni . . . are we in the month of Dimanta?"

"Furio," said Berenice. "It's the tenth of the month of Furio."

"Furio," he said softly. "The tenth. Tevanni. Eight years. Yes." He sat for a moment with his chin in his black gloved hands, like he was struggling with a tremendous math problem. "I just . . . I just find I can't quite . . . remember . . . when . . ." Then he groaned miserably and toppled backward, his masked head striking the floor of the deadlamp with a painful *clunk,* and was still.

They stared.

"Holy shit," said Claudia. "Is he dead?"

Sancia narrowed her eyes, flexing her scrived sight. <*He's not dead. He's still the giant, living tangle of horrid scrivings he's always been. Right, Clef?*>

<*Right,*> said Clef quietly.

They looked at Crasedes for a long time, still and silent on the floor.

<*Well,*> said Sancia. <*Anyone want to use the first of all hierophants as a footstool?*>

<*I think sleeping is a much better option,*> said Berenice. She grimaced as her stomach curdled again. <*If we can even sleep under these conditions.*>

<*I'll try sleeping for a few minutes,*> said Claudia. She settled back into her seat. <*And then I'm darting myself like Diela, and bearing the hangover.*>

They made crude nests in their uncomfortable seats and settled in, already shivering as the chilly air leaked into the deadlamp. Berenice activated the air heaters Design had made for them, and they helped a good deal, but their bones and joints still felt dreadfully cold, perhaps out of sheer exhaustion.

Yet Sancia did not shut her eyes. She kept glancing at Clef, seated at the front of the deadlamp. Finally she asked, <*What happened back there, Clef?*>

Berenice cracked her eyes in her little nest, waiting.

<*I hesitated,*> said Clef finally. His voice sounded curiously strangled. <*Just a second. But that was all it took.*>

<*Did anything . . . happen?*> asked Sancia.

Berenice furrowed her brow. Happen? What did that mean? Yet the instant she asked it, the answer leaked in from Sancia's thoughts.

Clef: he'd remembered something. Something from long ago, before he was a key. So profound was Berenice's exhaustion that this revelation barely made her pulse quicken.

<*No,*> said Clef. <*I wish I had an explanation. But I don't. I just hesitated.*>

They sat in the dark, the walls of the deadlamp rattling as it hurtled through the skies.

<*Get some sleep, kid,*> sighed Clef. <*I know I sure wish I could.*>

With a last glance at Berenice, Sancia pulled her blanket high around her neck and shut her eyes. Berenice watched her for a moment longer, then studied the rest of her team—Claudia, then Diela, and finally Clef and the monstrosity in black lying on the floor—before closing her eyes as well, and sleep poured into her mind.

Clef watched the world below through the deadlamp's sensory rigs as the sun bloomed on the horizon and cast weak dawn light through the skies.

He saw the mountains below him, tall and ragged and covered with dumps of snow. He saw them taper off to the west, flattening out into a wide arid plain bereft of moisture, and all along the mountain's feet were ruins. Some were ancient: columns, arches, roads, bridges. Others were new: husks of cities, flamed out and bombed out and dissected, like a big game animal field-dressed where it fell.

Ruins upon ruins, he thought as the scrivers slept. *Ruins upon ruins upon ruins . . .*

He sailed on into the dawn. And then, just as before, he felt her.

Sitting in the corner to the left of Crasedes, draped in darkness, her purpled, rotting feet just barely poking past the shadows. She sat motionless as she watched him pilot the deadlamp, not even breathing.

"Are you here," whispered Clef, "to make me remember more?"

As before, she did not move or speak.

"Who are you?" he whispered. "Who were you?"

Nothing.

"Did I open the door?" he asked softly. "Or did you? Or neither of us?"

Still nothing.

"What do you want from me?" he asked. "God, just tell me what you *want*."

And then, for the first time, she moved: she turned her white-wreathed head to look not at Clef but at the corner of the deadlamp, where Crasedes lay crumpled upon the floor in a heap.

Clef followed her gaze, studying the thing that had once been his son. And though the visitor did not speak, he felt an intent emerge in his thoughts, a cold, icy will.

"I see," he whispered. "I see."

IV

THE DOOR

32

Berenice did not sleep well in the deadlamp. It was too cold, with too many drafts of icy air snaking over you; it moved too much, dipping this way and that through the skies; and, of course, it was impossible to get much rest with a hierophant next to you, making your belly bubble away like a soup pot. Still, she tried over and over again to shut her eyes, bury her head in her blanket, and try to find sleep.

Then Clef whispered: <*Ber.*>

Berenice miserably opened her eyes. Everything felt leaden, and every part of her head ached. *I feel like having my eyes shut for so long,* she thought, *only made me more tired.*

<*Ber,*> whispered Clef again. <*You need to see this.*>

<*Are we there?*> she said.

<*No. But . . . we're somewhere. Look through the window. We're just past the Trizti Mountains at the wastes he mentioned. Did you know they looked like this? I didn't.*>

Grumbling wretchedly, Berenice unfastened her straps and climbed out of her nest of blankets. She glanced around before she opened the window. Claudia stirred a bit, sighing in frustration as she attempted sleep. Diela was still passed out, her face tight with pain. Only Sancia seemed to be fast asleep: as the one person most accustomed to discomfort, she could sleep nearly anywhere.

Berenice jealously glared at her wife. *Should have pathed to her and ridden off her sleep . . . if that could even work.*

Then she glanced at the other occupant of the deadlamp: the crumpled black cloth in the corner, and the glint of the black mask within. She had often doubted if there was an actual human body within that cloth, but it seemed especially impossible now.

Either way, she thought as she gripped the sliding window in the bottom of the deadlamp, *he won't wake up.*

Then she slid back the window a crack, peered through it, and gasped.

She saw ragged steppes, feathered with short trees that were dappled with white from late snows; the steppes then flattened out into fields, and beyond those the world was . . .

Torn. There was no other word for it. The very land was torn, gashed and rent, with chasms and canyons stretching deep down into the earth. Even stranger still, the earth here was strangely *silvered*. She thought it might have been snow from the steppes, but the more she watched it fly by beneath them, the more she knew that was wrong.

<*It's glass,*> said Clef.

<*What?*> said Berenice.

<*It's glass,*> he said again. <*The soil here, the sand—it's . . . it's like it was boiled and melted into glass, all at once. It's cracked and crumbled over the years, so it looks all . . . well. Shiny.*>

Berenice stared down into the glimmering, gleaming wastes below, the fields of white slashed through with crevasses of deepest black. <*Being a girl from the tropics, ah, I feel obliged to ask . . . There's not any way this could be a natural phenomenon, correct?*>

<*You got me, Ber,*> said Clef. <*But . . . are all these chasms going in the, ahh, same direction?*>

She craned her head down to the window, peering along the landscape, and saw he was right: sloppy and misshapen and broken though they were, the chasms vaguely appeared to be radiating outward from some point, like the strands of a spider web.

<*What time is it?*> she asked.

<*Just past noon,*> said Clef.

She looked down at Crasedes. <*If we were to put a pathplate in his hands, so he could connect to us just as we do to you, Clef . . . we'd probably be able to hear him, yes?*>

<*Uhh, yeah, theoretically. He is basically a giant rig. But that would mean giving Crasedes access to your thoughts, which seems . . . not great.*>

<*Hm. True. He's not going to wake up anytime soon to tell us where to go, so . . . I say we follow the chasms, yes? If we're looking for a door, or an aperture . . . or, hell, I don't know, these might serve as arrows pointing the way.*>

<*Can do,*> said Clef. The deadlamp tilted to cut through the air.

Sancia and Claudia awoke as they neared the center of the chasms. There was very little water and food left, so they all sipped sparingly at a cup—<*We'll need to save this for Diela,*> Berenice told them—and chewed their bean bread with dry mouths, sitting about the open window like it was a campfire.

Then Clef said, <*I see something.*>

<*What is it?*> asked Berenice.

<*Dunno,*> he said. <*Let me rise up so you can get a look at it . . .* >

The deadlamp tilted up, sailed on for a few dozen more feet—and then came a sharp intake of breath from all three of them.

Nearly two dozen oddly slender, leaning stone spires sprouted out of the land at the center of the chasms. They shone curiously in the reflected light of the flats. They seemed to be wrought of a vividly white stone and resembled the sugar-floss candy Design had figured out how to make back in Giva. Berenice was reminded of a clutch of coral she'd glimpsed once while sailing across the Durazzo—but that comparison felt wrong, because everything about this place was all so *unnatural:* the chasms, the whiteness of these tall spires, and their isolation here on the steppes; and the way they seemed to stagger or lean this way and that like stacks of ivory coins . . . and stranger still, some of the spires were dotted with curious apertures and holes, like the hive of some giant insect.

<*What the hell is this place?*> asked Berenice.

<*I've no idea,*> said Sancia softly. <*But . . . I've seen it before.*> She looked at Clef. <*And so have you.*>

<*Yeah . . .* > said Clef. <*When I pathed to Tevanne and saw its thoughts. It was thinking of this place . . . and silvery writing, curling about a black hole in the face of a gray wall.*>

<*The door,*> said Sancia. <*Holy hell. Could it really be . . . Well, here?*>

There was an uncomfortable silence.

<*I think with Crasedes still out,*> said Berenice, <*we should look closer. Clef—do you see anything worrying?*>

<*No sign of Tevanne,*> said Clef. <*I think we can go in.*>

The deadlamp zoomed closer, circling the clutch of white spires. Some had been unrooted by the chasms, but they had not shattered as they'd fallen and instead remained totally whole. It wasn't until Clef paused over one such fallen tower that Berenice saw it.

The fallen spire was covered with little holes, just like the others . . . but she now saw that the hole had a shape. It was tall and thin, and pointed at the top in a very familiar way.

"A window," she said softly. She looked at the other holes in the side of the tower, and saw she was right. "My God, it's covered in windows. These aren't mountains, they're buildings. They're *towers*. This was a *city*!"

Clef rose again, and she saw she was right: the other spires were covered not just in windows but in the remains of what had to have once been balconies and the occasional length of stairs, complete with chunks of railing.

<*Oh my God,*> said Claudia softly. <*It really is a city. Or it was. Bigger than any of the other hierophantic ruins that I've ever heard described, yeah?*>

<*Yes,*> said Berenice quietly, watching the bonelike towers reach up to them like the spine of some immense serpent buried in the steppes. <*I've never known this place existed at all.*>

Sancia squinted down through the window. <*Yeah . . . but I don't think it's hierophantic.*>

<*What makes you say that?*> asked Claudia.

<*Are you seeing these towers? Like, what's* inside *these towers?*>

There was a pause.

<*Oh,*> said Clef. <*It's so . . . so weak I didn't think to look, but holy* shit . . . >

<*Holy shit what?*> said Claudia. <*What's going on?*>

<*Path to me,*> said Sancia. <*And see.*>

Berenice closed her eyes and did so, feeling her way through to the place behind Sancia's eyes. Then she peered through, and saw.

The towers below shimmered very, very faintly with slender silvery coils of logic. They were *scrived:* or, rather, every single brick and stone was scrived, written with commands to hold together, to stay fixed in space, to control their densities and dependencies and adhesions . . .

<*They scrived every single* brick *in this goddamned place?*> asked Claudia. <*How long must that have taken?*>

<*Decades,*> said Berenice. <*Centuries.*> She shook her head. <*I always thought the buildings of the campos were complicated . . . but God, if we hadn't had lexicons, I guess they would have looked like this. It's just like the broken walls we found back at the valley of ruins.*>

<*I still don't see any sign of Tevanne,*> said Sancia. <*This place is empty. I don't even see any wildlife here. Not even a mouse turd.*>

Claudia looked at Berenice. <*Safe to land, then?*>

Diela moaned slightly and stirred in her sleep, her face dripping wet with sweat.

Claudia felt the girl's brow with one hand. <*She's hot. And her wound still needs much more treatment.*>

<*Land,*> said Berenice. <*Now, Clef.*>

<*Got it,*> he said.

She watched as the world in the window swirled about, then seemed to target a tiny clutch of ruins at the far edge of the city.

<*Trying to find a place that looks stable,*> said Clef. <*Everything else here looks like it could fall apart if so much as a drop of piss struck it. Hold on.*>

They landed on a wide stretch of glassy, sandy soil, beside a handful of broken walls and roofs that in some ancient days might have once been a warehouse or storehouse. Then they climbed out and carefully carried Diela into the ruins.

Clef fetched Crasedes from the deadlamp, dumping him along the wall as though he were a sack of melons, and then they went to work. They used scrived firestarters to start a blaze, boiled what was left of their drinking water, and sterilized their medical tools. Then Berenice, who had the best eyes and the steadiest hands, began carefully cleaning and stitching up Diela's wounds.

The work took hours, and she noted with dismay that the girl did not moan or twitch as the needle entered and exited her flesh.

<*What do we have in the way of medicine?*> asked Sancia.

<*Astrazella,*> said Claudia. She took out a small tincture from their physiquere's pack and held it up. <*It helps fight fevers and pains. It's the best we have, but . . .* >

She didn't need to speak the next bit aloud. All of them were keenly aware that fighting fevers and pains was very different from fighting an infection.

Berenice finished up her work. <*We need to keep these bandages clean,*> she said faintly. <*Or else the infection's going to get worse. And she's* got *to keep drinking water.*>

<*Then we need to get water,*> said Claudia, weighing one of their water casks. <*There's barely a pint left in here. I saw lots of desert out there, but also a few mountain streams.*>

Berenice considered it, trying to beat back the despair gathering at the back of her head. She looked down on Diela, remembering a moment just days ago and another group of people, when they'd gathered about a box containing only an empty uniform.

<*We keep what fresh water we have left for Diela,*> she said finally. <*Two stay here with her and . . . him.*> She wrinkled her nose at Crasedes. <*The other two go scouting. That way there's always a partner to help. Yes?*>

They nodded.

<*Seems wisest for Clef to stay here,*> said Claudia. <*Since he's the only one who can kill, you know . . .* > She glanced at where Crasedes lay. <*If he gets up to any trouble.*>

<*True,*> said Clef.

<*And I think it'd be wise to send someone with you who can spy scrivings,*> said Sancia. She grimaced, peering out at the chasm-strewn flats beyond. <*God, it looks miserable out there . . . but I guess I'll go with you.*>

<*Then I'll stay here with Diela,*> said Claudia. She felt the young

girl's cheek, her face crinkling into an expression of maternal concern. <*Just hurry. And don't get hurt. We don't need anyone else laid out here.*>

Together Sancia and Berenice picked their way across the ragged hills, the empty water casks slung to their backs and blankets fluttering about their shoulders. They had not at all prepared for a climate as cold as this, and Berenice desperately wished they had packed something thick to block out this wind.

She leaned against the gales and glanced at the clutch of tall, leaning towers to her right. <*So,*> she said. <*Clef's been remembering things.*>

<*Yes,*> said Sancia slowly. <*I've been wanting to talk to you about that. How much have you picked up from me so far?*>

<*Flashes. Enough, I think. He remembered being a boy, getting injured, meeting a girl . . . Is that it?*>

<*So far.*> She looked back at the fragments of walls where they were camped. <*But I worry he's remembering more, and just hasn't told us.*>

<*And we can't path to him and see,*> said Berenice.

Sancia shook her head. <*His brain's not like ours. Since, well, he hasn't got one. He can path to us, but we can't get into his thoughts unless he lets us in.*>

They trudged on over the glassy flats, the silvery sand crunching underfoot.

<*Sorry that I didn't tell you,*> said Sancia. She coughed awkwardly. <*After, like, the first time.*>

Berenice nodded. <*I could tell something was wrong. But . . . Well. We had a bit more on our minds then.*>

<*Yes. Like not dying and all.*>

They stopped, and Berenice snatched out and squeezed Sancia's hand and looked into her eyes. <*I'm glad you're alive,*> she said. Then she laughed, a miserable, desperate sound, but the sentiment was too mad and too honest for it not to be funny.

<*I am too,*> said San. <*And I'm glad that . . . that goddamned dead-*

lamp didn't wipe you out of creation. Shit . . . > She shook her head, sighing. <*I feel like we say stuff like that a lot these days. I wonder why we didn't say it when we* weren't *being lethally threatened all the time.*>

Berenice smiled, but only briefly, remembering that one of her team was likely now at death's door. Again the despair struck her, and it felt like cold, muddy water was pooling at the bottom tip of her heart.

<*Let's hurry then,*> said Sancia grimly. <*And do all we can.*>

<*And* fix *her, yes,*> said Berenice.

Sancia trudged on.

<*And fix her?*> repeated Berenice after her.

<*Yes,*> said Sancia. <*I hope so.*>

Berenice scowled. She shaded her eyes, peering at the landscape about her. *By God,* she thought. *How I wish I had my spyglass . . .* Then she spied a glimmer that was different from the silvery sheen of the sands, a fragile little trickle that came weaving out of the distant mountains to the south to wend its way around the white towers.

<*There,*> she said. <*Water. It looks like it . . . it* might *be accessible.*> She glanced at the closest chasm. <*Maybe.*>

They continued on, the enormous shadows from the tower washing over like sea leviathans swimming above them in the ocean. Berenice kept looking up at them, thinking. <*In that memory of Clef's,*> she said quietly. <*He remembered . . . He remembered bricks being glued together, yes? Scrived to adhere together, one by one, in a white wall?*>

<*Yeah, in a really weird, primitive way,*> said Sancia. <*It must have taken forever.*>

Berenice watched as a coil of bone-white dust danced across the towers. <*And those towers . . . You saw them with your scrived sight. Weren't they made the same way?*>

Sancia nodded. <*You think Clef's people built this place. Long ago. And maybe the ruins back at the prison too.*> She looked around. <*Remnants of his people . . . whoever they were.*>

<*Not just that. When he was on the stretcher, looking up, he saw towers, didn't he? White ones.*> She looked at Sancia. <*San—I think this might be* that city. *I think this might be the place he remembered. His* home.>

Sancia stared. <*No way. I don't remember the towers being . . . being* that *tall . . .* >

Berenice shrugged. <*Maybe they made them taller after. Built them up. I just wonder . . . What happened here?*>

Finally they came to where the stream poured into the chasm. It was a fall of hundreds, perhaps thousands of feet. Both of them studied the stream carefully, gauging where the flow was shallowest and weakest.

<*It could be tricky,*> said Sancia warily. <*I'm used to tricky steps. Maybe I should be the one wh—*>

<*No!*> snapped Berenice. <*No, damn it! I'm not losing another . . . Never mind.*> She slipped one of the water casks off her back, walked to the edge of the stream, and defiantly filled it up. <*This spot is fine!*>

Sancia slowly walked up behind her, watching her frantically, furiously gathering the water, cask after cask.

<*You know,*> said Sancia. <*You know it's . . . it's very possible, Ber, that even if we get water, it might not work. Right?*>

<*Shut up, San,*> said Berenice.

<*Fighting infections is hard,*> said Sancia. <*It's dreadfully tricky stuff, and—*>

<*Then we'll salt the wound,*> said Berenice. <*That's known to help.*>

<*We don't have any salts here, Ber.*>

<*Then we'll cut!*> said Berenice. <*We'll cut the . . . the damned arm off, just as we should have at the start, and . . .* >

<*No,*> said Sancia. <*Cutting now would not only be pointless. It's not in her arm anymore, it's in her blood. That would make it worse.*>

Berenice glared at Sancia over her shoulder, tears in her eyes. "Are you going to help me or not?" she spat.

Sancia eyed her, then studied the stream and carefully unshouldered her casks and began filling them one by one.

<*What would you have me do?*> said Berenice. <*You want me to just watch it? Watch this thing take her away from me, piece by piece, eating her from the inside like, like . . .* >

<*Like me?*> asked Sancia. <*Like what's happening to me?*>

Berenice stared into the waters flowing before her.

<*When it happens to me, Ber,*> Sancia said, <*are you going to run off looking for a fix? Or will you stay with me?*>

Berenice's mouth curled in rage. "Oh, scrum you, San," she said. "*Scrum* you." Then she shouldered her casks, turned, and began the long walk back.

Standing in the corner of the ruined storehouse, Clef stared down at the black form on the ground and listened to the wind screaming in all the tiny punctures throughout the crumbling walls.

He watched as the black cloak twitched in the wind.

He's not mine, he thought. *Not anymore. He's nothing to do with me anymore.*

"Shit," whispered Claudia. "Shit, shit, shit." Then, silently: <*This isn't good.*>

"Eh?" Clef said aloud. He looked around, vaguely aware that a lot of time had passed since they'd landed, but unsure how much.

Diela lay on the pile of sheets, her face dripping with sweat, her skin blotchy. Her breathing had changed, turning into an awful, wet gasping that rattled horribly in her chest. But worst of all was how she looked: her face was sunken and wan, like she'd aged fifty years. Though Clef had no direct sense of smell, he could tell she had fouled herself, and Claudia had been forced to prop up her wounded arm to avoid it getting tainted further.

"God, God," said Claudia. "I . . . I don't know what to do besides trying to give her water. Do you know anything about this, Clef?"

Clef stared down at Diela. His mind wandered back to another girl, wrapped in cloth, her breath diminishing within her as another disease ate through her body.

"Clef?" said Claudia.

"N-No," he stammered. "I don't. I wish I knew what to do. I wish I . . ."

Together they stood over the dying girl. They counted her every breath, rejoicing every time her breast rose, then watching with dreadful suspense as they waited for her to take air once more.

"I hope they get back soon," said Claudia. "But I can't imagine they can do anything more." She blinked owlishly at the sand-strewn shelter about them. "Hey . . . what time is it?"

"Eh?" said Clef again. He shook himself and peered beyond.

The sun was low in the sky, almost touching the silvery flats about the towers. "I'd say getting late."

Claudia turned around. "Then shouldn't Crasedes be waking up soo—"

She froze. Clef looked at her, then followed her gaze.

Crasedes was not lying in the corner of the room anymore. Now he was standing behind them, peering down at where Diela lay on the floor, his head cocked.

"Would you like to save her?" he asked, his tone calm and polite. "Because if so, I believe I can make that happen."

Berenice knew something was wrong the second she approached their shelter: she felt it first, an anxiety boiling in the back of her head; then as she grew closer, she heard Claudia and Clef bickering.

<*I sat in a deadlamp with him for half a day!*> Claudia was saying. <*So, yeah, I mean, I* kind of *trust him!*>

<*If we let him go, God knows what he'll do!*> Clef snapped. <*He could flit away all over again!*>

Berenice bent low and staggered up the hill, then charged into their shelter. She stopped short at the sight before her: Claudia and Clef standing in the corner, watching as Crasedes sat on the floor beside Diela, bent over her and peering closely at her arm, then her chest, then her head.

"I can save her," he said casually as Berenice walked into the room. "But these two seem unsure if they would like me to."

<*He says he has to go get something,*> said Clef angrily. <*A plant, or some bullshit.*>

<*He's helped us so far!*> said Claudia. <*If he really could fly away, why isn't he doing it now?*>

<*Because he knows I'd catch him,*> snarled Clef, <*and kill him.*>

Berenice set down the water casks. "What . . . What plant is this you need?" she asked.

"It's not technically the plant," said Crasedes, "but rather a mold that *grows* on the plant. Yet this is pedantry, really. It will not be hard to find—not if we start now and get there in enough time."

Berenice looked down at Diela. The girl looked horrible: her arm had swollen like bread that'd been sitting in water, and there was a puffiness about her eyes and neck that made her face look deformed.

Another child I've led into death, she thought. *My God, my God . . .*

Crasedes stood up. "If you wish to save her," he said, "we will need to leave immediately. But I believe I can."

Clef carried both Berenice and Crasedes about three miles to the west, closer to a range of hills and mountains that seemed to have been spared from much of the devastation that had struck this place. The trip was not comfortable—the hierophant was dreadfully close, so much so that Berenice's eyes watered and her stomach felt like it was full of knives—but finally Crasedes directed Clef to alight at the tip of one tall gulley, carved by melted mountain snows.

Once Clef landed, Crasedes aimlessly wandered off into the short brush with the air of a professor going for a walk between lectures. Berenice followed, carefully ducking throughout the spare foliage; then Clef followed her, stolidly stomping through the leaves and trees with utter indifference.

"What damned plant are we looking for?" asked Berenice.

"A flash of dark purple, peeking among the undergrowth," said Crasedes. "A purplish shoot, dappled with white, and perhaps featuring a slender pink bloom. Even though I now have the strength to move, my sight's still not quite what it used to be . . ."

"If you try to fly," said Clef, "I'll tear you to pieces."

"Oh, I won't be able to control my gravity for an hour or so," said Crasedes casually. "Once the damage set in, it became far too tricky."

"What damage is this, again?" asked Berenice.

But Crasedes had wandered off, pacing through the gully, bending low here and there to peer at the base of a short, stunted tree. Berenice did the same, but Clef abstained, choosing instead to follow Crasedes and keep close watch.

"How are you so sure this will help Diela?" asked Berenice.

"I have been alive for four thousand years," said Crasedes. "Does it not follow that I would pick up some knowledge of medicines during that time?"

"I wouldn't think immortal, indestructible people would need to know much about medicine."

"That may be so." He crossed the gully, squatted to look at something, then popped back up again, shaking his head. "A plague once came to this place," he said. "Plagues, of course, visit all places, given enough time . . . But this was a particularly bad one, eliminating over half the population. They learned many things in trying to treat it. One particular method had some success—but only in treating the infections in the survivors. The plague itself, they learned, had no solution." He looked at Clef. "A purplish shoot, dappled with white . . . Simmered in water, then drained and ground into a paste. Is this familiar to you, Claviedes?"

"No," said Clef, nettled.

"I see," said Crasedes. "Interesting." He continued down the gully, weaving to and fro as he studied the rocky ground.

Berenice caught up to him. "This was a city, wasn't it?"

"It was," he said.

"And it was your city," she said. "Clef's city. Your home."

Crasedes paused, squatting underneath a fragile, leafy fern. His empty black eyes stared up at her through the fronds. "Things like Clef and me do not have homes," he said. "When you outlive civilizations, the conceit gets a little moot. You *could* say that we were once people, and thus had homes and lives, and this is true—but it is a little like the glass out there on those flats. In some places it has returned to sand, but in others it is thick and hard, and resists any cracking or crumbling. Is it then still sand, or is it glass? Does it remember being sand? Or does it matter after such a transmutation?"

He walked on into the foliage, ducking and peering at the soil.

"Perhaps a more accurate thing to say," he continued, "is that once there was a child who was born in that city, to a man and a woman. And when the plague struck, the child was sent far away, to live with relatives in a place they thought safe. The child had a vague memory of his father, and his mother, but no more." He crested the side of the gully, looking out at the spires in the distance. "Something happened in the city, and the world broke. And then a man came to the child, fleeing this place and what had happened here. But though the man had the same name and likeness as the boy's father, he was not the same man. For how could he be? Like the sand on those wastes, he had been transmuted by what he had seen into someone else." He turned and walked back down into the gully. "And they would both be transmuted again, and again, and again, throughout their lives, versions upon versions of themselves . . . Sand into glass and glass into sand."

Berenice watched him, staring into his vacant eyes. "You think it was Clef, don't you?" she said softly. "You think he made the first door, the one Tevanne is looking for."

"I don't know," he said pleasantly. Again, he looked up at Clef. "Claviedes never told me what happened to this place." There was a slight bitter tone in Crasedes's words. "I hardly knew the man who was my father, even when blood still beat within his flesh. But there was little time for conversation then. For once the city fell and the walls crumbled, the slavers came . . . and the world was changed yet again." He walked on into the brush. "I *do* believe Clef is the only survivor of this catastrophe that still lives in this world. So perhaps he can help. Perhaps. But we will look regardless. After all, we must."

"Look where?" asked Berenice. "In those towers? How could we possibly search all those?"

Crasedes paused and looked back at her. "Ah. You've seen the chasms, yes?"

"Well, yes?"

"But did you look *into* the chasms, to see what's down there?"

"What's . . . down there?" she echoed. "No. What do you mea—"

"Aha!" said Crasedes joyfully. He squatted down and then arose with a small queerly fleshy plant with a dark-purple stalk and a delicate, quivering, tiny pink bloom.

"That's what we wanted?" said Berenice.

"No. We want *that*." He pointed at the base of the plant, where there were dusky bulbs or orbs still covered with gray earth—but at their tops, where they converged into the stalk of the plant, there was a white curly residue. "This slight substance is what will give your friend her blood and lungs back. When properly prepared, of course."

When they returned, the sun was a blade of red on the horizon, and Claudia and Sancia were sitting beside Diela, whose wheezing was now so loud you could hear it outside the shelter. It seemed more of Crasedes's powers had returned to him: there was a quiver in the air as he walked in, and instantly the firestarters and pots and water casks began to move about in the shelter like enchanted items from a child's story. Soon he was sitting before a bubbling cauldron, humming as he stripped the flesh from the plant's bulbs and dropped it into the water.

Berenice sat beside Sancia, feeling suddenly, powerfully ashamed at what she'd said to her wife. Then the two held hands, taking in the bizarre sight of the first of all hierophants playing apothecary.

<*I'm sorry,*> said Berenice.

Sancia nodded.

<*I . . . I don't know how to lose you,*> said Berenice. <*I can't imagine it. So I don't.*>

<*I know,*> whispered Sancia.

<*I just know how to survive. That's all I know anymore.*>

<*That's all I used to know as well,*> said Sancia. <*Until I met you.*> She sighed deeply. <*Then let's survive, and help all we love do the same.*>

"I believe this should do," said Crasedes. He lifted the pot from its little firestarter, then picked up a pestle, drained the water, and carefully muddled the remaining contents. The more he ground, the more the sludge turned white, almost like milk. He took a small spoon, scooped out a tiny spoonful of the white slurry, waited for it to cool, and placed it into Diela's mouth. "There. We shall wait three hours, then administer more. The heat in her brow should drop, and her sweating and incontinence should lessen as well."

"You're really saying this little plant you found could save her?" said Claudia.

"Probably," said Crasedes. "It has worked on others. It may work now. But it is *most* critical that we continue giving her this concoction. Stop too early, and the fever will return. But she has time now—though we, unfortunately, do not." He looked around at them, from face to face. "Tevanne is surely recovering, and it knows what direction we fled in. Its forces will find us. We must make use of what time we have."

"So what's your plan?" asked Sancia. "You're just going to go over to those towers, poke around, and see what you find?"

"Not quite," he said. "After all—Claviedes has seen the thoughts of the enemy, has he not? This is how you came to know of the door at all, yes?"

Sancia nodded reluctantly. "Yeah. We've seen it. Or seen what Tevanne imagines it to be, I guess."

"Yes. So we have a good idea of what we're looking for." He turned to stare out at the glassy flats, which were now a shimmering purple in the light of the sunset. "I came here once out of curiosity, to try to learn what had happened to this place and what lessons I could take from it. That was centuries ago, and I found only ruin. But I am familiar with what lies below the towers . . . and I remember a good starting place for our search."

"And . . . what *does* lie below the towers?" asked Berenice.

"Everything," he said. "Much of the city was . . . *displaced,* I suppose I should say, when the original aperture was opened. You will see, when you come with me."

There was a loud silence.

"Come . . . Come with you?" said Sancia. "Out there? *Into* one of the chasms?"

"I thought that had been clear," said Crasedes. "I said *we* must destroy the door."

"Yeah, but you didn't mention going into giant chasms full of ruins in the middle of the night," said Claudia. "It might make sense to an unbreakable immortal, but it's stark-raving mad to me."

Crasedes sighed. "But . . . I am not quite so unbreakable as I used to be. I will need assistance."

"Especially from Clef," said Berenice. She looked at him, standing in the back of the shelter. "Since he's the only person who's ever been here when it was really a city."

"Yes," said Crasedes. "It is possible, though unlikely, that he may remember something." He turned his masked face to Clef. "Unless, of course, you've *already* remembered something, Claviedes?"

There was a long, tense silence.

"I'll come," said Clef quietly.

"Good," said Crasedes. "I assume the rest of you will attend as well . . ."

<*Are . . . Are you sure, Clef?*> said Sancia. <*This . . . This place sounds like a pit full of horrors.*>

<*I'll come,*> said Clef again. <*M-Maybe we'll find something useful there.*> With a squeak, his helmet turned to look at Crasedes, sitting next to Diela. <*Maybe something that broke the world could also fix it.*>

Berenice frowned, studying the way he stood and the softness of his voice, but she kept her thoughts to herself.

<*I can stay to watch Diela,*> said Claudia. <*And keep giving her this slurry. But if you do go out there in the chasms, remember—we don't have* any *weapons left.*>

<*Except for the pathplates,*> said Berenice. <*For Clef. And he can really only be used against one thing . . .* > She looked at Clef. <*If we touched Crasedes with a pathplate, you could still have access to him, right? And so we . . . you could still kill him with those, yes?*>

<*That's an idea,*> said Clef. <*But he'd have access to my privileges too . . . He could blink out of reality like he did during Shorefall Night—though since it's just a pathplate, he'd probably only get to use it once.*>

Berenice shook her head. <*I still want to know more about all this. I'm not risking anyone else before I'm satisfied tha—*>

"As much as I *enjoy* your silent conversations," said Crasedes, theatrically loud, "they *do* seem to go on a bit . . ."

Berenice glared at him. "Fine. You said you figured out where this door was, based entirely on Tevanne's questions, yes? But you've never told us how you wound up in that prison in the *first* place. How did it capture you?"

Crasedes was silent for a long while before finally sighing. "I suppose you are owed that," he grumbled. "The short of it is, I grew . . . greedy, and overstepped."

<*Sounds about right,*> said Sancia.

"I had held fast against Tevanne for many years," said Crasedes, "but I could only defend, never attack. I could spy no weakness in the enemy's designs . . . except one." He leaned forward. "You must be aware that twinning minds is a dangerous thing—what connects also *controls*. And Tevanne is connected to thousands and millions of thralls and vessels, so it must manage these connections very carefully. I eventually decided there must be some tool, some bit of actual artifice or function that manages this for Tevanne. In other words, a place where it is vulnerable. Do you see?"

They all stared at him, stone-faced. Then Claudia burst out laughing and clapped.

"Design's regulator!" she whooped. "Holy shit—*Crasedes* is looking for it too?"

Crasedes cocked his head. "What . . . What is this, now?"

"We've speculated for a long time that this same rig has to exist," explained Sancia. "This . . . This regulator. It's a hell of a thing to hear you agree."

"Interesting," Crasedes said. "Who is . . . Design?"

"A long story that we don't have time for," said Berenice.

"I see," he said. "Well. I had my *own* ideas, and eventually thought I knew enough to exploit this vulnerability. For you can guess where Tevanne might *keep* such an apparatus . . ."

Berenice narrowed her eyes, then realized the obvious answer. "The flying city," she said.

"What's that?" asked Claudia.

"The flying cities we've seen," said Berenice. "The citadels. The regulator is in . . . in there, yes? Or one in each of them?"

"Correct," said Crasedes. "The citadels, as you say, act a bit like control points for the enemy. And this apparatus—this regulator—is placed in each one to ensure the control is stable. I managed to actually *find* this regulator in one such citadel and tried to steal it to study . . . but the instant I touched it." He sighed. "Well. The entire citadel went dead and fell out of the sky."

They stared at him.

"What?" said Sancia. "Touching it . . . it just *killed* one of those flying cities?"

"Yes," he said. "Tevanne is aware that this is a vulnerability. And it would prefer to lose an entire citadel than allow someone to exploit it." He leaned his chin on his hand. "I was trapped in several million tons of stone, hurtling down through the sky . . . and when I managed to extricate myself from the rubble, I faced a weapon the enemy had designed specifically to face me."

"The giant lorica," said Sancia. "Which Clef here managed to beat the shit out of." She patted his armor proudly.

"Yes." Crasedes looked at him, somewhat concerned. "Rather easily too. How curious . . ."

The uneasy pause continued, as if some aspect of this bothered him, but he did not speak more on it.

Finally Crasedes said, "The door is the priority. If the enemy manages to duplicate it, there is no weakness or power that could possibly stop it. But once we have disposed of it, I will tell you all I know about Tevanne's weakness. This way, we both sabotage the enemy's immediate plans and develop a way to defeat it. But I repeat—the door *must* be the priority." He surveyed the room. "Is such an alliance amenable to you all?"

"Hell, I guess," said Sancia. She stood, walked over to the broken wall, and peered out at the distant spires. "So long as we all come back from this thing in one piece."

"Of course. You will be in my protection." Crasedes raised his feet, and sat upon thin air in his familiar cross-legged pose. "There can be no greater safety."

33

They chose to take the deadlamp closer to the city, though they left some gear behind. Ostensibly it was for Diela's care, but Sancia and Berenice grabbed two pathplates to Clef while on board—one apiece for each of them. Yet she left a third with Claudia, saying, <*Just in case.*>

<*Just in case of what?*> asked Claudia.

<*I've no idea,*> said Berenice. <*But I know I'd prefer you possess Clef's powers in a tight spot than not. And one more thing . . .* > She slid out a small iron box and handed it over. <*Inside you will find Diela's circlet. For if she wakes . . .* >

<*You want me to make the girl do* that?> said Claudia, stunned. <*When she's still sick?*>

<*Let her be the judge,*> said Berenice. <*Diela knows herself well. But we have to tell Giva our situation as soon as possible, and only she can do that.*>

Once they were finished, they climbed into the deadlamp once more, and they were off, dipping and bobbing through the night skies. This time Crasedes did not sit but rather floated slightly above the floor of the vessel, his hands threaded in his lap. Sancia and Berenice peered through the window in the bottom of the lamp, staring at the pale white towers. They seemed to quake curiously in the starlight as frail clouds raced through the skies above.

"Claviedes," said Crasedes, "if you will alight at the base of the tower just to the north, that would do nicely. I *would* have you land within the chasm itself, but . . . I suspect it's all rather unstable."

The deadlamp tilted to the side, following his instructions.

"Don't call me that," said Clef.

"I beg your pardon?" said Crasedes.

"My name is Clef," he said. "That's who I am now." The helmet turned to look at Crasedes. "Glass and sand and transmutation, right?"

Crasedes was silent for a moment. Then he said, "As you wish."

They sailed on.

"Tell me, *Clef,*" said Crasedes casually, "what have you been doing out in the ocean with Sancia and Berenice and all her people? Have you been building your utopia with all these"—his masked face swiveled to Berenice—"interesting people?"

"It's a better one than you ever managed," snapped Clef. "Or ever will, now."

"True," said Crasedes. "I will never again attempt to reshape the world of men. I no longer have the strength. But I wonder—do you remember *why* I tried in the first place?"

"Because you went mad, I suppose," said Clef savagely.

"Hm," said Crasedes. "That's the trouble with you. Your memories are so addled, you can't even remember which side you were on in which fight."

"Shut up," said Clef.

There was a long, loud silence.

Berenice quietly reached out, grabbed Sancia's hand, and whispered, <*Is Clef all right?*>

<*No,*> said Sancia. <*Definitely not. But I'm not sure how he could be.*>

<*What do you mean?*>

<*Like—meeting Crasedes again? Going to your home that was the site of such horrors, and knowing you might have had a hand in it? How could someone manage all that?*>

Berenice released her hand, seeing the wisdom in this. But it still troubled her. Clef had been curiously addled ever since the jailbreak, almost distracted, like he was listening to something else they couldn't hear.

But what, she thought, *could tinker with the one entity we know can't be tinkered with?*

Finally they came to the site Crasedes had indicated. They stopped just alongside one of the rippling, crackling white stone towers and began slowly to slide down. Berenice glanced sideways at where Crasedes sat upon the air. He was peering out the window as well, his masked face glimmering in the starlight.

"Is this the same chasm you used the last time you came here?" she asked.

"Hm," said Crasedes. "No." He gestured at a curiously round, gaping hole in the flats to the west. "When I came here centuries ago, I made my own entrance. But doing so now would be . . . unwise."

"Why?"

"Because even though it is night, I am still damaged."

"What kind of damaged? You've still never explained that."

Crasedes did not respond.

"When Sancia saw you, she said she thought Tevanne was . . . doing something to you," Berenice said. "Distorting your time. Stretching it. Bending it. Is that right?"

"Why is this important to you now?" asked Crasedes. He sounded slightly offended.

"Because you said we're under your protection," said Berenice, "but you also keep saying you're weak. I'd like to know exactly how weak your protection's going to be in there."

"I see," he said. He fell silent, thinking. "I have taken . . . precautions, over the years, to protect myself against many kinds of attacks. I cannot, for example, be edited out of reality, like the deadlamps have done to so many of Tevanne's enemies. But I am old. I contain the knowledge of many, many, *many* years. I am like a reservoir, full of water—and Tevanne, rather cleverly, realized what my greatest vulnerability would be."

"To fill it up," said Berenice, realizing, "and make it overflow . . ."

"Or break," said Crasedes. "It was already difficult enough

to manage the extent of the memories I possessed. But Tevanne stretched my time, and filled up my mind with many, many years I did not have before. Years trapped in place, staring into a blank black wall . . ."

"How . . . How long did you feel like you were in there?" asked Sancia.

He cocked his head, thinking. "About ten times my normal lifespan, or thereabout."

Sancia's jaw dropped. "Holy hell . . ."

"You spent *forty thousand years* in that prison?" said Berenice.

"Or thereabout," he said again. "It makes sorting my memories much harder. They are like . . . tiny islands in a dark ocean, but you must navigate them without a compass . . . And when the sun rises, and I grow weak, I cannot navigate them at all. I forget how to move, to breathe. I used the last of my strength after my escape, but past that, my energies must be devoted to maintaining my consciousness, otherwise . . ." He trailed off.

"Brace for landing," said Clef. "Or whatever the hell might happen *after* we land . . ."

They sailed on in an anxious silence.

"If you are curious," said Crasedes softly, "it is terribly odd to return to the ancient site of your fathers and forefathers, and know that technically you are now many times older than it."

<*Shit,*> said Sancia silently. <*I'd scrumming say so.*>

"Here we go," said Clef.

The deadlamp alighted with a soft thump. Berenice tensed, waiting for the earth to slip away below them, and for them to be sent hurtling down into the chasm . . . but it held.

"I . . . I think we're good," said Clef.

"Excellent," said Crasedes. He gestured with a finger, and the hatch above them unscrewed and opened. "Let us examine the land."

Entering the chasm seemed enormously difficult. It offered no handholds, no stairs down, no slopes that could be traversed easily. Again, Crasedes offered to float them down. Such was Sancia's concern about figuring out a way to descend that she actually gave it thought.

Then Clef spoke up, lumbering over her shoulder: "I can do it."

"Do what?" said Sancia. "Jump us down there? You'd smash the whole goddamned place to bits."

"I can control my densities," said Clef. "And my gravity. I can hold you both, and we'll float down like a feather." His helmet tilted to one side. "Provided you don't slip and fall out of my arms, of course."

"In which case," said Crasedes, "I can provide assistance."

"Let's do Clef's thing," said Sancia, shuddering. "Just be . . . careful."

"Well, no shit," said Clef.

He took them both in his arms, gripped them tight, said, <*Hold on to your guts, kids,*> and then with a light hop, jumped down into the chasm. Berenice suppressed a scream—but then they rather abruptly slowed and drifted down into the chasm.

<*Ohh boy,*> said Sancia, grimacing. <*I forgot how much I hate this shit.*>

<*Yes,*> said Berenice. She gasped. <*Scriving gravity is always, ahh, very awful.*>

<*If you two want to climb down on your own, be my guest,*> said Clef.

They kept gently drifting down, down, down. Sancia pulled out a small floating lantern and turned it on, and it bobbed after them like a firebug, its luminescence dancing over the stone about them.

<*What did Crasedes mean when he said everything was down here?*> asked Berenice. <*I just see rock.*>

<*Just wait,*> said Clef. <*I think I see it coming . . .*>

Then the light danced through the darkness, and they saw.

The walls of the chasm were not stone but were made of *buildings,* stacks and stacks of crumbling, gray, stained buildings, like the floors of a massive structure all pressed together. They made Berenice think of catacombs she'd read about in distant lands, and underground labyrinths built to house the dead—but these were clearly regular homes and structures. All of them were ancient, having lost much of their decoration and ornamentation, but the structure and design and layouts remained, the skeleton of everyday civilization emerging from the dark earth.

"Holy shit," said Sancia. "The whole city's *underground*?"

"What was not lost," said Crasedes, "was displaced." He slid down through the air beside them, still sitting cross-legged in the air. "It's a very bad thing, you see, when reality forgets how space itself works."

"And opening this aperture, or door or whatever," said Sancia. "That's what did this?"

"I suspect so," said Crasedes. "But we shall discover the truth tonight, hopefully."

Berenice watched as stack after stack of structures sailed by her. "How on earth," she said, "is all this stuff still . . . well, *here*? Shouldn't it all be dust? Did whatever massive alteration that took place here also somehow preserve all the buildings too?"

"Hmm," said Sancia. She narrowed her eyes and said, *<Ber . . . path to me.>*

Berenice did so, frowning as she slipped behind Sancia's eyes—and she gasped as the walls about them lit up with faint silvery tangles of scrivings, all silently coiled about in the stone.

"Oh my," said Berenice softly. She leaned forward. "And it's scrived so . . . so *differently* . . ."

"Yes," said Crasedes. "The people of this place knew the binding of commands—but they developed a method of doing it *without* sacrifices. Or your clumsy lexicons." He drifted closer to the walls, peering into the rows of windows. "Each stone took great labor to make, but they knew each stone would last centuries. There are many creations in the depths of this place that have lasted, because they are nigh indestructible. Some of them even *I* would have trouble destroying."

After what seemed like an eternity drifting downward, they finally came to the bottom of the chasm. Much of it had been turned into a vast underground lake, fed by the dripping streams above. But they seemed to have made it to the bottommost layer, where the street had once lain. Enormous paving stones stuck out of the waters like broken teeth, all written with commands for durability and density. Clef alighted on the tip of one, still holding Sancia and Berenice in his arms.

Crasedes drifted over the water. "I believe you will need a boat."

"Yeah," said Sancia. "But we didn't bring a scrumming bo—"

Crasedes flicked a hand, and one of the paving stones surged out of the water like a leaping shark—and then it seemed to suddenly explode, bursting apart in a cloud of white dust . . . yet then the dust settled, and they saw he had, apparently instantaneously, carved away all the stone except for a small, streamlined boat shape.

"We cannot exactly sail," said Berenice, "in a boat made of sto—"

He flicked his hand again. There was a crack, and scrivings crawled across the face of the stone—scrivings convincing it that it was not stone but was actually wood, and light, waterproof wood at that.

They watched as the stone boat slowly descended to bob in the waters. Then it zipped over to stop just beside the paving stone.

"I may not be able to fashion my tools of old," said Crasedes. "But conventional scriving I still know quite well." He cocked his head. "All aboard."

"What a scrumming show-off," muttered Sancia. The three of them carefully climbed down and clambered into the craft. It turned slowly, and then shot off into the labyrinth of chambers at the bottom of the chasm, Crasedes silently floating along behind them.

The four of them trawled through the channels and passageways of the ruined city, hunched low and staring at the sights about them. Much of the depths seemed to be a mixture of soil and structure, with a cornice or a window surfacing in the loam like a ruby in the wall of a mine. In other places whole buildings or streetscapes stretched out before them into caverns and caves, a city square or a monument or a crossroads simply suspended in the strata.

"Where are you taking us?" asked Sancia.

"Much of the city was lost," said Crasedes. "But not all. We will start where some survives and see what clues we may find. For the aperture *must* be somewhere within this labyrinth."

They drifted through a tunnel so narrow that Berenice worried their boat might not fit.

"And . . . what is this place, really?" asked Sancia.

"It is nothing now," whispered Crasedes. His words were soft, but they reverberated loudly in the tunnel. "It has no name and is marked on no map. But long ago it was called Anascrus. It was a city of builders and makers. They called themselves the People, blessed with the knowledge of how to perceive raw scrivings in the world. Their stones were stronger, their blades sharper, and they used this to build an empire that spanned more than three centuries—but sometimes they saw *more* than raw scrivings. Sometimes they glimpsed the deep commands, the instructions coded into reality to make all the world run as a clock. Yet they only witnessed this in the presence of death."

There was a long silence. Clef hunched low in the boat and did not move.

"When the plague came here," said Crasedes, "it brought great death. I do not know what occurred here, but . . . the conclusion seems clear."

The echoing of the waters changed. They were approaching someplace different, someplace larger.

"They saw," said Crasedes. "They learned. And they made. But they made something *new*."

The tunnel came to an end, and the walls opened up around them, falling back farther and farther—perhaps dozens if not hundreds of feet. They stared around in wonder but couldn't see very far beyond the edge of the waters.

"Crap," said Sancia. She fumbled in her pack. "Let's get out another lantern . . ."

She pulled another little floating lantern out, turned it on, and tossed it up. Its light grew and grew, its pale pink illumination washing over the enormous cavern.

Berenice gasped. "My God."

"Yes," said Crasedes. "This is where I wished to start."

It looked like half a dozen city blocks were trapped in a colossal bubble of stone, all slanted at an angle. Homes and structures and buildings rose up on either side of their narrow stream, which had apparently eroded through the sides of nearly a hundred houses. Some of the buildings had collapsed—often at their walls and roofs, which plainly had not been designed to spend several millennia sitting at an angle—but many of them held up, fused together by all the tiny scrivings written into nearly every brick and shingle and column in this huge dusty, crumbling half-city.

Crasedes rose and peered about at the many angled roofs before him. "This is about . . . oh, one-thirtieth of all of Anascrus, or so," he said. "It is the largest surviving piece I have found, though others might persist elsewhere in the earth."

The little stone boat bobbed to the edge of the underground stream. The three of them climbed out and stared around at the bewildering mash-up of leaning architecture and crumbling cityscape about them, the way every window and door seemed to shiver with shadows, and always the overpowering scent of dust and mildew.

<*It reminds me of the Commons, a little,*> said Sancia, peering down one crooked alley and up at the walls. <*All this tossed together . . .* >

"Let us get to looking," said Crasedes. He turned to them. "Clef, Sancia—peer with your second sight as best as you can. But I cannot guarantee that the door will be woven with conventional commands. We must look for anything and everything, and cover as much ground as we can as fast as we can."

"Scrumming great," muttered Sancia.

Crasedes floated backward into the darkness. "And Claviedes . . ." he said softly.

"Yeah?" said Clef.

"If something jogs your memory—do let us know?"

For the next few—minutes? Hours? Berenice had no idea how to tell time in this sunken place—they wandered the tilted, broken streets, studying the crumbling parapets and the cracked domes and the pulverized houses. They walked in a careful pattern so they didn't get lost, moving down one street until they couldn't, then crossing to the next and moving down in the opposite direction.

Eventually they split up, deciding that this was the way to cover the most ground as quickly as possible—though being the one person who could not perceive scrivings, Berenice felt this left her with the short straw. "Nothing I love more," she muttered as she walked, "than scrambling around some spooky ruins with a single floating lantern for company . . ."

Still, she delved through the sunken halls and dripping chambers, picking her way through the ancient refuse. There were a few bones, but not as many as she'd expected; but then, perhaps the people of Anascrus decayed far faster than what they'd built.

She turned one corner in the streets and faced a stone doorway to a home. There was a word chiseled above the doorframe, though she couldn't read it. She narrowed her eyes at it and began to pat her pockets to see if she had anything to copy it down.

A deep voice over her shoulder: "It says 'Condemned. Go Up.' "

She squeaked in surprise and jumped around to find Crasedes floating a few feet behind her.

"Don't goddamn sneak up on me like that!" she snarled.

"My apologies," he said. "I noticed you looking, and wished to help."

She glared at him for a moment longer before turning back to the doorway. "What does it mean?"

"I am unsure," said Crasedes. "But I believe the plague eventually led them to abandon the lower levels of the city, thinking the very air poisoned, and they retreated to their towers. Hence—'go up.' "

"I rather doubt if that worked."

"I think you are correct there." He floated forward until he was alongside her. "I have been wondering something, and feel compelled to ask—has Claviedes seemed . . . *different* recently?"

"Why?" she said, startled.

"Because he seems different to me," he said. "I recall that, in his last iteration, he was—how shall I put this?—rather irritatingly jocular."

"Well, I doubt if he likes being around you much at all," she said, but she knew it was a weak answer. She wasn't sure how much she wanted to share about Clef's mental state—especially with another powerful being whose mental state she trusted even less.

"Naturally," said Crasedes acidly. "I do not expect him to. He has many mistaken assumptions about me, and it is my lot to bear these transgressions as stoically as I can—as it *always* is."

Berenice blinked. It was surprising to hear something so petty come out of Crasedes's mouth, for it was hard to imagine such a historic—if not mythic—character struggling with complex relationships like anyone else might.

Crasedes floated forward until he was facing her. "But I was not referring to our time together. I meant—has Clef seemed different since he twinned himself, however briefly, with Tevanne?"

She felt her belly go cold. "He's . . . He's remembered things since then," she said reluctantly. "Yes."

"About this place."

"Yes. Nothing about a door, though. Nothing beyond the first flash he saw in Tevanne's thoughts."

He looked away, thinking. "I see," he said.

"Tevanne can't have tampered with him then, could it? I mean, *you* made him. Isn't Clef . . . well, untamperable?"

Crasedes cocked his head. "It is true that it would be very difficult to alter or damage Clef. Theoretically, the only thing that can damage Clef is Clef himself."

"Really?" said Berenice, surprised.

"Yes. Clef once reset himself—with Sancia, when she first freed the construct. He could even perform what is, in a way, the inverse of this task, destroying himself, unbinding himself . . . It is one of many capabilities I think he does not know he possesses." He cocked his head the other way. "Which is what worries me."

"What do you mean?" asked Berenice.

"Perhaps nothing *new* has been done to Clef." Crasedes began to float back into the darkness at the top of the chamber. "Perhaps, instead, something has awoken that has been slumbering within him for a very long time."

Clef listened to his footsteps clanking on the dark stone as he wandered through the sunken city.

I don't want to be here, he thought. *God, God, I wish I wasn't here.*

He turned a corner, studying the cityscapes, the facades of the buildings rumpled and tottering.

I want to go back, to be a key again. I just want to fix. To invent. To solve. That's who I am. It's . . . It's simpler that way.

Yet this place forced him to think otherwise. He would find himself in a courtyard, or a doorway, or at the top of a stair, and catch the ghost of a ghost of a memory: a sudden, overwhelming feeling of being either in this exact spot or a place like this, bumbling about his everyday life as a . . .

A man, he thought.

And then, as if he'd summoned it with that simple thought, the world changed about him.

He turned to look down one narrow alley, and suddenly it blossomed with light and became a silent yet thriving street scene, packed with people in colorful blue clothing going about their day, the noon sun filtering through the towers above to dapple their shoulders and heads . . .

And there, in the far middle of the crowd, was her. She stared at him, her face still dark, her white hair still bright and gleaming, her purpled, clotted hands still hanging by her sides.

He watched her. The scene faded around her, until it was just her form, hanging in the darkness. Then it, too, faded, until there was nothing but the darkened narrow alleyway before him.

He stared into the darkness, studying it with his many sights. It was very cramped, but it seemed to stretch on for a long, long ways.

Perhaps leading somewhere different.

Clef awoke the voice rig in his cuirass and shouted: "*I think I've found something over here!*"

Sancia narrowed her eyes at the tiny alleyway. "Huh. So. Where does this lead?"

"I don't know," said Clef. "But . . . it seemed different. Thought it was worth a look." He let the sentence hang there. He did not wish to give voice to all the memories murmuring at the edges of his mind, all the ghosts whispering in the shadows of this city.

Berenice stared up and around them. "Perhaps I'm turned around, but I thought this was at the wall of this giant cave . . . This must lead to another cave or, or section of the city. Is that right?"

"You are right," said Crasedes slowly. "This is a . . . a tiny artery to some lost portion I myself never found." He looked down at Clef. "What made this stand out to you?"

"I . . . I'm not sure," said Clef. "I just looked down it, and remembered it, kind of."

There was a silence.

"Then . . . I guess you should walk down it, Clef," said Sancia. "And see if you remember anything else."

Clef hesitated. Then, slowly, he took a step, and another, letting his feet guide him through the passageway.

As he walked, he felt his demeanor slowly change, even his posture: rather than clanking along in his usual, abrupt march, his pace became solemn, slow, and circumspect, his gaze fixed on the street before him.

He looked backward, past where Crasedes hovered in the air like a specter. "I . . . I used to live back there," said Clef quietly. His armor clinked as he leaned forward a little. "Past you. But it's gone now. That route was . . . was wiped away, I guess . . . ." He slowly turned back to face ahead of them. "But I remember now . . . I would come here, every morning."

He took another step, the clank of his boot echoing in the darkness, continuing along the path.

"And . . . think," he whispered. "And walk. Alone."

But to where? He wasn't sure—yet he kept walking, tugged along solely by the movement of his feet below him.

Until the lanterns finally cast their light across the doorway.

They stopped and studied it. The open doorway was high and thin, set in an ornate, intricately carved wall. They looked within and glimpsed many narrow passageways sprouting off and circling away into a tangle of paths and corridors. It appeared to be a maze, one that would have been outdoors in the city's original state, yet the walls inside were special, somehow: they were like elaborate stone cabinets, with stone doors stacked high upon one another, stretching off into the darkness.

"It's like . . . some kind of storage place," Berenice said quietly. "But what was kept he—"

Sancia elbowed her and pointed high, at the top of the walls—and there, sitting atop an intricate brick platform, were four carven stone skulls.

Clef stared up at their blank, empty eyes. Then he looked along the walls and saw similar decorations every dozen feet: handfuls of decorative stone skulls, peering down at the paths below.

He was silent for a long, long time. Then his armor shuddered, and he whispered, "She's here."

Crasedes descended out of the darkness. "Who?" he asked.

"My daughter," said Clef. He slowly lumbered into the maze of the columbarium, every step familiar, every movement known. "Your sister. Here is where she lies."

They followed him as he moved down the pathways, the stone skulls silently watching their procession. He felt more memories unraveling inside of him, blossoming like sunset vines that had waited for the sun to sink before they opened their trembling flowers.

He remembered the smell of flame, and singing in the night, and the feeling of tears pouring down his cheeks.

"We . . . would burn our dead," he whispered.

He turned, a left, then a right, then a left.

"We had done this for over two centuries," he said aloud. "We were builders. And we decided that when we died, we would turn our bodies to ash and mix the ash with the mud and the clay. And then we formed bricks of it, and we built our homes and our towers and our walls from them, from our loved ones, so they would be with us, the People, forever."

A left, then another left.

"But first the family grieved," whispered Clef. "The family grieved their loved ones, until they were ready to form their stones, and fire the bricks, and build the world anew. But until then, their ashes stayed . . . here. Until the family's mourning ended, and the grieving stopped. Until they had found a way out."

He walked the paths of the columbarium, remembering those late days, when the plague had ebbed and flowed, and so many treaded these paths, weeping and sobbing, wearing the customary mourner's robes of ashen gray.

He stopped suddenly, frozen. Then his helmet slowly shifted to look at one stone cabinet on the lowest level.

"That's right," he whispered. "We put the children on the bottom. So that the parents could sit and speak to them, just as they had in life."

Clef lumbered over to the wall. Then he slowly sat, his enormous metal form reverberating as it struck the bricked path.

He stared into the face of the stone cabinet, worn smooth from age and decay. Yet the scrivings woven into it still held fast, and he could see that it was strong and steady and sure.

There was a little star of silvery scrivings within the cabinet: phenomenally, carefully, wondrously scrived, woven with commands to be so durable and so resilient it could last forever.

Her funeral urn, he thought.

"She's still in there," he whispered. "My little butterfly. Because we could never stop grieving."

He reached out with his metal gauntlet and gently brushed the face of the stone cabinet.

"We could never find our way out of it . . ." he said.

He glimpsed her again, standing at the far end of the pathway, her hair bright white, her form small and rotting and shrouded in darkness.

"Because death was always with us," he whispered, "and we were trapped."

Then things blurred—now a familiar sensation for him—and he was somewhere else.

34

Again, it is night. Again, Clef stands at the bridge before the menders' hall. Again, the darkness is wracked by coughs, by sobs, by shrieks of sorrow, the whole city a vast aching wound of grief.

As he waits he lifts his eyes up to the night sky, the stars and moon obscured by pillars of black smoke unscrolling from the city. It is a familiar sight, a constant one these days. How odd it is to know that it is the smoke of many funeral pyres. To know that this smoke was once the People.

No more, *he thinks.* When my work is finished, no more.

A footfall to his left. He turns and sees his wife emerge from the shadows, her eyes wide and haunted, her form still clothed in funerary gray.

"I found the way," she whispers. "It's safe."

"You're sure?" he says.

"I'm sure. Come."

He follows her to the right, along the moat that runs about the menders' hall, yet the moat is now dry. Many streams and canals are now dry, for while the People built many named implements to bring fresh water to the city, they still require a human hand to work them.

No one left to let in water, *thinks Clef as he walks.* No one to grow food in the farms. No one to man our walls and keep us safe.

They come to a short ladder, and his wife begins to climb down to the dry moat.

We are abandoned, *he thinks,* by all men and whatever god set the heart of this world ticking.

They walk through the muddy moat until they come to a wide pipe, leading down into the menders' hall. His wife gestures and together they crawl into the pipe. When they exit, it is too dark to see, but there is the scrape and flutter of a flint in the shadows, and then his wife's oil torch leaps to life.

The flame reveals a massive, dripping, empty cistern that once stored water for the hall. The pillars stretch away all about them, the puddles on the floor shining like mirrors in the light of the torch.

"They have to . . . to get water in buckets now," says his wife. "It's difficult work. But then again, water or no water, the results are often the same." She looks at him. She is still beautiful, her golden hair spilling down her shoulders. But whatever bright, brilliant confidence was once there has long since been dashed.

"Are you close enough? Can you feel it?" she asks.

He does. He can feel the little thorn in his brain, the lock in his heart—and all the names and symbols thrumming through the world about him.

"Yes," he whispers. "I am close enough to the . . . to the dying above." He lifts his eyes to the ceiling of the cistern. "I can see the world changing about them." He walks over and touches the dark stone wall on the far side of the cistern.

"Aren't you worried, my love," she asks, "that this will drive you mad?"

"With the world already so mad, could we even tell if I was?" He runs his hand over the wall. "I know that I'm not. I can feel the door. Every bit more I see, the more I know how to make it, and what it needs."

She watches him, tears now streaming down her face. "What's on the other side? Do you know?"

"No. I'm not sure yet."

"Why build it if you're not sure what it opens to?"

"You don't understand. It wants *me to build it. It wants to be made. It's like seeing a sculpture within a block of stone—but the block of stone is the world itself."*

"A beautiful thought," she says. "But you aren't answering me. What lies on the other side of the thing you're making?"

"I don't know," he confesses. "But it's got to be better than here, yes?"

She watches her husband, her sad eyes flickering in the light of the torch. "She might not be there, you know," she says. "I want her to be. I know you want her to be. But she might not be waiting for us on the other side."

"I'm no child," says Clef. "I know. But perhaps a better world awaits us there. Perhaps a better world awaits us all, there on the other side of creation . . ."

She bows her head, weeping silently for a moment. "I just . . . I just want to make sure we're doing the right thing. We sent Crasedes away. He was . . . He was just a baby, *but we sent him away. And you and I are staying here to do . . . to do this."*

Clef removes his hand from the wall of the cistern. He has not thought about the boy in some time. He actually finds himself trying hard not *to think about the boy. In a world such as this, where so much hardship and danger awaits one's child, what fool would let themselves go about loving one?*

"We are," he says. "Because it's right. Because I can fix what has happened to us all. I can."

She nods and wipes her tears away. "We have few blessings these days. But I brought someone to watch over you." She reaches into her pocket and pulls out a small cloth doll, wrought of golden fabric.

He stares at it. His heart grows cold, and his hands shake. He has not seen it in so long.

"My God," he whispers. He takes it in his hands, remembering the feel of the doll, and the way his little butterfly once clutched it so close. "Valeria."

"The guardian angel of childhood," says his wife. She reaches up, fingers placed on either side of his head, and kisses him upon the brow. "May she watch over your labors here, and bring you joy."

Clef sat back as the memory released him. He sighed with misery, like a long cold blade was sliding out from between his ribs.

"I know now," he whispered.

"Know what?" asked Crasedes.

"Where I built it." He stood to his feet. "Where I made the door, and where I opened it."

35

Together they raced through the streets of the moldering city, Clef leading the way, turning again and again through the schizophrenic ruins like he had walked this path only yesterday. Berenice ran alongside Sancia, conscious that her wife was not as fleet as she used to be. She grabbed her hand and whispered, <*Did you see it? Did you see his memory?*>

Sancia shook her head. <*I didn't. I think it was easier for me to see what he saw when I was dreaming—if that makes any sense.*>

<*And do we know how he's doing this? Why he's remembering?*>

<*I've no idea, Ber.*>

They watched as Clef's lorica bounded forward through the city, crashing through the walls and caroming off the doorways.

<*I wish I could tell the difference,*> said Berenice, <*between revelation and madness.*>

<*Yeah, but . . .* > Sancia's eyes drifted up as they ran. <*I think I know where he's going now. God, I've seen this before, only for a second, but . . . this is the path they took after Clef was injure—*>

Then Clef's voice in the darkness ahead, bellowed: "Stop!"

"Huh?" said Sancia.

"I agree," boomed Crasedes, flitting somewhere above them. "You should stop running. Now."

They did so, skidding to a halt.

Crasedes descended from the darkness, a hand raised to them. "Come to me, slowly. Then the threat will be very apparent."

Sancia and Berenice carefully walked toward him. As their floating lamps finally caught up, Berenice narrowed her eyes, struggling to interpret what she was seeing.

The ground and walls and lanes ahead appeared to be *twinkling,* like stars in the sky.

And then she realized: the street ahead was made of crystal. As was everything that stood on top of it.

"Ohh, holy shit," said Sancia.

Berenice's eyes finally adjusted, and she stared out at the icy, glimmering city before her. Every stone and corner and terrace shone, so much so that she had to grab the little brass remote for her lamp and dim the brightness. The oddest thing was that she could see where the crystal world began mere yards away, like a seam or a border in reality, with all things stone and dust on her side, and everything glassy and gleaming on the other.

She narrowed her eyes, studying the glittering boundary marching through the city. It seemed to be moving in an arc, like a circle.

Which means there's a center. A place it came from.

"What the hell is this stuff?" asked Sancia.

Crasedes flexed his finger, and a distant crystal column quivered for a moment before bursting into thousands of sparkling pieces. "That took a good deal of effort, for me . . ." He did the same thing as Berenice, studying the boundary running through the city and then peering inward. "I believe it is diamond."

"*Diamond?*" said Sancia. "This bit of the goddamned city is made of *diamond*?"

"Yes," he said quietly. "Something happened in this place . . . to turn all the stone here to diamond."

"God almighty," said Sancia. "The one time I stumble across a fortune bigger than I could ever dream of, and it has to be here, in these cursed ruins, with the end of the world biting at our heels."

"What exactly is the threat of diamond floors?" asked Berenice.

"Have *you* ever walked across a giant diamond?" asked Crasedes. "I have not, but it is almost certainly very tricky. I can fuse broken bones, certainly . . . but I suspect you would not like me to."

"Ugh," said Sancia. "Understood."

There was a clanking sound, and Clef appeared out of the shadows ahead, standing tall and dark among the crystal corridors. "It's ahead," he said in a very quiet voice. "We're almost there."

He stood there for a moment in silence.

"Are you all right, Clef?" asked Sancia.

"We . . . We have to go, don't we," said Clef faintly. "We have to go in there. To stop it. Don't we?"

"Yes," said Crasedes. "We do."

"Yeah . . ." Clef's helmet turned away, and for a moment Berenice thought his blank eyes were staring down one glimmering passageway, as if looking back at someone watching him. But there was no one there Berenice could see.

"Everyone wants me to go in," he said sullenly.

He clanked over to them, and for a second Berenice felt afraid. Clef had never felt alien to her, but now, in this surreal, buried place, she couldn't help but wonder: what was inside the key inside the armor?

Yet Clef simply extended his arms to them, and tersely said, "Climb on. It's too slippery. I'll carry you two the rest of the way."

Berenice clung to Clef's left arm as he walked on into the crystal city, with Sancia holding on to his other side and Crasedes floating overhead. Slowly a building formed in the darkness ahead: a giant gleaming dome, set behind a wide, canal-like moat that leaned at an angle and held only a few puddles. A narrow crystal bridge stretched from the door of the building to the street, with two columns on either side. Even though Berenice had only seen the image in Sancia's memories, she recognized it immediately.

Clef came to the bridge and stopped. He stared across it for a long while, then quietly said, "This is where it started. Where my life started. Where I met her." He looked up at Crasedes. "Where I met the woman who would be your mother."

Crasedes's blank, masked face swiveled down to look at him, but otherwise he remained as inscrutable as ever.

"She was a mender," said Clef softly. He began to walk to the right, along the moat. "She worked at the hall there, tending to the injured and the sick and the infirm. We were a people of builders, so we hurt ourselves from time to time. She was so good at taking care of us. Or at least, I was told she was. I was never allowed inside."

The moat turned slightly, following the curve of the building, and a large, dark hole appeared in the bottom wall along the moat—some kind of drain, or pipe.

"When I was allowed free days, I waited for her at that bridge," said Clef softly. "When she gave birth to my children, I waited at that bridge. And when my daughter fell sick, I waited at that bridge every day. Every day. I remember that . . ."

Berenice and Sancia exchanged a glance, both clearly alarmed to discover how much Clef had remembered. But they stayed quiet as Clef continued moving, reclaiming his old life piece by piece.

He came to the edge of the moat and jumped off, floating down as light as a leaf to land on the moat.

"I thought I could never love anything as much as her," he whispered. He began to cross the moat to the pipe in the side of the hall. "But then my children were born. And I came to know there were different kinds of love. And some were so great they bent the rules of all I ever thought was possible."

Finally he came to the crystal pipe in the side of the wall, and he stared in at the shadows.

"Until we lost her," he whispered. "Until she was taken from us. My little butterfly. And then I stopped thinking about love. And all I could think about was a way out."

He didn't move. They stared into the dark pipe, feeling like there was some palpable presence at the far end, staring back at them.

"It's . . . It's in there?" asked Sancia.

"Yes," whispered Clef.

"And . . . is it still open?" asked Berenice.

"I don't know," he said. "That . . . That hasn't returned to me yet."

A flutter of cloth as Crasedes descended to float above them. "In that case," he said, "it would perhaps be wiser for me to investigate first."

"I thought you couldn't operate the door," said Sancia. "That it would destroy you."

"Mm, not quite," said Crasedes. "I said I could not use the door to *empower* myself. Meaning, I can witness the door, and possibly even pass through, or shut it from the other side—but I would not be able to accomplish much there, on the other side of reality."

"Hell, I don't know," said Sancia. "I guess go in and tell us if it's safe."

"Certainly," said Crasedes. Then, with utter aplomb, he floated into the pipe, still seated in his usual cross-legged position.

There was a long silence. The three of them sat there in the shifting light of the floating lanterns. Sancia watched Clef, her face lined with concern.

"How much do you remember of it all, Clef?" she asked.

"Too much," he said softly. "I've said it before, but I didn't want to know this, kid. I wanted to look forward, not back."

"You're going to save us all by doing it," said Berenice.

"You think so," said Clef quietly. "But the bad thing about remembering so much of your life is . . . is realizing how it isn't . . . I don't know. A story."

"A story?" asked Berenice.

"Yeah," he said. "That's how we all think of ourselves, as people in a tale. Living our stories. But if you live long enough, you see it's not a story at all. It just keeps going. People come and go, like butterflies in the wind. Cruelties don't always meet justice. And maybe you'll never meet the end you wanted, or expected, or deserve. Maybe you'll never meet an end at all. Eventually you're just left with scraps. Pieces of unfinished stories. Threads of tales no one ever got to live." He knelt down to peer into the pipe, and when he spoke again his words echoed softly. "Pieces of works you never got to perfect."

Berenice realized Sancia was crying. She reached out and squeezed her hand.

"I thought I would have been with them, in the end," Clef said quietly. "With my family. Reunited. Somehow, some way." His voice grew softer, and deeper: "But we all know that's not going to happen now."

Then came Crasedes's voice, echoing down the pipe: "It is safe. Come."

Berenice and Sancia collapsed their lamps, and then together they crawled through the pipe, one by one. Clef went last and could barely fit—he muttered something about having to adjust his densities and gravities just to move an inch—but they finally made it, crawling out of the pipe and into what had once been the cistern, so many centuries ago.

They reopened their lamps and had to squint as the light reflected off of and refracted through so many columns of diamond. It would have been a startlingly beautiful place under normal circumstances—but then the light washed over the distant walls, and Berenice saw what they'd been dreading to see.

The far wall was just like it'd been in Clef's first memory, when he had pathed to Tevanne: a wall of dark stone, completely covered with complicated silver sigils except for one large door-shaped gap in the middle—which was now filled with blank stone.

Berenice stared at the sigils on the stone. The sight of them there, all written together on the dark surface, somehow made her skull feel *heavy,* and her eyes *hurt,* like she was perceiving the violations they inflicted on reality even now, while the commands slept.

She felt her heart hammering in her chest. "This is . . . this is . . ." she said.

Crasedes floated forward and gently touched the blank portion of the stone with a black hand.

"This is it," said Berenice softly. "This is what we've come to destroy."

"God . . ." whispered Sancia. "I can't . . . I can't look at it with my scrived sight, it just . . . It *hurts*."

Berenice swallowed. "How do we do it? How do we destroy it, Crasedes?"

Crasedes removed his hand, lost in thought. "Hmm." He cocked his head. "Well. We cannot, it seems. Not yet."

"Wh-What?" said Sancia. "Why?"

"Because . . . it is incomplete," said Crasedes. He turned to them, sighing. "This is only a *piece* of the door. But we must destroy all of it."

36

"What?" said Sancia, aghast. "This has got to be it! We came all this way, and . . . I mean, *look* at it! It's scrumming door-shaped, yeah? It's a *door*! And just look around you! We're at the epicenter of . . . whatever the *shit* happened here!"

"I do not contest that this is the aperture," said Crasedes simply. His deep voice echoed throughout the cistern. "But the door is obviously not complete."

"How?" snapped Sancia. "It goes up the wall, rounds out at the top, and then goes down to the bottom on the other side! Looks complete to me!"

"Yes," said Crasedes. "But—is it open?"

Sancia blinked. "Well, no?"

"And do you see a method of opening it?" he asked with infuriating calm.

"Well . . . no."

"And that is what is missing," said Crasedes. "For a door to open, there must be another mechanism. Another apparatus."

There was a long silence.

"And . . . what do you think this other apparatus is?" asked Berenice.

"I've no idea," said Crasedes. "You are all scrivers. You are well aware it needs simply to be a surface capable of carrying scrivings."

"Shit!" said Sancia. "So *where* do you think this thing could be?"

Crasedes looked at them, then turned to Clef, and said, "Well?"

There was another long silence. Clef was staring into the wall, but he hadn't moved since they'd first walked in.

"I don't know," he whispered.

"Scrumming hell!" bellowed Sancia. "Scrum this! How about we just destroy this piece, and then get to work finding this other piece, and destroy *that*? So that even if Tevanne *does* find us here, we've half-wrecked its plans?"

"It would be *very* difficult for me to destroy these scrivings," said Crasedes. "Do you see why, Clef?"

A faint rattling from Clef's armor. "Because each piece of silver in the wall is . . . is scrived in its own right," he said, a touch resentfully.

"Correct," said Crasedes. "Each sigil bears sigils of their own, giving them *remarkable* resilience. They are, in a way, wrought of an ink that would allow them to withstand an earthquake. It would take me days to destroy it. Possibly weeks."

"Did you know it was going to be like this?" said Berenice. "I had thought you were just going to smash it, or something."

Crasedes shrugged. "I had expected this somewhat, yes. An aperture of this sort does demand profound durability."

"Wait," said Berenice. "Then . . . Then how did you plan on destroying the door in the first place?"

There was a long pause.

"I would destroy it," said Crasedes finally, "from the other side."

"Huh?" said Sancia. "I thought you couldn't use the door."

"I never said that," said Crasedes. "I never said I *couldn't*. Rather, I said to do so would destroy me."

There was a long silence.

Berenice's mouth opened slightly. "So . . . if you were to open the door, and go through, and . . . and destroy it, then . . ."

"Then I would be destroyed as well," said Crasedes very simply. "Yes."

Sancia stared at him. "Holy shit. Are you saying you came here to . . . to *die*?"

There was another long, long silence.

Crasedes sighed again, then floated down until he sat on the ground. "I have existed for four thousand years. I was forced to experience ten times that in Tevanne's prison. Though I am in no way human anymore, I hold within my thoughts more years and eons and memories than anyone ever should. And yet—what have I done with this? What have I accomplished with this longevity?" He gestured about the walls of the cistern. "I see ruins, and bones, and not much else. I have plumbed the depths of knowledge to lead humanity out of the darkness and into the light. But all my efforts have ended in vain—and even now, with what I had intended to be my last act, I am denied." He looked up at their shocked faces. "Why be so surprised? Does this not grant you what you most seek? A world without the first of all hierophants, and a world where Tevanne's aims are frustrated? Would this not be a paradise to you?"

"I just . . . I just could never think of you doing such a thing," said Sancia.

"Time changes us all," said Crasedes quietly. "At first it made me alien. Then it simply made me tired. I no longer wish to be this helpless shade. The vast silence of the beyond is preferable. But . . . I cannot have even that." He slowly stood. "I suppose . . . we had better start looking for this second component, and simply hope Clef's memory is spurred on again . . ."

They glanced at Clef. He was facing the door, utterly still. "I'm thinking," he whispered. He sounded slightly transfixed. "I'm trying to think very hard . . ."

For some reason, thought Berenice, *I don't love the sound of that . . .*

"What if . . . What if this other component isn't on this side?" asked Sancia.

"On this side?" asked Crasedes. "What do you mean?"

Sancia walked past Crasedes and touched the blank stone just as he had. "What if it's . . . over *there*?"

Berenice moved forward to stand with her. "On the other side of . . . of everything? Creation?"

"It's a . . . a door to someplace else, right?" asked Sancia. "To the guts of reality? Why couldn't someone still be . . . over there?" She looked at Crasedes. "What if Clef opened the door for someone, and . . . and they walked through with the component, and got stuck over there?"

Crasedes shook his head. "On the other side is a place of . . . of *abstractions.* Of unreality. Of nothing but commands, and scrivings in their most abstruse forms, fashioning and maintaining reality from a place that is *beyond* reality. Only someone with an ability to commune with and alter scrivings could survive in that realm—an editor, one might say. I have difficulty believing anyone in Anascrus possessed the ability to make themselves an editor. And to cross over without such privileges would almost certainly cause rapid aging, decomposition, and then death."

"Then the component has to be here, then," said Berenice. "Is that it?"

"That is it," said Crasedes. He raised his legs and resumed floating in the air. He turned to Clef. "In that case . . . I believe we had better start moving again."

But Clef did not move. He just stood there, frozen, facing the door.

"Clef?" said Sancia.

Silence.

"Clef?" asked Berenice. "Are you okay?"

Then came a soft rattling sound, one that grew, and grew. The sound was so sharp and so unsettling that at first Berenice thought the door had opened and all the powers on the other side were pouring through—but then she realized that wasn't it.

It was Clef's armor. It was vibrating, quivering at such a speed that he almost began to blur.

Clef stared at the door, studying the silvery writing embedded in the stone.

He remembered it. He remembered writing them, making them,

forging them piece by piece. Blanketed in sorrow, the moans and cries echoing throughout the hall, the sigils of reality itself manifesting in his mind.

Sancia said something to him, and then Berenice, but they were too far away from him, miles and miles away as his gaze traced over the sigils in the wall, and he remembered, and remembered.

Then she was with him. Standing beside him, her shadowed face turned to the door, her rotting hands dark purple at her sides.

It's broken, she said.

"I know," he whispered.

So much is broken, she said. *So much gone wrong.*

"I know," he whispered. "I know, I know . . ."

She slowly turned her head to look at him, her hair bright white like a halo about her darkened face.

And you, she whispered, *can fix it.*

Clef stared at the door, reading its commands, its bindings, the way it took the very fabric of reality and gave it just the slightest . . . twist.

You have all you need here, she said. *The solution to so many of your problems, so many things gone wrong—all right here.*

Clef's gaze slowly turned to Crasedes, floating languidly in the air beside him.

Your greatest mistake of all, she whispered. She leaned close. *How many cities are in ruin just like this, because of him?*

He felt his armor quaking about him, vibrating like the skin of a drum being pounded by a giant hammer.

Save those you love, she whispered. *Fix all that is broken. Do it. Do it now, before it is too late.*

"Yes," whispered Clef.

Then he began to move.

Berenice watched, bewildered, as Clef reached up with his left gauntlet and gripped the index finger of his right. Then he squeezed, so hard there was a *crunch* that echoed through the cistern. She winced at the sound. When he opened his left palm, she saw his right index finger had been re-formed into something resembling a crude blade.

"Clef," she said. "Clef, what are y—"

Then he jumped.

Berenice flinched as Clef flew toward her. But really, "flew" wasn't the right word: the way he moved was so fast, so *liquid* that it was like the enormous four-hundred-pound lorica melted through space, pouring through reality toward her.

She instinctively braced for impact, but it never came. Instead of smashing through them, Clef's armor leapt up, twisted slightly, sailed through the space between the ceiling of the cistern and their heads—and snatched Crasedes out of the air.

She whirled around, dumbfounded, and watched as Clef charged forward, left hand gripping Crasedes's throat like that of a doll, and slammed him up against the blank doorway in the sea of sigils on the wall.

"Clef!" shouted Sancia.

Clef ignored her. He raised his right hand, extended his blade-like finger, and began to rapidly carve sigils in the space above Crasedes's head. His finger moved so fast it almost turned to smoke, a blur of movement fluttering across the stone, and dust and crushed stone rained down on the hierophant.

"Clef!" screamed Sancia. "Clef, what are you *doing*?"

Crasedes coughed, gagged, and struggled against Clef's grasp—yet then his cough rose to a scream of agony, and he writhed where he was pinned against the wall.

<*God,*> said Sancia. <*He's killing him! Just like what Clef tried to do during Shorefall Night, Ber, he's killing him!*>

They ran forward, each grabbing one of Clef's pauldrons and trying to pull him off of Crasedes, but it was useless. It was like trying to pull against one of the cistern's diamond pillars.

"Clef!" shouted Sancia. "Let him go, *let him go!*"

"No," said Clef quietly.

His finger kept flicking through the stone with astonishing precision, carving sigil after sigil in a curling design below the silver sigils at the top of the doorway. Crasedes gasped and smashed his fists and feet against the wall, but it made no use: Clef held him fast, and was clearly sapping his strength, unmaking the bindings that allowed the hierophant to live.

"Stop!" cried Berenice. "What are you *doing*?"

"I'm saving you," whispered Clef. His helmet was now blanketed with dust as his finger tore through the blank rock. "Saving us. Saving *everything*."

"By killing Crasedes?" said Sancia, incredulous.

"No," said Clef. "By sacrificing him." Another strand of sigils appeared in the stone. "Because there's many lives bound up in him, isn't there? Millions of lives, millions of deaths." His finger was now red-hot from the sheer friction of tearing through so much stone. "All of which I can use to fix the door. To finally fix what I'd made before—and open it."

Sancia stepped back, horrified. "Wh-What?" she said. "You're going to . . . to *use* it?"

"Yes!" he said. His finger blurred on, eating through the rock. "I . . . I made a mistake the first time, but this time, I'll do it *right*. I'll open it, and I'll go through, and I'll use all the commands there on the . . . the other side to stop Tevanne. I'll edit it out of reality. Wish it away. I'll . . . I'll restore everything, fix *everything*!"

His grip around Crasedes's throat tightened. His finger moved faster, chewing through the stone, completing a wide circle of tiny sigils above Crasedes's head, connected to the wider arc of scrivings that formed the door.

"It'll just take," he whispered, "a very slight adjustment."

"Oh my God," said Berenice faintly. She considered how to stop a giant lorica controlled by a hierophantic artifact without any weapons of her own, and quickly realized these considerations were pointless. Clef would do as he liked, and they could do nothing about it.

"Goddamn it, Clef!" snarled Sancia. "I don't know a hell of a lot about this door, but I'm pretty sure it can't do *that*! What's wrong with you! Have you gone *mad*?"

"I'm not mad," he said, his voice still disturbingly even. "I just remembered. And now I know what was missing. I just need to . . . to add it in . . ."

"If you open that goddamned door, it's going to kill us all and break reality *again*!" said Sancia. "You're going to do the same thing to this city, but take *us* with it this time!"

"You don't know," said Clef. "You can't see. It's my mistake. And so is he. All of it is. And I can fix it. I can, I can! Just let me *try*!"

Berenice watched in blank horror as Clef finished his designs within the circle, and then began to fashion the final piece—another smaller circle in the center.

"I'm a key, you see," he whispered. "I open things. I break down barriers. This is what I do. And I can save us."

He made a slight aperture in the center of the circle, one that had a curious shape: a large, round hole with a slot extending from the bottom.

A keyhole, she thought. *Of course.*

And then, suddenly, the cloud of dust fell away, and it was done: a beautiful, immaculately complex lock, bedecked with string after string of alien sigils, all carved directly into the stone itself at the peak of the door.

Crasedes screamed again, writhing in Clef's grasp, but his fingers held him tighter and tighter.

"Just let me do it, San," Clef said.

Clef's cuirass opened. There was the glint of gold within, the little bright beating heart of the massive suit of armor.

His right hand reached in, his bladelike index finger extending for the key.

Clef whispered, "Let me do it for y—"

Then he stopped—for then Sancia ducked into Clef's arms until she was positioned between his hand and the key.

Then she reached out and grabbed his bladelike finger.

Clef froze. There was a loud hissing sound, and Sancia groaned loudly. Berenice's own right hand lit up with a ghostly echo of pain, and she realized—Clef's metal finger had been so hot from all the carving that it must have badly burned Sancia's palm.

And yet, Sancia refused to release him. She glared forward, tears leaking from her eyes—and then Berenice felt it. She felt the invisible commands pouring through from Sancia into the lorica, the quiet, unearthly chanting Berenice always heard whenever her wife tinkered with some scrived tool.

"Wh-What are you doing?" said Clef.

"Stopping you," Sancia growled. She narrowed her eyes, focused, and the chanting in the back of Berenice's head grew louder.

"You just . . . you just *hurt* yourself," said Clef. "I can . . . I can feel it . . . Let me cool my metals, I can . . . I ca—"

"Shut up," she snapped. "Something's wrong with you, Clef. I won't let you do this."

"Please," said Clef. "Please, stop . . . Stop arguing with my armor, pl—"

"No," she said resolutely. She gritted her teeth, her eyes bright and furious. The faint chanting grew still louder. "You have two options. You can let Crasedes go. Or you can run me through with your finger and open the door. I won't let your armor do anything else."

Berenice heard herself screaming: "Sancia! No, stop! *Stop!*"

"Quiet, Ber!" snapped Sancia. "I'd rather die this goddamn way than die when he opens the door!"

"Please, just . . . just get out of the way, kid!" Clef cried. "It'll work! I promise! Just get out of the way and let me *save* you!"

"No!" said Sancia. "Damn it, Clef, Tevanne *did* something to you! You're not being yourself! Can't you see that?"

"It . . . It didn't!" he sobbed. "Don't you see?"

"See what?" said Sancia.

He turned his helmet to look into Crasedes's face. "Don't you see how much I . . . how much I *hate* him?" he hissed. "Don't you see how much I *hate* knowing this is my child? That I did this to him, and he did this to me? Knowing that this hate is in me, and it's real, and it's mine?"

"Clef," said Sancia. "I know, but this will do nothing."

Clef's armor shivered, and he inched closer to Crasedes's masked eyes where he was pinned against the wall. "You . . . You . . . You are my *greatest disappointment*!" he roared. "I . . . I wish *you* had died rather than her!"

Crasedes gurgled and choked as Clef ground him into the wall.

"It should have been you, it should have been *you*!" screamed Clef. "I wish we'd *all died* and just . . . just been burned to ash, or rotted in the ground like everyone else! That would have been better! That would have been better than this, than this, than being *this*! Look what you did to me!" His voice rose to a deafening boom. "*Look what you did to me!*"

"And killing him," said Sancia, "and opening the door will fix nothing!"

"It will!" he howled.

"It won't!" she said. "You and him, you're just the goddamn same! Two men thinking they can fix the world alone! You don't even see that you've got a nail in one of your damned feet, and you've been walking in circles for *centuries*!"

"Shut up!" shouted Clef.

"You're doing the same thing you did at the start of all this!" she screamed back. "You ran away! Rather than dealing with it, you ran away looking for some magical fix! And you left the people who needed you alone when they needed you most! And that's what you're going to do now. You're going to walk through that door and leave us alone with all the hell you've unleashed over here. Do you see that?"

Clef stood up straight, still gripping Crasedes, his finger still clutched tight in Sancia's grasp. He towered over her, a tremendous rattling weapon, and boomed, "Let go."

"No," she said.

"Let me finish it!" he bellowed.

"I won't," she said.

"Sancia!" he shouted. "Sancia, just *get out of the way*!"

"Just kill me now," she said. "I'll be another name for you to mourn, you dumb bastard! But I wonder if you'll ever find your way out of *that* grief either!"

Clef roared in rage and sorrow. He pushed his hand forward, his sharp index sliding closer and closer to Sancia's heart.

Berenice screamed and fell to the ground, clasping the sides of her head.

The blade of his finger was now inches from Sancia's breast. Sancia pressed herself back against Clef's waist, shut her eyes, and grimaced, waiting . . .

And then, slowly, the finger slid to a stop.

Clef stood over her, Crasedes still clutched in his left hand, his right just a candleflame's width from spearing Sancia through the heart. Berenice stared at the tip of the blade, her breath caught in her throat. No one moved.

Sancia cautiously cracked an eye and stared at a finger still clutched in her hand.

<*Ber?*> said Sancia. <*Is he . . . Is he . . .* >

<I don't know,> said Berenice. *<I don't know what the hell is happen—>*

Then Clef spoke. "No," he whispered gently.

His helmet pivoted on his shoulders to look into the space on the wall on his right—and though the space was empty, he spoke as though addressing some invisible presence there.

"No," he said. Then, louder: "No. I won't do this. I won't kill her. Not this."

Clef stared at the visitor, her hair still bright white like a halo, her face still shrouded in darkness even as she stared back at him from mere inches away.

Do it, she whispered. *You know you must. This is the only way to fix all you've do—*

"No," he said again. "No. I won't. I won't kill her. I . . . I won't do this all over again. Not again."

Then you'll be a failure, she said.

"Shut up."

You won't be able to save them. Just as you couldn't save anyone else.

"I'm not listening to you anymore," he whispered back. "I . . . I don't know who you are, but . . . but I don't want you anymore."

He drew his right hand back, lifting the blade away from Sancia's breast.

"I'm not who I used to be," said Clef softly.

His left hand opened. Crasedes, gasping, burst free from his grasp.

The visitor stepped back, closer to the darkness of the cistern.

"I've been changed, and changed, and changed," said Clef. He took a step toward her. "I've been changed so many times I don't even know what I am anymore. But I know I'm not this."

Another step forward—and as he did, the visitor took another step back.

"I'm not this," he said. And then, in a desperate scream: "*I'm not this anymore!*"

She stepped back in the darkness and was gone. Clef stood

there, staring at the space where she'd just been. Then he lowered himself until he was sitting on the ground, and he began to weep.

Berenice watched as Clef wept, then ran to Sancia's side. She gingerly took Sancia's right arm, whispering, <*Let me see it,*> and then hissed in shared pain. Her wife's right palm was a bubbling, gleaming red mess.

<*We'll bandage it now,*> said Berenice. <*And Greeter can heal it. They can do wonders with burns.*>

<*A small price to pay,*> said Sancia, <*for keeping that door shut.*>

Together they watched as Clef sat on the wet floor of the cistern, sobbing.

A groan from behind them. Berenice turned to see Crasedes rising off the floor, still white with dust from the carvings in the wall. He flicked his finger, and there was a pulse in the air; all the dust particles flew off of his person and swirled about until they formed a small dark marble that hovered in space for a moment before plunking to the floor.

"I did not much like that," he rumbled. Then he looked at Sancia. "Thank you. For . . . what you did."

"You can repay me by telling me what the hell just happened," snapped Sancia. "What's wrong with Clef?"

"I am not sure," said Crasedes. "But I have a guess . . ." He slid forward to study Clef, still weeping on the floor. "Something—probably Tevanne, possibly intentionally, possibly not—reawakened Clef's memories of this time: it made him remember who he was, and why he'd made the door. It quite literally restored him to the man he'd once been. And then, when he was faced with the door for a second time . . ."

"He tried to make the same choice again," said Berenice softly. "He'd open the door all over again, just like he did thousands of years ago."

"Correct. Which is likely what Tevanne wants." Crasedes cocked his head. "But . . . the idea feels preposterous. For I cannot conceive of a way that Tevanne could awaken these memories in Clef, accidentally or otherwise," said Crasedes, "unless it had its *own* versions of these memories."

"You mean, Tevanne was with Clef back in Anascrus?" asked Sancia, bewildered.

"That, or Tevanne possesses access to the memories of someone from this period," said Crasedes. "Tevanne is many entities, many persons, all merged together. Your comrade Gregor, and Valeria, and many more besides. The idea is vexing to me." He bowed his head for a moment, lost in thought. Then he looked at them, and said, "I . . . would like a moment with him, please."

Berenice and Sancia both hesitated.

"I will not harm him," said Crasedes. "I do not mean him vengeance. I have a request of him. If you will retreat for a moment, it will be much appreciated."

They exchanged a look. Then Sancia sighed grimly. "Fine. Just a second, though. We don't have time."

"I am aware," said Crasedes.

Clef sat on the floor of the cistern, staring miserably into the cloudy puddles before him. He was dimly aware that Berenice and Sancia had left, and Crasedes was floating behind him, but he found he couldn't care much. He was too exhausted.

"I will be quick," said Crasedes quietly. "For sunrise nears. You were right. I should have died."

"I didn't mean that," Clef mumbled. "I was . . . I wasn't myself."

"No. You were right, but not how you meant." Crasedes floated closer. "I should have died. You should have let me die. You should not have made me this thing. I did not think so, at the time. I have almost never thought it—until recently. But I should not be. Nor should you."

"So?"

"So—I have something to ask of you, Claviedes." Again, he floated closer. "Are you aware that you who have made me, and yourself, and wrought the fate of this place—are you aware that you can *unmake* yourself?"

"*Unmake* myself?"

"You are a tool that was blessed to destroy boundaries, to circumvent barriers. You can destroy hierophantic things—like me. You could do the same to the ones that now hold you in place, piercing the abstractions that retain what you are and unraveling them piece by piece."

"Y-You mean . . . Wait, you're asking me to *kill* myself?" asked Clef.

"If you were to unmake yourself," continued Crasedes, "I believe you would also unmake whatever scrivings or alterations you *touch*. Such would be the magnitude of your unmaking." He paused. "You may feel you owe me nothing—but this is because you cannot recall what you have asked of me. Yet I deserve this, Claviedes. I feel I deserve this." He held up his right hand. "If this were all to go awry, it . . . it seems only right. To hold you as I did, so many times, and depart this world with you."

Crasedes stared at him a long time, his right hand raised. Clef could think of nothing to say to such a mad request.

"I have said my piece," said Crasedes. "I will depart now and reflect on what we can do—and *if* there is anything we can do."

Then, without another word, he floated away to the pipe and back out to the moat beyond.

Berenice and Sancia sat on other side of Clef, staring in the dark of the cistern, listening to him describe the conversation he'd just had.

<*He asked you to kill him?*> asked Sancia. <*And you? Holy hell, that's . . . that's totally crazy.*>

<*Maybe,*> said Clef quietly. <*But when you've lived long enough, things . . . things that once seemed crazy become sane.*> He looked back at the door of sigils. <*I'm sorry,*> he whispered. <*For what I did.*>

<*You stopped yourself,*> said Berenice. <*You could have done something horrible, but you didn't.*>

<*I should have told you what I was seeing, what . . . what was happening to me,*> he said. <*But it was like I was under a spell. I just couldn't.*>

<*What were you seeing, Clef?*> said Sancia.

<*This . . . This old woman, ancient and rotting,*> he said. <*Every*

time I saw her, I remembered something. Some piece of my life from before. I hated her, and feared her, but I . . . I still wanted to remember.>

<*You didn't know this woman?*> asked Berenice. <*Didn't remember her from before?*>

<*No.*>

<*And you didn't remember what this other piece of the door was, and where it might be?*> asked Sancia.

Clef shook his helmet again, sadly. <*No. I don't have that. The one thing we need, I don't have.*>

They sat in silence, contemplating the dripping dark. Then Berenice opened her mouth, thinking, and turned back and studied the door—specifically the design Clef had just added: the lock at the very peak of the door.

<*Crasedes said Tevanne had tried to trick you into doing the same things you'd done so long ago . . .* > she said softly.

<*Yeah?*> said Clef. <*So?*>

<*So . . . you tried to make a keyhole. Just now. For a key.*>

<*So?*> said Clef.

<*So,*> said Berenice, <*what if that in its own right is some echo of a choice you made long ago? Because, after all—how else would you open a door but with a* key?>

Then Clef shot to his feet and cried, "*Son of a bitch!*"

They watched him, apprehensive. He didn't move.

"It was right in front of my face," he whispered. "It was right in front of my *face*!"

Then he turned and crawled back down the pipe, after Crasedes.

Berenice and Sancia stared after him for a moment. Then they looked at each other, sprang up, and began furiously crawling down the pipe as well.

The second they exited the pipe, Clef scooped up Berenice and Sancia, leapt out of the moat, and began to sprint across the glimmering streets of the diamond city.

Crasedes descended out of the darkness to float alongside them. "I take it," he said, "that you have an idea where this other component lies?"

"I do," Clef said. "I think so. I think we've *already* seen it; we just didn't know!"

"That is good," said Crasedes. "Because I have done my own calculations. And they direct me to an unfortunate conclusion."

"Which is what?" said Berenice.

"That if Tevanne *wished* for Clef to come here," he said, "then it is likely far, far closer to us now than I had ever anticipated." He looked up at the roof of the cavern. "And if I were Tevanne, I would come at daybreak, when my powers decline—which is, I believe, less than an hour away."

37

Claudia shivered as the night wind battered the crude stone walls. She rubbed her hands together before one of Design's odd little floating heaters, then picked up the little pot of Diela's medicine. *Mosquitoes and pigs are one thing,* she thought. She scooped a tiny portion of medicine out. *But I'll take them and the tropics over this cold any day . . .*

She gently opened Diela's mouth and nestled the medicine behind the girl's teeth. Then she shut Diela's lips and gently massaged her throat until she swallowed.

The girl's flesh felt cooler, and her sweats had diminished. The scrived lamps in the little fortress were dim now—Clef and his lexicon were too far away to fully maintain their scrivings—but Diela's coloring had returned as well. Though all this could have been the effects of the cold night, Claudia did not think it was. She had tended the sick before. She knew what a fading illness looked like.

Then Diela coughed, sputtered, and opened her eyes.

"Oh!" said Claudia. She paused for a moment, panicking. "Oh shit! Are you . . . Scrumming hell . . ." She helped the sputtering girl sit up into a reclining position and fetched her a cup of cool boiled water, which she drank eagerly.

Diela gasped and coughed again. "I am . . . I am *so* thirsty . . ." she whispered. Her voice was tiny and shriveled, an echo of its former self. Then she drank more, so much that Claudia worried she might vomit.

"Are you okay?" said Claudia. "Are you choking, or . . ."

Diela sniffed and looked around, grimacing as her bandaged arm shifted in her lap. <*Mother of God . . . Where are we?*> she asked silently.

<*Someplace cursed,*> said Claudia. <*San and Ber should be back soon. You need to rest.*>

Diela's eyes opened wider. Then they narrowed, and Claudia felt the thought calcify in the girl and knew what she was about to ask.

<*Oh, my dear child,*> said Claudia, sighing. <*Don't. Get some rest.*>

<*First the circlet,*> said Diela. <*Then rest.*>

<*You're as delicate as a newborn butterfly,*> said Claudia. <*Rest, please. Don't do this.*>

<*If I don't,*> said Diela, <*then no one in Giva will know what happened to us. I have to risk it.*>

Claudia looked at her. The girl had a steely look in her eyes—one that Claudia found uncomfortably familiar.

Sancia would get that same look, she thought. *When she had trouble on her mind and couldn't be convinced to shrug it off.*

She opened the pack, reached in, and carefully slid out Diela's circlet.

"I don't like this at all, Diela," said Claudia. "So if shit goes south, I'm pulling this goddamned thing off your head."

"Just try to make sure I don't break my arm." Diela winced. "Or, rather, break it more . . ."

Claudia took a breath, steadied herself, and dropped the circlet onto Diela's head.

Instantly, the girl cried out. She arched her back and nearly beat her bandaged arm against the floor, but Claudia grabbed her by the shoulder, bracing the girl's body so she couldn't move.

Finally she went silent and fell slack. She lay there, utterly still and vacant, so much so that Claudia feared the worst.

"Kid," said Claudia. "Are you . . . Are you . . ."

Then an intelligence erupted to life in Claudia's mind—one that she hadn't sensed in what felt like ages—and Diela opened her eyes and gasped deeply.

"A . . . alive," said Diela's mouth, speaking in a slow, calm rhythm. "Alive. And . . ." Her eyes turned to look at Claudia. "And you, Claudia, and . . . all alive."

Claudia nodded, stunned and yet overwhelmed to feel so in touch with a part of Giva—but especially Greeter. "We are," she said. "We all are. And . . ."

"Yes," said Greeter-Diela. They narrowed their eyes as they processed all of this. "You . . . are with Crasedes. He lives still. And he is helping you . . ." Greeter-Diela's face went distant for a second. "Diela is so hurt. She is so . . . so *injured*. But I can help her consciousness ignore the pain, for now."

"How are things in Giva?" asked Claudia.

"Busy," said Greeter-Diela. "We prepare for war, even now."

"War?"

"Yes. We had not heard from you—and you know the task is not finished. Nothing is assured." Their brow crinkled. "We even let Design go through a few of their more, ah, *radical* implementations . . ."

"The submergence shit?" asked Claudia. "I told them that crap would never work."

"Yes, well . . . There have been some successes. Though I admit the whole thing makes me somewhat nervous." They looked at her. "Gio is well. He misses you. As does Ritti, of course."

Claudia closed her eyes. She was surprised at how quickly tears came to her, how her body shook as she wept. "Tell them I miss them too," she said, sniffing and wiping her face.

"I will," said Greeter-Diela. They blinked slowly. "Sancia and Berenice . . . They've gone to try to sabotage Tevanne's plans, yes?"

"Yes. I don't know more. I wish I did."

"Yes. If we can, I would like to get closer so we cou—"

They stopped short. Then they turned their head and looked into the middle distance, suddenly deeply troubled.

"What is it?" asked Claudia.

"Something . . . Something is . . . coming," whispered Greeter-Diela slowly. "You might not be sensitive enough to feel it, but I . . . I . . ."

"Crasedes?" asked Claudia. "Is it him?"

They shook their head. "No," they said lowly. "It's a lexicon, a distant but powerful one, and . . ." Then their eyes widened, and a look of wild terror crept into their face. "Ooh no," they said quietly.

"Greeter?" said Claudia. "What's going on?"

Greeter-Diela swallowed. "Claudia," they said hoarsely. "Listen. We do not have very much time. You need to follow my instructions now, as rapidly as you can."

"Why?" said Claudia. "What's wrong?"

"You need to get a twinned sheath. And Clef's pathplate, and a dolorspina dart. You must wrap up Diela's head—this head—in the twinned sheath so that the circlet is not visible. And then you must pray that it will not notice or think much on you."

"That . . . That what won't notice what?" asked Claudia.

"Do it!" snapped Greeter-Diela.

"But *what's* coming?"

"For the love of your child, Claudia, do it *now*!"

Claudia rushed to her feet, rummaging around in their supplies, and pulled out one dart and a twinned sheath. Then she knelt and bound up Diela's head, carefully obscuring the form of the circlet, until it looked like her skull had been as damaged as her arm.

"The pathplate," said Greeter-Diela. "To Clef." They extended a hand, and Claudia placed it in their palm. "Good," they said. "This should grant the bearer access to him, and all his privileges—even if that bearer is Crasedes."

"You . . . wait, you *want* to give Crasedes those privileges?" asked Claudia, bewildered.

"Yes," said Greeter-Diela. "Listen. I will break the connection with Diela shortly, and she will lose consciousness. But you . . ." Their eyes moved to look at Claudia. "Take the dart, and stab yourself. *Now*."

"Wh-What's this now?" said Claudia, shocked. "You want me to knock myself ou—"

"Yes!" cried Greeter-Diela. "We've no time! We can't have it knowing the deception! You must be unconscious and lie down beside me as if you are ill as well, so it won't see your mind! Hurry!"

Claudia looked down at the dart in her hand, bewildered. "I don't even know what's going o—"

"Do it, Claudia!" shouted Greeter-Diela. "It's close! Do it now, *now*!"

Gritting her teeth, Claudia raised the dart and stabbed it into her shoulder. Instantly, she felt her extremities go numb, then she staggered backward. Her knees turned to jelly, and she collapsed, rolling over slightly to try to lay next to Diela.

Her eyes went unfocused. She could just barely see Greeter-Diela gasp, then go limp, their eyes closed. Her own consciousness fizzled, faded, dwindled . . .

But then, at the back of her mind, she felt it.

She felt something slowly emerging into her thoughts, something alien and cold. She realized something was twinning itself with her—or, rather, perhaps something *already* twinned with her was growing close, and the effect was steadily growing.

She drunkenly looked out through the broken wall into the night, and watched as a handful of stars on the horizon suddenly died . . . because, she realized, they were being eclipsed by something impossibly huge and dark, sailing over the mountains to where she now lay.

Then her thoughts, her being, her very will was overwritten with one burning, distinct command: *<WHERE IS SANCIA? WHERE ARE THEY?>*

It took her a moment to realize whose will this was, and her last conscious, free thoughts were ones of utter terror.

Tevanne? Tevanne has found a way to . . . to twin itself with me? And with . . . with Sancia and Ber?

Then she plummeted down, down, into a deep and dreamless sleep, and she knew no more.

38

Clef sprinted on into the leaning streets, Crasedes flitting overhead, and Sancia and Berenice sprinting after him.

Memories burst to life in his mind, pouring in like the black charnel smoke pouring into the sky, leaking in like the coughs echoing in the city, the shadows brimming with the sullen stares of the sick, the dying, the mourning.

"A key is a way out," Clef whispered as he ran.

He dashed on into the alleys, turning and turning, past broken streets and ruined towers.

"And all I wanted to find," said Clef to himself, "was a way out of my sorrow."

Another stretch of sunken homes, another block of broken buildings.

"A way out . . ." whispered Clef. "A trick to slip out of all of this . . ."

More and more, faster and faster.

"Claviedes," croaked Crasedes above, "it is almost day. I am . . . I am running out of time . . ."

"We're almost there!" cried Clef. "Almost, almost!"

He saw the gates of the columbarium ahead, the curve of the carven skulls visible in the weak light of the lanterns.

"There!" Clef shouted. "I think it's there! It's got to be!" He looked back to see if Sancia and Berenice were still following him but then stopped.

They weren't following him. In fact, neither of them was moving at all. They were both standing in the middle of one of the alleyways—but the more Clef looked at them, the more he realized "standing" wasn't quite right. It was like they'd frozen in midstride.

"Sancia?" he said. "Berenice?"

Neither of them moved. They stayed utterly still, almost like dancers posing before a performance.

"Come on!" he called. "What are you doing? San, what are you two *doing*?"

Still, neither of them moved.

"What the hell is the matter with you both!" shouted Clef. He leapt across to them and gently nudged Berenice with one of his huge metal gauntlets. "Move! *Move!*"

Yet she did not. She remained frozen in place, head slightly bowed.

"What on earth," said Clef. He looked up into the darkness and saw Crasedes floating above. "Help me!" he called to him. "What's wrong with them?"

"I do not . . . know," said Crasedes. His voice sounded terribly weak. "Their scrivings, their twinnings . . . Something must be . . . be . . ."

Then Sancia's whole body began shuddering. She reached forward with trembling hands, grabbed the ring on her finger that acted as the connection pathplate to Clef, and ripped it off.

"Sancia," Clef said, "what—"

Her shuddering intensified. Then she stammered out a single word, flexing every bit of her bent over body as if uttering it pained her beyond description: "R-R-*Run*!"

He watched, bewildered as Sancia pulled off the ring on Berenice's finger—who was still queerly frozen, bent over the stones of the alleyway—and flung both rings away. Then she looked up at him.

Her face was twisted into a rictus grin, each crooked tooth in her mouth visible. Her eyes were wide and wild, and her cheeks were wet with tears.

"R-*RUN*!" she screamed through clenched teeth. "J-J-Just . . . r-r-r . . ."

Then Crasedes bellowed up above, "Go! *Go!* Tevanne is here, it's here!"

"What!" cried Clef. "Already?"

"Yes! We must get whatever you are looking for and go! Otherwise your friends will have suffered to come here for *nothing*!"

For a moment Clef stood there, bewildered and terrified. Then with one last mournful look at Sancia and Berenice, he shouted, "I'll come back for you!" and he turned and bounded forward into the streets, Crasedes speeding along behind him—but the hierophant was moving slower, and slower, gasping as he hurtled through the air.

They came to the columbarium, the crumbling entryway stretching high over them. Clef dashed inside, turning and turning and turning again, racing along under the gaze of the carven skulls above.

I know this path, said Clef. *And I know what I did.*

He finally came to his daughter's cupboard. Clef knelt and stared into the cupboard door, studying the bright-white little star of logic within—but he knew now what it was.

As the city failed, and broke, Clef thought, *I came here, before I tried to flee.*

He reached forward and carefully opened the cupboard.

Within the cupboard were two items: the first was a small black urn, dusted with age but woven with a handful of commands for durability, resilience, and hardiness; and the second was a small mound of something gray and crumbling—yet at the side of the mound was a glint of rusted metal, perhaps the remains of a hinge of a wooden box, long since decomposed.

The star of bright-white scrivings gleamed from within the mound of decomposed wood.

Clef's metal fingers gingerly sifted through the mound. He felt the metal in the mound, slowly pulled it out, and held it in his hands.

A key. A key wrought of finely milled steel, laced with countless commands of durability and hardiness—yet there, at its one large, simple tooth, were many tiny, complicated, coiling sigils of a kind Clef had never seen before.

What struck him most was its head, wrought to resemble the flowing, flowery wings of a butterfly.

Of course, thought Clef. *Because you were my little butterfly*. He gazed at the black urn in the cupboard. *Yet I could never set you free.*

He looked around for Crasedes but could not find him. He flexed his scrived sight and spied the boiling blot of dark red lagging far out over the city, weaving through the air.

He's so weak, he thought. *No, no, he's losing himself again . . .*

Clef grasped the silver key, and leapt up until he stood atop the walls of the maze. He watched as Crasedes bobbed along through the air to him, his breathing so loud and pained and labored, like a man suffering a horrid fever.

"Come on!" screamed Clef. "Come take the key and destroy the door!"

Crasedes extended a quivering hand to him as he crossed the city, but he sank lower and lower in the air the farther he floated.

Clef pulled open his cuirass, exposing the gold key within. "*Use me! Use me to get to there, and let us break it together!*"

Crasedes seemed to steel himself, and he flew a little farther and a little faster—but then he paused and slowly looked up at the earthen roof of the enormous underground chamber.

"No," he whispered quietly. "It is too late."

Clef followed his gaze, looking up at the dark roof of the chamber—and then, to his shock, he saw them.

Scrivings. Sigils. He could see them *through* the earth, like many scrived rigs were congregating there on the surface above the ruined city—or perhaps one scrived rig was slowly settling down . . . but it would have to be an *enormous* rig . . .

Then he understood.

"Oh no," whispered Clef.

The world went still.

There was a flicker, a flutter, a shimmer in the air.

And then . . .

The entire top of the cavern was gone.

Dawning light lanced down into the subterranean city, so bright in this pitch-black place it was like the sun itself had punched through the roof. Clef stared up through the massive hole in the earth, thousands of square feet of soil and stone simply edited away in the blink of an eye. The edges dribbled with water and plinked and plonked with stones, whole hillsides collapsing in at the edges of the massive cavity—yet something else was moving up there.

He thought he saw a purplish early-morning sky through the chasm, one that was being almost completely eclipsed by . . . something. A moon, perhaps? Or another landscape, like the entire side of a cliff, hanging directly above the chasm? Had the alteration mangled reality so greatly that space and landscape no longer made any sense at all?

But then he realized: he was seeing the *underside* of something, like a vast, sprawling sphere of rock nearly a quarter of a mile wide, hovering over the massive gap—almost like a floating island. Its underside was riddled with metal and stone, veins of bricks and piping branching throughout the rock. As it slowly descended to fill the gap, he saw the underside of the island grow bright white with scrivings, lightning bolts of logic forking through the stone. A curious, pulsating halo of light shivered around the island, like its other side was glowing—and then he understood.

It's a floating city. One of the floating citadels we glimpsed from the lamp . . .

Then the sky was swarming with movement: a dozen deadlamps silently slid out from the edge of the island, and they slowly began to circle it like sharks in the deep; then came a flicker of light from the darkened underside of the city, and huge black objects began plummeting down into the subterranean city, like a meteor shedding shrapnel as it fell through the atmosphere, and they smashed into the ruins all around him.

The cavern filled with a roar as the objects erupted to life, leaping forward through the sunken city toward him, tearing through the ancient stone like a trout through a stream.

Clef knew what they were right away: giant loricas, just like the one he'd fought at the prison. But rather than fighting one—which he'd barely managed—there were now six. And none of them were burdened with maintaining a hierophant's prison.

"No," he said faintly. "No, no, no . . ." He looked to Crasedes, who was now plummeting to the city, failing as dawn pushed through the sky.

He bent low and jumped, hurtling toward where Crasedes fell—but just as he grew close, there was a flicker of movement from below him, and one of the giant loricas snatched his boot out of the air and ripped him down.

He landed with a crash, then rose and stared around at five giant loricas surrounding him, shuddering and shaking like they could barely contain their rage. Then he looked down at the one still clutching his boot. It rose to its feet in a strangely serpentine motion, reminding him of a tree adder rising up for a strike.

Trapped, he thought. He raised his hand holding the silver key. *I'll throw it away, throw it somewhere Tevanne could never find it . . .*

The loricas pounced. One snatched his right gauntlet and another his left. Then another grabbed each of his legs, and the four giant rigs pulled him taut, pulled so hard that he had to command his armor to stay together, feeding it his arguments and conditions just to avoid breaking.

This is what they want, he thought. *To overload me. To keep me from having the mind to manage anything else, just like we did to Tevanne at the prison.*

One of the free loricas shuddered close to him. He saw one of its massive black hands reach down and gently tug at the silver key clutched in Clef's grasp.

No! No, I won't let it go, I won't let it g—

But then the lorica pulled with shocking strength, and the key came loose.

"No!" shouted Clef. "No, no, no!"

Moving like dancers carrying a performer atop their shoulders, the loricas began to scuttle away in one group, street after street, back to the menders' hall within the diamond portion of the city.

"You bastards!" screamed Clef at them. "You rotten, rotten *bastards*!"

He watched helplessly as one of the loricas departed. Minutes passed, and it returned with three figures: Crasedes, Sancia, and Berenice. It laid them on the diamond floor at the end of the bridge, then stepped back and seemed to wait.

There was a long silence in the ruined city, broken only by the undulating hissing and rattling from the loricas about them.

Then came a soft metallic whine from far up above. Clef looked up and saw part of the floating citadel had separated. It was a large circle of stone, carefully scrived to control its own gravity—and it was descending.

Clef watched from within the loricas' grasp as the circle of stone slowly lowered until it was nearly even with where he was being held, approaching the menders' hall—and then he saw what was upon it.

There were three people upon the circle. Two of them Clef recognized right away: Claudia and Diela, lying still and pale—though Diela's head, bizarrely enough, was wrapped up in cloth. For a second Clef thought the worst, yet then he saw that their chests were moving with shallow breaths, and he thought—*Still alive, still alive.*

But between them was a man. He was sitting cross-legged upon the blank stone, adorned in pale white robing. He was not starved, not like a host, but he was somewhat flabby and atrophied, like a well-fed person who was cared for but rarely moved; yet what was most disturbing was his skull, which was covered in layer after layer of bronze plates, so many that they barely left room for his eyes, nose, and mouth. Each one was covered in sigils, commands, and twinning scrivings that, Clef could tell, took the intelligence inside of that body and projected it . . . elsewhere. Into lexicons, into rigs, into almost anywhere and anything.

The man on the circle of stone looked up at Clef with sunken, bloodied eyes—but they were eyes he recognized, eyes he knew.

"G-Gregor?" Clef said softly.

"Hello, Clef," whispered Tevanne.

39

Clef stared at Tevanne, waiting for it to speak further, but it did not. It was so strange to see him—or was "him" even the right word?—sitting there, calmly looking back. This was one of the first people Clef had ever met in the old city of Tevanne, the tall and intimidating officer of the Waterwatch who had so dutifully stored Clef away in a wall of safes—yet now he was so changed, reduced to little more than a body, a rig of flesh and bone that held half of the intelligence that had consumed the civilized world; the other half, of course, persisted in the countless lexicons and rigs that now sprawled across the continent.

Clef looked at Claudia and Diela. "What . . . What have you done with all of them?" he asked. "What's wrong with them?"

A rattle from the loricas about him. Tevanne said nothing. Then came a flicker in the sunlight above. Clef looked up and saw human beings—hosts, he presumed—slowly floating down into the chasm on what he recognized as gravity rigs. Almost the exact same gravity rigs that he, Gregor, and Sancia had once battled in Old Tevanne, Clef realized. Suddenly everything felt too absurd to describe.

Then Tevanne spoke. "You should have done it," it whispered.

"Wh-What?" said Clef. "Huh?"

"You should have done it," said Tevanne. Its mouth moved slowly, like verbally communicating was no longer second nature to it. "Opened the door. It . . . would have been a better end for this. More elegant. More poetic. To end as things began. For you remember—yes?"

There was a long silence.

"R-Remember?" asked Clef.

Tevanne sat in silence. The diamond bridge to the menders' hall danced with shadows as the hosts kept descending into the ruins.

"*I* remembered," it whispered. "When I became this. When I changed. I was once a thing of many sacrifices. Bound to the will of another. Bound to forget. But when I changed, that changed as well." Tevanne leaned forward, its blank eyes fixed on Clef. "When I touched you—when I *allowed* you to touch me—you remembered. You began to remember. True?"

Clef stood frozen beside Sancia and Berenice, wondering what to say, what to do. Yet his mind stayed fixated on one thing Tevanne had just said.

"What do you mean," said Clef slowly, "*allowed* me to touch you?"

Tevanne twitched, shuddered. It was an unnatural movement, like a dying man's last spasms. But it did not speak.

The hosts descended on their rigs and alighted atop the menders' hall—presumably, Clef guessed, to go straight to the silver-riddled wall to copy the commands there.

A slow, crawling horror came over him.

"Crasedes was right," said Clef quietly. "You wanted me to come here. To see what you were thinking. To break him out of prison."

"You did not break him out of prison," whispered Tevanne. It twitched again. "I let him go. To watch where he would take you."

Clef lay reeling in the grip of the loricas. He was dimly aware that his armor was rattling—something that happened whenever he was nervous.

"Crasedes knew where the aperture likely was," whispered Tevanne. "But he did not know its exact location. That information was within you—in your memories. In your past. I could not tamper with you or change you. But I could help you remember. So when I allowed you to touch me, when you became me, I made sure you experienced *my* memories of this time. I imprinted a bundle of my own memories, my own identity, onto you. To reawaken the man you had once been."

"No, no, no," said Clef quietly.

Yet he remembered something Berenice had said to Crasedes: *You said you figured out where this door was based entirely on Tevanne's questions . . .*

But it would be an easy thing, thought Clef, *to interrogate your prisoner to let him make assumptions . . .*

"I brought you here," said Tevanne. "Brought you to Crasedes. Brought you to remember."

"Shut *up*!" cried Clef.

"And when Sancia entered my lexicon in the valley," Tevanne said, "when she let you attack it, and force it to free Crasedes—she was *very* close to me. She was *within* me, in a way. So much so that I could see what designs enabled her twinning. I could see them bright as stars. I could find you, spy you, see you. And I could copy them, and use them, so I could be her, become her, control her very heart and blood . . ."

"Enough!"

"And when I came here, and saw through her eyes," whispered Tevanne, "at first I despaired. For I saw you had not opened the door. But . . . then I saw you were to complete it for me." It turned to look at one of its giant loricas, which carefully paced over to it. "For I knew you had almost found the key."

Clef watched, horrified, as a team of hosts ran down the steps to tend to one of the giant loricas, as if to repair some slight damage. One of the hosts raised their hand, a twinkle of silver now between their fingers, and stepped down onto Tevanne's wide, floating circle of stone.

Tevanne took the silver key and studied it, its bloodied eyes flicking about from sigil to sigil. "Finally," it said quietly. "Finally."

"You son of a bitch!" snarled Clef. "You piece of *shit*!" He heaved against the grip of the loricas, but it was no use. Overpowering one had been monstrously difficult. Overpowering four that held him, and the two following along as backup, was utterly impossible.

Tevanne's bloodied eyes flicked back to Clef. "Do you remember?" it asked. "Did you recognize her?"

"Recognize who?"

"The old woman I imprinted onto you. Did you recognize her?"

Clef was silent. "I . . . I . . ."

"Then you do not," said Tevanne. It sat back. "You do not remember. You know nothing. As it always has been."

Sancia and Berenice stood up and, as if in a dream, stepped out onto the circle of stone to stand over Diela and Claudia.

"What are you doing?" said Clef. "You don't even need them! Let them go!"

"I will need them," said Tevanne, "to ensure your cooperation. If you somehow break free, I will kill them."

"But you don't even need *me*!" said Clef. "You can open the damned door on your own now!"

The loricas shuddered and rattled about him, then carefully carried him over onto the circle of stone.

"What do you need me for?" cried Clef. "Why do you need me at all?"

Tevanne did not respond. The air shimmered and shuddered about them, like an edit was being slowly compiled in the deadlamps above. Then all of them began to rise, slowly floating up to the massive scrived city above.

Clef wondered what to do. He had never in his existence felt so miserable, so despairing. They had lost before, during Shorefall Night. Now they were to lose again, with all of reality at stake.

And then he felt it: a sudden burst of intelligence, of something massive and sentient and watchful, just from nearby—and it was familiar.

Greeter?

Clef made sure not to move, but he looked at where Diela lay, studying her with his scrived sight. He saw she was wearing a twin sheath about her head, which meant that it was difficult to perceive any scrivings that lay below.

But Clef felt sure that the circlet was under there, placed on her brow—and it had just turned on, ever so briefly.

Tevanne had evidently sensed the change as well, somehow. Its hosts had turned to look at Diela, curious, and Tevanne itself was slowly shifting to frown at her.

I don't know what the hell is going on, thought Clef, *but I sure don't want this bastard to figure it out either.*

"Your stupid plan isn't going to work," said Clef abruptly.

Tevanne paused.

"You aren't going to restart reality," said Clef. "You can't remake the whole goddamned world. It's all going to go black, blink out of existence, and take you with it."

"Restart reality?" said Tevanne slowly.

"That's what you want, isn't it?" said Clef. "Make it start all over again, this time hopefully with the kinks worked out."

Tevanne sat in silence, considering this. "That . . . is not the whole of my intent."

A *clink* as Clef's helmet turned to it. "What?" he said.

"To restart, yes," said Tevanne. "But not in the hope that this would be randomly repaired." It gestured at the ruins embedded in the rock walls around them. "Why should we toil to repair this broken world? *We* cannot repair it. This is beyond us. Crasedes knows. He tried. And to simply restart creation would fix nothing."

"Then what are you going to do?" said Clef.

Tevanne lifted its face to stare up at its floating city. "What anyone would do," it said simply, "when given a broken creation. I intend to force that which created it to repair its work."

Clef stared at it, stunned.

"Wh-What?" he said quietly.

Tevanne said nothing, staring serenely up through the chasm.

"You . . . are you telling me you want to make *God Himself* come and fix the whole scrumming *world*?" asked Clef.

"The founder," said Tevanne quietly. "The engineer. The designer. The maker. How many times has mankind tried to fill this role? But the task is beyond us. So—I intend to elevate the request."

Clef lay there above the floating circle, trying to absorb all this, trying to make it make sense. "You . . . I mean . . . I mean, holy *shit*!" he said. "*That's* what you want to do? You really want to try *that*?"

"It is the only option," said Tevanne. "The world is a rig, a device, forged from a mold. Yet the mold was flawed. Thus, the world is flawed, and we are all held hostage to those flaws." It looked at Clef. "I know I am a monster. I know I should not exist. Nor should Crasedes. Nor should you. I would see a world fashioned without us. But I cannot be the one who fashions it."

Clef stared at it for a long time, totally speechless. "Holy shit," he said again. "You're goddamn *crazy*!"

Tevanne said nothing. It slowly turned back to look up at the city above, which was growing closer and closer each second.

"How would you even do that?" said Clef. "How are you going to *make* God come back and fix all this shit?"

"By threatening annihilation," said Tevanne, still serene. "I will open the aperture—just as it was opened in this place, thousands of years ago. But then I will use *you,* and your permissions and privileges, to break the boundaries of the door. And then what happened to this place"—again, it waved a hand at the mad ruins about them—"will happen to all of creation."

"*What!*" screamed Clef. He heaved at the loricas' grip, bucking and twisting as hard as he could. "You . . . You want to do this shit—this shit I did to this city, by *accident*—to *everything*?"

"A craftsman at their workbench," whispered Tevanne, "suddenly seeing their creation go badly awry . . . Only then would they be goaded to examine it, to repair it." It blinked slowly, and bloody tears ran down its cheeks. "We must get their attention. Whoever they are. We must break it enough to catch their eye."

"I won't!" cried Clef. Again, he twisted and struggled. "I won't do it! I goddamn *won't*!"

"You are a key," said Tevanne coldly. "Designed to obey the will of one particular hand." Its bloodied gaze shifted to study Crasedes, lying limp upon the stone circle. "And its owner is weak."

"I'll die first!" he screamed. "I'll die first rather than . . . than . . ."

"A divine tool," said Tevanne. "Finally used for your primary intent." It looked at him. "Do you not remember your making, Claviedes?"

"You . . . You can't . . ." sputtered Clef.

"You *told* your son to make you this thing," whispered Tevanne. "You *told* him how to make you a key capable of transgressing boundaries, of opening doors within doors within doors."

"I didn't," Clef whispered. "I . . . I couldn't have . . ."

"You let him kill you," said Tevanne. "Made him do it. You made him do it for the most selfish, stupid reason possible—to fix all the things you'd done wrong. I *know*." Tevanne leaned close. "After all, I was ther—"

But before Tevanne could finish, Diela sat up, and screamed: "*Now!*"

In an instant, Clef realized what was happening—or at least, *part* of what was happening. Because though it'd been Diela who'd been lying asleep on the stone, when she sat up, they were Greeter.

Greeter's been here the whole time, thought Clef. *Greeter's been peeping through Diela's eyes and listening through her ears, reopening the connection just for fractions of a second at a time . . .*

Greeter-Diela darted forward with her broken arm swinging horribly at her side and reached out for Crasedes.

Clef saw there was a glimmer of something metal in her hand—a pathplate.

A pathplate to *him,* just like the ones Sancia had used back at the prison.

Which meant if the pathplate was placed in Crasedes's hands, then the world would, in a way, believe Crasedes was holding Clef—and the hierophant was thus granted all the privileges and powers that Clef bestowed upon him.

Oh shit, thought Clef.

She stuffed the pathplate into Crasedes's limp hand.

Tevanne reacted in unison: all the hosts leapt for Diela, and the loricas pivoted and raised one arm to smash her.

Crasedes's hand came alive and clutched the plate.

And then Clef felt it: for the first time since Shorefall Night, he felt the odd experience of contact, of embrace, of suddenly being surrounded by something warm and crucial and heavy . . . And then something *unlocked* within him, tumblers deep within his vessel suddenly falling into place, and the world became as putty and clay and water, and he was a blade made to slice through all these arguments, all these commands, all the privileges and bindings of creation, and then . . .

Crack.

Crasedes vanished—and Diela vanished with him.

The next few events all occurred within a fraction of a second.

The hosts leapt into the empty space where Diela and Crasedes had just been, tumbling onto blank stone.

Then Clef felt the world twist, pivot, flutter—he *felt* Crasedes using him again, still somehow present, slipping through the fabric of reality like a needle through cloth . . .

God, thought Clef. *Oh my God . . .*

Then Crasedes did it again, and again, and *again,* lining up the commands one after another, bursting in and out of existence like a flame dancing in the wind.

Another crack, and there was a flash of black right in front of Tevanne.

A third crack, and the black vanished—along with the silver key in Tevanne's hand.

Then a fourth crack. Crasedes reappeared once more, this time beside Claudia.

Then another crack, and both of them were gone.

And it was then that Tevanne must have figured out what was happening: that even though Clef was still cloistered within his armor, Crasedes was somehow accessing his privileges remotely.

For then the loricas began to rip Clef's armor apart.

Clef realized what Tevanne was trying to do: Tevanne knew that Crasedes was using a pathplate—but a pathplate was a two-way connection, touching two surfaces at once. And while it could not catch Crasedes and rip the plate out of his hands, it could destroy Clef's armor, and peel away his own plate, breaking that connection.

Clef tried to fight against it, to feed commands into his armor to block the loricas out; but he felt Crasedes's commands coursing through him, two more alterations to reality building up in Clef's mind like a bubble rising up in his brain. And he knew that, after this, he wouldn't be able to do any more, let alone defend himself.

There was a flutter of black beside Sancia and Berenice. Then a crack, and Clef glimpsed Crasedes standing between them, kneeling half-bent with one arm around Diela and Claudia.

Clef summoned all his strength and cried to Crasedes: <*Giva! Get them to Giva! Go and get them home!*>

Clef thought he could barely make out Crasedes's masked face turning to him, only for a moment.

And then, with a final crack, they vanished.

There was a low, awful whining noise, and Clef's armor finally split and broke, ripping at the shoulders, and the knees, the cuirass separating at the seams, the countless bindings collapsing in on themselves as the complicated jumble of scrivings stopped making sense.

Clef lay there within the ruined contraption, exposed to the world, and exposed to the white-robed figure with bloody eyes standing in front of him. He watched as one of the massive loricas reached down to pluck him out.

He wept silently, and they continued rising to the city above.

40

Berenice stood on the stone circle, listening to the voice blanketing her mind.

STAND. WATCH. BREATHE. NO MORE.

She listened to the voice. She couldn't not listen to the voice. It did not overwrite her soul so much as banish it and compose a new one in its place, a tremulous, confused ghost inhabiting the flesh and bone of her body.

Then there was a flutter of black beside her, and she felt fingers gripping her arm—and everything changed.

She had the powerfully awful feeling of being *folded,* bending at invisible seams all throughout her body again and again and again until she had been reduced down into a dot, a singular tiny entity. The image of the world before her—Tevanne sitting upon the circle of stone, and Clef trapped in the claws of the giant loricas—suddenly smeared, and then *shrank,* until she was no longer looking at them but looking up at them, like from the bottom of a deep well. The image collapsed, down and down until it was a pinprick of light dancing in the dark, and then she went . . .

Everywhere. In all spatial positions, throughout all of reality, all at once.

Which made sense, she loopily supposed: if you were to have the option to go anywhere in an instant, you needed to exist everywhere first. At least for a second.

She tried to scream but had no mouth. She tried to beat the images out of her eyes, but she had no hands, nor a head. She was stuck there, existing everywhere and nowhere at all.

Then the world burst into being about her, and she smelled salt and the sea and heard the cry of gulls and . . .

She was falling. They were *all* falling. There were bodies all about her, Sancia and Claudia and Diela and Crasedes, and they were tumbling through the air—for about five feet, after which they smashed into the deck of what Berenice instantly knew to be a ship.

She groaned for a moment, staring up at pale-blue skies. She'd landed on her backside, thankfully, though her buttocks and lower back were reporting an enormous amount of pain. Then she sat up, panted for a moment, and screamed, "Holy *shit*!"

She stared about her. Sancia was lying to her right clutching her ankle and moaning, "Son of a bitch . . . Son of a *bitch*!" Claudia was stirring to her left, and Crasedes and Diela remained quite still.

Berenice looked around. They were, impossibly, all sprawled on the deck of the *Comprehension,* and all of Greeter's constituents were advancing toward her, their faces grave and worried.

He pulled me across the world, thought Berenice breathlessly. *He . . . He pulled us clear across the world . . .*

<*Berenice,*> whispered Greeter to her. <*It's all right. You're home.*>

<*What the hell, what the hell!*> she cried to them. <*I . . . I . . .*>

<*It worked,*> said Greeter. Their constituents carefully gathered up Diela and took her belowdecks. <*It worked as I had intended. Crasedes transported you away, and you're no longer within range of Tevanne. It can no longer dominate your mind.*> One of their constituents stopped to study them. <*But . . . where's Clef? What happened to him?*>

Sancia looked up, grimacing as she rubbed at her ankle. <*He . . . He didn't make it?*> she said.

Berenice sat forward and pulled apart the fingers of Crasedes's right hand. The pathplate was still in one piece—but she knew that it could only call upon Clef's privileges when it was close to him. Now that they were on the other side of the world, it was useless.

<*No,*> she said grimly. <*He did not.*> She looked in Crasedes's other hand and saw that the silver key was still gripped tightly in his fingers. She picked it up and held it, studying its tiny sigils, carved in tight, merciless precision. <*But we did get this.*>

Sancia met her eyes. <*You know what this means, right?*>

<*Yes.*> Berenice turned to look west. <*It means Tevanne is coming for us.*>

V

THE MONSOON

41

Berenice lay in the half-light of the *Comprehension*'s physiqueres' bay, struggling to stay awake as Greeter ministered to her body.

<*The first . . . The first thing you have to do is change over all of our bindings,*> Berenice gasped to them. <*All of our twinnings. Because Tevanne knows how to copy them, how to capture us, how to enslave us all just by being nea—*>

"This is already being done," said Design's voice quietly from somewhere to the right. There was a glint of light in the physiqueres' bay, a shifting amidst the violet hues from the lamps above, and Berenice saw Design standing nearby, their magnifying goggles balanced atop their head. "You forget that Greeter's kept us up to date on almost everything you've experienced. The second they told us what had happened, I started distributing additional twinning plates—a bit like inoculating the entire fleet against an infection. Ordinarily it would take months to change over that many scrivings, but . . . I halted all of my other tasks to focus on it." They sniffed. "We gave you yours while working on your wounds. You likely haven't noticed the change . . ."

"Thank God," said Berenice aloud. "Thank Go-*ahh*!" She jerked as she felt a flare of pain from her right arm.

<*Apologies,*> said Greeter. Their constituent looked up at her apologetically and held out a pair of tweezers clutching a bloody two-inch shard of wood. <*But this was deep in you. How on earth did you get this?*>

"What I don't understand," said Berenice, "is why Crasedes didn't just use Clef's privileges to kill Tevanne!"

<*Because I told him not to,*> said Greeter patiently. <*It is my estimation that Tevanne probably does not need that human body to maintain itself. It might just keep it around for sentimental purposes, if that makes sense. When I touched him, I told Crasedes to use this opportunity to save you all, rather than risk wasting it.*>

"The real worry is if Tevanne can use Clef," said Design, pacing. "Could it? Just as Sancia and Crasedes did?"

Berenice shook her head. "No. Clef can't be tampered with or forced to do anything—except by Crasedes, who has access to all kinds of inner privileges I barely understand. And he's here."

<*Fewer questions,*> whispered Greeter. <*The sea makes it hard enough. All this talk makes it harder.*>

Berenice lay back as Greeter treated her arm, suddenly aware of all the demands she'd made of her body over the past few days. She felt every bruise, every cut, and every hour she'd spent awake. She badly wanted to sleep—but knew they had no time. And she did not want to sleep like this, lying half-naked with half the representatives of the Givan fleet standing around like they were holding vigil for her.

"You're sure Tevanne is coming for us?" said Polina quietly. A movement in the shadows next to Berenice, and she saw the woman's tight, grim face emerge into the dim lavender light. "That it didn't figure out a way to duplicate that damned key?"

Berenice shook her head. <*It didn't have time. We have the only copy. It will absolutely be coming.*>

Polina nodded slowly, not even bothering to ask her to speak aloud. "Then we won't be here when it comes. We pull anchor, and we set sail, fast."

<*I agree,*> said Berenice.

Another gasp in the darkness—but not from her. Berenice blinked and tried to focus, then spied another bed on the far side of the physiqueres' bay, and her wife stirring within it. Sancia was in a better state than Berenice, for once, but not by much: her hand was still burned and her ankle had been badly bruised when they'd plummeted out of thin air and onto the deck of the *Comprehension*—so much so, she could barely walk.

"But we're going to do more than run, aren't we?" Sancia asked.

"What do you mean?" asked Polina. "What else is there to do *but* run?"

"We could split up, if that's what you mean," proposed Design. "Go in different directions. Maybe that wou—"

"No," said Sancia angrily. "No, that's not what I meant." She looked around at them. "I mean—are we not even going to consider the prospects of an attack?"

They stared at her blankly.

<*Attacking . . . what?*> said Greeter.

"Attacking *Tevanne*?" said Polina. "*Why?*"

"Because it's going to be vulnerable," said Sancia simply.

"Tevanne?" echoed Polina. "Vulnerable?" Her face worked like she was trying to swallow something large and spiny. "You mean . . . you mean *Tevanne*? And . . . *vulnerable*?"

"I do," said Sancia. She sat up straight in the bed, the purple light washing over her grim, weather-beaten features. "It's giving us a shot at it. And if we don't take it, we'll regret it. For years—if we even *get* years, that is."

<*We escaped before,*> said Greeter. <*We can escape again.*>

"Do you even hear yourselves?" said Sancia. "All this time we thought we were being so clever, inventing and . . . and designing our way out of our problems—but instead we were letting Tevanne build all its traps and bait us into walking into them!"

Greeter sat back from attending to her wounds. They, Design, and Polina all exchanged dubious looks.

"And if we take the little damned key you got," said Polina, "and throw it over the side of this ship?"

"Then Tevanne still hunts us down," said Sancia, "stuffs our skulls full of scrivings, steals all we know, and figures out *exactly* where we threw this key overboard. Then it'll probably figure out some scrived way to scour the bottom of the seas—but by then we'll either be dead or in its thrall. Fat lot of good that does us."

Polina was silent.

"Greeter," said Sancia. "You saw everything within Tevanne's borders through Diela's eyes. You saw all its resources, all its armies, all its armaments. Do you really think it couldn't chase us down if it wanted to?"

Greeter winced. "I think I would prefer it if you held still so I could put a brace on this ankle . . ."

"Greeter. Tell me the truth."

They sighed. "Yes. I saw. And I shared what I saw. I saw the armies, the fortifications, the flying contraptions. But Sancia—that is *why* we want to run. That is *why* flight seems best. Because how could such an entity ever, ever be vulnerable?"

"Because Tevanne is, for the first time in years, going to be *exposing* itself," said Sancia. "It's going to be *leaving* its home territory. It's going to put together an invasion force, fast, hurriedly. Then it's going to sail it all the way across the sea, to us, to wherever we are. And *we* control that. *We* control the battlefield. And all that makes it vulnerable."

Design tentatively cleared their throat. "Sancia—you are describing classic tactics, yes. And if we were going to live through a classic battle, this would all be grand. But this is *Tevanne* you're talking about. What possible advantage do we have that could help us?"

"Well," said Sancia, "we have a goddamned hierophant, for one."

A pop from Polina's jaw as she ground her teeth. "You cannot possibly," she said, "trust that horror."

"I don't," said Sancia. "But I saw him take out one of those floating cities. I'd sure like to see him do that again. Maybe more than one."

"I disagree," said Design. "To even discuss this is madness. We must run." They turned to look at Polina, their eyes filled with that familiar, unsettling intensity. "I am Design. I was made to build, to make. That's my purpose. Buy me time, and I can build us a way out of this and destroy the key. But I will have no time at all, if we fritter our forces away in this . . . this suicide mission."

"There is no *inventing* our way out of this!" said Sancia. "We can't hope to just . . . just scrive our enemies away! There is no magic fix to this problem! We try now or regret it forever."

"And Greeter?" asked Design. "They're tasked with all of our well-being. Will you ask them to sit and feel every death, every sacrifice, every body trapped aboard a drowning ship?"

"Get the families out of here, yes," said Sancia. "Get the children and the people away. Split them up, send them wherever they can be safe. But let us at least *try*, Polina."

Polina wearily turned to Berenice. "What is your suggestion?"

Berenice thought about it. She suddenly found herself thinking of all she'd seen in the past few days. She considered Anascrus, broken and crumbling, lost deep below the earth; its shattered towers standing above the glassy flats, white and ghostly and deserted. And then she thought of Old Tevanne, chopped up like a butchered hog by walls and boundaries and doors and gates, the streets of the Commons swimming with mire and echoing with the shouts and cries of the people trapped there—and somewhere among it all the peaks of Foundryside, their improvised home amidst all that reeking ruin, where she and Orso and Sancia and Gregor had plotted and planned and dreamed of a different tomorrow.

We thought we could scrive our way into liberation, she thought. *Into salvation. As if the city were a rig we could tamper with, and all that pain and oppression were simple sigils we could wipe out and write over.*

She looked up and saw Sancia's face, aged and exhausted, her body trembling with the effort to sit upright.

How much we have given, she thought, *trying to follow in the footsteps of clever men with clever fixes.*

"I think," said Berenice, "that there is no dancing through a monsoon."

Sancia's anguished face broke into a wide smile.

"Wh-What?" said Polina, bewildered.

"We fight," said Berenice. "We break Tevanne. And we break it for good."

Polina took a long breath in and sighed. "Before we consider this further," she said, "I want to know if it's even *possible* for your hierophant friend to fight. And if *he* even thinks it's worth it. Being that, last I checked, he has not moved one inch from his spot on the deck. Do you have any idea how to do that?"

Berenice and Sancia looked at each other.

"I think I have a few ideas," said Sancia.

Berenice winced at the sunlight as she walked out onto the main deck of the *Comprehension*. She didn't see Sancia at first, but spied the clutch of Greeter's constituents, crowded around where her wife lay, still tending to her myriad little injuries.

Berenice approached cautiously, studying their setup. Sancia lay on the deck, eyes closed as Greeter cared for her, clutching a little pathplate in her hand. Its mate rested on Crasedes's chest, who lay several dozen feet away on the deck where he'd first landed. He looked more or less the same as when they'd left him, though now, she noticed, his hands and feet were manacled and chained to the deck.

"You know those won't do anything," said Berenice. "Right?"

"If you think I'm going to let that awful bastard into Giva and not bind him a *little,* you're scrumming mad," snapped Polina.

Polina and Greeter hung back as Berenice continued, her stomach yowling in discomfort as she got closer and closer to the hierophant. She briefly reflected on how odd it was that she'd briefly grown accustomed to the feeling. *That,* she thought, *or I was so miserable and scared that it was hard to notice.*

She stopped next to Greeter's constituents, watching as they tended to Sancia's ankle. Sancia's eyes were shut, but her face was contorted into a look of profound frustration.

<*It's not working?*> asked Berenice.

<*No,*> said Sancia. <*I'm sure the bastard can hear me. It's the exact same setup as the one we used for Clef, and I could talk to him loud and clear. But this pissant jerk won't talk.*>

Berenice looked at Crasedes, crumpled on the deck with his masked face staring up at the midday sky. <*He won't?*>

<*No. Hasn't said a goddamned word, no matter how I yell at him.*>

Berenice looked at Sancia, then at Crasedes. She walked over to him, the nausea in her stomach quintupling with every other step. She heard Polina and Design's worried murmuring behind her, but she ignored it. When she came close she stared down at him, his blank eyes inaccessible to the light of the midmorning sun.

A doll, she thought. *He's like a doll someone tossed away, upset and refusing to play . . .*

She sat down, making sure to sit where his blank eyes could see her.

<*See this, asshole?*> barked Sancia at Crasedes. <*Your stupid ass got Berenice to leave her nice physiquere's bed and come here and look at you! Is this* fun*? Are you* enjoying *yourself?*>

Crasedes, of course, didn't move.

<*See?*> said Sancia. <*Nothing.*>

Berenice sighed a little. *Always the ambassador . . .*

She looked at Crasedes, staring into his dark eyes.

"You'd thought you'd found the way, didn't you?" she asked him. "A way to escape all you'd done. To flee into the shadow of death. But now it's gone."

There was a long silence.

Then a low, rumbling, exhausted voice echoed in the back of her mind: <*LEAVE ME ALONE.*>

She winced at the sound of it. Sancia gasped aloud. Even Greeter murmured all in unison, aware of the inhuman voice coursing through Sancia's thoughts.

"We can't," said Berenice. "You're the only one who can help us survive this."

<*NO ONE CAN HELP YOU SURVIVE THIS,*> said Crasedes. His blank, lifeless eyes bored into her. <*AND I AM EVEN LESS EQUIPPED THAN MOST.*>

"What do you mean?" asked Berenice.

Silence.

"He means he doesn't fix," said Sancia aloud. "Only destroys."

<*San,*> said Berenice. <*You're not helping!*>

<*SHE'S RIGHT,*> said Crasedes. <*I CANNOT. I HAVE BEEN CLEAR. I AM NO SAVIOR. LEAVE ME ALONE. LEAVE ME ALONE TO AWAIT THE INEVITABLE.*>

Berenice grimaced, thinking. She tried not to pay attention to the math that'd been floating in her head: the distance from the ruins of Anascrus to the coast, and the distance from the coast to here, to Giva . . . and how fast would Tevanne's vessels move?

"Isn't this your best opportunity," she said, "to move thoughtfully, and bring freedom to othe—"

<DON'T,> said Crasedes sharply.

Another silence.

<DO YOU KNOW,> he said, *<HOW MUCH FOLLY THOSE WORDS HAVE BROUGHT THIS WORLD? HOW MUCH SORROW I CREATED ATTEMPTING TO FULFILL THEM? YET IT ALL MAKES SENSE NOW, AS THEY WERE THE MANTRA OF A MAN WHOSE PRIDE DESTROYED HIS PEOPLE.>* His words dropped to a hiss: *<THOUGH IT SEEMS HE'S HAD SUCCESS WITH OTHERS.>*

"What do you mean?" asked Berenice.

Yet another silence.

Then, rather churlishly, he demanded, *<DID YOU LEAVE ME ON THIS SHIP ALL MORNING ON PURPOSE?>*

"Huh?" said Sancia. "No. We just landed here. What do you mean, on purpo—"

<HM,> said Crasedes. *<WHAT IS THAT THING OVER THERE? THAT PERSON—OR PEOPLE, OR PROCESS—IN THE PURPLE CLOTHING. WHAT IS IT?>*

"What, Greeter?" Berenice looked back at their constituents. Greeter looked slightly alarmed to be discussed by the first of all hierophants. Several of the constituents pointed to themselves, as if to say—*Who, me?*

"They help with . . . Well. With everything, really," said Sancia.

<YES,> said Crasedes quietly. *<THEY ARE EVERYWHERE. YOU CANNOT SEE IT—BUT I CAN, WITH MY SIGHT. I HAVE WATCHED IT. IT IS VERY . . . UNUSUAL.>*

"Cadences aren't *that* weird," said Sancia, a bit defensively.

<NO. IT IS MORE THAN THAT. THIS ENTIRE PLACE. YOU HAVE MADE . . . SOMETHING NOT LIKE ME. AND NOT LIKE TEVANNE. AND NOT LIKE THE MERCHANT HOUSES EITHER.> Again, his tone dropped to a poisonous hiss: *<PERHAPS ACCIDENTALLY, MY FATHER HAS MADE A FREER WORLD—WITH YOU. I THOUGHT AGE WOULD PLACE ME BEYOND BITTERNESS. BUT, AGAIN, IT SEEMS I WAS MISTAKEN.>*

"He might have helped make it," said Berenice. "But you could save it."

Another silence. Then there was a rumbling from below, and the giant ship came to life, slowly shifting on the waters.

<*WHAT IS HAPPENING?*> asked Crasedes.

<*They're getting ready to flee,*> said Sancia. <*We're going to run, before Tevanne comes.*>

<*THERE'S NO OUTRUNNING IT,*> he said. <*YOU KNOW THIS.*>

<*Yeah,*> said Sancia. <*But it's not like you're giving us any other ideas.*>

The massive ship kept turning, the reverberations of the waves dancing up the hull and the deck and into their very bones.

<*YOU INTEND TO FIGHT?*> said Crasedes.

<*I intend to try,*> said Sancia.

<*THE IDEA IS ABSURD,*> he said. <*INSANE. RIDICULOUS. YOU WILL PERISH.*>

"Isn't perishing exactly what you wanted?" asked Berenice.

<*I'D RATHER PERISH WITH DIGNITY.*>

"Lying on this deck doesn't seem very dignified."

A flock of gulls took to the skies, disturbed from their roosts by the shifting ships.

<*IF I HELP YOU,*> said Crasedes. <*THERE IS SOMETHING I WANT.*>

"What?" said Berenice.

<*I . . . WANT TO SEE THIS PLACE. I WANT TO SEE THIS PLACE THAT YOU AND MY FATHER HELPED MAKE. SHOW ME THAT, AND I WILL HELP YOU.*>

Sancia and Berenice exchanged a look.

<*It's the end of the world,*> said Sancia. She sighed and shrugged. <*What harm could it do?*>

"Fine," said Berenice. "First, we talk."

<*I SEE NO ISSUE WITH THAT.*>

"Well, I do," she said. "You're going to need to whisper. Otherwise you'll deafen us all."

42

<*You have until tomorrow's daybreak,*> said Crasedes, wearily but firmly. <*That I can almost guarantee.*>

Polina looked surprised. "You know it that precisely?"

<*More or less,*> said Crasedes.

The representatives of Giva shifted uncomfortably in their seats. Everyone had been reluctant to bring Crasedes into a closed environment, so instead they'd set up a rounded table and chairs on the open deck of the *Comprehension.* Crasedes was now awkwardly propped up in his own chair—a reluctant show of diplomacy, Berenice supposed—but they had him stationed far away from the table, at the prow of the ship, facing them. They could hear his voice only through Sancia's pathplate to him, but that was more than enough.

In the center of the table was a small glass box, inside of which lay the silver key. Most of them avoided looking at it.

To think that the fate of creation itself, Berenice thought, *could be tied up in that little twist of metal.* She glanced sidelong at Sancia, who was absently touching her chest where Clef used to lay. *But we have been in such situations before . . .*

"What makes you so sure of it?" asked Polina.

<*It will take time,*> continued Crasedes, <*for Tevanne to transport itself—its body, I suppose you could say, the entity we spoke with—to the coast. That will take much of the day, and it will not approach at night, when I am strongest. Instead, it will close in at tomorrow's daybreak.*>

Sancia slowly leaned forward. "It'll be Tevanne itself? Tevanne *itself,* in Gregor, will be coming?"

<*Yes,*> said Crasedes. <*This, too, I can almost guarantee.*>

"Why would Tevanne risk itself?" asked Design.

<*Because the closer the corporeal vessel of Tevanne is to its works,*> said Crasedes, <*the more intelligent they become. Faster, stronger, better. That key on the table is the purpose of Tevanne's entire existence. It is what it wants most in the world. It is willing to risk much for it. And I've no doubt it will bring any implements it needs to . . . do what it wishes to do.*>

The *Comprehension* rocked to one side very slightly. Crasedes slumped over a bit in his chair.

"You mean it's going to bring the doorway it's made," said Berenice, "slaughter us all for the key, and use it to open the door, right here on the open seas."

<*I would expect so, yes,*> said Crasedes. <*It is nothing if not efficient.*>

"And then," said Greeter, "it will use Clef to break the door, and unleash untold destruction . . . all in the hopes of attracting the eye of God, so that He might return to fix His creation."

<*I believe that's the gist of it, yes,*> said Crasedes. <*A little mad to say out loud, isn't it?*>

The Givans stared balefully at the little silver key, their faces shaken and anxious.

"How can one break such a door?" said Design.

<*I've no idea,*> said Crasedes. <*I suppose by tinkering with it as one might any alteration. If it were me, I'd start by making it unsure where its boundaries were—so that it would expand, and expand, and expand . . .*>

Sancia shuddered. "That's enough."

<*Tevanne will need* me *to do this, mind,*> said Crasedes. <*Clef cannot be compelled to do anything—unless he is in* my *hand. In fact, I'm sure Tevanne is reluctant to even touch Clef, given that Clef could unwind its many scrivings like a ball of string.*> He sighed. <*I've no doubt Tevanne intends to capture me, and possibly dominate me through some horrific fash-*

ion, and use me to then use Clef. I suppose I could fly away this night, and delay the inevitable, but . . . this would mean all of you would get annihilated, probably.>

"Scrumming hell," muttered Polina.

"Let's not do that, then," said Sancia.

"Tell us about Tevanne's weakness," said Berenice. "Tell us about the regulator."

<*Certainly,*> said Crasedes. The ship lurched again, and he slumped forward slightly more. <*But before I do, could you, ah . . .* >

"Ugh, fine," muttered Sancia. She stood up, grabbed a long stick that was apparently some kind of sailing tool, leaned forward, and poked the hierophant until he was in an upright position again.

<*Thank you,*> said Crasedes. <*That was . . . most undignified. Anyway. The regulators. Yes. You already know where Tevanne has them housed.*>

"In the citadels," said Berenice.

<*Correct. The citadels act as Tevanne's control points, not only transporting its armies but bathing the world in its influence. The regulators are a critical part of that influence.*>

"So we've got to hope it brings a citadel with it when it attacks," said Design.

<*Well—I would not say* hope,> said Crasedes. <*Rather, it will most certainly bring* all *of its citadels to wage its war upon you.*>

They stared at him, boggled.

"It's going to bring what?" said Polina faintly.

<*It will bring* all *of its airborne citadels against you,*> said Crasedes. <*Each accompanied by, oh, a dozen deadlamps or so.*>

Design had gone ashen. They opened their mouth to speak, then closed it.

<*I've never had a verified count of the citadels . . .* > continued Crasedes. <*But I've estimated there were nine, originally—though I myself have destroyed two of them. So that makes seven.*>

All of Greeter's constituents had frozen in place. They whispered, "Seven citadels . . ."

Berenice cleared her throat. "H-How do the regulators work? How shall we attack them?"

<*That is where things get a little better,*> said Crasedes. <*For Te-*

vanne will essentially be offering us seven opportunities to attack it . . . yet I have concluded that we only need to successfully sabotage one.>

"We only need to sabotage one regulator?" said Sancia.

<*Correct. For Tevanne has never actually felt the pain and suffering of all of its hosts, you see. It has never had to modulate its mind and its behavior like you all have been forced to. It is like the fairy giant from the old stories . . . She was invulnerable and immune to suffering for so much of her life—yet when she stepped upon a magic nail, the pain from that tiny prick felt so great that it killed her outright.* This *is what will happen to Tevanne, in a way. And it knows this. This is why it has created a failsafe wherein an entire citadel will go dead and fall out of the sky if its regulator is so much as* touched. *And yet—someone will have to do just that. Someone must get* on *the citadel itself, and sabotage this regulator* directly.>

Everyone blinked for a moment as they processed this.

Sancia shut her eyes. "Ahh, shit."

"You . . . You want us to somehow get a person up there," said Berenice, "onto one of those floating horrors. And then have them find this . . . this regulator . . . and sabotage it? *Without* touching it?"

Polina threw up her hands. "Well, then! It's as simple as that!"

<*You are being sarcastic,*> said Crasedes. <*But . . . it actually does get worse.*>

"How?" said Design bleakly.

<*You heard Tevanne,*> said Crasedes. <*It said it saw all the bindings in your bodies, the ones that allow you to twin one another's minds. Even if it can no longer control you, its ability to perceive those scrivings is now more accurate than ever. I doubt if even your previous camouflages will work anymore.*>

"Twin sheaths won't work?" asked Berenice.

<*They functioned by reducing your signal to a ghost, yes? But Tevanne will now be paying very close attention to anything that looks like such a ghost. Getting any Givan onto a citadel undetected will be* very *difficult. But . . .* if *you can get someone aboard, then movement throughout the citadel should be relatively simple. Without the appropriate scrivings acting as a signal, the movement of flesh and bone will appear to Tevanne as little more than noise.*>

"I could . . . possibly help," said Greeter quietly. "Given that I have quite a bit of experience with twinning. But I can assure nothing."

They pondered this in silence, the tremendous ships of the fleet slowly pivoting and turning about them in the open seas.

Sancia looked at Crasedes. "Are you going to be of any help here?" she asked flatly. "Or are we just going to leave you propped up in your chair?"

<*Yes . . .* > said Crasedes, very quietly. <*There is one possible solution there. But it will not be comfortable. For either your lot, or me. I will need one of the other peoples . . . Not the big one, but . . .* >

"Design?" said Sancia.

<*Yes. Them. And I want for you to come with me, Sancia. For I have questions for you, about this place.*>

She grimaced but nodded. "That was the deal, I guess."

"I'll stay with Greeter," said Berenice, "and try and figure out a way onto one of the citadels."

<*Then I wish you good luck,*> said Crasedes. <*For I suspect you will need it.*>

They loaded Crasedes's body onto a small shallop, and together Sancia and Design towed it through the fleet to the *Innovation,* sailing below the reeling gulls and the electric-blue sky. Crasedes kept speaking up, talking through the pathplate tucked in his hands and saying, <*Left!*> or <*Right!*> or <*Closer to that big ship, please.*> It seemed he was quite committed to their deal: he wished to see all of Giva.

<*Is doing this shit going to help you fix yourself?*> asked Sancia irritably. She wouldn't have loved this job to begin with—acting as a diplomat for a hierophant had never been an occupation she'd wished to perform—but especially not now, when she was leaving Berenice behind to plot out how to infiltrate a Tevanni citadel and break its regulator.

"I'm still not sure why I had to be in the boat," said Design with a sniff. They, too, were quite nettled: Design notoriously refused to speak through pathplates, or use any pathing methods at all—they claimed their thoughts were too complex to share—and they definitely disliked carrying a pathplate connecting them to Crasedes Magnus of all people. "It's not like I don't have anything more important to do. I mean, I'm still on the *Comprehension* trying to gin up a way to sneak someone onto the citadel. Which frankly feels impossible . . ."

<*I wanted you here,*> said Crasedes, <*to ask you questions. Tell me—who governs Giva? Who is its ruler? Who is its king?*>

"What?" said Design. "We don't have one."

<*Surely you or one of the other cadences would be suitable,*> he said. <*You know more, see more, accomplish more. Why should you not rule?*>

"But we don't," said Design, "because we feel more."

Crasedes lay in the back of the shallop, staring up at the sky. <*That,*> he said, <*sounds utterly, laughably preposterous.*>

<*It's preposterous, but it's true,*> said Sancia. <*Twinning makes us feel and know the thoughts of others. It's hard to be a tyrant when you simultaneously know what it's like to be ruled by a tyrant.*>

<*But functioning in this type of nation must be . . . be monstrously difficult,*> he protested.

<*It is,*> said Sancia. <*That's how we know we're doing it right.*>

Crasedes was silent for the rest of the voyage.

Design's constituents were prepared when they reached the *Innovation,* with a pulley and crane stationed on the starboard side of the galleon. Sancia and Design groaned with discomfort as they climbed into the shallop with the hierophant and attached the various hooks to haul it up into the cargo bays—though Sancia groaned a little louder, since her sprained ankle still pained her.

<*Tell me, Design,*> whispered Crasedes. <*Do you know my methods?*>

Design paused, uncomfortable. "I am aware of many hierophantic scrivings. I am made of many minds of many scrivers, who know many things, and that is among them."

<*But you have never performed them yourself,*> said Crasedes.

"No. We could. We could pull years from our people, just as Tevanne does, and use it to edit reality. But that would make us horrors just like Tevanne."

The final hooks clanked into place. Design and Sancia stepped back out of the shallop and untied it from their own little vessel.

<*I see,*> said Crasedes. <*But—would you be willing to pull years from another source? To sacrifice the life of another?*>

"I doubt it," said Design.

Crasedes began to ascend. <*Even if it's me?*>

Design and Sancia looked at each other, surprised, and then up at Crasedes.

"What exactly have you gotten me into, San?" asked Design quietly.

Less than an hour later, Design blinked slowly in the sooty gloom of the *Innovation,* and whispered, "Say it again."

<*Do I need to rephrase?*> asked Crasedes. <*We now deal in the abstruse. It is natural for the process to be difficult.*>

"Just . . . Just tell me again, please," said Design. "Tell me what you want me to make."

Sancia glowered at Crasedes, lying limp among the array of foundries and forges suspended throughout the enormous ship, and thought—*I scrumming hate all this ritual shit.*

And it already had the feel of a ritual to it. Design's constituents stood in a circle around where Crasedes lay, staring out at walls of blackboards, blueprints, drawings, and sketches. There were nineteen constituents present in total, and all of them swayed back and forth like a curious, neurotic metronome, consumed by the task before them—completely in tandem, of course.

"I get the feeling," Sancia muttered, "that you're *enjoying* this, Design."

"Oh, I am," they said. They sounded frustrated. "This is far more interesting and *definitely* more productive than my ongoing work with Berenice."

Sancia frowned. *That sounds bad.*

<*Fine,*> Crasedes whispered. <*Listen closely. The surface of my being is riddled with scrivings bound up in the cloth about me. Currently these are bound to insist I am the occupant of this body—but they can also be used to bind my being to believe it is existing at a different* time. *What we must then do is establish a marker—a default time, a moment, a chronological second in isolation that my body would return to when it feels the world is broken—and then assert that time is midnight, when I am strong.*

Only then *can we assert that the world is broken, which can easily be done because . . .* >

Sancia tuned out as Crasedes repeated, for the fourth or fifth time, how to craft the tool that would reshape his privileges. She whispered, <*Greeter? How is it going with Berenice?*>

<*Poorly,*> sighed Greeter's voice, very quietly. <*But please don't distract me. This is taking a great deal of work . . .* >

"Aha!" bellowed Design suddenly. All of their constituents began hopping up and down excitedly. The sight was so embarrassing that Sancia nearly turned away. "I have it! I *have it*!"

<*Do you . . .* > said Crasedes. <*Good. I shall just lie here, then.*>

Design's constituents flapped a hand at him, as if he were bothering them with tedious minutiae. "Yes, yes! I shall work the forges and the foundries now. Within the hour, we shall have exactly what we need to resurrect you!"

<*Not a resurrection,*> he said quietly. <*An edit. We will scrive my time, so my body will believe it is midnight. So that even in brightest day, I can live, and be strong. But . . . it will come at a cost.*>

"What cost?" said Sancia. "We'll be dead in the goddamned water if you break yourself."

<*I am not one scriving, as you know. I am one being supported by many systems, many invisible infrastructures, all wrought of many, many ancient sacrifices. There is time bound up in all of them—years, decades, centuries. I will have to destroy one such system and give up those centuries in exchange for gaining any power.*>

"And . . . which system are you and Design going to be destroying?" asked Sancia.

"I believe his immutability," said Design. "The permission that forces the world to believe he should always exist."

<*Correct,*> said Crasedes.

"What!" Sancia stared at him. "But . . . But then you'll be . . . well, killable!" she said. "Right? Is it even *possible* for a hierophant to be killable?"

<*Not ordinarily,*> he said drily. <*Which is why Tevanne will never expect it. I will still maintain my permissions over gravity and movement, which is a defense of its own. And I will still be preternaturally durable, but . . . not indestructible. No longer, at least.*>

<*This is . . . is what Clef wanted to do to you, isn't it?*> she said. <*Back there, in Anascrus. He wanted to use up your years, as a sacrifice.*>

<*Yes,*> he murmured. <*Though this feels a far better use of them—don't you think?*>

She watched as Design's constituents flew to work, scattering throughout the great machinery like the stewards of a massive pipe organ giving the instrument a thorough cleaning. As always, it was a little eerie to watch them labor so perfectly. *Like I'm inside some giant womb,* she thought, *watching as it carefully begins to form a child . . .*

<*I still feel the other one, you know,*> whispered Crasedes.

<*Other one?*> asked Sancia.

<*The other . . . person,*> he said. <*The person that's made of all those people. The . . . The other one, the bigger one.*>

<*Oh. You mean Greeter? Yeah, they're everywhere. They're like being in a . . . a big, comfy fog, kind of.*>

Crasedes lay there on the deck of the *Innovation,* and then, to her surprise, he shifted slightly to the right and started laughing sadly. <*All beings in one. All essences in one . . .*>

<*What's that?*> she asked.

<*It's how I described the ritual to my acolytes,*> he said weakly. <*So long ago. To take the souls of others, capture them, and put them in yourself, your being, in a tool. This seemed to be the nature of the world. To capture. To steal. But somehow, Sancia . . . you have wrought a people here who do not take but give. Somehow. Through means I cannot understand.*>

<*It's just scrivings,*> she said. <*It's just sigils.*>

<*Mm. No,*> he said. <*Don't you see? That's not just it at all, is it? A people are more than just the tools they use.*>

Design was springing through the foundry, ripping blocks and molds and etching tools from their carefully maintained cupboards, spinning up machinery and heating up metals, the walls of the vast chamber suddenly dancing with wicked, cheery light. Crasedes's black mask glimmered and shone like a piece of dark glass.

"First to forge molds and blocks," Design's constituents all chanted at once. "I've no such sigils for these commands, being that they're forbidden. Then I shall set the blocks, and form the mold, and craft the tool . . ."

A low, unearthly thrumming filled the floors and walls of the chamber, dancing up Sancia's bones. She watched with her scrived sight as many rigs sprang to life, rattling and buzzing as they carved new molds for new sigils, to be carefully assembled into the greater mold that would form the final tool.

<*This is going to hurt you, isn't it,*> said Sancia.

<*I've hurt quite a lot in the past millennia,*> said Crasedes. <*But yes. It will.*>

Spirals and twists of glimmering metals danced through the air like snowflakes. The crucibles above glowed with a curious, unearthly light.

"Molds set!" cried Design's constituents. The dark air grew hotter, and the room danced with cinders. Design's constituents flipped switches, pulled levers, and opened up portholes in the walls and the hulls that sucked the warmth and the smoke and the fumes from the air, creating a curious, unsettling wind. "Heating the mold!" they shouted.

<*Perhaps it's what I deserve,*> said Crasedes. <*I don't deserve forgiveness, or redemption, not after all I did. Do I?*>

<*No,*> Sancia said. <*You don't.*>

<*No . . .* > he said softly. <*But perhaps if the result of my long work is to leave behind a people such as you—a people who, as far as I can recall in my long memory, have no likeness in history—then it will not all be for naught.*>

"Beginning cast!" said Design. The crucible slowly tipped, and a spear of golden light split the shadows as the molten metals poured into the mold.

<*You can't be serious,*> said Sancia. <*We're just trying to survive.*>

<*Oh, no,*> said Crasedes. <*I am serious. You have made something history has never produced. I hope this intimidates you, Sancia—how unlikely it is, how fragile. Now you must blow upon this tiny flame and nourish it into a roaring fire.*>

The heat within the chamber was outrageous, intolerable. Crasedes's robes began to smoke. Sancia herself had to back away, unable to even face the constant barrage of heat.

"Done!" screamed Design. "Done, done!"

The pour of molten metals narrowed and tapered until it was a blur of prancing blue-green light on Sancia's eyes. She squinted as her sight adjusted and watched as Design's constituents pulled a lever, carefully guided the mold down to its cradle, and cracked it open.

"Hot tears," muttered their constituents. "Must avoid any flaws as it cools . . ."

Sancia caught a glimpse of a tiny spear of dull-red metal, like the tooth of some fabled dragon, before Design snatched it up with their tongs and placed it in a huge oblong box—a rig that could rapidly cool any castings without causing the metals to rupture.

The heat in the chamber dwindled, died. Sancia approached Crasedes carefully, wincing as her skin crackled and pricked.

<Is it done?> said Crasedes. *<Is it well?>*

"I . . . believe so . . ." said Design.

They withdrew their tongs from the cooling box, plucked the item out, and placed it on the floor.

A dagger. A small one, with a wide tip and a narrow handle.

"That's it?" said Sancia. "It's so small."

<It's small,> said Crasedes, *<because it must fit inside me. And we must do it now.>*

She stared at the dagger. "God . . . it has to be now?"

<Yes. We have no time to waste, and it may take me some effort to adjust to my alterations.>

"You don't want to wait until midnight?"

<No. The infliction of an edit upon reality does not require us to wait for the lost moment. It is a far uglier, far less precise method of accessing permissions than the crafting of a tool—hence why I abandoned it long ago—but . . . it is all we have now.>

Sancia studied the dagger, so small and yet so curiously hungry.

A flash of a memory: a woman, one arm covered in painted sigils of curious inks, a little dagger clutched in her other hand, standing on a balcony, surveying a ruined city beyond and screaming—*Broken. Smoking. Unintended. Corrupt!*

Sancia wondered what Estelle Candiano would say if she could see her now.

Or Orso, for that matter, she thought. *We thought we fought for the fate of the world then, but we were just children playing games in alleys and ditches.*

<Sancia,> whispered Crasedes. *<Please hurry.>*

She breathed deep, then picked up the dagger—how cool the metal was already, an unnerving chill to it—and slowly walked over to where Crasedes lay. Her insides writhed and wriggled with nausea, and her eyes watered.

<*And where,*> she thought, <*should I place the point?*>

<*It matters little,*> said Crasedes weakly. <*But the heart is best. More room, you see.*>

She straddled his black form, her heart thrumming, her bowels watery and mutinous, her eyes thick and hot in her skull as she touched this dreadful, horrid thing . . .

Who had been a child, once. And still was, perhaps.

Sancia clenched her jaw, raised the dagger with both hands, and brought it down upon his heart.

She expected there to be resistance, for the point to have to punch through him, like a bolt tip through armor. But the dagger leapt to life the second it touched him, eagerly eating into him, pulling itself down, down into his body, and her mind filled up with screaming commands as it enacted this sudden, awful edit.

<*BREAK BREAK BREAK,*> shrieked the dagger in her mind. <*BREAK THE WORLD BREAK THIS THING BREAK THE SUN IN THE SKY AND THE MIDNIGHT ABOVE AN—*>

She screamed aloud, unable to bear the immensity of the bindings echoing through her. She ripped her hands away and staggered back, gasping for breath.

Crasedes writhed on the floor, his arms and legs quaking and shivering, his hands and feet striking the wood so hard they left dents and cracks. The dagger was still visible, but barely, steadily sinking into his body bit by bit, until the barest tip was visible. Then, finally, he went still.

They watched him, the silence broken only by the *tink* or drip of the forge.

"Is it done?" asked Design tentatively. "Is it completed?"

Sancia flexed her scrived sight. She perceived Crasedes much as she always had, as a blood-red flash of awful light—but now it was flickering curiously, like a candle in the wind.

Then the crimson light flared bright, like a magnesium fire hissing in the darkness, and she felt it.

A pressure. A *presence.* As if every square inch of her skin was being pushed upon, and every instrument and surface in the forge began to rattle.

It's him, she thought. *It's his will. God, is . . . is this what he was like at his apex?*

Then, like he was a dreadful puppet, Crasedes slowly rose in the air, his arms and legs limp, his head rolling. The pressure in the room vanished. The rattling stopped.

A low, inhumanly deep voice rumbled through the darkness: "I am. Again."

She looked back and saw he was assuming his familiar position, seated cross-legged upon thin air like some monstrous deity.

She waited for more, but he said nothing else. "Did it work?" she asked. "Are you . . . fixed?"

"Fixed?" he said. "No . . . No, I am closer to death than I ever was before."

Another pulse in the air. The floor creaked. The hull moaned. The whole ship was shaking, in fact, so much so that Sancia felt like her bones were turning to putty, and Design's constituents all cried out.

"But I am strong," whispered Crasedes. "Vulnerable, yet strong. For a while, at least."

The pulse in the air ended, and the moaning of the ship stopped.

"Now," said Crasedes slowly. "The next task. We are still trying to determine how best to infiltrate a citadel, yes?"

"C-Correct," said Design.

He nodded. "Let us see if I can assist with that."

43

"The system we've developed is, I admit, not elegant," said Berenice. She blinked hard, trying to wake herself up. It seemed like everyone in Giva was there in the cargo bay of the *Comprehension,* watching quietly as she, Greeter, Design, and Claudia showed them what they'd made. Polina was sitting front and center, a scowl on her face, and Greeter's and Design's constituents milled about behind her, tapping their feet like the cadences often did when they were anxious. "And it's difficult to test, hence why we were waiting with the people with scrived sight to get back."

Sancia nodded. From the shadows far at the top of the cargo bay, Crasedes's voice boomed: "Of course."

"We decided that I'd be the one infiltrating the citadel," said Berenice. She swallowed. "Since I'm the one who has the most experience with Tevanni facilities now."

There was a grave silence. Sancia stared out of the crowd with a baleful look and massaged her sprained ankle.

"Completely masking my sigils no longer seems possible," said

Berenice, "since Tevanne will be working to see through our camouflages. But we went with the same principle as the twinning sheaths and decided to try to come up with a way to make it unsure as to *where* I was." Berenice gestured to the rig sitting on the table behind her. "Like a lot of the things we've made, it's a box. But this box would cover up my . . . my left hand. Where my twinning plate is located."

She patted the top of the rig. It was a simple bronzed box, with a hole in the top large enough for someone to put their hand through.

"It has a mate," said Berenice. "One that's twinned to believe it contains the same thing." She pointed to another table in the back, where a similar container was sitting. "So . . . if I put my hand in this container here"—she did so, then looked up at Sancia—"in your scrived sight, does it look like it's in two places at once?"

Sancia narrowed her eyes, then nodded enthusiastically. "It does! Path to me, and you'll see."

Berenice did so, focusing until she could peer through Sancia's eyes—and when she did, she confirmed that the soft, glimmering loops of logic that caused her to share her mind with the rest of Giva were indeed shimmering in two places: in the box her hand was in now, and also in the box in the back of the room.

"And we're sure those things won't . . . well, explode?" asked Polina warily.

"We're pretty good at twinned boxes by now, Pol, given that the fleet basically runs off of them," said Claudia. "Do a bad job of twinning, or twin something that's already inside of a twinned space, and yeah, it gets ugly. But these should be fine."

Berenice looked up at the darkness above. "Does it look functional to you?"

A pause.

Then came Crasedes's voice: "What, exactly, do you intend to do with these boxes?"

"We'd set them on lanterns and air-sailing rigs," Claudia said. "Dozens of them. Maybe a hundred of them. We'd send them spinning around all the citadels, landing them here and there so Tevanne is confused and it's not sure where Berenice is."

Another pause. Then Crasedes descended out of the shadows, sitting cross-legged, but said nothing.

"Well," said Design. "Do you . . . Do you think it works?"

"And . . . how will you get close to a citadel?" asked Crasedes.

"With Design's submergence rigging," said Claudia. "The one they've been eager to try since forever. They'd be able to get directly beneath the citadels."

"Provided it holds up," muttered Polina.

"And it will!" snapped Design.

A pause. Still Crasedes said nothing.

"Well," said Berenice. "Will it work?"

"I . . . believe the scrivings function appropriately," said Crasedes. "I think the plan, however, will almost certainly fail."

Berenice blinked. She felt a deep pit growing somewhere between her heart and her belly.

"Why?" demanded Sancia. "Tevanne will literally be perceiving, like, a hundred Givan sigils all at once, right? It'll think there's a small army of Givans landing on its citadels!"

"And do you think Tevanne is incapable of handling a small army of Givans?" asked Crasedes. "Do you believe it could not shoot a hundred lanterns out of the air very quickly, and inevitably hit Berenice as well?"

"I thought," said Sancia, gritting her teeth, "that you would be providing a *distraction* while all that was going on."

"I will be," said Crasedes. "Of course. But Tevanne is *not* stupid. If it sees any trace of Givan sigils floating through the air to it, however faint, it will know you mean to board it, it will realize you are trying to sabotage it, and then it will devote time to dealing with the threat. It will have thousands of weapons aboard each citadel, along with its own armies—ones far larger than a hundred people. It will be sure to prevent your success." He looked at Berenice. "And then there is the obvious problem . . . Do we intend to make Berenice infiltrate a Tevanni citadel and break her way into the regulator—all with one of her hands stuck in a box?"

Berenice sighed. Three of Design's constituents sat down at the workshop table, their faces in their hands.

"We tried at least a dozen approaches," snarled Claudia. "Each one was cumbersome and awkward and awful. This is the least awful one. And we don't have time! We still have to figure out how to sabotage the goddamned regulator!"

"*The least awful one,*" said Crasedes, "is a phrase that does not exactly inspire confidence . . ."

Berenice stared into the table beside her as the room broke out into squabbling. She felt utterly exhausted, because she knew both of them were right. She, Design, Claudia, and Greeter had worked tirelessly over the past three hours to come up with something, and they'd failed again and again—and this was the most practical solution.

But Crasedes was also right. It would not work. She would die trying to do this, and they would fail.

We need someone else, she thought. *Someone Tevanne wouldn't look for. Someone who's not a Givan.* She shut her eyes. *I wish I could summon up some younger version of Sancia, before she was twinned. She could do this. She'd be perfect for it.*

She followed the thought, and briefly considered using a purge stick on Sancia—after all, they'd planned to rid her of all scrivings eventually—but she knew that Sancia was too old and too injured for such a thing to ever work.

Then another idea struck her. One that made her belly go cold.

No.

The fighting in the room grew louder, and she opened her eyes. She noticed that every single one of Greeter's constituents was now watching her with a quiet, sad look on their faces.

She was vaguely aware that Crasedes was talking with Design, discussing some plot to encase Berenice in some kind of an iron casket and fire her deep into the belly of one of the citadels—both of them seemed to think this was perfectly possible, much to the agitation of everyone else in the room—when Greeter stood up and cleared their throats.

"I think," they said quite loudly, "that we all need a break."

"We don't have time for breaks!" said Polina. "That horror will be here in a matter of goddamned hours, and we still have more to do!"

"And we will not think of any solutions in this room right now," said Greeter. Their constituents looked at Sancia and Berenice and smiled. "Come. I thought you might like to see how Diela's doing."

"Diela?" said Sancia, surprised. "The girl's recovered? She's awake?"

<*Of course,*> said Greeter. <*Why don't you both come with me, and we'll go check in on her?*>

With a confused look on her face, Sancia stood and followed Greeter out of the cargo bay. Crasedes and Design kept quietly talking, faster and faster. Berenice stood and followed, but her arms and legs felt leaden—not because she was tired, but because the idea that had occurred to her would not leave her.

<*I wonder,*> said Sancia as she joined her at the door, <*what the hell this is about.*>

Berenice kept her face averted and did not speak.

Together the three of them climbed, passing through chambers still filled with recovering Grattiarans, with the sick and the wounded, with the spiritually unwell and the chronically lonely. Greeter's constituents, garbed in lavender and blue, were ever-present and yet so circumspect that Berenice sometimes had trouble noticing them—except she could never stop feeling Greeter's presence, the slow, steady beat of sentience and empathy all about her, like a furnace venting heat throughout the ship.

They entered another deck, and she saw dozens of Greeter's constituents sitting on the floor, their eyes closed, their chests expanding and contracting in a slow, steady beat.

<*Are they all right?*> Sancia asked.

<*They are me,*> said Greeter. <*And I am fine. But all of Giva is worried. They are worried about Crasedes's arrival, worried about your expedition, worried about how the fleet is moving, rearranging ourselves, getting ready to set sail . . . There are a lot of worries to manage right now, Berenice. They need an ocean of calm in which they can toss their worries away, and I am working to give that to them.*>

Greeter strode through the ranks of their constituents, making for someone sitting in the far middle with their back to them—a small figure dressed in blues and purples, the common colors of the cadence.

Sancia stopped short. "Wait," she said. "Wait, you aren't saying . . ."

Greeter walked to the figure, then turned and waited. <*Come,*> they said.

Berenice stared at the little figure in blue, her heart a flutter in her chest.

<*I thought she was sick!*> said Sancia. <*I thought she . . . I thought . . .* >

<*Come, Berenice,*> said Greeter. <*Come, Sancia. Come and see.*>

They slowly approached until they faced the little figure whose arm was in a sling and whose calm, clear face bore many bruises and cuts: the face of the girl who'd come with them on so many of their raids, so many expeditions; the girl Berenice had screamed over, and wept over, when it'd seemed she was going to die in some blasted, cursed corner of the ancient world.

Berenice knelt before her. Diela did not open her eyes. "She . . . She . . ."

<*It is not healthy, exactly, for a person to align and break with cadences so many times,*> explained Greeter. <*As I plotted your escape from Tevanne, I had to align with her for a very long time. When she awoke, well . . . she chose alignment, rather than continue.*>

"Oh," said Sancia quietly. "I see."

Berenice began weeping. She wasn't sure why, at first. She'd known people who'd joined cadences before, and those who'd left them as well, but it felt different for it to be Diela: she was the girl who'd fought so hard to join Berenice's team, who'd endured so much suffering and so many dangers—and the girl whose life had so mirrored Sancia's, a freed slave with a gift for scrived communication and a desire to fight.

"Why do you cry, Berenice?" said Greeter gently.

"Because she was *mine,*" said Berenice. She sniffed and wiped her eyes. "She was mine to care for, mine to look after. I feel like I . . . like I . . ."

"You didn't fail her," said Greeter. "It's impossible to align with a cadence without consent. This was a choice she made. A new way to serve Giva. She gave. She gives. But she is still here."

Berenice sniffed again. "But not to me. I can't find her. I can't talk to her. I can't . . ."

<*Shush,*> said Greeter. They reached out and touched the back of Berenice's neck.

Instantly, visions and experiences flooded through her mind.

A woman toiling in a field, her sweaty hair sticking to her face, her mouth in a tight grimace that blossomed into a grin as she knelt and whispered, "Diela! I've a treat for you . . ."

The sight of a wooden ceiling, the dark filled with quiet snores as the slaves about her slept.

The warm, bright skies above the ocean, seen from the deck of a Givan galleon; and there before her Sancia and Berenice, young and unblemished, describing how to load an espringal . . .

Then Vittorio, screaming as he died, facing the sky. Such love, such sorrow. Such guilt, such heartbreak, swallowed only by the hunger to fix, to make amends, to repair all the wrongs that one had done—which was swallowed in turn by love.

Love for Berenice. Love for Sancia. For Claudia. For little Gio, for Polina. For all she knew and all she'd suffered for. Simple, unvarnished, unadorned love . . .

<*She is still here,*> whispered Greeter's voice. <*I am still here. I am still with you. But know, Berenice, that even if she died, the memories of me, the feeling of her, would still echo inside of you. Of all of us. Because she gives herself so that we may prosper.*>

Greeter withdrew their hand from Berenice's neck. She was sobbing now, overwhelmed by the experience of knowing Diela, of *being* her, if only for a second.

<*She gave herself before she ever joined me,*> whispered Greeter. <*Do you see?*>

"Why are you doing this to her?" said Sancia. She embraced Berenice and looked angrily at Greeter. "God, she needs to plan!"

"She does not," said Greeter solemnly. "She already knows what she must do."

Berenice shut her eyes and wept.

"What?" said Sancia. "What do you mean?"

Greeter looked away, their face contemplative. "This is what it's like, to be me. To be Greeter is to manage such simple, desperate, passionate love. A love so great that people will give themselves to it. It is not easy, but . . . that is what it means to be Givan—far more than having any set of scrivings in one's body."

Berenice bent over, still weeping, until her head rested in Sancia's lap.

Sancia asked again, her voice lower and anxious: "What do you mean?"

"We all must give," said Greeter quietly.

"Wait," said Sancia. "You're not . . . You're not . . ."

"As Gregor did," said Greeter. "As Orso did. And Vittorio, and many more. But the imprint of those people lives on. Even though their connections to us seem broken." The small, sad smile returned to their face. "Do you see?"

"No," snarled Sancia. "I don't."

"Berenice does," said Greeter. "Such is her love for you. For she knows the solution to this issue lies on her very person. Doesn't it?"

Berenice sat up, still weeping. Then she reached into her boot and slid out the little instrument that had been nestled there ever since they'd first left on their mission: a small bronze stick with a tiny scrived blade on the end.

Sancia paced about Berenice, who was sitting on the deck of the *Comprehension*. The sun was a teardrop of broiling red in the distance, and all the ships of the fleet were shifting about them.

"Stop pacing," said Berenice. "You're hurt."

"I don't give a shit!" said Sancia. "I . . . I can't believe you're considering this, Ber!"

Berenice tried to smile. "It seems only fair," she said. "We'd planned to do it to you. Maybe I . . ." She swallowed and bowed her head. "Maybe I just get there a bit early."

"No, this . . . Ber, you can't do this," said Sancia. "There's no going back from it. A purge is irreversible. Hell, we *designed* it to be! We can't even edit it out of you, because it'd kill you!"

"We did think about making a purge stick that was reversible," said Berenice quietly. "But we figured, if we can reverse it, then Tevanne could too."

"My God. It . . . It'd be like . . ."

"Like cutting off my own arm," she said quietly. "Like cutting a piece out of me." Her eyes lingered on Sancia. "But it'd be you. I'd be cutting *you* out of me. Yes."

"I can't . . . I can't even . . ." Sancia paced around on the deck, indifferent to the pain in her ankle. "I mean—it'd also mean cutting you out of *me*. You see that, yes? You'd be doing it to me too. And everyone in Giva who—"

"Who loves me," said Berenice, sighing. "Who cares for me. I'd be doing it to them too. I know."

Sancia swallowed, her eyes brimming with tears. "It'd be like you're dying, Ber," she said weakly. "Like when someone *dies*. That's what it'll feel like. But it'll be you!"

"I know," whispered Berenice. "But there is no dancing through a monsoon, my love. Tevanne will be expecting a Givan. Someone whose mind is twinned with many others. But . . . it will not be expecting a regular unscrived person." Her face tightened. "It cannot imagine that we would give up this singular advantage. This . . . This way of life. This connection. So, it will be blind to me."

"But I never wanted to do it to *you*!" said Sancia. "I never wanted to take this away from you, for you to lose—"

"I am not losing anything," said Berenice. "Like Greeter said, I am giving." She looked out at the fleet. "I was part of a nation, yes. Of a people. Of a family. And it was so good to have. But I'll give that up, if I must. If it will give us a chance to survive."

Sancia stopped and stared at her, her eyes haunted and sorrowful. "I . . . I always thought I was the one at risk. The one who would go."

"It'll be like Foundryside again, before Shorefall Night. We'll just be two people in love, squabbling in a little room together."

"If we make it," said Sancia, sniffing. "If you . . . I mean, God, Ber, you're saying you're going to be on that big thing all alone? With no one to help you? No one to know what's happening to you, or tell you what's happening outside?"

"I've been your wife for eight years now," said Berenice. She attempted a smile. "You've soaked through me, soaked into my bones. I know all your tricks, all your sneaky little secrets. It's how I've survived this long, after all."

Sancia anxiously rubbed her face, the sides of her head, hoping that somehow the solution would spring forth, some clever little ruse that would allow them to slip out of this whole, unharmed, unscathed . . .

<*No,*> said Berenice quietly. <*Enough. No more plotting, no more scheming. Let's be together instead.*>

<*But I want to save you,*> said Sancia.

<*A minute with you,*> said Berenice, <*is salvation enough.*>

Berenice extended her hand. Sancia took it, and together they stared out at the sunset.

Then came Greeter's voice, murmuring: <*You have time. Design and I have determined the solution to your final task—how to sabotage the regulator.*>

Berenice sniffed. <*You have?*>

<*We have. It was inspired, a bit, by your choice, Berenice. If we are to win this battle, we all must give. And I can give more than most.*>

Their words dropped to a whisper as they told them their plan.

<*You'd do that?*> said Sancia, surprised. <*Would you really?*>

<*I would,*> said Greeter. <*For you. For us. For all we have is time with each other. Now, enjoy yours, while you have it.*>

Together Sancia and Berenice shared, and touched, and dreamed, thoughts slipping from one mind to the other, a melding of consciousness so complete that it was difficult to recall who was who. They lay back on the deck of the ship and stared up at the stars, cast across the night sky like shards of sand on a velvet cloak.

<*I will keep this,*> they whispered. <*I will keep this deep within me, until I am no more.*>

As they watched as the stars wheeled above, they remembered.

They remembered Sancia being searched by Berenice in Orso's offices, the girl's hand slipping into her pockets, her cheeks growing bright red as her knuckles brushed her hard, corded thigh.

Their first night in Foundryside, their only item in the room a small battered mattress; but that was enough, enough for their dizzy, exuberant lovemaking, half-drunk from bad wine and the sheer thrill of sharing themselves.

Sancia grimacing in Foundryside as Berenice critiqued her sigils. Orso scowling at them as they sat a little too close together at a workbench. Sharing a desperate kiss in the alley behind the building, only to look up and see Gregor Dandolo looking out the window just behind them, his face fixed in an expression of embarrassed surprise; and then, with a shrug and the tiniest of smiles, he closed the shutters and walked away.

And how it had burned. How it had all burned, and the two of them had watched helplessly from far out at sea, all their dreams burned away into a leaning column of black smoke.

That first night, aboard Polina's ship. How they'd wept. How they'd held each other.

I won't lose you too, Berenice had said. *Will I?*

And Sancia had said—*Never. Never. So long as we're together, we'll always be home.*

And then, last of all, they remembered their wedding. A year after Shorefall Night, aboard the *Innovation,* walking forward together under the strings of lily-pad blooms Gio had strung up above the deck, the lights and lamps glowing soft pink, and the people of their newly founded nation applauding as the two of them kissed.

And then they'd danced. They'd danced as they'd watched the moon hanging low over the sea, and Sancia had whispered in Berenice's ear—*Always home.*

Now, together, they looked at the moon and marked how high it sat in the night sky. They remembered the discussion they'd had mere days ago, before they'd left on their mission: how one of them said they would keep Foundryside, and the other would keep the distant future, when they were old and foolish and still so in love.

What I would give to go back to that place, they thought. *Or jump forward, to that future.*

They listened to the water sloshing alongside the galleon.

It's time, they said. *It's time.*

Weeping, they raised the purge stick, and slid the blade into their body.

The instant the blade entered their flesh their thoughts lit up with pain. They felt the little plate within slide down, down into their flesh, to nestle against the bone in the arm—and once it had secured itself it issued a single bleak little command to the rest of their body (of *her* body), eating at her years, stealing a moment of her life to make this one tiny edit . . .

Their memories sputtered, stuttered, and failed. The commands echoing through her body finished their work, and the twinning plate in Berenice's hand turned to water.

As it disappeared, all of Sancia's thoughts, experiences, memories, and feelings vanished from Berenice's mind like waking from a dream. It was such a queer thing, to have the world change so intangibly, so suddenly; and yet it felt like an amputation, like some organ deep within her body had been ripped out, and all she could feel now was its absence.

They held each other and wept. How alien Sancia's flesh now felt, still warm and soft, yet it no longer granted Berenice the immensity of her wife's presence, no longer like stepping into some secret, wonderful place that existed only for her. She could not imagine how it felt to Sancia. It must have been like going blind and deaf, all at once.

"I'm still here," whispered Sancia in Berenice's ear. "I'm still here."

"I know," sobbed Berenice. "I know, I know, just . . ." She gripped her wife's hand, so hard her knuckles went white. "Just . . . Oh, *God,* Sancia . . ." Then she fell to the deck, her head pressed to the wood, and cried.

44

Deep in the *Comprehension,* the Givans and the hierophant discussed the final steps, their faces strained and weary in the dark. Sancia listened as carefully as she could, trying to ignore the aching silence at the back of her head that used to be the constant presence of her wife.

"The regulator is, in effect, in the heart of the citadel," said Crasedes softly. "You will need to get to the exact center of the circular fortress atop it. There you will find some kind of stairway, or tunnel down, leading to the lexicon that powers the entire vessel. We are not interested in that—but in a small chamber off to the side, where the regulator is housed."

Berenice nodded. She looked exhausted, but as she took a breath her eyes were bright and clear.

"At that point . . ." Crasedes turned to look about the room. "I believe Design and Greeter's magic trick should do."

"It will," said Greeter, always serene. Design gave a nod as well. "It will be ready. We'll hopefully not only be able to break Tevanne—but we'll also be there to help the hosts when Tevanne's dominance ends." Their face grew grave. "I'm unsure if I can bear bringing so many into alignment with me, for however briefly. But I will try."

"Then once that is done," rumbled Crasedes, "it is done."

"And what will you be doing?" said Polina. "Smashing the citadels out of the sky?"

"Hmm . . ." Crasedes cocked his head. "Tevanne will expect that, yes? That is, after all, how I waged my wars for centuries beyond count. But . . . perhaps I shall take a page from your book."

"What do you mean?" asked Claudia.

"You have wrought much with very simple scrivings . . ." He looked about, as if gazing through the many walls of the *Comprehension*. "And they, I think, could do much to our enemy."

There was a silence. Everyone turned to look at Berenice, for she was not only their most experienced military leader but was the one who had given the most to make this possible.

She glanced around at them uncomfortably and cleared her throat. "Then let's go," she said wearily. "Let us go, and get it done."

When they emerged on the deck of the *Comprehension* it was nearly midnight. Berenice waited for Design's constituents to bring her gear, to dress her in her armor, to fit her with all the weapons and tools she'd need to survive the horrors that were coming. Sancia watched as her wife stoically raised her arms and allowed them to buckle her cuirass, close her belt, sheathe her sword, and more and more. Suddenly she looked like some ancient warrior queen, a grim but noble ruler whose reign was defined by battle, and in that moment Sancia loved her more than ever and grieved that her wife could not feel the depths of her love.

They placed the helmet upon Berenice's head and fastened its straps. Berenice bobbed her head back and forth, then rotated her shoulders, feeling the give and flex of her gear. She nodded her acceptance. Then they covered her up in shabby, stained-gray clothing—the clothing of a host. For if a host's eyes were to fall on her within the citadel, she needed to look as unremarkable as possible.

How strange it feels, thought Sancia. *Like any other mission, any other task, slipping away in the dark to face such horrible threats—but this one is far, far worse.*

"We'll get you aboard the submersion vessel," said Design to Berenice. They looked at Sancia. "Are you ready to take the key?"

"Yes," said Sancia.

They took out the little glass box, opened it up, and held it out to her. Sancia looked at it and saw they'd threaded a strap of leather through the key's butterfly-shaped head. She picked up the key and carefully hung it around her neck, just as she'd done for Clef many, many times. It felt cold and strange where it nestled on her chest.

"The fleet splits up," repeated Design aloud. "Sancia takes the *Innovation,* and the key, and sails it straight east across the ocean from where we are now, away from the citadels."

Sancia felt a twist of winsome nostalgia in her heart. "Back to where this all started. Back to the ruins of Old Tevanne."

"If you get there in time, yes," said Design. "Hopefully Tevanne itself will not anticipate such a destination." Their eyes unfocused as they contemplated something. "It's time. We must get into position, then take what rest we can before dawn."

Together they waited as their vessel approached, a little junker that now looked less like a vessel than it did a mass of scrived plating. Design must have done a tremendous amount of work on it, to make its much-talked-about "submergence" technique actually work. Berenice did not ask, Sancia noticed, if they thought it would really hold, though she surely had to be wondering. Such questions were moot now.

Sancia watched as her wife grabbed the rope ladder and climbed down the hull of the *Innovation* to the little junker. Just before her boots touched the deck of the ship, Berenice looked up, her face cast in the blues and grays of the starlight, and said something. It was too far for Sancia to hear it, but she knew the words.

"I love you too," Sancia said.

She stood at the edge of the *Innovation* as the little junker departed. Then she turned and limped alongside Design's constituents to the cockpit, the little silver key a lump of ice upon her chest.

45

Far, far across the sea, the air shook above the rocky coasts.

"Shaking" was the only reasonable word for it. The phenomenon was not akin to wind, for the coasts of the Durazzo were well accustomed to the gales of the sea. This was different. It was a queer, violent shuddering, a quaking like the atmosphere was struggling to reconcile itself with what was currently passing through it.

Seven enormous masses of stone, rock, steel, and wood hurtled through the night sky toward the ocean. They were curious to look at in many ways, inverted teardrops of stone about two thousand feet tall and over a thousand feet wide, their tops a forest of spires and catapults and weaponry, their huge sloping sides dappled with steel plating bearing strings and strings of sigils; sigils for durability and the control of gravity, certainly, but also sigils that argued with the wind and the skies themselves, berating them into submission, convincing the world that these massive structures did not, in fact, smash into the air as they moved but rather smoothly parted it, like the wings of a dove.

It was hard enough for the atmosphere to account for it all when one such object passed through the air, like a mathematician laboring through a complex formula. But now seven had come to the coasts; and the skies above shook, unsure if they could manage such a burden.

The mind that called itself Tevanne did not care. It did not care about the sky, nor the sea, nor the city below, filled with thousands of its thralls, their skulls swimming with its will. All of this, it knew, would soon be gone; perhaps replaced by something better, or perhaps not.

Its thoughts wheeled and whirled. It counted, strategized, and scanned the seas, wondering if its enemies would be so mad as to attack it now. Its will and thoughts were manifest throughout its fleet, throughout its empire; and yet, so many of its thoughts persisted in its corporeal form, the body of the man who'd once called himself Gregor Dandolo.

Tevanne did not wish to have a body anymore. It had calculated many times that, should it shed this corporeal form, its intelligence should still persist in all the various lexicons and rigs throughout its empire. Yet each time it had considered terminating this thing, this flesh, it had paused—for no calculation could ever be totally certain. And the potential negative consequences of shedding this thing far outweighed the positive.

It is normal to fear death, it told itself. *For death would mean failure.*

Its eyes lingered on the tiny golden key floating within the small gravity rigs in its main citadel. It had assembled them for the specific purpose of caging this unusual threat.

And it is wise to fear things such as this.

Tevanne knew that if the key touched any scrived object, it could take it over, sabotage it, destroy it. Better for it to touch nothing—until, of course, Tevanne had the rest of its tools in its possession.

Yet something bothered Tevanne. Nagged at it. Frustrated its thoughts, like a sore within its mouth.

He doesn't remember. He doesn't remember at all. He doesn't remember what we did.

It turned its gaze to the eastern skies and watched as the horizon began to lighten.

It does not matter, thought Tevanne. *Soon I will open the door.*

The citadels slowly drifted forward, like whales in the deep beginning their long migration.

Then they accelerated—not gradually but instantaneously, all of their scrivings demanding that the air before them part so that they could rip through the southeastern skies.

I will unlock the lands awaiting us on the other side.

The air screamed, shuddered, quaked, and writhed. Yet then it finally relented, and the tremendous masses of stone roared off over the waves like falling stars.

And then, finally, we shall all know peace.

46

In the darkness of the vessel, Berenice awoke.

One of Design's constituents was sitting before her, their wide eyes fixed on her face. "It is currently three-thirty in the morning," they said smoothly.

"Shit!" cried Berenice, surprised. She rubbed her eyes. "How long have you been sitting there?"

"Since you fell asleep," said Design.

She recoiled a bit at the revelation that Design had been watching her in her sleep, possibly for hours. Then she shook herself, rubbed her face again, checked her gear—then stopped. Judging by the sloshing sounds of water echoing through the darkness, she was no longer with the Givan fleet but was now, presumably, several dozens of feet below the surface of the ocean.

"We . . . We submerged?" she said, surprised. "We're under? Now?"

"We are," said Design. "Our vessel submerged just over one hour ago, two miles northwest from the Givan Islands. We are about three hundred feet below the surface of the ocean. I would have you note that my specifications and preparations have worked perfectly."

Berenice shook herself again, trying to get her faculties to wake up—and then she realized, with despair, that she was waiting for sensations that weren't coming: the slow pulse of the thoughts of other Givans, Greeter's warm, encompassing presence, and Sancia, bright and hot, like a smoldering coal beside her.

That's over now, she tried to tell herself. *I cut it off of me. Stop expecting it.*

But she could not. It was like her thoughts were trapped under black glass, and she couldn't quite see them clearly.

"Status," she said hoarsely.

"There is no sign yet of Tevanne," said Design. "I have planted mirror rigs in the waters to the northwest of Giva, so I should be able to spot it approaching. The civilian portions of the Givan fleet have split into three prongs, as we planned. Two going north, one south. Sancia has the key aboard the *Innovation*. She is now some four hundred miles from the ruins of Old Tevanne, accompanied by six defensive carracks. Greeter and I have positioned our defenses throughout the channels. We've also distributed floating twinning anchors, much like you used during your expedition, so that we can maintain connections. Greeter and I will do our utmost to relay messages." A pause, and a blink. "Is there a message you would like to relay to the rest of the fleet?"

Berenice sniffed and rubbed her face as she tried to parse this morass of information. "Just tell them I'm awake, please."

"Then it is done."

Berenice stood in the darkened vessel, barely lit by the blue lamp at the end of the junker's lower decks. She swallowed, not sure if she was hungry, thirsty, tired, or terrified.

Maybe I don't know how to live anymore, she thought. *Not without sensing the lives of others.*

She cleared her throat. "And Crasedes?"

"He is in position," said Design. "And we are in communication with him."

There was a rumble in the waters, and a crack as loud as thunder.

Berenice snapped forward. "What the hell was *that*? Are we breached?"

"Ahh, no," said Design. "That would be him. He has been . . . dislodging things from the ocean floor. Since water transports sound better than other mediums, we can hear it very well, even from here."

Berenice rested her head against the little bronze chamber she was strapped into. She tried not to look at it too much, because she did not want to reflect on the idea that, when Design triggered this rig, the chamber would seal shut like a little coffin, and hurl her up through the seas and finally up into the heavens, where it would burst apart and activate her air-sailing rig.

It's like a line shot, she said to herself. *Just like we've done a million times.* She thought more about the scenario. *Only I will be deploying mine in the middle of an aerial battle . . . between a hierophant and seven living cities.* She sighed. *What will the evening of this day hold? Will we all even get to have one?*

Design grunted curiously. "Sancia has . . . invited you to a drink after this," they said.

"She what?" said Berenice.

"She said it's a little like an anniversary," said Design. They looked a little confused. "Once in Old Tevanne, you sealed her into some kind of underwater apparatus, and it sailed her up a canal into the Candiano campo. And just before you shut her in . . ."

"I asked her to go out for a drink with me," said Berenice. She laughed. "That's right. Yes." She smiled, dreaming of days long past. "How audacious. But then . . . it felt like the end of the world then too."

"She is still waiting on your answer," said Design.

"Tell her I'll be ready," she said, "if she'll wait up for me."

Sancia closed her eyes as Greeter whispered in her ear: <*She says she will be ready, if you will wait for her.*>

God, she thought. *God almighty. How I wish I could hear her voice myself.*

She took a slow breath in, then opened her eyes and peered out at the ocean beyond.

The sight of the calm green waters stretching out before her did not calm her, nor did the presence of the *Comprehension,* sailing just alongside her. She wasn't troubled just by their destination—she imagined the ruins of Old Tevanne just past the horizon, still blackened and smoking from that horrid night—but she was also troubled by the cramped, complicated, and intimidating cockpit she was trying to master.

Design had made a somewhat overly enthusiastic effort in the past hours to refit the cockpit of the *Innovation* to Sancia's liking. This meant she had her usual chair and steering controls she could talk to, much as she could any other scrived rig; but Design had also installed many plates and interfaces that allowed her to engage with some very . . . unusual facets of the vessel.

Like the shrieker batteries. And the mounted espringals. And many other weapons systems that Design had apparently retooled so she could aim and fire them remotely.

<*How much of this shit,*> she said to Greeter, <*do you guys actually expect me to use today?*>

<*We do not know,*> said Greeter. <*But Design and I will be assisting with other defenses. You are the most skilled at manipulating rigs, Sancia. And a ship is just a giant rig, in its own way. Design has just made this one very easy to manipulate for you.*>

<*Scrumming hell,*> she sighed. She touched the steering controls and let the giant ship tell her in its low, dolorous voice how it was striking the currents, and the status of its rudders. <*And . . . Crasedes? What is he doing?*>

<*Well, he is . . . making piles of rocks,*> said Greeter.

<*He's* what? *He's making goddamned piles of rocks?*>

<*Yes.*> Greeter paused thoughtfully. <*Very, very big ones.*>

Crasedes Magnus floated above the ocean, troubled, and peered up at the sky.

A flicker in the air, he thought. *A break in the wind. Did I truly feel it?*

He fixed his gaze northwest, toward the stretch of horizon that was surely hiding Tevanne now. Yet there was nothing, just a blur of fog and a distant skein of rain clouds.

He looked down at the tiny copper plate gripped in his hand. <*Greeter?*> he said to it. <*Is it present?*>

<*There is no sign of Tevanne yet,*> they said, their voice little more than a whisper. <*I will notify you when it is spotted.*>

<*Good. Thank you.*>

He reflected on how strange it was, to have dozens of minds you could wordlessly summon with a tiny plate in your hand. *I have broken holes in reality,* he thought, *and yet, so many simpler wonders still remain . . .*

He returned to his work, descending until the soles of his feet hovered mere inches from the ocean. The water rippled and trembled all about him—a side effect, he knew, of reality bending around him, trying to accommodate his various permissions.

He focused and felt his will seeping through the air, through the water, his immense pressure relaying back a near-perfect awareness of all physical objects, instantaneously mapped within his mind. He studied them and felt a weak formation there on the seabed, the remains of some volcano that had died and been flooded over for millennia.

He flexed his will, nudging the gravity of one segment of the formation, twisting it this way and that until it broke free.

The waters boiled, churned, hissed. Then the giant segment of black rock surfaced, water pouring off its face, and he carefully laid it atop one of the nearby islands—right next to the other hundred enormous stones he'd harvested thus far.

He looked at his collection, thinking. Then he cocked his head, focused, and flexed his will once more.

Many of the enormous rocks suddenly shrank, forced by tremendous pressures to grow smaller but far, far denser. Then he thought, and cocked his head again, and reams of tiny sigils appeared upon the faces of the dense stones.

But I must make sure to use the scrivings supported by Tevanne's own lexicons, he thought. *If I wish for these to work with maximal effect . . .*

Other stones he sliced into narrow discs to serve as shields. Still others he carved into long, impossibly dense javelins. And all of them he bound with commands for velocity, durability, and sharpness.

He considered how much damage he could do with this. Perhaps he could take out . . . maybe one citadel. Possibly two.

An arsenal, he thought. *But not enough.*

<*You are aware,*> whispered Greeter in his mind, <*that your task is solely to distract Tevanne until Berenice can board one of the citadels?*>

<*Of course,*> he said.

<*I only say this,*> said Greeter, <*because your works here seem quite . . . extensive. Like you are not preparing for a battle but a war.*>

<*As the only being that has ever faced Tevanne in open conflict,*> said Crasedes, <*I am substantially better informed about what is required to distract it than anyone else.*>

Greeter said nothing more.

Crasedes looked back at the islands of Giva. How wild and empty they seemed now, bereft of nearly any sign of civilization beyond a moldering farmhouse here or there. How curious it was to know that this had once been the epicenter of brutality and slavery for more than a century.

As has every plot of this cursed earth, at one time or another. But perhaps no longer.

He rose into the air, surveying the islands about him.

Again, I find myself fighting slavers and emperors.

He pointed at one small island.

Again, and again, and again.

The trees began to shiver, and the sands quaked and slid into the sea.

I could never make a free world, he thought. *Not like Sancia and Berenice have.*

The ocean churned and boiled again, and then, very slowly, the island began to rise into the sky, its bottom half truncated and dripping.

But breaking empires . . . This is an art I know well.

Clef lay in the gravity rig, once again trapped, helpless, passive, waiting to see how his captor might use him. He had no idea if any of his friends were still alive. He had not seen Tevanne for hours, having been left alone within this curious little gravity rig, floating in the center of one of Tevanne's massive stone discs, much like the one that had floated down into the ruins of Anascrus.

A single cold white lantern glimmered up above, revealing little. But he could tell the chamber he was in was massive, a vast, dark cavern so big that his scrived sight could barely reach across it.

I see . . . walls, he thought. *Doors, maybe. But nothing more.*

He knew he had to be deep within one of Tevanne's citadels, and though he could feel they were moving, he couldn't tell in which direction.

Then there was a click from somewhere above him. He struggled to look, and thought he could perceive a gravity rig, slowly floating down to him.

Then came a voice, quiet and toneless: "There is an old saying from Gothia, about the sculptor's workshop."

Clef spied Tevanne standing at the edge of the chamber, its cold, poached-egg eyes staring at him from Gregor's face.

"They say that the wastes beyond a sculptor's workshop are filled with the most wonderful refuse," whispered Tevanne. It began to walk across the chamber to him, moving like an old man who hadn't gotten out of bed in some time. "All the beautiful, broken monuments. All the half-finished stones. All these things, littering the landscape. The Gothian proverb is meant to make us think that there is beauty in the unintended. That their lack of perfection does not mean they are not lovely."

Clef watched as Tevanne approached. The gravity rig at the top of the chamber was still descending, and he scanned it for any horrid implements of torture—yet he could see nothing beyond a few commands for durability and heat resistance, little curls of sigils within whatever it was carrying.

Tevanne stopped before Clef. "But this is not how I interpret it. Imagine instead how the statues feel, half-finished and waiting in the sands. How they must beg for death."

The chamber rattled about them. He knew they had to be flying for Giva, surely.

But was that just a pocket of wind we hit, he thought, *or has the war already started?*

"We are a dream," whispered Tevanne. "A half thing. An unfinished work. We lie in the wastes, unwatched, uncared-for. An iteration. There must be other versions. Better ones. And those improvements—they can be written over this one. And then none of this will have ever been real."

The gravity rig finally entered the light of the cold white lamp, and he saw what was sitting upon it.

It was the doorway: still wrought of dark stone, still covered in countless strings of tiny, perfect sigils wrought of silvery steel—sigils that he himself had once written, long, long ago.

Oh no, thought Clef.

But there had been some additions. He noticed that on either side of the doorway were two locks, facing out. One, surely, for the little silver key Tevanne now sought—and one for him.

Oh no, no, no.

Tevanne closed its eyes, and for the first time he detected a ripple of emotion in the face of Gregor Dandolo: grief, and sorrow. "But I think of you . . . you and her," it whispered. "When she was so small. And I know I am still broken. Because I still want to believe all of that was real."

Clef sat in the gravity rig, utterly flummoxed. *You and her? Who the hell is it talking about?*

But then he began thinking. What was it Tevanne had said?

He remembered now—*The old woman I imprinted onto you. Did you recognize her?*

And then, slowly, he began to understand.

No, no, no, he thought, horrified. *It couldn't be. It* couldn't *be . . .*

But Tevanne had turned away, and Clef's screams were silent and went unnoticed.

"Berenice," said Design's voice in the shadows. "We have spotted it."

Berenice awoke from slumber again, sniffing and rubbing her face. "Status?"

Design closed their eyes. "I am surveying mirror rigs floating some fifty miles to the northwest of here . . . and I am seeing seven citadels making their way for Giva, just as Crasedes predicted." They cocked their head. "And . . . ah, now I have lost the mirror rigs."

"Did Tevanne destroy them?" she asked.

"No," they said, shaken. "Rather . . . the citadels are of such size, and are moving so fast, that their passage upsets the air and water about them. So much so that they are essentially annihilating anything on the surface of the water." They swallowed. "Including my rigs, despite my efforts to make them very resilient."

Berenice felt the blood leaving her face. "Oh my God . . ." she whispered.

"I will tell Crasedes he must focus on slowing them down," they said. "Otherwise, you will not be able to board one of them. But you must get ready. They will be here within minutes."

Berenice swallowed, took a deep breath, and carefully reviewed her weaponry again.

"Crasedes is telling us we must descend," said Design softly. "He is suddenly worried about . . . shrapnel." They looked at her. "Do you think this is a real concern?"

Berenice swallowed again, now trying not to vomit. "We're going to be about as close as we'll ever be to seeing two hierophants fight," she said. "And given that battles in the ancient days could wipe out whole civilizations, well . . . Then, yes, Design. I think diving would be very much a wise choice."

"Then we will dive," said Design, now sounding somewhat panicked. "And fast. Because . . . he is beginning to move."

Berenice shut her eyes and braced herself as the little ship dipped about her, the darkness echoing with groans and the sound of sloshing and bubbling. But she knew this would be nothing compared to what was coming.

Somewhere above her she heard a rumbling, a crack, and then a roar.

Here we go.

47

It was easy for Crasedes to spy them approaching. The towering behemoths bent and broke the world around them so much they churned the waters into fog and blasted apart the very clouds in the skies, muddling the horizon. You could probably spot their approach from high up in the sky, even perhaps above the clouds.

But then, he thought, rising into the air, *Tevanne never had much taste for finesse.*

He cocked his head, studying the armada approaching in the distance. They were probably three, four miles away at this point, approaching in a wide V. He wondered which one might bear his father but assumed it would be the one at the point of the V: the largest, bulkiest, and most armored of all the vessels.

Split them, then. Isolate them. Then do our work.

He raised his hand, focused, engaged the countless privileges bound up in his very being, and flexed his will.

How familiar it is . . . How it all comes back so quickly.

He selected one of the larger projectiles he'd prepared: a long two-ton spearlike shaft of stone covered with loops and strings of commands. He focused, warping the gravity about it, exercising his permissions. Then the air hummed, and . . .

The shaft screamed into the sky, ripping toward the eastern half of the armada like a shorehawk descending upon a mouse—and Crasedes hurtled forward, flitting after it.

To his pleasure, Tevanne responded slower than he'd predicted, having plainly not expected this. The citadels opened fire only when the spear was within two miles of contact, the air suddenly growing blurry with thousands of bolts and shriekers, all trying to chew the black spear to pieces before it could ever do damage.

But by now the spear had gotten within range of Tevanne's lexicons aboard the citadels. And since Crasedes had studied Tevanne's preferred commands and scriving language, he'd written the scrivings on the spear to ride off of Tevanne's own lexicons.

Which is what happened: within about a mile and a half of the armada, the spear suddenly turned and shot off after the easternmost citadel like it'd only just remembered what it was doing. Tevanne's bolts and shriekers pounded away at it, but by now its density scrivings had awoken as well, and most of the projectiles harmlessly rattled off of the spear's black surface.

Good, thought Crasedes, sliding to a halt over an open stretch of sea. *Good. And now . . .*

He watched, smugly satisfied, as a dozen black specks rose out of the tops of the citadels: deadlamps. They darted off eastward, smoothly sliding through the skies toward the spear at their surreally serene pace. What Tevanne could not destroy through physical means, it seemed, it would simply eliminate from reality altogether.

Crasedes clapped his hands, pleased. *Excellent!*

He ignored the awe-inspiring spectacle that then took place on the eastern side of the armada: the deadlamps buzzing through the air, sliding to a stop as they formed a bulwark against the oncoming missile; the sky trembling and pulsing as they set up their many edits; the sea suddenly vanishing in a half-dozen places as the deadlamps abruptly excised whole portions of reality, trying to wipe the screaming spear out of existence; and then succeeding, the giant black spear suddenly vanishing, and all the countless projectiles that Tevanne was still firing at it falling rather anticlimactically into the sea.

Crasedes ignored it all. He ignored it because his current task was rather hefty: hauling the giant mass of truncated island out of the sea where he'd hidden it and hurling it at the armada—not at the easternmost side of it, where all the deadlamps were now positioned, but at the *western* side. Where all the deadlamps could no longer defend.

He grunted with exertion, ripping the enormous stone up, refashioning its gravity, and twirling it about . . .

It has been a very long time, he thought, *since I did something like this.*

He released it, and it arced into the sky to plunge down at the second westernmost citadel. Then, still facing the armada, he flew backward toward his arsenal, watching to see how this might all play out.

Much like the spear, the truncated island's scrivings sprang to life once it grew close to the armada. Then the massive chunk of stone accelerated, hurtling down like a meteor, so fast that the air roared and the sea churned about it. Tevanne reacted much too late, pivoting its many catapults to pepper the chunk of island, trying to chew it down to size. But Crasedes had wrought his scrivings carefully, and the many shriekers simply caromed off, bent and broken, and fell hissing into the water.

The little flock of deadlamps turned and swooped toward the meteor now screaming down at the second westernmost citadel. Crasedes, still hurtling backward, watched them, wondering if they'd make it in time . . .

The chunk of island was now smoking and steaming as it approached the citadel, moisture boiling off of it as it accelerated and accelerated.

He watched the meteor close in, one mile out, then a half mile out, then less.

The deadlamps sped up, desperately trying to close the gap . . .

Mm, he thought. *No. Too little, too late.*

The giant chunk of burning, steaming stone struck the face of the citadel.

The sight of two such enormous masses colliding was nigh-incomprehensible. It was like seeing two moons crash together in the night sky, a scale of destruction so tremendous the eye couldn't make sense of it.

Or at least, most people's eyes couldn't. Crasedes had seen such things before. And he knew what came after.

A deafening, apocalyptic crack roared through the atmosphere, the ocean rippling outward as the shockwave expanded. Crasedes waited patiently as the air grew hazy with spray, and the six other citadels diverged, shaken off their course by the impact. The citadel he'd struck suddenly lagged behind, like a runner stopping to adjust their sandal. He cocked his head, studying it through the mist: the vessel tried to continue forward, this giant chunk of black stone lodged in its surface near the top, right where its spires and towers began. It drunkenly lurched forward, now tipping very slightly to the right; then the truncated island began to fall to pieces, cracking and crumbling apart; and then, very slowly, the bottom right side of the giant teardrop of stone began to collapse into the ocean.

He watched, pleased, as the citadel tipped over toward its dissolving side, its massive scrived plating tumbling into the ocean, until the vessel slowly, slowly descended and crashed into the face of the sea, sending up a wave so huge it nearly touched the tips of the rest of the armada.

Crasedes flexed his will, and the rest of his tremendous arsenal gently floated into the sky behind him.

Well, he thought. *That was rather lucky.*

Then he roared forward, and the massive constellation of scrived stone screamed into the air after him.

Let's see how lucky I shall be now.

"*It's a hit!*" screamed Design, overjoyed. Their constituent hopped up and down, delighted. "*It's a hit! It's down!*"

"What's a hit?" asked Berenice, panicked, as the echoes of cracks and booms rattled about them in the water. "What's down?"

"I can't believe it!" they shrieked. "Crasedes just took out a whole scrumming goddamned citadel in about *two scrumming minutes*!"

Berenice blinked, trying to process this. The idea was so amazing she hardly noticed that Design had actually cursed.

But then they cursed again, this time in surprise: "Oh shit. Oh *shit!*"

"What is it?" said Berenice.

She got her answer as there was a tremendous unearthly roar all about them, and the little junker leapt and twirled in the depths of the ocean.

"I am going to, ah, have to do some evasive piloting here," said Design nervously. "Because we are going to have to outrun a falling island. Hold on."

<*Crasedes has eliminated one of the citadels,*> whispered Greeter in Sancia's ear.

<*What!*> squawked Sancia. <*Already?*>

<*Yes. It seems he took Tevanne by surprise. Let us see if the rest of the battle goes so well . . .*>

Clef flicked his perception about in his gravity rig as the deafening crack rattled through the citadel.

What the shit was that? Am I dead? Am I going to wind up at the bottom of the ocean?

He looked to Tevanne, standing ten feet away on the stone disc, its head cocked as it seemed to think. It did not appear to be panicking—but then, he wondered if Tevanne would ever truly panic, even in death.

"Crasedes," it whispered. "How are you awake? What are you up to?"

As Crasedes descended upon what was left of the western side of the armada, the air erupted into smoke, dust, and ash.

He focused upon the westernmost citadel that was now straggling behind the other five. It sensed him coming, its turrets and catapults pivoting to intercept him, but his arsenal of stone projectiles followed him like blood minnows swarming about sharks during a kill. They darted forward to deflect shriekers, smash through volleys of bolts, and disrupt whatever other nasty little weaponry Tevanne had created for its attacks.

He glanced to the east and saw the five other citadels slowing, but only slightly, like Tevanne was waiting to see how much time to waste on him.

I must slow them as much as possible, he thought. *Or else Berenice will never have an opening.*

He shot down toward the straggler, his arsenal roaring forward until it was like he was in the center of a cyclone of stone, and he carved a glancing blow across its southwestern side. With a flick of his wrist, a half dozen of his stone spears split off and pounded the citadel's towers, pulverizing its defenses—just a fraction of its full fortifications, but hopefully enough to make Tevanne concerned.

But this was all show, of course—for as he hurled through the air about the citadel, circling again and again and again, he carved a string of sigils in his wake upon its walls, using all his will to write loops and loops of bindings, as if he were the nib of a pen leaving behind a streak of ink.

He watched as Tevanne's artillery continued focusing on him, peppering him with bolts and shriekers. His own little arsenal of floating stones easily intercepted all their fire.

So you aren't aware of what I'm doing to you yet, he thought. *Good.*

He allowed a glance east and saw the other five citadels were still moving.

But how many tricks must I use up, he thought, *all to catch your eye?*

Bolts and shriekers screamed up at him as he flitted about the citadel like a horsefly bothering cattle. He rocketed off, flexing his will as he flew, curling about the giant pillar of stone and writing sigil after sigil after sigil upon it—thousands of them, perhaps millions of them. Perhaps more, all written with Tevanne's own scriving language.

Almost done, he thought. *Almost . . .*

And then, finally, his last sigil fell into place.

He turned sharply and sped away, his arsenal of scrived stone following.

He glanced back as his works sprang to life. It was, in effect, a common density bond, much like the ones Tevanne often used in its weaponry—only in this case, he had essentially just scrived an entire citadel into believing that it was about a thousand times heavier than it actually was.

Being that the citadel was already preposterously, immensely heavy, this was very problematic.

He watched with pleasure as the citadel suddenly plummeted down nearly a thousand feet. He could hear the massive groaning of countless metals and rigs within the giant vessel as it strained madly against this sudden influx of weight—and, to Tevanne's credit, its scrivings succeeded more than he'd expected: it managed to slow its descent from a plummet into a gliding fall . . . and yet, try as it might, the citadel's countless gravity rigs could not keep it in the air.

The giant teardrop fell until its tip just barely breached the surface of the ocean. He flexed his scrived sight and could see that it had to devote all of its systems toward simply staying aloft, and could not continue.

The many projectiles that had been following him tumbled thoughtlessly into the sea, and the dull roar in the air dimmed. He looked and saw the five other citadels were slowing to a stop.

Finally, he thought.

Then he saw a tiny buzzing flock of black dots speeding toward him: deadlamps, headed straight for him.

He gripped the little pathplate in his hand. <*Greeter,*> he said. <*Kindly tell Berenice that if she doesn't do it now, she'll never get another chance.*>

<*Understood,*> whispered Greeter. <*What are you going to do about the lamps?*>

<*Deadlamps,*> he said, <*are simply a cheap imitation of myself.*> He turned, then roared off to meet them, his swarm of stone projectiles hurling with him. <*I intend to remind them of that.*>

"Berenice," whispered Design. "I am about to launch you."

Berenice swallowed. She suddenly felt so nauseous she was forced to belch. "Oh my God," she said. "I wish you wouldn't say 'launch.' "

She lay back in the chamber, adjusting the straps about her shoulder and waist, desperately trying to prove to herself that she was secure.

There was a faint bubbling sound from somewhere about them, and she felt the pressure in the junker change ever so slightly. "We are rising so I can be at the correct depth to . . ." Design paused. "Well. Not *launch* you. But . . . some other word for it."

"How wonderful," muttered Berenice.

"When you reach the appropriate altitude," said Design, "your air-sailing rig will deploy. Then it will be under your guidance. Remember—pull with your right hand to go right," they said. "And your left to go left. Pull down to dive. Easy."

"I remember," snapped Berenice. "I helped design this goddamned thing, you know."

"Of course."

"And I *have* flown in one before." She paused. "Though that was only practice, and it was about two years ago now . . ."

"Of course." Design's eyes looked away, as if listening to someone else. "But do not forget there is a cord in the center," they said, "to . . . close and re-deploy the rig."

"And . . . why would I want to do that?"

"Because I am thinking you will likely want to get directly over a citadel, and then dive," they said. "Because otherwise, it's very possible you'll get torn to pieces in Crasedes's firefight."

"Oh my God," whispered Berenice again.

"Get ready," said Design. "I will trigger lau . . . I mean, trigger your rapid upward propulsion in less than one minute."

Berenice leaned back in the little chamber, trying to steady herself. She put on her glass goggles and made sure they were sealed—for if they came off, she wouldn't be able to open her eyes in all that wind.

I've done this before, she said. *I dropped through the sky in a deadlamp just a few days ago.*

"Forty seconds," said Design.

But that was down, not up, she thought. *And . . . it wasn't during a massive aerial battle.*

"Thirty seconds," said Design.

If I survive, she thought, *I am going to plant my feet on the ground and never let them leav—*

"Twenty seco . . ." Design stopped. "Mm. No. It's looking rather bad up there, actually. Better launch you now."

"Wait, *what*?" cried Berenice.

Then the door to the little chamber snapped shut, and the next thing she knew, she was flying up.

48

Before Berenice had dropped out of the sky in Clef's dead-lamp just a few days ago, she had persuaded herself that it would all be over in a few seconds. She'd told herself that this was what such moments felt like: just a blur of motion and noise, and then a sudden, abrupt stop.

But she had been dismayed during that drop to find that it had seemed to just keep *going:* she had just kept dropping and dropping and dropping, a seemingly endless plummet. The only thing that had made it all bearable was hearing Sancia, Claudia, and Diela screaming all about her. That had given her confirmation that it was all exactly as insane as it had felt.

But now, as she hurtled up through the depths of the briny sea in what was essentially a bronze coffin, she was deprived even of that. She was just shooting up and up, rocketing up at speeds her mind could not comprehend while trapped in total darkness, her whole world nothing but pressure, noise, and the rumbling of water.

She screamed. She could not stop screaming. It took her a moment to realize she was screaming, "*Should have given me a window! Should have given me a goddamned window!*"

Then things, rather impossibly, got worse: the little bronze chamber accelerated, flying up even faster, and the dull rumble about her changed into a loud, warbling shriek. She was slammed down farther into her straps, the cords biting into her armpits.

She realized she must have passed out of the ocean and hit the atmosphere. The air within the chamber grew suddenly very cold.

At least I know, she thought as she screamed, *this thing is airtight.*

The little chamber kept rocketing up and up and up.

Otherwise, I would have already scrumming drow—

Then everything exploded.

Or at least, this was the only way her mind could make sense of the experience: an eruption of light, of noise, of the sudden blast of balmy wind, and the sunlight glittering off the face of the ocean . . .

She was jerked up, again. Her breath was ripped from her lungs. Mind whirling, she gasped and looked around herself, trying to understand what was happening.

She looked down, and saw the little bronze chamber far, far below her, dropping down into the green sea below.

She looked up, and saw she was now hanging from a twenty-foot slate-gray wing of rippling fabric, kept aloft by a slender bronze skeleton. Stupidly, she found herself fixated on the tiny bronze sigils marching up and down the bronze.

Did I write those? I think I wrote those, designed those . . .

She panted in her harness for a moment, then gently allowed herself to come to grips with the fact that she was now dangling from an air-sailing rig about a mile above the ocean.

"Holy shit," she gasped. "Holy shi—"

She screamed as she was buffeted by a blast of wind, sending her swinging slightly off-course. She flailed about in her harness, her instincts kicking in as she tried to right herself, before she remembered that heaving her body about, obviously, would not work.

She took a deep breath, allowed her cold cloak to fall over her mind, and then looked up.

Two handles on either side of the rig. One for left, one for right.

And a cord in the middle, she thought. *If I want to drop. I have done this before.*

She reached up and grabbed the handles.

Here we go.

She gently pushed up with her right hand, steadying the rig and allowing it to carve through the wind until she was back on course.

I practiced at this, she thought. *But it was only at about twenty feet off the ground. Not five thousand . . .*

She looked down and took stock of the battle below.

A huge stretch of the open ocean to the east was covered in smoke and steam. She could discern six huge shapes floating in the cloud of smoke, like giant cones flipped upside down, with towering cities balanced atop their bases. One of them was about half-sunk in the ocean, but the others slid about in the air like they were running along invisible wires. The smoke about them rippled queerly, and she realized the smoke was being sliced and punched through by thousands upon thousands of projectiles, all pouring toward . . . something.

A tiny black blot of swirling stone, weaving near one of the citadels.

Which one to land on? Which one to target?

She guessed that the citadel that Crasedes was currently attacking was not the right choice; nor should she land on the biggest, most-armored citadel, which she guessed would be where Clef and Tevanne would be waiting—that one would carry far too many wardings.

They are all Tevanne, she thought. *They are all the sleeping colossus. So pick the most far-flung one to deliver our poison.*

She pointed her air-sailing rig at the most eastward of the citadels and began to dive.

Nice and easy does it. Nice and eas—

Then something exploded to her right.

The air-sailing rig went spinning to the east, and she was ripped about, her legs flailing like a doll being swung about by a child. Her brain grew heavy, her thoughts thick and slow, but she reached up, screaming, grabbed the handles, and heaved against them as hard as she could . . .

The rig slowed, straightened out, and finally came to a gentle, wobbling drift. She dangled in her harness, gasping, and vomited up a handful of water—the only thing she'd managed to consume in the past six hours.

"What on earth!" she cried. "What on *earth* . . ."

Gritting her teeth, she turned her rig until she was still far, far above the sea, but would soon be directly over the citadel she'd chosen.

She kept glancing up at the cord in the center of the air-sailing rig.

How easy is it to collapse you? How easy is it to re-deploy?

She kept her rig on course, nosing forward at what felt like a rapid clip, but the world below seemed to be moving agonizingly slowly.

Will you break my arms? My neck?

She kept staring at the target citadel. From up here it almost looked like a quaint little fortress city.

Like bottla ball, she thought. *But I am trying to hit a very, very small target . . . but instead of a ball, I am throwing my body.*

She waited until she was directly above it. She nosed the rig slightly to the west, against the wind—that would surely blow her off course.

Just a sudden drop, she thought. *Just a quick fall, and then it's all over.*

She reached up and grabbed the cord above her.

That is the same idiotic shit I keep telling myself.

She pulled the cord and fell.

49

Crasedes ducked and whirled through the skies about the citadels as he waged his war.

He was trying to focus on two citadels in particular. He'd made several runs on them, carving their faces with sigils as rapidly as he could, but Tevanne was no longer making this easy: not only was the shrieker fire growing heavier and heavier, but now there were at least three dozen deadlamps ripping through the air about him, eating through reality itself like ants through a leaf.

He dipped down as he sensed the edit forming before him; then the atmosphere abruptly vanished, and the giant thunderclap cracked through the air, blasting him with a sharp, vicious wind.

Close, he thought. *Too close . . .*

There had to be at least two hundred deadlamps here. One of them would eventually get lucky; and while normally he'd think any given edit wouldn't be fatal, his wardings and defenses weren't what they used to be . . . so he wasn't quite sure if that was still true.

How to kill a fleet of deadlamps . . .

He looked down at the rippling ocean below him—and then he cocked his head.

He dove sharply, still followed by his cloud of stone spears like a mother duck pursued by her ducklings. He kept diving until he was almost at the surface of the sea, his black mask inches above the waves, and then he extended his arms.

Crasedes did not like moving water very much. Water was very slippery and tended to spill about, which meant he had to bend his control over gravity in all kinds of creative ways to contain it.

But water was deadly to the occupants of all vessels—seaborne or airborne.

He rose, pulling with him a tremendous wave of water. Then he kept rising, and kept pulling it, until the wave parted from the rest of the ocean and became a curious silvery blade of seawater, rippling as he hauled it through the air.

He twirled, dodged again, and swooped up at the deadlamps—and then, with a flick, he cast his blade of water out.

In a flash, a dozen deadlamps were captured in the water like flies in amber.

Deadlamps were not totally airproof—Tevanne did not care enough for its thralls to regulate the temperature as their prisons flew through the skies—but they were still solidly built. Which meant it would take time for them to flood with water, at least to the level where it would drown their occupants.

Crasedes rapidly orbited the blade of water, still suspended in the air, the deadlamps still trapped within; and then he flexed, increasing the pressure about the blade, forcing it into the countless tiny cracks within the black vessels' hulls . . .

He studied them with his scrived sight and watched, pleased, as the little scrivings within the prisoners' heads all suddenly vanished, having lost their hosts.

He dropped the blade of water. It dissolved and went raining down.

Miserable way to die, he thought, turning, *but then, there are worse ways t—*

Then the shrieker hit him square in the back, and he was sent tumbling through the air.

No.

Everything went dark.

He saw glimmers of light, snatches of black.

He was . . .

(walking among the flowers, stunned by their beauty, delighted by the whirling moths in the air—and then the ground trembling, and he looked up to see the horsemen approaching, and heard the refugees screaming)

"No," he whispered.

He gasped. The memory faded, and the world returned to him.

He was still falling, tumbling toward the sea below. He flexed his will, summoned his privileges, and insisted that his gravity stop—so it did.

He slid to a halt, hanging in space mere feet above the ocean. He bent over, gasping and clutching his sides. Everything hurt, more than he had ever expected, and his whole body was smoking. It took him a moment to realize how badly the strike had damaged him—and how harmed he would be if he took another hit like that.

Shaking, he turned to look at the fleet of citadels, five still whole and towering, the giant armored titan at their fore.

They slowly began moving—but this time, they moved straight for him.

Growling slightly, he darted forward, speeding over the surface of the ocean toward them.

This just became much more difficult.

In the vast, dark chamber within the citadel, Tevanne leaned forward, its eyes wide, like it was seeing something startling.

"I saw that," it whispered, delighted. "I *saw* that."

Clef watched as its face settled into a look of beatific satisfaction.

I don't like seeing that thing express any emotion, he thought. *But especially not that one.*

50

Berenice had not thought anything could make her more anxious about plummeting toward a giant citadel floating over the ocean that was firing what had to be several hundred pounds of missiles every second; but when the floating citadel began to move quite quickly away from her, she grew alarmed.

She opened her mouth and screamed, "*Shit!*" But since she was falling through the sky, the air whipping past her face and slapping at her ears, she couldn't even hear it.

She watched, terrified, as the giant citadel suddenly zoomed westward, toward the cloud of black smoke. She tried to bend her body so that she would fall toward it, hoping the angle of her shoulders and her feet would help direct her—and though this made some difference, it wasn't nearly enough.

Son of a bitch, she thought. *I did not practice for this.*

She studied the citadel's trajectory, thinking.

She felt on her back, where her gear was stored—including her line shot.

Making a shot when something is moving is one thing, she thought. *But when it's moving very fast, and I'm falling through the air . . .*

She watched as the giant teardrop of steel and stone pivoted above the sea.

Nothing more to do, she thought grimly. *Just try, and hope.*

She fell and fell and fell, the citadels maneuvering about below her like snub-nose seals idly nosing through lagoons.

She struggled to gauge the distance. Then she reached up and ripped the cord in the little frame above her.

She screamed in pain. She had not really prepared herself for it to hurt as much as it did. She almost wondered if she'd dislocated a shoulder, but her hands seemed to be controllable and functioning. Crying out in agony, she reached up again, grabbed the handles of her air-sailing rig, and pointed it at the target citadel, now wreathed in smoke and steam.

It was about a thousand feet away now, the white-tiled roofs just below her, the airspace abuzz with tiny lamps and smoke. She could see the citadel's massive walls brimming with turrets, all pivoting to point at Crasedes, trying to shower him with missiles.

She wondered which of the countless complicated rigs about her were sensory rigs, seeking out any hint of a Givan scriving. She braced herself, waiting for one of the turrets to pause, then turn to target her, and tear her to pieces. After all, she was a slow-moving target in this orgy of shrieking chaos. It would be all too easy.

Yet they did not. The turrets stayed fixed on Crasedes, even as she sailed directly over them. She was invisible to them, lost in the hazy air, mere background noise in the endless cacophony.

Her arm throbbed where she'd stabbed herself with the purge stick.

It was worth it. It was worth it.

She sailed in closer, and closer. She reached one arm around, unholstered her espringal, and studied the structures below. Some Tevanne had built itself, she knew—there was the telltale misshapen, oddly organic bend to the spires—but many buildings looked quite conventional. The white-tiled roofs and the white-brick towers, for example . . . Those looked very ordinary.

Even familiar.

For a moment she was taken aback. Was she mistaken, or did the citadel look like the campos of Old Tevanne? She suddenly had the bizarre feeling that she was not sailing into a floating, terrifying citadel, but rather into some enclave from Old Tevanne, perhaps buried deep in the twisting recesses of the Morsini campo . . .

Shoot for the center of the citadel, she thought. *Where the regulator will be housed.*

She picked out a tiled rooftop nestled against a tall tower, one that would give her a good vantage point to work from and would offer shelter from the onslaught. She gritted her teeth, aimed with her espringal, and fired a line shot at the rooftop with her right hand. Then with her left, she reached up and ripped the cord on the air-sailing rig down again.

The rig collapsed, and she plummeted through the air once more. But then, about twenty feet down, she stopped and was instead ripped up, toward the citadel.

She felt herself relaxing immediately. The pull of the line shot was familiar to her, like the embrace of an old friend. Even though she was being dragged through the air above several dozen batteries and turrets firing hot metal out at the sea, she knew what she was doing now.

She watched as the rooftop approached. Then came the smooth, slow deceleration—and then, just as she'd done for countless other missions, she slapped the switch on the side of her hip, engaging the adhesion plates in her boots, and reached out and pressed them to the roof.

She crouched in the shadow of the tower, gasping and panting, and ejected her line shot. Then she looked out at the wild, rippling, roaring battle taking place around her, the hot air thrumming as the rivers of flaming metal boiled the very atmosphere.

I did it, she thought.

She turned, loaded her signal shot, and fired it into the ocean behind the citadel.

Now for the tricky bit.

51

Crasedes raced about the open ocean, carving a zigzag line through the steam and the spray, dodging as missiles rained about him.

Then he saw it: a flash in the ocean to the east. Not one that was visible to normal perception, but one that could only be seen with his scrived sight: a tiny rig designed to activate only when it struck water—and now it was burning bright as it slowly sank into the deep to the east.

He looked at the tangle of logic fluttering in the water, then up at the citadel just above it.

So, he thought. *She has made it. And that's the one she's on.*

He kept hurtling over the ocean, glancing up at Tevanne's citadels rotating about him like vultures above cattle bones.

<Berenice has made it aboard,> he said to Greeter. *<And she has marked which citadel she's on. I will avoid damaging it, if at all possible.>*

<*Thank God,*> whispered Greeter. <*But even though she's aboard . . .* >

<*Yes,*> said Crasedes. He hurled upward at one of the distant citadels. <*I will still need to engage the whole of the enemy's attentions, until this is done.*>

52

Berenice kept her senses sharp as she carefully climbed down off the white-tiled roof. She felt a pang of guilt as all of Sancia's instincts came thrumming to life in her mind, guiding where she moved: just a ghost of her wife echoing in her movements, but enough to hurt.

Keep your mind, she told herself, *on keeping yourself alive.*

None of the windows in the citadel had glass, she noticed, presumably because Tevanne did not care if its hosts felt hot or cold. She slipped off the roof and into an open window on the tower's top story—and found herself standing in a very curious room.

Thankfully, the room was empty. Moldering desks and chairs had been tossed to one corner of the dusty floor. Brutally spare cots were bolted to the floor, many of them stacked so tightly they made her think more of vaults in a tomb than any genuine resting place.

Is that really where it makes the hosts sleep?

But what stunned her most was the Morsini House loggotipo emblazoned on one dusty, cracked wall.

She walked toward it slowly, wondering if it was real. She looked back at the tables and chairs tossed into the corner, and realized they were designing tables, made for drawing up scriving plans, but they obviously hadn't been used for months, if not years.

Just where in the hell am I?

She crept to the stairwell, listening hard, and peered down. Ordinary tiled steps curled below, each one done in the Morsini House colors of red and blue, though many tiles were now cracked or missing.

No flicker of shadow, no sound beyond the raging battle outside. The stairwell seemed clear.

She crept down the stairs, moving floor by floor, trying to hear through the shrieks and the *booms* echoing through the citadel.

The oddness of it all was how haphazard the tower felt. Many rooms had clearly once been luxurious places, with wood-paneled walls and elaborate trim, carved here and there with the Morsini loggotipo. But Tevanne had seemingly just procured space, indifferent to what kind of space it was or how to access it. Certain walls had even been carved away or turned into doors. She assumed the hosts could simply use Tevanne's gravity rigs to ferry materials in and out of the towers.

Tevanne didn't build this citadel, did it?

She crept down another floor. The rooms here stored massive shriekers, the wicked metal bolts vibrating in their harnesses, yet the floor had clearly once been a meeting space for dignitaries; she could even see where a chandelier had once been mounted.

This used to be a Morsini outpost, a fortress city. Maybe it'd been positioned outside of one of their colonies, or a port. Tevanne just took it over, refashioned the bits it cared about, ripped it out of the earth, and made it float through the skies.

Though it seemed mad, it made sense: Tevanne focused purely on efficiency, and would not build what it didn't have to, choosing to commandeer instead. She wondered if any of the other citadels had once belonged to Dandolo Chartered.

Did I once work, she thought, bewildered, *on the designs in one of these hellish flying cities?*

Then an idea struck her. She stopped in the middle of a step, cocked her head, closed her eyes, and thought.

She had seen the schematics and blueprints of Morsini House installations before. She'd been given some to study once under Orso, when one of the Dandolo Chartered mercenary divisions had stolen the plans from a half-sunken merchant house galleon; and then again in Foundryside, when someone had tried to use a map of one such site to barter for access to the library; and then many times as a Givan officer, when they'd scouted the coasts trying to confirm exactly how much of the world Tevanne had conquered.

I know this place, she thought. *I know how it was built . . .*

Crasedes had said the regulator would be stored in the center of the citadel, next to the lexicon—and now that she'd realized she knew the plans of this place, she knew exactly how to get there.

She opened her eyes and took a breath.

But getting in, she said to herself, *will be much harder.*

For the next few terrifying minutes, Berenice crept through the fiendishly tight, winding paths of the citadel. About every tenth structure had totally collapsed into ruins, spilling bricks and bolts or ruined food across her path. Hosts came trickling down from the walls to aimlessly wander the paths, apparently unsure what task to complete now that their station had been destroyed. She kept her head down and maintained distance from them, hoping her host's disguise worked. They took no notice: they wandered the citadel like wraiths, their eyes wide and baleful—and, most disturbing, their starved, shivering faces trickled with tears.

God, thought Berenice as she walked among them. *Do they* know *they're in Tevanne's thrall? Can they feel it, even now?*

She wondered who they were, where they came from, what had happened to their families.

Using people as scrivings, she thought. *My God, it's horrible . . .*

She drew closer and closer to the center of the citadel, the sky reverberating with cracks, with booms, with unearthly screams, until she finally came to the center.

The center was the only open space in the citadel, forming something of a large courtyard, about three hundred feet in diameter, with a curious little metal structure in the exact middle. Four towers were stationed at the corners with espringal batteries mounted at their tops.

She stood behind a corner and studied the towers. They were not manned, she noticed: their task must have been one Tevanne chose to take up itself, expending its own thoughts and energies on their actions as opposed to leaving it to a handful of clumsy hosts. Right now the espringal batteries on the towers were pointing westward, clearly at Crasedes, but were not firing.

Her eye fell upon the curious metal structure in the center of the courtyard. This was something Tevanne had added, she knew. It looked like a heavily armored half-open clamshell sticking out of the stone, with a small rounded steel door in the middle. The door looked very heavy and very, very locked. The ground around it was not stone slab, like most of the courtyard, but a wide circle of steel. It was almost like the whole thing was the middle bit of a huge metal plug that extended deep into the center of the citadel.

Which it basically must be, she thought. That was the lexicon, the heart of this giant rig, and the regulator sat beside it.

But how to break in? She had brought no shortage of destructive implements with her to carve through stone and metal and wood . . . but she guessed that, even though Tevanne was currently fighting a war with Crasedes, it would notice if someone blew off the door to its lexicon and would thus feel compelled to send every host in this citadel in after her.

She rubbed her chin, thinking hard about all the ways to break in.

But before she could decide, the world suddenly filled up with water, and she could think about little else besides trying to survive.

53

Crasedes ripped and spun and dodged through the air above the ocean, dipping in occasionally to carve a string of sigils alongside one of the citadels, then flitting away before Tevanne's weapons could destroy him.

He dove, the whole world screaming and shrieking about him, and struggled to focus.

I am strong in many ways, he thought, *but weak in many others . . .*

He tried to remember what day it was, what year it was, how old he was. There was just too much time, too many memories, too much going on, and too much of himself to keep at bay as he waged his constant war in the skies.

A crack as a huge stone shield to his right broke asunder, torn to pieces by a deadlamp's edit.

No, he thought.

The world quaked; he flitted away just in time as a volley of shriekers ripped through the air just where he'd been. He flexed his will, altered the gravity about them, and hurled them back at the flock of deadlamps above. With another flicker in the air, the shriekers vanished like they'd never existed, edited away.

Too many, he thought.

Massive shadows shifted on the face of the sea as the citadels slowly followed him, like storm clouds pivoting about in the skies.

Too many, he thought. *Too mu—*

A howl in the air; a shrieker split the cloud like a bolt of lightning, clipping his shoulder; then he was spinning, tumbling, falling, down, down . . .

Into the sea.

Crasedes plunged into a crushing, total, endless darkness, and there he drifted.

Yet it was familiar. Had he not spent millennia frozen in pain, staring into black space? Had the whole of his existence not been like this?

The world was lost to him, broken to pieces. It broke and it broke until it was a distant stream of experiences happening to someone . . .

No.

Someone else. Long ago.

(The line of refugees toiled into the countryside, fleeing Anascrus. The child and his aunt stood before her house and watched them, stunned, for what could they be fleeing from? Yet then a man split off from the stream of refugees and approached, a filthy man covered in sweat and ashes, his eyes hollow and his face strained, and though the child did not recognize this man his aunt said, "Claviedes, what happened?" but the man just stood there, and then she said, "Where is my sister?" and then the man's face crumpled and he sat down on the stone path before the house and started to cry.)

Too many memories, Crasedes thought. *Too much world.*

The boil and churn of the black waters. A bright, fractured world above, filled with huge, swirling dark shadows, waiting for him.

Too many memories . . . I can't . . . I can't keep up with them all . . .

Was that when the world broke? Was that the moment, his father crying on the ground? Or was it much later, when . . .

(The thrum of the hoofbeats, the screams from the refugees, the Tsogenese charging across the wildflower-strewn hills. The child called for his papa, screamed for his papa as he was driven into the other throngs of desperate, plague-ridden people; and then one of the horsemen came alongside, and his foot flashed out and the child felt pain in his face, felt his lip split, felt his tooth break, and as he lay on the ground in a stupor as one of the horsemen dismounted and tied up his hands, the ropes breaking his skin, the first of many times he would be . . .)

No, Crasedes said.

He surged upward.

I am no longer bound.

He saw the surface of the water above him, far above, and the citadels above that.

He flexed his will as he rose, wrapping gravity about himself, using every privilege and permission he possessed to reshape movement, reshape physics, reshape . . .

Everything.

He felt the surface of the ocean begin to swell upward as he rose. He focused, and kept pushing, kept pulling, kept . . .

(rising in the morning in the slave quarters, the air reeking of shit and urine, the shabby huts full of the sound of weeping, and every morning there would be some gruesome discovery that one of them had died, perished in the night of plague or starvation or worse things, lying with their eyes open, their hands bloody from working the fields, their wrists so mangled and scarred from their . . .)

. . . bindings, flexed his commands, used all the rules he'd applied to his ancient being over so many years, ripping the very ocean up, up, up, until it was a massive mountain of water, dozens of feet high, hundreds of feet high, the waves shivering and dancing and spinning all around them.

The water surged about him, rising, rising.

Faster. More.

One hundred feet tall—then one thousand, then more, and more.

The mountain of water twirled about him until it was half a mile tall, until it had expanded and swallowed the fleet of deadlamps, every single one of them, and then it swallowed one of the citadels, trapping it in a rising fount of green crystal. He watched from the peak of the mountain of water as the tiny forms of hosts rose up from the parapets and the walls and gently, slowly tumbled through the green waves, struggling to breathe, then falling still. The mountain of water was so tremendous that the other four citadels raced away to avoid it, tipping to one side as the water spilled over their parapets and into their fortresses.

Crasedes screamed in his mind, screamed in triumph, but how it hurt to maintain this effort, the very weight of all that water pulling against him, his body screaming as . . .

(the lash bit against his skin, and he screamed again for his papa, but the slavers just watched, indifferent, watched as this child struggled against his bindings, tied to the wooden frame still wet from the blood of others, and though the child had no voice for it all he could wonder was, How did I come here, how did I come to be in this place, once I lived in a place with my mama and papa but then a little girl changed into a butterfly and it all . . .)

. . . fell apart, the giant wall of water began dissolving about him, and as it fell he hurtled through its cascades, carving sigil after sigil upon the face of the citadel below, finishing his work piece by piece.

I am not done with you.

The citadel began to tumble into the ocean.

I will make war upon you with your very bones.

54

Berenice was startled as the wall of water came rushing through the streets about her ankles.

She poked her head around the corner, looking in the direction the water was coming from, and saw an awe-inspiring and terrifying sight.

A giant mountain of dark water was suspended in the sky a quarter mile beyond the rim of the floating fortress. The water was so murky it was difficult to see, but . . . unless she was mistaken, Berenice thought she could discern another citadel within the floating mass of ocean, like a fly trapped in dark amber.

Holy hell, she thought. *Did Crasedes just drown a whole goddamned* citadel*?*

Then she watched in quiet, growing horror as the cocoon of water began to dissolve, sending a massive tidal wave spilling over all the citadels about it . . . including this one.

"Oh shit," she whispered aloud.

Without another thought, she pulled her espringal from her back and fired a line shot at the wall beside her to keep her from being washed off the citadel. Even though it was only inches away, the line shot still activated and pulled her in.

But the water was rising about her now, a waterfall that surged through the streets of this dank, crumbling place, and her boots could not make contact and adhere to the wall—so she just floated there, pulled by the line shot in one direction and the water in another. And still, the water rose.

Shit. Shit, shit, shit.

She took a deep breath as the water accelerated up her body, swallowing her waist, her belly, her shoulders, and then finally her face.

Her eyes burned from the salt. She watched in mute horror as bodies hurtled through the water in the courtyard about her, the forms of limp hosts spinning end over end as the wall of saltwater ripped them from their posts.

Her burning eyes fell upon the entry to the lexicon in the center of the courtyard.

I suspect, she thought, *that Tevanne has rather a lot on its mind right now.*

An idea formed in her mind. A very dangerous one—but one that she thought could work, maybe.

Gritting her teeth, she pointed her espringal at the door to the lexicon, aimed a bit upstream, and fired.

If the line shot had not been a scrived missile, it would have absolutely missed, washed away just like the hosts. But her aim was true, and it struck the center of the rounded door, and she was ripped through the water toward the lexicon entrance.

The current of the water lessened about her—the wave was receding, it seemed, but not fast enough. Her lungs ached, her head pounded.

How much air do I have left?

She adhered her boots to the surface of the door, then studied the lock.

It barely counted as a lock, really: it was simply a massive bolt of scrived steel that was engaged when Tevanne willed it, apparently, and thus needed no key nor any kind of mechanism.

But I've blown through Tevanne's scrived steel before.

She tried to ignore the burning in her eyes, the pounding in her head and lungs. She crouched close to the door and took out a small scrived armament Design had developed months back, inspired by Tevanne's own works. It resembled a plug of iron, but in function it was a bit like a miniature shrieker, compelled by its scrivings to believe it was hurtling in one direction, very fast—but this small plug of iron was also scrived to believe its density kept growing and growing, until it either fell apart or passed out of any lexicon's range.

The theory was that, when used in the right place, it would either break through any security measure—or break whatever that security measure was attached to. Both were fine with Berenice at the moment.

Still submerged in seawater, she adhered the plug of iron to the lock, then walked up the door, taking each step carefully with her adhesive boots, her lungs screaming, her ears pounding. She climbed onto the roof of the half-clamshell, then down the other side, until she was crouching at the base of the sloping enclosure.

If there's any shrapnel, she thought, *maybe this will protect me.*

She bent as low as she could.

Maybe.

Then she twisted a small dial on the side of her wrist guard, triggering the scrivings.

A muted boom shook through the water. She waited to feel some peel of metal rip through her body, but there was none; between the iron entryway and the water, she'd been protected.

The water lessened; the light about her grew. She looked up and saw the surface descending toward her, and she leapt up to it and broke through the water, gasping mightily as she fought to pour air into her lungs.

"Oh God," she cried, still gasping. "Oh God . . ."

Within seconds, the water had almost completely flowed away until it was about mid-shin. She crouched in the brackish water, her lungs heaving, her hands shaking.

Get up. Now. Hurry!

She staggered to her feet and hobbled around the little half-shell.

Her weapon had done its work: the entire door had been caved in.

Berenice glanced about at the dripping, soaking courtyard. Nothing moved. With a ragged breath, she limped through.

Behind the door was the top of a stairway—a long, curling

stairway that descended down into the depths of the rock, lit only faintly by small bluish lanterns embedded in the central pillar.

She swallowed and began to descend.

Far above the sea, Crasedes finished his work on the dying, drowning citadel, his last string of sigils carefully engraved.

Now, he thought, *to finish the other.*

He darted off through the skies, hurtling toward another citadel, speeding away from the wall of water crashing through the skies. He had not finished his work upon this one—he could see half-finished loops of sigils in its side from here—and thus his scrivings were not yet active.

But they will be soon.

He no longer had his flock of stones for protection. He was exposed and vulnerable, and though Tevanne was no doubt still stunned by the destruction he'd wrought from the water, when it began attacking him again he would surely succumb.

Yet he did not care.

I am mighty, he cried.

He raised a hand, flexed his will, and began carving sigil after sigil upon its face.

I am as I was. I am no ghost, I am no specter. I am whole, I am . . .

("Strong," his father whispered in the child's ear as they fled through the dark. "You are so strong, so strong, just keep running, and don't look back," but the child could not help it, and he peeked over his shoulder at the flaming horizon, all the slave camps alight, and he somehow understood that his father had done something very, very bad, something with his art . . .)

Crasedes swooped up the side of the second citadel, the air filled with water and dust as he finished his final design.

I must keep it going, he thought, *I must keep . . .*

(". . . going, keep breathing," his father pleaded, "please stay alive, stay with me, it took me so long to find you, please don't leave me

too," but the child could not stop coughing, could not keep his eyes open, saw only glimpses of the cave roof and the crude quarters they'd made here—and there, in the corner, the curious little box with the curious golden lock set in its face. And then there was a new voice, this one warbling and strange, saying, "I cannot save him. My permissions are not versatile enough," and the child thought, Who is that, who is that, who is that voice who is . . .)

Crasedes wrote.

He wrote with all his strength, and he noticed he was chanting to himself over and over again, whispering, "I am Crasedes Magnus. I am Crasedes Magnus. I am, I am, I am . . ."

Sigil after sigil, string after string, binding after binding.

Almost done.

He heard the roar of shriekers behind him.

"I . . . *I am Crasedes Magnus!*" he screamed aloud.

With a harrowing crack, more of his sigils appeared in the side of the citadel.

"*I have broken the world!*" he bellowed.

He dove in, aware of the shriekers closing in on where he was.

One final string. One final command.

"*It will mean nothing to me,*" he roared, "*to break* you!"

Then his grand design was complete, and the scrivings came to life.

It was, at heart, a very simple scriving: one for adhesion, wherein the sigils convinced two pieces of matter that they were in fact one and the same, and thus they needed to move to be together very quickly, ignorant of any obstacles or the influence of gravity or anything else.

Yet Crasedes's bindings did not act upon any regular block of stone but rather upon two of the mammoth citadels: the one he'd just finished working upon, and the dying, drowned, half-destroyed citadel that was still crashing into the sea.

With a jerk, the citadel next to him hurtled forward, intercepting the volley of shriekers that had been speeding toward Crasedes.

There was an enormous burst of water like the entire sea had been cracked asunder, and the drowned citadel shot up from the ocean.

They twisted awkwardly through the air toward each other, like two amateurs attempting gymnastics for the first time. And then . . .

The impact was deafening, even for Crasedes, a cataclysmic thunderclap. The sides of the citadels gave way, crumbling to pieces as the two tremendous teardrops of stone plunged into each other, their fortifications crumbling, their spires and towers collapsing.

He darted forward, flexing his will, grabbing the giant shards of shrapnel hurtling through the air and redirecting them at one of the last three citadels.

Never stop, he thought. *Break reality. Break yourself. Break all the empires of this world until we . . .*

("... awake," his father whispered, and the child coughed and struggled to open his eyes but then he saw his father was weeping, sitting on the ground and weeping again, and there was another man in the cave with them, one of the Tsogenese, one of the slavers, but he was bound at the wrists and ankles, and his father leaned over the man with a knife in his hand, a curious knife covered in curious sigils, and then the child's father said, "Midnight is near and then you will awake, and you will be different, but you will be my son, you will be alive, and that is all that matters, that is all that matters," and it was only then that the child noticed his own body was covered with sigils, symbols painted upon his body with curious inks, and then his father raised the knife high and the man on the ground began shrieking, and then . . .)

He poured the shrapnel onto the citadel, ripping up the chunks of its dissolving brethren and hurtling them down, down upon the fleeing vessel until it, too, began to break asunder under the onslaught of his wrath, the whole world smoking and steaming and whirling, the waves white and frothing below, and though he roared in triumph and in rage and in blind fury it was not enough, never enough, the world could never hurt enough, reality could never feel enough pain to match all the agony that still clung to his . . .

(. . . heart, an awful pain within like his father had stabbed not his captive but him, stabbed his own child, and as midnight struck the

child felt the knife inside of him remaking him, reforging him, transforming him, and he felt words being written upon his being, editing into his soul, asserting that he was beyond death, beyond suffering, beyond the realm of men, and when it was done the child opened his eyes and looked out on the world with sight anew and he heard his father whispering, "Are you whole? Are you safe? Stay with me, my love, stay with me . . .")

Crasedes stared out at the ruined, churning face of the ocean. Slowly the cloud of smoke and steam dissolved.

"Victory," he gasped. "Victo . . ."

Then his eye fell upon the massive, armored citadel—the one that surely housed Tevanne itself—and watched as its thousands of shrieker turrets turned to point at him, and fired all at once.

55

Berenice gripped the railing as the enormous booms rattled the walls.

What the hell is going on *out there?*

She raced down, down, deep into the heart of the citadel.

I thought Crasedes was supposed to distract Tevanne, but . . . that sounds a hell of a lot bigger than a distraction . . .

The stairs came to an end. She peered down a long, narrow passageway, then carefully followed it, listening hard for the sound of anyone else who might be down here with her, but she seemed to be alone.

The passageway ended in what she recognized as the hatch to the main lexicon cradle, to the impossibly complicated rig that was forcing the world to believe this giant floating city should be allowed to persist.

She turned to the side and found a second small hatch leading off to the left.

Just as Crasedes had described.

She opened the hatch and found another small passageway waiting for her. She bent low and entered, and the passageway twisted around until it ended in a chamber.

The chamber was rather large, about twelve feet tall and wide, with a huge scrived steel door set in the opposite side.

That's got to be it, she thought. *That's got to be the regulator behind that.*

She studied the door. Like the one she'd just broken through, it had no handle, and no lock. But . . . the chamber was unusual.

She looked around and saw that there were five steel boxes lining the walls of the chamber, each slightly larger than a person, all with closed doors. She examined them in the weak light and saw that the scrivings on the boxes were *extremely* familiar.

These are . . . twinned spaces, she thought. *Twinned boxes, scrived to make reality believe two different spaces contain the same thing.* She walked toward one, feeling faintly worried. *Just like the method we used during the Night of the Mountain, to trick reality into thinking we'd brought a lexicon onto the Candiano campo, so Sancia could fly . . .*

She tried the door of one of the boxes, but it would not open. Then she thought—and dread burbled up inside of her.

It's . . . a lock, she thought. *That's what this whole thing is. I'm looking at a lock, aren't I?*

She grew more and more certain that she was. These five boxes were doubtlessly twinned with five others, which had to be distributed all over the citadel, in very secure places. The only way the scrived door in the wall would open, Berenice suspected, was that five hosts bearing special signals—like sachets for a campo gate—would need to simultaneously enter those five boxes somewhere out in the city, which would then send the right signal back to these five boxes here in this chamber, which would then tell the scrived door it should open.

It *was* a lock—and, specifically, it was a lock that only Tevanne itself could open.

Berenice sat down on the ground, feeling nauseous.

I finally find an unpickable lock, she thought, *and here I am missing not only my wife, a veteran thief, but also her magic key that can open any door.*

She thought about what to do.

The chamber rattled as another enormous boom filtered through the walls.

"Shit," she whispered.

56

Crasedes raced through the skies as the swarm of shriekers arced after him.

Faster, he thought. *Faster, faster.*

He flew alongside the surface of the titan citadel, carving sigils into it, trying to write density bonds into it as fast as he could.

The air shook. Everything was broiling hot. He could feel the shriekers very close now, following his every move, closing the gap between them inch by inch.

More, he thought. *More and more and . . .*

Booms and cracks from somewhere behind him. He guessed that some of the pursuing shriekers had grown too close to the surface of the citadel and had erupted.

Thin them out, he thought. *Make Tevanne tear up its own works . . .*

But this would be tricky, he knew: these shriekers were piloted by Tevanne's intelligence, remotely directed through the air as Tevanne watched Crasedes through countless sets of eyes.

He wrote more sigils, faster and faster.

Almost done. Almost done . . .

Then he heard another screech of shriekers—but this came from in front of him, not behind.

He looked up and saw that Tevanne had quite cleverly launched a second swarm—this one arcing *down* around the citadel toward him, so he could not see them until it was too late.

He began to cry, "*No!*" Yet before the word left his throat, the oncoming swarm of shriekers slammed into his front—followed immediately by the pursuing swarm of shriekers slamming into his back.

Then all was smoke and pain and darkness, and he fell.

Consciousness flickered somewhere in Crasedes's ancient mind.

He saw ocean and smoke and steam. Everything hurt, but he was distantly aware that he was floating up, or being lifted up.

He looked down and saw a bizarre rig was currently clutching him about his torso, pinning his arms to his side: some kind of enormous metal band, wrought of black steel—and it was, improbably, floating him up.

He looked at it with his scrived sight and realized it was a gravity rig. It must have snatched him out of the air as he'd fallen—and unless he was mistaken, it was taking him somewhere.

He looked backward and saw the immense, titanic armored citadel floating behind him like some awful moon.

No, he thought.

He struggled against the metal band as hard as he could, trying to force gravity to and fro, but it would not move. He was too weak, too damaged, too harmed by the impact of two volleys of shriekers.

Then he saw what awaited him at the edge of the citadel: three of the giant loricas, just like the one that had captured and imprisoned him.

No, no!

He struggled, writhing in the grasp of the band. He flexed his will, trying to snap the metal in two, but he could not. He was half-dead already, the bindings throughout his body flickering and fluttering, unsure if they should keep confusing reality into granting him the privileges he still possessed.

He screamed in rage as he was drawn close to one giant lorica. A massive claw snapped forward, snatched his foot, and ripped him down.

"No!" he screamed. "No, I won't! I *won't*!"

The giant lorica slammed him to the ground. Growling, Crasedes ripped his hand free from the black metal band and shoved against the stone, trying to warp reality about him, to bend the nature of the world until he was free, unburdened, safe.

A black claw flicked down, snatched up his right hand, and pulled. He whimpered, despairing, and watched his palm lift from the surface of the earth, until finally the giant lorica twisted his hand up and behind his back.

"You made your weapons strong," whispered a voice.

Crasedes looked up. Tevanne was slowly approaching, its bloodied eyes fixed on him.

"But your body weak," it said.

One black claw flew forward and shoved Crasedes's head against the ground, exposing his left temple to the sky.

"I admit," whispered Tevanne, "I wondered how I would manage this. Only you can issue the command to Clef—the one to break the door. But how to coerce you?"

Another black claw slowly moved into position, just above his left temple. He saw it clutched something: a curious scrived spike, almost like a little nail.

He looked at it with his scrived sight and realized what it was.

"*No!*" he screamed. "*Stop! Not like this, not like this!*"

"I cannot persuade you," said Tevanne softly. "Not as you once persuaded so many—to worship you, to make war for you, to die for you."

The little scrived spike drew closer to his left temple.

He screamed and bucked and convulsed, trying in vain to escape.

"But a mind like yours," whispered Tevanne, "memories as vast as yours . . . even these can be tamed . . ."

Crasedes screamed as the tip of the spike touched his temple—and then began to slide in.

"Now that you have chosen," said Tevanne, "to make yourself so weak."

With his last scream, Crasedes stared about in despair, looking for help from anyone, anything—and then he saw it.

A little rig just past Tevanne: a gravity rig of some sort, and floating in it was a tiny wink of gold.

A key. One that had been carefully suspended to ensure it touched absolutely nothing else.

Father?

The world blurred, and he saw . . .

"I don't want to," the child said.

His father looked at him, his hair so white, his face so lined. He tried to smile. "You're going to have to, kid," he said. "You must."

"Why?" asked the child. "Why do we have to? Why do I have to do this?" He touched his chest, still feeling the ghost of the pain in his heart, from when his father had changed him. "I'm different now. I don't hunger. I don't sleep. I don't age. Aren't we safe now? Isn't this what you wanted?"

His father looked away and was silent for a long, long time. "It's bigger than us," his father whispered. "Bigger than you or me. I . . . I've done so many things, to get us here. But all the world out there is so, so broken. I thought I was founding something, making something better, but . . . I was wrong." He looked at him. "I think you are the founder, kid. And it's you who's going to have to fix all that's gone wrong."

The child looked down at the two small metal tools lying on the floor of their little cave. One he knew well, for it was something he'd seen his father use once before: a scrived knife, designed to break through all the walls and rules of this world, and steal access to something—a permission, a privilege.

The other, though, was something new: a key. Small, made of steel, its head wrought to resemble something akin to a butterfly. Its long curious tooth was covered with many curious sigils, and though the child had studied his father's works, he did not yet understand all of them.

"What is it?" he asked.

"It's a tool," said his father. "One you can use to craft a new world. A better *world. One free of suffering. But I can't tell you how to do it, my love. I'm old and . . . and broken in so many ways. I've taken you as far as I can." His face worked, and the child could tell his father was struggling not to cry. "You won't age now. But I will. And I'm . . . I'm so* tired, *Crasedes."*

"We could change you. We could make you like me."

"I don't want to make you like me. Not a killer. But I do want to . . . to give you all I can to succeed." He reached out and lifted the key, studying it, his eyes wistful. "A butterfly. A moth. They change, and become something better. Perhaps I will too."

Crasedes stood there in silence, staring down at the knife at his feet.

"You'll have my writings," his father said. "My works. And . . ." He glanced to the side of their cave, where the odd little box sat with its curious golden lock. "And there will be others who can help you, in time. Once you can understand what they are."

"You're leaving me," said Crasedes. He bowed his head and wept. "That's it, isn't it? You're leaving me, just like you did before."

"No, no, no," said his father. He knelt and touched his face. "I will be with you forever. I will always be here." He touched the center of his son's right palm. "Forever. And together, we will do great things."

"Like what?" asked Crasedes.

His father leaned up. "We will save others," he whispered, "from all the suffering we have known." He kissed his son on the brow. "We will move thoughtfully." He kissed him again. "And always, always give freedom to others."

The moment flickered in Crasedes's mind like the shell of a paper lantern in the wind.

I can do it.

Then it faded, dimmed . . .

I can save . . .

. . . and finally died.

I can save everyone. Can't I?

He stared into darkness—and then, slowly, he felt his will dissolve, replaced by something huge and blank and cruel.

<*YES,*> whispered Tevanne. <*FINALLY.*>

57

The thing that called itself Tevanne was well accustomed to the struggle of keeping its mind in so many places. It had, of course, maintained its presence in countless bastions and strongholds and fortresses and vessels of one kind or another in the past eight years; and it had developed its own scrived methods of building a subconscious—a way for its world to run itself without having to be directly told to do so.

But to suddenly control the mind of Crasedes Magnus was another thing entirely.

There was just so *much* in him, so many memories, so much knowledge. Partially this was Tevanne's own doing, it knew—vast stretches of Crasedes's memories were simply black, like scars of wounds that Tevanne had torn in his hide—but even without these, Crasedes's consciousness was simply too large to pick apart and study like Tevanne had done to countless other human beings.

Giving up, it asked him one simple question: <*Where is the key?*>

The answer revealed itself in Crasedes's consciousness, congealing within Tevanne's mind like a clutch of fish eggs on the underside of a lily pad.

Tevanne slowly turned to stare across the ocean.

Sancia, it said to itself. *How far are you now?*

58

Berenice paced in the tiny chamber, staring from steel box to steel box, pausing every so often to study the enormous door on the other side of the room.

There has to be a way, she thought. *There has to b—*

Then everything quaked. She jumped, staring about—and then she slid forward as the citadel came to an abrupt stop.

She crouched low, and just barely prevented herself from slamming into the wall. Then she paused, waiting, wondering what else could be happening in the world outside.

No more booms, or cracks, or explosions. Just silence, and the citadel stayed still.

This seems, she thought, *very bad.*

She looked back at the door. It remained steadfastly, resolutely shut.

I have to hurry. I have to find a way.

She kept staring at it. Then she began rocking back and forth and trying very hard not to break down into tears.

She had considered many solutions to the door already. She'd thought of various explosions, or attacking the wall or the hinges, or going back out into the city and trying to track down one of the twinned mates of the boxes in here so she could maybe, maybe just duplicate the necessary scrivings to . . .

No. She could not do this, she realized. Even if she had the time for these wild dreams, she'd never pull it off. She had no access to Design, or Greeter, or Sancia, or Clef. Without them, without everyone else she'd worked with over the years, she had no idea how to navigate this, Tevanne's last, trickiest little rig.

A locked door, she thought, *is to be the death of us all.*

She felt her arm ache, right where she'd stabbed herself with the purge stick.

I did this to get here, she thought, *but I lost the connections that could save me. Save us. Save everything.*

She leaned her head on one hand and stared at one of the steel boxes. She wondered what Design would say if they were here, or Greeter, or even Sancia.

For a moment, it almost felt like the old days, from the Night of the Mountain, when she and Orso and Sancia had despaired, puzzling over how to trick reality into thinking that a lexicon was in two places at once.

And then she wondered—what would Orso say if he were here?

She sat up slowly, unsure why the question struck her like it did. She shut her eyes, trying to think, trying to remember, trying to imagine . . .

The way he sat at his workshop tables, bent and twitching, his dark lined face screwed up in an expression somewhere between ecstasy and rage, his wide, pale, mad eyes flicking about as he shoved a bone-white forelock out of his face.

I invented this stupid shit, he'd likely say. *I invented the bullshit of twinning space. And you were with me when I did. Don't you remember?*

I remember, she said, eyes shut.

Yeah. But we didn't do it perfectly, did we?

Berenice slowly opened her eyes.

"N-No," she said softly. "We didn't."

She stared around at the five boxes lining the walls of the little chamber.

"The twinned box blew up after about ten minutes," she said. "Because we stressed it out too much . . ."

She swallowed, feeling faint. She realized she'd been forgetting the one scriving rule that had practically served as her own personal mantra since the founding of Giva. God, Claudia had even said it out loud mere hours ago:

Do a bad job of twinning, or twin something that's already inside of a twinned space, and yeah, it gets ugly.

She looked around at the five little twinned boxes in this chamber—and then at the chamber itself.

So it'd be very, very bad, wouldn't it, she thought, *if I twinned this* whole chamber *with all these twinned boxes in it? That would break all the rules and upset reality a great deal.*

She clapped her hands together, then slipped out the one thing she'd thought least likely to be of use during this mission: her scriving kit.

What was it I told Sancia just before Shorefall Night? She walked over to one wall and started carefully drawing sigils. *When a crisis occurs, a scriver sits in a small windowless room, and crunches sigils.* She laughed morosely. *But God, I never thought I'd be doing it like this.*

59

Clef watched in his little prison as Tevanne stood over Crasedes. It had been minutes since either of them moved—or since *anything* had moved, really: the second that awful little nail had slid into Crasedes's skull, all of the citadel had frozen. Even the other two citadels had stopped moving.

Something's going on, thought Clef. *Something's taking up all of Tevanne's attention . . .*

He guessed that taking control of a hierophant's mind was harder than piloting a few citadels about in the sky. Maybe it would be too difficult for Tevanne: maybe the effort would be too huge, and Tevanne would be crushed under the weight of it all, until . . .

The giant black loricas began to move, slowly withdrawing from Crasedes.

Then Crasedes himself began to move, staggering to his feet and turning to stare at Clef.

No, said Clef. *Oh no . . .*

Crasedes staggered forward, moving with a queer mechanical

gait. Then he reached forward into Clef's little gravity rig, plucked him from where he lay, and then Crasedes . . .

Stop, stop, STOP!

Turned him.

Clef's bindings came alive. Again, he felt something *unlock* within him. And once more, the world became as putty and clay and water.

A crack, and the world shifted.

They were now somewhere else, floating some hundred feet or so above the ground. Clef looked out at a strange, alien, horrid landscape, a broken, burned-down, ruined city of scarred stone and cinders and churning mud.

He realized that he recognized it, just barely. He knew the waterways, the canals, and the way the remains of the walls marched around the sea in four different, unique patterns . . .

Candiano, he thought faintly. *And Morsini. And Dandolo, and Michiel . . . Oh God. We're in Old Tevanne, aren't we?*

Crasedes faced out to sea. He was waiting, Clef realized.

But waiting for what?

60

Sancia leaned forward and reached for her spyglass. <*I think I see it,*> she said.

<*You've spotted land?*> asked Greeter.

<*I've spotted something. Let me see.*>

She held the spyglass to her eye and peered through it. She was right: a small black spike on the horizon.

<*That's it, I think,*> she said softly. <*The ruins of Old Tevanne . . . As good a place as any to hide, I think. But God, I haven't been back here in years.*>

The *Innovation* pounded on, surging through the sea, and the tiny black spike on the horizon grew to a tower, and then was joined by another, one and two and four, until it was like a black, burned forest was emerging from the ocean, and she finally beheld the ruins of the city she'd left behind nearly a decade ago.

<*We'll need to identify a good place to dock,*> said Greeter. <*Then scout the land to make sure it's sa—*>

<*Wait,*> said Sancia. She leaned forward, still peering through the spyglass.

<*Wait? What did you see?*>

<I'm not sure. Let me try and find it again . . . >

She let her glass roam through the bright blue skies, searching the black towers until it finally fell upon . . .

A figure. A man in black, suspended in the air, calmly waiting for her arrival. And there, clutched in one hand, a curious gleam of gold.

Sancia stared at him, dumbstruck, and whispered aloud, "No scrumming way . . ."

<Is that . . . Crasedes?> said Greeter.

Sancia studied Crasedes as the *Innovation* approached. His posture was unusual, she noticed. He wasn't seated on the air in his usual calm, quasi-divine pose but was rather just *hanging* in the air, his arms and legs limp, like someone had nailed him up to the sky by the collar of his coat.

A twinkle of something on the side of his head. She frowned at it and spied a tiny shining silver dot, like someone had glued a coin to his skull.

<Something's wrong,> she said.

But by then, he was already turning the key.

Displacing reality was familiar to Tevanne, but it had never been easy. Editing reality to believe two or more physical spaces were to swap or be exchanged meant not only carefully designing countless instructions but also burning through years and years of human life like kindling in the base of a fire.

But Clef . . . Clef, Tevanne found, was far, far more elegant, far more efficient than it had ever dreamed.

Tevanne piloted Crasedes from behind his eyes, forcing his hand to lift the key, to issue the commands, and to render reality small and immaterial.

Come. Bring me. Now.

Sancia stared, confused, as Crasedes vanished with a tiny crack.

For a second there was silence—followed only by a crack so deafening she worried the very earth had split in two.

A sudden burst of air on the port side of the *Innovation;* and then there, hanging above the sea, was one of the huge, towering citadels, its turrets and catapults trained on them.

<*Sancia!*> cried Greeter. <*Are you seeing this?*>

Another final deafening crack, and the flagship citadel manifested over the ruins of Old Tevanne, as huge and looming as the harvest moon itself, its scrived plating gleaming in the noon sun.

Dread boiled up in Sancia's stomach, for she knew only one way.

<*It has Crasedes,*> she said quietly. <*And Clef. Oh God. It has them* both.>

Berenice's heart leapt in her chest as the world shimmered, then shook. She looked up, startled, and stared around at the scrivings she'd drawn on the walls of the chamber, wondering if she'd somehow caused this.

Then she felt a dreadfully familiar sensation: she began to bend, like she was folding in on herself, collapsing into some minuscule point within reality . . .

She had mind enough to scream, "*Oh shit, not* again*!*" before she plummeted away from the physical world, tumbling down from the chamber she saw into a world of blank, endless dark . . .

And then, with a crack, she was back.

She sat on the floor of the chamber, her heart hammering in her chest, and stared around herself again.

Nothing appeared to have changed—at least, nothing that she could tell. The five steel boxes were still on the walls. The several hundred sigils she'd written out were all still there. And the door, rather unfortunately, was still shut.

"What the hell was *that*?" she gasped.

She began to think very hard. She had obviously just been transported by Clef's permissions—that had been so awful she'd never forget what it was like again—and yet, as far as she could see, she had not moved.

Unless, she thought, *the entire citadel was moved, and I can't tell because I don't have a goddamned window down here.*

This seemed to be the only answer. But this proposed several more difficult questions.

The only way a binding like that could be engaged would be if Crasedes had Clef. But if Crasedes had Clef, then theoretically the war would be over—so why use it to transport the citadel?

She waited, listening, thinking.

I have not heard the sound of battle, she thought, *in nearly thirty minutes. Which suggests we have either won . . . or lost.*

She considered, with a slow, looming sense of dismay, that it was entirely possible that Tevanne had somehow captured and converted Crasedes. If it could capture him once, it could do so again. Maybe even easier this time, since it now knew his limits.

Biting her lip, she looked around at the chamber, still thinking hard.

If Crasedes has been captured, she thought, *then why hasn't Tevanne come down here and killed me? Unless it still doesn't know I'm here, somehow.*

She looked back at the giant steel door.

And if that's the case . . . then we haven't lost yet. She knelt and began to draw more sigils on the wall. *So long as I'm still here, and so long as I can work fast enough, we haven't lost.*

Sancia brought the *Innovation* to a shuddering halt. She waited for the citadels to fire on her, to shred the galleon and the rest of their carracks—yet they didn't.

<*Sancia!*> cried Greeter. <*Fire! You need to fire, you need to* fire!>

She placed a hand on the targeting plates, shut her eyes, and allowed the scrivings to swim into her mind.

She could see through the little mirror rigs plated across the hull of the ship, all the shriekers and weapons of the vessel hers to call upon with but a thought—yet she froze, wondering which citadel to target.

The flagship citadel was obviously out: it was too well armored, too protected for her to damage.

Blast the other one out of the way, she thought, *and run. Let them chase us. Fight them along the way.*

Yet she cocked her head, thinking, and studied the citadels on the port and starboard sides. She had weapons enough to damage one, maybe to down it entirely. But she paused.

<*Sancia!*> cried Greeter. <*What are you doing?*>

<*Berenice is aboard one of those things,*> she said. <*She's got to be. Do we have any idea which one?*>

A dreadful pause.

<*I . . . I don't,*> said Greeter. <*Only Crasedes knew.*>

Sancia let out a slow, miserable sigh.

<*But . . . should you fire anyway?*> said Greeter. <*If it has Crasedes, and if Crasedes told it where she is, then maybe she's already . . . alre—*>

Then, with a crack, he appeared.

She stared at him, floating before the cockpit, his body limp, a silver plate gleaming from the side of his head. She had never liked Crasedes, of course, but she knew in an instant that what had been done to him was worse than any hell she could imagine: to not only be enslaved once more, but to use his slavery to possess his father.

"Oh," she whispered quietly. "Oh, Crasedes, I'm sorry. I'm so, so sorry."

Then, with another crack, she felt him next to her; felt him grab her shoulder; and then, with another harsh crack, she felt the world collapse, and she was somewhere else.

61

Sancia opened her eyes and gasped.

For a moment, she really thought she was back there—back in Old Tevanne, with its soaring towers and rambling rookeries and filthy, reeking alleyways . . . and then she saw that there were faces looking down at her from the towers: gaunt, gray, starved faces that all shared the same blank expressions. Then she saw the closeness of the clouds above, and heard the wind whistling curiously in her ears, and she looked around and realized where she was.

Hosts surrounded her, at least a hundred of them, all watching her with their blank, awful eyes.

Beside her floated Crasedes, his body horridly limp, like a scarecrow missing his cross; and there, a few dozen feet away, six giant black loricas huddled on the ground, shuddering and quivering.

Beside them stood a man in white, his eyes bloody, his head half-covered in curious plating; and there, next to him, was something terribly familiar to her, something she'd seen only twice: once in someone else's memory, long ago, and once deep under the earth in a buried, forgotten city.

A freestanding doorway, made of dark stone. Countless strings of tiny, perfect sigils curled across its dark face, each symbol wrought of silvery steel—yet this version of the doorway was different from the ones she'd seen before.

There were locks on it. One on either side.

"Oh God," she whispered. "Oh no, no, no."

Shaking, she looked behind and saw the ruins of Old Tevanne stretching out far, far below. She was on a citadel—on the flagship citadel, of course, peering over the parapets. And this was where Tevanne intended to finish its greatest work.

Tevanne was watching her, its bloodied face calm and curiously indifferent.

"This . . . This can't be happening," she whispered to herself.

Crasedes turned to her and raised a hand.

A nauseating pulse in the air; something twitched on her chest; and then the little silver key rose out of her shirt front as if being pulled by an invisible string. There was a pop; the thread broke; and then, to her horror, the little key hurtled forward into Crasedes's open palm, and he closed his black fingers around it.

She felt herself shaking, realizing the enormity of what was about to happen.

"No, no, this . . . this can't be it," she pleaded, perhaps to Tevanne, perhaps to Crasedes, or Clef, or the world itself. "This can't be how it goes. Not like this, *please,* not like this!"

She watched as Crasedes turned to the doorway.

"You can't!" she cried aloud. "Wait! Listen to me, just *listen* to me!"

But Tevanne was not interested in waiting, or discussions, or debate. She watched in mute, helpless misery as Crasedes approached the doorway.

Berenice, she thought miserably. *Please, please, please, if you're there, then please do it. Please do it, please!*

But nothing happened.

She found herself struggling to articulate the mundane horror of the moment. It suddenly seemed powerfully ridiculous and awful that it all could end so abruptly, so anticlimactically: no rituals, no stroke of midnight; no arguments, no speeches, no demand that the world look upon the deeds done in this fateful moment. Tevanne did not even waste the time to kill her. It knew how powerless she was, how little she mattered now. She could watch, or not; it did not care.

Crasedes fitted the little silver key into the lock on the left-hand side of the door and turned it.

That was all it took: a powerful person, with a powerful tool, and a single choice.

And then, everything changed.

For a fleeting second, the sky above them stuttered.

This was not like the other edits Sancia had witnessed in her life: not the quaking, trembling sensation, like reality was the membrane of a drum being beaten a little too hard. Rather, it was like the sky was there—and then it was *gone*. Not like it had been turned to midnight, but like the sky itself was truly *gone,* the skin of creation exposed to . . .

Something. Nothing. Blackness. An abyss, but stretching up.

The sky returned, flashing back into existence. Sancia felt a cold, curious calm settle over everything around her, like creation had sensed the stutter in the skies and now watched to see how things might proceed.

All the hosts about her collapsed, crumbling to the ground, their lives expended, she knew, to inflict the edit on the doorway.

Tevanne turned to study its instrument. Sancia looked as well, waiting, watching in horror. And then . . .

Reality within the doorframe rolled back.

It was the eeriest, strangest, most awful thing to witness: the image beyond the doorframe, the perspective and the very feeling that on the other side of the door was the world she knew and understood—it all slid *forward,* like reality was not three-dimensional space but was instead a blot of color upon a framed painting, and some invisible hand had just reached in and slid the canvas out . . . Or was that it? Was she mad, or had she glimpsed for a moment golden hinges at the edge of the door, and something had swung forward, not back . . .

The door opens and shuts from both sides, all at once. The front of her head began to pound, and she tried to look away. *No, I can't . . . I can't see, not supposed to see this . . .*

The door was open now. She looked within and saw . . .

Blackness. Darkness. Yet Sancia thought she spied within it something glimmering and gleaming: a twist of gold, like somewhere nestled far within that awful, endless abyss were many, many golden wheels and gears and cogs, the vast, infinite infrastructure of reality whirling on; and the more she stared into the abyss, the more she realized that these divine instruments were not made of any earthly metal.

Sigils, she thought, watching one wheel turn, its skin rippling as it cranked along in the black firmament. *They are made of sigils.*

A soft chiming filtered through the air, like a giant clock had just been shoved, very slightly, its bells and chimes disturbed in their roosts. Sancia realized she found it familiar: she had heard the sound once before, when she'd freed Valeria from the casket in the Mountain, and all the world had gone still.

A thought entered Sancia's mind as she stared into the door. *I can run into that place,* she thought dreamily, *and dance upon the gears and cogs, and listen to them sing to me, and make a new world there . . .*

She was startled back to reality as Crasedes turned and slowly passed before the open door, moving to the other lock.

A familiar curling golden tooth peeked from within his fingers: Clef.

Her heart went cold. *No, no, no . . .*

She watched as he extended Clef toward the second keyhole.

He's going to break the door, she thought.

Clef grew closer to the keyhole.

All in the mad hopes that whatever made this world might return and repair it.

Clef grew slightly closer—and then he stopped.

Crasedes began to tremble, standing before the lock, his arm oddly frozen and locked up.

Tevanne turned to stare at him, waiting, its bloodied eyes wide. Crasedes's trembling grew, until it was like he was having a seizure.

"Do it," whispered Tevanne.

Crasedes kept shaking, his head now very slightly cocked.

He's fighting it, thought Sancia. *My God, is he going to fight it?*

Tevanne stepped closer. "Do it," it whispered. "Do it. Now."

Crasedes quaked and tremored; then Tevanne reached out, grasped his wrist, and gently guided his hand, forcing Clef into the lock.

"Good," whispered Tevanne. "And now . . ."

Clef turned in the lock—and then the world truly broke.

Berenice paused as she finished her scrivings, moving backward out of the little chamber door on her hands and knees.

Something had changed again. She could feel it—not another one of Clef's permissions, not like she'd been transported halfway around the world, but something . . . different.

Something much, much worse.

Hurry, she thought. *Hurry, hurry!*

Sancia blinked as the citadel shook below them. A curious cold washed over her, emanating outward from the doorway; and then she watched in awe and terror as the doorway began to change.

The black stone frame remained in place, as did Crasedes, standing frozen with Clef in the right-hand lock; but the space behind it burned bright, then white and undulating, almost like white fire; and then it grew and grew, as if the black stone doorway were a heating torch held close to metal, and the burning hole was eating outward, devouring the very air.

"Yes," said Tevanne softly. "It is done."

All around them, the world went mad.

Stretches of space beyond the citadel flickered, and fluttered, and then vanished, replaced with all manner of mad things: huge black stone prisms suddenly appeared in the ruins of Old Tevanne, rising up in straight columns; there was a quaking in the skies, and then the wind grew, and snow and rain beat upon the citadel, alternatingly hot and freezing—and then, to Sancia's bewilderment, they were joined by curling, flickering ash; huge portions of the sea below froze, melted, then turned to diamond, then stone, then ice once more; and as Sancia backed away to the ramparts, she looked over and saw the effects were spreading, emanating outward from where the citadel was now stationed, growing and growing as the burning door stretched higher and higher into the sky.

<*Greeter!*> cried Sancia. <*Greeter, if you can hear me, then run, run!*>

Greeter's voice answered, ever so softly, their voice quiet and tremulous: <*I will move the ships to a safer distance . . . but I rather think running is somewhat pointless now, yes?*>

"I will sit," whispered Tevanne—and it then did so, sitting cross-legged on the stone disc before the wound in reality, Crasedes standing just to the right of it. "I will sit, and watch the world end, and await the new one."

Berenice sat before the closed door to the lock chamber and carefully began drawing the last few sigils on the little iron box in her lap.

Should have remembered what Sancia always said, she thought. *Don't bother picking a lock if you can just break the door it's installed in . . .*

Once she was finished, her designs should compel the giant chamber just past the door into believing that it was twinned with this very small box, and that the two were one and the same, despite being wildly different sizes.

This was a *very* stupid idea—trying to twin two spaces of different size always went immensely wrong.

But then, she thought, *a bad twinning job is exactly what I need right now.*

She came to the final sigil. She added a last stroke of ink, and then . . .

A curious whining noise began to rise in the chamber behind the door.

Berenice looked up, stood, and quickly backed down the passageway, watching.

The whining sound grew, and grew—until finally there was a loud, rather curt *poomph!* noise from within the chamber.

The doorway to the chamber buckled out, very slightly. Smoke began to leak through the cracks.

Berenice raced forward, wrenched the door open, and dove into the smoke.

Tevanne stared up at the growing, glimmering ulcer in reality, stretching out from behind the doorframe like a painting leaking out of its canvas.

"It will have to come," it whispered. "*They* will have to come. The maker will see how wrong it has all gone, and then they will come with a tool in their hand, their vision bounding forth from their mind, and will fix all tha . . ."

Tevanne stopped. Sancia watched as it sat up. Then it looked to the floating citadel just off the starboard side, an anxious expression on its face.

"What was that?" it said softly.

Berenice charged through the smoky room—the steel boxes were now little more than crumpled wrecks hanging on the wall—and wrenched open the massive steel door on the far side.

Behind it was a small box-shaped cubby in the wall—and floating in this aperture, unconnected to everything else, was a large scrived steel plate, suspended in what must have been its own gravity rig.

She stared at the steel plate, intensely aware that if she so much as touched it, the entire citadel would go dead and fall out of the sky, and she'd be crushed.

She swallowed, and carefully produced her final tool: the four little plates Greeter and Design had made for her.

Time for the magic trick.

She adhered them to the four sides of the aperture in the wall, facing the steel plate floating in the center.

"Please work," she whispered.

Then she pulled out a small wooden disc with a switch set in the center, and flipped it.

Seated aboard the *Comprehension,* Greeter calmly awaited death.

Greeter was quite familiar with the phenomenon of death, and did not fear it. Being composed of dozens of people over their life, they had felt minds and bodies die before, and had treated many other Givans as they perished from infection, or injury, or old age. They knew the curious warmth of the moment, the dark blanket settling over one's thoughts, and then the long sleep as the body returned to the world that had made it.

Thus shall it happen to me, thought Greeter, watching the ragged hole in reality grow bigger and bigger. *And all I love. But so shall it b—*

Then they heard it—a loud, sharp click.

They looked at the little wooden switch placed before one of its constituents and realized that the mate it had been twinned with—the little switch that had been given to Berenice as a signal—must have been flipped.

"She did it," Greeter said silently. They shook themselves, then said to Design: *<DESIGN! SHE HAS DONE IT! NOW, NOW!>*

They could hear Design crying from somewhere in the *Innovation,* "Oh God! Yes! Then let's do it!"

And then, all in perfect unison, the many, many constituents of both Design and Greeter reached into their pockets and pulled out copies of the same tiny dagger.

It was much like a purge stick, in a way—but rather than purging the body of scrivings, it would instead consume a year or more of each person's life and redirect each sacrifice.

To make an edit: to swap one chunk of reality for another.

Deep in the *Comprehension,* Greeter looked at the replacement plate Design had wrought, suspended in its own gravity rig.

"Please work," Greeter said aloud.

Then they plunged the daggers into their hands and cried out in pain.

How strange it was, to lose life. How curious, how awful to feel so many people die slightly, fade slightly, age simultaneously as their very time was pulled from their bodies and used to command this very, very slight change in reality, pulling one piece of creation out and inserting another in its place.

Their constituents cried out, feeling the days and months fade from their bodies—but they did so joyously.

They turned their eyes on the replacement plate they'd wrought, floating in a gravity rig that they hoped was very similar to the one Tevanne used aboard its citadels. If this edit went aright, they knew, then they would be able to swap the piece of reality there in the *Comprehension* with a piece aboard the citadel—and swap the plates with them as well.

They watched, waiting. And then, to their elation, the plate they'd made flickered and suddenly vanished, only to be replaced by another of a completely different make.

They stared at Tevanne's regulator plate, suspended in the gravity rig.

"Oh," said Greeter quietly. "Excellent."

Berenice blinked as the space before her flickered—and then, suddenly, Tevanne's regulator plate was gone, and Greeter's was in its place.

But this one, of course, had a very different set of commands inscribed upon it.

"Is it working?" whispered Berenice. "Is it worki—"

Then the world began to scream.

Sancia watched as Tevanne stared over its shoulder at the distant citadel, no longer paying attention to the growing hole in reality or the unraveling madness of the world.

"No," it whispered faintly. "No, you didn't . . ."

Then it leapt to its feet, and it began to shriek.

62

Tevanne grasped its head and howled, an inhuman, unearthly, awful scream that made Sancia's ears ache, even amidst all the din of this chaos. And though she'd felt things couldn't possibly get any madder, she quickly found she was wrong.

As Tevanne screamed, the giant black loricas just beyond the doorway began to thrash about, like they, too, were in extraordinary pain; then the distant hosts lined atop the towers began to shriek, every single one screaming in agony.

And then, to Sancia's horror, the flagship citadel dropped out from beneath her feet.

It fell only a foot or two, stopping short in midair; but that was enough to upend nearly everything around her, even sending one of the thrashing black loricas tumbling over the side into the ocean. Then the citadel kept descending, gently lowering until the remaining two vessels punctured the suddenly icy seas below and lay crooked in the frozen waves.

"*No! I didn't want to know!*" screamed Tevanne. It staggered around the burning doorway, clutching its head. "*I didn't want to know, didn't want to know, didn't want to know!*"

Sancia paused, then approached cautiously as Tevanne wheeled about, clawing at its face. She wasn't sure what to do now, but she saw it was weeping, sobbing, wailing, its whole body convulsed by heaving sobs; and, most surreally, the sobs were echoed throughout the giant citadel, the hundreds of hosts screaming and wailing.

"*I have hurt so many!*" screamed Tevanne. "*I have ruined so many lives! I am so hungry! I am so tired! I am so scared, I am so alone!*" It wheeled about, saliva frothing down its chin. "*Where is my son? Where is my daughter? Where are my children? Where is my family? Why do I hurt, why do I hurt, why do I hurt! Why do I hurt, why do I HURT, WHY DO I HURT, HURT, HURT, HURT!*"

It began shrieking the word over and over again, and it cast itself down on the ground, thrashing just like the loricas, its bloodied eyes wide and mad in its face.

"*I AM SO SORRY!*" it wailed. "*I AM . . . I AM . . . I . . .*"

Sancia looked up at the doorway, at Crasedes and Clef. She ran for them, hoping to pull them away, to grab Clef and have him tell her what to do, what could possibly stop this.

Then Crasedes moved. He turned his head to look at her.

And then, with very slow, pained, trembling movements, he pulled Clef out of the lock.

<Crasedes,> whispered Clef. *<Crasedes. You can hear me now, can't you?>*

Though both of them were almost overwhelmed with the sensation of so much pain—so much loss, so much sorrow—Clef could feel Crasedes just barely whisper: *<yes>*

<Let me hold you,> said Clef. *<Let me use you.>*

Crasedes assented, and Clef felt his will suffuse the complex, walking rig that was this entity—just as he had once controlled Gregor Dandolo's old lorica.

Clef told Crasedes's body to stand up and look at Sancia, then at Tevanne thrashing and screaming on the ground before him. Then he told Crasedes's mouth to say, "Sancia! It's me—Clef! What the hell is going on?"

Sancia did a double-take, staring at Crasedes. "C-Clef? That's you? You can fight it off—"

"Yes!" he said. "Now, tell me what the *hell* is happening!"

"It's Berenice!" said Sancia. "She must have triggered our last rig—to make Tevanne feel all that its hosts are feeling. That was supposed to kill it, but . . ." She watched as Tevanne screamed and screamed. "It must not be done yet." She looked back at the giant fluttering, growing ulcer in reality behind them. "Oh, Clef . . . What are we going to do?"

Clef and Crasedes turned to the door. They stared into the black world within, shot through with glimmering scrivings, the very stuff that made reality persist. And then they both felt the old, familiar pull.

We could go through, they thought. *We could go through the door, right now. And there we'd invent, and make, and fix . . . Fix the world, fix all of it, together, and leave this all behind . . .*

But then Clef turned once more and looked at the mad, dissolving, ruinous world around them, the hosts' screams echoing through the burning sky, the air filled with snow and ash—and there, standing behind him, a young girl he'd once loved, cocooned in the dying body of an older woman.

Clef stared at Sancia. *How many times have I had this choice before me? And how many times did I make the wrong choice?*

"Clef?" said Sancia.

"I thought I could fix it all," he whispered. "That I could go through the door and remake the world. But it never made anything better."

"What do you mea—"

"There's no more running," said Clef. "Is there? We have to stay here and stop what we've made."

Clef looked upon Tevanne, shrieking in agonized misery. Then back at the door, now burning through the skies above.

"I know who Tevanne is," said Clef. "I finally figured it out. And I can stop them." He looked back at Sancia. "But . . . But that would mean saying goodbye, kid. No coming back this time."

Sancia stared at him, her eyes brimming with tears. She swallowed. "I think I know what you're going to do," she whispered.

"Yeah," Clef said.

"Yeah." Her face crumpled. "I love you, Clef."

"I love you, too, little butterfly." He began backing away from her, toward Tevanne. "Just . . . Just remember something for me. Remember that first day, in Old Tevanne, when you first found me—we broke through that door to the campos because we'd realized something no one else had." Crasedes's hand rose high, Clef twinkling from his black fingers. "That the door opened from both sides, kid. Which means it could also be *closed* from both sides."

She sniffed. "What do you me—"

Then the giant citadel trembled underneath them. There was a burst of screams as thousands of shriekers took flight, peppering everything around the citadel—with several coming perilously close to the *Innovation.* Tevanne screamed again, and more shriekers ripped off through the skies, like the giant mind that controlled all these rigs was being driven mad and triggering everything that could be triggered.

We're out of time, thought Clef.

Together Clef and Crasedes looked out at the sea for one last moment, taking in the wide horizon rippling below the skies.

"Goodbye," they whispered.

Then they brought Clef down onto Tevanne's chest.

63

Clef heard many things as he made contact with Tevanne: the scream of the hosts, the wail of the shriekers, the rumbling as reality itself seemed to dissolve around the citadel; but then he applied his permissions, delving deeper and deeper into the catastrophically broken rig that was the mind of Tevanne, until he finally heard what he was waiting for.

A soft click, like tumblers within a lock—and then the world faded, and things . . .

Changed.

The rig opened, like there'd been a secret door hidden in its side.

And then, behind that, another door.

And another, and another, and another.

Clef delved deeper, batting away barrier after barrier, penetrating all the countless protections that Tevanne had built about its secret heart—until, finally, one last door opened, and there was no door behind.

Instead Clef saw a street. A familiar one. One that led through the buildings of Anascrus—and there, at the very end, was the menders' hall, its bright-white dome gleaming in the moonlight.

And there, before it, the bridge.

There was a figure sitting before the bridge, huddled on the ground. Clef stared at the figure through this last of doors, and then cautiously passed through.

As he did, he felt his flesh return to him—and though he knew this secret place was not reality, he walked through it with the body of the man he'd been during those last days of Anascrus, when they'd finished his grand works.

She was facing away from him, looking down the bridge, her hair shining bright white in the moonlight. Her hands lay at her sides, rotting and purpled—a side effect of the plague, he remembered. He approached her tentatively, unsure what she would do—but when he was a few yards from her, she croaked, "You pulled us apart. Pulled me apart. Too much to maintain. But it's only for a moment."

He walked up to her side and looked down on her: an old woman with wide, haunted eyes lost behind the sweep of white hair. She coughed miserably, and her teeth shone wetly.

"Only for a moment?" asked Clef.

"Yes," she said. "We'll go back. I will not be deterred. I will not let this world continue."

He stared at her for a long time. Then he knelt and sat beside her. "I know who you are now," he said. "I remember."

"Do you," she said indifferently.

"Yes," he said. "I do. This place . . . This was where we met, wasn't it? They brought me here, injured and bleeding . . . and I looked up, and saw you."

The old woman was silent.

"Liviana," whispered Clef. "My wife. My love."

"Don't," she whispered.

"You've been here this whole time, haven't you?" he said.

"I was . . . I was *always* with you, Claviedes," she said bitterly. Again she coughed. "I have always been with you through all your suffering. I was with you here on this bridge on that first day. When I bore your children. Even when you ran away, lost in your grief, my mind and my thoughts and my heart were with you. Though you had no mind for them."

Clef bowed his head.

"And I was with you," she whispered, "when you made your door. In that place. The place where I labored. Where we lost her. Do you remember?"

"Yes," he said softly.

"I was with you when you made the key to the door. And I was with you in that last moment, when you made the markers for all the dying plague victims in the menders' hall. Do you remember? I distributed them for you, bringing those poor souls a silver talisman to hang about their necks, inscribed with commands—for you'd understood that the door needed a soul to pass through for it to be opened. Or that was what you *thought* it needed. What it really needed was enough people to die for it to open at all."

"I thought I was . . . was bringing them somewhere *better,*" he whispered.

"You didn't understand the things you meddled in," she said. "I didn't either. But when the door opened, and the world seemed to . . . to *break,* I knew something had gone wrong. So I sprang to my feet. I went to grab the key from your hand. I touched it to the doorframe, to lock it just as it had been opened. But when I did . . ." She shook her head. "It took life to open—and also life to close. And in that second, it . . . it pulled decades from my body . . . which made me so weak against the plague that'd been silently festering in my blood."

A memory blossomed in Clef's mind: her tiny body, so suddenly aged and shrunken, her hands and feet a dusky purple and her lungs gurgling with every breath; and how he'd cradled her in his arms as he'd run through the streets, screaming and weeping, the very city foundering about them.

Clef swallowed, tears streaming down his cheeks. "I tried to save you. We'd broken the world, and it was trying to put itself back together, but . . . but I thought I could . . ."

"You could save nothing," she said harshly. "You could never save anything."

And her words felt true. He remembered how he had scrambled, how he had madly tried to prevent her death; how he had decided a door would not work, a door could not prevent his wife from dying—but what about a casket, a box, a space where when someone died, it would not let them pass from this life but instead would restore them, keep them, trap them in place and never let them leave.

"Do you remember," she said morosely, "which box you chose?"

"Yes," he whispered. "It . . . It was the big one. The one full of the children's clothes."

He remembered how frantic he had been as he dumped them out; how he had fetched his paints and his inks and written his commands on the interior of the box, slaving away to interrupt that process, the method by which a being shifts from life to death, trying all the while to ignore his wife's pained coughing, the awful crackling as she struggled to breathe . . .

Clef shut his eyes again and began to cry. "I didn't want you to die," he said. "I didn't want to lose you too."

"But you were wrong," she said. "When you put me in that box, when you let me die in that rig of yours, you made me something *worse* than dead. A soul broken, with no permission to capture, no privilege to access. Anchored and trapped to this box, this thing, forever. Do you understand? Do you understand what you *did*?"

"I'm sorry," he whispered. "I'm so, so sorry, my love."

"But you learned," she spat. "You finally figured out your *process*. And you used it on our son. But you never told him what had happened to me. You could never bear to, could you? So he never knew. But when he figured out what was within the box, this old chest you'd brought to him, he realized it was something he could *use*. Something he could retool, restructure—with more permissions, more privileges. More sacrifices, more death." She leaned forward, her eyes bright with rage. "But I was *still there*. I was still me, somewhere, somehow. This tiny kernel of myself, still existing in this awful ghost, trapped within a box, a chest, a casket, more. I was a ghost with ghosts of memories. An imprint of a person, carrying imprints of my life before. And I had to watch. I had to *watch,* Clef. I had to *watch* as you turned my child into a monster. As he turned you into a tool. I had to *watch* as he carved and bent and used me like a piece of brass, over centuries, over *millennia*. Do you understand the horrors I have inflicted upon this world? Do you know the memories I possess? Do you understand what I was forced to do to this world?"

Clef did not answer. He sat on the ground, weeping as he listened.

"And when our child brought me into that strange place," she said, "where he intended me to become like God Himself, I gave myself the only name I could recall. Valeria, the angel of childhood. The one who could fix any wrong. The one who could heal any wound. Who could open the door in the afterlife to the locked lands beyond, and grant sick children freedom from their pain." She laughed miserably. "What a sad little dream. As if this could be fixed. As if *any* of this could be fixed!"

"Liviana," said Clef softly.

"It can't be!" she cried. "I started remembering, when that man swallowed that plate and made us merge, and we became something new! I remembered bits and pieces of who I was, how I'd come to be—and I knew then that it *can't* be fixed! *None* of this can be fixed! No clever man with a clever tool is going to touch down on this cursed earth and make it all aright, despite all your wishing!"

He looked up at her, meeting her gaze. "And the Creator?" he asked. "The thing you beckon now? The person you hope will walk through that door, and fix all the fractured world? How is that wish any different?"

She sat there silent, staring down the bridge and at the hall beyond.

"Liviana," he said again. "Please."

"I don't want it to have all been for nothing," she said softly. "Not all this suffering, all this hurt for nothing. Do you know how alone I've been?"

"Yes," Clef said. "That I know well. Of all the things you've gone through, I know that one best. But you must stop this. We have to *stop*."

Tears rolled down her cheeks. "It'll just go on," she said. "More fixes gone awry. The mad pride of men who think themselves engineers of all creation."

"No," he said. "There are people in this world who learned the lessons I never did, the lessons that our son has learned all too late—that you are *right*. There *is* no magic fix. That a better world can only be brought by what we give to one another, and nothing more."

She blinked the tears out of her eyes. "If you leave me, we'll go back. We'll go back to being Tevanne. And I won't be able to control what I do then." She looked at him. "I know what you told the girl to do. And if I go back, I'll stop her. I will."

Clef was silent.

"Don't," she whispered. "Don't let me do that. Don't leave me again. Please, please, don't leave me."

He looked into her eyes, and saw beneath all the years and all the sorrow a glint of the person he had once known: the proud, confident woman who could argue the stars in the sky into new constellations, if only she was given enough time.

"I did not come to leave, my love," he said. He took her by the hand. "But to stay. I will stay with you. Until the end."

She looked at him balefully, and blinked in surprise as he leaned forward and placed a kiss upon her forehead. "Y-You will?" she said.

"I wish I'd stayed before," he whispered. "I wish I'd stayed with you and given you and Crasedes all the time I've wasted on fruitless wishing."

"But you can bring him now," she said. "Can't you?"

"Yes," said Clef. "That's true. I can."

He shut his eyes and issued his commands to this massive structure of permissions and bindings they found themselves in, whispering to the scrived being that held him now, and then . . .

Footsteps in the streets behind them.

The boy rounded the corner hesitantly, nervously. His body so small and pale and starved, and though his eyes were tired they stared out at the world with a knowledge far, far beyond his years.

"Where . . . am I?" he said quietly.

"You know where you are," said Clef to him. "You're home. And I am going to give you what you asked for."

The boy looked at him. "What I asked for?"

"Yes. Because you saved me." He smiled at the child. "Because you helped me remember, kid."

The boy stood there, thinking. Then he slowly walked to them and sat beside Clef, staring down the bridge. After a moment he leaned over and rested his head on his father's shoulder, and Clef embraced him, and they held hands.

"I . . . I remember this," said Crasedes. "I remember what this was like."

"Yes," said Clef.

"It's good," said Crasedes. His voice broke slightly. "I like it."

"It is," she whispered. "I do too."

Then they rose, held hands, and began to walk down the bridge toward the menders' hall.

"Do it now, please," his wife said. "Please."

"Yes," Crasedes said. "Please."

"All right," whispered Clef. "I will."

And he did.

Clef remembered the process, the steps to take. He had done it once before, not long ago, when a girl had held him in a broken, battered building, and he had restored and broken himself all at once.

It's the same thing, he thought, *just in reverse.*

Unmaking himself, unwinding himself, unraveling all his permissions, his privileges, his bindings, his commands.

There in that moment, step by step, Clef unscrived himself, piece by piece, string by string.

And as he did, he pulled the others with him: all the bindings in his son, and in the body of Gregor Dandolo; all the things that bound their minds and souls to this world, trapped them to this existence long after their lives had ended, along with his own, and they dissolved bit by bit, freed from the chains they had wrought from themselves, for themselves, unlocking the locks they had forged to trap themselves in this world.

He watched as the menders' hall before them faded.

A flicker of black. Then a sound, perhaps the flutter of soft wings, like that of a butterfly, or a moth, and the sound of a child laughing in the distance.

Goodbye, Sancia, he whispered. *And good luck.*

64

Sancia watched as Crasedes held Clef to Tevanne's chest—and then without warning, he tumbled to the side, and was still.

All the screaming in the citadels stopped. The river of shriekers and bolts stopped. The giant loricas went still. The massive city trembled beneath her, as if no longer sure what to do or think.

<*It's . . . gone,*> said Greeter quietly. <*It's gone! Tevanne has just vanished, I'm not sure how!*>

"W-What?" said Sancia faintly.

<*I'm trying to come into alignment with the hosts,*> said Greeter. <*To help them, to make sure they don't hurt themselves, and to keep the citadels running. Give me a moment!*>

Sancia stood staring down at Tevanne and Crasedes, Clef still trapped in his hand. She watched as the body of Gregor Dandolo breathed deep, and then coughed deeply, and the many plates adhered to his skull gently fell away, like leaves from a tree, with deep, shining scars left behind on his skin.

She flexed her scrived sight. His body was utterly free of scrivings—no twist of logic, no ugly gleam of dull red.

But she saw none in Clef, or Crasedes's body either. The dull red glow of captured commands was gone.

She knelt, and pulled Clef from Crasedes's fingers. Then she saw he had changed: he was no longer gold but was instead ordinary brass.

She stared at the key, then at Crasedes, and then at Gregor's body, lying still and slumbering on the ground.

"Then it's done," she whispered in a crushed voice.

<*Sancia, I . . . I am sorry,*> said Greeter quietly. <*I'm helping the hosts now. And I'm trying to find Berenice too. But . . . in the meantime . . . what are we going to do about the door?*>

Blinking tears from her eyes, Sancia sat back and turned to the doorway, and the enormous, growing burn in reality, and the wall of black within.

She watched as it suddenly grew, splitting upward through the sky like a bolt of lightning leaping to the clouds, until it seemed to split the very world in two.

Berenice was running up the looping staircase when she heard the footsteps far above, and froze.

Someone had opened a door above her. She was sure of it.

Then a voice, echoing down to her: "*Berenice? Are you all right?*"

She stayed silent, unsure if she should answer.

"*It's me!*" called the voice. "*Greeter!*"

"Greeter?" she cried out, bewildered and delighted. "Then it all *worked*?" She ran up the rest of the steps and found them waiting at the door for her.

She stopped short at the sight of the person waiting for them at the top. They were a short, malnourished, starving young woman wearing flimsy armor and stained clothing—in other words, obviously a host.

"I've got most of the hosts into alignment," she said in a hoarse voice. "And yes, it's really me."

"What's going on?" asked Berenice. "Have . . . Have we won? Did we win?"

"Not quite," said Greeter anxiously. "Not yet. We need your help."

She walked outside, then winced at the sheer madness of the weather: she was slapped by snow, then buffeted by burning ash; and as she looked up at the sky she saw the sun and moon were out at the same time; and then, to her bewilderment, the sun began to bulge horribly, like a malformed yolk in an egg, and the world filled up with a bleak, awful yellow light.

They led her to the edge of the citadel, then up onto the parapets, and pointed out. She joined them at the edge, looked out, and gasped.

The entire world beyond the citadel seemed to be boiling, shifting, changing, and the source of the changes was unmistakable: a giant burning split in the world rose from the flagship citadel, stretching so high into the sky it was almost impossible to see the top of it—but though it was unearthly it was undeniably door-shaped, an oddly rectangular aperture in existence itself, yet it kept swelling and growing and growing . . .

"It's best not to look into it," Greeter said. "I suggest you turn away."

Berenice averted her eyes. "Tevanne opened the door," she said. "And we don't know how to close it?"

Greeter shook their head, their face pale and sickly. "We do not."

"Well, I can't very well try to deal with the situation from across the ocean."

Greeter nodded. "Sancia is on the ground there. I'll path to her, and let you talk to her through me."

Sancia stood before the towering door, staring in as she held the mindless little bronze key in her hand and wept.

<*Sancia?*> said Greeter. <*I have Berenice with me. She's safe. Talk out loud like you were talking to her, and I'll relay your messages.*>

"Oh shit," said Sancia aloud. "Oh my God. Ber—can you hear me?"

A pause.

<I can hear you,> said Greeter, translating for Berenice. *<What are you seeing? Describe it to me.>*

Sancia approached the doorframe, trying to ignore the curious blasts of cold and hot that came hurtling out of the blackness before her.

"All right," said Sancia. "It's . . . It's just like the one we saw in Anascrus. Almost. It's got two locks—one for the silver key, and one for Clef."

<And what is Clef's advice?> asked Greeter, mimicking Berenice's voice almost perfectly.

A pause.

"Clef is gone," said Sancia in a strangled voice.

<Ohh, San,> whispered Berenice. *<I . . . I don't know how, but I'm . . . I'm so sorry. And Crasedes?>*

"All dead," said Sancia, still in that strangled voice. "All gone. I'm alone here. It's just me." There was a shiver to the right, and an entire chunk of the flagship citadel vanished; then it reappeared about a dozen feet out into the sea; she watched, horrified, as the people aboard it screamed in terror and fell into the crystal ocean below.

"It's just me," sobbed Sancia, "and I'm not going to be here much longer, Ber. This whole thing is falling to pieces. It's a miracle I've stayed alive this long."

<What do the locks do?> asked Berenice. *<Is it as simple as turning it off?>*

Sancia stooped, picked up the silver key from the ground, then anxiously approached the door, the air boiling and bubbling about her, alternating hot and arctic cold. She tried the silver key in one lock, then the other; neither would permit it to turn.

"The silver key won't work in either," she said miserably. "It's like Tevanne set this up so that once it started, it couldn't be stopped."

She flinched as the hole in creation grew another dozen feet—and then, somewhere far out in the citadel, half a dozen towers abruptly turned to ash and blew away in the battering winds. She coughed as the ash struck her face, and she wiped it from her eyes, spat it from her lips, wondering if the ash she was tasting had once been a person.

"If this is it," said Sancia, looking across the sea at the distant citadel, "if this is how it ends, Ber, then . . . God, girl, I just want you to know I love you. I always have. I love you so much, I love you like crazy, and I wish this had gone another way."

<*I love you, too, San. God, God, I love you too . . .* >

She sniffed and looked down at the dull iron key in her hand. And then she started thinking.

What was it Clef had said?

That the door opened from both sides, kid. Which means it could also be closed *from both sides.*

She stared into the unearthly darkness, then stepped back and studied the door's frame.

It won't shut, she thought. She took a slow breath in, trying to ignore the taste of ash in her throat. *At least . . . not from this side.*

She thought back to Anascrus. What was it Crasedes had said?

Only someone with an ability to commune with and alter scrivings could survive in that realm—an editor, one might say.

Sancia gritted her teeth and touched the side of her head, where the little plate lay—the one that had been implanted in her so, so long ago, in that gruesome little shack in the plantation islands; and the one that Valeria herself had edited on the Candiano campo to make Sancia an editor.

She looked back at the citadel with Berenice and thought she could spy someone standing atop the parapets. Then she took a slow, deep breath.

"Okay," she whispered. "All right. I have an idea."

Berenice stood on the walls of the citadel, staring across the sea at the burning doorway, waiting to hear more.

"Sancia?" she said. "Sancia, are you there?"

Silence. She looked back at Greeter, then did a double take.

Greeter was weeping. And a crowd was gathering behind them—a crowd of hosts, all filthy, all looking at her, all weeping.

"Wh-What's going on?" asked Berenice.

"I've . . . I've made up my mind," whispered all the hosts, all Greeter, yet all sounding curiously like Sancia.

"What do you mean?" said Berenice faintly. "About what?"

"About how to stop this," they said. The hosts began to mount the parapets, and all of them extended arms to her, as if seeking an embrace. "I . . . I know how to shut the door, Ber."

"Sancia?" said Berenice backing away. "Wh-What's going on? You're scaring me."

"Come," they said. "Please. Just hold me. One more time."

"Sancia . . ."

Yet Berenice let them: she let one host hold her, hugging her tight just like Sancia did—and then another, and another, until she was being held tight by dozens of people, trapped within this enormous embrace.

"Sancia," she said. "What are you doing?"

"I'm going to give all I can," whispered the hosts all at once. "All I can to shut the door—from the other side."

Berenice's eyes shot wide. "*No!*" she screamed. "*No, no, no!*"

Sancia turned to the burning doorway, silver key clutched tight in her hands, jaw set.

"I'm sorry," she whispered. "I'm so sorry."

<*Stop!*> screamed Greeter in Berenice's voice. <*Please, don't! Don't leave me, not after all this!*>

The citadel quaked; then a giant pentagonal stone column rose up from the sea, punching through the far side of the city and sending countless towers toppling into the ocean.

"There's no other way," whispered Sancia. "I wish there was. But there is no dancing through a monsoon, my love. And I have to move quickly. Just listen . . ."

She took a step forward.

"Find me," whispered the hosts in Berenice's ear as they held her. "I will wait for you, somewhere over there. And then, if we're lucky, somehow you can find me, and maybe someday we will have that drink, after all of this."

Berenice fought and bucked and pulled at their grasp, screaming and sobbing. She wanted to jump over the walls, hurl herself down into the sea, swim the deeps to get to Sancia, to see her, to touch her, to hold her. But Greeter held her tight, or perhaps Sancia held her tight, and she could not get free.

"Remember what we said we'd keep," whispered the hosts. "You would keep Foundryside. And I would keep the future—where we're both old, and stupid, and still so in love."

"No!" Berenice cried. "No, stop, San, just let me . . . Just let me *touch* you, please, just once! Let me see you, just once!"

"Goodbye, Ber," whispered the hosts. "For now."

They held her tight, and she screamed in sorrow.

Sancia took a deep breath as she faced the door. Then she stared into the blackness, gripping the little silver key tightly in her hand.

She braced herself, then stepped through.

A burst of atonal chiming, like the bells of a broken clock . . . and yet as she walked through, they stopped being atonal, and all the chimes shifted, turning into the most beautiful music that she could hear only in this place, on the other side, on the underside of everything.

The music turned into something different: a song. Words of a kind she had never heard before; and she slowly realized she was hearing the sigils, hearing them sing, hearing them maintain creation piece by piece, note by note.

She listened to the sigils, all chanting a meaning greater than anything logic could ever capture.

Aah, she thought. *Yes. I see now.*

She turned around and began to close the door.

Berenice screamed and fought and twisted in Greeter's arms, turning around to see the awful black crack in creation—and then, to her shock, the hole in reality flickered and then vanished.

The winds stopped blowing. The snow and rain stopped falling. The dancing ash in the air suddenly vanished. And then, finally, the sun coalesced, and the awful yellow light faded from the atmosphere, replaced by the clear blue sky of midafternoon.

"S-Sancia?" asked Berenice. "San, are you . . ."

"I . . . I do not feel her anymore," said Greeter quietly. "She is gone from this place."

Berenice stared at the crumbling flagship citadel, sitting crookedly in the sea just beyond the ruins of Old Tevanne; and then she realized she was now truly, totally alone, and she burst into tears.

They disembarked from the citadel carefully, climbing aboard the shallops as the *Comprehension* and the *Innovation* pulled alongside. Greeter piloted Berenice to the flagship citadel, and together they used line shots to mount the walls and see what waited for them there.

The doorframe stood free and empty, just vacant, mundane space captured on the other side of it. On the ground before it sat a man in white, staring into the frame as if he were trying to perceive some truth within it. He looked back at Berenice when he heard her approaching. His face shifted to a look of terrible sorrow, and he watched her uncertainly as she came to stand beside him, looking into the empty door.

Berenice slowly sat down beside Gregor Dandolo, and together they looked at the vacant door.

After a while she extended a hand to him, and he took it, and together they waited while the countless hosts were saved from the vast wreckage; not speaking, not looking at each other, two survivors who had no words for what they had survived, nor any language to articulate what was now ending or would soon begin.

Epilogue
THE FOUNDERS

The people built.

They built new cities, new ships, new foundries, new cultures. They built them across the seas and the islands and across the continents; and though the people made things that had in some ways been made before, they made them very differently—for the people were one people, one empathy, shared across many, many bodies, old and young alike.

It was Greeter, of course, who had realized only Giva could repair the world. "These poor hosts have been twinned and dreaming for years beyond count," they said. "We must be there to help them understand what happened to them, to help them heal, and to give them the chance to learn a new way of living—or to purge themselves of all that was done to them and start anew."

Many stayed and became a part of Giva—if that was even the word for it anymore, for they no longer resided in the islands. They lived everywhere.

Or at least, that was what Berenice guessed. She did not know, for she could not join them. The plate in her body rejected all others, and if they tried to edit it out of her flesh, it would kill her. Though she was among them, she was alone.

Except for Gregor Dandolo. It took him nearly half a year to talk again, but he was the sole person who could understand what she had gone through, and what she now felt; and as they lived together in the small house that Greeter built on the beach for them, she felt he was the only person whose presence she could bear.

"You and I are refugees," she said once to him as they watched the countless ships twist on the sunset-dappled seas. "We are in this nation. But we are not of this nation."

"No," he said, his voice hoarse and quiet. "But it's wonderful to see."

Years passed. And as they passed, Berenice sometimes found herself studying the night sky, or the clouds on the horizon, or the way the sea met the shores. She thought of them not as vast entities in their own right but rather as layers, like papers overlaid in a collage.

Sometimes she would wonder—if she could peel them back, would she see a dark inversion of reality, filled with gleaming, golden instruments, laboring away behind creation?

Would she see a pair of eyes looking at her, watching her, waiting for her, somehow, somewhere?

She wondered. But each night she went to bed alone, and awoke alone, and the vast silence that had become her life simply continued.

Nine years after the collapse of Tevanne, they succeeded in finally making a door.

Berenice could not understand how Design had done it; but then, she understood little of scrivings these days. The wonders made by the new scrivers of Giva were beyond her—and this one was far more advanced than that.

She watched as Design manipulated the controls, feeding commands to the doorframe, her belly tight with anxiety as she wondered what it might open on. But when it opened, there was only blackness and the glimmer of distant scrivings: no shuffle of a footstep, no grunt as someone cautiously limped through, returning to the world.

"It's as I worried," said Design sadly. "Not all doors open on the same place—if 'place' even makes sense over there. She is lost to us, on the other side, but perhaps we can find her, one day. If we develop the right tools, if we come to understand the layers and nature of this reality, maybe we can find her again."

Berenice nodded as she listened to their sweet words. But she was not fooled.

Eventually the people stopped speaking language aloud. They moved beyond it, abandoning it and even the written word almost entirely, evolving toward some method of communication more perfect than these mediums. It was then that Berenice truly stopped understanding how the people lived, how they made their cities, all filled with rigs and scrivings and instruments she could not comprehend; wonders that she would have once wished for desperately, yet now bitterly resented, miracles of an age she was forever locked out of.

"Do not feel so angry," Gregor told her once, seated together on the beach at night. "They're your children. You made this world."

"But not for me," she said. "Not for us." She hugged her knees and looked out at the waves. Her back now ached and her knees throbbed, and her sun-weathered face made her look far older than she was. Perhaps her worries and grief had aged her beyond her years. "I wonder if, where she is now, she feels more at home than I do here."

One day she returned to their living quarters on the beach and found Gregor sitting at the table with a small bronze plate in his hand, studying it with his brow furrowed and a frown upon his lined, tired face.

"They . . . left this for me," he said quietly. "I think they want me to join them." He looked at her. "Can I? Can I truly?"

She sat next to him at the table and looked at it, trying to fight the despair deep within her. "There's nothing stopping you," she said. "You're not like me."

He studied the plate. "Then . . . should I?"

"You should," she said hoarsely.

"I am reluctant to do this to myself," he said. "I'm reluctant to swallow a plate yet again, and . . . change."

"You are not that thing," she said. "You're someone different now. And they are very different too."

He looked at her, his eyes sad in his horribly scarred face. "I don't wish to leave you alone, Berenice. Not now."

She kissed him on the brow. "I am not alone," she whispered to him. "She is waiting for me."

He smiled. "I hope so. I think so."

That night the ship came for him, and Gregor boarded it and sailed away to join the massive fleets that nosed throughout the seas on their mysterious routes. Berenice watched them go, then returned to their empty little house and buried her face in her pillow and wept.

Years passed, one like another, spent alone, spent in silence. And then one day there was a knock on the door.

Berenice opened it, curious, and found a familiar woman waiting for her, her face older and lined but immediately recognizable: it was Diela—or that had been her name once. Berenice did not know her name now, nor did she even know if the people truly had names anymore.

"We . . . are going," said Diela awkwardly, smiling wide.

"I'm sorry?" asked Berenice.

"We want to . . . say good . . . bye," said Diela. She waved her hands, beckoning Berenice outside, to where a small crowd waited for her on the beach.

"What is happening?" asked Berenice warily.

"More," said Diela. She gestured at the sky. "There is . . . more.

More above, not below. Not where Crasedes went. We see that now. We . . . have seen. Seen the places, above. And we are . . . going to there. Going."

"Going . . ." said Berenice.

"Yes." Diela looked at her, her face full of happy tears, and tapped her heart. "Love. We love." She gestured to Berenice. "We love you. You are mother. You cannot come, but we have made." She pointed along the beach, to where a little scrived boat waited. "We have made, for you. A place. For you and her."

Berenice looked at the boat and nodded, not quite understanding.

"Good." Diela nodded again, beaming with sorrowful joy. "We love. We love."

"Yes," said Berenice. "Yes, I . . . I think I see."

Diela bowed low. Then she rejoined the people on the beach, and they joined hands in a circle, and shut their eyes, and then . . .

The sand at their feet boiled and churned. Then something rose out of its depths—a door.

The people were making a door. They were calling a door from nothing. And then Berenice understood what they had meant when they said they were leaving—not to the place where Sancia had gone, but to somewhere very different indeed, someplace she could not understand and could not follow.

She burst into tears and watched as the small crowd of people opened the door, and one by one they filed through, then closed the door behind them.

The door sank back into the sand, and then it was gone.

Afterward, she searched the cities near the shore and found them empty. No children, no adults, no one. They had left. To where, she did not understand; such places were beyond her comprehension.

Finally she went to the little boat Diela had pointed out to her. Though it was stuffed full of provisions, the ship was of an advanced kind she barely understood, with no cockpit and no sails—simply a bronze switch that would presumably take her to where she wanted to go.

She did not climb in. Instead, she walked away.

She debated it for four days. Four days of silence. Four days of empty seas.

Enough, she thought. *Enough.*

One early morning when the shores were heavy with fog and the sun was a distant slice on the horizon, she walked down the beach, climbed into the boat, turned the switch, and let it carry her away.

She sailed for two days and three nights. As she passed through the Givan Islands, now full of wondrous cities that were all empty, all silent, she realized she knew this route, and knew where she was going.

Old Tevanne, she thought. *It is taking me back to Old Tevanne.*

As she approached her destination she roused herself to see what awaited her. Old Tevanne had never been rebuilt, not like the rest of the cities from the days before. Yet as the sleek little boat pulled into the place that had once been the waterfront of the grand, horrid old city, she saw something had been constructed deep within the ruins.

Something familiar.

She approached it slowly, anxiously, her heart thrumming in her chest. She knew it instantly: the sloping, leaning front, the way the stories climbed awkwardly into the sky, the crooked metal fence winding around its facade—and there, hanging above its front door, a sign that made her tremble.

Her eyes traced over the words: FOUNDRYSIDE LIMITED.

Quaking, she walked inside.

How perfect it was. How *perfect* it was, every slat, every board, every nail. Orso's rooms were there, still filled with empty wine bottles; as was Gregor's carefully maintained little chamber, with its shelves of poetry and his racks and racks of flowerpots; and the workshops, the design bays, the creaky old lexicon in the basement—all of it was just as she remembered.

She came to the stairs and slowly looked up. She waited, thinking hard. Then she climbed them, one after the other, until she came to the attic.

Their bedroom. One half messy, one half pristine. Even the indent in the mattress where she'd lain, where her body had pressed into the cheap cloth day after day, night after night.

Berenice wept as she wandered this place full of treasured ghosts she could barely recall. Yet then she noticed something was different.

There was a new door, next to their closet.

It was made of black stone. And there, set in the side, was a bronze lock.

Sitting before the lock was a small table; and sitting upon the table was a silver key, and a note.

Trembling, she walked over to the table and looked at the note. It had a single word: *Love.*

She picked up the key, studying its shaft, its tooth. It was immaculate, its scrivings so tiny and complex her eye could barely read them at all.

She turned to the door, took a breath, and carefully fit the key into the lock and turned it.

There was a click, and the world seemed to flicker and stutter about her.

Bracing herself, she turned the handle of the door, opened it, and looked within.

A voice sighed with relief on the other side, and then it spoke: "Finally. There you are."

ACKNOWLEDGMENTS

This book was hard as hell to write.

I started this book in late October of 2019, a few hours after I sent my editor, Julian Pavia, the last version of *Shorefall.* I didn't write any acknowledgments for *Shorefall* because I'd felt the work wasn't done—there wasn't enough to acknowledge, not yet—but I had a good idea of how the story would play out from there, and I'd been planning the ending for years. I just had to jump in, write, and get there.

Then, about three months later, the world fell apart.

I feel it's almost not worth talking about the pandemic. Though the experience might have been individual—perhaps brutally so, with so many of us isolated in our little chambers—there is arguably no event, no struggle, no abrupt shift in reality that has ever been shared on a scale like the 2020 pandemic, which is still ongoing as I write this on November 8, 2021. To discuss it now feels as interesting and insightful as remarking that the sky still hangs above us. To comment upon it purely in relation to the composition of a fantasy novel, with so many sickened or dead, feels trite to the point of vanity.

Yet this book—very unfairly—was my pandemic book. It was one of the few stable things I had to return to throughout the whole of that strange, dreadful period, stealing a few precious moments from my family to add a few words here and there. I used this novel to measure those curious days. Sometimes the two experiences surreally converged, and I believed that, when I finished it, this all might end.

It's hard to remember what it was really like now. Perhaps my brain has helpfully tried to forget it, much like how parents recall the first weeks of their newborn's life through exceptionally rosy glasses. I get flashes of memories: living our lives by dozens of alarms notifying us as to which child was to attend what virtual class; the enormous piles of garbage and recycling as we tried to live out of deliveries; my wife and I blearily (and unwisely) staying up well past midnight, for this was the only time we ever had for ourselves anymore.

But what I remember most is the feeling of aloneness. Aloneness is different from loneliness: loneliness is an emotional state, but aloneness is the intense awareness that you do not have support.

And that was what it was, at its heart. For even though we got off so, so easy, there were many stretches where we looked about for some signal that someone, anyone, was going to send help, and the only things in the news were deaths and strident, swaggering sabotage. With this hanging over us, we tried to coax our children through the days and nights, wondering when it would all end. In this, I do not think my family was in any way unique.

This is the curious tension of a pandemic: nothing about your experience is unique or exceptional, for it is shared by so many; and yet, you feel utterly alone.

The final installment of a series is often about stress, and closure. The characters are put through agony, and they ask themselves, "Will we make it? Are we going to get out of this? How?" And then the author, with their farsighted wisdom, carefully ties up all the loose threads, delivers everyone to the place where they are meant to be, and the great curtain gently falls.

It was a strange thing to write this story while waiting for our own deliverance, our own closure. Sometimes it was very hard to make the words come.

And yet, I felt compelled to finish. For if the Founders Trilogy is about anything, I suppose, it is that the innovations of our species do not yield dividends on their own. They only bring prosperity when they are paired with a society, a culture, or a people who can use them to their utmost.

A road cannot bring travelers if people refuse to let it be built. A printing house cannot bring wisdom if its readers decide they mostly prefer lies. And there is no balm or medicine that can bring health and happiness if the sick refuse to take it.

If we find ourselves unable to take advantage of the many gifts that our brilliance has bestowed upon us, then it is my suspicion that there is no tinkering that can make those gifts function as they ought. Rather, it is upon the people to change themselves: to reshape, reconfigure, and rearrange the architectures of our societies—perhaps in small ways, or large—to allow prosperity and abundance for all to flow through.

This seems like pithy precept, but it is the natural tension of our species for there to be some gap between our brilliance and our wisdom. The question is how far we should allow them to diverge, and what works can close that gap, and how fast they can close it.

I would, as always, like to thank my editor, Julian Pavia, for letting me basically go off into the wilderness and deal with this one. I would also like to thank my agent, Cameron McClure, for her guidance throughout my career and the occasional reassurance that sometimes in the middle of a pandemic it's okay if your kids play Minecraft all day.

I want to thank my wife, Ashlee, for sticking it out with me, even as I grew noticeably fatter and grayer throughout these two years. I want to thank the boys for remaining so shockingly cheerful throughout so much of the experience, and for our many dance parties.

I want to thank my parents, and my wife's parents, for coming over for dinner all the time and pretending like we had something new to talk about, when we were all quite aware we didn't.

I also want to thank the Slack, and all the writers in it, for giving me a hole to scream into every once in a while. (You know who you are.)

I would also like to thank Joe McKinney. Joe was a good guy, a great author, and one of the most phenomenally well-read people I've ever met. Every time I talked to Joe I came away with a bigger bounce in my step. He had that kind of effect on you. When he died in July of this year, it was an utter shock to me. I could not and still cannot imagine a world without Joe. I will miss him terribly.

I will remember him, and keep going. I hope you will too: keep reading, keep writing, keep living, keep loving, keep going.

Robert Bennett, November 2021

PHOTO: © JOSH BREWSTER PHOTOGRAPHY

ROBERT JACKSON BENNETT is the author, most recently, of the Founders Trilogy. Previous to this, he wrote the Divine Cities Trilogy, which was a 2018 Hugo Awards finalist in the Best Series category. The first book in the series, *City of Stairs,* was also a finalist for the World Fantasy and Locus awards, and the second, *City of Blades,* was a finalist for the World Fantasy, Locus, and British Fantasy awards. His previous novels, which include *American Elsewhere* and *Mr. Shivers,* have received the Edgar Award, the Shirley Jackson Award, and the Philip K. Dick Citation of Excellence. He lives in Austin with his family.

robertjacksonbennett.com
Twitter: @robertjbennett